FROM THE RUINS OF WAR, THEIR LOVE,
LIKE THE WOUNDED LAND,
WOULD BE REBORN ...
WOULD RISE UP TO PURSUE A SOARING DREAM.

Adam Tremain, the legendary Black Swan, had won honor in battle—and the undying pledge of Dulcie Moran, Savannah's most dazzling beauty.

Born in defiance, their love withstood trial and separation. Now it would endure a perilous test in the bitter aftermath of the Civil War.

Many would sell their souls to survive. But Adam and Dulcie were bound to each other and the ravaged land. The pillars of the South would stand proud against the sky once more. Their love would burst into bloom anew. Fired by the finest dreams, emboldened by the vision of a glorious destiny, they would reclaim their cherished heritage ...

MOSSROSE

Also by Day Taylor

THE BLACK SWAN

MOSSROSE

Day Taylor

A DELL BOOK

Published by
Dell Publishing Co., Inc.
1 Dag Hammarskjold Plaza
New York, New York 10017

ISBN: 0-440-15969-5

Printed in the United States of America
First printing—July 1980
Second printing—August 1980
Third printing—August 1980
Fourth printing—October 1980

CHAPTER ONE

Once it had been a beautiful land, an Eden soothed by flower-scented breezes, serenaded by the twilight songs of birds. It had been a land of lush greenness springing from the bounteous earth, of vaulting blue skies reflected in silver waters. A land of languor, chivalry, and charm. Its drowsy summers never ended; its bold heroes always triumphed.

Now Eden had been destroyed, and the scented land stank.

The year: 1865. The land was called the United States again. The War of Secession had ground to a halt. The days of Reconstruction were upon the mortally wounded South.

Leroy Biggs and Lyman Matthews mustered out of Lee's army along with 27,803 other men. The Southern warriors had marched off to battle amid a flurry of brilliantly gay pennants, marching bands, and dreams of killing ten Yankees for every Confederate. Now, war-weary, mostly on foot, mostly hungry, they turned their faces South, toward home.

Leroy and Lyman joined a procession of crippled men, ragged, barefoot, faces gray with fatigue and defeat, eyes bitter. The days of April walked on the heels of May and the men straggled along country roads, avoiding towns where they could, succumbing only when their bellies were so empty that begging, even from Yankees, seemed excusable.

They followed the roads through burned land. They gazed across fallow fields; blue skies mocked them through gutted plantation houses. They stepped off the road for soldiers—black soldiers, white soldiers, Federal-blue soldiers, empowered to enforce a new order on their homeland. They listened to the songs, the laughing, jeering songs of the victors.

As the last of a lurching gaggle of blue-clad soldiers passed, Leroy grabbed Lyman's arm. "You better hol' tight onto me, Lyman, 'cause I swear to God I'm gonna kill me every damn stinkin' sonofabitch in that line."

Lyman stared after the soldiers. "Wouldn't be no use, Leroy."

Leroy spat. "No use." His voice was low, sensual. "Sure as hell'd pleasure me. Sure would. Leastways we can git off this road. I've had a bellyful o' steppin' off into the dirt for any black Yankee bastard."

They stumbled across a field toward some woods. Leroy, the stronger of the two emaciated men, held the rope that served as the skeletal horse's bridle. Suddenly he stopped, bent forward, and with his fingers dug something faintly shiny from the earth.

"Son of a bitch if that ain't a button, Lyman."

"You gonna eat buttons, Leroy?"

Leroy polished his find on his filthy jacket, taken off a dead Yankee at Briscoe Station, Virginia. "I ain't had a button on my uniform in two years. What'll the home folks think if we come back lookin' like po' white trash? We're goin' home in *style,* boy. You ridin' that fine snortin' stallion, an' me with my button shinin'."

Lyman grunted. "One thing you got a-plenty is ee-magination."

Leroy looked around, his eyes red with fatigue and starvation. "Yes, sir, my button shinin'," he muttered. "The folks home gonna know there's some o' us ain't surrendered nothin' to nobody." His eyes began to sting and water. Must be the haze. "God damn them!"

Around them burned trunks of trees twisted pleading limbs to the sky. On the ground sprawled the debris of battle: broken harness, canteens and rifles and pikes, metal, bones, splintered wheels, stiff-legged dead horses and cows, ragged bits of clothing still on their decomposing owners. A little distance off, vultures tore at the carcass of a Confederate soldier. Over all hung a gagging stench.

Leroy's lip curled. "Tell you one thing, Lyman, there's only two kinds of dead men I ever want t'smell again—black an' Yankee."

Warily, Lyman examined his festering wounded leg. "I'd like to get the bastard that shot me. I'd make him dance all the way acrost Jawjuh."

Leroy chuckled softly. "We got us plenty o' Yankees, didn't we? I drew bead on fifty of 'em befo' I quit countin'. Ain't no Yankee knows how to fight like a Reb."

"I never thought 'bout countin'. How many you s'pose I killed, Leroy?"

"I donno."

"You want t'ride a while?"

Stumbling, Leroy moved doggedly into the woods. "After a bit. I'm jes' gonna stop an' rest befo' we go up this hill."

Leroy sat against a big dead tree, folded arms on his knees, head down. Laboriously Lyman dismounted and sank to the ground beside him. The two sat side by side, dozing then waking to sudden alertness. The spirit of caution, which had protected them through four years of war, was as vital in them as ever.

The South was a land of refugees. Starving men and women, frightened displaced Negroes, arrogant, bitter ex-slaves, deserters of both armies, men demented by war, all roamed the roads and the woods and the villages searching for food, raping, robbing, killing, maiming out of hatred and loss and need. The War of Secession had ended, but the war of survival toiled on.

The hot, steamy afternoon wrapped slumbrously around the two men. The horse, its head nearly touching the ground, breathed shallowly. Insects buzzed around them, crawling in their ears and around their crusted mouths. The pitiless summer sun beat down on them.

Leroy lifted his head. "Lord God, but I am thirsty. We got t'find us some water, boy."

Lyman touched his thick dry tongue to his cracked lips. "Wouldn't mind havin' a jug from yo' daddy's still."

Leroy helped Lyman mount, then entered deeper into the woods. They found no water. The walking seemed endless. Leroy was no longer sure if he were leading the horse or if only his hold on the bridle kept him upright. It was near dusk when they stumbled out onto a dusty, rutted, red clay road. A hundred yards away, two elegantly dressed women waved to him. He rubbed his tired eyes.

"Lyman . . . tell me I ain't seein' things."

Lyman moaned as he pushed himself upright on the horse. "Oh God," he sighed. "They're dressed fit to kill. Oh, God, Leroy, if they got garb like that, they got to have grub. They got to, don't they, Leroy?" He gave a pathetic laugh. "They got to!"

The two women stepped out onto the road, waving in joyful greeting. As the men neared, the smaller woman turned toward the house. She returned with another girl and an older woman, both bearing hastily picked bouquets of wildflowers. "Welcome! Welcome home!"

"Jee-zus, we got us a greetin' party, Lyman. I ain't seen anythin' like that since the War started. Makes a man feel good, don't it."

The older woman walked up to meet them, holding a tin of life-giving water. The sight of it made Leroy's throat hurt so much that he feared his eyes would begin their mysterious watering again.

"Thank you, ma'am," he managed. He drank deeply, tempted to empty the cool refreshing liquid from the cup, but he turned and offered the remainder, more than half, to Lyman.

"Ah am Mrs. Castleton, widow Castleton that is, since Vicksburg, an' these chawmin' young ladies are

mah daughters. Heah's Ruth, mah oldest, an' Mary
Kay—she's been so good to her mama since her daddy
went down—an' mah baby Lucinda. Now gentlemen,
y'all will honor us by stayin' to dinner, now won't
you?"

"Colonel—Colonel Leroy Biggs of Savannah, ma'am,
an' this here's Cap'n Lyman Matthews."

Lyman looked dumbly at Leroy. "Leroy, you ain't
no colonel—you—"

"Like hell I ain't! He's burnin' up with fever, ma'am,
shot in the leg at Petersburg an' ain't quite himself. We
sure would appreciate it if we could wash up, an'
maybe do a little for that wound he got in battle."

"Of course, gentlemen. Why, whatever am Ah thinkin' of, lettin' y'all stand out heah in the hot sun. Why,
come on in. Dinner'll be served just as fast as Bessie
Mae can dish it up. Can't tell about nigras today.
Things aren't what they once were, but we manage
heah. We try to keep the true Southern way."

Leroy and Lyman gratefully washed the dust and
filth from their faces in the basin provided them in the
back yard. Ruth stood off to the side, watching Lyman
as the men cleaned themselves and murmured with
pleasure at the feel of the cool water on their hot
parched skin.

Lyman was of average height and build. That his
family tended to fall in love with each other showed in
his rabbity look, the washed-out blue eyes that slid
away from a gaze, the lusterless sandy hair. His attempt
at a beard and mustache was a wispy disaster. Unlike
Leroy of the legendary grim smile, Lyman seldom
showed his pleasure or his uneven teeth.

Lyman Matthews had been Leroy's shadow and sidekick since he was ten. Early on, Leroy had become
Lyman's ideal. For his idol Lyman choked back apprehension and dread, and faithfully followed in footsteps
larger than his own.

Unlike Leroy, whose mind for all its narrowness was

lightning quick, Lyman did very little thinking, and no
planning at all. His idol told him what to do. Lyman
sprang unquestioning to obey.

Lyman, whose ablutions were brief, had begun to
dry himself. Leroy rose from the basin, his head streaming water. "Gimme that towel, Lyman." Lyman handed
Leroy the towel. He dried his hands on his dusty
trousers, looking apologetically at Ruth.

She smiled tentatively. "Y'all fought at Briscoe Station?"

"Yes ma'am, we sure did. Took out a pack o' Yankees too."

"Y'all weren't at Lookout Mountain too, were you?"
she asked hopefully.

"Why, ma'am, did you lose somebody there?"

She looked down the road, then shook her head
vigorously. "Oh, no! My brother was there, but he's
comin' home. Any day now. I just thought maybe
you'd heard tell of him. Jason. Jason Castleton."

Lyman looked at Leroy, who said, "No ma'am, we
haven't. Never happened to hear about him. You must
be mighty proud of your brother."

"We sho'ly are. We're proud of all our Confederate
boys." She turned toward the house. "That's the dinner bell. Ma's ready now. Bessie Mae—" she began,
then let her voice trail off.

Lyman and Leroy flanked her, pleased and anxious
to be gentlemanly. Leroy smiled appreciatively at her
attempt to look pretty. Her dress was a collection of
patches; the skirt front was mostly mauve taffeta, the
sides and back patched with scraps of calico, black
velvet, red silk, white brocade, pieces of lace, and bits
of indescribable color and texture. Each of the four
ladies was dressed so. Leroy wondered how many
dresses had gone to make up one. It didn't matter, he
decided. What mattered was that they had the pride
to look good for their menfolk. It was never giving up
that mattered most. He smiled as they entered the
ruined house.

The table was set with a pathetic attempt at grandeur. The marred mahogany table was partially covered by a tattered Irish linen cloth. Sèvres china was mixed with wooden bowls salvaged from the burned slave quarters. A six-branched candelabra, broken, warped by fire, graced the center of the table. Bessie Mae, the serving girl, entered bearing a cracked platter of yams, turnips, and greens.

Mrs. Castleton smiled apologetically. "Ah am so sorry that we have no meat for you gentlemen. The Yankees left us none."

Leroy said graciously, "Ma'am, there's no need to apologize. After what we been eatin', or should I say not eatin', this looks to me like it came straight from the hands of the angels."

For the first time he looked at the serving girl. His mouth opened in astonishment. The girl looked at him pleadingly. Leroy glanced at Mrs. Castleton, eating with exaggerated delicacy. Too frequently she dabbed at her small mouth with her ragged napkin. The Castleton sisters talked quietly and politely, their voices soft, their laughter flirtatious and musical.

Leroy looked back to the servant. Not Bessie Mae—Lucinda, the youngest daughter. Her face and hands, up to the long sleeves of her osnaburg servant's shift, were blackened with smeared charcoal. Where she had touched the platter her fingers had left small black smudges, which her mother and sisters ignored. Her young, red mouth quivered, and her hands shook as Leroy continued to stare. He looked away, forced himself to smile and answer the question Mary Kay had asked him.

Lyman was still staring at Lucinda–Bessie Mae, his eyes full of questions and revulsion. Leroy kicked his friend's ankle, caught his eye, and frowned warningly to keep quiet.

Mary Kay smiled broadly at him, as Bessie Mae bustled around the table, serving them.

Leroy could barely keep his eyes from her, but he

managed to say, "Sure is good, Mrs. Castleton. Lyman an' me ain't tasted food like this since we left home four years ago. My compliments—to your nigra."

"Why, how kind, Colonel Biggs. I'll certainly tell her that. It's a real pleasure to have this ol' hall of ouahs full of guests again. Theah was a time when he had guests every night of the week, impohtant guests. Mah late husband, Colonel Castleton, was a *very* close friend of the gov'nah. They worked together on many an' many an impohtant project." Her laugh tinkled merrily. "So we know it won't be long till we have things back to nohmal. Isn't that so, Ruth honey?"

Ruth's grave face lighted briefly. "Oh, yes, Mama! I can hardly wait till we have a ball again! That'll be such fun!"

Leroy said, "I used to be a pretty fine dancer myself, befo' the War. I bet I'd still be good at it now. When y'all send out invitations, jes' be sure to send me one!"

Mary Kay's look was plainly invitational. "I jes' bet you'd be good at *anything,* Leroy."

Mrs. Castleton interrupted deftly. "Mah late husband, the colonel, used to say. . . ."

Later, after the dinner mercifully ended, Mrs. Castleton apologized again, this time for not having bedrooms for her guests. "The Yankees—such crude, disgustin' men! They came right into this house an' went upstairs, pourin' coal oil on everythin'. Mah family antiques, heirlooms, they jes' burned everything! They'd have burned the house right down around ouah eahs, hadn't been fo' mah fine daughters carryin' watuh. Ah was so frightened, Colonel, you just can hardly imagine. We barely saved the main floah."

Leroy murmured sympathetically for a while, then said, "We saw part of a barn out back, ma'am. That'd do us mighty fine."

"Mama," said Mary Kay, the second oldest, "I'll just show Colonel Biggs an' Cap'n Matthews where they can sleep." She turned, smiling appealingly to Leroy.

Leroy Biggs was a big man, close to six feet tall and massively muscled. Mary Kay's teeth closed over her lower lip as she restrained the impulse to reach out and touch him. Her brown eyes warmed softly as she met his gaze. There was a rugged attractiveness about him, about his hard mouth with the little lines like parentheses at the corners, about his sensual hazel eyes with their heavy brows, and his dark brown hair that fell in a curl over his forehead. Mary Kay wanted to brush back that lock for him, wanted to feel the texture of that coarse masculine hair in her fingers.

She walked slightly ahead of the two men, hips swaying provocatively as she led them to the single horse stall still in fit condition. Lyman spied a meager supply of hay, walked the few paces to it, and slumped down, exhausted.

"Why, Cap'n Matthews, we can do a little better by you than that."

"I thank you, Miss Mary Kay, but I swear I'm too tired to move. This feels mighty good." Lyman's eyelids were drooping as he spoke. A small smile played around the edges of his mouth, then vanished in weariness.

Leroy smiled, a slow sensual curving of his mouth, his eyes watching Mary Kay. He touched the curl that caressed her high cheekbone. She closed her eyes, leaning into his hand. She suddenly looked forlorn and terribly vulnerable.

Leroy was unprepared for the rush of his own emotion. He stroked her throat, then bent down and kissed her tenderly. He murmured, "You make a man mind how much he's missed his home, Miss Mary Kay."

She leaned against him longingly. "Oh, Leroy, pretend—pretend just for a li'l bit that you're somebody I love."

His arms went around her tenderly. "Why, honey,"

he said softly, pressing her head to his chest, his fingers moving gently through her soft, silky hair. "You pretend anything you like. Is there somebody you loved, ain't comin' home?"

Mary Kay nodded, and clung harder to Leroy.

He rocked with her in his arms. His eyes sought the night sky. "I been awful lonesome too. Out there on the battlefields for four years sometimes you git to wonderin' if that's all there'll ever be." The moon suddenly blurred, and seemed brighter. He blinked several times. More self-possessed, he said, "It'd be nothin' but pure enjoyment to hold a sweet li'l gal that's wishin' fo' somebody, jes' like I been wishin' fo' somebody. Somebody an awful lot like you." He stroked her throat.

She gave a little gasp.

Leroy kissed her hard, his hand closing over her full breast. Mary Kay whimpered, struggling weakly against him, then her mouth parted under his, and her body moved closer to him.

Leroy felt a great surge of desire. He held her tight, kissing her until he was breathless.

Mary Kay, her head back, her eyes half shut, pushed at his chest. "Colonel Biggs—what makes you think I—" She was panting.

"Hush, sweet darlin'. Hush. I got somethin' fo' you, Mary Kay."

She moved her mouth against his, their breath mingling, then she pulled away. "I can't—it wouldn't be—"

"Don't say no to me, honey. Don't say no—" He pressed her hand against his bulging trousers. "I got that all fo' you." His lips found hers again and he pulled her to him, her hand between them. "Where can we go, honey?"

"Oh, Leroy, what we're thinkin' about's wrong," she moaned.

"Ain't wrong, li'l doll," he murmured. "Ain't wrong at all."

Trembling, she took his hand and led him across the

faintly moonlit yard. He followed, and they were in a small place entirely enclosed by greenery.

"This is it," said Mary Kay in a small voice.

"You picked a purty place." Soothing her with his voice, he boldly put his hands on both her breasts. "Don't you worry none, honey, it's gonna be all right. It'll be good—you'll see."

Mary Kay smiled tentatively, her eyes misting. "I get so lonely . . . sometimes I pretend he'll come home —but he won't. He'll never come back, will he."

"I'm gonna do somethin' so fine you ain't gonna need to pretend I'm anybody but me," he declared. "You lay still, sweet darlin', an' ol' Leroy's gonna make us both happy again." He pulled her skirts up and put his hands greedily between her thighs. She moved one knee, to give him room. He caressed her a few times, then began to work his penis inside her.

It had been months since he'd had a woman; it was no time for finesse. He stroked hard, then harder, then with a great sigh of relief he came, shuddering with pleasure, until he lay flat on the girl. Still panting, he said, "Did you like that?"

To his consternation he realized she was crying. He stroked her tears away with his fingers. "Now honey, now honey, it ain't that bad. We'll have to do somethin' about it—can't have you cryin'."

He withdrew from her and skinned off his trousers. Pity he looked so scrawny now, he thought, he'd look a lot better with twenty-five pounds back on him. He dropped his jacket to the ground and bent over her.

It was late when he returned to the stable. He didn't know how late. A melting golden moon had been rising when he walked out with Mary Kay, and a brilliant white moon had silvered her naked body when he became aroused the second time. He had forgotten to see where the moon was when she left him.

He stretched his long body out, his arms placed under his head as a pillow. "You awake, Lyman?" he asked softly.

Lyman murmured, then raised up on one elbow. "Yeah, yeah, I'm awake. What's wrong, Leroy?" He looked warily around the stable.

Leroy gently pushed him back down. "Nothin' like that." He laughed. "I jes' felt like talkin' a little. How's your leg?"

Lyman moved the leg gingerly. "Not bad. Mrs. Castleton put some nasty-smellin' stuff on it."

Leroy laughed again, his voice low and musical in the night. "Mrs. Castleton. Now there's a true Southern lady. Did you see that daughter of hers? Black face an' all, servin' dinner jes' like she was a darky. Thought I'd bust up when I saw that, an' her settin' there pickin' her dinner off her plate like we was eatin' in high style."

"Makes you a little bit sad, don't it, Leroy? What's that lady goin' to do?"

"Keep right on puttin' blackface on her daughter, I s'pect, until she got her a right smart nigger to do for 'er again."

"Is it goin' to be like that back home too?"

"Hell no, leastways not soon as we get there. Only reason Mrs. Castleton's makin' do is her menfolk ain't around to git them black bastards in line. Damn uppity niggers. Let th' men git home, an' there'll be a lot o' things put right." Lyman murmured sleepy agreement.

"That Mary Kay set me t'rememberin' good times we ain't had for a long, long time. Remember the tournaments? Lawd, there wasn't a man in the County could outrun me, outfight me, or outyell me." He let out a soft shout. "Lawd, Lawd, if I wasn't somethin'. 'Member, Lyman?"

"Sure do."

"Remember Dulcie Moran?"

"Yeah. Run off, didn't she?"

"I coulda had her. Damn, if she wasn't mine for th' takin'."

"You didn't? I al'ys thought—"

"Nope. Might jes' be the biggest mistake of my whole life."

"Well shit, what's one girl? She said no when you asked her to marry you. No point in buzzin' around a flower that says no. An' you got Camille."

"She was some piece o' female," Leroy mused. Then he laughed harshly. "Camille. I only married her 'cause o' my son, Royal. Camille's a good sort, but she ain't no Dulcie Moran."

"No use thinkin' 'bout it," said Lyman, disturbed. "She married that Tremain boy, an' anyway she's gone, left home, I heard."

"Tremain. Damn bad-assed boat driver. I al'ys knew he was a no-good bastard. There was sumbuddy that ever' nigger in the South called the Black Swan. Whoever it was hauled the niggers North, an' nobody can tell me he wasn't sellin' th' Yankees guns an' food. I told you so. See if I ain't right. Cap'n Adam Tremain had his fingers in the pie right up to his elbow, an' I'll bet money he was the Black Swan."

"I heard it was us he was runnin' guns for."

"Now, ask yourself this. If you was wantin' money an' willin' t'do anything t'git it, who'd you go to? Our side, or the Yankees?"

"Well—"

Leroy turned on his side, now sullenly silent. He thought of the past, and how it had been, and wondered what it would be like to go home. Before the war he had been a planter. At age twenty-one he received, as his patrimony, one fourth of his father's plantation. His twin brother Conroy having fallen in battle at Chickasaw Bluffs, Leroy looked to own half the land, if not all of it, on his arrival home. He didn't know if his parents, his wife, or his son were alive. He had had no news from Georgia for more than two years. A lot could happen in two years. A whole lot had happened to him, and none of it good.

As though to make up for the failings of reality, his

mind turned to producing pictures of his wife Camille
at her most seductive, and then sometime or other they
changed to Mary Kay, then to a whore in Tennessee,
and finally to Dulcie Moran Tremain. In his dreams
he both pleasured himself with the woman and punished
her husband.

Two weeks later Leroy and Lyman bid farewell to
the Castletons. The June sun, an enormous blister on
the blue sky, glared down on them as they walked
slowly and painfully across South Carolina. Once more
their bellies wrenched in empty pain, and their mouths
were dry with the hot, moist, dust-laden air they
breathed.

It was mid-June before they neared the Georgia
border. Only Leroy's unflagging determination kept him
on his feet, and Lyman's pathetic idolatry kept him
following. Their eyes were hollow and haunted. Lyman's leg, improved by Mrs. Castleton's poultices, was
once more festering, his head hot with fever.

Leroy labored up a hill. The horse, nearly as spent
as the men, moved slowly and irregularly. On the top
of the hill, with a little breeze blowing, the stink of the
battlefield through which they had passed was left behind them. Below them, supported by a tangle of rusty
wires and burnt trees, was a nest of shacks.

Leroy lifted his head. He touched Lyman's thigh,
their means of communication in battle. Without speaking he sniffed. Lyman did the same. Their eyes met,
and relief flickered over their faces.

"Catfish!" Leroy whispered hoarsely, and moved
several paces, sizing up the area.

The shacks had been hastily built of materials scavenged after Sherman's men had burned the town and
marched on to the sea. In the red dust of the crooked
street several black children were playing a game with
sticks and stones.

One child suddenly looked up. He pointed to the
scarecrow tableau on the hill. In a wink the children
vanished, swallowed up like gophers into their holes.

The little murmurs of conversation in the dwellings stopped. A waiting stillness lay over the settlement.

"Looks like we got to capture us a town."

"Don't do nothin' rash, Leroy. You know I can't hardly walk. I can't help you none."

"Why, boy, we'll stroll right in, bold as brass monkeys. If they got supper cookin' they'll have to ask us in. It's no more than Southern hospitality. They'll say—" He swept off an imaginary hat and bowed low— "They'll say, would you two fine gentlemen care t'partake of some refreshments? An' we'll say, hell yes!"

Lyman briefly bared his crooked teeth. "What do I do?"

"Stay right with me. On your horse, 'n case we have to run."

"You know how niggers love to snuggle up, Leroy, there's goin' t'be a hunnert in them shacks. An' only jes' two of us."

"They ain't organized, an' we are. C'mon." Leroy jerked on the horse's bridle and they plodded downhill.

The clip-clop of the exhausted horse's hooves sounded strangely muffled in the hollow where the shacks stood. No birds sang nearby; only insects hummed. A shiver went over Leroy, a premonition that things here were not what they seemed.

Lyman leaned down. "Think we oughta go on, Leroy?"

For answer Leroy called loudly, "Hey! Anybody home?" He knocked on the side of an open shack. "We're Confederate soldiers, comin' home! We're unarmed, an' all we want is a little somethin' t'eat!"

The stillness grew. Leroy motioned to Lyman to guard the empty street. He ducked under a low door, his hand near the long knife in his boot. A pile of brush in one corner served for a bed. A small fire was still hot. Leroy looked quickly around, keeping his back to the wall, but no one was there. A rat scuttled across the floor near the rear, leaving through a big hole at a corner.

Leroy peered into the hole, and smiled. The holes, man-sized, led from one shack to another, a secret passageway, so they could all escape out the rear if necessary. But where did they go? There was no hiding place among the trees and wire. They must be in a cabin at the end. He went back outside, conferred with Lyman, then silently entered the farthest cabin. It was empty, and there was no escape hole. No trapdoor. Mercifully unaware of the reeking stench of his own body, he continued aware of the scent of blacks.

Moving soundlessly, he looked into each shack. He came out into the dying sunshine and minutely examined the landscape around them. A hill or two, hardly enough to hide a child behind, a few more trees. That was all.

He sighed, scratching at his scalp as he spoke to Lyman. "They're hidin' someplace. Must not be very many of 'em, or they'da stayed."

"It's goin' t'be dark pretty soon, Leroy."

"Yeah, but they got food. I'll take one more look."

In the last shack he found what he should have seen before. The brush pallet, instead of being flattened by sleepers, was piled loosely, concealing the entrance to the blacks' hiding place. In a fury, knife glittering in his hand, Leroy kicked the brush aside.

"You black sonsabitches get your black asses up here right now, or I'm goin' to set this brush on fire an' burn you out! I'm countin' three! One . . . two . . ."

The first to come up, eyes wide with fear, was a tall, rangy man dressed in a breechclout of gunny sacking. He was followed by a fat man of about thirty, and three others. All were in rags, oddments, or sacking.

"Where's the women?" Leroy rasped. "Where's the pickaninnies?"

The first man answered. "We ain't got no 'oman, massa. Gen'l Sherman done rode off wid 'em."

Leroy glared at the five. "Where's the other bucks? I ain't b'lievin' you're all. I seen the pickaninnies with my own eyes."

The dark brown eyes in the black face shifted slightly, but his voice remained respectful, evasively apologetic. "We done lef' Uncle Tom down de hole, massa. He mighty ol' an' sick, an' he lib dere."

The others nodded, their eyes sliding away from Leroy's. "Yassuh, yassuh, Uncle Tom got a baid in de hole."

"I smelled catfish cookin'. I'm gonna count ten, an' then I want t'see that spider full o' fish settin' in front o' me."

They began to babble: there was only one fish and it was all they had.

". . . two . . . three. If you ain't bringin' me catfish, it better be somethin' good, or I'll kill the whole damn lot o' you. Four . . ."

Out of the corner of his eye Leroy saw that Lyman had come to stand behind him. In his hand was a bayonet. Wounded though he was, he would fight with Leroy.

The smallest black dropped into the hole and returned, holding a skillet in which lay some dead earthworms, ants, and crickets. With a smile he said, "Dis whut we eat, massa." The other blacks nodded. "Eat 'em in de cotton fiel's, massa."

The skillet of insects flew across the room, bouncing crazily off the wall. Leroy, his rage full-blown, glanced sharply from one innocently smiling face to the next. Poised to knife one of them, or at least to kick somebody, he exhaled deeply and simply shook his head. "Christ. You dumb idjuts. You deserve t'be slaves."

As though some magic word had been spoken, the charade was over. Every black man was suddenly in possession of a weapon, a knife or rock or club. The fat man spoke with great dignity.

"We are free men. No man owns us. You came here to rob and kill us, to steal our women and harm our children. You are fortunate that we are black men, sir, for we do not right one wrong with another. Go now, and you will not be attacked."

"Le's go, Leroy."

"You God-damned niggers, where d'you get off talkin' to a white man like that! I'll come back here with a posse an' clear out your rats' nest for you."

Hard lines showed at the sides of the black man's mouth, but he spoke calmly. "I will count to twenty-five. That will give you time to get off our property. One . . . two . . ."

As the heavy man counted, the four others moved quietly forward, a step at each count.

Lyman stood his ground, then with the tall black only three feet away from him, he moved with awkward haste to mount the horse. His face suffused with impotent fury, Leroy followed. They started walking.

Behind them the Negroes chanted:

> "De bottom rail is on de top
> An' we gonna keep it dere."

A hundred yards out, Leroy turned around to shake his fist at the little settlement, and saw behind them several rows of men, marching as toward battle. Drums banged, women and children chanted:

> "De bottom rail is on de top
> An' we gonna keep it dere."

He sucked in his breath. "Look at that, Lyman."

Lyman turned, and his eyes popped wide. "Jesus! They never made a sound. Maybe they're waitin' till we get way out someplace an' kill us! We gotta hurry up! Oh, God, Leroy, we gotta get outta here!" He pounded on the horse's neck with his fist, but the weary beast just plodded on. They continued, looking back nervously, until fatigue, the fear of what might lie ahead, and the inky darkness stopped them.

Lyman lay on the ground with his wounded leg stretched out. "I feel like I got eyes all over me t'night. Seems like it's worse than fightin' the Yankees, don't it? Leastways they was friendly over the pickets some-times. Is this what it's goin' t'be like now, Leroy?"

"Shit no," Leroy said, the bravado of his words hid-ing the fear beneath. "Bunch o' slaves like that wouldn't have the guts t'kill two white men. Why, you know well's I do, their black hides'd be stretched out over ten counties for touchin' a white man."

All the same, one kept watch while the other slept.

The sun came out late the next morning, shining through a cottony layer of fog. Around the men's sleep-ing place scuttled the small life of the woods—squirrels, chipmunks, voles. Leroy had been sleepily watching a squirrel and trying to wake himself enough to devise a snare. Suddenly he hissed, "Lyman!"

Lyman woke up feeling sick, his head hot and hurt-ing, his leg throbbing. "Huh?"

"We're near water. See that squirrel? Let's go get some." He bent over his friend. "C'mon, gimme your hand."

He got Lyman on his feet, wavering, glassy-eyed. "I got t'lean on you, Leroy . . . I can't hardly stand up t'day."

One half-carrying the other, the two men walked several hundred yards to a small stream. They lay face down and eagerly drank their fill. "How come we didn't hear this las' night, Leroy?"

"With five hunnert black savages doggin' our foot-steps? Here, set on the bank an' soak that leg. Sure wish I knew what that muck was Mrs. Castleton put on it. We got to get you cooled off, boy."

Lyman's teeth were chattering. "I'm cold a'ready. I wish we was home, Leroy. Ma'd put me t'bed. She'd know how t'poultice me up. She'd use hot bread an' milk, maybe, or hot turnip greens." His voice trailed off.

"Show you a bowl o' bread an' milk, you sure as hell wouldn't waste it on a bullet hole. Stay awake, y'hear? I'm goin' after that horse."

The horse had made its way a hundred yards up-

stream, cropping the long, sweet grasses that grew
along the banks. Leroy jerked the bridle, but the horse
balked. Like the men, it had not eaten for several days.
Then, his body wet with perspiration, his temper short
in weary frustration, Leroy began beating the horse. Reluctantly the beast began its customary slow movement.

Then it stopped, and pricked up its ears. Leroy, his
stick raised to strike, listened. Some distance away, he
heard the easy hoofbeats of a horse trotting. His animal
made its first sound in days, a low whinny. Leroy
grabbed the horse, tightly clapping its jaws shut. He
looked quickly around.

The red earth was still. Here on the rolling plain the
sparse grass still grew in thick tufts. White cabbage
butterflies fluttered aimlessly over the wild mustard. To
the north, where the hoofbeats had seemed to be, nothing was visible but small green hillocks. The settlement was hidden from view.

When he got back, Lyman was lying asleep, curled
up beside the branch, breathing shallowly. Leroy said
softly, "Hey, boy, you got to get movin'. You'n'me's
goin' t'lie low t'day. C'mon now, c'mon."

With greater difficulty than before he got Lyman on
his feet. Panting, sweating, furious at his own weakness, he heaved his friend across the horse. He stumbled
along, his eyes flashing from side to side and occasionally behind them, wondering where in this wide
plain there was a tree big enough to hide a feverish
man and a broken-down animal. For himself he'd fight,
even if he went down. Dying wouldn't be too hard for
a man about to starve to death anyway. But he couldn't
leave Lyman all alone. Lyman was counting on him.

He heard the hoofbeats, galloping now, coming for
them. And the sounds had multiplied. The one horse
nearer. Others making a muted pounding in the background. Sweat hung heavily on his upper lip. He ran
his tongue over his lips, tasting the salt, wondering if
the blacks at the settlement had decided to come after

them. He let go of the bridle and, knife in hand, went back to stand by Lyman. His eyes were trained on the blank horizon to the north. Finally a figure appeared. "It's a Yankee," he said softly. "A black Yankee in a spankin'-clean uniform. A sonofabitchin' nigger!"

Lyman, lying on his stomach over the horse, raised his head. Light-headed and silly with fever, he said, "M-maybe you oughta give'm your—your button, Leroy."

Leroy stared at him, then grinned, his teeth white in his dirty face. "Maybe I'll jes' take his horse an' outfit." He said nothing about the drumming sound of other hooves, the sound that grew stronger. Leroy waited, his hand still touching the horse.

The Yankee officer pulled up before them. In a swift, lithe motion he was down, pointing his pistol at the two of them, just a bit too far away for Leroy to try jumping him.

The Yankee stalked around them silently for a while, cocking his head on one side then the other as he looked them over. He was a bigger man than Leroy, taller, heavier, better nourished.

"Stan' ovah heah, so's Ah kin git a bettah look at you," he ordered. His hard brown eyes looked into Leroy's, held for a long moment, and passed on to the man hanging over the beast's neck.

Sneering, he holstered his pistol. "Well," he said. "Well, well. Whut do we got heah? Why, Ah b'lieve we got us two Reb soldjahs. Po' fellas, all tuckered out fum de Wah, an' cain't wait till dey gets home. Ain't dat so?"

Leroy glared at him in silence.

"De propah ansuh, soldjah, is yes suh!"

"My answer is go fuck yourself."

Leroy did not see the lightning-like kick, but felt the agony on his wrist as his knife sailed through the air. In spite of his pain, he tried to kick back, but the black Yankee caught his foot, turned it, and threw Leroy joltingly to the ground.

He lay there, the breath knocked out of him, his shattered wrist stabbing with sickening pain. He opened his eyes. A satisfied smile played across the officer's handsome brown face. Black soldiers, all on fine mounts, all dressed in clean Federal uniforms, looked down at Leroy on the ground. At a gesture from their officer, the soldiers moved, their animals forming a loose circle around Leroy and Lyman. Leroy craned to see what they were going to do. The sun, peering over the fog now, caught him in the eyes and blinded him. Gasping, holding his wrist, he tried to sit up. Suddenly a boot was on his windpipe.

The black Yankee's smile mocked him. He said conversationally, "Y'all know de Oath?"

Leroy ground out from between clenched teeth, "What Oath?"

"De Iron Clad Oath." The boot pressed carelessly harder. The Yankee officer waited.

"I—don't know!" So far, he and Lyman had never had a Yankee ask them this. The Oath was something new to them.

"Y'all want me t'tell you?"

Leroy tried to nod. The air around him was bright with colored sparkles. It seemed to be getting dark.

"De Oath is fo' de Southun gent'mens comin' back fum de Wah." The Yankee, observing that his captive was losing consciousness, and that Lyman was struggling to rise from where he had fallen off his mount, lifted his foot fractionally. He nodded at one of his men, who immediately pointed his pistol at Lyman. "Th'ow dat stickah behin' y'all, Reb," the black soldier ordered.

The Yankee officer continued talking to Leroy. "Dat mean you. Unnerstan' me? You sweahs to suppo't, proteck, an' defen' de Const'tution of de United States an' de Union of de states, an' abide by an' suppo't all de laws an' proclay-mations made durin' de Wah consuhnin' ee-mancipation, else you doan git to be a citizen o' nothin'. You unnerstans? An' you has to say each an' every word, an' sign yo' name in de groun' 'cause we ain't got no papuh."

Leroy, allowed to breathe a little bit said, "We did all that. When Gen'ral Lee signed up t' Gen'ral Grant, he did it fo' all of us. That's what they told us."

"You has t'say each an' every word, or Ah jes' might stomp you till you's dead. Now you say whut Ah say. Ah solemnly sweah befo' God . . ."

When Leroy had finished, his tormentor made him crawl to a place the Yankee found suitable for signing one's name to an oath. Painfully Leroy crawled on his knees and one hand while the black troops twittered and laughed among themselves.

The Yankee officer said, "Move quickah, soldjah, 'lessen Ah might have to gut-shoot y'all."

Leroy had had enough. He stopped crawling and sat on the ground, looking up. "What in the hell have you got against me, Yankee? I never saw you befo' in my life."

The Yankee grinned hugely. "Leroy. You'n'me's got a lot o' things to talk about, lots o' good ol' times in Massa Jem's fiel's. Doan say you doan 'members, you like to hu't mah feelin's. Times like when Fellie make free—'member dat? Times like when you picks me out an' say y'all gwine shoot me—gut shoot me—iffen de Massa doan fin' Miss Dulcie. You 'members dat, sho'. You had me boun' up like a ol' hog, down on mah knees in de yahd, jes' waitin' fo' dat ol' gun o' yours t'go off. 'Member now? Sho' nuff, Ah sees you do."

Leroy stared at him appalled. That had been years ago, when Dulcie had helped some of her father's slaves run off. She'd damn near caused an insurrection. "You can't hold that against me! Lawd God, it was a emergency—the whole damn plantation was—"

"Ah 'members bein' in Miss Trishy's church, prayin' an' singin'."

"But—" Leroy had kicked in the blue door of the

chapel and selected six of James Moran's best field
hands, threatening to shoot one for each hour it took
to get Dulcie back. But which one was this? They all
looked alike—on his knees. " 'Pollo?"

The huge black stared at him for a long time before
he said, "Now you knows whut Ah got 'ginst y'all.
Staht crawlin', *Massa* Leroy, so it mek me sm-i-ile."

For half an hour Leroy crawled in and out between
the nervous legs of the prancing Yankee horses as
Apollo bid, then was reminded of the Oath by having
to take it again. The soldiers laughed, as did Apollo
as he ordered Leroy to sign his name in the dirt. He
did so, scrawling unevenly with his left hand.

Apollo inspected his work. "Y'all jes' stay theah." He
went over and looked closely at Lyman. "Look like he
done swooned." He glanced at Leroy again, then spoke
to the unconscious man. "You looks like sumbuddy
Ah know, but Ah doan know who, an' iffen Ah doan
know who, Ah doan b'lieve y'all done me bad. Ah
ain't gwine wake you up fo' nothin'. But now, dese
weapons, an' dat dere nag, dey b'long t'de United
States govament. Ah takes dem in de name o' Mistah
President Johnson." Apollo gathered up the knife and
the bayonet and mounted his horse. "Leroy, Ah specks
Ah see you agin. Yas suh, Ah do!"

He lifted his pistol and shot Lyman's wretched
mount straight through the eye. As the beast crumpled
to the ground, he touched up his fine horse, signaled
to his men, and rode off, his rich laugh floating through
the foggy morning air.

Leroy struggled to his feet. He grasped his throbbing
wrist with his left hand. The pain shot up his arm and
through his shoulder, pulsating, spreading. His teeth
clenched, his face red, Leroy screamed his hatred and
agony. He screamed and screamed until he had no
voice and his throat was raw and tasted of blood and
dust. Looking around him in misery and despair, he

saw Lyman unconscious, his face white, his hair wet with fevered sweat, next to the dead horse. In front of him lay a long stretch of land, all uphill, endless and forbidding and hiding home. He fell to the ground and cried, his sobs sounding loud and racking in his strange, strained, croaking voice.

It was night when Leroy awakened to Lyman bathing his brow with water from the branch back in the woods. "Leroy?" Lyman asked fearfully. "Oh, God, Leroy, you awake? I thought they'd killed you. You all right, Leroy? Tell me you all right!"

Leroy could barely see. His eyes were covered with film and swollen almost shut. "They ain't killed me, Lyman."

"I never been this scared before, Leroy. We gonna make it home?"

Leroy looked out into the blackness, thinking of the long uphill climb. Slowly, painfully, he got to his feet. "We'll get home. We'll get home."

They began to walk. Their progress was slow, and their pain hindered their efforts. Lyman had to stop and rest every few yards, and Leroy grunted in anguish each time it was necessary for Lyman to support himself by taking hold of his arm.

The black night began to quiver with nameless color as they came to the top of the bluff. Panting, no longer trying to keep rational thought, Leroy struggled up the last few steps. Spent, the two of them stood there looking down into Georgia. On the horizon the sun began to light the sky.

They stared down from the steep bluff and saw the ruins of Savannah. Houses lay destroyed, the windows in shards. The city was blackened with the scorched reminders of fire and guns and bombs and mortars, mementos of the Cause that failed.

Leroy thought of Mrs. Castleton, and of Mary Kay. He remembered his wife and son. The faces of the blacks at the settlement haunted him, as did Apollo's bitter smile. What were they all to do? How would they live? How would they survive?

Together Leroy and Lyman entered Georgia, their faces lit by brilliant lavender and gold, a dawn of the damned.

CHAPTER TWO

It was spring, 1866. From the northeast bank of the Potomac, Washington City rose looking more like a mud-spattered army encampment than the proud capital of the newly reunited United States of America. Remnants of army artillery stood rusting in open fields. Tattered men in nondescript uniforms, both gray and blue, trudged along the yellow-clay scars awash with mud and water that served for roads.

But it was Pennsylvania Avenue that held the attention of the sleek, well-groomed man ensconced in the back of a luxurious black coach. From the Anacostia's banks, past the Capitol with the statue of Freedom atop its graceful ribbed dome, through Washington's business district, this four-and-one-half-mile street symbolized power to the man. Edmund Revanche loved power. He schemed for it, he gloried in it. Power was plaything, mistress, *raison d'être* for him.

Having leisurely traversed the spacious avenue from one end to the other, he pulled his pocket watch from his vest, noted the lateness of the afternoon hour. Impatiently he rapped his walking stick against the ceiling of the coach. Without further instruction, his driver headed for the most famous eating place in Washington. For several blocks as they approached, Pennsylvania Avenue was clogged with lines of hacks, as hired cabbies vied for curb position with the liveried coaches owned by the wealthier. With deft maneuverings while the footman screamed imprecations and made way, Revanche's driver pulled the coach into the curb near the corner of Sixth and Pennsylvania, right in front of the door to Pete Dubant's restaurant.

Edmund Revanche waited impatiently until his foot-

man opened the coach door. Then with a smooth grace
seldom seen in a man of his height, Edmund, dressed
in black relieved only by his immaculate white shirt
front, emerged from the coach. He stood for a moment
in the street, serenely indifferent to the hacks that
threatened to crush him, while his snapping alert eyes
caressed the length of Pennsylvania Avenue once more.
Then, jauntily twirling his gold-headed walking stick,
he smartly entered Dubant's.

The *maître d'hôtel* seated Edmund immediately at
the table kept reserved for him at all times. Near the
back of the room, but in plain sight of all who entered,
the table afforded Edmund command of view and the
luxury of private conversation. He assumed his throne,
comfortable and proprietary in his arena of power.

If one wished to wield power in this city, one must
have a base from which to exercise it. In Washington
City, deals were made in the dram shops of the Capitol
and in the saloons, restaurants, bars, and faro rooms
of the select establishments. The fineness of Pete Dubant's cuisine was not its only boast. On its upper floor
was housed Ike Jones's Faro Bank. Nearby was Robert
Teel's Faro Bank, where one might find Thaddeus
Stevens. In all ways Pete Dubant's suited Edmund
Revanche. He sipped a fine sherry as he waited for
two of his associates, Albert Seldon and Talbot Channing, to join him.

Edmund liked neither man nor did he trust them.
Trust and liking were not in Edmund's nature. He did,
however, believe he controlled their loyalty, for he knew
all the secrets, the cravings, and the illegalities each
man was immersed in.

Under hooded lids Edmund's brown eyes roved with
seeming casualness, missing nothing, noting everything
that occurred in the restaurant. He smiled in satisfaction as he observed two men he knew with their heads
close together, talking privately. Over cards and whisky
this evening, the younger of the two would reveal much
of interest. A calculating, ambitious man, Edmund was

graced with a cynicism that allowed his morality to shift with the needs of expediency.

He was superficially attractive, having inherited dark good looks from his French Creole father. From his high, narrow forehead sprang fine black hair, now distinguished with gray at his temples. He was a man of exquisite tastes with ample means to indulge them, thanks to a sizeable patrimony and lucrative war contracts he had fulfilled for both North and South. He was discreet and secretive, with a constitution that shrugged off as nothing the most flamboyant of his excesses.

He rose, hand extended as Talbot Channing came to the table. A Yankee kingmaker, he gave the impression of a dignified, upright man, yet exercised his fortune and power with brutal directness. He was tall and beefy, with coarse blond hair that lay in tight waves, and a careless mustache drooping down over the petulant lines that ringed his mouth.

"Good evening, Edmund," he said, seating himself and reaching for the wine decanter. "Traffic is damned bad this evening. Dubant's isn't the high-class establishment it once was, I fear. They seem to allow any rabble to come here these days. Did you see the carriages outside? Fit only for hacks. I must have seen a dozen that couldn't have cost near twenty-five hundred."

Edmund smiled indulgently. "You are a snob, Tab. Those rabble are the bemused little men who will keep you and me living like kings so long as we succor their illusions of grandeur. Everybody wants to be somebody, dear man. Those who foster that desire are nearly always wealthy." Edmund raised his glass, touching it to Talbot Channing's. "To little men with big illusions."

Sourly Channing raised his own glass, then drank thirstily. "Where is Albert? He's always late."

"He will be here shortly. I had him stop off to send a wire to Lloyd Henry in New Orleans."

Talbot Channing sat straighter, glancing hastily around.

Edmund laughed heartily. "Dear God, Tab, you are impossible. We are completely private here. That is why I have chosen this table. In any case, who would know or have any interest in a fraudulent Louisiana colonel by the name of Lloyd Henry Grooms?"

Channing looked piqued at his companion. "Your arrogance will be your downfall one of these days," he said in a low voice. "I do wish you would keep in mind that I have a reputation to uphold."

Edmund raised his brows. "Haven't we all."

The blond man finished his wine and refilled the goblet. "Well? How is the Georgia project coming?"

Edmund smiled. Deliberately, slowly, he lit a cigar, his dark, cold eyes never leaving Channing. He remained silent until Channing had begun to feel unaccountably guilty and took out an immaculate white monogrammed handkerchief to mop his brow.

"It is slow progress, Tab, but then one can't be too careful. Lloyd Henry has contacted a Jabez Hooks. The Reverend Jabez Hooks. He has a strong reputation for his ability to lead the blacks, and he maintains good standing among the whites in the Savannah area. The Reverend Hooks has been known to lend a helping hand in time of trouble, and at a later date has extracted payment in most ingenious ways. He made a suggestion to Albert, one that will be to our advantage."

Channing looked frightened. "Albert and I were never to be directly involved," he said quickly. "You gave your word on that, Edmund. We were to provide . . . whatever supplies required, and in return share in the profits. We were not to be connected."

Edmund's dark eyes bored into his companion's. "I am aware of our agreement, but there are certain facts you should be cognizant of. The first is that the South is open ground for those who move the most swiftly. We may see opportunity in all directions, but so do thousands of other men. If we want the South for our own purposes, then we move on all fronts in whatever way we need." Edmund stopped talking as Albert Seldon, a small, rotund man with perpetually wrinkled clothing, hurried on short legs to the table.

"Edmund! Tab!" he said heartily, his pudgy moist hand outstretched first to one then the other. "I stopped by the hotel. Good news from Lloyd Henry. He's found the perfect piece of land. It's just outside of Savannah, belonged to a planter named Cal Saunders."

Talbot Channing looked confused. Seldon glanced at Edmund. "You haven't told him yet?"

"We were just getting to it when you arrived, Albert. Why don't you go ahead and enlighten Tab. He is quaking in fear that his name will be involved in some despicable connivance—far worse than the aphrodisiacs and stimulants he now imports and sells."

Seldon's bald head shone as he laughed heartily, thinking it a joke. He began enthusiastically, "Lloyd Henry said we can pick up this Saunders plantation for next to nothin'. The father and sons got shot all to pieces in the War, and the family plan to live with relatives or somethin'. So Lloyd Henry got in touch with this Reverend Hooks—you know, Edmund, Hooks looks like he might turn out to be an ace up our sleeves. He's the crookedest, most devious man I ever heard tell of, exceptin' present company, of course." He roared laughing, glancing at each to see if he got the humor of it.

Edmund waited patiently for the loud laughter to subside. "What is Reverend Hooks going to do for us, Albert?"

"Hooks figures that I buy the land, and then he goes through the area tellin' all the darkies an' whites who might be hurtin' for cash that out of the kindness of my heart I've permitted him to open a general store on a hunk of my big ol' plantation, see?" Albert Seldon grinned. "Then, again out of the kindness of my heart and through the saintly influence of our beloved Reverend Hooks, he's going to persuade me to extend unlimited credit, and *then*—"

Edmund smiled coolly. "Then when the bills become out of hand, naturally all or part must be collected, and in lieu of money, children or perhaps land will be accepted."

Seldon's jaw sagged. "Right! Right—how'd you know?"

Edmund laughed silently to himself. "And naturally all these transactions can be handled without a ripple on the surface."

"That's what Lloyd Henry tells me," said Albert.

"Has he found a suitable house in Savannah yet?" Talbot asked. "I must know when to begin shipments and how much he'll be needing."

"That's a different matter entirely," Seldon said hastily. "Hooks doesn't want his name attached to any house of ill repute, naturally, and we don't either. Seems to me the general store is more important than having Hooks run a house for us. Don't you agree, Edmund? So I'm going to telegraph Lloyd Henry about that sidekick of his, Bret Tully. Tully ought to be able to own that house. Him bein' tucked away safe in Loosiana, if there was any trouble brewin', he could claim he didn't know what his tenants were up to. Hooks can keep an eye on things from time to time, make sure nobody's dealin' behind our backs. What d'you think, Edmund?"

"I think you have everything well in hand, Albert. Did you send Lloyd Henry the telegram as I asked?"

"Yes, on my way here. Told him you'd be in Savannah once we've got this business cleared up. He knows he's got to have everything in order and workin' by the time you get there. I put a fire under his butt, that's for sure. How soon you figure we can leave here?"

"Another ten days, perhaps two weeks. I talked to Jubal Lerner today. He is too prone to let the girls get the best of him. I'd like to see him replaced before I leave. And I have caught wind of one more difficulty, at least a potential one."

"Nothing we can't handle, Edmund," Seldon boasted.

"Today when I went to see about my pardon and the return of Gray Oaks to my possession, a sergeant in the Attorney General's office told me that two applications for pardon have arrived in the mail, with the applicants to follow soon. One is Captain Adam Tremain, and the other James Moran. Moran is Captain Tremain's father-in-law. And Tremain is a dangerous man." The lines on either side of Edmund's thin lips deepened. "I want you to arrange it, Albert, so that Captain Tremain is taught immediately that in this new era, everyone plays the game or he goes nowhere, not even into the slip to dock his ship."

"Just so our names aren't mentioned," said Talbot Channing.

Seldon said eagerly, "If you want him stopped from entering Washington, I'll stop him. I know a few people who'd be happy to do me a favor." He laughed loudly again. "Just don't you forget to tell Jubal that I'll be sendin' a few men down to his place for a night on the house, an' to be damn sure to give 'em clean girls."

Edmund gave Albert Seldon a cold, hard stare that made Seldon regret his having taken so peremptory a tone. His voice was hard. "Albert, I'd like you to go a little further than that. Make certain that neither Tremain's nor Moran's application gets to the President's desk unless both men come across. You might also find out where they're staying, and arrange for small annoyances—lost trunks, misplaced reservations—until money changes hands. Captain Tremain is a bright man. He'll understand soon enough. I am curious, however, to find out how long it takes him to play to our rules."

"What kind of man is this Tremain?" Talbot asked. "I don't recall you ever mentioned him before. Is he someone we could use?"

Edmund laughed. "Not with his knowledge. He is one of those rare men who actually try to live by their ideals, a truly moral man. He has somehow made it all work to his advantage. But that kind always folds once they have had to besmirch their high principles. Therefore we shall teach the good captain right from the start that he will get nowhere in Washington or in the new South unless he observes the new criteria. We shall utilize him, or we shall neutralize his effectiveness. He could become a political force in the South to our detriment unless we carefully guide him to unknowingly do our bidding."

"You mean make him think that what he wants is really what we want him to think?" Albert said in confusion.

"Something like that," Edmund said. "Shall we order dinner, gentlemen? I am eager to get to the gaming table. I feel lucky tonight."

CHAPTER THREE

The *Black Swan,* a sidewheel paddler with several new coats of white paint replacing its wartime camouflage gray, had entered Chesapeake Bay during the night. As dawn crowded through thick morning mists, Adam Tremain steered into the busy Potomac River at Point Lookout. Through the growing warmth of a Virginia spring day they steamed upriver. Most of the time Dulcie stood on deck holding their infant son Beau and chatting gaily with Adam, and drinking in the sights visible from the river. When on the crown of a gentle hill they saw the pillared porch of Mount Vernon, they knew that within the hour the *Black Swan* would be docking in Washington.

A few hundred yards out from the Maine Avenue docks they were hailed by a small boat of the port authority, and told that no berth would be available for the *Black Swan.*

Adam, astounded, gestured toward the docks, nearly empty at mid-afternoon. He called through his megaphone, "What do you mean, no berth? I can see plenty of space from here."

The man in the port official's uniform shrugged. "Port authority orders, Cap'n. No berth for the *Black Swan,* Adam Tremain, Captain."

Adam lifted his megaphone again. "How much? Whom do I pay?"

The official smiled. "Five hundred. You pay me for the port authority."

"What's your name?"

"Smith—Orville Smith."

Baffled and angry, Adam demanded an explanation,

but the official only said, "It's my orders, Cap'n. No
free docking for you."

"I'll see your supervisor about this!" Adam shouted.

"Cap'n," came the voice across the water, "I *am* the
supervisor."

Adam turned away, as near fury as he had been for
a long time.

Dulcie came near so they could talk quietly. "What's
happening, Adam? Is there a dock fee now?"

His vivid blue eyes were dark with rage. He said
shortly, "Yes, there is, and I won't pay it. We're going
back downriver to Alexandria." He barked out orders
to the first mate and stood glaring at the retreating
back of the port supervisor.

They tied up at Alexandria in late afternoon. Adam
leaped off while the gangplank was still being lowered,
and strode quickly up King Street. Inquiries at two
shipping-line offices yielded no information about the
Washington City port authority. Frustrated, he arranged
for coaches and drays to take their party to Washington
the next morning.

Late that night he stood on his quarterdeck, looking
out across the quiet river, thinking. Speculatively he
considered that he should have bribed the man and
saved his family the jouncing trip by coach into the
city tomorrow. In the next moment, however, he re-
jected the thought. He had learned long ago that one
did not play any game without knowing the stakes and
the identities of the other players, especially not when
one had a reputation such as his. Above all, he had to
be certain that his wife and son were safe. This over-
land route was time-consuming and annoying, but it
afforded the best safety in an unknown situation.

He turned, instantly alert to an almost imperceptible
footfall. His black hair stirred in the soft evening
breeze, falling to gentle curls on his forehead. The
moonlight cast highlights on the strong, broad planes
of his face. His vivid blue eyes lost their pensive tension
as he observed his wife coming toward him. His full,

sensual mouth curved softly in a warm smile. Without speaking, Dulcie walked into his arms. He stood holding her to him, his face hidden in her scented auburn hair.

Dulcie let a shiver of pleasure course through her. It had been a long day, vaguely frightening at the end; and Adam would not tell her anything. She had been tired and apprehensive, yet now she felt secure, well loved, and happy. She would never be immune to this man. His strength, his strong, lean, muscular body, the intensity that showed in his face, in his movements, in his passions, would always move her as they had when she first met him. Together they had been through danger, sorrow, parting, pain, and ecstasy; every corner of their lives had been shattered at one time or another, yet Adam, the man, had never changed. They were as they had been from the first, and she loved him with all her soul.

They arrived by coach at Whitney's Hotel late the following afternoon. As they entered the lobby, Tom Pierson leaped up from a chair and ran forward, embracing Adam and pounding him on the back at the same time. "My *God,* it's good to see you again."

Adam, laughing, drew back and looked at his old friend, at the mild blue eyes which had grown colder with the years, at the scarred face which yet managed to be genial, at his wildly waving sandy hair, at the shoulder slanting toward his misshapen left arm. Tom had changed subtly since Adam had last seen him in the fall of 1864. He seemed less indrawn, more sure of himself than Adam had ever known him. There was even a perkiness about his beautifully tailored suit, as though its elegant pastels were an invitation for everyone to inspect its wearer.

"How long have you been here?" Adam asked, but he received no answer, for Tom's attention was caught by Dulcie and the baby.

Adam left them in order to talk to the desk clerk about their suite and the whereabouts of James and

Patricia Moran, Dulcie's parents, who were expected from New York City, where they had lived during the War. He encountered the same resistance he had at the dock. The clerk knew nothing; he would arrange to know something for a fee. Adam's face hardened into authoritative lines, his piratical black mustache accentuating the set of his mouth. Adam Tremain was unaccustomed to having his orders ignored. "I have a suite reserved for myself, my wife, my child, and my staff. I will be taken to it within the next ten minutes, or you, sir, will have a hotel filled with no one. I will personally see to its emptying." With a final scowl at the indignant clerk, he turned, pleased with himself and grinning as he returned to Dulcie and Tom.

"Well now," Tom said merrily, "what have you been up to? I'd know that ornery look anywhere. If I didn't know better I'd say you just busted through a Federal blockade."

"I may have. Seems we have a hidden detractor who'd rather not have us in Washington. You wouldn't have heard anything to that effect, would you, Tom?"

"Yes an' no. I heard talk about you an' Mr. Moran, but not a hint about who's behind it. I wouldn't be surprised if you an' I are gonna want t'look into it." Tom nudged Adam and glanced behind him.

Dulcie let out a squeal of delight as she and the baby were swallowed in Jem Moran's embrace. More greetings were exchanged, with Tom meticulously monitoring his language in deference to Patricia. Every inch a Southern lady, Patricia's perpetual look of little-girl helplessness covered an iron will and a whitleather constitution.

Jem, stocky, his red hair now muted by a plentiful supply of gray, wrung his son-in-law's hand. "This rebellion's changed everything. Have you noticed, Adam? Folks aren't the same at all. A man can't get a cab, can't get his baggage loaded, can't get a seat in a restaurant without putting something in somebody's hand."

"I've run into that," Adam admitted.

"Ever since we got here, I've felt like somebody's layin' for me."

Adam's glance caught Tom's. Patricia said, "Jem dahlin', youah not used to this crass commercialism. It's the Nawthun influence. Southun men ah so much moah polished in theah dealin's. You'll see when we get back home to Jawjuh."

Jem swung his head in a stubborn negative. "This whole place is runnin' on money. I can smell it, I can feel it. There's renderin' to Caesar on every corner, and a man better watch he gets the right Caesar or he's in trouble."

Tom interrupted smoothly as Patricia was about to disagree again. "You're right, Jem. Everything's for sale in Washington City. Land, precious stones, preferments, pardons, honor—even souls have got their price. And here at Whitney's Hotel, there's more damn, uh, more blessed talk floats around, and I'll give a dollar for every truthful word." He turned to Adam. "One thing's sure, Adam. We'd better get our pardons and get out as fast as we can."

"Why?" Jem asked, alert to the possibility that someone besides himself was being balked.

"You been here a while now, Jem, you ought to noticed there's hardly a body in Washington that ain't after the President's hide. Why, they're callin' Andy Johnson everything from a drunk to a loony. They just about got him finished now. He can't get anything passed in Congress, nor get anything stopped. 'Bout the only thing they haven't been able to touch are the pardons, an' they're workin' on that next."

"It's that bad?" Adam, looking to Jem for verification, saw unusual consternation on the older man's face.

"Pretty close to that, Adam," Tom answered. "The Radicals thought they had a real fire-breathin' Dixie hater when he first took over for Lincoln. You know, he was yellin' how he was gonna hang all the Southerners responsible for the War. Well, it seems like we all read Andy Johnson wrong, 'specially the Radical Republicans."

"Who are the Radicals, Tom?" asked Dulcie.

"As a political party they're powerful. And dangerous," Tom said. "They've got more fanatics and abolitionists in their ranks than you can count. They tried to keep Lincoln from the nomination in 1864. And now we've got a maverick Democrat in the Presidential seat, they're tryin' t'run the country over his head. They hate the South. In their eyes the War was all the South's fault, and they're tryin' to make sure we never get it back again. That's what I mean about the pardons, Adam.

"But Andy Johnson's not runnin' in their tracks," he went on. "Johnson's first love is the Constitution o' the United States, and he'll uphold that as he sees it no matter what the parties want. Now you know damned —sorry, ma'am—you know well's I do that no damn . . . politician is gonna take kindly to somethin' like the country comin' before his party and his pocketbook. This town is no place to be if you're Andy Johnson or if you're Southern."

"I'd better wire Ben West and tell him not to put off getting his pardon any longer than he must," Adam said. "I can't have my best friend and business partner a man without a country."

Jem said, "Adam—and Tom—if you don't mind a little unasked-for advice, there are ways of gettin' around this problem of pardons. In fact, I used it myself only a few days back. I'm expectin' my own pardon, and my Mossrose land back, any time soon."

"How is that, sir?" asked Adam.

"Whah, Jem, you nevah tol' me anythin' about youah pahdon—"

"I'm tellin' you now, Patsy," James Moran said testily. "I get around when I'm in a city, see, and I sit in the taverns and the bars an' listen to the talk in all the hotels. The best place I've found for information—"

He leaned forward, touching Adam's lapel confidentially. "—is Sweeney's Tavern, next to Saunderson's Hotel. I've heard a lot about President Johnson, and what Tom says is right. The Radicals are out to steal our lands. But I found out about pardon brokers."

Pardon brokers, said Jem, were influence peddlers who could obtain a pardon for any Southern gentleman more quickly than he could get it for himself. The era Jem had known was gone. In this new era, the pardon broker sounded to him like an answer to prayer.

"So I visited a Mrs. L. L. Cobb," he explained. "She has an excellent reputation for results, boys; you'd do well to consider her. She's a hardheaded businesswoman, but not ugly, if you follow me. I thought her price was a mite steep, but gettin' Mossrose back is worth anything I'd have to pay—"

"And how much was her price?" Patricia asked frigidly.

"Five hundred dollars—but I only paid her fifty, on account. It's for Mossrose, Patsy—our Mossrose!"

Patricia smiled, seeing on Jem's earnest red face all the things he felt about the plantation in Georgia they had left early in the War. Regaining Mossrose was everything to him. Mossrose represented the sum of Jem Moran's being, the accomplishment of his life. He had brought it back from a played-out tract of red clay to a flourishing plantation, and no damned Yankee War was going to take it from him. It was his, was his daughter Dulcie's inheritance, and Dulcie's son Beau's.

"Ah'm suah that's a very fayah price," Patricia agreed.

"And she's to let me know on Friday. Now how's that for quick work?"

As Adam and Tom seemed to agree with him, he gave them particulars about getting in touch with Mrs. Cobb. But there was more that he did not tell them.

He had been feeling pleased the day he left Mrs. Cobb's office-sitting room. He was even smiling to himself as her butler showed him out through the parlor.

"Good day, Moran," said a deeply cultured Southern voice from the depths of a leather wing chair.

Jem swung around toward the voice. His smile froze as he gazed at the dark, lean features of Edmund Revanche. Quickly his face reddened with anger as he recalled the heartache this man had caused his daughter. He nodded curtly, muttering, "Revanche," then hurried on.

Without apparent haste, Edmund caught up with him at the door. "You have chosen well in a pardon broker," he said judiciously.

Jem didn't answer, but nearly catapulted himself into the street. Anxiously he looked up and down for a cab.

Edmund smiled. "Let me take you to your hotel, Mr. Moran. After all, we are two grown men, perhaps not friends, but surely not childish oafs who must vent their spleen at each other publicly."

Nearly rigid with dislike, and angry at having his manners questioned, Jem thanked him and entered Revanche's carriage. Edmund directed his driver to the Whitney.

"How do you know where I'm staying?" Jem asked, then his eyes widened. "Why were you at Mrs. Cobb's? Were you waiting for me?"

"In a manner of speaking. I had business with Mr. Cobb, and was informed you were seeing his very talented wife." Edmund kept his eyes on the road. "As an old friend I thought I'd wait to greet you. I've heard you've been having some trouble since your arrival."

"Have you now?"

Edmund laughed softly. "Surely you haven't forgotten my line of business during the War? I still hear things that others might not."

"I imagine you do," said Jem sourly. "Like how to take a man's property away from him." It was one of Jem's fears, now that the War was over, that someone already had taken, or would take, his beloved plantation before he could return to restore it to its former bloom himself.

Edmund answered, "Occasionally, Moran, though that is not my main concern. As I told your daughter a few years ago, my main interest is and always has been the well-being of the South. Do we not at least share that interest, Moran? White supremacy?"

Jem grumbled an unintelligible sentence into his coat collar.

"I thought we did," Revanche said confidently, then he looked seriously at Jem. "However, I wonder what your son-in-law will think. How will you keep that headstrong reformer under control?"

Jem remained silent. Seeing Edmund Revanche was disturbance enough, but the questions he raised about Adam were as bad. Jem did not know how Adam would view the new situation in the South. Nor did Jem know how he was going to live with the ideas his son-in-law lived and breathed and fought for with his very soul. Jem felt only relief when the carriage mercifully stopped in front of Whitney's before he had to think further along these lines.

Edmund graciously offered him any assistance he might require, and bade him good day. Jem stopped off at the Whitney's bar and had several bourbons and branch water before he felt prepared to return to his rooms to consider what the presence of Adam Tremain in his life was going to mean.

For the first time, Jem connected his difficulties in Washington with his son-in-law.

Adam Tremain, a New Orleans-born Southerner, had distinguished himself in the hearts and minds of Southerners by running the Federal blockade throughout the War with audacious recklessness. He had also made innumerable enemies. To the Negroes he was widely known as the Black Swan, a man who would come in the dead of night to transport them away to freedom. To whites he was Captain Tremain, the daring blockade captain. To Southerners he was supplier of needed munitions and medicines. To Northerners he was abolitionist. To those who knew something of all his reputations he was the most hated man alive.

One of those men Jem knew to be Edmund Revanche.

The following morning Adam and Tom went to the stables next door to Whitney's, hired two horses, and rode to the Capitol.

"First thing we got to do is mosey round to the dram shops and see the lay of the land," Tom said.

As Tom talked, Adam was looking with dismay around him. "This city still looks as if it's dug in for battle." Washington bore the scars of war. Troops still marched through the streets before being mustered out. Cannon and drays and other war equipment were still in evidence. "You'd think they'd want to clear this away as quickly as possible."

Tom laughed. "Boy, you been holed up in Nassau too long. Nobody wants this war forgotten. It's the best damned political tool ever to come down a pike. Breeds hate like a swamp breeds mosquitoes, an' hate used proper is money in certain banks. Rumor, hate, fear, that's the coin of the day, Adam. There's a whole passel o' bigmouths sayin' the President is just waitin' for the right time t'arrest all the Radical leaders. And then he's goin' t'call a new Congress of Southerners and Copperheads."

"My God, what for?" Adam laughed.

So did Tom as he added, "It's not so funny when you figger these men are playin' for keeps. 'Course, the mule kick in all this is that after all this happens, then ol' Thad Stevens an' his cronies are supposed to set up a rival Congress o' the West, an' boom! Another Civil War."

Adam shook his head disbelievingly. "Looks like a man had better be careful choosing friends here."

"Damn right. These boys will steal your pants an' then point out your bare ass. If it's money or a deal,

they'll eat out o' your hand, but if you're talkin' Reconstruction—popular word hereabouts—you better make
sure you know who you're talkin' to an' what game he's
playin' in."

Adam looked over at the Capitol. On the lawn there
were great canvas tents. They covered enormous columns that were to form the portico when they were
finished. For now, it was a workshop of canvas with
men laboring industriously to finish the columns under
the tents. Though Washington was a city bright with
excitement and activity, Adam was filled with a cold
distaste for it. He wanted only to complete his business
and leave immediately.

Adam and Tom went to the dram shop in the south
wing, on the Representatives' side. It was the hub of
the House. Located on the main floor, it was busy from
early morning on. The "boys" were lined up at the bar,
their feet polishing the smooth-worn brass rail. Tom,
smiling and ready for business, sidled up to the bar between two men. With relish he chewed on his wad of
tobacco, then spat ferociously into the spittoon with a
resounding ping. Grinning now, he said, "Mornin',
boys, did I ever tell you the story 'bout a man I knew
in Loosiana could spit a wadda 'tabacca twenty feet an'
hit a squirrel in the eye? Well, this fella, Welkins by
name—"

For a few minutes Adam stood in quiet awe as Tom
wove his stories, every now and then pausing to greet a
newcomer and ask a casual question which, unknown
to the man who answered, supplied information he
sought. After a while Adam winked at Tom and moved
down the bar to try his own hand at information gathering. Washington, he realized, wasn't merely a city. It
was a state of being, a whole way of life. These men
played games, very deadly games that decided the fates
of millions of people who never even knew the games
had been played.

Adam also quickly realized that no treaty, no finely
drafted piece of paper, had ended the War Between the

States. The War still flourished, but its nature had changed. The war this new breed of politician fought was one of subterfuge, of mind pitted against mind.

By the time Adam and Tom met for lunch in the Senate dining room, he knew that his reputation as the Black Swan would hold him in good stead—if he was careful. It had been driven home to him that he was regarded as a man who could be used by certain interests. Adam hadn't needed to be told that anyone who could be used could also be a user, nor that, like it or not, he was already involved in the power struggle that would take place, with the South itself as the prize.

The two men settled back after a lunch featuring Baltimore oysters, enjoying a snifter of brandy and a cigar.

"I feel like I put in a full day's work," Tom groaned. "Can't say I'll be sorry to see the last of this place." He fell pensive.

"What's eating you, Tom? You've got something more than politicians' talk on your mind."

"You know me too well. I always did say you poked in where you shouldn't, didn't I?"

"I never learned. Tell me what you're thinking of."

"Not sure I can say. Mebbe I lived too long lookin' over my shoulder, Adam. I jes' got that feelin' I'm bein' observed, if you know what I mean. Somethin' ain't settin' right here."

Adam nodded agreement.

"I heard a piece o' news t'day . . . been wonderin' if I should do somethin' about it or forget I ever heard it."

"Which is?"

"Jubal Lerner. Jubal Lerner's right here in Washington runnin' a house down in the district for some bigwig I can't get a handle on. Son of a bitch. That's the first I heard of him since Angela run off with him. I was thinkin' . . . wonderin'. . . ."

Adam was silent for a moment, reflecting on the torment Angela, Tom's daughter, had caused his friend.

Finally, he asked, "If Angela is one of the women in his house?"

"Holy Jesus, Adam, I know I said I didn't give a rat's ass what happened to that little girl o' mine when she run off, but seems like I do. Only thing is—I don't know if I could take it if she's there. Can't stand not knowin' either."

"When you go, I want to come with you, Tom." Every time Adam thought of Angela he still saw a sunny little golden-haired girl he used to take for rides on her pony, or in his bugboat. They were all to blame for what happened to Angela; they had all acted as if she were white and everything open to them would be open to her. Then Angela had found out hard and fast that her mother's Negro blood made her a "nigger" too.

Tom shook his head. "You never did blame her for what happened, did you? Damn, I wish I could see it that way. The things that girl didn't do."

"She did do it all, and threw it right in our faces too, but it doesn't change anything. She's still Angela, still your daughter, and we all still love her. Sometime we've got to make peace with ourselves, and with her. The sooner the better."

"If we can find her," Tom growled.

CHAPTER FOUR

The following day Adam checked the status of his application for pardon. All Southerners owning property or having wealth in excess of $20,000 were required to apply for a presidential pardon requesting that any lands they had owned before the War be returned to them, and justifying their right to regain their citizenship and its privileges. This sometimes was complicated and frustrating, as many lands had been confiscated and later sold; other properties had been turned over to the Freedmen's Bureau and had been leased to Negroes for crops.

Adam went to the Attorney General's office and spoke to the pardon clerk there. The clerk, one of the men Adam had met the day before and spent the evening wining and dining, smiled as Adam entered. "Your application is on its way, Captain Tremain. I hope you haven't too long to wait." He indicated that there might be more hands to be dealt with. "We seem to be moving along rather quickly this morning, one hopes."

Adam clapped the man's shoulder, saying low that there were tickets for him at the box office of the Canterbury Theater and an envelope in the man's mail slot. Then he went to the anteroom of the President's office to wait with two dozen other men.

Two days Adam sat in the waiting room from nine in the morning until the President saw the last person at three in the afternoon. It was a short period of time compared to what some had had to wait, including Jem Moran, whose pardon had still not been granted.

Jem had finally decided that Mrs. Cobb was not for him and had filed another petition. Now he waited

along with Adam and Tom. Washington was aflutter
with gossip about Mrs. Cobb, which did not ease Jem's
discomfort. It was rumored that Mrs. Cobb, whose
reputation for prompt action on pardons was well
known, had influence of a sort that no woman should
have with the President, and in the heated anti-Johnson
atmosphere the affairs of Mrs. Cobb were quickly becoming the scandal of the year.

When Adam was finally ushered into the President's
office, he saw a rather sad, dignified gentleman. After
hearing tales of the speechifying drunk in the White
House, Adam was surprised.

President Johnson sat erect, his stockiness giving the
impression of a powerful man. Yet Adam's gaze was
drawn to the President's small, deceptively soft-looking
hands—nothing else about the man appeared soft or
vulnerable. Sensitive, yes; dignified, even punctilious,
dressed in perfectly cut dark broadcloth, here was no
backwoods tailor confounded at being suddenly ele-
vated to the highest position in the nation. Andrew
Johnson knew exactly what he was about.

The President listened but offered no comment on
Adam's opinions. His silence, his amiable demeanor
left it too easy for a man to assume Johnson agreed
with a policy about which he had actually stated nothing.

And this, thought Adam, is why the Radicals are
trying to destroy him.

"Yours is an unusual case, Captain Tremain. I don't
often receive petitions from men whose record is so
clearly a service to both sides. Your allegiance, however, seems to have been with the Confederacy."

"No, Mr. President, my allegiance was and is with
the South."

"Not with the United States of America?"

Adam smiled slightly. "As I see it, Mr. President,
the South *is* the United States of America, or at least
a sizable part of it. Our best men have dedicated their
lives to forming this nation. We haven't stopped now.

Most of us didn't stop during the . . . rebellion. There were those caught up in a fever of war and revolt, but most men, I think, fought honorably for what they believed was right."

The President's small clasped hands moved impatiently on his desk. "Slavery? Do you feel that slavery should have been continued as a necessity to the well-being of the South?"

"I have never believed in slavery, Mr. President. But neither do I believe in methods of abolishment that were designed to disrupt and destroy. Slavery could have been ended without waging a costly civil war."

President Johnson's eyes met Adam's, but he said nothing. Adam's interview was over. He left unsatisfied as to whether his mother's property in Smithville, North Carolina, would be returned to him; but more important, whether all his citizenship privileges would be restored, including the right to hold office and to vote.

As Adam left, the doorkeeper, his salver piled high with calling cards, opened the door wide. "Single file now," he called out in vain, as several dozen people elbowed and shoved to reach the President's desk. Adam, amazed, watched the noisy throng of buck-skinned woodsmen, uniformed ex-soldiers, suavely dressed politicians, and women clad in everything from silks to patched cottons.

Thoughtful, he joined Tom and Jem.

They returned to the hotel together. That evening, they were all to attend a ball. As Dulcie and Patricia chattered excitedly about it, Tom got up to leave. "Evenin', folks," he said loudly.

Adam grinned and winked at him. "See you down in the lobby in about an hour, Tom."

"Could be," Tom said, "but I got a little business to tend to first. I'll jes' catch up to you all later at the dinner, or at the ball."

Adam released himself from Dulcie and walked over to Tom. He spoke in a low voice. "I don't want you going down to Murder Bay alone, Tom. We agreed I'd go with you to look for Jubal."

"We didn't agree on anything. You told me what we was goin' to do. I never said a word. You and President Johnson got the same problem. You think you know what's goin' on, but you don't. I'm goin' alone. Angela's my daughter, and if she's there with that no-good black bastard, I'll take care of it my own way. See you later, Adam."

Adam growled, "Tom, you bullheaded son of a bitch, you'll get your skull bashed in. Why in the hell did you wait until now to tell me you're going there tonight?"

Tom grinned. " 'Cause I knew you couldn't do a damn thing to stop me now."

Shortly before dark, Tom strolled down Tenth Street, passing a group of young men of the Sons of Temperance. Politely Tom doffed his hat. "It's a blessed mission you're after," he said in a deeply serious voice.

A heavyset man near the front of the group nodded agreement. "It is indeed, sir, and if there were more souls such as yourself around, we'd have Demon Rum on the run." He smiled happily at his turn of phrase, looking to his compatriots for appreciation.

"I'd surely like to hear a verse or two of my favorite song."

"I know just the one you have in mind, sir," the man said, pleased. " 'Father's a Drunkard and Mother Is Dead.' "

"You are right. Would I be wrong in thinking you boys know that one?"

The man turned to his fellows. They grouped more tightly together and raised their voices in ragged harmony.

"I thank you, boys, that was mighty touching, mighty touching indeed," Tom said as they finished, and tipped his hat once again. He moved down the street chuckling to himself. Temperance people. They were all

over this city, a whole passel of fools who didn't know
what else to do with themselves. But they were good
for a minute's entertainment now and then. Father's
a Drunkard and Mother Is Dead. He laughed to himself,
then sobered as he thought of Angela. Her father was
no drunkard, but he sure as hell hadn't been there for
her, and her mother was dead. Then he banished those
thoughts as well. What had happened to Angela was
nobody's fault, and everyone's. He wasn't taking too
much of that burden on himself. He was looking for
her, that was enough.

To help push away the disturbing thoughts and pass
the time, he hailed a cab, directing the driver to take
him to Robert Teel's Faro Hall, near the National
Hotel.

Tom played faro until nearly ten o'clock, then he left
and headed for Fifteenth Street.

Between the canal and Ohio Avenue on both sides
of Fifteenth Street was Murder Bay, a settlement of
shanties and shacks and a few more substantial buildings, inhabited mainly by contraband Negroes who had
come to Washington in droves and then had nothing to
do and no money. They had congregated in Murder
Bay, attracting a retinue of thieves and criminals.

Tom walked past one sordid, dingy saloon and dram
shop after another. Streets with ominous names like
Hell's Bottom and Louse Alley were crowded with
humanity. Drunken soldiers, deserters from both armies, displaced blacks, sharpers out looking for a mark,
all moved along the darkened, mud-laden streets. Tom,
accustomed to taking care of himself in the roughest
company, shoved his way along the street.

Without needing to give it thought, he turned and
swung at a man who was nimbly reaching for his
pocket. The man sprawled in the muck. Not looking
back, Tom hurried on, his eyes hard and wary, meeting
the bitter, crafty glances of the men and women he
passed without fear or hesitation. A woman came up

to him boldly, her breasts outthrust as she rubbed
against him. "Buy me a drink, mister," she purred.

Tom shoved her aside. "Not tonight, sister. Beat it,
I got business with a man."

Undaunted, the woman came at him again. "Business with a man ain't as much fun as I can make it for
you, honey."

"You know Jubal Lerner?" he asked suddenly and
harshly.

"Mebbe I do, mebbe I don't."

Tom's fingers bit into her flesh. "Where do I find
him?"

"What d'you want him for?"

"He got a woman with him?"

The woman smiled, thinking she now understood
Tom's business. "I'm better than Jubal's ol' bitch. What
you want her for? Tell you what, make you a bargain
price. What d'you say?"

Tom reached into his pocket and pulled out a gold
piece. "I say you tell me where I find Jubal, and you
an' I got a bargain."

The woman shrugged, her eyes on the gold. "They
say he's in Five Gun Battery. Don't know no more
about him."

"That's enough," Tom said, and tossed the gold
piece into the air. He caught it, and looked at the
woman.

She sighed. "My place is up the street a ways."

He put the gold piece in her hand. They walked a
way together, then the woman turned in at a leaning
shanty. "Well?" she asked as Tom didn't follow. "Ain't
you comin'?"

Tom touched his hat, shook his head, and walked on.
Again, he was disturbed by thoughts of Angela. The
woman was not much older than Angela would be, he
guessed, though it was hard to tell, for she looked to be
as old as he was. He was sorely tempted to turn back
and never go near the row of houses called Five Gun

Battery. He wasn't sure he could bear seeing Angela if she had fared as poorly as the woman he had just left standing outside her shanty. He couldn't picture his beautiful fair-haired daughter walking the streets asking a man if he'd buy her a drink and meaning would he buy her body. He kept seeing his beloved Ullah's face on Angela. Ullah . . . oh, God, what would she do if she knew what had happened to her daughter.

Tom's pace was slower now, his steps more reluctant as he neared Fourteenth Street. He walked along Ohio Avenue, his eyes seeing nothing, his mind showing him pictures of horror. Now he was afraid, not of the filth or the depravity or the men who milled in the street, but of what he would find in the row of brick houses in the next block. As he neared Fifteenth Street, he saw the buildings. He stopped four streetwalkers before he learned in which of the rows of houses he'd likely find Jubal and his woman.

Tom mounted the steps and entered, wondering suddenly if he could recall what Jubal looked like. He'd only seen him once, the day Angela had run off with Lerner, and he was in such a rage then that he'd hardly looked at the man. Tom shoved his way into a room crowded with men and women, mostly black. It was smoky, filled with loud, drunken talk and the reek of unwashed flesh. At every table a game was being played: faro, three-card monte, the shell game, roulette, poker. Tilted back on his chair in a far corner was Jubal Lerner.

Tom stopped dead still. It seemed like yesterday that this man had sat on the sofa in Zoe Tremain's house, waiting to take his daughter away from him. He had screamed at him that day, called him a black nigger buck, and then had allowed his only daughter to walk out the door with him never to return. Once more Tom almost turned away, wanting to flee to the clean safety of his hotel and his ignorance about Angela. Gritting his teeth and setting his jaw hard, Tom approached the table where Jubal was sweeping in a meager pot.

In his deep rasping voice Tom said, "Get up, Lerner. I want to talk with you."

Jubal Lerner, a cigar clamped tightly between his teeth, smiled broadly. His eyes were hard and black and cruel. "I'm busy. You want to play, set down. You want to talk, go fuck yourself."

Infuriated, Tom smiled coldly. Easily and slowly he uncovered a small derringer in the palm of his hand. "I said I want to talk. You don't want to talk to me, then damned if you ever talk to anybody again. You get my meaning, boy?"

Jubal smiled at the other men at the table. "Seem like I got a little business with this man. Y'all keep my seat warm. I'll be back. Gonna take a little bit more o' your money yet tonight." He smiled grandly, bowing and walking over toward Tom. "Who the hell are you, man? I don't know you from some *other* piece o' shit."

"You got a woman with you?"

Jubal looked more closely at him. "What you want to know for? You don't need no gun if all you wants is tail."

"I want to see the woman."

"She's workin'."

"I don't give a damn what she's doin'. I want to see her. Now." Tom nudged close to him, the gun still concealed, but known to Jubal.

Jubal shook his head, but led him toward the staircase. "Up there. Second floor."

"Come on. You show me, and make damn sure you show me the right woman, or by God we're gonna open every fuckin' door in this house."

"Who are you? What you want with me? I don't know you."

"You do now," Tom snapped.

Jubal stopped at a door. "She's workin'," he repeated, pleading.

"Open it!"

Jubal opened the door. The room was pitch black. "Light the lamp," Tom snapped.

A shout of enraged protest came from the bed. Jubal struck a match. A large black man, naked and angry, sat up in the bed, his hand clenching a knife. Beside him, her leg still under his, was a woman. She was about twenty, still shapely, and blacker than Jubal. Tom let out a gust of trapped air.

The woman looked questioningly at Jubal. She seemed calm and unafraid. "Whut you doin' bustin' in like that, Jubal? He paid."

Jubal cocked his head at Tom. "He wanted to see you, and he's got a talkin' piece."

The girl smiled. She arched her back, moving her body provocatively. "Well, you seen. You like?"

"You his only woman?"

The girl's face twisted in anger. "I ain't good enuf fo' you! Pigs is too good fo' you, you beat up ol' piece o' shit! Git outta heah afore I cut up the rest o' yo' face fo' you!" She threw a metal-based lamp at him. Tom deflected it with his forearm. The girl leaped forward, grabbing the knife from her bedmate. Tom jumped back as she hurled herself at him. Teeth bared, her eyes wild with rage, she came at him again.

Tom bared the gun and pointed it at her.

She screamed her laughter. "That doan scare me!" She dived at him, knife outthrust. Tom drew his arm back and hit her backhand, the gun adding weight to his fist. The woman grunted and fell against the wall. Jubal and the naked man leaped on Tom, pummeling him. They beat him semiconscious, and Tom saw only flashes of faces and fists mixed in with bright explosions of red and pain within his head and body. Loud noises of men screaming in anger and anguish thundered in his head.

When he came to in the wet filth of the alley behind Five Gun Battery, he was being hauled to his feet by a rumpled, bruised, and hard-breathing Adam Tremain. "How'd you fin' me?" he murmured through split lips.

"It wasn't easy. Can you walk, Tom? Jubal and com-

pany have a few aches and pains at the moment, but
it won't take long before their friends are after us."

"Don't know," Tom said weakly. He remembered
being thrown down the stairs and little else. His coat
was gone, and of course, every penny he'd had on him.
His watch and gun were gone as well. He hurt all over
and his face was a mass of blood. His nose was broken
again.

"She's not there, Adam," he said, ridiculously happy.

Adam laughed softly. "I know, Tom. I didn't think
you'd find her in a place like that. Angela's got too
much of her mama in her to do that to herself." He
placed Tom's arm over his shoulder and took his
weight. "If that damned little scamp I paid to hold the
horse hasn't sold the beast, we'll be all right."

"Well, you can't trust a pickaninny, Adam. Not
hereabouts."

"I damned well better be able to. The little Turk
wants a ride on my ship, and gold as well."

Tom, almost giddy with relief over Angela, laughed
too. "Oh well, if it's the Black Swan himself rescuin'
me, I guess we could trust the devil to hold the horse."

It wasn't until they had returned to the hotel, and
he had made certain Tom was all right, that Adam
allowed himself to think about the more disturbing
aspect of the evening.

As Adam had tried to revive Tom in the alley, Jubal
Lerner and a white man who had come in at the end of
the fight had gotten into an argument. In the beginning
Jubal had defended himself boldly, but had ended
pleading with the man not to report to Mr. Revanche
what had taken place in his house that night.

Edmund Revanche. In Washington. It made Adam's
many petty annoyances with port officials and clerks
take on a different character. And it gave him the cold,
wary feeling he had had during the War. He knew
Edmund Revanche well; primary to the man's nature
was an economy of motion. Edmund did not harass, he

did not intimidate aimlessly; everything the man did was done with thought and purpose.

His concern turned immediately to Dulcie and Beau. He'd leave Washington by the end of the month, with or without his pardon.

CHAPTER FIVE

Leroy Biggs sat morosely on what remained of the sofa in his front parlor. He had returned home to Georgia to find that his fields lay fallow, grown thick with scrub and grass, or were burned, ruined by wide scars of permanently scorched earth, the soil hard-packed and unyielding. His wife and daughter were dead, and his son was lost.

He had gone to war brash and confident. He had fought with a bravado and competence that did credit to the Confederacy. And he had made his long trek home expecting to begin again. But his homecoming had held nothing in it of hope. He had found reasons to hate, but none that made him want to go on, none to make him want to rebuild and start over.

He found a galling humiliation that black soldiers who still paraded the streets enjoyed pressing upon him publicly. He found antagonisms of Northerners who flocked South to pick at the carcass of the defeated land. He found in those Northerners a need to punish the South. He found reasons to make him feel mean and resentful, but none that returned to him the sense of pride he had known before the War. Wherever he looked, whatever he heard and thought, gave him a sense of desolation and abandonment. What there was left of his pride turned inward, a secret thing to be expressed by sullen resentment.

Mostly his thoughts turned to the past, a long past that contained the promise of his young manhood, the enticing anticipation of love and success. Mostly his thoughts were of things as they might have been if the Yankees hadn't won the War. He thought of himself able to outrun, outride, outwrestle every other young man in the County. He thought of himself claiming for his queen of the tournament the most beautiful girl.

Often his fantasies placed Dulcie Moran at his side. Again and again he visualized her glowing beauty and vitality, and the joyous smile that warmed her lovely amber eyes. And often it was her image that forced him from his pleasant daydreams back into the harshness of reality. She had refused him. She had been the first to make him doubt his own superiority, and now the damnyankees had taken away even the illusion of it.

He ran his hand across the upholstery, feeling the rough edges where it had been slashed by bayonets and dirtied by Yankee bummers who had camped in his home. His eyes moved across the ugly burn marks on the fine hardwood floor that had once shone golden and rich with wax. The windows, those that were not broken, were clotted with filth and lined with rivulets left by the most recent rain.

Lyman Matthews came shuffling down the stairs. He lived with Leroy now, since his own house and land had been confiscated because he refused to take the Iron Clad Oath. "They here yet, Leroy?"

Leroy shook his head. "Won't be long, though. You all packed?"

"Yeah, my Sunday best. Mighty sorry best."

Leroy said nothing, thinking of his own Sunday best. The blue outfit thin at the seat, with a tear down the leg. A mustard frock coat that he would never have worn with those trousers in days past. He would look like a country bumpkin. Suddenly he sat up straight, his face contorting with frustration.

"Shit, Lyman! I'm so God-damned sick o' bein' low man on the totem, I could break every damnyankee head person'ly."

Lyman laughed bitterly. "Y'all git your chance. Ain't that why we're goin' to Pulaski?"

"Damn right it is! I'm goin' t'relish fightin' again. Damn if this war is over yet, we'll make those—" He stood up. "Billy Bob an' Todd are here. C'mon, no sense in them comin' in. Let's ride."

Leroy, Lyman, Billy Bob Acton, and Todd Saunders rode to Pulaski, Tennessee, stopping only to rest their horses, to eat and sleep. With each mile traveled, Leroy felt some of his self-respect returning. Finally he would be doing something. He was going to meet and join with other men who knew and understood the hideous vindictiveness of the North. It made him feel good to know that there were still people willing to fight for the values the South had been built upon.

When Pulaski was in view, he felt his heart ease. A feeling of purpose and importance made him square his tired shoulders and straighten a back that slumped.

Following the directions they had been given, the four men made their way to an isolated house on the outskirts of Pulaski. The house stood strange and eerie against the evening sky. Ragged edges of ripped-away walls, damaged by a cyclone, were silhouetted stark and forbidding.

"Gawd," Billy Bob drawled. "What the hell we gittin' into, Leroy?"

Leroy assumed a bravery he didn't feel. "Think they can just meet anywhere? This is a perfect place. We're goin' t'have t'find ourselves one like it when we get home."

Todd Saunders coughed, spewing spittle. "They don't call it a den for no reason." He spurred his horse. "C'mon, get it over with."

Leroy urged his horse forward, retaking the lead from Todd.

They were within two hundred yards of the house when four hooded, white-robed figures emerged from the darkness of the trees.

A hollow voice commanded, "Dismount."

A hooded figure escorted each man on foot to the house. Billy Bob, who had lost a leg in the War, maneuvered his crutches over the uneven ground. Suddenly, another hooded man stood before them. "Who goes there?"

Leroy, Lyman, Todd, and Billy Bob stammered they were candidates, and begged entry.

The white-hooded Lictor faced them, his eyes unreadable behind the dark-trimmed slits. He raised his hand to his mouth and emitted a loud, piercing whistle.

Instantly, the Night Hawk emerged from some hiding place in the gloom. He blindfolded the four men and led them into the den.

There, the Grand Turk asked them a series of test questions. Leroy, with the others paraphrasing what he said, told of his feelings about the South, the inequity and injustice of placing the freed Negro over the white. He was feverishly pasionate about the behavior of the black and the Yankee toward Southern women.

The Grand Turk expressed his approval of every satisfactory response, and as a reward Leroy, Lyman, Todd, and Billy Bob were draped with the royal robe. After another series of questions and pleasing answers the regal crown was placed upon their heads. Around each of their waists was strapped the sacred sword belt.

The four blindfolded, honor-bedecked men stood proudly and blindly as they repeated the Ku Klux Oath of Obligation.

"I, Leroy Biggs, before the immaculate Judge of Heaven and Earth, and upon the Holy Evangelists of Almighty God, do, of my own free will and accord, subscribe to the following sacredly binding obligation:

"We are on the side of justice, humanity, and constitutional liberty, as bequeathed to us in its purity by our forefathers.

"We oppose and reject the principles of the Radical party.

"We pledge mutual aid to each other in sickness, distress, and pecuniary embarrassment.

"Female friends, widows, and their households shall ever be special objects of our regard and protection.

"Any member divulging, or causing to be divulged, any of the foregoing obligation, shall meet the fearful penalty and traitor's doom, which is Death! Death! Death!"

The men's voices grew in strength as they promised to abstain from alcoholic beverages so long as they remained active Klan members; never to reveal the signs, symbols, grip, or secrets of the order. They pledged never to reveal their membership in the Klan.

Once they were sworn in, the blindfolds were removed. Before them was a large mirror. All four faces registered shock and surprise. The mirror reflected them draped with robes that were donkey skins. Their crowns were fashioned from old torn hats bedecked with donkey ears. Their sword belt was a common saddle belt. Leroy's jaw jutted out. Here, of all places, he didn't expect to be mocked. He spun around and glared at the hooded men watching him. Then one by one they began to laugh, and the laughter was good humored. Some of them began to caper in boyish antics, and soon the tense seriousness in the room dissolved into horseplay and ribaldry.

The next several days were spent with more serious concerns. Leroy, Lyman, Todd, and Billy Bob would return to Chatham County and begin a den of the Klan there. As new members, they would be called Ghouls. The Grand Turk, a kind of master of ceremonies and their questioner of the night before, turned them over for indoctrination, to a man he called Radcliffe, not his real name. Radcliffe was a Grand Magi, the chief lieutenant to the Grand Cyclops.

Dressed in borrowed Klan robes, Leroy, Lyman, Todd, and Billy Bob watched silently as the Grand Magi sat erect and self-contained, his body covered from head to boots with impressive garb. On his head was a tall, pointed white hat with large red horns sticking out at either side. From the hat depended a mask of white hair with black-rimmed eyes and a long, pendulous purple tongue. His robe of calico was red, trimmed with white. On his left sleeve was a five-pointed star surmounted by a crescent moon.

Leroy felt a surge of kinship and pride when Radcliffe stood up. The Grand Magi rose gracefully to a broad-shouldered height over six feet. His voice was deep and cultured, with the softness of the South. "Good evenin', gentlemen. It's mah distinct privilege to have y'all here."

The men murmured responses.

The Grand Magi cleared his throat and drew a paper from under his robes. He paused, looking closely at each man present, then began to read. " 'We recognize our relation to the United States government, and the Union of the States thereunder. . . .' " He read to them again the Oath of Obligation they had taken, strongly emphasizing the inclusion of widows and orphans of Confederate soldiers. "Their men fought and laid down their lives for us," he added, his voice quivering with emotion. "No decent man is goin' to forget his compatriot died fightin' for him." He went on reading: the Klan supported and defended the constitutional laws; they would protect the people from invasion, from unlawful seizure, and from trials by other than their peers. "We are and shall remain in conformity with the laws of the land."

As he spoke, the Grand Magi paced the room, letting the men digest what he had read thus far. All of them looked puzzled, but none dared voice questions. None wanted to risk making a mistake, thereby placing his suitability as a Klansman in doubt.

Radcliffe waited until they became uncomfortable, then said, "Now, there are all kinds of invasions. Ah'd say the Freedmen's Bureau and its agents are an invadin' force. Any military govament comin' in to run the affairs of a sovereign state—what would a man call that but an invadin' force?"

Light dawned in Leroy's eyes. "Peers! We're the peers!"

The horned hat nodded. "Ah see you are a thinkin' man. And you can surely see the peers, in protectin' the weak and injured, must judge with hard and equal justice. An eye for an eye. Far's I know the Bible still reads the same. Yankees haven't rewritten that yet. The most impohtant thing for you to recall is that the Klan is an institution of Chivalry, Humanity, Mercy, and patriotism. We are the men who haven't given up. We are the men who still have the courage to say *we will not turn our land over to the infidel.*"

He returned to the tract in his hand. " 'This noble organization has been formed to regenerate our unfortunate country and to relieve the White Race from the humiliating condition to which it has lately been reduced in this Republic. Our main and fundamental objective is the *maintenance of the supremacy of the White Race* in this Republic. History and Physiology teach us that we belong to a race which Nature has endowed with an evident superiority over all other races, and that the Maker, in thus elevating us above, has intended to give us over inferior races a dominion from which no human laws can permanently derogate!' Now that, gentlemen, should be your guidin' principle. We are pledged to be the guardians of justice, and our Maker will be our guide."

Leroy couldn't help laughing in his pleasure. He understood perfectly what was being said to him. Finally someone cared. Someone was speaking to the horror of the aftermath of war that ate at him. The Klan was offering a method to do, under a cloak of secrecy, what a Southern white man could no longer do lawfully. Finally someone was speaking and implementing a kind of justice Leroy knew and understood, and with it would be returned his sense of pride, his cloak of authority.

The Grand Magi sat down again, relaxed, pleased with the excitement he sensed in the initiates. "Now you know and Ah know that the Radicals have got control of the United States govament, and are doin' a lot of

things that don't set too well with us. There are out-
rages bein' perpetrated right now, and we don't have
to tolerate them, boys. That's why we have the Klan.
And there are more of us than a man could count if he
was to sit and figure all day and all night. We are
everywhere, in every town, every plantation, every
street, and every buildin'. We are the Invisible Empiah.
A fittin' name, as y'all will soon see. The Ku Klux
is named for the Greek word *kuklos,* meanin' a band
or circle. And that's what we are. We are invisible, and
we are as unbreakable as a circle. No one knows us,
no one sees us in our true identity. We are the spirit
of righteousness . . . of the South. Ah'll tell you how
secret we are. Even mah wife doesn't know Ah'm a
Klansman."

"That's 'cause youah invisible!" said Billy Bob, and
they laughed.

The horned hat and the matted white hair swiveled
to look hard at each one in turn. The swollen purple
tongue bobbed threateningly. "The secrecy of the Klan
is not somethin' for levity. Ah will not have. levity.
These are serious matters. Ah believe we'll ad-journ
until tomorrow. Y'all better have a serious talk among
yourselves. Ah'm not sure a mistake hasn't been made
in allowin' you boys to wear the robes of the Klan."
He stalked from the room.

"Shit!" Leroy exploded. "Why'd you have to go say
a fool thing like that? Look what you done!"

"You laughed! What'd you laugh foah if you thought
it was so fool? It ain't all mah fault, Leroy—Todd, tell
him it ain't."

Todd Saunders, the most cynical of the group, said
slowly, "He's puttin' on a big show. Radcliffe ain't
mad, he just talked his throat all dry. Most likely he's
out back swillin' down some good whisky."

"He ain't drinkin'," Billy Bob said earnestly. "A
man can't indulge an' be a membah."

Todd snorted. "Shee-it! You got to be the dumbest

thing still walkin'. Hey, Lyman, you gonna give up your bottle?"

"I'm gonna say I am." Lyman laughed. "But hell, a man can't get mean enough t'do justice without a little juice to spur him on, can he?"

Leroy stood up. "Look, this ain't gettin' us anywhere. No more jackass comments, Billy Bob, y'hear? I swear, I'll ram my fist down your throat up to my elbow if you open that mouth of yours again. We got our den ridin' on this. We got to get home an' start this thing rollin'. This is our way to pay back those sonofabitch Yankees for what they done."

The following evening the Grand Magi, in all his regalia, returned. The four men were properly somber and attentive. Billy Bob tendered his apology.

Radcliffe said, "Ah'm pleased to hear ya'll take this as seriously as Ah do. The Klan is only a few months old, but our members are very powahful in their desiah to help the South. We are on the side of justice, humanity, and Constitutional liberty. Not Radical Yankee justice, but true Constitutional justice that is fair to planters and farmers and workin' men.

"The South has lost a great deal because of this damnyankee War we fought so gallantly. Ah've got some money here." He pulled a wad from under his robes, and flipped the edges. "Confederate money, the currency of a sovereign nation, and it's not worth a God-damn. Ah can't buy bread with it, Ah can't buy ham or potatoes or lamp oil. And that's your money too. Now the Yankees say it's worthless. The currency of the Confederacy worthless! Ah'm not talkin' just to make you discontented, boys. Ah don't want to do that. What Ah want is for you to see the truth about what the Yankees did."

"They sure as hell did steal our slaves."

"I know a God-damned Southerner who did that," Leroy said viciously.

The Grand Magi paused, tempted to pursue what Leroy said. Finally he said, "Ah'd like to speak to you

after the meetin' about that matter. You may already
have a problem at home that demands the Klan's
attention."

"Sure, I'll talk. Be glad to, only he ain't from Chatham County. He . . . visited there once. For all I know
he's dead. But he sure as hell made enough dirty Yankee money stealin' other people's property."

"Ah would still like to discuss it with you. But now,
gentlemen, back to the matter at hand. The Yankees
stole our slaves. They took our darkies right out of our
fields, our kitchens, and our parlors. Those damned
Yankees said, 'Cuffee, you're free. Sambo, you don't
have to work. Liza, lay up that shuttle and fold your
hands.' They turned those niggers loose. But they didn't
turn them loose on Northern land. No, suh. They
turned them loose on us, encouragin' 'em to wander
around and steal. They left nobody on our great cotton
and rice plantations but the old, the sick, the infants,
and the dyin'! Now y'all know what one slave costs.
Throughout the South—now this is true—we lost between two and *four billion dollars* because the damnyankees freed our slaves!"

"God a'mighty," Todd breathed, making himself
cough. Regaining control, he went on, "Some astrono-
mer said there must be a billion stars in the sky. A man
can't count 'em. And you say we lost four times as
much money as there are stars. God damn those Yankee cowards! Somethin's not right when one man can
take that much away from another."

The masked, horned head nodded. "We had cotton
stored up, wharves full and warehouses bulgin' with it.
United States Treasury agents confiscated that cotton.
They stole it from us. By 1865 they had stolen thirty
million dollars' worth of Confederate cotton. We grew
that cotton, boys. Our sweat was in every fiber. We
owned it. Is it justice for the damnyankees to steal thirty
million dollars of another man's sweat and blood?"

The men muttered among themselves, but the Grand
Magi continued. "And now Congressmen refuse to

recognize Southern senators and representatives! In March, just last month, they passed a joint resolution that Congress has to readmit each state to the Union before they'll recognize us! Now, I ask you, can they have it both ways? *They say there was no sovereign Confederacy.* They say we were *states in rebellion.* If we're states, where are our constitutional rights? Where do they get the authority to deny us what the Constitution guarantees?"

Todd said wearily, "By now, they've undoubtedly decided we were at war."

The Grand Magi moved excitedly. "Then, gentlemen, the man seated in the White House as sworn President of the United States is *not a citizen!* President Andrew Johnson is a native of this great state of Tennessee—*a proud member of the Confederacy of the United States.* I ask you again, can they have it both ways? If Johnson can legally be President, can a duly elected senator from the same state be denied recognition on the floor of the Senate? Think of that, gentlemen. Think of that, and you'll know why the Ku Klux Klan is the hope of the South!"

Radcliffe went on quickly. "They are working to elevate the nigger above us. That's the only way they can see to keep us down, keep us under their mercy."

"They're goin' t'have one hell of a time doin' that," Leroy protested. "Any time a white man ain't better'n a nigger—"

"How come I got niggers squatted all over my land?" Lyman demanded belligerently. "He's right, they are puttin' niggers above whites. I can't get my property back. You know that, Leroy. What about that?"

"That's goin' t'change—damn quick," Leroy said angrily.

Lyman let out a low, anguished growl. "I jes' want t'go out an' burn up some nigger's shack, or—" He seemed to recollect where he was, and fell silent.

"What makes me boil," Todd said, "is that the darkies aren't accountable to anyone. We touch one of the bastards, and we're hauled into court. The damn no-'count niggers can do as they want."

"Not quite. The Freedman's Bureau holds them accountable—but for a purpose. No Yankee does anything without a purpose, remember that. They want that nigger votin' right. Votin' Radical. Why do you think the Freedmen's Bureau is around if not to control the votes?"

"And that means they're goin' to try to get all the niggers to the polls come this November election . . . God a'mighty, can they ram that Fourteenth Amendment down our gullets?" Todd asked.

"No, sir!" said Leroy quickly. "We still got the Georgia Legislature. We ain't lost everything yet."

The Grand Magi laughed harshly. "As long as the Radicals win elections they control Congress, and so long as they control Congress, they can throw out legislatures faster than we can elect them. This will be one hell of a fight. It's not going to be won or lost in one election.

"Here's what's in that Fourteenth Amendment. One, before any state can be readmitted to the Union, it has to pass this Amendment. They got us on the outside of the govament and helpless. That's where they want to keep us. Two, the Civil Rights Bill is part of the Amendment. Civil Rights!" he snorted. "Whose civil rights? Ours? No, suh! Three, they get to enforce nigger votin'. Four, any Southern man who was anybody or anything before the War, or who was a brave leader of men durin' the War, can't hold office until Congress pardons him. They are tryin' to incapacitate our leaders. What nation ever did great things without its leaders?"

"Shee-it!" Todd intoned, making a gesture with his fist.

"But there's more, boys. The Yankees don't stop until there's nothin' left of a man's pride. This Fourteenth Amendment says out and out that the war debt of the South shall *never be paid,* and that the Union

debt *can never be repudiated.* We got to *pay* the damned
Yankees for invadin' our land, for burnin' our crops,
for rapin' our women, for beatin' us. *We got to pay
them! That same* Amendment says *no slaveowner will
be paid for the slave property taken from him!* All
that's in the Fourteenth Amendment."

The men began talking angrily. The Grand Magi held
up his hand. "Now we've got to keep movin' on, boys.
As Ah was sayin', the Yankees steal our property,
destroy our land, hamstring our leaders, call our money
worthless, and then *demand* we pay their debt! Every
single provision of this Amendment is an insult to
the pride and common sense of every Southerner who
ever loved the Constitution and this nation." Radcliffe
stretched his arms out as if to embrace them. "Ah've
told you but a small part of the Radical threat to this
great country, but Ah think it is enough for you to see
how impohtant the Klan is to the South, and to the nation. We have an obligation, a duty, and by God we
will pufform it!"

The four men left Tennessee the next morning. They
had come there hardened, disillusioned men, men who
lived with a hollow pit of emptiness and defeat within
them. They were returning to Georgia filled with an
inflamed sense of mission, and a burning hatred for
the enemy.

"One Rebel is still worth ten Yankees," Billy Bob
said.

"One Rebel isn't worth a shinplaster if we don't fight
the right way. We got to learn to ferret out the enemy,
use his own methods against him." Todd laughed,
triggering another spasm of uncontrolled coughing. He
gasped as he went on. "And when they don't work we'll
burn the bastards in their own cookfires. We'll hang 'em
from the tree stumps, and beat the shit out of 'em."

"Damn, that'd give me pleasure," Lyman sighed. His
hand went to his crotch. "I can feel the pleasure runnin'
right through me."

Todd stared straight ahead of him. "You know,

there are a lot of us that don't see things like the Klan."

"What the hell are you talkin' 'bout?" Leroy snapped. "We all swore loyalty. We all agreed."

"Not us four. I mean back home. Some folks won't cotton to this. Take my brother Glenn. He's up to his neck in the Union League. He says the only way for us to come back is to teach the nigger how to live free. Make him a worker, a voter."

"That God-damned Loyal League. We oughta burn them out," Lyman said. "Let's make the Freedmen's Bureau and the Loyal League our first—no, damn it, I want to burn up Israel Jackson's family that the Freedmen's Bureau put on my land. Black bastards are raisin' corn an' turnips all over my property. I want t'run 'em off."

"There's a lot o' work t'do," Leroy said. "The Grand Magi said we're not to act alone. We got to act together. So we'll get our den organized first off. I was thinkin', you know the cemetery out on Thunderbolt Road? Caleb Wells is caretaker out there. He's got a shack. I'm for makin' that our meetin' place. Nobody's goin' t'bother us in the graveyard, an' no darky's got the balls t'come there at night. When we go visitin' some nigger bastard, we could take him out there. Lawd, I can see him turnin' white with fear soon's his eyes catch hold o' those tombstones."

The other three chorused raucous approval.

Then Todd asked, "What did Radcliffe tell you about that man you said was stealin' slaves? Who were you talkin' about anyway?"

"He goes by the name Black Swan," Leroy said thoughtfully, chewing on a piece of long grass. "I got a suspicion who he is."

"Well, who is he?" Billy Bob asked when Leroy didn't continue.

"I'll tell you when the time comes. Radcliffe told me how t'take care of bastards like him. We'll hold a trial, see, and I'll name the man, and present the evidence against him. Then you—you're his peers—

will decide a fittin' punishment for his treason. You get the hang of this Klan business, an' it makes things seem sensible again, don't it."

"Leroy, don't do that to us," Lyman whined. "Tell us who he is now."

"No, not now. I got to give it some more thought." Leroy's eyes narrowed. It had never made sense to him how Dulcie Moran was able to spirit away ten of her father's slaves. It was difficult enough for one to get away alone, but for ten it was almost impossible unless she had powerful help. There was only one man Leroy could think of who would have given her that kind of help. It didn't figure that a man who would take runaways once was likely to stop, or that it was his first time.

Maybe he couldn't prove Adam Tremain was the Black Swan, but he'd be damned if anybody in Chatham County could prove he wasn't.

One day, Leroy was sure, Dulcie would come back to Mossrose. If she came, Adam would come too. "Yep," he said aloud, "soon's we got a good den back home, we're goin' t'hold that trial."

CHAPTER SIX

Adam stood on the quarterdeck of the *Black Swan,* his eyes scanning a calm, teal-blue sea. The Potomac River, Washington City and its politics, Edmund Revanche, all were behind him. Before him was the open ocean, clear sea lanes to New York City and his future. His blue eyes turned hard and deeply gray. He slammed the heel of his hand against the smartly polished brass rail. That was the way his future should be: clear, open. He had fought for it. He had earned it. But he knew as well as he knew his own ship that that was not the way it would be. Edmund Revanche would see to that.

Impatient, unwilling to allow Revanche to consume his thoughts, Adam told Rosebud McAllister to take over, and went below to the officers' mess. Tom sat alone at the captain's table. As he saw Adam enter, he raised a flask. "Have some. You look like a stepped-on bug."

Adam took a swallow and returned the flask. He waved an impatient hand at the mess boy who had appeared instantly. The boy disappeared, hurrying to bring the captain's supper.

Tom shook his head morosely. "Adam, you ain't actually gonna live with Miss Nellie Sunbeam, are you?"

Adam looked at him blankly, then laughed. "Patricia?"

"Yeah, Patricia," Tom muttered. "That woman could drive a saint to drinkin' an' carousin'."

"She's not so bad. I can stomach her a lot better than I can take Jem's talk about the blacks. He must realize he can't go back home and be master any more."

"So why are you gonna do it? You don't need to go to Mossrose."

"It won't be for that long. I'll be set up in New Orleans in a year or so. By then the house will be re-built, and Jem and Patricia will be settled in." Adam leaned back as the boy served his supper. He picked up his fork and began to push the food around his plate. "Soon enough Jem will recognize that there is no life as it was before the War. He may be a stubborn old mule, but he's a realist. He must be. He brought that plantation back from nothing once."

"Don't sound good to me. None of it."

"Dulcie would like to be with her parents for a time, Tom. She's the only child they have."

Tom took a long swallow of whisky. "Your ma's only got one child. You gonna live with her a while too?"

Adam gave up the pretense of eating. "What are you getting at?"

Tom sipped. "I ain't too sure, boy. I jes' don't like the lay o' things. Nothin' feels right to me. I don't like Edmund sneakin' around behind the scenes, and I don't like the idea o' you livin' in the same house with two people who haven't even started to approve o' you yet. That whisper-voiced ol' woman's gonna drive you loony, as well as know ever' speck o' your business. An' be tellin' it. An' somethin' about that house bothers me. There's an ol' sayin' about not buildin' a new house where the ol' one caught fire."

Adam raised his eyebrows. "You're stretching a little for that one, aren't you?"

"Yeah?" Tom asked gruffly. "That's what I said when Ullah told me she'd dreamed o' muddy water. You know what happened then. And there's another thing I don't like about this whole setup. Why in the hell ain't you gonna be on this ship doin' what you know best?"

"I will be," said Adam irritably. "Ben will be setting up the shipping line in New Orleans as soon as he's pardoned. I won't exactly be idle while I'm in Savannah either. They say shipping is starting to revive there. Could be I'll open an office there, too, if I can find a trustworthy man to run it. It might work out well."

"Maybe. Here, have another snort before I drink it all."

The two men fell silent. Adam began to eat his cold meal.

Suddenly Tom shoved the empty flask across the table. "Damn him!"

Adam looked up, but said nothing.

"That son of a bitch. He's always there. Trouble, and he's always there. I shoulda known the bastard was in town the night I went lookin' for Jubal an' Angela. Couldn't be a hellhole like Murder Bay without a Revanche. Someday I'm gonna get that bastard. There ain't nothin' in my life he hasn't made dirty."

Angela sprang vividly into Adam's imagination—blond, tall, and willowy—as she had looked when they had last walked along the beach together. "She'd be nineteen?"

Tom grunted. "If she ain't dead."

Adam looked away from Tom. "She's all right," he said tightly.

"I don't know. I just don't know what to think. Sometimes I'm more afraid to think she's alive than to think she's dead. What's she likely to be now?" Tom's expression was pained and remote.

Adam remained silent, and Tom went on. "Y'know, lately, I can't remember what her mama looked like. Only woman I truly loved, and I think about her an' I see a kind of blur. Ullah's jes' a feelin' to me now. Don't seem right the years can take her face from me." He turned toward the port, swallowing hard.

Silence engulfed the room. Adam was remembering Ullah too. She had been dead for fourteen years, long enough that the usual man would have remarried. But, Adam reflected, Ullah was an unusual woman, and Tom had an unusual reason for remaining widowed.

Tom cleared his throat. "I'm gonna kill that son of a bitch."

Adam said nothing. Edmund Revanche. He wondered how much pain, bitterness, and hate one man could generate in the hearts of others and never pay. Sometimes he thought Edmund would go on forever, not dying like other men, not aging, nor ever experiencing remorse.

Tom's face was set in bitter lines, his eyes staring into space, a space occupied by the vision of Edmund Revanche.

They entered New York harbor in late spring, 1866. South Street was clogged with traffic, ships were anchored three and four abreast, hull to hull in crowded berths. Warehouses were overflowing into the street with goods from all over the world. Taxis, buses, drays, carts zigzagged in dizzying confusion along the roadway. Irate longshoremen, drivers, hawkers, and merchants shouted commands until a steady hum of human voices rose and rivaled the clatter of steam engines and the cart wheels that never stopped.

Adam settled his family at his parents' new and fashionable home on Murray Hill. For the next few days the women supervised temporary unpacking for the Tremains and made plans to purchase the imported china, crystal, and appointments Patricia and Dulcie would want for the rebuilt plantation house at Mossrose. Adam spent a leisurely first week enjoying the company of his father.

Long before he had known Roderick Courtland to be his father, Adam had known him as friend and business partner. Before the War Rod, Tom Pierson, Adam's uncle Garrett Pinckney, Ben West, Beau LeClerc and Adam had begun a shipping firm with lines connecting the South, North, and Europe. Under the cover of this firm, Adam, Ben, and Beau had begun hauling slaves by sea to freedom for the Underground Railroad. During the War their operation had become more clandestine, with Adam, Ben, and Beau running slaves North and supplies of medicines and ammunitions to the South. The dashing Beau, for whom Adam's son had been named, had died valiantly during the occupation of New Orleans. Now, Adam and Ben were going to begin again. Through the experiences, dangers, successes, and tragedies of their mutual venture, Adam and Rod had grown closer and more aware of the depth of their love for each other.

The weeks spent in New York were filled with pleasant conversation, visits to Rod's clubs, and the more serious business of preparing for Adam's move to Mossrose and the connection that would be formed between the New York branch of the shipping firm and the one Adam would form first in Savannah and later in New Orleans.

One evening in August after Adam had seen to the purchases of Italian marble for the new mantels in Mossrose, Adam, Tom, and Rod sat comfortably in a private lounge of Rod's club, sipping cognac and discussing what faced them in the South.

Adam pulled at the end of his mustache. "If we don't play the political game right—if we guess wrong, even once, we're never going to get a ship loaded in New Orleans or any other Southern port. Those small-time politicians can think up a rule to cover anything faster than you can swallow. It's going to take a lot of thinking to figure out just which party shoe we should be wearing."

"Maybe the thing to do is stay out o' the damned politickin' until we can see what's ahead," said Tom. "Ol' Thad Stevens don't want any o' the old Southerners to have a say in where they piss. He has his way . . . I'd sure like to steer clear o' him an' that Sumner."

Rod shook his head. "We can't avoid the Radicals, Tom. We're going to have to work with them. No one in Washington, and few in New York, are going to listen to logic or reason when it comes to Reconstruction in the South. It was too bloody a war. Hatreds have been aroused that won't die out for years."

"He's right, Tom. The North wants our ass. They're victors and they want to feel that victory. We'll crawl on our bellies for a long time before they ever let the South rise again."

"Adam, what you're saying is that you're going to work with the Radicals in Savannah, like it or not. That is going to put you in opposition to most of the Southern leaders in Georgia. That state is Democratic."

Adam laughed. "I learned a great deal in Washington. You don't know what the shell game is until you watch those boys operate. Anyway, I am not entirely opposed to the Radicals. It may be that the only way the black man will ever have a voice in the country is if the Radicals hang on long enough to give him some experience with voting and working in the Legislature. The Democrats, while they are willing to be fairer to the South as a section and are willing to see her reinstated in the Congress, are also willing to put the blacks back under the overseers as a token gift to the planters. My objection to the Radicals is their ranks are riddled with the damnedest bunch of crooks and opportunists this country has ever seen."

Tom grumbled, "Ain't nobody interested in Reconstruction 'ceptin' those who want their slice o' the pie. Brings to mind the carrion crow in Loosiana—ol' black birds jes' waitin' to pick on the carcass."

"We'll rebuild if we can," Adam said. "But Southerners won't get the opportunity. The bitterness and vindictiveness of the North is strong, Rod, you've said so yourself. Lincoln's death did the South tremendous harm. Several men have told me to my face that if it hadn't been for slavery he'd be alive today."

Rod said, "Nobody wants to remember that Lincoln wasn't always in favor of abolition. He's become a martyr to a cause that wasn't his."

* * *

It was early October when the *Black Swan* made
her easy way down the Atlantic Coast to Georgia.
Dulcie stood on the quarterdeck with Adam, admiring
both her men as Adam held their infant son Beau up
for his first look at his mother's homeland. The child's
unknowning eyes scanned the Tybee Lighthouse, still
in ruins from Confederate action during the War. The
sixteen-mile voyage up the Savannah River to the city
was broken by beautiful lagoons and long, low sea
islands covered with swaying, wind-caressed salt
marshes. At the approach of the long, sleek ship, peli-
cans, cormorants, and ibises lifted themselves up and
flapped lazily away.

Well forward at the ship's rail stood Jem and Patricia, their faces alight with the expectation of homecoming. Behind them stood Ruel Jordan, tall and dignified like his father Fellie; Kyra, his wife, whose cool
beauty did not disguise a fearless determination; and
Jothan, lanky and awkward beside his small, plump,
giggly wife Mindy. The women were a contrast. Kyra
was all control—smooth, tailored clothing, smoothed
hair pulled back into a bun low on her neck. Mindy's
clothing was fluffy, ruffly. Her hair was curly, bouncing
all over her head when she moved. Her dark eyes
shone with good humor and amusement.

The Jordan brothers were dressed alike in con-
servatively cut business suits; but Ruel had the ascetic
look of a man whose life is foreordained and he has
accepted it. Jothan, like Mindy, was a jokester, apt to
find some incident inappropriately humorous. Although
their looks differed, in their work both men were competent and calm, which was why Adam had especially
wanted them along.

On the bridge, Adam kept a sharp eye forward, as
though challenging the river to have changed since he
had last steamed up it. In the distance he saw the city,
set on a hill on Hutchinson Island, the buildings
grouped around the river's curve on a bluff crowned

with trees. Tugboats fussed around in the oily red waters at its feet. Drawing nearer, they passed lowland market gardens, looking shriveled and depleted at this time of year. They docked opposite rough brick four- and five-story warehouses.

Adam breathed deeply of the satisfactory tang of salt winds, the hint of sulphur in the waters, the sturdy smell of tar and cording and fish. Once they were secured, he and Tom and Jem would go ashore. He knew Dulcie wouldn't want to stay aboard a minute longer than she had to, nor would the other passengers.

"Adam, you won't be gone long, will you?" Dulcie asked.

"Only an hour," he assured her. "Two at the most. I want to locate a decent hotel with a restaurant. And I want to walk around long enough to see if the streets are safe for beautiful ladies." His eyes sparkled as he looked at her.

Dulcie was not taken in by his smile. "You *will* be back in time to escort us to dinner?" she asked tartly.

"Temper, temper. I promise to be speedy. If I happen to get tied up, I'll send a boy with a message." He kissed her lightly, and went down the gangplank. A series of long, steep flights of steps took the men up to Bay Street and Factors' Walk.

Jem sat down abruptly on the nearest bench, his face dangerously purple. He was puffing mightily. "My God, Adam," he panted, "haven't you any regard for an old man? We should have taken a hack up here." He mopped his face with a bright blue bandanna, took off his hat and wiped his forehead. "That climb like to killed me."

Adam was breathing heavily himself. "My apologies, Jem. I had forgotten how steep that is."

Jem recovered shortly, and the three of them moved sedately down Factors' Walk, a row of narrow buildings along the river bluff, a commercial center and the meeting place of cotton merchants. The huge Cotton Exchange building with its brick red façade blackened over with the years and soot stood imposingly midway down the walk.

Jem pointed to it grandly. "Remember when that building was full of Mossrose cotton, Adam? You were shipping on the *Ullah* back then." He glanced over at Tom. "That's how he met my daughter. Came out to my house on business on her sixteenth birthday. Damned rogue took my cotton and my only daughter. She couldn't think of another man after that. Wasn't for want of suitors, either." He pointed to several old brick buildings. "See those? And the cobblestones in the street? They were built from stones brought from England as ballast in the early sailing ships."

Adam nodded, feeling content and charmed by the city. Whenever he came to Savannah he was impressed by the muted, weathered bricks and heavy ironwork dark against the waters, and was reminded of European seaports. On the north side of Factors' Walk the upper stories of the warehouses whose foundations stood at the foot of the cliff were connected with the bluff by wooden platforms that formed a sidewalk. The walk spanned a narrow, steep roadway leading at intervals, by a series of turns, back down to the wharves.

Soon they had found suitable hotel rooms for the families and quarters for the Jordans. Since they saw a few women on the streets, poorly dressed and unaccompanied, but holding their heads like ladies, Adam decided Dulcie and her mother would be safe. The city hadn't the lively commerce he had been accustomed to as he was growing up in the South. The children who would normally be swarming the street corners, playing games, and dodging carriages and wagons, were missing. All Savannah was quiet.

Musing over his observations, he left Tom and Jem to tend to their own affairs and made his way back to the *Black Swan*. On his way he stopped at a dry goods store, always a good place to collect information. The merchandise, he noticed immediately, was scanty and high priced.

A neatly dressed male clerk helped him select some cigars and began to measure ribbon Adam was buying for Dulcie. "We jes' got some lovely ladies' handkerchiefs in today, suh."

Adam smiled to himself. He was beginning to know Patricia well. Soon, she'd be wanting to visit her old friends and of course she'd need to bring a gift. Nothing too ostentatious, but nice. "That won't be necessary. I'll take the box."

"Six dozen. Theah's six dozen in a box, suh. Do you—"

"I'm sure my mother-in-law will want all those and more. Just wrap them with the ribbon."

"Yes indeed, right away." Nervously the man wrapped Adam's purchases. "You must be from the Nawth, uh, suh?"

"I didn't know my accent had deteriorated to that extent." Adam smiled. "No, I was born and grew up in New Orleans. I've been . . . out of the States for several years."

The clerk's voice was very soft and courteous. "I expect you missed the War entirely then."

Adam usually found no reason to justify himself; but he would be doing business in Savannah for some time to come. If the mousy clerk thought he was a draft dodger, he might start a rumor that could harm his family or his business. "I wasn't in the military. I ran the Federal blockade until the last port was closed, bringing in blankets, food, guns, and medicines."

The clerk's eyes widened. "Theah was a man—the Black Swan—you didn't happen to know him, suh?"

"He sailed out of my home port, Nassau."

"He's a wondahful man. He saved my mama's life. Not personally, undahstand, but he brought in quinine —an' she was real sick—an' we bought some. She'da died without it. I wish I could thank that man."

Adam smiled. "That's very gratifying to hear. By the way, where are all the children?"

"They're in school, suh. Weah proud to say that

Savannah's schools are open this fall. Weah the fust
city in Jawjuh t'do that." He made a face. "Even the
darky children are in school. Put this on youah bill,
suh?"

Adam reached into his pocket. "No, I'll pay cash."

"Th-thank you, suh. We get so much bahtah—"

Adam glanced quickly around and out into the
nearly empty street, and surmised that even the barter
customers weren't buying much these days. "How is
business?"

"Poor, suh, damn poor," the clerk admitted. "Weah
havin' a depression just now. A lot of businessmen've
had to sell out this fall, just take any price they could
get for their goods." He shook his head, his eyes glaz-
ing over wistfully. "Last yeah we looked like a boom
town—new businesses on every corner, people buyin'
like they used to. The merchants bought with the prices
high, an' now that they've gone so low, an' there ain't
many jobs—well, a few of us are still hangin' on. We
need cash customers like you, suh. Then of course,
gettin' goods to Savannah is mighty hard."

"I've heard that freight costs are very high."

"Not only that. The only railroad open its entire
length is the Western an' Atlantic. Oh, the Jawjuh Railroad an' the Central of Jawjuh are bein' rebuilt. The
Freedmen's Bureau had darkies workin' all along the
lines. But between heah an' Augusta the only route so
far is by water. Shippin' cotton from Augusta to Savannah costs eight dollahs a bale. Ain't that a sin now?"

Adam shook his head. "I'll be hiring next week.
What's the labor situation?"

"White men who need work'll be glad to heah that.
As for the darkies, they either work or starve."

"I thought they were getting federal relief."

"Well, they got quite a bit last yeah. But General
David Tillson—he's in charge of the Freedmen's Bureau—is cuttin' that down, said no rations would be
furnished able-bodied men if he could find 'em work.

He's forced the darkies to make contracts and keep 'em."

"You've been very helpful. Sorry, I didn't get your name."

"Osgood Baxter, of Baxter's Since 1799. And youah's, suh?"

"Captain Adam Tremain. It's been a pleasure to talk with you, Mr. Baxter." Adam picked up his packages to go.

"Captain Tremain," said Baxter as though he knew the name. "Of what ship?"

"It's that white paddlewheel steamer down in the harbor, alongside the *Mersey*. You can't miss it, Mr. Baxter. Good day." Adam went out, hearing the bell tied to the door tinkling behind him.

Early the following day the men headed for Mossrose. The trip out was relatively easy. They had bought a new wagon and mules to pull it. The broad wheels rolled readily over minor obstructions. Sherman's Army had passed this way in December 1864, but the rubble left in the wake of a marching military force had been scavenged. In the road were still holes, wallows, and wheel ruts, but the men had come prepared with planks and shovels.

Going north on the River Road they passed former plantations, now gone back to sandy clay tufted with briars and burned cotton and cornstalks. Many of the plantation houses that had crowned broad acres rich with rice and cotton were gone—demolished by Federal shells or fire, or by Sherman's wanton vengeance on a land that lay sprawled already helpless. Here and there a chimney stood gaunt against a crisp October sky. They passed shacks where in the golden times only blacks or poor white trash would have lived. Where shelter still stood, sometimes a child would wave timidly, to be quickly jerked back out of sight by an unseen adult.

Eventually they neared a yellow frame house with its paint peeling off. "The Tweed plantation," Jem said.

"Old Man Tweed was a hell-raiser if one ever lived. Oversaw his own darkies and made 'em miserable, but he grew the finest rice in ten counties. Had two daughters, Phoebe and Zenobia. He never let those girls marry. He wanted somebody to care for him in his old age."

As Jem paused, Tom said, "Did they?"

"Well, he gave them every opportunity. The old man had softening of the brain, and his last ten years he ran 'em ragged. But you'd never have known anything was wrong over there. Cheerful as crickets, they were. Patricia'd call on 'em, and she'd always pull up in front and wait till one of the ladies came to the door. That gave the other one time to get everything inside prettied up. Patsy's heard some pretty serious yelpin' an' bellers coming from the house, and maybe a holler or two from Zenobia. She was the strong one. Phoebe now, she's as strange a little thing as you'll ever meet—kind of fey, always spoutin' poetry. I reckon they're both dead now. They'd have to be in their eighties."

Farther on there was evidence of wealth, or at least of enterprise. Close to the road on Saunders plantation land stood a homey little general store, recently built of new milled lumber. On its broad veranda sat a few chairs, sacks of grain, and barrels of molasses and flour. A middle-aged woman came out. She stared at the wagon for some moments as at a rarity.

"Well, I always said if anybody came back rich, it'd be Jem Moran. Mr. Moran, don't you recognize your old neighbor?"

The men quickly doffed their hats and climbed down. Ruel and Jothan stood, but not quite facing the woman. Jem smiled, hiding consternation as he realized this poorly dressed woman had once been his elegant Patsy's best friend and rival. "Why—Mrs. Lydia Saunders. How are you, ma'am?"

Mrs. Saunders gave him a one-armed hug, hanging on to her parcels. "Fine, thank God. And yourself?

You're lookin' splendid. And can this be Captain Tremain?"

Adam bowed, kissing her hand with a flourish, which made her blush richly. "May I present my partner, Mr. Tom Pierson?"

She stared at Tom's scarred face for a moment, pity dawning. "Mr. Pierson, I'm—I'm so pleased to meet you." She looked away.

"It's a fine store you and Cal have here," Jem began.

She said baldly, as though telling it any other way would make her weep, "Cal died at the Battle of Frayser's Farm, Mr. Moran, early in the War."

Jem stammered condolences, and she went on, "When Glenn and Todd came back we couldn't pay the taxes, so we had to sell the plantation to a Yankee, a Mr. Albert Seldon. It doesn't matter too much. My children are all settled now. Glenn and Birdie live nearby and Blythe went to Arizona Territory with her husband. I live with my daughter Blossom and her family. My youngest boy, Ferron, is five now." She laughed shyly. "Some of Blossom's younguns are older than he is."

"I have a fine grandson too," Jem boasted. He looked up the long hill to the Saunders plantation house. Among the stumps of trees stood a relatively undamaged dark red brick house with double Ionic scrolls over the recessed doorway. He wondered if he could face the loss of his property as well as she, or what Patricia would have done in Lydia Saunders' place. "May we give you a ride home, ma'am?"

"That'd be a treat, thank you, Mr. Moran." She climbed into the wagon assisted by Adam, and sat looking very pleased with herself. She explained, "The Yankees took all our rolling stock. Where are you gentlemen going? Mossrose is ruined, you know."

"So Adam has told me. But we're going to build again."

"I'd invite y'all to stay with us, but we're so crowded,

nine of us in four rooms without even a kitchen. We have to cook in the back yard. That south wing's all that Sherman left of Blossom's house. I expect you know Blossom's husband, Jan Chilcote?"

Adam remembered him: a fresh-faced, pleasant, black-haired man he had done business with before the War.

"Jan works hard, but he's the only man on the place, and there's so much to be done." She said this cheerfully, stating another fact of her new life without rancor. "Grandad Whitaker helps him out sometimes. Goodness knows *they've* got plenty of men around." Her voice had turned faintly sour.

"How are the Whitakers faring?"

"Better than the rest of us. They hung on to their money somehow, and the Yankees used their house as a hospital for a time. Imagine Emma Whitaker nursing Yankee soldiers? And that freckle-faced young Enid? With Andrew dead at First Manassas, and the other three boys fighting under General Longstreet! Well, maybe I shouldn't talk. After all, we sold to a Yankee."

"He's running the store himself?" Jem asked.

She looked puzzled. "No, he isn't. Mr. Seldon bought our land through an agent. No one's seen him. Reverend Jabez Hooks runs the store. He's a Southerner, and if one ever lived, a truly dedicated man of God. He talked Mr. Seldon into letting him run this store to help the folks out around here. I don't know what we all'd do if it weren't for the credit he gives us. He's a fine, pious man." She laughed softly. "Every Saturday night he preaches hellfire and damnation at the store. He has a church somewhere else that he goes to on Sunday mornings. Never heard of the place myself."

Jem, starting to look a little dazed at the flow of her chatter, interrupted. "Isn't that Ned Whitaker chopping firewood?"

Adam pulled into the Whitaker plantation road. Jem hopped down from the wagon before it had stopped, and approached his former neighbor, who came joyously to shake his hand. The two older men fell deep into conversation. Mrs. Saunders greeted Ned and asked to be remembered to Emma Whitaker. Then she excused herself, preferring to walk the rest of the way home rather than wait.

"As long as you'll be in the neighborhood, Jem, why not stay with us?" asked Ned Whitaker. "We have plenty of room, and I'd be pleased to have the company and catch up on all the news. The quarters are gone, but your boys can sleep in the kitchen."

The two black men, standing at a distance, exchanged glances. A little grin played around Jothan's mobile mouth. Under cover of the conversation he said, "Now you knows you is nigger, Ruel boy."

Ruel darted a look at the whites, then at his brother. "Sshh."

"Man, doan dey got no baids? We'ns cain't sleep on de flo'!"

"Jothan, quiet, they'll hear you."

Jothan shook his head and sighed. "It's not going to be easy putting up with these folks. Daddy told us the truth when he said it would be different down South."

Ned tossed his tools onto the back of the wagon and climbed on beside Jem. Adam drove toward the Whitaker house, smiling at Jem's quickly renewed vigor.

Emma greeted her unexpected guests with pleasure and grace. She turned the house into a maelstrom of activity as she directed scurrying maids to prepare rooms and haul fresh linen upstairs. By dinner time all was serene and in order once more.

Emma set a table of plain but plentiful fare: rabbit stew, hot biscuits, and apple cobbler. She sat proudly at the foot of the table overseeing the service and occasionally glancing at each of her sons, her daughter-in-law, her daughter, and her husband. All except the daughter-in-law, Pearl, were blond, all plain but strongly masculine in looks. Unfortunately that also included her daughter, Enid. Grandmother Whitaker, a stiff-necked old lady dressed in royal-violet silk, sat across from Adam. Next to her was her husband, a crumbling reprobate in his late seventies who still had a wandering eye for attractive young girls.

"Where's that pretty little wife of yours?" he crowed at Adam. "I wouldn't have let you in the door if I'd known she wasn't along." With an ornery twinkle in his eye, he nudged his rigid, long-suffering wife.

Adam smiled, uncertain, as Grandmother Whitaker fixed him with a withering glance. He cleared his throat, quickly hiding his mouth with his napkin. "I am sure Dulcie will want to visit you and Mrs. Whitaker as soon as she is able. She'll want to show off our son Beau."

Grandmother softened at the mention of Adam's son.

Cutler Whitaker, sitting beside Adam, murmured under his breath, "You've got the sight, or you're a shrewd man with women, Tremain." He laughed gaily. " 'Bout the only thing Grandmother approves of is a man who likes his children. Keep playin' her, she's hummin' like a rusty ol' fiddle."

The conversation remained peaceful and pleasant. Brock Whitaker, Adam noticed, was a grim man whose drinking kept him at the edge of inebriation. Cedric was more outgoing and far more outspoken. He questioned Jem and Adam hotly on every aspect of their plans for Mossrose, and the use of free black labor. "You're goin' t'have to be cautious, Mr. Moran," he said. "Those darkies are in the kingbird's seat right now, and they know it. They'll steal a white man blind. We've got a mighty problem with them."

"You've got problems with everything," Cutler said cheerfully. "Shoot, Cedric, you're not happy 'lessen you got somethin' to fight."

Cedric lifted his wineglass to his brother. "I can get a fight outta you any time I'm feelin' ornery, Cutler, what do I need anything else for?" He looked over at Jem. "My brother's turnin' into a flamin' liberal, Mr. Moran. Could you ever think a thing like that of a

Whitaker if it wasn't a Whitaker tellin' you it's so? Why, he's even joined the Loyal League." Cedric whooped, and Brock joined in. Together they shouted, "Liberty! Lincoln! Loyalty! League!" then dissolved into laughter.

Adam looked at Cutler with greater interest. "You belong to the Union League?"

Cutler glared at his brother before turning to Adam. "I do. It's a damned good thing, and it's needed. We can't undo Emancipation. We've got to live with it. The smartest thing we can do is teach the darkies what votin' and legislatin' is all about. They're free and we're burdened with all their problems. These damned idiot brothers of mine think they're going to turn the clock back and make everything the way it was before the War." His eyes went back to his brothers, his jaw jutting out. "It will never be the same again."

Cedric laughed. "You might be in for a big surprise, brother."

"Sure as hell's hot, one of us is," Cutler said. He stood up. "Anyone care to come out for a breath of fresh air?"

Adam, Tom, Enid, and Brock joined him. The bickering was left behind as the four of them took a pleasant walk around the grounds. Adam puffed slowly on a cigar, enjoying the feel and the scents of a Southern night. It was good to be home again.

Over the following weeks the men visited around the countryside, gathering information, learning about available craftsmen, and studying the Mossrose acres. The immense live oaks that had sheltered the house had died, been hacked down, or burned. There was only a blackened hole where the three-and-a-half story house had stood. Even the bricks had been salvaged by neighbors. The distinctive pinkish-brown rectangles had been used to mend Whitaker's parlor wall, and a neat pile of them stood in Jan Chilcote's side yard.

Jem was stunned. He had tried to prepare himself for

whatever he might see, but neither his imagination nor Adam's description of the house had readied him for this.

Adam instructed Ruel and Jothan to begin work, hoping that would bring life and color back into Jem's ashen face. Jem walked aimlessly onto the lawn, his hands unconsciously caressing the dead bark of his lifeless trees. Ruel and Jothan began taking rough measurements of the old foundations. Tom took Jem by the arm and led him out toward the fields. As with most Southern land not in use, the scrub growth was creeping back.

Slowly Jem began to take practical notice of what was around him. He sifted a handful of the red-brown sandy soil in his fingers. "Just look at that, Tom. Played out. And there'll be no barns full of manure to enrich it this time. We'll have to plow under every blade of green and hope for the best."

"How about some other crop besides cotton?"

Jem wasn't listening. The bewildered look on his face had become determined, then pugnacious. "I'll have row after row of field hands chopping, picking Mossrose cotton. Mossrose cotton was the best. It will be again. We'll do it somehow."

CHAPTER SEVEN

By the time Adam, Tom, and Jem returned to Savannah, Adam was beginning to realize the enormity of the tasks he had set out for himself. The trip to Mossrose had demonstrated clearly that Jem would need his assistance far more than Adam had anticipated. Jem Moran, though he was game and determined, could not do the labor he had done as a young man or accept the changed position of the blacks. To Jem a black man was still a creature meant to serve, far down the ladder from the white man, and in Jem's eyes he had the Bible to back him up.

Beyond the problems involved in the rebuilding of Mossrose, Adam had his own shipping office to open and run in Savannah, and a trip to New Orleans to meet with Ben West on the establishment of the Tremain-West Line there and the purchase of the sugar plantations in St. Mary's Parish.

Instead of a sense of Southern leisure, Adam felt harried, felt the need to move quickly in several directions at once. During the next two months he leased office space in Factors' Row and moved in the furnishings he had brought from New York on the *Black Swan*. For this work he hired several blacks who had just finished digging the foundation for a commercial building nearby. They did their work well, and he paid them in cash.

He stood outside his office building in the January sun talking with them, knowing they felt more at ease out from under a roof.

"Where'd you come from?" Adam asked the straw boss of the group.

"Chatham County, suh—de Ribbah Road."

"What's your name?"

"Mah name Albatross, suh."

Adam's lips twitched. "Albatross. Who named you that?"

Albatross moved his feet back and forth, raising dust, then he looked squarely at Adam. "Ol' Miss like bu'ds, suh. She name me."

Fleetingly Adam thought of the albatrosses he had watched at sea, their twelve-foot wingspan and their effortless flight. "Well, Albatross, how would you like to live near the River Road again?"

The black man eyed him suspiciously.

"I'm offering you a job. I'll be building a house in the country soon. I'll need builders and men to work in the fields. I can see you're strong and you work steadily."

"How fah out on de Ribbah Road, suh?"

Adam knew the man was thinking of his woman, or his family. He smiled. "Only a couple of hours ride from Savannah, Albatross."

The men exchanged looks: doubt, distrust.

"How you gwine pay us, suh?" Albatross asked finally.

"I'll pay each man standard wages, three dollars and fifty cents in silver every Saturday night. Besides that, you'll get three outfits of work clothes each year and a cabin to live in. That's clothing for every member of your family who can work, that's a place for you to live, and it's money for you to spend on food and clothes for your children."

The men muttered and nodded among themselves.

"I expect a full day's work from anyone I hire. Your contracts will be ready to sign tomorrow. Albatross, can you read?"

"Mistah Sweet he'p us out."

"Who's Mr. Sweet?"

"He a gub'mint man whut he'p us out."

Adam nodded. "Then we understand each other." His eyes rested momentarily on each of the men. The black men milled around, then moved off in the direction of the wharf.

As Adam turned to go back into his office, someone yelled, "Hey, *you!*"

He was straightening the line of his desk when a short, fat man came bustling in, panting with choler and exertion. "Hey, didn't you heah me callin' you? Ah want you t'pay attention t'me!"

Adam glanced at the red-faced man. "Good afternoon, sir. If you'll have a chair, I'll be with you as soon as I get this desk positioned." He bent over again, taking more time and care than reasonable. He expected to hear more explosions from the fat man, but evidently his cool response had stopped him in his tracks. His visitor's breathing, however, had become more stentorian.

Deftly Adam produced two glasses and a bottle and silently poured. "Have a drink?"

"Ah doan want no drink, boy. Ah come to 'rest you."

Adam sat down and stretched his long legs out. "I'm not going anywhere. Sit down and have a drink and tell me about it."

"Now looka heah, boy, youah makin' me mad, an' when Ah git mad Ah doan have good control o' mahseff. Iffen Ah was you, Ah'd pay mo' 'tention t'the law."

"I have a high regard for the law, Mr.—uh—"

"Sweet. Laban Sweet. Ah'm Jestis o' the Peace round heah, boy, an' doan you fo'git it."

"Justice of the Peace?" Adam said with evident admiration. "I've often wondered, is that a good job, Mr. Sweet?"

Sweet absentmindedly picked up his glass and found a soft chair. "Naw, boy, t'tell the truth it's a hell of a job. Doan know why Ah evah took it. It's moah work than Ah evah thought it'd be. Jes' 'bout run mahseff ragged some days." Then, suddenly brisk, he set his glass harshly on the desk. "But talk doan git the work done. Boy, you ah undah arrest."

Adam winced. "Don't say that, Mr. Sweet. I thought we were having a friendly chat. Here, soothe your liver."

Sweet resisted for a moment, then took the bottle. "Much 'bliged. As Ah was sayin', you ah undah arrest fo' hirin' illegal."

"Uh?"

"You got them niggers offa one job an' put 'em to haulin' youah funnituah, an' that's illegal. They got t'go thoo the Beero."

"The Freedmen's Bee—Bureau?"

" 'Sright. An' as Jestis o' the Peace heah in Savannah, Ah'm a delegated agent o' the Beero. Ah'm in chahge o' refugees, freedmen, an' abandoned lands. We treat them niggers good—get 'em jobs, feed 'em if we cain't find jobs, put 'em in school—we treat 'em fust rate. Ah read all the job contracts. Ah fine 'em when they doan puffawm. Ah 'rest them that hire illegal. Youah in trouble up to youah bellybutton, boy."

"Mr. Sweet, I'm a newcomer—I didn't know—how could you expect me to know when you didn't come around to tell me? I ask you man to man, do you call that fair?"

"Fair ain't paht o' mah duties, boy. Jes' touch up mah glass a tad. Ah'm a mighty busy man, a mighty impohtant man heahbouts, an' Ah doan have time t'visit with every Tom, Dick, an' Harry jes' so's Ah doan have to 'rest 'em latah."

"I'm afraid I don't understand your duties, Mr. Sweet," Adam said innocently. "Those men had been paid off their previous job. As far as I knew they were free to engage in other activity. Surely your Bureau doesn't place a limit on the amount of work a man is allowed to perform."

"Paid off, huh? That means they finished up theah contracts. Mebbe Ah woan haf to 'rest you aftah all. Mebbe you an' I can reach an agreement."

Adam watched Sweet's small calculating eyes narrow speculatively.

Sweet took a long swallow from his glass. He licked his lips. "You see how Ah got to be diligent in mah work, boy. These darkies ain't got nobuddy t'perteck 'em. We have a hell of a time with one plantah hirin' out from undah anothah, an' then not payin' on the contract. You pay? You did. Ah heard you talkin' to them blacks 'bout hirin' agin. S'pose you tell me all 'bout that?"

"I'm sure a man of your station has heard of James Moran of Mossrose?" Adam began as he explained his plans. "So you see, we'll be hiring a considerable number of men, both black and white."

"Y'all still got t'go thoo the Beero. You cain't jes' git up contracts an' staht carryin' men out theah to work. You already got youahseff on mah wrong side, an' fah's youah concerned, Ah *am* the Beero. See wheah that leaves you, boy?" Sweet smiled broadly.

Adam's blue eyes were direct and guileless. "I see where that leaves me, Mr. Sweet. I also see how valuable your time is. I don't want to delay you a single moment, so perhaps you'll tell me the right way to work with the Bureau."

Sweet sat back, relaxed. "We each of us got a problem. Ah know youah's, now Ah'm gonna tell you mine. Ah got a nigger buck ah cain't git settled. Now, if you could see youah way cleah t'take that nigger offa mah hands, mebbe Ah could almost fo'git you violated the Beero's authority by hirin' them niggers."

"And if I agree to take on this man, that will *almost* make you forget. That leads me to believe there is more to satisfying the requirements of the Bureau."

Sweet's eyes gleamed avariciously. "Theah's a li'l chahge fo' every nigger you hire."

"And if I cannot afford—"

Sweet's piggish eyes jerked around the well-appointed office. "Boy, ya'll didn't git heah on Factors' Row with shinplasters. Ah smell Yankee dollahs. Y'all kin pay."

"You're an astute man, Mr. Sweet," Adam said silkily. "How much did you have in mind?"

"Ten dollahs per nigger."

"And I make out a check to the Freedmen's Bureau?"

Sweet's lips tightened. "Ah already told you, *Ah am* the Beero t'you, boy. An' Ah doan want no checks. Gold or silvah. You jes' turn it ovah t'me an' Ah'll see the Beero gits it."

In one swift fluid motion Adam was standing, his arms braced on the desk, his body thrust toward Laban Sweet. "Dave Tillson, the man in charge of the Georgia Bureau, is a friend of mine, Mr. Sweet. I've known him for years, and he's never done a dishonest thing in his life. I think he'd be pretty unhappy with you if he found out you've been putting a price on freedmen's labor."

"Boy, jes' who the hell do you think you ah?"

"I'm Captain Adam Tremain, but to you, Mr. Sweet, I'm the Black Swan."

Laban Sweet's mouth sagged open. "You ain't," he breathed. "He's dead!"

"I am, and he's alive." Adam refilled Sweet's glass and gave him time to assimilate his astonishment. Then he went on, "You and I can do business, Mr. Sweet, but not at your prices. I'll give you a hundred dollars— and that's my final payment."

"Youah jes' tryin' to be hard to git along with—the Beero doan pay nothin'—" Sweet whined.

"If you'd rather, I can send a check to General Tillson for a thousand dollars, with a letter detailing your activities here."

Sweet squirmed under the fire of Adam's merciless blue eyes. "Ah'll take the hunnert in gold," he mumbled. Then, regaining his self-confidence, he added, "An' you bettah keep youah trap shet, boy. Mebbe you got me by the shawt hairs, but Ah ain't without frien's around heah, an' doan you fo'git it."

"Well, I do have to get along with the law, don't I?" Adam's eyes were mild and innocent again. He counted out the money and laid it in the middle of the desk.

"One never knows, Mr. Sweet, you and I may find need of each other's cooperation in the future. We do well to understand each other now."

Sweet, flushing, got up and pocketed the money. Turning to leave, he bumped into a lanky towhaired man lounging in the doorway to the office. He said through his teeth, "Sonofabitch!"

Adam, smiling, called after him, "By the way, my two partners will be hiring too. Don't try to charge them anything."

Sweet turned to glare at him, his face mottled red, his breathing loud and hoarse.

Adam said quickly, "Send your man over whenever you want. What's his name?"

Laban Sweet had difficulty talking, but finally said, "'Pollo Justus Sherman," and walked quickly into the street.

"Come on in, Cutler," Adam said, motioning toward the chair Sweet had vacated. As Cutler sat down, Adam said ruminatively, "Apollo—Apollo Justus Sherman. There used to be a field hand on Mossrose named 'Pollo. It couldn't be the same man?"

Cutler took the glass Adam offered him, smiling. "It could be, and it is. You're not thinkin' of hirin' him, are you?"

Adam raised his eyebrows. "As you heard, Sweet and I have just reached an amicable arrangement. Hiring Apollo is part of my agreement."

Cutler laughed. "Ol' Laban pulled one then. 'Pollo is a hothead, always was. He joined the Yankee Army and rose to captain. Since the War there's no holdin' him back. But the most tellin' thing about 'Pollo is that he's stayed South, right here in Savannah. He's smart as a whip, but he's not so much interested in advancin' himself as in makin' us see him as equal. Laban's been tryin' to get someone to hire him for near a year, ever since he mustered out of the Army."

Adam listened attentively. "Does he hate whites, or is he just trying to prove his own worth?"

Cutler threw up his hands dramatically. "Damned if I know." Then, looking around the room, he held his glass up toward Adam. "You've got good taste, Captain. Lookin' at this office a body'd never know we lost a war. Makes a man feel prosperous just to sit here."

"I didn't think you'd take to an office, Cutler. I think of you, and I think of the plantation."

Cutler made a face. "That's the way of things. A man's daddy gets a plantation a couple hundred years back, and every man in the family gets tied to it."

Adam leaned back in his chair, thoughtful and silent. He didn't know Cutler well yet, but he liked him. Until now he had never thought of Cutler as anything but a casual friend because of the proximity of the two plantations. Now, he couldn't help allowing his imagination to roam and his hope to stir. He picked up a letter opener, playing with it, balancing it on his finger. "What would you do, if not plant, Cutler?"

"Oh, I don't know. I never gave it much thought, to tell the truth." Then he laughed. "I think I might make a shopkeeper. Yeah, maybe I'd run a shop . . . an import business, or . . ."

"Ever think of a shipping line office?" Adam asked.

"Like yours?"

"Yes, like mine."

"Naw. I don't know the first thing about ships. My heart belongs to those beautiful columns of numbers. Now you can see why I didn't give it much thought." Cutler drained his glass and stood up. "I've got to be hurryin' on, Adam. I was due back at the plantation hours ago, and they're waitin' for supplies. My brothers'll be ready to hang my ass out to dry. I stopped by to ask if you might be interested in attendin' a meeting of the Loyal League with me tonight. The other night at dinner, you seemed to take interest in it." Uncertain, Cutler went on tentatively, " 'Course, if your sentiments are runnin' elsewhere—I mean, if you don't believe in the work of the Loyal League, I understand. I'm not tryin' to force my views on you, Adam."

Adam stood also, and began to walk to the door with Cutler. "You read me right. I'd like to come, Cutler. I'm going to be involved more deeply with the rebuilding of Mossrose than I expected, so I'll want to be active in the district."

Cutler smiled and extended his hand. "I'll stop by your hotel about nine."

That evening Adam and Cutler stabled their horses at the livery and walked to the meeting hall. As they entered, Cutler muttered under his breath, "I don't go for all these trappin's." He nudged Adam, and pulled a face that was piously sincere.

Adam nearly burst into laughter at Cutler's long, narrow face, drawn into an expression that made it seem even longer. Somehow he, too, managed to look serious and earnest.

At the central altar were displayed a Bible, the Declaration of Independence, and the United States Constitution. In the front of the room a tall bony man with sallow skin raised his arms as if to encompass every man present. Slowly a hush fell over the room, and all eyes fastened on the Lincolnesque, black-garbed preacher.

Reverend Jabez Hooks waited for silence, then from deep within his chest his voice rose and grew in volume until it filled the room, vibrating, as he intoned the evening prayer. Hooks, his arms still heavenward, trembled, his straight black hair falling over his forehead.

"O great an' gracious Lawd! We beseech Thee t'look with favah on these Youah humble suhvants, gathered heah in a labor of loyalty to the United States Govament. We ah assembled heah undah Thy eye, O Lawd, with the solemn puhpose of maintainin' freedom an' gainin' equality foah all Youah people, the white, the black, an' even the Red Indian!

"Lawd, undah Youah mussiful guidance the black man's prayah foah freedom fum bondage was an-

swered. It's only one step moah befoah the freedman
gets to live in that exalted state o' bein' able t'vote, o'
bein' as well educated an' as well paid as the white
man. They ain't had the oppohtunities, Lawd, an' we
aim t'see that they get 'em!

"Lawd, Ah doan need t'remind You that there's
some serious enemies in ouah very midst. These enemies of loyal American citizens want us t'go back, they
doan want us managin' on what we got an' lookin' to
the future t'bring these United States back united. This
nation is in-di-visible, Lawd, an' with Youah almighty
hand upon us, helpin' us, weah gonna keep it that way!

"We ask Thy puissant hand on them domestic traitors, too. Hold 'em back, Lawd. Stay 'em fum intuh-
ference with God-lovin' Constitution-lovin' men who
want t'make this nation a mighty force foah freedom
an' equality! Stop theah feet, Lawd. Hol' theah hawses
fum movin' aginst loyal people who ain't got nothin' in
mind but the good o' everybody!

"We thank y'all, Lawd, foah bein' with us in ouah
endeavohs. He'p us t'devote ouah hands t'Thy holy
suhvice. Amen. Amen."

After the meeting had opened, new candidates came
up to the central altar. Adam, with a quick, wary glance
at a grinning Cutler, followed three other men who
dutifully marched to the front. In his turn Adam placed
his hand on the open Bible and repeated the oath of
membership, which bound him to support the Declaration of Independence and the Constitution, to help
maintain freedom, to vote for men sympathetic to the
League, and never to tell League secrets. After the
oaths had been taken, the secrets of the League were
shared, the most important of which were the four L's:
Liberty, Lincoln, Loyal, and League were divulged and
learned by the new members.

Adam returned to his seat beside Cutler. Arthur
Redgrave, a gentle-mannered man with softly waving
brown hair and an attractive smile, took his place before the central altar. He said pleasantly, "From all of

us, Ah extend a welcome to ouah new membahs, especially at this time, when weah goin' to need every bit of assistance in a impohtant fight in the votin' place. As y'all know, the Fouahteenth Amendment to the Constitution will be put befoah the people of Jawjuh this Novembah. That leaves us mighty li'l time to make suah all ouah people ah registered as legal votahs an' will be goin' to the polls.

"Weah goin' to get strong, heavy opposition from suhtain quahtahs. Without mentionin' any names, we know weah goin' to have to guard against attacks of a pernicious natuah, especially against ouah black membahs. Ah want to see a show of hands of those men who ah ready an' willin' to do what they can to protect ouah loyal membahs from night rides, an' harassments on the streets."

Adam looked around the room, mildly surprised at the willingness of so many men to guard their black neighbors. He raised his own hand.

Arthur smiled and said, "Ah see we ah all in accord. Last, Ah'll remind y'all that early in the week befoah the election, we will all be assigned to groups of men. It will be the duty of every group leadah to make sure his men get to the polls an' ah given theah constitutional right to vote. Once we've won this victory, ouah way to reinstatement to the United States Congress an' ouah rightful place of dignity and influence will be neahly accomplished.

"We can't look back. We, the membahs of the Union League, ah dedicated to lookin' forward, to bringin' the South a new vitality, an' preservin' the best of the South. This isn't the time foah any of us to foahget the men who wrote this Constitution. We can't turn ouah backs on the men who conceived an' formed the govament we all revere. Those were ouah daddies an' granddaddies. We ahn't goin' to do less in ouah time. Things ahn't the way we'd like them, but no Southun American worth his salt lets a little opposition upend him.

"We've got a mission—to pass that Fouahteenth Amendment, an' get on with the business of rebuildin' ouah country. It's a healin' mission, an' weah goin' to win it!" He raised his fists, and the men in the audience cheered.

A few other men stood up and spoke briefly. Only one caught Adam's interest. A tall, powerfully built black man sauntered arrogantly to the front of the room. The soft yellow glow from the lamp highlighted the broad planes of his handsome face. Unusually poised, he waited for silence. Then in a deep voice which showed the efforts he had made to correct his dialect, he introduced himself.

"Ah am Apollo Justus Sherman," he said proudly, his head raising a bit, as he looked with bright dark eyes at the men. "Ah ain't Jim or Bob or Tom, or none of those kind of people names, 'cause somebody jes' picked a name fo' me out of a book, an' it wasn't my mama. My mama nevah had no choice of who Ah am called. So when Mistah Linkum made me free, Ah made mahseff who Ah wanted to be, and that was Justus. In the ahmy Ah meet Gen'l Sherman, an' that man do some things Ah was wishin' mah whole life Ah could do. He humbled some mighty high mens, so Ah took his name too.

"Ah'm standin' heah now to tell you, Ah tends to live up to mah name. Mistah Redgrave, he doan want to name no names, but Ah do. It's them mens callin' themseffs the Invisible Empiah that wants to keep us from the polls. Justus doan mean nothin' to them. Fightin' an' shootin' is the only thing they knows. This Union League al'ys say we doan carry guns. We doan use no violence. We be the peace savin' kind. Ah'm standin' heah to say we can't keep no peace an' we can't get ouah peoples to the polls next month iffen we doan staht lookin' like we means business." Apollo stopped talking, and an awkward silence fell. He moved hesitantly, then halted, looking directly at his audience. "Ah thanks you fo' listenin', an' Ah'm makin' a—a movement fo' a vote on the carryin' of guns." Then he strode down the aisle to his seat.

Adam turned to Cutler. "That's Apollo?"

"That's your boy," Cutler said cheerfully. "Can you picture him back under Jem Moran's direction?"

"God, no!" Adam breathed. "But damn, Cutler, he'd make one hell of a leader, given some time and an opportunity."

"No question, but he's as prickly as an ol' sticker bush. What are you going to do about him? Laban Sweet is here tonight. Maybe you can talk him out of that part of your agreement."

Adam shook his head. "No, I like Apollo Justus Sherman. Damned if I know how to handle him, but I'll give it my best shot."

Redgrave pounded for quiet, and asked for a hand vote on the question of carrying firearms. As in the past, the motion lost.

Soon after, the meeting broke up and the men gathered into groups, talking of crops and commerce and the high tariff on freight. Several were discussing what to do about the burned-out sections of Savannah. With Sherman's occupation of the city in 1864, six of the lovely city squares were burned out. Savannah, the largest city in Georgia, with a population of 25,000, was isolated because of the destruction of railroads and access routes. Trade had suffered, and recovery was slow.

Adam made his way to Laban Sweet. "Mr. Sweet, I was hoping to have a word with you."

Sweet, remembering his humiliation earlier in the day, looked warily at Adam. "If it's business, Ah'm off duty. Ah got t'have some time t'mahseff."

Adam smiled and put his hand on Sweet's shoulder companionably. "This is business, but I give you my word, it will ease your mind."

More suspicious than ever, Sweet moved with Adam to an isolated corner of the room. He said in a low whisper, "Whut you want, Tremain? We made ouah bahgain. Ah ain't givin' back youah hunnert dollahs."

"No, no, nothing like that, I assure you. I would like you to send Apollo Justus Sherman to my office first thing tomorrow morning. As he is here now, I thought it might save your running yourself ragged if you could tell him tonight."

Sweet beamed cherubically. "Why, that's mighty kind o' you, Cap'n. Could be we'll get on aftah all. Ah'll jes' do that."

As Laban Sweet bustled off, Adam returned to Cutler. "He'll be sending Apollo to the office tomorrow." Adam smiled in satisfaction.

Cutler looked at him curiously. "I think you're looking forward to it, but damned if I can figure why. You know he's going to cause trouble. First time Jem gets his Irish up and starts yellin' at those darkies, 'Pollo's goin' to be agitatin' like a bull in the cow barn."

"I know, but I like his spirit. Men like that are worth a little trouble now and then."

Cutler made a sucking sound through his teeth as he shook his head. "I gotta say you're one man whose acquaintance I'm happy to have made, Tremain. Next to my brothers, you got to be the contrariest man ever born. It's pure entertainment to see you work yourself into and outta the darndest troubles."

Adam grinned. "I'm good at getting myself into trouble . . . never too sure about the getting out part, though," he said. But he had a feeling the troubles were just beginning.

Apollo appeared in Adam's office the next morning before Adam had his eyes fully open or had rid himself of the headache he had acquired along with his pleasant conversation with Cutler over brandies.

Apollo had no sympathy for a groggy white man. His back militarily rigid, his full, sensual lips pressed into a firm line, he said, "Laban Sweet sent me ovah heah. Said you was hirin', an' 'specially ast fo' me."

Adam winced at the loudness of his voice and said softly, "Sit down. I'll be with you in a minute."

Apollo smirked, and took the seat offered. "Befo' you get to thinkin' Ah'm jes' a darky willin' to do anythin' 'cause I doan know no bettah, Ah'm heah to tell you Ah ain't gwine—*goin*' to be no fiel' han' evah agin."

"I don't expect that of you," Adam said, still trying by example to get Apollo to speak softly. "What can you do—carpentry? Have you ever worked with brick? Stone?"

Apollo hesitated only a fraction of a second, then said defiantly, "Ah ain't done none o' those things, but Ah kin learn."

Adam managed to control a smile. He could imagine this man talking in such a manner to Jem or Ned Whitaker. No wonder Laban Sweet was eager to have Adam take him off his hands. "You think I should pay you for learning?"

Apollo sat straighter, his mouth became firmer. "You'd pay a white man iffen you believed he could learn."

Adam laughed aloud.

Incensed, Apollo stood up, his fists clenched. "Ain't no white man gwine make fun o' me. Ah kin learn good as anybody. You gwine tek that smile offen youah face, else ah'm gwine do it mahseff."

Adam jumped up and rounded the desk. Of a height with Apollo, he stood squared off. "Don't you ever talk to me like that again, and don't ever try to second guess me, mister. Sit down and shut your mouth until you hear what I have to say."

Apollo's face was hard and set. "Ah doan tek ordahs from you or nobuddy Ah doan choose."

"You'll take orders from me if you ever want to work around Savannah, or if you meant what you said at the Union League."

Apollo hesitated, allowing curiosity to creep in.

"I heard you. Was it all hot wind, all that talk about taking the name Justus because justice meant something to you?"

"Ain't no hot wind!" Apollo said loudly. "Ah'm goin' to—"

"With that chip on your shoulder you're not going to do a damned thing. You won't get the chance. Laban Sweet can't unload you on anybody—except me. I want you, because I do think you can be somebody."

"Then why you laughin' at me?"

"I laughed because I felt good when you said you could learn. I like a man with pride and spirit. Sit down, and let's get on with this. I can't hire you just because I like you. Now, what can you do and what is it you want to do?"

Only slightly mollified, Apollo remained standing. When Adam leaned back in his chair, unwilling to talk until they were both seated, the black man sat down. "Ah . . . ain't sure what Ah want to do. Whut you hirin' fo'?"

"You may like this no better than you liked my laughter. I am hiring men to rebuild Mossrose. You'd be working there."

Apollo looked dumbfounded at first, then began to laugh. "Ah ain't goin' back there," he said, still laughing. "Y'all got to have bats upstairs, man. Ah jes' got free o' that place. Ah he'p burn down whut's lef' of it."

"Well, now I'm offering you a job to rebuild it. And later, if you want to, go a lot further than that. You can stay on here after it's rebuilt, or you can come with me, or go off on your own. The choice will be yours. Right now you don't have much choice, Apollo. No one wants to hire you except me, and unless you make a start for yourself, you'll never be free to do anything. Slavery isn't the only thing that held the black man down. Lack of opportunity is a worse kind of slavery."

Apollo stared hard at Adam, then asked him to continue. Adam explained his plans for Mossrose, told Apollo something of his shipping line and about the black man who was now the captain of one of his ships. Finally he spoke of his intention to settle in New Orleans once Mossrose was reestablished.

Apollo was quiet for a moment. Then he said, "Ah doan believe you. Ah ain't heard o' no white man, Nawth or South, evah let a nigger become a sea captain. You lyin' youah white ass off."

Adam held back his flaring temper and said calmly, "I don't lie. I have no need for lies."

Apollo's upper lip curled in disdain.

"I'm offering you a job, Apollo, you can take it or leave it. But I want you first to verify that I have told you the truth. I was known during the War as the Black Swan. Anyone who knows of me will tell you my first mate was a black man. His name is Rosebud McAllister; he was a slave from Gray Oaks plantation in New Orleans. He now captains his own ship, one of my line."

"You ain't the Black Swan," Apollo said quietly.

"Good God, man, what do I have to do with you, prove every word I utter? My ship is docked right below us in the Savannah River. Go look at it with your own eyes, then come back in here."

Apollo went out. Adam waited, expecting him to return promptly, but it was nearly an hour before Apollo sauntered through the door to the office again. "Ah'd like to work fo' you, Captain."

Adam smiled. "Took your damned sweet time about it, didn't you?"

Apollo grinned and shrugged. "Ah did some checkin'. You the Black Swan. Ah ast a couple people. One them was Ludy's sistah. You 'member Ludy?"

Adam thought back to the time during the War when he had returned to Mossrose hoping to find Dulcie, or at least learn something of her. The house still stood then, broken by shell fire and all but abandoned. But Ludy had been there. He remembered Ludy and her axe.

"She tell her people 'bout the Black Swan. Willa, she

Ludy's sistah, an' she tell me whut the Black Swan looks like, an' you the Black Swan. Ah works fo' you —iffen the res' o' whut you say is truth."

Adam put his head in his hands. "I didn't think that sudden humility of yours could last."

"Whut's humility?" Apollo asked immediately.

"For now it isn't important. I'll draw up your contract. Can you read?"

"Ah was a fiel' han'. Nobuddy wants me t'read. But Ah kin—a little."

"Well, Laban Sweet will help you with it. Once we get settled, I'll see that someone teaches you."

Apollo grinned. "Y'all goin' t'pay me fo' learnin' to read?"

"Hell, no!" Adam barked. "Get your black ass out of here, before I change my mind."

"Yes, suh!" Apollo saluted smartly. "Suh?"

Adam looked up, smiling. "Yes?"

"You jes' hired yo'seff the best damned nigger evah was borned."

CHAPTER EIGHT

All Jem's good New Year's resolutions about treating the blacks properly blew away the first day he interviewed men for hiring. He was unwilling to go out on the street, where men could be found between jobs. He wanted to conduct his business from his home, which was temporarily the hotel. It was not the best atmosphere to put Negroes, who were normally not allowed in the building, at ease.

Jem couldn't bring himself to take on new ways, for all his determination and hope. Though he strove gamely, he couldn't overcome the feeling of displacement that came with his return home. Blacks on the street didn't step aside for him to pass; in fact, they crowded him a little. Savannah had lost her refinement, and looked like a burned-out remnant of herself. And so did her people. The gracious sidewalk conversations filled with balls and soirées and tournaments were gone. Everywhere he looked he saw women who appeared not to have eaten in a week. Men missing arms and legs. Faces that bore scars of the War. Eyes that burned with bitterness, eyes grown dull with the emptiness of unaccepted loss.

He was determined to bring Mossrose back to its former elegance, but there was a part of him that knew an alien fear, a sense of despair that no matter what he did, or how authentically he rebuilt, Mossrose would never be the same, he would never be the same, the South would never be the same. Jem felt a longing that ate deep inside him, for the days that were no more.

He could hardly face what he saw in Savannah, yet he couldn't give up. He had to have workers. He compromised by sending Jothan to the Freedman's Bureau to bring back men for him to look over.

The first morning Jothan had returned with three field hands who were acutely uncomfortable in Jem's small hotel office with its beautiful furnishings. Jem addressed the closest one, a wiry man who stood slowly turning his battered hat. "What's your name?"

The black's accent was so thick he was nearly incomprehensible. He said, "Job, suh," keeping his eyes down the way a field hand should.

Jem felt some satisfaction that things were still basically as they should be, and, unaware, began to slip back into the old master-slave frame of mind. "Job, what kind of work do you do?"

"Chops, suh."

Jem's limited patience was already strained. With a rush of blood that darkened his face, he thought of the truth that blacks were like ignorant little children needing to be guided each step of the way. He looked at Job and felt he would burst his skin when he thought of men in Washington and New York blithely stating that these blacks were his equal. "Speak up, man! *What do you do?*"

"Chop de cawn an' cotton, massa," Job said.

After an hour Jem dismissed two of the men. He puffed out his lips in exasperation as he viewed the last applicant. He was tall and heavy, dull-looking but strong. As Jem examined him by eye, fighting the impulse to look into the man's mouth at his teeth, and poke and prod at his muscles, as he would have been free to do before the War, Tom Pierson walked in and sat down.

Jem nodded to him, and pounced on the black man. "What do *you* do?"

"Ah does whut you tells me, suh."

"Well then, what are you good at?"

The freedman scratched his head but didn't answer.

Jem's face grew dangerously red. "Can you drive mules?"

"Mules. Hawses. Ah kin plow. Chop."

"Hmph. What's your name, boy?"

"Mah name Boy, suh."

"Haven't you got any other name?"

"Dey ain't gib me none, suh."

"Where did you work last?"

Boy's gaze slid down to his shoes. He stood silent.

"Speak up, man, you must have worked somewhere."

"Ah bin sick, massa." Jem noticed for the second time that when blacks got scared, they fell back into slave usages. Damned abolitionists should be here with him, now, and they wouldn't be so hot to call a black a man at all. In fact, the Yankees called the blacks niggers, and hated them like they did the rats that ran the streets. It's only in the South, Jem thought vengefully, that black men were supposed to be white men's equals. He snapped again at Boy. "How long were you sick? What were you sick with?"

Confronted with two questions, Boy retreated into an indeterminate crooning that showed he was trying to form words to please this white man.

Jem glared at him. Finally he said, "I don't think you'll make a good worker, Boy. But you seem to be the best the Freedmen's Bureau has to offer. You're hired."

"Yassuh." He stood there, waiting.

"Well, go on. Go!"

Jem turned to Tom, complaining that the damn niggers were as stupid and ignorant as when they'd been slaves, and that if they wanted to be treated equal with white men, then they ought to start acting like them.

Tom's mild blue eyes twinkled briefly. "Jem, you ever catch one of them darkies actin' like a white man, and you're gonna shoot him. You don't want them actin' like anything but niggers."

"Right now they're neither one," Jem said inconsistently.

"Maybe you're workin' the wrong end of this thing, Jem. It don't seem to be your style to deal with the

bottom man. You've always had overseers to do that
for you. Why don't you just leave the hiring up to
Adam and his two clerks?"

Jem brightened. He knew as well as Tom that he
was being offered an easy, face-saving way out of a
situation he couldn't tolerate. "Just between us, Tom,
I wonder if you could be right. A planter is a leader
of men. I believe I would do better if I had a competent
work force assembled for me. I'll speak to Adam about
this."

Jem was not alone in his dilemma. Dulcie was having
her own difficulties with the new ways. In her mind,
and Patricia's, it was natural to expect that the black
women would assume the accustomed roles of servant
and maid. To eighteen-year-old Mindy, being trained
as a nurse to active young Beau, her position was
several steps up from maid or dishwasher; therefore,
she was delighted.

However, Dulcie experienced an entirely different
and perplexing situation with Kyra. At twenty-eight
Kyra, a Northerner, had been a schoolteacher for ten
years, respected and obeyed in her own realm. She was
both unhappy and inept in the role of lady's maid. She
had tried, and Dulcie had begun her training, but by
early spring their combined efforts had resulted in frustration and pain for both of them.

"Kyra, you're pulling my *hair*," Dulcie cried sharply.

"I expect I am," said Kyra with some heat. "I told
you, I don't know how to do this. What am I to do
with this hair of yours—it flops all over your head."

Dulcie bit her lip at another brutal tug. "I'll be bald-
headed if you keep up. Can't you be more careful?"

"I'm tryin', Miz Tremain."

"*Ouch!*" Dulcie grabbed the brush and threw it across
the room. In a rage, she turned to face Kyra. "I don't
know *how* many times I've *told* you to learn to do
things right, Kyra. Can't you learn anything?"

Kyra's expression was a mix of hurt and anger.

"Well, answer me! Can't you learn?"

"Yes, Miz Tremain, I can learn."

"Why don't you, then?" Dulcie, not expecting an answer, was prepared to say more, but Kyra began to speak.

"Miz Tremain, I'm not a maid, or a laundress, and I'm not used to your ways down here. I've been trying to do what you want of me, because I like you, and Captain Tremain is giving my husband a chance most black men never get. But I've been used to—used to having folks listen to me, not taking orders, Miz Tremain."

"Oh. Really! And would you mind explaining to me just why you think Captain Tremain furnished *you* passage down here?"

Kyra was taken aback, but only slightly. "Ruel, Jothan, and I are to help the freedmen and women learn to cope with their freedom."

Dulcie, hands on hips, tried to control her temper. She had never been confronted by a black woman like Kyra. In her waged a war between reluctant admiration of the woman's independence and knowledge that her own authority with all the servants was at stake if she allowed Kyra to have the upper hand in even the slightest way.

Momentarily at a loss for the logical solution, she said sarcastically, "I'm sure you're very well equipped to help your people, Kyra. And when the time comes, no doubt you'll try. Meanwhile, how do you propose to earn your living? Shall Captain Tremain and I provide you with room and board and await your desires?"

Kyra's eyes sought the solace of the sky outside the window. Her face was sad and troubled. "I don't want you and the Captain ever waiting on me, Miz Tremain. I don't know what to say . . ." She turned dark eyes filled with tears to Dulcie. "My people mean everything to me, Miz Tremain. I'm one of the lucky ones . . . I can read and write . . . and I was a teacher. There aren't so many black women who've been educated. I want—I was hoping there'd be some way I could work for the Freedmen's Bureau. I don't mean to be disrespectful to you, Miz Tremain, I—"

Dulcie slumped onto her vanity seat, her hands between her knees. "Oh, Kyra. No one will ever let a black woman do the things you want to do in the South. I don't want to hurt your feelings, but better I do than someone else who doesn't care about you. You're going to have to take a menial job whether you want it or not."

Unable to look at Kyra's face, Dulcie turned to her mirror and concentrated hard on fixing her own hair. But her feelings for the black woman wouldn't rest. Her mind flew on, forming arguments for Kyra. Why couldn't she teach her own people? Didn't the men always complain that the blacks couldn't vote, couldn't participate in the Legislature, couldn't even live up to work contracts because they were ignorant, untutored? *Why couldn't this woman help her people?*

"Why do I have to, Miz Tremain? Why must it be that way?"

"Because black women in the South have always been slaves, and people still think of them that way."

"Do you?"

"Who cares what I think!" cried Dulcie, nettled and upset, because her own position was little better than Kyra's, and because she felt helpless for them both.

"And another thing," she said with irritable quickness, "a black woman can't call a white woman Mrs. anything, the way another white woman would. I've told you before to call me Miss Dulcie."

Kyra lowered her head. Her eyes were fixed on the carpet. "Yes, Miss Dulcie."

Dulcie's large, golden-brown eyes grew moist. She clenched her small fists and wished momentarily she were a man and could take out her pent-up feelings in some physical demonstration as Adam might. It was difficult being a woman sometimes. There were so many means of accomplishment closed to her. But her very frustration gave her a new and burning determination to do something for Kyra. She didn't know what, and she didn't know how. But *something*.

She looked at Kyra and said softly, "I'm sorry, Kyra. You may have been emancipated, but you are not free. When the Yankees were passing out promises, they neglected to tell us that there is a great distance between emancipation and freedom." She turned from the pain on Kyra's face. "I'm facing facts."

Unable to continue the conversation, Dulcie went to Beau's room. Her young son gave a squeal of joy as he broke away from Mindy and toddled to his mother, his arms outstretched. Smiling broadly, Dulcie stooped down and let him run into her embrace. For the next hour Dulcie played with her son, repeating to him the names of the letters on his slate. But as pleasurable as her activity with the child was, it did not take her mind off Kyra.

It seemed that everything she did and thought only accentuated the inequity of Kyra's position. She couldn't forget that there were black children who would never learn their letters, for there was no one to teach them. But Kyra could read and write and figure.

Kyra could teach.

Her mind made up and her heart pounding with the audacity of it, Dulcie returned Beau to Mindy's care and went to her sitting room. She began to write a letter to General David Tillson, requesting that Kyra be permitted to do work for the Freedmen's Bureau from the Tremain home. Perhaps Kyra could not take a job in Savannah, but it should not mean that her services would be lost entirely. Finally satisfied that she had said everything she needed to say in the letter, Dulcie set it aside.

She took great care in dressing that afternoon, and was as nervous as a young girl awaiting her first suitor when Adam came to their suite. He had barely closed the door when Dulcie ran from her sitting room to face him.

"Adam! I would like to talk to you, please—right

now," she said breathlessly, the color in her face heightened, her eyes bright.

He paused, his hand still on the doorknob. His eyes raked over her, seeing her as he had not seen her for a long time. She was vibrant and beautiful; excitement emanated from her. He went to her, taking her hands in his. He wanted to kiss her, but waited, increasing the wanting, enjoying what he saw in her. It was said that marriage took the romance out of love, but he had never noticed a paling in their marriage.

Now he understood what that warning meant. She had changed. The Dulcie he saw and held in his hands was subtly different from the wife he had left this morning, and she excited him in a way she had done before they were married. He prolonged the moment of greeting, relishing the difference, the smooth feel of her skin, the moist bath fragrance of her.

She began to laugh softly at the look on his face. She kissed him lightly on the cheek, then received his not so light kiss on her lips. She pushed at him playfully. "Stop it! You're going to make me forget what I want to talk to you about, and it is *very* important."

He laughed with her, teasing her with his lips. "How important?"

"It's very important to me," she said more seriously.

He pulled back from her, looking at her carefully. A look of worry and uncertainty had crept into her eyes. He smiled gently. "No, Dulcie, I don't think you are refusing me. Come. Let's talk. I'm sure we'll get back to the other soon enough."

She began to smile brightly again. "Come into my sitting room. I have something I want you to read. You must be completely honest with me, Adam. I need to know if this is done properly. You must tell me."

"I will, but it would be helpful to know what it is."

She handed him the letter, and stood tense with anticipation. As soon as he saw the salutation, he looked up at her, his eyebrows raised. A question formed on his lips, but he began to read. "The letter is clear, to the point. It is a good letter, Dulcie. But why are you doing this? You could have asked me to take care of this for you."

This was the part Dulcie had feared. Would she ever be able to make him see that it wasn't his help she was refusing, but her own need to accomplish that she was succoring? She didn't know what to say, so she said the most inept thing possible. "I wanted to do it myself, Adam."

"But why? I've never refused you anything—"

She came to his side, wanting to be near him, but unwilling to touch him, for she would not use that aspect of their love to mollify him. "Kyra has told me of the things she wants to do for her people. She's capable of so much. She is, Adam. I wanted to help her. It isn't right that just because she's a woman and black, she must be a maid or—or some other thing that any one of a hundred women could be. She's different—special. I wanted to—I want her to have the chance to try."

"I can give that to her," he said, still uncomprehending. "Why didn't you ask me? You still haven't explained."

The thoughts were too new to Dulcie to be clear. She looked at him troubled, struggling for lucidity. "It's because you can just *give* it to her, and I can't—or maybe can't. I want to try too. Sometimes, Adam, it is very hard to be a woman, and—and want to do things—and not be able to." She bit her lower lip angrily. "Oh, I can't say what I want! I'm asking you to allow me to do something, and I can't even say what it is!"

Adam was looking out the window, his mind and heart full of memory. He didn't know what she had said that had brought a time long ago in his life back to him. Perhaps it was her inability to say what she felt at a time when she felt it so strongly that it permeated the air between them. She couldn't say the words, but he could feel her need and her desire to follow the things she believed in.

He remembered when that had happened to him. He had been no more than sixteen or seventeen years old, and he had tried to tell his uncle, Garrett Pinckney, what he felt about slavery and what he wanted to do about it. He hadn't been able to talk then either, only to feel. But Garrett had listened and had been moved by the teenager's stumbling attempts to take on a man's ideals.

He looked back to his wife, and loved her more than he had ever known it was possible to love another human being. "I understand what you are trying to say, Dulcie."

"You couldn't," she said angrily. "I've been wanting to tell you about Kyra and me and the things I've been thinking all day, and now I'm more tongue-tied than— than some old field hand." She was nearly crying with frustration.

He picked up the letter. "Put it in its envelope, Dulcie, and mail it."

"No, I'm not going to send it."

He stood up and walked away from her. "Why? Because you fear I will think you are headstrong and unfeminine?"

She didn't answer.

"Perhaps you even think I'll feel you are trying to undermine my masculine authority."

"Well, won't you?" she snapped, then regretted it. "Oh, Adam—I didn't mean that!"

He laughed, and came to her, hugging her to him. "Of course you mean it. Don't be such a coward. Idealists always must be very brave—it makes up for the sense of caution they lack. And until you can see it for yourself, just believe me when I tell you I do understand what you were trying to say."

"How could you?" she asked, looking up into his deep blue eyes.

He smiled at her. "Umm, when you are more certain of what you feel, I'll tell you all about it."

"Tell me now."

"Uh-uh. This is your time. We'll exchange views later. Go mail your letter, or all your good intentions will be for naught, and Kyra will continue to pull your hair out in great brushfuls."

Dulcie waited in an agony of uncertainty until the reply from General Tillson finally arrived. She flayed herself with every worry she could dream up. She worried that General Tillson would think her too bold, or worse, a silly, favor-seeking female. She fretted over having declined the usual method of asking her husband to petition for her, and worried even more greatly that she had damaged Adam's image in General Tillson's eyes by not even mentioning his name in the letter. What would he think of her? Would he assume Adam could not even control his own wife? Would he write to Adam first to see if answering her was agreeable with her husband? A dozen new worrisome questions plagued her each day.

When the letter came bearing General Tillson's name, she couldn't bring herself to open it. She walked through the suite carrying it, her eyes devouring it, her fingers poking at the seal, but unwilling to make the final push that would unlock the contents. Finally unable to endure it any longer, she went to her sitting room and locked the door so she could cry in private if necessary.

She held her breath as she slowly drew the letter from the envelope. She read only the first three lines before she let out a shriek of joyous laughter, jumped up from her desk, and ran from the suite. With her hair coming loose from its pins, she hailed a cab, and directed the driver to Factors' Row.

She burst into Adam's office, her hair flying, her cheeks red. "Adam, I haven't any money with me—will you pay the driver, please?"

She ran beside him as he went to the street. She was

fairly hopping by his side waving her letter. "It's come! Adam, he's said Kyra can work for the Freedmen's Bureau out of our house—even when we go to Mossrose. Adam, look!"

With one arm around Dulcie, trying to hold her reasonably still, Adam paid the disapproving driver, then, with a wink, scooped her up into his arms and carried her back to the office.

"Read my letter," she giggled. "Read it, read it, read it. It's a beautiful letter! He said *yes!*"

"Why don't you tell me what it says, and I'll look at you."

"I can't," she said, throwing her head back and laughing harder. "I only read the yes part. I don't know what it says."

Together they read the remainder of General Tillson's letter.

". . . I can't tell you how pleased I am to know that a lady such as yourself is concerned and interested in the plight of the freedmen. Our staff is pathetically inadequate to handle all of the needs and requirements of these people.

"Many of the Negroes have been separated for generations because of the peculiarities of the slave system. We would be most grateful to have your woman, Kyra Jordan, write letters of inquiry in an effort to reunite them. These letters are sent to churches and are read aloud. When someone in the congregation knows of a name, then there will be a reply. In that happy event a separated family member is reunited. The original letter is sent on to church after church. In this way, entire families have been brought together again.

"I have sent instructions to Mr. Laban Sweet of Savannah to provide Kyra Jordan with all the information and materials she will require to perform this task of mercy. May I also send you my warmest admiration, and to Captain Tremain my deep personal regards. I am yours sincerely,

> David Tillson
> General, United States Army
> Supervisor, The Freedmen's Bureau
> in Georgia

Adam kissed her, and bowed low before her. "I think this calls for Captain and Mrs. Tremain to celebrate long and boisterously into the night. I'll escort you home, and then we'll be out on the town. Come, my lady."

Adam closed the office and took Dulcie back to the hotel. Taking only enough time to tell Kyra of the news and instruct her as to what she should say and do when meeting Laban Sweet, Adam and Dulcie dressed and left to celebrate, saying that they would be back tonight or tomorrow or maybe next week. They left Jem and Patricia with looks of consternation on their faces. Kyra and Ruel, however, wore grins as large and happy as Adam's and Dulcie's.

By the first of April, 1867, Adam and Ruel had hired men, mostly blacks, to prepare the soil of Mossrose for the cotton so dear to Jem's heart. Adam had waited patiently until Laban Sweet finger-read his way through the contracts.

"Now whut's it mean heah, y'all goin' to funnish bed an' boahd? That come out o' theah pay?"

Adam pointed to the paragraph in question. "Bed, board, clothing, and three dollars and fifty cents per week for each man. Standard pay. The other items are spelled out here, three meals a day, three outfits per year, an attached cabin for each family."

"Attached to whut?"

"To the next cabin. Row houses."

After a few more questions, Sweet pronounced himself ready to accompany the men to the job site. "The

Beero puhvides transpohtation fo' the workers," he explained proudly.

"Why Mr. Sweet, how kind!" said Adam, sensing another flimflam.

"Ain't no special thing, Cap'n. Ah jes' want t'see whut the sitcheeation looks like. An' every now an' then, Ah pay you a s'prise visit. Ah want t'see you keepin' youah word, boy."

"No wonder you run yourself ragged, going from one end of the county to the other."

Sweet smiled grimly. "When Ah git paid enuf, Ah doan haf t'check up all the time like Ah'm goin' t'do with you."

"Well, we'll be pleased to have you. If you'll be coming often, you can take Kyra's letters of inquiry back to the Bureau with you and bring her fresh work. It'll save her occasional trips to town," Adam said cheerfully.

Sweet looked sourly at him. "Sonofabitch! You got a smart-ass answer for everything!"

"Could be." Adam waved at Tom. "Let's get these men moving."

Laban Sweet, not to be outdone, bustled around, prompting the workers to greater speed. A stream of black men moved down the steep stairs to the dock. Boxes, barrels, sacks of supplies were taken from the *Black Swan* and loaded onto heavy drays.

Finally, the lengthy procession of wagons, guarded by Adam, Tom, Jem, Ruel, Jothan, and Laban Sweet, began the trip to Mossrose. Adam was reminded of his trip there during the War. He had been wary of every moving creature, every sound, for it meant the possibility of attack. It was difficult to think that this was peacetime, and still they had to guard against plunder —or worse.

This area of Georgia suffered and would suffer from a food shortage all winter long. So few acres had been planted, and those not all harvested for lack of workers.

The Freedmen's Bureau handed out emergency food supplies, but even those were hard to come by.

The distribution of food in Georgia had been cut in half from last year. Hordes of black refugees had come to the cities from rural areas, and were moving north from Florida, crowding the streets of Savannah, existing hand-to-mouth in paper shacks they built wherever they could. Starving and destitute Confederate soldiers were still straggling home over dusty country roads only to find burned-out houses, empty fields, and families scattered or dead.

The contingent of workers and supplies on their way to Mossrose was a tempting oasis of plenty in the midst of famine. The Negroes were jittery and tense as the wagons rumbled along the rutted River Road, having to stop frequently to dislodge a wagon wheel from a pothole, or clear the road of debris or fallen trees.

Albatross, driving the lead wagon, for which Jem rode guard, raised his hand, shouting for the wagons to halt. Jem looked far down the road in front of him and saw nothing.

"What are you stopping for?" he shouted as he rode back to the driver. "Get this thing moving again!"

Albatross pointed ahead. "Doan look so good, suh."

Jem squinted into the distance. "What? What?" he sputtered.

"Trees down, suh. Look to me like sumbuddy put 'em dere. Ah doan like de look of it. Bettah ride up dere an' see."

"You damn well better be right. If I stop this train for nothing, I'll skin your hide right off you, boy." He cantered briskly back to the rear of the train. "Adam! Albatross thinks he sees something up ahead. I can't see a blamed thing, but he says there's trees down. He thinks we're riding into something." Jem scratched his head. "I don't think we'd better take a chance. I don't trust that black buck at all—he came off the Borens' plantation, Mallow. Every overseer and manager they had over there was a born cheat and liar."

"We'd better make sure. Jothan! Call out ten men and go up ahead to clear the road. You and Ruel ride guard. Give us a warning shot if you see anything amiss."

Jothan and Ruel walked their horses beside the ten laborers, their guns ready, their eyes moving quickly from one side of the road to the other.

Adam, Jem, and Tom rode slowly around the wagons, a small but constant cordon of armed men ready to defend the supplies and workers. Throughout the countryside, in the remote areas, bands of armed ruffians and former Confederate guerrillas called bushwhackers roamed—plundering, burning property, committing atrocities, and frequently killing blacks and whites they thought were loyal to the Union. A man such as Jem Moran who had lived North during the War then returned so flagrantly prosperous was a ready target for these thugs. Adam knew that sooner or later they would be visited by the hungry or the vengeful, desperate men, willing to kill for the food the wagon train carried.

Jothan, Ruel, and the men returned to the wagons. Ruel rode up to Adam. "We didn't see anything, but I don't like the look of it either. Those trees are cut fresh. Sure thing somebody put them across the road."

"But you saw nothing—no one?" Adam asked.

"No, Captain, but if we can see their trees from here, they can see our wagons too. They don't want us, they want the supplies. They're most likely just waiting."

Adam nodded.

Laban Sweet joined the small group. "You goin' thoo anyway?"

"We have to pass that spot sometime," Adam said simply.

"Lissen heah, Ah got t'perteck these men. Y'all ain't carryin' enuf perteckshun. Go on back to Savannah."

"And start out again tomorrow? No. We'll go through now." Adam rode over to one of the wagons. "Apollo. You said you were in the Army?"

"Yes suh, Ah was a Cap'n mahseff, like you, only Ahmy."

Adam tossed him a pistol. "Can you ride a mule?"

Apollo smiled as he jumped from the wagon. "Ah kin ride anything with laigs, Cap'n. We got us some bushwhackers up yondah?"

"Not sure," Adam said, his eyes on the distant road.

"Y'all give me a *good* mount, an' Ah find out fo' you. Ah stahted out as a scout. Ah'm still the best scout evah."

Adam looked hard at the tall, massively muscled man before him. Apollo's broad high cheekbones glistened in the cool sun. He had Indian blood in him, Adam thought, noting the high narrow-bridged nose, the firm line of his jaw.

"Ah'm standin' heah to tell you, Cap'n, you kin trust me. Ah nevah lies. Ah'm a good scout. Ah kin flush 'em out fo' you. If they's heah, Ah'll find 'em."

Without replying, Adam dismounted and handed Apollo the reins. "Don't be a hero. Call for help if you need us."

Apollo rubbed the horse's nose and neck, then mounted, his voice soft, crooning to the animal. Deftly he maneuvered the horse through a series of dancing steps, then trotted across the field away from the road.

Jem was at Adam's side in a moment. "Where's he going? What are you doing, Adam? What are we going to do about moving on?"

"Just hold on, Jem. Apollo knows what he's about."

" 'Pollo! My 'Pollo? I'd never have recognized him. He was just a boy—" Jem's voice trailed off.

All eyes riveted on the River Road as Apollo, with a bloodcurdling war cry, burst from a copse of trees. Before him, running in ragged confusion, were a man and several boys.

Albatross and several of the others jumped from the wagons and ran up the road. Apollo, walking the horse, brought to the wagons the several scrawny whites. "Heah's youah bushwhackahs." He dismounted, handing Adam the reins. "They's hardly worth the trouble."

Adam looked at the man with his emaciated face and bloated belly. Three of the boys were obviously his sons. The other two were probably wanderers, or neighbor children. The oldest could be no more than fourteen, Adam guessed. "What's your name?"

The man spat in the dust at Adam's feet. "Ah ain't tellin' you nothin'."

Laban Sweet came up. "Youah undah 'rest!" He fumbled for his badge. "Ah'm a swawn offisah o' the law, an'—"

"Take it easy, Laban. The man hasn't done anything yet."

The man looked up at Adam, then at Sweet, shrewd comprehension dawning in his eyes. "That's right. Ah ain't done nothin'. This hyah man had his man 'tack me an' mah boys. 'Res' him. Ya'll the law, 'res' him. He 'tack me. Y'all seen it."

The boys parroted agreement.

Sweet grew red in the face. "Ah ain't nevah heard the like. Y'all bettah git youah asses outta heah befo' Ah lose control o' mahseff. Ah see you layin' in wait agin, an' Ah have you in the jailhouse fo' the next hunnert yeahs."

After the man and the boys had scurried back to cover, Jem asked, "Why did you let them go? You know they were laying for us."

"Sure Ah know it," Sweet shouted irritably. "But the suckah's right. He didn't do nothin'. We 'tacked him. Sonofabitch!"

With much talk and confusion, the wagon train began to move again. They had all looked forward to arriving at Mossrose and what seemed like safety. The first few moments after their arrival told them how mistaken they had been. Working at Mossrose in these early days, there would be constant danger. Several of the men were put to patrolling the vast, empty fields day and night. Tents were erected on the exposed, unprotected lawn. Until shelter could be built, the men would sleep in the tents. Despite their numbers, each man felt lonely and vulnerable working on the empty land without shelter and against time and the marauding, hungry men who skulked in the countryside beyond their sight.

Jothan became an overseer under Jem, while Ruel took charge of stores and accounting. The three men developed priorities for the labor. Before the rebuilding could start, it was necessary to house the workers and, as soon as possible, the horses and mules. Of equal priority was the erection of a substantial storage building for the foodstuffs.

Mossrose stood in the open countryside, exposed and tempting. Adam worried constantly about protecting the workers. He turned again to Apollo, placing him in charge of a cadre of men who would do nothing but patrol and keep watch. It was an impossible task. There were too many acres, too many ways they could be attacked, and too few men and guns for them to be properly prepared. But he felt Apollo would do all that any of them could do.

The field hands, in spite of their numbers and the animals and their daily efforts, were making very slow progress. Jem and Patricia had left Mossrose to survive on its own in early 1862. The five intervening years had done nothing to soften the red clay soil, which turned to harsh, thick crust with every downpour. Jem, to whom getting ready for planting meant nearly as much as the erection of his house, surprisingly blamed no one for the delay.

Under Jothan's supervision and Albatross's leadership, cajolery, threats, and outright two-fistedness, the storage room and stables were built during the following months. They began on the row houses, each of which was to be sixteen by twelve feet, partitioned into two rooms. After a heated argument between Adam and Jem, the size was increased by two feet each way; each cabin would have a chimney and hearth.

By the end of each day, the men were exhausted and

happy to be able to crawl into the damp, drafty tents. Aside from Apollo and his vigilant crew, Mossrose looked abandoned at night.

They had been at the plantation for two months and there had been no further attempts to steal food or animals. Slowly the tension began to fade, and the men to feel secure in their outpost. Apollo was in a fury, frustrated that he couldn't make his small army of guards understand that it was now that they needed to be most alert.

"'Those bushwhackahs been in the Ahmy theyseffs. They knows what to look fo','" he preached, marching up and down before his night patrol. "They ain't gonna come fo' you when you's lookin'. They gonna sneak up on you when you ain't watchin'."

Dark, sleepy, bored eyes looked back at him.

Apollo stuck his face up close to the first black man in line. "Iffen they doan come sneakin' up on you, Ah will! Ah'll be out theah, an you woan see me or heah me till Ah'm right up youah ass! You keep awake, you heah!"

He sent them all out to their posts and then began his own restless, wary prowl of the land. The rest of the men went to sleep. Jem, Adam, and Tom kept watch over the newly built storage and stables.

With the closing twilight they listened to the *jo-clack* clatter of the guineas, the frantic squealing of wild pigs, and the last evening song of the mockingbird. In the darkness there were sounds less identifiable. It was a peaceful November night, one meant to lull a man to sleep in its cool, embracing arms.

As dawn neared, the shadows of moving creatures blackened the dark earth. Slow, stealthy disturbances of the soil and the grass could be heard. Apollo, his head raised high and cocked to one side, was tense and alert, trying to locate their sources. The men's snoring blurred the keenness of his hearing. Silently he crouched and moved like a shadow himself along the outskirts of the area where the men slept.

Suddenly there were streaks of light, and screams cut through the night air. The tent nearest the food storage blazed up in a bright golden pillar of flame. Men leaped up and ran through the dark, flaming pieces of tarpaulin clinging to their backs.

Apollo fired a warning shot, waking those few who were not already racing around the yard in confusion and fright. Adam placed himself at the door to the storage house, his guns drawn.

The noise and tumult seemed to go on forever, but nothing else was happening. No attack was made on the storage building, and no one could be seen but the terrified workers of Mossrose.

Slowly the light crept up from the east, staining the night sky with morning colors. Adam and Jem began to tend to the men who had been burned, none badly. Tom and Apollo checked the property for damage, still on guard, still expecting an attack.

Tom returned to Adam, his face grim. "Well, they got what they wanted, or at least part of it. Three of the mules are gone, and two of the horses."

Adam ordered Apollo to take some of the field hands and double the guard.

Several days later, Laban Sweet returned to the plantation.

"You coming to check up on us already, Sweet?" Adam asked.

"Not this time, Cap'n. You promised t'escort these folks to the votin' polls. Y'all didn't fo'git, did you?"

Adam rubbed his forehead. "To be honest, Laban, I had forgotten. I'll have the men at the polls. The Legislature may vote down the Fourteenth Amendment, but they won't be able to stop it at the polls."

With the help of Ruel and Apollo, Adam escorted the men into Savannah to the polls, in groups of ten, made certain that each man knew what was stated on the ballot, and that the votes were placed in the proper box. Crowded election workers relied on the Negroes' inability to read. It was an easy matter to reposition the candidates' names on the ballot, thereby misleading a Freedman into voting for someone he didn't mean to. And outside the voting places, men were always waiting, ready to pay any man whose vote could be purchased.

By sunset, when every Mossrose worker had voted, the men were chattering excitedly among themselves, pleased with their new experience.

As November ended, order was coming to the desolate plantation. The row cabins were finally finished. With great relief the men quitted their uncomfortable tents. The following day Adam brought their wives and families. Jem, in a seizure of generosity, gave them all two days off to celebrate, and declared there would be a frolic at Mossrose the second night.

The blacks prepared with zest. The largest hog in the pen was slaughtered and put to roast over a long pit fire. A wide area of the lawn was trimmed for dancing. Every man and woman who played a musical instrument readied himself. Those who owned none made some musical apparatus out of anything from bones to empty barrels, or bits of tinkling metal. Through the day there could be heard the toot, saw, and boom of bone flutes, gourd fiddles, and hollow-log drums.

Adam had expected to leave Dulcie, Beau, and Patricia in the hotel in Savannah until the house was built. But the ladies insisted they all be present at the first party the new Mossrose was to have. However, Ned Whitaker approached Adam with the proposal of lodging his family in his twenty-two-room house for the year or two it would take to rebuild Mossrose. Adam seized on the idea. He suggested a price, a procedure that would have been insulting and unthinkable before the War, still would have been between less practical men. But Ned agreed. The Whitakers headed the list of neighbors who would come to the frolic.

Emma Whitaker helped them settle into the six spacious rooms of the north wing. Then the women all fell to planning what they would wear. Emma and Patricia tried to outdo each other with reminiscences of frolics the slaves had held on their respective plantations years back. With great giggling they discussed how before the War they would never have dreamed of going to a frolic, much less be eager for this one. It seemed as though a part of the Old South they had thought never to see again was returning, if only for a night.

On the night of the frolic, there was a great, orange harvest moon. The pungent smells of barbecued hog, fried fish, and hush puppies hung in the air. On plank tables were dishes of baked beans, cornbread, applesauce, peas, and potatoes. Nearby stood kegs of cider and whisky, presided over by a watchful Ruel. At first the blacks and whites, scrupulously polite to one another, kept their distance. Then as the music struck up a few blacks started to dance.

During the first dance, the women stood stock-still while the men danced around them, kneeling, making faces, and doing acrobatic contortions, writhing like serpents. Swiftly, then, they changed into another dance in which the men twirled the women around, the women waving gaily colored handkerchiefs over their heads. Ruel and Jothan and their wives watched avidly, for these dances were as new to them as to most of the County neighbors.

Between dances Ruel called out, "Can you boys play 'Shoo Fly' or 'Dolly Day'? We'll show you how to do a polka!"

The makeshift orchestra began a rousing version of "Dolly Day." Ruel and Kyra skipped nimbly, gracefully, to the lilting music. Then Jothan and Mindy joined in, whirling over the grass. Soon other couples were trying the new dance. Ruel and Kyra bowed to each other and separated, Ruel choosing as partner a young black woman who stood nearby. Kyra, reaching out at random, found her hand in Apollo's.

The big handsome man put his arm around her and kept it there while she showed him the basic steps. Smiling, they danced for a number of measures. Then suddenly their eyes held, and warm color heightened in Kyra's face. It was not long before she and Apollo took other partners.

Adam and Dulcie were nearby, each teaching someone the polka. Gradually almost everyone joined in.

Once the ice had been broken, only the music was needed to keep people smiling, talking, and dancing until they were happily exhausted. Then they all ate and drank, merry in the frosty air.

Apollo came over to Adam afterwards, his face wrinkled. "Cap'n, Ah'm right worrit 'bout you. Dat hog you et died o' mallitis, an' it might mek you sick."

"It'll make us both sick then, for I saw you eat your share. Why'd you wait so long to tell me, Apollo?"

Apollo laughed, pleased. "That's jes' a joke, Cap'n. Ah had a darky sahjint in the Ahmy name Ol' Cooch. He tell me his mastah doan feed his darkies very good. But he got sebben hogs fattenin' in the pen fo' wintah. One mawnin' Ol' Cooch rap on the back do' an' tell his mastah them hogs all daid o' mallitis. Mastah look, an' they all daid, an' the darkies all standin' 'roun' lookin' mighty sad 'bout all dat good meat daid. Mastah doan waste nothin'. He think the daid hogs good enuf fo' suhvants, so he tell them to fix up the hogs anyhow. So the darkies git to eat hog meat an' the mastah doan. What happen was, Ol' Cooch go out early in the mawin' an' bash them hogs in they head with a big ol' mallet. So they died of mallitis, like Ol' Cooch say."

Adam chuckled. "That's a good joke, Apollo. I'd like to pull it on Mr. Moran, but I don't think he'd enjoy it."

After the late supper, guests began to take leave. When the neighbors had gone, the frolic went on until daybreak. Adam did not go to bed at all, but kept watch with Apollo and Ruel well into the following day. He was thankful that no armed thieves had taken advantage of the merriment to cause trouble.

The frolic had an effect on Emma Whitaker no one had anticipated. The War and its aftermath had left such an emptiness, no one had tried to recover the grace or the joviality of times past. But now Emma felt a renewed vigor and hope. With all her energy she threw herself into plans for a Christmas party. Dulcie and Patricia became eager accomplices. Kitchen, storerooms, and trunks were plundered for every scrap of material that could be made to look festive. The Whitaker house came alive with decorations.

Christmas seemed almost like the old days when all the neighbors gathered for an evening of celebration, carol singing, and a buffet supper. Dulcie hesitated before putting on her third-best dinner dress of lilac silk trimmed with heavy, cream-colored lace.

"Do you think I'll look overdressed, Adam? I've hardly seen anybody yet who wasn't in rags and patches."

"Well, my love, since you don't have rags and patches, why not wear something in which you look beautiful?"

Dulcie, standing in her French-lace chemise and pantalettes, grinned at him. "It's hard to look poor when we're as rich as we are."

Adam agreed, thinking still with some surprise of the several million dollars he had earned as a blockade runner. He had risked his life time and again only for love of the South, but the money had come rolling in. It was safely deposited in English and Swiss banks, waiting to be used for the benefit of the South. Long ago he had determined he would put back into this land he loved all he had gotten from it.

At the party the Tremains, Morans, and Whitakers were the only obviously prosperous people. There were the Tweed sisters, Phoebe and Zenobia, pink-cheeked and sturdy as peasants, smiling, animated, seeming to share some hilarious secret. Jan Chilcote, his wife Blossom Saunders, and their children arrived. Blossom at twenty-six was the mother of five. She was still pretty, with her curly blond hair and delicate features, but poor nutrition had given her a pasty fatness. Mrs. Saunders followed with six-year-old Ferron, plump, rosy-cheeked, and more girlishly pretty than any of his sisters.

Glenn and Addie Jo Acton Saunders greeted the Tremains formally, and Glenn again thanked Dulcie for visiting him while he was imprisoned on David's Island in New York. Glenn's older brother Todd, haughty and dark-haired as a youth, now was surly, graying prematurely, and had a moist cough he was careless about covering up. Lung fever, he said, from too many months in the hole in Capitol Prison in Washington City.

Billy Bob Acton and his wife Birdie Saunders arrived. Dulcie was shocked to see Billy Bob on crutches, his right leg off above the knee. He explained jovially that ex-soldiers could get free wooden legs from the state and that he was still waiting to get his. Dulcie flew to hug Birdie, her dear companion in girlhood mischief. Birdie alone of all her friends looked the same. Her dark hair still curled around her pleasantly pointed face, her blue eyes still sparkled with love of life. Even the dimples at the corners of her mouth still deepened with every smile. They had no children, Birdie said, adding that she didn't think now was a good time to bring up children. Dulcie thought of plump Beau, rocking himself to sleep on his hands and knees in his crib when she had left him in Mindy's care.

The Whitakers' house became livelier with every moment. Old friends renewed friendships and remembered stories and happy times from the past. Ned Whitaker, dressed in the regalia of an earlier day, served wine to all his guests. Small groups of people began to sing the old Christmas songs, and applaud themselves.

Phoebe, the smaller of the Tweed sisters and unusually shy, declared herself willing to recite—after downing a generous glass of blackberry wine. Scarcely five feet tall and ninety pounds, her hair white as snow and her face as innocent as a newborn's, Phoebe folded her dainty hands before her, and in a fluting voice recited:

"Oh, Ah'm a good old rebel
Now that's just what Ah am;
For the fair land of freedom
Ah do not give a damn;
Ah'm glad Ah fit against it,
Ah only wish we'd won,
And Ah don't want no pardon
For anything Ah done."

Everyone in the room burst into laughter and applause. Phoebe blushed ferociously and looked for her stronger sister.

Zenobia, her lips pursed and eyes snapping, hauled Phoebe from in front of the harpsichord. "Sister! You've drunk more than you can hold!" she whispered fiercely.

Phoebe's eyes widened until they looked as if they might pop from her head. She drew in breath until she was puffed up like a little pigeon. "Why, Zenobia, I never drink anything! Not even water. Why, you know I never allow a drop of liquid to pass my lips!"

As the two sisters argued in hisses, three men arrived together. Slender, quiet Arthur Redgrave lived with his elderly parents on a dead plantation that adjoined Mossrose. Now he kept bread on their table by scavenging bones, metal scraps, and the lead from bullets left lying on battlefields and selling them to the Federals at fifty cents a hundredweight. Lyman Matthews, filthy, morose, and already drunk, followed Arthur. Last to enter was Leroy Biggs.

Dulcie's eyes were drawn to Leroy immediately. She had been saddened tonight by the effect of the War on some of her old friends. But looking at him, she thought he had changed the most of any of them. He still carried himself defiantly, walking with a swagger, but the buoyant antagonism, the animal meanness that once had characterized him, seemed to have vanished.

The Leroy she saw tonight was a sad and defeated man. He did not notice her; she watched him greet the Whitakers, his parents-in-law, with grudging cordiality. Dulcie wondered if Leroy's wife was ill, or if she hadn't recognized her. Certainly Camille had not come in with Leroy.

Beside her, Adam and Cutler were discussing the interest rates, which currently ranged from eighteen to twenty-four percent throughout the South. Idly, still trying to figure out what made Leroy different, she watched him take a cup of punch, make some comment that caused Zenobia Tweed to snort with laughter. Then he turned his head toward her. The motion was as smooth and purposeful as that of a snake preparing to strike. He had known she was there all along.

Dulcie moved a step closer to Adam. She was accustomed to large, muscular men. It was not Leroy's size that made her feel apprehensive.

He worked his leisurely way toward her, stopping to chat with Jem, who smiled and wrung his hand in welcome, and to tease Grandmother Whitaker before kissing her dry, wrinkled cheek. He waited until Adam and Cutler moved toward the buffet table. Then he stood before her, a rough-hewn gallant in torn blue trousers and mustard frock coat. "Dulcie, it's good to see you."

"Leroy—it's been—a long time, hasn't it?"

Leroy's smile was broad and genuine. "Glad to see

you brought your boat driver home with you. I heard you finally got married."

Dulcie ignored the barb; that was more like the old Leroy. "Yes, we have a son now, a year old."

Leroy's face darkened. "I had a son."

Dulcie looked down. "I'm sorry, Leroy. Is that why Camille isn't here? I didn't see her with you. Is she—I must stop by—"

He said harshly, "Camille's dead. Died in the swamp."

Dulcie drew in her breath quickly. She put her hand on his arm. "Oh, Leroy, I didn't know—I'm so sorry—I'd never have brought it up—"

He seemed to need to say it to her, tell her how his wife had died. "There was renegades come through—Yankee deserters stealin' whatever Sherman left. My maw and paw—maybe you remember 'em, Dulcie, they were as tough as me an' Conroy—Maw and Paw fought it out with 'em. They killed half a dozen of 'em before they got killed theirselves.

"Camille, she was livin' with 'em while I was gone, an' she ran out the back with my son Royal to hide in the swamp. I guess she—got lost. Then the new baby was comin', an' she had to lay down to have it. Nobody knew where she was. She had a baby girl all by herself. Then she bled to death all alone in the swamp."

Dulcie, tears in her eyes and a painful lump in her throat, squeezed his arm for want of words.

"Her daddy, Ned, found her there after three or four days o' huntin' for her. She an' the baby girl were layin' in a pool of blood. They don't know what happened to Royal. They couldn't only track him so far before they lost the trail. Ned even went over to S'vannah an' hired dogs, but it wasn't no use. They didn't even find his little bones."

"What a terrible blow for you—"

He looked hard at her, his eyes speaking words his mouth was not. "It was. I was countin' on raisin' that

boy up. I married so's I could have sons to carry on
for me. But don't want you mistakin' me, Dulcie. It
wasn't Camille I loved."

Dulcie suppressed a shiver.

His hazel eyes were steady on her face. "No, it
wasn't Camille I wanted. I married her, an' she had
my younguns for me, but it was like I said."

Dulcie's mind seethed with unformed questions about
Camille and pity for the dead woman; but all she could
think of was the hard, cold man before her.

In a calm, separate part of her mind she realized
what his sensual gray-green eyes were telling her. The
woman Leroy wanted was herself. He wanted her to
know it. Had Adam remained by her side, Leroy would
have risked a duel, or a fight, to let Adam know it.

Determined she wouldn't let him see he had succeeded in frightening her, she said, "What are you
going to do now, Leroy?"

"Oh, I got my plantation back, an' I'm workin' it
some. I got a still. I barter a little whisky for bread an'
beans. I make out."

Dulcie smiled and expressed her pleasure that he was
coping all right. As quickly as courtesy allowed, she
excused herself, saying she was going to join Adam.

The evening passed pleasantly as Dulcie caught up
with news of her old neighbors, exchanged promises to
keep in touch, and planned visits. Of the Whitakers
her age, four were left. Enid was twenty-four, a sallow
and bitter old maid; it was whispered that she had
fallen in love with a Yankee she nursed, who promised
to marry her, recovered, and left her. Cedric, the middle son, had married black-haired Pearl Carson in Tennessee and brought her home with him. Cutler and
Brock, at ages twenty-eight and thirty, were bachelors.

All the Whitaker sons had served the Confederacy
with grace and gallantry. Once home, Cutler and Brock
had seen their chances at marriage diminished to almost
nothing. If they married a girl of their station, it was
likely they would also marry her family's postwar

poverty. Neither man felt able to take on the burden of another plantation. Though the Whitakers had come through the War with a sizable fortune intact, it would take all they had and more to return the land to its former productivity. Neither Brock nor Cutler felt he could afford to marry. They were tied to a ravaged piece of earth.

Dulcie noticed again and again that the people who had been robbed of the most and had the most to be bitter about did not talk bitterly. She had heard far more bitterness from Northerners in Nassau, New York, and Washington than she heard from these Southerners. Ned Whitaker did not openly mourn his son Andrew or his daughter Camille, or mention his two grandchildren. Jan Chilcote did not sigh for his freed slaves who had once made life so pleasant; Billy Bob Acton joked about his lost leg and spoke with perfect naturalness of his brother Jim Ed who had died beside him in battle. It was as if by not grieving for the days and things that were gone they might still be made to return.

But, she thought, some of them must be bitter, seething with rage and frustration, boiling inside with a fury that had no outlet. Surely some of these men want to get even—with somebody.

When the party ended, Dulcie and Adam stood with the Whitakers at the door wishing each person well on his way home. Leroy took Dulcie's hand in both of his. His face was flushed from the warmth of the fire and from the wine. He looked at her for a moment, then, still holding her hand, he turned to Adam. "Y'all got your butt beat when we voted down the Fourteenth Amendment, Cap'n. That oughta tell you somethin' about the people hereabouts. We don't cotton to Yankee ways or laws."

"Perhaps the Legislature feels that way, Leroy, but apparently the people don't. It was a Radical sweep in the popular election."

Leroy's lip curled into a semblance of a smile. "Sure,

you won that. You corralled every darky in the county
and told 'em how to vote. Put the white trash an' the
niggers together an' you can fix any election. But it
won't last, Cap'n. Things will go back to their rightful
balance. Good night, Dulcie. I hope—no, I'm *promisin'*
—I'll see you again. Soon." His last look was for Adam.

Adam and Dulcie waited until the last guest left
before going to their rooms. Together they looked in
on Beau, then undressed for the night. Adam was unusually quiet.

Dulcie rubbed his back. "What are you thinking,
Adam? Is anything wrong? I thought it was a nice
party. Did you see Birdie? She hasn't changed a bit.
I'll be so glad to talk with her again—"

"I want you to stay away from Leroy Biggs."

"Adam! You've never asked anything like that of
me before. What did he say to you? Surely you're not
jealous of him."

Adam didn't know how to tell her what he was feeling, for that was all it was: feeling. The War had given
all men who lived through it a sixth sense. He felt the
evil of Leroy and could smell the hate and bitterness
turning the man rank. But Dulcie didn't know that and
wouldn't understand how deep a man's feelings could
run in politics, even deeper when his masculine pride
was at stake. Adam didn't know by what means, but
somehow Leroy had made it plain that he was Adam's
adversary, and that if he could win no other way, he
would try to win through Dulcie.

He remained silent and awake. He would be leaving
for New Orleans the first of the year, and some things
had to be settled before then. If he could just find the
words to impress upon Dulcie the importance of her
own safety. He had left her alone many times before,
but that had been in Nassau, where she was compara-
tively safe. And that was during the War, which in its
own peculiar way had far more honor in it than the
aftermath had.

Here in Chatham County they had come back to a frontier, where a man's life and goods must continually be fought for. He would be leaving his goods and, so long as his wife and son were here, his heart; but he would not be present to fight for them.

He did not want to persuade her to come with him against her own desires, for she seemed to feel a genuine duty to stay with her parents. Not, she assured him, that she didn't prefer being with him. But just now her parents needed her more than he did.

"I'll be gone several months, you know," he said, finally, "and Tom will be leaving too. He'll live in New Orleans again."

Dulcie pressed her cheek against his comforting bare shoulder. "I'll miss you so much. It seems as if we've been parted more than we've been together. It's nice that you still get jealous." She giggled in pleasure.

He said softly, "I do," and let her think it the reason he wanted her to stay away from Leroy. "You promise you won't see him until I've come home?"

"I promise," she said happily, snuggling closer to him. "I won't have time to bother with Leroy anyway. We're both going to be so busy, Adam! And I'll be thinking of you all the time. Maybe by the time you've returned Mossrose will begin to look like something. And you'll have news for me. When you buy the plantation down there, make sure we have a lovely house. I want a house that is—is gorgeous, with lots of trees and a place for Beau to play."

Adam chuckled. "I couldn't overlook your house and Beau's yard. What kind of planter would I be if my children didn't have a yard?"

She poked him lightly in the ribs. "And give Ben and Glory my love. I miss Glory. She is such fun. I haven't been on a real shopping spree since we left Nassau. No one can raid a shop like Glory. Will Ben be running the shipping business from New Orleans?"

"I hope he's already got it well in hand. Right now

everything looks good, with Cutler running the Savannah office. That means I can keep the line open here when we move to New Orleans."

"Oh, Adam, that's wonderful. And Cutler—Cutler can get married, if he wants to."

Adam groaned. "I think I may have done a good friend a disservice. When will you and your mother begin the matchmaking?"

"As soon as possible! And don't make fun of it either. After all, I matchmaked us."

"You matchmaked us, huh?" he said, and turned onto his side, pulling her close against him.

Dulcie moved into his arms, her hands smoothing across his broad chest. She arched her neck back so she could look at him. His smile was soft and loving. She nibbled at the edge of his mustache, playfully tugging at it, then her lips touched him. She shivered in pleasure as his hand moved slowly, searchingly across her breast, and down the curve of her hip. As she snuggled closer to him, she could feel him smiling.

The world that they alone shared began to emerge, bright and warm. Dulcie gave herself up to it totally. His lips were warm on her breasts. She ran her hands through his curly black hair as she looked down at herself, noting happily how dark and masculine he looked against the light fairness of her skin.

She couldn't resist the impulse to laugh, and the sound was gentle and joyful. Adam moved to cover her with his body. He kissed her face, her ears, her neck. She began to rotate her hips, touching him, teasing him. He kissed her nipples, his tongue working around the deep pink aureoles until they stood erect and hard. Both of them were breathless, caught in a maelstrom of pleasure and need for each other. Slowly Adam lowered his weight onto her, and Dulcie raised herself to meet him. With long slow motions they moved together, the rhythm increasing, the urgency heightening, and they both held on, wanting the moment to be endless, a zenith to be approached, but not passed.

Finally unable to hold back, they clung to each other, letting the passion envelop them, wrap them together as one. Long afterwards, when their tremors had ceased, they fell asleep still embracing.

CHAPTER NINE

Dulcie looked down at her plate, then from the corner of her eye watched her husband. It was the morning Adam was to leave, and they had awakened early to have breakfast together before the household began to stir. "Are you and Ben going to be talking about new ships?" she asked.

"What makes you ask that?"

"You said the *Black Swan* isn't built to carry enough cargo for what you now have in mind. I was just thinking—new ships mean a trip to Europe, don't they? I want to go with you when you order the new ones."

Adam laughed. "If I go, I promise to take you along." Then he said, "You didn't have it in your head that I am going to Europe after I've seen Ben in New Orleans?"

Dulcie's eyes twinkled. "I know you and Ben when you get together. The next I hear from you, you could be halfway across the world."

"Well, set your mind at rest. I am coming back to Mossrose as soon as I can conclude my business. I don't want you left alone here with the burden of running things any longer than necessary."

"Oh, Adam, you make it sound so—so serious. I won't be doing anything. Of course, I will have to keep Daddy from noticing Kyra. He does have a fit over the idea of a black woman not working his way. To him, her work with the Freedmen's Bureau avoids real work."

"She's not his nigger," Adam said sharply. Then, more softly, he added, "Dulcie, you're going to have to stand up for what you believe in. Your father will back down when someone in authority sets him straight."

"Authority! Me? I don't have authority!"

"Yes, you have. I've seen you use it many times. When a shopkeeper cheats you, for example. When one of your Nassau friends failed to keep her word. You may not know you do it, but you have a very fine way of telling people what they've done wrong without turning to pettiness. I have great confidence in your ability to handle adverse situations, Dulcie mea, or I'd never leave you on your own."

"That's the nicest compliment you ever gave me, Adam."

"Furthermore, if I hadn't seen this in you I'd never have married you."

"Hindsight," she said, and giggled.

"Be that as it may, you have the necessary backbone to survive in this wilderness, which brings me to another point. I expect you and your mother will begin visiting the neighbors. Gossip is an important way for you to learn about local situations. Keep your ears open. Pay attention to the darkies too, for you learn from them when they don't know you're listening. And I want you to go nowhere without an armed guard."

"Oh, *Adam!* This isn't the Wild West!"

"Dulcie, except for the items Reverend Hooks and Nemo Whitelaw carry in their little store, we have more articles of value than anyone else around here. Anyone who watches your movements will soon know you carry food and other gifts on your visits. Never underestimate what will tempt a desperate man, my love."

Dulcie shuddered. "I can't even imagine . . ." She looked at Adam. "There is something more that you haven't told me."

"I was getting to it." He told her of the roaming bands of blacks and whites, and of their burning and killing. "I don't want you to be frightened, just wary. You won't be besieged, but you must learn to be on guard even against people you know."

"You're talking about Leroy again, aren't you?"

"Yes. And Lyman Matthews. Don't trust either one, or let them in the house."

"Adam, I can't keep Leroy out. He's the Whitakers' son-in-law. Emma Whitaker would have to have a very good reason for keeping him out of her house."

Adam made a gesture of annoyance. "I had forgotten. Well, keep him out of the north wing."

"I will," she said, her heart sinking. Her responsibility for the family in Adam's absence was beginning to take on monumental proportions. "Is there anything else?"

"I won't be too surprised if the blacks start wandering off. Try to keep your father on an even keel with them. They've worked faithfully so far, contrary to expectations."

"Reverend Hooks preaches to them a couple of nights a week, Kyra tells me, and they end up having a frolic."

"They've got to have their fun. But if we lose too many workers, or they get drunk and start causing trouble, put Apollo in charge here, and send Ruel to the Bureau to fetch Laban Sweet. He's crooked as a dog's hind leg, but he'll do his job."

"There are nearly always some blacks who are sick. Is their care our responsibility or the Bureau's?"

"We've been fortunate so far. Some of the other districts have had smallpox outbreaks. And as you know, so many of our people are malarial and have intermittent fevers. But I don't want you nursing them. Find out what's wrong and give medicine and instructions, but no spending time in the cabins. If you have this kind of trouble, let Ruel and Kyra handle it. Will you promise? These aren't our people. We don't really know them."

"Adam, you never used to talk this way about darkies. You always trusted them. Why don't you trust them now?"

"Before the War there was a rapport between most

blacks and whites. There were also clear lines of behavior. A white man had a personal interest in his darkies, and the darky was a part of a family. Now neither black nor white has tie or obligation to each other. The blacks have been told they are going to be equal to the whites. They're bolder without being correspondingly more responsible. And the whites—you know well enough the attitude of most whites, Dulcie. I don't know just which way the cat is going to jump. I don't know whom to trust."

"I'll be careful, I promise."

"I'm probably being overcautious, to appease my conscience for leaving you."

"You mustn't feel that way, my darling," she assured him. "I'm a survivor, remember? The person who undergoes terrible tortures and lives to tell all about them in gruesomely rich detail."

He pulled her closer to him. "Dulcie, don't."

"Besides," she said, much less flippantly, "you must have room to fulfill your own goals and obligations. You have to have freedom, just as I do. I need to grow more. I know that. I need to find out what I'm capable of when I'm the one making decisions."

"There's nothing you can't do, my love," he said confidently.

"I'll make you proud of me," she boasted. "As I am proud of you."

Reluctantly Adam said good-bye to her, took his carpetbag, and left the house, heading for Mossrose. Still worried and uncertain about leaving her alone, he spoke with Apollo and Ruel. With them, he was specific about his worries.

"Laban Sweet tells me he's had reports from all over the County of a band of hooded men burning cabins, robbing, and intimidating blacks and whites who don't agree with their views. No one knows much about them. I've heard they call themselves the Ku Klux."

"We can be sure they aren't going to like us," Ruel said. "How long will you be gone, Captain?"

"Several months."

"Doan worry none, Cap'n. Me 'n' Ruel look aftah Mossrose."

"I'm counting on you, Apollo, for that and more. In my absence, Mrs. Tremain is in charge. I want you to help her. She'll have no trouble with you men, or Jothan, but others will try to take advantage of her because she is a woman. Make certain one of you is always with her. Back up her authority, and for God's sake, keep her safe."

"We woan let her go nowheah without one o' us bein' with her, suh. Ah sweahs it as a offisah an' a gent'man," Apollo said sincerely.

"It isn't going to be easy. One man I don't want near her is Leroy Biggs. I don't want him to step foot on Mossrose or go near the north wing of the house. Ruel, I want you to see to that. Apollo, I want you to guard Mossrose—and do what you can to keep Mr. Moran from, umm, from—"

Apollo laughed heartily. "Ah knows, Cap'n, Ah knows. Ah can't give mah word Ah'll keep him from steppin' in the shit, but Ah'll guard Mossrose fo' you."

Adam remained indecisive, reluctant to leave.

Ruel finally said, "Have a good journey, Captain Tremain."

"Ruel," Adam began slowly, "be certain Dulcie learns to . . . to take care of the plantation. If I were not here, she'd have to manage the family by herself. She needs to know so many things I've never had the chance to teach her."

"Lawd, Cap'n, you ain't feelin' the weight of a evil eye?" Apollo breathed.

"No, Apollo, I have no premonitions. I'm being realistic. I've made many enemies. I expect to outlive them all, but it is stupid to be blind to the possibility that I won't. I want Dulcie prepared to go on if . . . in the event something should detain me."

Adam touched his hat, said good-bye to them, and walked briskly to the stables, where Albatross was waiting to drive him to the Savannah docks.

Dulcie stood at the upstairs window staring at the long, narrow drive that led from the Whitakers' to the River Road. She knew Adam had already gone to Mossrose and that she couldn't see him pass by on his way to Savannah, but it made her feel better to watch the road. She had been very brave while he had talked to her, and she had even felt a warm glow of capability. But now that he was actually gone, she felt small and alone. This was not like other times he had left her, as he had during the War. This was different, and somehow more threatening.

As she pondered the reasons, Kyra entered the room bearing a tray. "Good morning, Miss Dulcie."

Dulcie turned quickly. "Kyra! What are you doing waiting on me?"

Kyra smiled, her lips slightly turned down at the edges. "Oh, I can manage a tray now and then. I thought you might be feeling a little lonesome about now. Let me pour you a nice cup of tea."

Dulcie moved from the window, constantly looking back as though Adam would miraculously appear if she just kept watching. She was mildly self-conscious when she sat down, allowing Kyra to serve her. "I'm being silly. He hasn't even left Savannah yet and already I'm longing for his return."

"Ruel told me the Captain was feeling the same way, ma'am. He doesn't want to leave, either."

Dulcie smiled, then her face grew serious again. "Oh, Kyra, I told him I'd be fine and I'd take care of things here, but I can't do it. I don't know where to begin, and . . . I'm afraid. I wish I could be more like you. You set your mind on something and do it—no fear, no breast beating, no whining."

Kyra shook her head. "Not so, Miss Dulcie. Most of the time I'm scared witless. But we can't let that stop us, we must keep right on trying and doing the best we can. If a man or a woman doesn't keep reaching for that goal just beyond his ability today, tomorrow he won't have grown a bit. We can't stop being scared, but we can't stop trying either."

Dulcie sat quietly listening. "But I don't know where to begin. How will I make men like Albatross and Boy listen to my orders? Even Daddy has trouble with the darkies."

Kyra glanced away briefly, but turned back. "Ruel will help you."

"Do you think I could do it, Kyra?"

"I wouldn't be standing here wasting my time if I didn't think you could do it, Miz Tremain. One thing for certain though, you can't do anything unless you're willing to try."

Dulcie made a wry face of agreement. "Try," she murmured. "Well—there are a few things I know I can do. I must visit all the neighbors. Somehow they must be encouraged to begin again. We can't have fields lying fallow throughout the County. Maybe we could help them with seeds, or. . . . And I can visit Mossrose every day. It's questionable whether I can be of any value in keeping the workers moving at the same pace Adam has, but as you said, Kyra, I can try."

Later that day Dulcie waited downstairs in the parlor for her mother to finish dressing for their afternoon visits. "Are you sure you won't come with us, Emma? We're going to see the Saunderses, and Lydia would be pleased to see you."

"Oh, my dear, there's nothing I'd like better than to gossip and tattle-tale for an afternoon, but this is our day to expect the Johnson brothers. They make me angry as sin, but still I can't bring myself to disappoint the old fools."

"They come regularly?" Dulcie asked.

"Once a month, no more, no less. I've told Ned it doesn't make a bit of sense for those two old fools to pretend things are as they were before the War. Why, they ride those two old horses around, dressed to their teeth as though they actually had something."

"Well, they must have. Surely they can't go from one neighbor to another always dropping in at dinner time. They'd starve."

Emma snorted. "Hah! When no white folks are available, they call on the niggers. *They* call it lookin' after their people. Even the darkies aren't fooled. The Johnsons are just too damn stiff-backed proud to let anyone see them do a lick of work. Instead they wander around all over the County, landing in someone's dining room *accidentally* just at mealtime."

Dulcie laughed lightly. "If they make you so angry, why not tell them? If they knew you think it's no better than begging, they'd stop soon enough."

Enid, tall and gaunt, walked into the room. "She won't because she can't stand to hurt the old geezers' feelings. Mama is as bad as they are." She turned to face her mother. "You realize you encourage them! There is no reason they can't go down to Reverend Hook's store and buy food like everyone else."

"They're too proud," Emma said placidly. "They'd starve first."

"Pride! You call that pride!" Enid said loudly. "Mama! They won't accept credit because Mr. Seldon is a Yankee. Not all Yankees are bad. Mr. Seldon has brought the Saunders plantation back to life. Cotton and vegetables are growin' in those fields again. Tell me Glenn or Todd Saunders could have done that so quickly. And Mr. Seldon has proved he has our interests at heart by allowin' Reverend Hooks to run that store on his property. Now what's so pride-savin' about refusin' the man's help?"

Emma sighed. "You are perfectly right, Enid, but the Johnson brothers don't agree with your thinking. I surely hope this Yankee War hasn't taken from us our right to have our little peculiarities."

Enid let her hands drop disgustedly to her sides.

"You're impossible, Mama, absolutely impossible."

"I know, dear, it's one of my peculiarities. Please go tell cook to have everything ready for them at one-fifteen. Also tell the stableman—what's his name? Ever since we've had to hire our nigras—I mean coloreds, that's what they want to be called now—I can't keep them straight. They come and go like the winter rains. Tell him that the Johnsons' horses are to be well fed with our best feed, y'hear?"

Enid flounced from the room, nearly knocking Patricia down in the hallway. "Mah goodness," Patricia breathed, straightening her hat. "Whatevah has got into dahlin' Enid?"

Emma laughed. "She's angry at her mama. You know how that is, Patricia."

"Well, Ah s'pose," Patricia said uncertainly. "Dulcie honey ah you ready to go? Is ouah basket all packed?"

"Yes, Mama, everything is ready."

Dulcie and Patricia spent most of the day with Lydia Saunders and her daughter Blossom Chilcote. Patricia gave them two of the handkerchiefs Adam had purchased. Then she unwrapped the basket filled with fresh pastries and breads she had had baked in the Whitaker kitchen.

Lydia Saunders was properly grateful, and practical enough to know that no return visit or gift was expected. She offered none, but instead invited the two women to visit again soon. With an understanding of misfortune that only women seem to manage gracefully, they hugged each other good-bye. Patricia and Dulcie were still waving and smiling teary, understanding smiles as Ruel drove off.

"Lawd, but Ah hate seein' Lydia so down at the heel, Dulcie," Patricia said, dabbing daintily at her eyes. "Do you remembah her when you were growin' up?"

"Of course, Mama. How could I not, I played at the Saunders plantation at least three times a week with Birdie and Blythe and Blossom."

"No one could dress as elegantly as Lydia Saunders."

"No one but you, Mama."

"No," Patricia said tearfully, her sympathy in full bloom now. "Ah was always second to her. Ah tried. Ah think Ah nearly bankrupted youah poah daddy buyin' Parisian gowns to outshine her, but Lydia was always the belle . . . well, almost always. Of course, youah daddy always made sure Ah had the best."

Dulcie smiled to herself and let Patricia's continuing monologue fade into the background. Visiting the Saunderses wasn't much of a feat, but she had done it. Before dinner she'd have Ruel take her over to Mossrose. She began imagining how she would act and what she would say. Finally she decided to ride rather than be driven. On horseback she would have an air of authority she could never achieve from the seat of a buggy.

Back at the Whitakers', Dulcie instructed Ruel to return the buggy to the stables and to saddle a horse for her and one for himself. Feeling surer of herself, she went inside to change.

Emma Whitaker caught them in the entry hall. "Dulcie, I'm so glad you and Patricia got back in time. Leroy came to visit this afternoon. He was so disappointed you weren't here." Her eyes twinkled. "Especially you, Dulcie. You and Camille and Leroy were such close friends. It makes me feel good to have that affection live on."

Dulcie touched Emma's arm. "I'm sorry we missed him, Emma. Perhaps we'll have another opportunity to talk."

"Oh, you haven't missed him. He was just gettin' ready to leave when you arrived. I just sent him back to tell cook he'd be staying for dinner." She giggled. "Can you imagine in the old days sending a man on an errand like that!"

Dulcie felt a tightening in her throat. "Emma . . . I'm sorry, but I—I can't see Leroy right now. I have to ride over to Mossrose. I promised Adam I would, and Ruel is waiting to escort me."

"Oh, honey child, that's nothing to worry about. Leroy would be happy to ride over with you. I'm sure Adam would feel safer with a white man ridin' with you anyway. I'll just call—"

"Emma, no!" Dulcie said hastily.

Both Emma Whitaker and Patricia looked curiously at Dulcie.

She said awkwardly, "Ruel is waiting. I must change." She ran up the stairs, leaving the two older women in the hallway perplexed and disturbed.

"Patricia, I thought she liked Leroy?"

"She always did, Emma. Ah sweah, Ah don't undahstand her half the time. Ah 'spect she's just missin' Adam. Dulcie isn't quite herself when he's not around. Ah sometimes wondah if it's good foah her to love a man that much. Maybe Ah ought to talk to her about that. What do you think, Emma?"

Dulcie dressed quickly, then went outside via the servants' stairs. She came around the side of the house, where she could call Ruel without anyone seeing or overhearing her.

"Ruel!" she called in a loud whisper. "Ruel!"

He brought the horse over to where she was. "Mrs. Tremain, what are you doing in the bushes?" he asked with a smile on his face.

Immediately she stepped out from her shelter. "Nothing," she said firmly. "I—I just didn't want to get into another conversation with Mama and Mrs. Whitaker. Everything is fine. Let's go, Ruel."

The smile remained on Ruel's face. He had seen Leroy's horse in the stable. This would make a gratifying story to tell the Captain. Dulcie might look like a sweet Southern lady, but she had resources she didn't hesitate to use. He wondered what story she had given to evade Biggs. "Did you tell Mrs. Moran where you were going?" he asked.

Dulcie's first instinct was to reprimand him for impertinence, but Adam had told her to rely on this man, to learn not to think of him as a Negro. "I told her the truth, that we are going to Mossrose."

Ruel said nothing, but he wasn't pleased. Leroy now knew she had gone to Mossrose. He could surmise she was not making an isolated trip there. Most likely, with Mrs. Moran and Mrs. Whitaker talking, he'd learn everything that Dulcie did.

As they rode over the plantation, Ruel introduced Dulcie to all the workers and their wives. She inspected the cabins, inquired about the health of the families, and asked if they needed supplies. It came to her easily.

Her first visit to Mossrose was mostly a matter of conversation and observation. But it was a start, and she felt satisfied with herself. "Ruel, where is Kyra? I'd like to see her."

"She's here. Captain Tremain gave permission to build a cabin just for her Bureau work and her teaching. You knew she is teaching some of the workers to read and write and cipher, didn't you?"

"Oh, yes, I knew. I suggested it to Adam."

Ruel smiled happily. "She's mighty proud of that little cabin. I can hardly get her to leave it in the evening to come home."

"Oh, yes! Adam told me you had leased three acres of the old Matthews plantation for yourselves. How do you likc it, Ruel?"

"I haven't gotten much of the soil turned yet, but by this time next year we'll have a nice crop put in. Kyra and I are very pleased with it, Mrs. Tremain."

"And your house? Is it finished yet?"

"Yes, ma'am, or nearly so. Jothan and Apollo helped me build it. But you know Kyra, she won't be satisfied until every stick of furniture is in place and pictures on every wall and a shelf built for books."

They laughed together in appreciation of Kyra. Ruel pointed out the cabin Kyra used. "I'll just let you visit for a while. I'll come by in half an hour and accompany you to Whitakers'."

"Better make it an hour, Ruel. I don't want to run into—I mean, I'd rather talk to Kyra a while longer."

"Yes ma'am." He touched his hat. "An hour."

Dulcie walked to the cabin and opened the door without knocking. "Kyra! Kyra, you were right. All I had to do was—"

Kyra and Apollo, heads close together, looked up in unison. "Why, Miz Tremain, what brings you here?" Kyra asked.

"Apollo, are you learning how to read?" Dulcie asked, feeling strangely as though she had intruded on something.

"Yes ma'am. Kyra the bes' teachah Ah evah had."

Kyra sniggered, and said bitingly, "Kyra de onlies' teachah you evah had."

Apollo smiled good-naturedly. "She mek fun o' me all the time. Ah tell her a teachah is s'posed to make her students feel *goood,* but she don't lissen to nothin' Ah say. She think Ah'm dumb."

"If you don't start paying attention to your lesson, Apollo, you are always going to be dumb. Go back to that desk and read this page. I'll come to hear you read in a few minutes." Kyra turned her attention to Dulcie.

"See, she doan pay me no mind, Miss Dulcie. Ah thinks Ah oughtta take this woman out back an' whup her," he said happily as he picked up the book and moved to the back of the room.

Dulcie couldn't shake the feeling of being somewhere she didn't belong. "I'm sorry, Kyra, I didn't mean to interrupt your work. Please go back to Apollo. I'll talk to you some other time."

"Now, now, Miz Tremain, you came in here all excited about something. Don't let that silly clown put you off. He just loves foolin' around."

"But you were teaching him."

She laughed, and walked outside the cabin. "He's as smart as he can be, but it will take a long time to break all those bad habits he's got. I can read anything to him and he understands with the first reading. He can read well too, but his talk is straight out of the Georgia cotton fields."

Dulcie nodded. "My daddy's Georgia cotton fields. Apollo was born right here on Mossrose. Mama used to teach our servants, but not the field hands. We thought they couldn't learn."

"They've got to learn, Miz Tremain. They've just got to learn."

"I know. I really am beginning to understand, Kyra. So you go back to teaching Apollo."

"But you haven't said why you came. I know you had a reason."

Dulcie smiled. "I just wanted to tell you you were right this morning. I'm still scared, but I haven't met with disaster yet."

"And you won't," Kyra said positively.

After that first day, Dulcie set a schedule for herself. She visited Mossrose daily, taking note of the amount of work done so that she could castigate the shirkers or offer encouragement and praise for each successful day. And she always had some treat with her from the Whitaker kitchen, to be distributed on good days. She learned to be both tough and gentle. For the most part, she felt the laborers liked her.

Twice a week she went visiting the neighbors. Late in the afternoons Dulcie went over the books with Ruel and Jothan. Slowly she began to learn all that was involved in the rebuilding of a plantation house and the running of the plantation.

Often Jem accompanied her on these sessions with Ruel and Jothan. Dulcie had expected him to be upset by her unfeminine interest in business, but instead he was delighted, taking her into his confidence. During these days she was closer to her father than she had been since she was a child.

Systematically, Dulcie and Patricia visited the people in the district around Mossrose, even calling on the Redgraves. Dulcie still had not been able to accept the idea of Arthur Redgrave's collecting scrap for a living.

She told herself repeatedly that the important thing was that he was keeping busy and supporting himself and his parents. But collecting scrap seemed such a comedown.

She pushed Arthur to the back of her mind. "Well, Mama, the only people left whom we haven't visited are the Tweed sisters."

Patricia giggled. "That, Dulcie honey, is goin' to take all ouah diplomacy."

"We'll just send a card over and tell them when to expect us. It will be all right. The Tweeds should be happy for company."

"They ah! But youah foahgettin' theah pride. Phoebe an' Zenobia do theah own washin'."

Dulcie looked dumbfounded. "Mama! What difference does it make who does their washing? We're only going to visit for one afternoon."

"You've got to learn to listen to the gossip, Dulcie. They don't want anyone to know. They do it in theah attic."

"Mama, that's ridiculous!"

"It's no such thing! If the curtain is down in the attic window we'll know they ah doin' theah dresses, an' we can't visit."

"Do you mean we are going to ride over there time after time until we see the curtain is up!"

"Of co'se. We sho'ly can't embarrass the poah ol' things."

Dulcie shook her head, not able to refrain from smiling. Visiting had more complexities than the plantation ledger books.

Late in February Dulcie and Patricia finally managed to arrive at the Tweeds' house when the curtain was up. Dulcie grimaced. "At last! They must be the cleanest women in the County."

"Dulcie Jeannette, don't be unkind."

"Come on, Mama, let's go in before they can get upstairs and begin scrubbing something."

Patricia and Dulcie stood on the front veranda, waiting for what seemed an extraordinary length of time.

"Perhaps they aren't home," Dulcie suggested.

"Theah home. Zenobia is cleanin' up, an' Phoebe is preparin' somethin' foah us to eat."

"How do you know all this?"

"It's theah way, everybody knows that."

Phoebe came to the door. "Why Mrs. Moran, Mrs. Tremain! What a pleasure to have you drop in on sister an' me. Come in, please. Ah'll just call Zenobia. She's workin' on her book. You know, of course, she's writing Papa's life story."

"Phoebe, I hadn't heard. When did Zenobia embahk on this task?"

"Last week, Ah believe. She's been plannin' it fo' a long time, though. She has the most interestin' collection of facts concernin' the folks hereabouts."

Patricia smiled. "Ah'm suah she does. Youah sistah nevah fails to surprise. Theah's no one bettah to know about everything."

Phoebe led the way to her parlor. It was a musty, stuffy room, its colors faded. There was an air of decrepit grandeur about the room and the two old ladies who inhabited it.

Phoebe saw her guests seated, then excused herself to call her sister. "Ah'll be but a minute," she trilled. "Ah do want Zenobia to tell you herself of the news hereabouts. Ah'm by fah the best reader, but no one can tell a story like Zenobia." Her voice dropped to an awed whisper. "It's her scientific mind, you know. She's very penetratin'."

When Zenobia appeared there were more greetings and a rather dreary tea served. Following her custom, Patricia presented her gifts. Scones from Whitakers' kitchen enlivened today's tea. "Ah don't know when Ah've tasted better," Zenobia declared.

"Ah envy Emma her Pauline," said Patricia. "Ah intend to do all Ah can to steal her away when Mossrose is completed. Ah've gotten used to this delicious pastry. Ah'm sure Ah'll die without it."

"Pauline," Zenobia said. "Pauline Jackson? Israel's wife? With all those children? The one whose family lives on the old Matthews place?"

"Why yes, the very one, Zenobia," Patricia said. "Why do you ask?"

Zenobia looked at her sister. The two talked in an undertone. "Shall Ah tell them, sister?"

"Ah think we can, Zenobia. Patricia has been our dear neighbor, hasn't she. She always respects our secrets."

Zenobia, dropping her voice even lower, looked sidewise at Dulcie. "What about *her*?"

Phoebe's eyes were wide, blue and innocent. She stared unabashedly at Dulcie. "Well, sister, Ah don't know. Ah don't think Mr. Whitelaw cares much for her husband."

Patricia stirred restlessly. "Phoebe, Zenobia, Ah think you ah bein' most discourteous talkin' like that in front of us. No one has evah questioned mah discretion befoah!"

"Oh, Patricia," they said in unison, "we don't question *you*. Mr. Whitelaw has been very good to us. He even delivers our goods to the back door so we don't have to be seen in his store."

"Have you been buying on credit at the store on Saunderses old plantation?" Dulcie asked. In response to their reluctant nods she said, "I'm not at all surprised that Nemo Whitelaw doesn't approve of Adam. Adam doesn't approve of his store. How are you ladies going to repay this debt you are mounting up?"

Phoebe giggled. "Oh, we don't have to pay. Nemo said we'd never have to pay a penny, an' Reverend Hooks was right there with him, an' he said we don't have to pay anything, an' we can buy whatever we like for as long as we live. Isn't that wonderful? You must tell your husband that he has misjudged poor Mr. Whitelaw."

"Miss Phoebe, no one's going to give you and Miss Zenobia whatever you wish indefinitely and expect no payment ever. You must have made some kind of agreement," Dulcie said.

Zenobia sat straighter, her shoulders squared, her breast out, making her look like an indignant pouter pigeon. "The Tweeds are an old, old family hereabouts, Mrs. Tremain. There are a few loyalists left who would see the founders of this region cared for an' protected. Reverend Hooks is a man of the highest values. He knows the Tweed name is important to the people around here. We bring hope to those who look up to us, isn't that what he said, sister?"

"That's what he said, Zenobia, an' all we had to do was sign a little piece of paper sayin' we gave our permission to be assisted in exchange for encouragin' the local people."

Despite their protesting innocence, Dulcie recognized this as something Adam would want to know about. She persisted, "That's all the paper said?"

"Well, we did give permission for Mr. Seldon to use our lands, but that is all to the good. With the nigras all run off we can't keep it in crops anyway. Captain Tremain has truly misjudged these good people, Dulcie. They are helpin' us," Phoebe said earnestly.

Zenobia waved her hand. "Ah don't wish to talk of this any longer."

Phoebe's eyes lit. "Oh, you've decided to tell Patricia what you saw through your glass."

"Your glass?" Dulcie said.

"Yes, Papa brought it to Zenobia after the last trip he made to Europe. We studied the stars and the phases of the moon together when he was alive, an' now poor Zenobia must look through her glass alone. Ah was nevah very good at it. But Ah read *Beowulf* to her as she studies the heavens."

"The other night Ah was studyin' the rings of Saturn, an' Ah thought Ah had performed a veritable wonder with my glass. It seemed the whole sky was alight."

"Mah word!" Patricia breathed. "Imagine seein' Satturan close at hand."

"It turned out not to be Saturn," Zenobia said with some irritation. "But it was just as peculiar. Once Ah realized it was *not* Saturn lightin' up the sky, Ah, of course, was curious. Now, ordinarily, you understand, Ah would never lower my glass to look upon mortals treading this earth, but this night . . . it seemed imperative Ah discover the source of this peculiar light."

"She saw the strangest sight!" Phoebe said shrilly, her small hands twisting in excitement.

"Israel Jackson was runnin' to beat the band down the River Road, an' after him came a whole pack of—of—*ghosts*! For a moment Ah thought it was Papa an' some of his friends comin' back. But it wasn't Papa. Papa never hollered in public like that! An' their heads were all pointy, too. Papa had a beautiful round-shaped head, like mine."

"Well, what happened!" said Patricia, her curiosity piqued.

"Israel ran right off the road onto our property, an' the ghosts made a big circle around him. They whooped an' howled an' beat at him with fiery rods, an' then they disappeared! Just were swallowed up in the dark. Gone!"

"What happened to Israel Jackson?" Dulcie asked.

"Nothin'. He fell down on the ground on his knees. Ah thought he might be hurt, but soon he got up an' ran back toward Matthews's land. You know he an' Pauline live on Lyman's property now."

"Yes, we knew that," Patricia said. "It's enough to make a puhson cry, when the Yankees won't let Lyman live in his own house."

"He has refused to take the Oath, Mama," Dulcie said.

"Ah don't see why that mattahs! It's his land. His daddy an' granddaddy an' his daddy befoah him worked that land."

"Well, there's no point in arguing about it now, Mama. It's the law, and Lyman could have asked for a pardon and return of his lands like everyone else—including Daddy."

"Not everybody is so flexible or cleah-sighted as youah daddy. Lyman most likely couldn't bring himself to say those awful Yankee words."

All at once Dulcie said, "They're about the Constitution—" and Phoebe said, "A terrible thing to do to a man—" and Zenobia said, "Well, Ah don't see how anybody could blame Lyman—" and a lively exchange of opinions continued for several minutes, until Patricia declared herself ready to go home. There was a flurry of good-byes, the sisters looking bright-eyed and zestful and sorry to see them leave.

Dulcie and her mother were hardly seated in the buggy when Patricia said, "Ah nevah thought Ah'd see the day when mah own daughtah would humiliate me! You contradicted me, Dulcie Jeannette. Right in front of the Tweeds! Now everybody in the County is goin' to know mah own daughtah doesn't respect me!"

"Mama, I merely disagreed with your views on the Yankee Oath."

"Ah know what you did! Ah expect an apology."

"I understand how you feel, Mama, but I'm not going to apologize. I'm entitled to my opinions. I'm an adult, not your little girl."

Patricia let out a moan and covered her face with her lacy handkerchief. "Oh, mah God, now youah denyin' mah mothahhood!"

"Mama, I—"

"Don't speak to me!"

Patricia managed to hold to her anger for a full week before she again spoke to Dulcie or consented to go visiting with her. By then Dulcie had decided to restrict her visiting to once a week. But she had begun to keep a journal, writing into it each day the news she thought would interest Adam. She listened avidly for any hint of the Tweed sisters' peculiar debt arrangement, hoping to hear something about Hooks's store that would make everything clearer.

From all quarters she heard tales of increasing violence; even the Union League had responded to it by voting that their membership would carry guns and parade in formation, making their power and intent obvious.

She had also heard many tales about the hooded riders Zenobia called ghosts. Terrible tales of burnings and beatings came from the Negroes, and occasionally a white. She learned that invariably those attacked were Radicals. She had not heard of one Conservative Democrat coming under the fire of the hooded horsemen. She was anxious for Adam to return. She missed him intensely; she had so much to tell him, and she felt miserable keeping it to herself.

He had been gone nearly three and a half months, and the weather was beginning to warm, with a gentle ocean breeze crossing over the sand and grass to Mossrose. Jem's newly planted fields were showing green. The foundation of the new house was complete. Even in Adam's absence, progress was made.

She felt terribly proud of herself. She hadn't failed. Adam had been right in all he said, in all the trust he had put in her. She could stand up to the tasks in front of her and for what she believed in. Every day she did a little better. In a way, it seemed to her she was being reborn just as Mossrose was.

On a beautiful April day she rode to Mossrose with Ruel to see the cotton fields. As they entered the long drive to the house, Dulcie grinned, and exclaimed happily, "Ruel! Albatross and his gang have planted the new trees. Oh, they look beautiful. Has Daddy seen them yet?"

"He certainly has. He was right here while they were being planted. He watched each one being put into the ground."

"He must be so happy. He loved this drive with the crape myrtles forming an arch over the roadway. How long will it take for these trees to be large enough to cover it?"

"It will be a long while, Mrs. Tremain. Too long for Mr. Moran, I'm afraid."

Dulcie looked at the small trees. "I hope you're wrong, Ruel."

Ruel wasn't listening to her. He turned quickly in his saddle, then spoke to her. "You go on ahead, Mrs. Tremain. I see a tree back there whose roots are exposed."

"But that isn't your job, Ruel."

"It must be taken care of, Mrs. Tremain. If you wouldn't mind, I'd appreciate it if you'd send Apollo to help me. Please tell him some animal's been digging at the roots. He'll know what tools to bring."

Dulcie agreed to send Apollo, and rode on alone. Ruel turned his horse back down the drive. He hadn't gone far when he met Leroy Biggs. Ruel situated his horse crosswise to the road. "Colonel Biggs, may I help you, sir?"

"Who the hell are you?"

"I'm Ruel Jordan, sir, Captain Tremain's foreman in his absence. If you have business at Mossrose, I shall be happy to assist you, sir."

"Git outta my way, nigger. My business ain't none o' yours."

Ruel blocked Leroy's passage. "I'm sorry, Colonel Biggs, but I'm afraid your business is mine if it has to do with Mossrose."

Leroy's face was mean, his eyes squinted to small slits, his jaw working. "You get your black ass outta the road, boy, or I'm gonna put a hole through you big as a cannonball."

"There's no need for violence, Colonel Biggs. I'm following the orders my employer left with me. No one is to come to Mossrose without reason of business. If you'll just tell me what it is you wish, I'll do my best to assist you."

"You God-damned sonofa—"

"Well, well, if it ain't the Colonel Mistah Biggs hisseff," an arrogant voice called from the side of the road.

"What's the mattah, Colonel Biggs, Ruel don't fight by your rules?" Apollo laughed. He stood with his muscular arms crossed over his massive chest, his handsome face cold and taunting. "You lookin' fo' youah kind o' trouble, Colonel, Captain Apollo Justus Sherman heah mighty willin' to give it to you."

Leroy looked from one man to the other. Ruel was impassive, reserved, unafraid. Apollo was strung like a taut wire, waiting for the slightest indication that Leroy would go for a gun or knife.

Leroy backed his horse a couple of steps. "What y'all got here, an armed fortress?"

"That's close enuf to the truth, Colonel," Apollo said, and moved his arm enough so that Leroy could see the gun he had tucked in his waistband. "Cap'n Tremain don't take chances with his people."

Ruel said, "Now, Colonel Biggs, if you'd care to state your business, I shall try to assist you."

"This ain't no business call, it's social. I come to see Dul—Mrs.—*Miss Moran.* Now get the hell outta my way."

"I'm sorry, sir, Mrs. Tremain is not receiving. You will have to visit her after the captain has returned home."

"Did she say that?"

"That is not for me to say, sir. My instructions are that she is not receiving."

Leroy's face was red with suppressed fury. As his hands grew firmer, then cruel, his horse began to dance.

"Didn't the Rebels teach you how to handle yo' hawssflesh, Colonel?" Apollo taunted.

"Shut up, you God-damned bastard!" Leroy shouted, in a rage, his hand pressed tightly against his pistol.

"Colonel Biggs, please take your leave," Ruel said gently.

Leroy jerked on the horse's mouth, whirling the animal around so he was face to face with Ruel. "You an' your purty speech, you think you're shit on a stick, don't you, boy. Think you're better than a white man—"

"That ain't too hard with some white men," Apollo said.

Ruel moved his horse forward, crowding Leroy's mount. Leroy gave ground. Enraged and frustrated, he pulled hard on the reins. The horse reared. Leroy dug his spurs into the animal and rode the frantic beast down the road away from Mossrose, shouting over his shoulder, "I'll get you, you slick black bastard. Both o' you. I won't forget this!"

Ruel let out his held breath.

"He's a mean bastard," Apollo said. "He most nearly had me gut-shot once."

"I'll be glad when Captain Tremain is home to handle him. I can understand far better now why he doesn't want that man on his property, or near his wife."

Apollo nodded. "He al'ys did take to Miss Dulcie. She told him what she thought of him that day he had us all tied up ready to shoot us. There was six of us—" Apollo stopped talking suddenly. "It was your mama an' daddy Miss Dulcie an' the Cap'n helped make free that day."

Ruel smiled. "I know. I wouldn't be sitting here now if it weren't for that day. Captain Tremain promised my father he'd find Jothan and me. He kept his word."

Apollo mounted Ruel's horse, and the two rode up to the main house. Both were shaken and disturbed by Leroy's visit, and neither believed it would be his only attempt. They were unsure whether to speak with Dulcie about it. Not only was it improper for a black man to be talking to her about such matters, they had no idea how to approach the subject without telling her things that would frighten her. As he so often did, Ruel went directly to Kyra to talk out with her the things that perplexed him. Without thinking, Apollo followed.

Kyra listened quietly, then said, "Ruel, the Whitakers are always happy when you have time to help out at the house. It makes them feel real good to have a butler answering their door and overseeing things. You're just going to have to take time and be there whenever Miz

Tremain is in the house. Colonel Biggs will likely try to see her at the Whitakers'. He knows we can keep him off Mossrose, but we can't keep him out of his in-laws' house. You guard her there."

Ruel rubbed his high, smooth forehead. "I can't be two places at once, Kyra. I'm needed here. The Captain wants this house built."

"Ruel, if he were here to choose between having his wife protected and having Mossrose rebuilt, you know what he'd choose."

"She's right," Apollo agreed. "The Cap'n sets great store by Miss Dulcie."

Ruel nodded. "You'll have to see to some of my work here, Apollo. I'll make a schedule for the men."

Kyra laughed lightly, her eyes fixed on the window. "Well, I guess this is not the time for my request."

"What request?" Ruel asked.

"I was just about ready to ask you if you could spare Apollo for an hour or so a day. Mr. Sweet brought me a load of papers to do for the Bureau. I've got so many reading students now, and all these letters of inquiry to write, I can't keep up with it all. I thought perhaps Apollo could help. He writes beautifully." She looked at Apollo, her face warm and full of pride, then she grimaced. "If only he'd learn how to talk!"

Apollo, for once, was speechless. His dark skin reddened, and he turned away. He liked Ruel, the best friend he had had since the days he had been Jem Moran's slave. Yet the thought of having an hour a day near Kyra was more than he could bear. He had learned never to think of Kyra as he did other women. Always he prefaced his thoughts of her with the words, Ruel's wife. He avoided her accidental touch as he would a hot stove, and still with all his efforts he could barely contain the rush of pleasurable confusion that assailed him whenever she was with him.

Finally regaining speech, he said throatily, "Ah can't be two places at once either. Ah better see to the men's work."

Ruel shook his head. "This other is important too—important for our people. You take the time, Apollo. Like Reverend Hooks says, where there is a will, there is a way. We'll manage."

Apollo said nothing, afraid that if he protested again, he would reveal the turmoil within; and if he remained silent—if he remained silent, for one hour every day he would be in this small cabin alone with Ruel's wife. His eyes darted to Kyra and quickly away. He remained choked with silence.

As Ruel had feared, his problems with Leroy were not over with that one meeting. His second encounter came on the River Road when he was making his fortnightly trip to Savannah for supplies. The better part of his day would be spent in buying goods, loading them, and repeatedly having to assure Osgood Baxter that Captain Tremain had given authorization and that Baxter would be paid.

Four of the field hands rode in the back of the wagon, with Ruel driving. They had gone only three or four miles when Leroy met them. In his flamboyant way he set his horse to rearing and made the animal prance, as though out of control, across the road in front of the dray. Ruel halted his team. After a suitable display of his horsemanship, Leroy brought the animal under control and came up beside Ruel. "Better watch out, nigger. You ever spook my horse like that again, an' I'll have the law on your ass."

Ruel held his silence.

"You hear me, boy? I'm talkin' t'you. When a white man talks you better listen. It's against the law for a nigger t'attack a white man. What d'you say to that, boy?"

"I didn't attack you, Colonel Biggs."

"I say you did!" Leroy said, leaning down from his saddle. He reached out and grabbed Ruel's shirt front. "It's my word against yours. Who d'you think a jury'll b'lieve? I can have your black ass any time I want it,

boy." Roughly he shoved Ruel back, letting go of his
shirt. He laughed loudly and began to ride away, then
stopped again, looking back. "I'll be seein' Miss Dulcie
soon. Don't you meddle in this time, nigger. Just remember I can have your ass any time I feel like it."

Ruel continued into Savannah, but his mind wasn't
on his business. He no longer believed he was capable
of keeping Leroy Biggs away from Dulcie Tremain indefinitely. When the Captain had spoken to him of
Colonel Biggs, Ruel had assumed he would be dealing
with a rough but reasonably honorable man.

He remembered Leroy only vaguely from childhood.
He had been fourteen when Jem sold him and Jothan.
As a youngster he had seen Leroy, but always at a
distance, and always as the Morans' guest, when Biggs
was on his best behavior. He remembered him only as
an able athlete. He did not remember the bitterness or
the hungry malice of the man.

Ruel began to watch the calendar as closely as Dulcie. He was anxious for the Captain's return, before
the situation was out of hand.

Apollo began to help Kyra with her Bureau work at
the beginning of May, 1867. Since Ruel had asked
him to help Kyra, he had tried everything he knew to
change his feelings for her into something decent, something he could live with. He and Ruel grew closer all
the time. It was to Apollo that Ruel confided his fears
about Leroy Biggs, and his hopes for the future. It was
to Apollo he told his dreams of the life he and Kyra
would lead, and of the children they would have. One
day, Ruel said, he and Kyra would have saved enough
money to build a little school of their own. They would
have their own home, and farm, and besides their own
children, they would take in some orphaned black
children.

Apollo listened, and he felt his love for Ruel grow
to that which he might have felt for his own brother
had they not been separated as small children. Occasionally Apollo dreamed about the brother he barely

knew, but Jupiter was the only one of his brothers and sisters he remembered at all. Sometimes, in his wildest thoughts, he imagined Ruel was Jupiter. Somehow it soothed the longing he had recently acquired to belong somewhere, to someone.

He entered Kyra's work cabin, determined to keep his mind on Ruel and the affection between Ruel and himself. He even tried to convince himself that he resented Kyra for intruding on that feeling. But he couldn't do it. He had only to look at her strong, lovely face, her eyes that burned with a warmth that he had never before seen. Kyra was love, he thought. She burned with a passion that encompassed him and all those she taught to read and all those for whom she wrote letters and even people she had never seen. He had taken the name Justus because that same hungry, burning desire was inside him, but he had never known what to do about it until he met her. She was all he wanted to be, and she was all he could ever imagine wanting in a woman.

"What's this work Ah'll be doin'?" he asked gruffly.

She looked up from her table. "Ooh! You are a mean man this morning!"

"Ah'm not feelin' mean," he said. "You're takin' me from impohtant work. What you want me to do?"

"You'd better pour yourself a cup of coffee first. Some is brewing over there on the hearth. I'm not talking to a bear."

Apollo poured a cup of coffee and stood facing the fire as he drank it.

Kyra watched him for a minute. She knew why he wouldn't face her, but he'd get over his feelings. She had learned to ignore hers. He would too. And she loved Ruel. He was younger than she, but he was all a woman could want in a husband. She liked their life together, and she loved him. It was natural to expect that a woman would meet other men she found appealing from time to time. She was sure this would pass.

She said softly, "Apollo, if you really don't want to

help me, it's all right. I can manage on my own, or I might find someone else who can help. Winnie is coming along with her reading and writing very well. Another month and she should be able to help out."

Apollo poured another cup of the strong coffee, then came to the table. "Tell me what Ah'm gonna do."

She smiled, touching his forearm. She realized immediately she shouldn't have done that. He pulled his arm away, spilling coffee over both of them. Kyra mopped them dry, then concentrated hard on the letters. Slowly her mind cleared, and soon she was afire with the joy she felt at helping her people. Apollo, too, sensed the change in her and began to listen.

"I can't tell you how good it makes me feel, and it will make you feel, to be actually helping freedmen! Look at our people, Apollo. They are so pathetic, and so hopeful. Did you ever notice that? Our people never give up hope. Even when we have nothing else, not family, or clothing, or food on the table, we have hope. It's in our songs, in our prayers, in our hearts. That's what you and I will do, Apollo. We'll make some of those hopes become truth."

Apollo's eyes glowed with love. He wished this woman would talk to him like this all day, and all through the night. Hope, she said. Oh, yes, he knew that hope.

She laughed, and he almost shivered as the sound touched deep inside him. "I know I'm not explaining very well," she said. "We'll be writing inquiring letters. They're terribly important in reuniting families who were separated years ago by being sold individually."

Apollo began to think of his brother Jupiter again. He had never mentioned Jupiter's name to a living soul but his mama and his daddy, old Simmon. Listening to Kyra, he began to wonder if he might find Jupiter again.

Kyra went on, "The letters are sent to churches and they're read aloud in services, and sometimes a name will be known to someone in the congregation. Then the letter will be answered quickly. Oh, Apollo, when one of our people hears from a lost father or sister, you can't imagine the joy! And we don't stop with finding one or two of the family. We keep sending that letter on to church after church. Entire families have found each other again."

"You want me to write those letters?" Apollo asked.
"Yes, I do."

Her warm brown eyes rested on him, and he was more moved than he cared for her to know. But it was as if she had touched something in him that would no longer be held back. He began to talk to her about Jupiter. Spoken aloud, his brother's name sounded strange, it had been so long. He told Kyra how he longed for his own family and how his mother had told him of her other children, but Apollo had never really known them.

"My mama an' daddy—they called him Simmon— had good, big sons. We all bring a good price, even when we was young, too young fo' too much work. We all get sold exceptin' me. Mistah Moran need me fo' the fiel's, an' he use me fo' a stud, figgerin' Ah'd sire big strong boys like old Simmon did. My mama tell me Ah had seven brothers 'sides me, but Ah only know Jupiter. Mistah Moran don't sell Jupe till he neahly twelve. Ah 'members Jupe, an' he al'ys come to me in mah dreams. Think Ah could find him?"

Kyra bit her lip. "We can try, Apollo. The letter will go to every church where black people worship."

Apollo bowed his head. "It ain't likely we ever fin' each othah again, but like you said, it makes the hoping mo' real."

"Yes, it does." Kyra hesitated. "Apollo, before, when you were talking about Mr. Moran and Mossrose in earlier years, you referred to yourself as a stud and to siring children?"

Apollo smiled proudly. "He set a big sto' by me."

"He treated you like an animal!" Kyra said heatedly. "And he made you think of . . . speak of yourself as though you were an animal. You're not! Don't ever refer to yourself like that again! You're a man, as good as Mr. Moran, as good as a dozen Mr. Morans!"

Apollo grinned in pleasure, then said, "Ah knows that, but Ah was his best stud. He wasn't lyin'."

She flared in anger, then saw the mischievous look in his eye. "I always fall right into your foolery, don't I?"

"You sho' do. There ain't—"

"Isn't!"

Undaunted, he said, "There *isn't* anyone Ah like funnin' bettah."

Kyra and Apollo began to work. He proved diligent, and as excited about the work as she. When Kyra was working in the cabin she was happier than she had been at any other time since coming to Mossrose. With Apollo helping her, it seemed so much more got done, and she had a sense of purpose she hadn't known before.

But when she went to the small house she and Ruel had built, she was uneasy and guilt-ridden. She threw all her energies into making the house comfortable, and to loving Ruel. When she was there with him, it wasn't difficult, for she did love him. Together they planned and dreamed about the times to come, the good times for them. She was happy in her house with him. It seemed peculiar and frightening to her that she couldn't keep the memory of that nighttime happiness with Ruel in the cabin where she worked with Apollo.

Ruel became Dulcie's shadow. If she wondered about his constant presence, she said nothing, for which Ruel was grateful. It was already mid-May, and the captain was expected home soon. If Dulcie remained accepting of his guardanship for just a short time longer, all would be well.

He kept the Whitaker home in perfect order. The house servants worked with an assiduousness Emma Whitaker hadn't seen even in slave days. Ruel was acting as butler when Leroy came to call one afternoon.

He opened the door to see Leroy's smirking face. "Well, well, if it ain't the fast-talkin' nigger of Mossrose." He shoved Ruel aside and entered the house.

"Mrs. Whitaker and Miss Whitaker are out this afternoon."

"Miss Moran is in!" Leroy snapped. "An' this time you won't stop me from seein' her. You mess with me here, boy, and ol' Ned'll toss you out on your black ass." Leroy took the stairs two at a time.

Ruel followed him. "Colonel Biggs! You may not enter the north wing, sir. Captain Tremain—"

Leroy turned, lunging at Ruel with his fist. He grazed the black man's chest, throwing him off balance. Ruel staggered back on the stair, his arms flailing as he grabbed for the rail. Viciously Leroy kicked at his hands.

Hearing the racket in the hallway, Dulcie came out of Beau's room. She stood horrified for a moment, then screamed Leroy's name.

At her shrill cry, he turned. "This black son of a bitch won't let me up to see you."

Recovered from her initial shock, Dulcie was angry. "How dare you speak to me like that! Leave here, Leroy."

"I'm sorry, Dulcie, truly I am. This nigger's been takin' on airs. He done it once too often. I jes' didn't have full control o' my feelin's. You understand that." His voice was sweet, begging for her understanding while assuming that she was prepared to give it. "You know how a Southern gentleman is when his honor is questioned. Sho'ly you won't hold my anger with a worthless darky against me."

Dulcie could barely speak for rage. "Ruel carries out my orders and my husband's orders. Neither of us wants your company here or elsewhere. Ruel, see Colonel Biggs downstairs. If he touches you again, I'll have Laban Sweet press charges against him."

"Why, you little bitch! You're raisin' this nigger over me."

"Yes, I am. He's far more the gentleman than you are right now, Leroy. You've changed, and not for the better. You're not the man you once were, or could have been."

Leroy's lips curled, his teeth bared in a feral semblance of a smile. "I ain't, huh? You'll regret sayin' that to me, Dulcie. Yes, by God, you'll regret every word of it. You an' me got an accountin' comin'."

"Oh, get out of here, Leroy, you make me sick!" she said, and turned back toward Beau's room.

CHAPTER TEN

Adam brought the *Black Swan* into Savannah at the beginning of June 1868. Taking time only for a hasty visit to his office to inform Cutler he was home and that the *Black Swan* was carrying goods brought from New Orleans, he rode directly to the Whitaker plantation.

Ruel opened the door for him, showing an uncharacteristic burst of extroversion. "Captain Tremain! It's so good to see you home, sir. I'll announce you immediately. We've all been waiting—"

Adam smiled. "I'm happy to be back, Ruel. It's nice to know I've been missed."

"You have indeed, sir. Mrs. Tremain will be so happy to hear—"

"Where is Mrs. Tremain?" Adam asked quickly.

"Why, she's with Master Beau, sir. Shall I call her?"

"No. Not a word." Adam went past Ruel and took the stairs of the north wing two at a time. At the top he began to walk stealthily. Quietly he entered Beau's room, moving silently across the floor until he came up behind Dulcie and his son. He grasped Dulcie around her small waist, and before she could cry out had her turned toward him, pressed against him, his eager mouth on hers.

Young Beau let out an initial squeal of fright, then manfully began to defend his mother by attacking his father's knee with rapidly moving little fists. Unsuccessful in this attempt, he sank his baby teeth into Adam's shin and gained instant attention.

"Dulcie!" Adam bellowed. "What have you taught this child—to beat up his own father?"

Dulcie laughed gaily. "He's protecting his mama. Isn't that what a good son would do?"

Adam smiled as he picked Beau up, then he looked into his son's mouth and back to Dulcie. "He's got teeth like needles."

"Give Daddy a kiss, Beau," Dulcie coaxed.

Beau looked suspiciously at the large man holding him. "Daddy?"

"Talk to him, Adam. He's only two and a half. You've been gone a fifth of his life."

Awkwardly Adam talked to his son, using a falsely soft, high voice, which sent Dulcie into peals of laughter. Beau was beginning to have fun, and joined in with his mother's merriment. His small, pudgy hands beat a tattoo on Adam's face, and then he rewarded his father with a wet, open-mouthed imitation of a kiss.

Dulcie put her arms around both of them and raised her face for Adam's kiss. She received one from each of them.

Adam, more at ease after his initial meeting with Beau, played with the little boy for half an hour before the dinner gong rang. Beau and Adam had just begun to know each other again, and Adam was reluctant to leave. "Just once more," he said, and Dulcie placed her son atop Adam's back so his father could give him another "horsey-ride" around the playroom. Beau's small arms wrapped around Adam's neck, and his childish giggles rang in Adam's ears. Supper seemed far less appetizing to him than this.

He stopped, kneeling upright, then grabbed hold of Beau and brought him somersaulting over his shoulder into his arms. He sat cross-legged on the floor with Beau in his lap. His hair was mussed and curling wildly around his face. He looked up at Dulcie, his blue eyes bright and sparkling. "Must we go down?"

He looked so young, Dulcie thought, no more than a boy himself, and yet he wasn't. She knew he wasn't. Still, she wanted to hold him as she would Beau, she wanted to be so near him that she would become a part of him. "Perhaps Mindy could—" she began, and was interrupted as Patricia appeared in the doorway.

"Dulcie Jeannette, Ruel just told me Adam is home. Adam! What evah ah you doin' on the floah? Dulcie, he's goin' to spoil that child rotten. Haven't Ah evah told you nevah let a man in the nursery?"

Dulcie adjusted the dazed, happy look on her face. It was as though her mother had shattered something fragile and beautiful by coming into Beau's nursery. But she hadn't. It was still there, just waiting to return the next time they were by themselves. "I think we'll eat up here, Mama."

"But Dulcie honey, you can't! Emma has suppah all laid out, an' everyone is waitin' to see Adam."

Dulcie looked at Adam, her eyebrows raised.

Beau, still joyous and excited, was chanting, "Horhee, horhee!"

Adam got up, placing the little boy on his shoulder. "See, Beau, you're bigger than Grandma."

Beau reached for Patricia's complicated coïffure. "Adam, don't you dare let that child muss mah hair! Dulcie youah goin' to regret the day you evah let that man in the nursery! He's spoiled Beau already. Not home an houah an' he's ruined youah baby." At the door she posed dramatically. "Ah expect both of you downstairs foah suppah."

Behind Patricia's back Adam saluted rakishly. "The queen speaks."

Adam and Dulcie went to supper with the rest of the family and the Whitakers. There was a great deal of excitement and curiosity. The first thing all of them wanted to know was whether Tom had found his daughter, and if he had decided to stay in New Orleans.

"Tom was originally from New Orleans," Adam explained for those who hadn't known him. "When I first met him he had just moved out into the bayou. When we came into the city this trip, he took me to see the house he grew up in. It's a beautiful old pillared mansion in the Streets of Nine Muses, Clio Street. The house has been badly run down, and Tom is bargaining for it. If I know him, by now he owns that house."

Jem nodded agreement. "I never understood why someone of Tom's background and breeding took to living in a pest-infested swamp. Why'd he give up everything he knew, to live like a no-'count?"

Because he loved a black woman and dared to marry her, Adam thought. He glanced at Dulcie, then he laughed. "Jem, that is a long, long story, one I'm afraid only Tom has a right to tell. Accept my word that there were powerful reasons for Tom's flight to the swamps."

Emma waited impatiently, then said, "You haven't told us if he found his daughter. Was she in New Orleans?"

Adam hesitated for a moment, then said quietly, "Yes, he found her."

"Well?" Emma persisted. "Surely that's not all you're going to say!"

Adam began to pay closer attention to his food. "There isn't much else to say, Emma. He found Angela, she's well and . . . safe."

"Where did he find her? What was she doing all these years? How did she manage during the war?" Emma asked in rapid-fire order.

"Is she married?" Patricia added.

All the women at the table were looking eagerly at Adam.

Dulcie, sensing his discomfort and his reluctance to talk about Angela, said, "Well, you know there were some strong ill feelings between Tom and Angela. I'm sure it hasn't been simple and easy for them. I think it is wonderful that he found her at all. What more could any one of us have hoped for in an initial visit?"

"Tom's been there for months, and if he's buying back his house, there must be more to tell. Adam, why are you so reticent?" Emma asked. "What happened that you don't want to burden us with?"

"I'm hiding nothing, Emma. Dulcie has stated it pretty much as it is. The bad feelings between Angela and Tom came from an incident long ago. Tom has seen her and they are in touch with each other again. That's a big step for them."

Enid's cold, disillusioned eyes sparkled with interest. "What happened between them? I've always wanted to know what could come between a father and a sixteen-year-old daughter that could be so bad that he would let her run off. Did she run away with a man?"

"Enid!" Emma said sharply. "That is an unfit subject for—"

"Really, Mama, what else could she have done? Where is a young girl going to go alone? What father would permit it? There aren't too many things a woman can do. It doesn't take much imagination to realize there had to be a man or—" She looked at Adam, her hard slate eyes filled with cynicism and contempt.

Adam returned her stare. He wouldn't tell them about Angela. No one at this table besides Dulcie and himself would even attempt to understand what had happened between Tom and his daughter. Not even Jem and Patricia knew that Angela's mother had been a quadroon slave, and they never would. Angela had already suffered too much at the hands of well-meaning whites, including his own mother and himself. He'd never again expose her to the horrible longing and alienation he unwittingly had before.

He ignored the pent-up silence at the table, with the questions about Angela still hanging in the air. He remembered her as he had first known her, a child little older than Beau, with whom he had played as he had earlier with his own child. And later as a tall, willowy woman-child who thought she was in love with him. He remembered sadly trying to explain to her that there was only one woman he would ever love, and that was Dulcie; but Angela by then had learned what it meant to be part Negro and part white, and she had thought his refusal was on that ground.

And he thought of her as he had seen her in New Orleans just a week ago. She was fully a woman now, experienced and worldly beyond her years. She was magnificent, poised, beautiful. She was rich. She had acquired a power of position and of personality that she didn't hesitate to use. There was nothing left of the hurt, confused woman-child who had run from her father with the black gambler, Jubal Lerner. There was only the woman who had learned to use her sensuality and beauty for her own ends, and who had learned to hate with a searing, passionate fire that was frightening.

Tom had found Angela, Adam thought, but what that meant was anybody's guess. He had no idea why Angela seemed willing to continue seeing her father. He couldn't tell if she still had some feeling of love for him or if she were serving some secret purpose of her own. Angela had become too skilled in the arts of deception to tell what she was thinking, or feeling.

"You aren't going to tell us a thing, are you?" Emma said in irritation.

Adam looked directly at her. "No, I'm not. I'm sorry, Emma, but there's very little to tell."

"Not even if she is married?"

"She isn't married."

"Adam, Ah don't think youah bein' very courteous," Patricia said.

"Patsy, leave the man alone," Jem growled. "There are more important things to talk about. Did you buy the plantation?"

Adam brightened immediately. "Yes, Ben West and I purchased fifteen hundred acres of prime sugar land in St. Mary's Parish. Ben will begin the planting this year."

"Then you and Dulcie will be leaving Mossrose for certain."

"Eventually, sir. We have always planned to do so."

"I know, I know," Jem muttered. "I was just hoping that when we got it built up again, you'd change your minds. Can't fault a man for hoping."

"No, sir, I can't." Adam looked over at Dulcie. He couldn't imagine a worse homecoming. There seemed to be no subject that wasn't touchy. And he was not even able to mention the incident that worried him most. Tom had not only found Angela, he had found Edmund Revanche. Edmund had also returned to his native city, and was once more living at Grey Oaks, his plantation just outside of the city. As was Edmund's custom, he was well established with all the important and powerful white men and black men of the city, and a staunch supporter of the Radical Republicans in New Orleans.

Tom was as brash and unpredictable as Edmund was cool and calculating. Edmund was in a nearly unassailable position in New Orleans, but Tom had sworn years ago to kill Edmund, his former friend and boyhood companion. Adam had no idea if Tom would practice common sense or restraint when it came to Edmund Revanche.

Adam had left New Orleans with reluctance. He had felt needed there, and there was an excitement in the city that he felt nowhere else. Perhaps it was because New Orleans was his city, but he thought it was more than that. No place on earth was like it. It had the fire and passion of its French and Spanish ancestry, the pride of the Creole and Cajun, the bawdy hilarity of its Gallatin and Perdido streets, and the quaint beauty of the Quarter. The city of New Orleans pulsed with a vitality unmatched anywhere else in the world. Were it not for Dulcie and Beau needing to be near the Morans at this time, he would have returned to Savannah after a week to take his family home with him to New Orleans.

Jem interrupted his wandering thoughts. "I suppose your shipping line is thriving there too."

"Ben has it going full steam. He's ordered two ships from an American shipyard. We've never used American-built ships before, but both of us feel that with the state the economy is in, we need to spend the capital here at home."

"Oh, Adam!" Dulcie wailed. "We won't be going to England?"

"Not soon, I'm afraid. But we don't need an excuse to go to Europe. Every once in a while, I'd like to make the Liverpool run myself. I've never been averse to beautiful lady passengers."

"Or spoiled little boys?" she asked impishly, her eyes on her mother.

"I love spoiling little boys," Adam said heartily.

Jem ignored the chatter between his daughter and her husband. All he could think was that they would be leaving far sooner than he would be willing to let them go. "I must get over to Mossrose," he said, and excused himself from the table. As he rose, his vision blurred temporarily, yet the candles on the table seemed to flare brighter. He said nothing, and the strange symptoms passed.

The Whitakers and Adam and Dulcie and Patricia continued talking. Dulcie basked in the look of loving pride on Adam's face as she displayed her knowledge of local politics and events. The Whitaker men were amused, and Emma, Enid, Pearl, and Patricia were shocked at her lack of femininity.

She was being inexcusably forward, but she loved every minute of it. Eagerly she said, "The Union League is armed now, Adam. They've reversed their policy against bearing arms and have formed military companies. They parade regularly now, and even at the meetings have posted armed guards."

Adam frowned. "Armed guards—are you sure? Why would they need guards at meetings?"

Ned said, "She's right, Adam. You've been gone a long time, and there's nothing that's the same as when you left. There's a group that calls itself the Ku Klux Klan now. They're terrorizin' the coloreds, and have more support than you or I'd think possible."

"I've heard of the Klan. There is a version of it in New Orleans too. They call themselves the Knights of the White Camellia down there. They're no more than a pack of hooligans, robbing, looting, and burning everywhere."

"The same thing is happening here," Ned said. "The Union League is one of their pet targets, along with any nigger who votes—unless, of course, he's goin' to vote Democrat. And these Klansmen are makin' a difference. If things keep on this way, it will influence the vote before long."

Brock Whitaker snorted and sat up in his chair. "You can thank the God-damned Yankee Congress for that. The War is over! Why don't they let us alone?"

Emma Whitaker quickly signaled it was time for the ladies to excuse themselves. Patricia gladly left, making a show of shock at Brock's language. Dulcie followed, though she was reluctant to lose this chance to learn more about County activities.

"You're referring to the military districting of the South?" Adam asked.

"I sure as hell am! D'ja ever think the Ku Klux might have the right idea? They're the only God-damned folks doin' anything to help the Confederate veterans. What right have the Yankees to come in here with their damned armies and tell us we've got to throw out everything we've accomplished in two years, just because they say our duly elected civil legislature is only provisional? Provisional! Hell, that only means we do it their way or they ram what they want down our gullets with bayonets while we sit here unarmed and undefended. Whose country is this? Are we part of it, or ain't we? When in the hell are they gonna make up their minds?"

"We had a military government in 1865. No one minded then," Ned said.

"Sure we did," Brock said loudly. "But there was one hell of a difference, Daddy. They were here then to protect property and help make the move from war to peace. That isn't what they're doin' down here this time. General Pope is not commander of the Third District for any good purpose. Them damned Radicals made their mark in the last election." He swiveled to look angrily at Adam. "An election *you* helped give to them! That was all they needed. Nothin's goin' to stop them now. They'll take away our right to decide anything for ourselves. There won't be any South, we'll have some damned carpetbaggin' Northerner up there in Congress tellin' those Radical Congressmen whatever they want to hear. There won't be any Southern voice left. They're gonna make raw meat out of us, unless somebody stops 'em."

"Like the Klan?" Adam asked.

Brock said belligerently, "Yes, like the Ku Klux."

"You a member, Brock?" Adam asked.

Brock sat back in his chair. "Member? Of what? Ain't you heard, Captain Tremain, there are no members. There ain't any organization. It's invisible. Everywhere. Nowhere. Everyone. No one." He put his hands up. "Poof! Nothin' there."

Disgusted, Adam looked away from him. "Ned, what has this done to the politics?"

Ned made a face. "Everybody is goin' every which way. I guess you could say we got three main groups. Some's in favor of followin' ex-Governor Brown. He wants to give in to Congress, put the niggers in the Legislature, and see what happens. And, of course, that means we'd meet Congress halfway on almost anything they have to say. Naturally, there's another bunch that feels givin' in to anything the Radicals want is suicide for the state.

"And then there's the folks who don't want to do a damned thing. They're for sittin' on their hands, standin' by President Johnson, and seein' what happens. I think that's just plain foolishness. One thing is sure— we've got to do somethin'. The Radicals aren't goin' to give our rights back to us until they have that Fourteenth Amendment ratified. We can't do anything as long as we're locked out of the Senate and the House. We've got to give in sometime, they're holdin' all the trump cards."

"Like hell they are," Brock said.

Adam snapped, "The Klan isn't going to stop anything. The Fourteenth Amendment will be ratified sooner or later, and the sooner it is, the better off Georgia will be."

"What the hell do you know about Georgia, or what's good for her? You're no better'n a carpetbagger yourself!"

"Brock!" Ned said sharply. "Captain Tremain is a guest in our house."

"He's a damned nigger-lovin'——"

Ned stood quickly, his hand raised. Brock also stood up. Sullenly, he left the room. Ned Whitaker sat down again and apologized to Adam.

"Politics is a subject better avoided, Ned. It was my fault. I was too eager to learn what had happened in my absence."

Jem rode over to Mossrose. He couldn't remember feeling like crying since he was a small child at his mother's knee, but he felt like it today. He had known all along that Adam and Dulcie and Beau would be leaving for their own home. He even admitted to himself that they should settle in their own place and live their lives together. What he had not known was how sorely he'd feel his own mortality, how badly he would want to cling to his daughter and his grandson for the years he had left.

He dismounted and handed the reins to Jothan.

"I've got the books all laid out for you, Mr. Moran. Mossrose is beginning to look like a thriving operation."

"Not now, Jothan. I think I'll just take a little walk first. I want to look at my fields."

Jothan nodded. "Yes, sir. Any time is fine. I'll have it ready for you whenever you want."

Jem was not feeling very well. He smiled weakly. "I don't know if I ever got around to telling you, Jothan, but you're the best overseer that's ever been on Mossrose."

Jothan blushed at this unexpected compliment. "Thank you, sir. I like working here."

"I should never have sold you away." He paused for a moment, finding it difficult in this first attempt to account for his actions to a black man. "I was wrong. Wrong about a lot of things."

Jem walked slowly across the lawn toward his beloved cotton fields. He didn't know what was wrong with him today. He was feeling mighty strange, and mighty sad about a lot of things. He seldom looked back, but he didn't seem able these last few weeks to think of anything but the past. Recent days seemed to run through his memory like water through a sieve; but the past, it was carefully displayed for scrutiny in some protected part of his mind.

Jem inspected the first field with care and pleasure; the healthy, green cotton plants stood sturdy and promising. Feeling somewhat improved, he walked toward the back field, which was being cleared of brush and tree stumps. A lot of planters didn't clear their fields of stumps, but Jem preferred it that way. He liked a clean regularity in his fields, no wandering rows of cotton to accomodate unnecessary obstacles.

In the distance a black man and a mule were working on a large tree stump. As Jem drew nearer, he saw that it was Boy. He increased his pace. He wasn't pleased that Boy had been left working alone. The man was strong enough, but Boy was a haphazard worker at best, and he was not bright. Problems were frustrations to Boy, incomprehensible obstacles that he repeatedly tried to attack with physical strength when a bit of figuring would solve them easily.

As Jem approached, watching Boy, the man threw down the pick mattock he had been using to break up the roots. He affixed a rope from the mule's hitch to the stump. Jem smiled, and said to himself, "Well, Boy, I guess I was wrong again. You're doing just fine."

Boy smacked the mule on his rump, then began to lead the animal away from the stump. The mule took several steps, then halted. Boy smacked him again and pulled. The mule remained stationary. Boy shouted at him, then in a fury kicked the beast. The mule kicked, his forelegs and rear legs thrashing. The mule's rear hoof grazed Boy's thigh. The big black man let out a shriek of pained rage. Clasping his hands, Boy raised his arms over his head, and brought his fists down on the mule's back like a hammer blow.

Boy and the mule were now two enraged beasts. The mule's thrashing became more frantic, and the black man was dancing around the animal, kicking and screaming. The mule turned, kicking hard, landing a sharp blow to Boy's hip.

Jem shouted and began running across the field.

Boy's trousers were torn, and blood began to seep and stain the jeans fabric. His whole attention was on the mule. He didn't hear Jem shouting at him, nor did he see his employer running and frantically waving his arms. Boy stood glaring at the mule, his face a dark sweating mask of primitive hatred.

Then, with a cry that came from deep within him, he lunged and grabbed the discarded mattock. Sweat glistened and rolled off his tautly muscled chest as he brought the pick over his head and swung, embedding it deep in the animal's flank.

The mule's enraged, piercing brays became wild, agonized screams. Eyes walling, teeth bared, the mule thrashed wildly, losing footing, flailing, and raising again to attack. Boy grabbed the pick handle, and with a gargantuan heave wrested it from the screaming animal's body. He swung the bloodied instrument again, plunged the pick into the mule's chest. With a scream and a final lunge, the mule threw itself at Boy. Boy leaped, twisting, and then fell, the mule crashing down across his pelvis. Boy lay on the ground screaming in pain, rage, and frustration, his powerful fists pounding the dying animal's body.

Jem ran up to them, his chest heaving, his face brilliant red from the unaccustomed exertion. He tried to speak, but couldn't catch his breath. His heart was pounding so hard it felt as if his ears and his temples

would burst with the pressure. He grabbed the lead
rope attached to the mule's harness, and began to pull
at the still thrashing animal. He dodged the weakly
flailing hooves and got a better grip on the animal's
neck.

"Pull that damn mule!" Boy screeched, angry now
at Jem's ineffectual efforts.

The strength in Jem's arms seemed to have gone.
Everything turned a hazy red, darkening at the edges.
He could hear nothing but the slamming of his heart.
The hammering of his own blood seemed to be everywhere, everywhere except in his limbs. As quickly as
he had felt the surge of heat and the mad pounding
come on him, Jem began to sweat, and the feeling
drained from his face. He let go of the rope, and the
mule, staggering back. He was nauseated, dizzy, and
weak.

Boy watched the purplish red sweep out of Jem's
face. He watched it turn gray-white, the mouth becoming colorless and outlined in an even deathlier pale
blue. Jem seemed to regain his balance, but he clutched
at his head, reeling sideways, then he crumpled bone-
lessly to the ground, his mouth open and drooling
saliva.

From different parts of the plantation Jothan, Ruel,
and Apollo all heard the crazed shrieks of the mule
and Boy, and had begun to run toward the sounds.
Helpless, they watched the entire episode as they ran
across the two fields.

Jothan was first to arrive, and he ran to Jem's side.
He straightened Jem's leg, which had crumpled under
him as he fell. When Ruel and Apollo got there, Jothan
had Jem's head cradled in his lap. Jem's mouth hung
slack, the left side of his face looking as though someone had hold of it and was pulling it down, so it no
longer matched the regularity of the right side.

As the three men came up, Boy was yelling, "Ah
din do nothin' to him! Wa'n't mah fault! Din do nothin'!"

Jothan and Ruel were bent over Jem. Ruel loosened his collar and spoke quickly to Jothan, who immediately sprinted toward the cabins to find something that could be used as a stretcher and to bring the dray so that Jem could be hauled back to the Whitaker plantation. Apollo walked over to Boy and the mule, which was still moving with feeble jerks. He drew his Union Army pistol out from the belt of his trousers and aimed it first at Boy.

Boy screamed in fright and renewed his efforts to free himself from the weight of the mule.

Then Apollo slightly adjusted his aim. "Don't bothah to move. Ah wouldn't mind havin' mah aim thrown off when Ah shoot this mule."

Boy let out a shriek. "Tu'n me loose! Doan shoot me! Doan hu't me! Ah din do nothin' bad!"

Apollo spat at him. "That pick jes' jump up an' dig itseff in that mule?"

Boy was weeping, his mouth open in a great red, gaping yawn of terrified misery.

Apollo squeezed the trigger, and Boy screamed once more. The mule gave one last spasm, then lay still across the struggling field hand. Apollo took the rope Boy had tied around the stump, and arranged it as a pulley.

Ruel, fanning Jem with his hat, watched as Apollo strained and heaved, slowly pulling the weight of the mule from Boy. Then he turned away as he heard the sounds of the dray. Jothan was driving the big wagon at breakneck speed across the fields. The wagon bounced dangerously behind the horses with Jothan clinging for his life to the seat, but he didn't slow down until he neared Jem and Ruel.

Carefully the two brothers placed Jem on a blanket, then lifted him to the bed of the wagon. Ruel climbed in beside Jem, and Jothan drove away, now taking the horses slowly, picking his way over the smoothest parts of the field.

Apollo was breathing hard before he got the mule

off Boy. As the animal's weight finally shifted, freeing
Boy's legs, Apollo slumped to the ground. He ran a
sweating forearm over his dripping brow.

Boy lay back, quiet for a moment, then with lightning swiftness he moved, gained his feet, and started to
run.

Apollo scrambled up. He ran a few paces then stood,
his feet parted, his hips thrust out, his pistol held in
both hands and leveled at the small of Boy's back.
"Halt, you fuckin' deserter!" Apollo shouted in a deep,
cold voice.

Boy slowed, twisting to see Apollo, but still running.
"Doan shoot! Lemme go, brothah, lemme go!" His
arms were outstretched, pleading.

Apollo fired.

Boy's eyes grew enormous. He felt nothing, but saw
his ring finger fly off into the air. He grasped his muti-
lated hand against his chest and began to howl.

"Walk back here—to me," Apollo said in a voice
devoid of emotion.

"Ah cain't," Boy screeched. "Dey gwine kill me. Ah
cain't. Lemme go. Ahh, Gawd, lemme go!"

Apollo leveled the gun again. "Walk back here,
nigger. Iffen you don't, Ah'll blow you apart a piece at
a time."

Boy fell to his knees, his words unintelligible now.
Apollo, his eyes still on Boy, reached for the rope.
With one hand, he cut the rope free of the mule, then
walked toward Boy.

He wound the rope around the man's neck, then
bound his hands behind him. "Git up. We're goin' to
the law."

"Dey gwine kill me! Mah blood on youah han's.
Lemme go!"

Apollo got the farm wagon and took Boy into Savannah. He turned him over to Laban Sweet, Justice
of the Peace.

"What's the Cap'n want done?" Laban asked.

"Ah don't know," Apollo said. "The Cap'n wasn't

there when it happened. Ah brought him in on mah own."

Laban laughed. "On youah own, huh. Looks like Ah got snookered by Tremain again. He hired you as a favah t'me—Ah thought. How come you nevah work fo' nobody else like you do him? Lawd, theah was a time Ah thought Ah'd nevah git you sitcheeated any-place."

Apollo stood proudly to his full height, then began to saunter away from Laban. Over his shoulder he smiled, saying, "Cap'n Tremain know a man when he see one. He treat me like a man, Ah works like a man. Treat me like a nigger, an' Ah works like a nigger."

"Sonofabitch," Laban muttered good-naturedly, then he yelled, "Hey! Hey theah, what you want me to do with this heah nigger?"

"You got a Pig Law, ain't you? See if you got a Mule Law."

Laban burst out laughing. "He didn't steal nothin'."

"No? What you call it? Mister Moran ain't got his mule no more, do he? That daid mule cost ovah ten dollars, didn't it?"

Laban looked from Apollo to Boy and gave the rope on him a heavy tug. "Looks like you goin' to be con-vict labah fo' the next twenny yeahs. Think Ah'll see if we cain't lease you out to a road gang. You can use that ol' pick o' yours as much as you like—on rocks. You got t'be the dumbest hunk o' goat meat Ah evah run into, Boy. Why'd you go do a stupid thing like stickin' a pick into Moran's mule? Didn't you know the critter'd get mad?"

Apollo climbed into the farm wagon again and headed back to Mossrose. By dusk he was within a mile of the plantation. An evening hush had begun to fall over the countryside. The human noises had dimmed, and the softer, rhythmic sounds of birds and insects emerged.

Apollo was limp with fatigue. He let the reins go

slack. "Go home, hawss. You got to be as hongry as me."

His hat was pulled down over his eyes, the horse moving along at a slow walk, when he heard the whine of a whip. His hat flew from his head, and silhouetted against the purpling sky was Leroy Biggs.

"Well, if it ain't 'Pollo Justus Sherman. Fancy meetin' you on the road, boy."

Apollo sat up straight. He picked up the reins, stopped the horse, and climbed down, walking back a way to retrieve his new black hat with a bluejay feather tucked jauntily in the red band. "What the hell do you want, *Colonel* Biggs?"

"You ain't afraid of me, are you, boy?"

"Ah ain't afraid of you, *Colonel* Biggs," Apollo said flatly.

"You an' that slick-talkin' nigger butler of Tremain's is two of a kind."

"Is that all you wanted to say, Colonel?"

"Don't you get uppity at me, boy! Where do you come off bein' disrespectful to your betters? Stand there, nice like, an' listen to me like a good nigger should."

Apollo ached to drag Leroy from his mount and fight it out with him as two men of equal standing. But he couldn't do that. He couldn't protect himself with his pistol. He wasn't on Mossrose property now. There was no Captain Adam Tremain to back him up. There was nothing to back him up. Leroy had him in the open, and any move he made in defense or provocation would be a black man attacking a white. Apollo said through clenched teeth, "Ah'm listenin', Colonel."

Leroy grinned. "That's better. You jes' stand there a while. I got to think about what I'll tell you."

Apollo stood in the road, his fancy black hat in his hand. Leroy walked his horse around him, the horse's hooves lifting little dust puffs in the dry road. Apollo remained standing for several minutes, with Leroy enjoying the sight of humbling this proud black man.

He laughed loudly. "You come a long way, didn't

you, 'Pollo? Yes suh, a long, long way—from Jem Moran's boy to Jem Moran's boy."

"Ah ain't Jem Moran's boy!"

"What are you, 'Pollo?"

Apollo whirled to face him.

"You're Jem Moran's boy! That's what you are, nigger!"

Apollo started for him, then saw the mean smile begin in Leroy's eyes, the lift of his sullen mouth. This was no different from a bear baiting, Apollo realized. He knew his only means of victory over this man was to hold his temper, endure the man's taunts, and do nothing in retaliation.

It was a bitter sort of victory, one that cast doubts on Apollo's ideas of manhood. If he tried to deal with Leroy on equal footing, he'd end up in prison as surely as Boy would, and Leroy would win. If he did nothing, Apollo won, but what did he win? The right to be free one more day? The right to keep trying to be equal, to be a man when so few would allow it?

With men like Adam Tremain, the way to free manhood was clear. One had only to prove oneself. But men like him were rare. Most of the white men Apollo had known, or ever would know, were Leroy Biggses, or Brock Whitakers, and they were too petty to ever allow another man to succeed, especially a black man.

With a crushing ache that tightened around his chest, Apollo Justus Sherman realized he had been freed to live in a new kind of captivity. He'd been freed only to be bound and shackled by white men's fear and black men's bitterness. Not in all his life would he be truly free. Then he looked at Leroy and realized Leroy was as much a captive as he was.

No longer caring what Leroy might do, Apollo, head down, walked slowly back to his wagon and got up on the seat. He picked up the reins, clucking at the horse. He didn't look back. Tears slowly rolled down his firm, handsome bronze cheeks. They were all damned. None of them free. All damned to captivity.

CHAPTER ELEVEN

Jem Moran hovered near death for three weeks. Patricia, a frail shadow of herself, was by his bedside day and night, shock and loneliness imprinted in every line of her face. She had thought Jem indestructible. She couldn't remember what life had been like before she knew him. She no longer knew how to live without Jem beside her. How did one draw breath without one's love to give reason for the effort? What did one talk about when the only ear desired was no longer there?

She didn't cry. There was nothing to shed tears for. Jem's quiet body did not present a loss to her. It ran far deeper than that. In Jem's comatose form lay Patricia's life. If Jem no longer breathed, Patricia no longer existed either. She couldn't cry, because Jem was unconscious and beyond tears. What he could not do, neither could she.

The Whitaker house was still. A pall lay over all of them. Emma went about her duties with a mute determination, her mind on Ned as Patricia's was on Jem. The War had brought many aspects of life and death closer to all of them than people normally experience. The men were equally affected. All of them waited for the daily reports of Jem's progress.

There was great rejoicing in the house the day, near the end of July, when Jem Moran opened his eyes. His speech was seriously impaired, and there would never again be life in the left side of his body. Jem would never walk his fields or anywhere else. But none of that seemed important to the Morans, the Tremains, or the Whitakers. Jem was alive. That was miracle enough for all of them.

Adam rode to Mossrose to tell the workers and Apollo, Ruel, Jothan, and Kyra the news, for they had been as concerned as the whites. Jothan blamed himself for not having accompanied Jem on his walk that day, overlooking the fact that Jem had wanted to be alone and would not have permitted him to go along. Ruel worried about having done the wrong thing to aid Jem.

It was a heartrending joy that Adam saw in the workers' faces when he told them Jem was conscious and would recover to some degree. He wondered from what depths love and loyalty such as theirs could come. Many of them were ex-slaves of Jem Moran, and yet they were capable of a feeling that Adam seldom found in his own kind.

Quickly the four of them left to spread the good news to the other workers. Some expressed pleasure, some didn't care, and some were pleased because it meant the work at Mossrose would continue, and with it their jobs. The reception of the news varied, but the mood of Mossrose lightened considerably.

Ruel came back to Kyra's work cabin. He walked in and took his wife into his arms. They stood in an embrace for along time, and Kyra felt a rush of protective love for Ruel flow over her. He was a good man, a sensitive man, whose feelings seemed to be bottomless. When she thought she knew him thoroughly, he was able to reach deeper within himself and find reserves of strength she hadn't expected. Together they walked from the cabin and took the farm cart to drive to their home on the neighboring Matthews land.

Later that night, Kyra sat alone in the living room of their new home, one lamp lighting the embroidery stretched taut on her hoop. A satisfied smile played across her regal features; lamplight accentuated her high cheekbones, high-bridged nose, full, well-formed lips. Occasionally she would look up from her work and survey the room. It was taking form. One piece of furniture at a time, good furniture, good draperies.

There was nothing makeshift in the Jordan home, for
Kyra had vowed when she and Ruel first decided to
lease a portion of the old Matthews plantation from
the Freedman's Bureau that there would never be
"nigger" furnishings here. They would have only those
things that truly reflected their tastes and themselves.
If they were to make a new world for the black man,
then it had to be something fitting and fine, or what
was the use? If the new were simply another version
of the past, was it worth the pain and the struggle it
cost them, would continue to cost them for God knew
how long?

Kyra's lips tightened. Much of what she was thinking came from her conversations with Apollo. Sometimes she wondered if she was quite right in the head.
The two men, Ruel and Apollo, sometimes merged in
her mind so she couldn't remember which one of them
had said what, which one of them had shared her sense
of mission over the work of the Bureau, or her dreams
of the future.

It had to stop, Kyra thought. She had one husband,
and she loved him. She'd make this a fine house, one
Ruel would be proud to call his. She'd have his babies
in this house. She'd bring them up, teach them, and
instill in them a knowledge of freedom and the peculiar
kind of courage which men who have known slavery
have in defending their freedom.

"Kyra!" Ruel called from their bedroom.

She smiled again. "Come on out here a minute. I
got something I want to show you."

"Come to bed."

It was amusing, and flattering, to hear Ruel's precise
diction take on the pained sounds of a small boy wanting attention. She laughed. "I'm coming, but I want
you to see this first. Come here, Ruel."

Sleepily, he stumbled into the warmly lit room.

She held up the cross-stitched panel. Ruel took it
from her, holding it closer to the lamp. "You finished
it," he said, smiling. " 'God Bless Our Home.' "

"Yes, it's finished, and it's true. He will bless us."

Ruel leaned down and kissed her cheek. "He blessed me. Come to bed, Kyra," he said softly, taking her hands in his. "I'll make a frame for it tomorrow, and tonight you and me—well, we'll lie down together and thing about those blessings."

"We'll think about them, will we?" she said, laughing softly. She blew out the lamp, then, holding his hand, she walked with him to their bedroom.

Ruel held her, his breath moist on her forehead as he spoke softly to her in the darkness of the many things he planned and hoped for them. Kyra sighed contentedly. Sometimes she thought she'd never stop smiling. Then Ruel fell silent, and his hand slowly began to move down her arm, over her breast. "Ruel," she whispered, "don't stop talking to me."

He raised up slightly, looking at her. "I thought you had other things on your mind."

"I did, but I like your talking."

"Can't make babies by talking."

"We'll make babies, but I know you, Ruel Jordan, and you're trying to please me tonight. But you please me when you make love to me with your voice and your dreams, too. It doesn't always have to be one way." She tried to see his face in the dark. "I just wanted you to know that I like all the ways you have of loving me, Ruel."

He pulled her closer to him, his lips against her neck. They talked and touched and made love, and sometime they fell asleep, their arms still around each other.

Kyra dreamed of people running, shouting. Darkened streets suddenly alight with torches, the pounding of the people running. New York. The dirty streets, the Negro section invaded by whites who didn't want to fight a war for the black man. She struggled in her sleep, frightened as she had been the night she lived through the draft riots—the night her brother had been hanged by a wild drunken gang, his body set afire as they danced in the streets like screaming banshees, bottles to their lips, evil grins on their frenzied faces.

She felt as though she couldn't breathe. Fighting the terror of the dream, she tried to awaken, but couldn't. She felt as though she had opened her eyes. She was in her own bedroom. Ruel slept beside her, but the room was a blaze of firelight. Outside where the moon should have been was a towering pillar of fire. Noise was everywhere. Pounding. Shouting. Wild screaming sounds. She couldn't awaken. Terrified, she stood up. She went to the window. She'd pull the draperies closed tightly.

Kyra reached for the heavy muslin undercurtain. The window pane shattered, spraying splinters of glass over her. She screamed and leaped back. She could feel the cool evening breeze and smell the kerosene of the blazing cross on the lawn. The hooded creatures rushed to the broken window.

"Oh, no! Oh, no! Sweet Jesus—no—no—" She cried, backing from the window. She backed up to the bed, sitting so she blocked Ruel from view. He stirred in his sleep.

One of the hooded men let out a deep, sepulchral howl, supposed to be the cry of the dead. Ruel sat up, startled awake by the loud, eerie wail.

Kyra grabbed his arm, her face a mask of fear. "Don't say anything," she whispered. "Oh, God, Ruel, don't make a sound. I don't think they can see in."

Outside the men called "Ruel—Ruel Jordan! Come out! Jesse! Jesse Cole, come out! The dead call you. Come out!"

Ruel reached for his shirt and pants.

Kyra grabbed him, holding tight. "Don't you answer them, Ruel! Don't go out there. They won't do anything. Don't answer them. Please, Ruel!"

Ruel got up, crossing the house to the window that looked out over the Coles' property next to them. Kyra was right behind him, begging that he remain silent and not answer the call of the Klansmen. The two of them looked out the window, watching as Jesse Cole, his wife, and their children came slowly into the yard of their house.

The Klan gathered in the open space between the two houses. Jesse Cole was prodded and threatened into the circle of men. Astride horses covered with black cloth and wearing masks of white plumes with the marking KKK, the black-robed riders waved Belgian muskets fixed with bayonets, first at Jesse, then at the sky. Tin buttons sewn all over their head-to-foot robes sparkled in the torchlight. Around their waists were bands of bright scarlet. Their faces were covered with white masks, the apertures for eyes, nose, and mouth lined with red cloth. Three men carried the Ku Klux Klan black silk banners. In the center was the banner of the skull and crossbones, with two lions rampant on either side. At the top of the banners was the mystic K.

Howling, laughing hollowly behind the masks, the men circled and circled until one came forward and reined his horse inches from a terrified Jesse Cole.

"A bucket of water," the hollow voice called out. "Water—a bucket of water—"

Rigid with fear, Jesse hobbled toward the well he shared with Ruel. He drew the water and with shaking arms lifted it up to the waiting Klansman. With a deep, strangled laugh, the Klansman hoisted the bucket toward his head and began to pour the water. He kept the bucket upturned until no drop remained. Then with a loud smacking of lips, the Klansman droned, "That's the first drink I've had since I was killed at Atlanta. Will you shake my hand?"

Jesse nodded his head, past the ability to speak. Hesitantly, he held out his trembling hand. From under his robe, the Klansman extended a skeleton hand. Jesse screamed and fell to the ground.

Ruel firmly removed Kyra's restraining hands from his arms. "I can't let this go by, Kyra. Jesse will tell every other superstitious Negro in the settlement about the ghost of the Confederate soldier. They kept us ignorant for a reason, and this is it. Let me go, Kyra.

If Jesse doesn't see right now that the man is no ghost, no one will be voting in any election. No one will do anything."

Tears rolled down Kyra's face. "I don't want you to go, Ruel. Talk to Jesse in the morning, when it's over. He'll listen."

"Tomorrow's too late," Ruel said, and walked to his front door. "What can I do for you gentlemen?" he said clearly in his distinguished, precise voice.

One of the Klansmen broke away. He rode up close, appearing to have no head. Under his arm he carried an outsized gourd, a face grotesquely painted on it. "Hold this for me, boy. It's a heavy burden."

Ruel took the "head," examined it, and called out laughing to Jesse. "Look at this, Jesse—clever, isn't it? Look, it's a gourd. Almost as clever as his bucket trick. Pouring water through a funnel into a container hidden beneath his fancy robes. Amusing, eh, Jesse? Well, gentlemen, we've enjoyed your visit and your show, but we are all working men, and if you'll excuse us now, we wish to retire for what's left of the night."

"Jee-zus! Listen to that black bastard!"

The Klansmen turned from Jesse, forgetting him entirely. The Coles hastily crept away through their dark cotton field toward the woods, where they would remain hidden forever if necessary.

Ruel handed the "head" back to the Klansman. The man didn't take it, and Ruel threw it to the ground.

Slowly the hooded figures began to ride around Ruel; then they spurred their horses to a quicker speed. From under the robes they brought their whips. Faster and faster they circled, the whips snapping threateningly in the air. Ruel stood straight-backed, determined to show no fear. Dizzily the men rode round and round, torches bobbing with the rise and fall of the horses. The Klansmen began to hoot. One of them lifted the bayonet then, jabbing, but at a safe distance from Ruel. "Kneel, nigger!" he shouted as he raced past. Another bayonet flashed in the torchlight, then jabbed in close to Ruel, but did not touch him. "Pray, nigger!" "Respect!" The horses circled and the bayonets flashed, more and more of them.

Dodging a misaimed bayonet, Ruel stumbled, falling to one knee. He rose immediately, off balance and too near another passing Klansman. The bayonet nicked him, drawing blood at his shoulder. Shouting in triumphant laughter, the Klansmen moved in slightly closer. The game became more dangerous. Ruel now jumped quickly to avoid one bayonet, only to be jabbed by another. Flecks of blood marred the pure white of Ruel's shirt in several places. The cross burned itself out on the lawn, the torches guttered. The men howled in a deathly screech now, excited and incensed at this black man who was unwilling to bow to them.

Kyra stood by the front window, crying, her hand pushed tight against her mouth. The white plumes of the horses bobbed up and down, the black banners streamed out behind the riders in the dark sky. Ruel cried out as a bayonet stabbed into his chest. Another hit him from behind. The pointed weapons moved in and out faster and faster, the spinning black mass of riders went by until they were a blur. Ruel staggered, to be thrust back by another bayonet. Lurching forward, he ran into one of the racing horses and spun around, bumping another horse. Frightened, the horses broke file. The KKK banner flew wildly to the ground as the horse threw his rider. Klansmen struggled to regain control of their mounts.

Ruel lay on the ground, rolling frantically to avoid the hooves of the thrashing horses. The leader, his horse rearing, brought the animal down, then, in command, moved the horse forward several paces. Again the horse reared, screaming, his head tossing, eyes walling. He came down with both front hooves on Ruel's back.

Kyra was out the door, screaming, her long-bladed kitchen knife in her hand. Wildly she lunged at the melee of horses and men.

The leader's big animal once more reared, and again the horse, with deadly accuracy, came down, front hooves on Ruel.

Kyra dived forward. She was hit hard by another horse, and fell to the ground. She was up again, pushing toward the lead animal. Screaming, out of her mind with rage and fear, she struck at the horse with her knife, missing and again being thrown to the ground. She rose again, attacking the horse or its rider. Her knife flashed through the air without care to what she touched, so long as it would back the frenzied horse away from Ruel.

Her knife went deep into the horse's throat. Blood spurted, and the crazed, wounded animal buckled, regained its footing, and plunged forward several yards, then fell rolling onto its rider. The man grunted in pain. The dying animal struggled screaming, tossing its head, its legs thrashing. The man yelled for help. Several of the Klansmen dismounted and ran to him, pulling him from under the now-still horse.

Kyra crawled to Ruel, covering his crushed body with her own. She lay silent, huddled over him, talking softly beneath her breath as though he could hear he.

The head Klansman was riding double now, his mask splattered with horse blood, his voice that of an enraged demon. He grabbed a torch from one of the men and flung it toward the Jordan house. The others followed suit. One by one the torches landed—on the ground, on the roof of the house, near the barn that Jothan and Ruel had just finished building the week before. Then they rode to the Cole house and threw the two remaining torches onto the roof. Screaming and howling, they rode off into the darkness, the hoofbeats sounding for what seemed hours. Then there was only the silence of the night.

Kyra stayed where she was, her arms around Ruel, her face turned away. She wouldn't look at him, because she didn't want to see what she knew she must see.

It was nearly dawn when the Coles crept back to their house. The Klan torches had sputtered and gone out on the roof of their house, but not on the Jordans'. Kyra and Ruel's house still blazed, lighting up the purpling, hazy sky.

Ethel Cole came up to Kyra, placing her arms around her. "He's dead, baby, he's dead. Let go o' him. Jesse, see to Ruel."

Kyra put her head down closer to Ruel, then looked up at Ethel. "You let him die," she said tonelessly; then her grief broke out afresh, and she screamed at Ethel. "Where were you? Where were you? You could have helped him! He died for you! Where were you?"

Ethel stepped back, frightened, then she put her hands over her face. "Doan take on, Kyra—we doan mean to hu't Ruel, we doan mean—Jesse an' me—we's skeered o' de dead."

With vicious strength, Kyra heaved Ruel's torso up. His head hanging, bloody, faceless, she thrust him toward Ethel. "*He's dead!* Are you frightened of him too? Is a black man so much less than a white man that he is nothing even when he dies for your worthless skin!"

Ethel screamed and ran toward her house. Kyra yelled after her, and then she got to her feet and ran after Ethel. The door to the Coles' house slammed shut. Kyra hammered on the door, screaming that the Coles had killed Ruel. Exhausted, she fell to the ground moaning and rocking herself to ease the pain. Over and over again, she cried Ruel's name.

The dawn rose full, and the sun began to light the lawn and the burned house. Drained of tears, Kyra sat up, her head resting against the Coles' door. Wherever her reddened eyes turned she saw destruction; her nostrils were filled with the scent of fire and death and evil.

Inside her, her stomach heaved in illness and grief, her heart hurt, and her mind couldn't contain the hate

that was there. Heavily she got up and walked slowly
back to Ruel where he lay face down in front of their
burned house. She dragged him out of the light, and
into the cooler, darker shade of the copse of trees between their house and barn. There she sat down beside
him.

Shortly, she got up again and dragged his body inside
the barn, which had not burned. She swung open the
heavy, scorched doors, got Ruel inside, then came out,
shutting the door behind her. Purposefully, she walked
to the fallen horse. She grasped the handle of her long-
bladed knife and pulled it free of the horse's neck.

Kyra, her dark mahogany face an impassive mask,
marched across her property and into the cotton field.
The sun climbed; the hot, humid heat pulsed around
her. Her blood-soaked nightdress clung to the generous
contours of her statuesque body. In her hand she carried the dark-stained knife. Oblivious to everything in
the world but Ruel's death, she walked along the side
of a narrow dirt road, looking neither left nor right,
not caring if she was seen by any passerby. On and on
she walked, into and out of woods, hunting, searching.
She wasn't sure for whom, or where she would find
him, but find him she would, and extract payment she
would.

It was midday when Kyra walked down another
narrow, hard-packed clay road. The road wound
through carefully planted lines of live oaks. Kyra never
slackened her pace, her face retaining the dazed look
of the night just past. Before her glazed eyes wavered
a vision of a hooded man. Demented with grief and
horror, Kyra pursued her ghostly image of the Klansman. She strayed off the road unknowingly, her wandering feet taking her into the woods and out again,
across the Tweeds' fields and onto Redgrave property.

She was nearly four miles from Mossrose when
Adam, Jothan, and Apollo found her. She didn't recognize them, nor did she stop at their call. She continued

her dogged pursuit of the Klansman, the bloodied knife still clenched in her fist.

Crying, Apollo ran to her. He threw his arms around her and forced Kyra against him. He took the knife from her, throwing it to the ground. She fought him; then slowly the fight drained out of her, and Kyra clung to him, the wall of her reserve breaking in a torrent of heartrending sobs.

Jothan, on a stream of held breath, burst into sobs. Ashamed, he hid his face. Adam, his own eyes streaming tears, watched Kyra and Apollo, then looked away.

It was dark when they finally drove back to Mossrose. Apollo took Kyra on his horse. Exhausted, she slumped against him, still crying in her sleep.

CHAPTER TWELVE

Apollo left Kyra in Mindy's care, then rode to the Jordans' house. He could smell the scorched wood long before he saw what was left of the small house. He dismounted and stood, hands on hips, his head thrust back as he looked down at the still-smoldering wreckage. His mouth was tense and turned down. He looked for a long time, then his face crumpled and he looked away. His eye was caught by a bulky mound of cloth lying near the woods.

The head Klansman's horse, shrouded from nose to tail, lay still, flies and gnats buzzing around it. Apollo walked over to the dead animal. The white sheet was stained heavily at the horse's neck where Kyra had thrust her knife deep. Apollo shuddered as he thought of Kyra, frightened and nearly mad with grief, fighting the Klansmen alone. With his horror was mixed a strong admiration. She would fight anything, anyone. Fearful or not, Kyra didn't give up. He admired that in her. He loved her for it.

He kicked at the horse, then knelt down beside it on one knee, his mind working fast and clearly now. "They gonna be wantin' you, ol' hawss," he murmured. "They sho'nuff ain't gonna leave you heah fo' anybody to see an' know." He looked up at the sky. The light was fading, and in the night they would come and take the horse. Apollo quickly shoved the sheet aside and examined the animal carefully. Before he uncovered it, he had been sure he knew its owner, but now there was no doubt. No man in the district would fail to know another's horse. And surely he, who had worked in nearly every stable around, could not fail to recognize Leroy Biggs's horse.

Apollo rocked back on his haunches. He wasn't surprised. But he wasn't happy about his certainty of Leroy's identity either. No lawman was going to listen to Apollo, and no jury was going to take his word over Leroy's in a court. There was nothing he could do legally.

And there was little he could do illegally. Just as he knew Leroy, Leroy knew him, and would kill him or have him killed if he tried to go after him. For some time Apollo remained in his cramped position, then he looked up at the sky again, and then at the trees. A joyless smile crept across his handsome bronze features. Quickly he got to his feet and remounted his horse. Within half an hour he was back again with a team of mules and a coil of heavy rope.

He gave no more thought to consequences, or fear. He was a study in purposeful motion. He bound the legs of the dead horse, making sure they were secure; then he rode into the woods as far as the length of rope would permit. There he threw the end over the highest tree branch he could manage, about twenty feet off the ground. His eyes constantly darted to the sky, noting the growing purple gloom of twilight. Running to the mules, he brought them into the woods. He secured the rope he had thrown over the branch to their hitch, then began to bring the mules forward.

Reluctantly they moved at his command, slowly dragging the Klansman's horse across the clearing in front of Ruel's and Kyra's house and into the woods. Apollo beat at the mules' flanks and shouted commands to them. The animals moved forward again, then as the horse was next to the tree and his weight began to pull more heavily against them, they stopped.

Sweating now and in a terrible race with the darkening sky, Apollo positioned himself in front of the animals to pull on their harness, then raced behind them to beat them into obedience. The Klansman's horse began to rise from the ground. Slowly, a foot at a time, the dead animal rose. When it was finally near the branch, Apollo tied the mules' hitch to another tree so they couldn't move or let the horse drop.

Momentarily perplexed, he stood before the tree with the dead horse dangling from its limb and realized there was no low branch for him to get hold of to climb up. Then he noticed the first sounds of the night birds' songs and a single lonely cry of an owl. With the agility of a small boy, Apollo shinnied up the tree and grabbed for the branch supporting the horse. With a quick, graceful swing he pulled himself over the limb. Working rapidly in the darkness, he took up the slack in the rope, securing that with another piece of rope which he tied to the limb. Holding his breath, he cut the rope attached to the mules.

The rope creaked, and dug into the bark of the limb, but it held. Apollo wound the cut rope around the limb as well, then with a laugh and a small glance up at heaven he prayed it would hold until the night riders came back hunting for the horse. He climbed down from the tree, ran for the mules, and took them back to Mossrose. Without taking time to clean or groom them properly, Apollo shouted for Albatross to do that, and went back to the Jordans' house on foot.

Stealthily he made his way across the open pasture, hunched down, taking what cover he could from scrub grass and the few bushes that grew wild. He moved like a shadow once he had gained the protection of the woods. He climbed another tree, as high into the branches and foliage as he could. From there he could see the murky silhouette of the suspended horse. He moved around until he was reasonably comfortable, then he prepared to wait.

He wouldn't permit himself to think about what had happened, about Ruel or about Kyra. He thought only of minutes, of the sounds of the woods animals, of the feeling of the night, of the soft perfume of the leaves and bark, of the deathly sweet stench of the rotting horse. He listened for the inevitable hoofbeats of the Klansmen, but he refused to think about them. He couldn't. He didn't dare. He would take what little satisfaction he could from watching them return for the horse, but he couldn't think, for justice wasn't open to him, and that was truly what he wanted. He wanted someone to be held accountable for what had been done, and that wouldn't happen. So he remained perched in his aerie and watched, thoughtless and alert.

He was cramped and sore and tired by the time he heard them coming. He stirred slightly to ease the aching in his hip and to be able to see better.

There were six of them, all looking like demons from a grave, their white robes beating in the night wind, their heads covered with pointed caps, the masks decorated with obscene grotesqueries. The riders burst into the clearing in front of the Jordans' burned, still-smoldering house. They went directly to the place the horse had fallen.

"Jee-zus! It ain't here!" one of them said in a high shrill voice. "Somebody's got your ass, Le—"

"Shut up, you God-damned souse!"

The men halted the horses, then milled around aimlessly as though they didn't know what to do. One of them coughed sharply.

"It ain't here," another said quietly, fear in his voice. "What we gonna do now?"

"It's got to be here!" the leader shouted. "Ain't nobody goin' to take a dead horse."

"They did it! Look! It ain't heah."

"God damn it! Will you quit pulin'! I'm tellin' you nobody took that horse. If it'd been somebody who counted, our asses'd be in jail right now. Wasn't nobody. One o' them God-damn darkies's hid it somewheres."

"You crazy! No darky's goin' to touch anything dead!"

"I know one black bastard'd touch anything alive or dead if he could do me hurt." The lead man wheeled his horse, then raised his arm and shouted, "Spread out. All o' you. Look fo' that horse. It's here, I'm tellin' you. Find the damned thing."

"How? How we gonna do that?"

"Christ! Use your nose if you ain't got no brains!"

Apollo clung to the tree trunk, pressing himself against it so hard it hurt, to keep himself from making a sound. He wanted with all his passionate nature to show himself, to fight like a man, to let it be known that he knew who and what the riders were. Below him the frantic hooded spectres spread out, moving like ghosts through the dark woods. White-blanketed horses and hooded men bobbed in and out of the black cover of the woods. Apollo watched the *danse macabre* from the corner of his eye, his head pressed against the bark of the tree.

"Ah smell the son of a bitch!" one man shouted.

"Shit! It smells up the whole woods. But wheah is it?"

"Ahhh, God damn!" a man screamed.

The others came riding over to the anguished sound. Then there was pandemonium as one rider after another pounded into the hanging carcass of the horse.

Apollo in his tree began to laugh, the sound soft and shrill, hysterical. Tears of laughter rolled down his face. He shoved his fist into his mouth trying to still the noise that pushed out from inside him.

The hooded horsemen moved erratically around the base of the tree from which the horse hung, their pointed hoods thrown back as they peered through the darkness at the decaying bulk of the animal.

"Who done that?" asked one man, coughing. "Who'd do a thing like that?"

"Shit, how're we gonna get him down?"

"Can you see up there—can we cut him loose?"

"Hell no, you ass. He'd come right down on us."

"Well, damn it, you got a bettah idea?"

"Yeah, climb up there an' cut him loose. The rest of us can stay clear."

"*You* climb that fuckin' tree an' cut him loose. Ah ain't. It ain't mah hawss."

The men began to fight among themselves, pushing at each other, their voices growing louder and angrier.

"You got us into this. It's youah hawss."

"Ah nevah wanted t'come aftah that Jordan bastard anyhow."

"We gotta get that animal down, damn it. Lyman, climb that tree, you're the lightest."

"You shut up! Don't call my name!"

"Aww fuck! Nobody's gonna hear."

"Hell's fire, *Leroy,* nobody's gonna put a fuckin' horse in a tree neither."

Another of the men moved toward the shadowy bulk of the horse. "I got a rope. Maybe we can put it on him an' hold him while we cut the other rope. We could let him down easy—mebbe."

"All right, we'll try it," Leroy said.

"Somebody still has to climb the tree," said the man. "And it ain't gonna be me."

"Ah'll climb youah damn tree," one finally said. The hooded man removed his hood and walked quickly to the tree.

Apollo strained to see who it was, but could see nothing except a dusky figure in white and shadow.

The white-robed figure embraced the trunk and to Apollo's eyes seemed to coil like a snake around the tree, going higher and higher into the dense foliage. Apollo rubbed his moist eyes, shaking his head. He looked back to the figure, which now seemed to be perched airily over the horse's carcass.

"Ah got him roped," a voice called down from the thickness of the dark leaves.

The other riders lined up and took hold of the rope.

"Wait till Ah come down," the voice called.

"Hell no! You got to cut him free!"

A garbled sound came from the tree, then the Klansman slashed the rope with which Apollo had secured the horse. The others were not prepared for the swift, heavy drag on their new rope. The first man in the line was thrown backwards from his horse into the man behind him. As the rope seared through bare hands, panic broke out among horses and men. The woods came alive with the shouting, frightened cries of the men and the piercing, shrill whinnies of the animals. Forelegs flailing the air, the horses wheeled as one and moved back toward the tree.

"Hold them horses fast!" a man shouted. "Hold 'em!"

The mass of men and animals was shoved against each other, moving closer to the swaying carcass. The closer they retreated to the tree, the lower the horse came. Seeing what was happening, Leroy slapped the flank of the horse nearest him. The animal bolted forward, butting the horse in front of him. The rope was torn from Cedric Whitaker's hand.

Apollo no longer tried to restrain the hysteria. He laughed senselessly now, letting his mind flow freely. He saw himself and Ruel together in the tree watching the spectacle below. Ruel, the man he thought of as family. Ruel, the only grown man Apollo had ever dared to love. For this moment, he and Ruel were one. What Apollo could see, Ruel's dead eyes could also see. Apollo felt his presence. In the warmth of his own heated sweat, Apollo felt the body of Ruel. He was there. With him. Apollo's laughter rose, blending insanely with the anguished cries of the night riders.

The crazily swinging carcass moved through the air like a broken pendulum, thudding into the tree, bumping into men and horses. Then with a suddenness it came crashing down.

Apollo wailed, his arms outstretched against the tree, his lean, hard body pressed against the cool, passionless tree, and his laughter turned to tears. All he could see was blood, and all he could hear were Kyra's sobs. Ruel's blood; Kyra's sobs. Blood and tears.

The hooded men yelled and swore, cursing God and man. They struggled from under the rotting corpse.

"By God, I'll kill that fuckin' black bastard when I get my hands on him!"

"Get this God-damn stinkin' horse offa my leg!"

"Where's the rope? Pull it off!"

Regaining some semblance of order, the hooded men got the lead rope on the dead horse again and began to pull the body off their leader.

Free, Leroy stood up.

"What now? What're we gonna do with it?"

"Shit, Ah'm sick o' this stink."

"Shut up. We're gonna get rid of it, that's what." He pointed to two of the men, now remounted. "Drag that son of a bitch to the stream. We'll bury him there. Ain't nobody gonna look for him now."

"Aww shit. I want t'go home. I need a drink worse'n I ever needed anything. I got horse stink all over me."

Leroy laughed heartily, aware he was losing control of his followers. "We're just about home free, boys. Come on now, and I'll stand y'all to the biggest drunk we ever had. How 'bout that? First man home gets a double drag every time 'round."

The men grumbled, but with better nature, and the work of secreting the telltale horse carcass went on.

Once more Apollo forced silence on himself. He watched in mute agony as the men began to drag the horse's body away. His eyes were bleak and glazed. This wasn't enough. It could never be retribution for a man's life. He needed more. But he stayed perched in his tree, watching, knowing he was helpless to do anything of real import to these white men who hid themselves beneath the grotesque robes and masks.

He waited until the sounds of their voices were gone and the woods echoed its own eerie silence once again. He climbed down from the tree and stealthily, carefully began to move in the direction they had dragged the horse. When he got to the bank of the stream, they had gone, but the muddy, disturbed soil showed clearly in the moonlight where the dead horse was buried. Apollo looked at the mound for several minutes, his body rigid; then, trembling with an emotion he couldn't identify, he flung himself onto the disturbed mud and began clawing at it. His fingers dug deep into the wet clay soil. His breath came in hard, scraping sobs as he exposed the bloated mound of the dead horse. The moonlight shone down on horse and black man covered with the sticky muck of the river. Apollo lay face down in the mud, his hands beating at the earth. He no longer held back, but cried aloud at the hideous, searing helplessness that was inside him and could never be released.

He had no thought, only feelings that ripped apart all the rational behavior he had ever known. He had learned as a slave and as a free man the way to live in the civilized world, but all he truly knew was how to die in it. He died daily, hourly, by minute and by second, and he couldn't stop it and he couldn't end it. There was nothing of civilization left in him in these minutes, only the pain of a man who knew what it was to be denied his humanity. He didn't count. It was as if he didn't exist, as if Ruel had never been, as if Kyra were nothing. But they were there, at least part of them was there. The part that felt and hurt and cried was there.

Little pools of river water, held captive by the soil, collected in the pits he dug with his clawing, grasping fingers. The invisible wriggling creatures that lived in the slime moved gently under his mouth. Apollo thought of the stories his mother had told him as a small child. Man had come from this slime, it was to this he would return. He pressed his head deeper into the soft mud, letting it creep into the hollows of his eyes, into his nostrils, into his mouth, until his lungs screamed for relief and forced him from it. Gasping, he drew in air, cool night air, made colder by the silver light of a cold moon. Exhausted, he fell back, lying on his back staring up into the black of the night. He wiped the mud from around his eyes, and slowly began to notice the stars.

Lights that he hadn't seen or hadn't noticed made themselves known to him. The night wasn't black, it was ablaze with hundreds, thousands of winking lights, streams of them, rivers of light across the sky. They mocked him, a man who could see only blackness in the face of a multitude of lights.

The lights had a calming effect on him. His breathing slowed, the pain within him diminished to an ache. He lay on the wet ground staring up into the sky, his mind at rest, thought free.

He couldn't remember sleeping; he was only aware when the color of the night subtly changed. The stars took on a new appearance, and Apollo began to think of himself, Ruel, Kyra, Leroy, the Klansmen, white men, black men, men and God. He could do nothing for Ruel. He would never be able to. He couldn't take revenge on Leroy either. And he didn't know if he could trust that God ever would. All he knew was that he could not.

His thoughts shifted abruptly to Kyra, and the ache within him stirred and became a pain once again. She was Ruel's wife. But she was Apollo's love. To whom did the living belong? To whom did love belong? To the living or to the dead? He didn't know the answer to that either. Deep within him the fear that Kyra would feel bound to Ruel for all time made him think that she belonged to Ruel. And deep within him the unquenchable spirit that made him love and hate with so unbearable a passion told him he'd never stop loving her, that she was his, and that he'd stay by her side no matter what God, man, or Kyra said.

Apollo's thoughts went round and round all night. The first streaks of multi-hued light raced across the sky before he sat up and began to think clearly. As the sun began its climb, Apollo felt a strong calm of determination and decision come over him. He had no answers, but he wouldn't forget this night for all his life, for tonight he knew his life meant virtually nothing.

A man was but a dot on the earth, impermanent, impotent, not worthy in the scheme of things.

But he also knew that if his life meant nothing, and Ruel's meant nothing, and Kyra's meant nothing, then Leroy's and the other men's lives were meaningful only falsely, only because they declared it to be so. And that much he could have, too. He could declare his own worth. And he would. At least in that small way his life and the lives of the people he loved would have meaning.

Apollo stood up and grimaced at the filth that covered him. He could only rise. No one could ever put him lower than he had been last night. No one could ever put him through a hell greater than that he had felt in the darkness. He could die, but even dying had a dignity he hadn't yet experienced in living. He looked again at the mud, and this time he smiled. He straightened his back, thrust out his broad, muscular chest, and threw his head back and laughed. Live. He would learn now to live without fear. There was nothing left to fear, but there was much to learn and feel; and there was Kyra alive and warm and his to love, *because he decreed it*. From the slime he had risen, and now he was going to walk upright on the earth as God had planned it.

He walked back through the woods and across the fields that divided the Matthews plantation from Mossrose. He didn't look back at the Jordans' burned house, and he didn't glance at the tree where he had hidden or at the tree from which he had hung the dead horse. His eyes were straight ahead. He walked to his cabin, drew buckets of water, and took them inside. He stripped himself, throwing the caked, filthy garments out the door. Naked, he strode around the room, feeling good and strong and for once whole. Then he washed, scrubbing his body with soap and water until it gleamed. Still wet, he threw himself down on his bed, arms behind his head. He was too wide awake to sleep, but he remained there until he heard activity in the other cabins. Then he got up and dressed in crisp, fresh clothing, a pair of black trousers and an immaculate white shirt. This morning was Ruel's funeral. For Apollo, it was the beginning of a new life.

CHAPTER THIRTEEN

James Moran was fretting. Something was afoot today, with the servants hurrying through their work and standing whispering outside doors. In the manner of the convalescent he had learned each person's routine, and when that routine was changed as it was on this day, he sensed the wrongness without knowing what was making him uneasy. Even Patricia, who stayed maddeningly the same except for looking constantly thinner, seemed to come near him only to fly away.

He felt terribly isolated inside his damaged body. No one seemed to know him anymore, or even recognize that he was still the same man he had been before his stroke. The servants couldn't, or wouldn't, understand his halting, mushy speech. When he asked them something, they'd answer something else. And he was sick of it.

Jem raised his voice. "Patsy!" In his mind her name echoed down the corridors, knocking on every door until it found the one where she was.

Patricia, standing looking out the far window, heard the weak whisper and, skirts rustling, came to his side. "Yes, Jem dahlin'? What can Ah do fo' you, sweetheart?" Her pale, thin hand reached out automatically to soothe his brow.

Jem jerked away. When he got better—and that would be damned soon!—he'd tell her he hated having his forehead rubbed. But just now the problem was to get his skittery mind to work properly, get his words in order and his tongue loose. After a small struggle he asked, "What's . . . going on? People rushing—"

Patricia bent down to straighten his coverlet. "Whah, nothin's happenin', dahlin'. It's just—Emma has got a

heap o' work fo' the coloreds to finish today, that's all."
Her eyes strayed out the window to the hazy morning.
"Wouldn't you like a drink of nice cool watah now,
honey?"

"No! Where Dul—Dulsh? Dulsha. Want 'er."

"Dulcie's busy with Beau now, Jem. And Adam is
at Mossrose." Her heart skipped a beat as she saw the
hectic color in Jem's cheeks. "Jem honey, you've got
to keep quiet. Please don't frighten me like this. You
might do youahseff hahm. The doctah said—" Patricia
shied away from what the doctor had said, that any disturbance might bring on another, possibly fatal stroke.
"He said youah to lie quiet. Heah, let Patsy fix youah
pillows foah you." Tenderly she poked and patted, re-
arranging the pillows that helped him to lie on one
side, then the other, in an endless routine of galling
monotony.

"Heard . . . racket other night. Horses. Yelling. Fox
hunt?"

Patricia tried to smile, to hide the cold fear inside.
"Not a fox hunt, Jem. Ah don't know jes' *what* it
mighta been."

Before she could guard against it, he asked the question she dreaded. "When . . . Ruel?" Up until two days
ago, Ruel had been coming in daily to report progress
to Jem, who understood far more than he was able to
express. Patricia busied herself with an imaginary task
at the bureau. She had known Jem would ask about
Ruel. She had tried to prepare herself to answer, but
no answer had presented itself. Her hand went to her
hair, nervously patting it into place. Jem must not find
out that Ruel was being buried within the hour. Jem
must never be told what had happened to Ruel.

But how could she hide it? What could she say? "Ah
don't . . . don't know wheah Ruel is, Jem." She kept
at a distance from him to hide her trembling hands and
the twitching smile that wouldn't leave her face. "It's
only nine o'clock. He . . . well, he . . . might be late.
Perhaps Adam is keepin' him busy. Yes, Ah'm suah

that's it. Ah think Adam did mention that he might be sendin' someone else to repoht to you—he needs Ruel's suhvices."

Jem struggled in bed. "Want . . . chair."

Patricia seemed to flutter in her protests. "Not yet, Jem. You know youah not as comf'ble in that ol' wheeled chayah as you ah right theah in the bed—"

"Chair! Get my chair!"

"All right, all right, now jes' wait a li'l while till Ah can get one o' the men to lift you. Please, Jem." Patricia placed both her shaking hands against her cheeks.

Jem's eyes were bright with annoyance and suspicion. Haltingly he said, "Patsy . . . don't pen me up. Want out."

She tried to smile soothingly. "Of cou'se you want out, Jem honey. But we have to be cayahful so you don't ovahdo. Ah don't believe it's good fo' you to be sittin' up so much."

His eyes moved around the room wildly. "Pris'ner." His hand gestured uncertainly. "Want to see . . . see fam'ly. Eat . . . table. Bed, no. No bed."

"Jem, youah gettin' all worked up!" Her hands went back to her cheeks.

"I'll get up!" Fruitlessly he thrashed in the bed, dislodging pillows and covers and nearly falling onto the floor. Patricia hastened to hold him still, but he flailed at her. His voice was strong enough then. "Get up!" he shouted.

Patricia's voice was high, on the verge of tears. "All right, Jem, mah goodness, ya'll don't have to *yell* at a puhson. Ah'll get you up. Jem, now you got to promise not to try to move till Ah get back."

In jerks he nodded his assent. His face was dangerously red, his breathing labored, but his eyes shone. Once he got out of this damned bed, they'd have the devil of a time putting him back in, he'd see to that! And today he'd go downstairs, see some sunlight for a change, see some carpeting instead of bare sickroom floors, handle his own fork instead of letting Patsy feed

him. He might have only one good hand, but by God
he'd show them he could use it!

He felt positively Olympian. In a nearly normal
voice he asked, "Where . . . is everybody?"

Patricia turned back to him. "Jem, Ah told you.
Dulcie and Adam ah busy. Ah'll jes' go see if Ah can't
find—" Her voice trailed off as she bustled out into
the hall. She sent black Lucy in to be with Jem, and
John for fresh linens and the wheelchair. Then she
hurried down the stairs and went out to stand alone on
the veranda for a few minutes.

Patricia let out a long, quivering sigh. She stood very
still, not trusting herself to walk to the edge of the
porch. She felt as though there were no part of her
body left that was not trembling in that insidiously
gentle way that made her sometimes feel she would
burst apart in a thousand small pieces. She closed her
eyes, and opened them again to stare out at the beautiful lawn of the Whitakers' side yard. Lush waves of
green grass rolled down the gently sloping terrain,
giving no indication of the aura of violence and threat
that Patricia felt all around her.

She didn't know how to deal with the horrifying events
that crept up on them and damaged their lives and their
beings before they even knew something was about to
happen. Nothing had prepared her for these new
tragedies, not even the War. In war one expects catas-
trophes as part of the nature of the times, but this was
peacetime. This was supposed to be a time of healing,
of binding the wounds. She wasn't prepared, wasn't able
to fit into her understanding the reality of hooded ghosts
riding with torches like fiery demons through the night,
attacking and killing and burning and maiming. She
couldn't fathom that Mossrose, Adam, Jem, Dulcie,
herself could be victims of something she didn't comprehend.

She took a few hesitant steps, forcing herself to remember the elementary laws of graceful motion and
poised posture her mother had taught her as a child.

She forced on her body the fluidity that all ladies must learn. By herself, she thought, for there was no one to help her, she'd get herself calmed and strong, and recover her determination not to break down, for Jem's sake.

He could not know how frightened or isolated she felt these days. For this once, she had to be the strong one and learn how to do on her own. Patricia had only recently learned how dependent she had become on Jem's guidance, Jem's thought, Jem's decisions. Faced with having to be the leader of their world, she felt a confusion and an inadequacy that was overwhelming. She didn't know how or when she had lost her own vital and strong will in the larger reality of her husband's will. And now that she needed the whole of herself, she couldn't seem to find it.

In her there seethed many and painfully contradictory emotions. She loved and depended on Jem for the very breath she drew, and she had become acutely aware that she didn't want to face living without him. Yet sometimes, just lately, she had the feeling she would faint if she had to stay cooped up in that room with him one second longer. Wanting out of his bed! Trying to talk, trying to move himself! Didn't the man have any idea how sick he had been, and still was? Didn't he know that he had to cooperate, obey implicitly the doctor's orders, or he and Patricia would be separated from each other? Didn't he yet realize how fragile life is? Didn't he need to be with her as she needed to be with him? She felt as though she were battling nature, and unseen threats, and added to that she had to battle Jem himself. All that thrashing around in bed—it was as if he didn't care if he were free of her.

Maybe she ought to send for that doctor in Savannah again, just to make sure Jem was all right. She didn't want him damaging himself and getting worse again, not after she'd stayed by his side night and day seeing that he never wanted for a thing.

She took one more breath of the morning's thick,

stuffy air. Briefly her mind touched back to the other
event of today, Ruel's funeral, then quickly closed the
door on that. With a brave smile in her dark-circled
eyes, Patricia trudged back up the stairs to be with
her husband.

The July morning was somber, with gray, ragged
clouds tattering the sky. Fitful gusts of damp, warm
winds brushed the straight rows of cotton plants, making
them dip their proud heads as though in sorrow. Across
the fields from the east, Adam and five of the strongest
men carried Ruel's hastily crafted coffin down the dirt
road toward the slave burying ground that had been
used for Mossrose servants for a hundred years. The
laborers walked behind them in twos and threes, dressed
in their best, speaking if at all in solemn whispers. In
the overcast sky several vultures hovered, circling with
unending patience.

They reached the graveyard at last, and the men
placed their burden on trestles and stepped back. The
Reverend Jabez Hooks stood beside the coffin, laying
a hand on it in blessing while he waited for the assemblage to settle.

Nearest the coffin was a trio formed by Mindy, Kyra,
and Jothan. Mindy's usual carefree giddiness had vanished; tears flowed freely from her eyes, and she dabbed
at them frequently with her handkerchief. Jothan's eyes
and face were puffy. Occasionally his mouth trembled
and he bit his lips.

Kyra stood between them, for her protection, for she
looked so depleted that she might fall at any moment.
Yet she stood curiously separate from Ruel's brother
and his wife, remained dry-eyed and rigid, staring un-
blinking ahead at her husband's coffin. Immediately
behind her, his face lined with grief, Apollo stayed
watchful. Constantly his eyes roamed the woods nearby,
always coming back to the woman so near him that his
breast almost touched her back.

Adam's grief and sorrow were overlaid with a great

burning anger—anger at himself for bringing Ruel down
here where he could be killed; anger at the men so
contemptuous of the law that they could do a thing
like this with no fear of retribution. But his greatest
anger was reserved for his neighbors, men who knew
the Klan members, knew the things they did, and would
not speak to the authorities of what they knew.

Reverend Hooks raised his hands, then the shuffling
murmur became silence. In a soft warning voice he
said, " 'Man that is born of a woman is of few days and
full of trouble. He cometh forth like a flower, and is
cut down. He fleeth also as a shadow, and continueth
not. And does thou open thine eyes on such a one?' "

He looked around, at Dulcie whose eyes swam with
tears she did not want to let fall, at Ned and Emma
Whitaker whose central emotion was fear for themselves, at the frightened blacks who mourned the loss
of a kind brother, at the family trio with their Cerberus
on guard. Hooks's voice adopted the peculiar singsong
that he reserved for funerals. "Mah chillun, we have
come heah today t'lay t'rest ouah black brothah Ruel
Jordan, a man whose lofty ambitions were greatah than
his poah human reach. He was cut down outside his
own home, in the full flowah of his manhood, in the
presence o' his lovin' woman. An' now, as Job put it,
ouah eyes ah dim by reason o' sorrow.

"Sorrow, mah chillun, because in the mi'st o' life we
ah in death. Sorrow because we place too high a value
on this life, fo'gettin' what the Lawd's will is fo' us.
Now a famous lady poet said it fah bettah than Ah can.
'Knowledge by sufferin' entereth, and life is perfected
by death.' Ruel Jordan didn't learn a awful lot while
he was alive, but he got a good deal o' knowledge in
his short houah o' final sufferin'. His life was imperfect,
like the rest o' you's lives, he did a lot o' things he
shouldn'ta did, includin' tryin' t'rise above his station,
an' now his imperfect life has been perfected by death.
Ah want y'all t'dwell on that, an' see if you can't improve youah own seffs some in this life, when youah

mournin' brothah Ruel. Y'all can perfect youahseffs without dyin' like brothah Ruel did. It jes' ain't the Lawd's will fo' black folks t'try t'be white folks, an' now brothah Ruel knows that."

Hooks's head swiveled on his long, skinny neck, surveying the quelled blacks and the fidgeting whites. "Now quotin' ol' Job, who suffered fo' many, many yeahs, 'My days are swifter than a weaver's shuttle, and are spent without hope.' Now we wouldn'ta wanted that t'happen t'Ruel, would we? We wouldn't want him lyin' injured an' beggin' God to call him home, would we? No suh, he was cut down befo' any o' that could happen t'him. 'O remember that my life is wind, mine eyes shall no more see good. As the cloud is consumed and vanisheth away, so he that goeth down to the grave shall come up no more.' "

Hooks cast a look of mild reproof at Mindy, whose sobs burst out afresh. He said, with somewhat more emphasis than seemed necessary, "No suh, he shall come up no moah. That ain't the Lawd's will t'have brothah Ruel back heah agitatin' an' talkin' fancy in front o' the white folks. No suh, the Lawd's got his own ideas 'bout a man's place heah on earth. An' it is ouah sorrowful duty t'heah the Lawd's voice, an' know what He is sayin' t'us.

"Brothahs an' sistahs, it is ouah duty t'learn how the Lawd's will worked in the takin' o' brothah Ruel. Jes' lissen t'what David said, when he was prayin' befo' all the princes an' the captains an' the valiant men in Jerusalem. Blessin' God, David said, 'For all things come of Thee, and of Thine own have we given Thee.' The Lawd's will has been done, an' in it we must learn o' His eternal, almighty wisdom. We done give Ruel back t'the Lawd now. The Lawd gave, an' the Lawd taketh away, an' blessed be the name o' the Lawd.

" 'We are strangers before Thee, and sojourners as were all our fathers, our days on earth are as a shadow, and there is none abidin'.' Nobody, brothahs an' sistahs, not even the blessed Lawd Jesus, abides on this

earth fo' long. When the Lawd sees ouah work is done,
He calls us home. Now it ain't ouah place t'judge or
question the will o' the Lawd when He done say,
Brothah Ruel, you done a plenty, youah time is up,
an' then He sends his divine messenjahs t'take care
o' brothah Ruel—"

Adam had heard enough of Hooks's bigoted oratory,
obscured and larded with quotations from the Bible.
His anger exploded. In a harsh voice he said, "Reverend Hooks, that is blasphemy. May we have the closing
prayer now."

The blacks, intent on Hooks's words, sent Adam a
shocked, hostile glare, and moved agitatedly among
themselves. Hooks, gesticulating grandly on the theme
of divine messengers, stopped in mid-stroke, his mouth
sagging open. "Who ah *you*, suh, to call God's work
blasphemy? We poah mortals know not what fawm it
may take—"

"Ruel Jordan was a good, God-fearing, able man.
His death was the work of Godless men, Reverend
Hooks, not by the will of God. No divine messengers
came to take Ruel from this earth. Hooded maniacs—
men—mortal, evil men—took him from us."

Hooks looked hastily at the circle of black faces
surrounding the grave site. The momentary hostility at
Adam's harsh intrusion was gone. In its place were
looks of consternation, pondering. Many dark eyes had
turned to the preacher in suspicious speculation. Hooks
quickly mopped his sweating face. These were his flock.
He had to keep their trust. He glanced back to Adam,
his eyes burning with loathing. His mouth formed con-
descending, placating words. "You misundahstood, suh.
Ah am the Lawd's devoted suhvant, an' with all mah
heart Ah am bringin' t'these dahk chillun of God comfoht an' undahstandin' o' theah brothah's dea—"

"Reverend Hooks, if you don't pronounce the closing
prayer immediately, I'll give one myself."

Lips pressed shut in a thin, enraged line, Hooks
hesitated only a second as he saw Adam move. " 'And

Jesus said unto Martha, I am the resurrection and the life; he that believeth in me, though he were dead, yet shall he live; and whosoever liveth and believeth in me shall never die.' 'For we know that if our earthly house of this tabernacle were dissolved, we have a building of God, a house not made with hands, eternal to the heavens. For this we groan, earnestly desiring to be clothed upon with our house which is from heaven. . . .' Brothahs, if you'll jes' lowah the coffin into the grave now."

At this Mindy cried out and began to keen sharply. Kyra, showing emotion for the first time, swayed toward the coffin. Apollo could bear no more. His strong arms came out and pulled Kyra back against him. They stood there, his hands on her upper arms, trembling in a common grief as Ruel's coffin was swallowed into the earth.

Hooks, his gaze flickering over the assemblage, then resting momentarily on Kyra and Apollo, continued, " 'The voice of thy brother's blood crieth unto me from the ground . . .' " Seeing Adam's fierce glare and his start forward, the preacher added hastily, "These words from Ecclesiastes: 'As he came forth of his mother's womb, naked shall he return to go as he came, and shall take away nothing of his labor, which he may carry away in his hand. And this also is a sore evil, that in all points as he came, so shall he go.' " He added emphatically, " 'And what profit hath he that hath labored for the wind?' "

Hooks raised his face to heaven, his eyes closed, arms spread out, palms open for celestial blessing. "Lawd, unto Thy tender mercies do we commend this spirit. We ask Thy blessin' on his friends an' relatives an' his grievin' widow, Amen." Hooks picked up a shovel and tipped earth onto the coffin. Kyra jerked, but Apollo held her. " 'Death is swallowed up in victory. O death, where is thy sting? O grave, where is thy victory? The sting of death is sin . . . but thanks to God, which giveth us the victory through the Lawd

Jesus Christ.' This ends the funeral obsequies, brothahs an' sistahs. Anybody who wants to can come fo'ward with youah offerin's fo' the deceased."

A few started forward, bearing small pots and pans and bright-colored ribbons that would decorate the filled-in grave. Suddenly Kyra was galvanized into action. "No—o—" her pleading voice rang out. She clawed toward the grave in supplication; she eluded Apollo's hold and rushed forward to throw herself face down on the ground at the edge of the grave. Over and over she cried, "No! No! Ruel, don't leave me! Don't! This can't be true! No!" Blindly she scraped at the earth, trying to clean off the coffin.

Mindy's keening reached agonized heights. Some of the blacks watched motionless, sharing in Kyra's pain. Some, in a gesture to grief older than time, drew up their aprons to cover their faces, and their voices shrilly echoed Mindy's. Others turned away, frightened and wanting to close from their consciousness what was happening today, and what could so easily happen to them.

Adam and Apollo acted as one, hurrying to Kyra, lifting her from the grave, forcing her to stand upright. Apollo circled her waist with his arm. Together they led her away, supporting her stumbling steps as she sobbed in a shuddering undertone, "No—no—no—don't let them take him away—" They lifted her into Adam's buggy, and he took the reins while Apollo held Kyra's head down against his shoulder.

Rapidly the laborers filled in the grave, and the women with heightened apprehension and reverence laid down their offerings. The mound of freshly dug earth decorated with the multi-colored and glittering offerings looked raw and obscene in the sweltering damp light of the day.

Dulcie stared in horrified fascination. She still could not comprehend that Ruel was lost under that fresh earth forever. His death was a fact to her, but his presence, his precise speech, his kind manner, his conscientious love of life did not belong buried under the weight of the soil. She stood, unable to move away until Ned Whitaker came over to her. He took her arm, silently directing her to the Whitaker carriage.

She sat beside Emma with a great sharp lump in her throat that would not go down. Angrily she dabbed at her eyes, her throat sore for Kyra, for Ruel and for his family, and for herself, and the nameless, faceless fear that seemed to permeate everything since they had returned to Georgia.

Emma patted her shoulder comfortingly. "Now there, dear, you just go ahead and let it all out and you'll feel better. I expect you and Adam will miss your servant, won't you? The good ones are so rare nowadays." She sighed, not noticing Dulcie's furious glare. She went on, "But I must say, I thought Kyra's actions were inexcusable. Throwing herself down in the dirt! Making a spectacle! Yelling like that where everybody could hear. What kind of a display was that? Just a show for the other darkies, if you ask me. They were all just carryin' on scandalous. Now I don't hold you responsible for Kyra's actions, Dulcie, I know you didn't raise her, but I declare, the nigras—I mean the coloreds—certainly aren't like *us*."

Dulcie could not say a single truthful word in reply that would not alienate Emma from the Morans forever, so she sat in stony silence. When they arrived at the Whitakers', she leaped from the buggy and ran into the house ahead of Emma and Ned. If she could not get onto a horse and ride somewhere for a long time, she knew she would explode into a million sharp slivers of rage.

In the hallway she nearly knocked down Enid Whitaker and Birdie Saunders Acton. "My goodness, Dulcie, what's your hurry?" Birdie asked cheerfully.

Dulcie had to stop. "Birdie—" She bit her lip and turned away, unable to master the fury churning inside. "I'm sorry, Birdie—Enid—I'm just so upset I—" The front door opened again. Dulcie saw the Whitakers entering, and she couldn't, couldn't speak to Emma now. She grabbed her skirts and ran up the stairs.

Enid said, "*Well!* She gets ruder every day!"

Birdie, looking up the staircase, said, "I must go up and see if I can't comfort her in some way—"

"Yes, Birdie, do that," said Emma. "We've just come from Ruel's funeral—can you imagine going to a colored funeral? It's as good as a play anytime, especially now that they can do what they like. I'm sure I won't forget this for a long while, and it upset Dulcie terribly, poor child. On the way back she was trying so hard not to cry. Adam should never have permitted her to go!"

Dulcie, at the top of the stairs, out of sight but not out of hearing, pounded on a chair with her fists.

Her sitting room door was closed when Birdie came upstairs. She entered the room without knocking. She said solicitously, "Is there anything I can do, Dulcie?"

Dulcie was standing in the middle of the room, her eyes blazing with unspent anger. Suddenly tears spurted from her eyes, her face grew red, and she clenched her fists again. "I hate them! I hate them!" Dulcie began to pace frantically around the room, her eyes streaming tears.

Birdie was taken aback by the vehemence of her friend's emotion. Timidly she asked, "Who? The darkies?"

Dulcie stopped her roaming, whirling to face Birdie.

Intimidated and unsure, Birdie stammered, "I don't know who you're angry with, Dulcie. I only want to—to help."

Dulcie angrily shoved at a table, toppling the objects on it. "Us! The Yankees! The Whitakers! The Klan! God! I hate them all! Look at us, we're becoming animals!" She began to laugh bitterly, her face stained with tears. "What's happened to us, Birdie? Where is the glorious, gracious South? I hate that War. Look what it's done to us! We hate each other, and we—we

—Southerners—ride around in the night hidden under bedsheets and kill helpless people!"

Birdie, speechless, edged away from Dulcie toward a chair. She slumped down into it. Birdie's pretty face was drawn, her eyes haunted. She listened to Dulcie, and her own fearful shame moved higher up into her mind.

Dulcie stared at her with pained eyes, then slumped onto the bed, her face in her hands. She said desolately, "It's me I'm angry with, Birdie. I'm sorry, I shouldn't do this to you. It's me. I listen to Emma and I don't even have the courage to say what I believe. I am as bad as the rest. I hate what is happening to us—all of us—but I don't stand up for what I truly believe. I keep saying and doing what's expected, what's proper for a nice Southern lady. Oh God, Birdie, I never knew it was possible to be such a traitor to your own soul. It hurts so much more than anything someone else could do to me, so why do I keep doing it?"

Birdie began to cry, her shoulders shaking with each wrenching sob.

Dulcie stopped short, her eyes widening. "Birdie," she said in a small, awed voice. She went over to her friend, kneeling at her side, her arm around her. "I'm sorry, I'm sorry. I didn't know I had upset you so much. Birdie, please, stop, it isn't that important. I shouldn't have said anything."

Birdie shook her head wildly; her face was twisted, her words nearly incomprehensible. "I know—" she said on a long wail. "I know what you're feeling. Oh, Dulcie, help me—"

Dulcie's face was now frightened and concerned. "I'll do anything I can, Birdie, just tell me. What is it? What's wrong?"

Birdie looked at her, pleading with her eyes. "You do understand, don't you? You do?"

"I—I don't know. Understand what?"

Birdie's voice rose to hysteria. "What you said!

What you said about being a traitor to your own soul! Oh, Dulcie, if I don't talk to someone I don't know what I'll do. I can't keep it inside any longer. I can't stand feeling this way."

Dulcie clung to her friend. "What's wrong? Is it Billy? Someone else? Birdie, you're not expecting, are you? I mean—Billy Bob—is it another man?"

Birdie shook her head. "I'll never have any children. God will never grant me children. I don't deserve them. It's His judgment on me. If I had let those men—if I had just loved my sister enough—but I didn't, Dulcie. I let it all happen to Blythe; then when the others blamed her, so did I. So did I! I've wanted to die of shame."

Dulcie got up and came back with a cold, wet cloth. She gently soothed Birdie and bathed her hot, feverish face. "Birdie, you've got to stop crying. I can't understand what you're trying to say."

Birdie took the cloth from Dulcie and mopped at her own face and eyes. Sniffing, her breath still catching, she said, "I know the hate you feel. I feel it too. For the War and the Yankees, and the Whitakers. I always act like everything is all right, like none of it bothers me, but it does. Inside it is killing me, Dulcie. I don't know how to feel that much hate. Every time I see Cutler Whitaker, I just want to kill him. I try not to feel that way, but I do. So mealy-mouthed, and just like the rest of them." Birdie's face crumpled, then she began to laugh, a pathetic, hysterical sound. Gasping, her hands clutching Dulcie's arms, she said, "But I'm just like you, Dulcie, I know I'm as bad or worse than Cutler and his family and the rest of our neighbors— even my mother, because I'm afraid they'll do to me what they did to Blythe if I say what I really believe. I'm awful, aren't I, Dulcie? I know it, but I can't stop."

"Birdie, what *is* it you're trying to tell me? You're not making sense. Blythe? What happened to Blythe? Your mother told Daddy she had married a Confederate sergeant and they live in the Arizona Territory."

Birdie laughed bitterly. Her voice was acid, mouthing the words she had often said sweetly in company. "Oh, yes, Blythe is so happy. She and Sergeant Jamison are just the most wonderful couple in Arizona—everybody loves them. And so handsome! There just isn't anyone can hold a candle to them. Why, we're all just waitin' and prayin' for that first Jamison baby. It's goin' to be the most beautiful child the Lord ever made."

"She's not married to Sergeant Jamison?"

"No, she's not married to Sergeant Jamison! She's not married to Sergeant anyone."

"Then what . . . where is Blythe?"

Birdie's false smile became a sneer. "She's right here, in Savannah. Yes, my sister is in Savannah walking the streets like all the other women—of that kind."

Dulcie opened her mouth to speak, but Birdie went on, her voice vicious and hard with bitterness. "Dear sweet Blythe opens her legs to anyone who'll pay her, because she can't live any other way. Don't look so shocked, Dulcie, or are you going to be like all the others and condemn her before you even know why she's there? If that shocks you, how do you feel knowing that I was the one who put her there? And Mama— her own mama—and Blossom, and Todd, her whole family, Addie Jo and all the good people who live right around us.

"The Whitakers—I don't even want to talk about the Whitakers. Blythe was supposed to marry Cutler when he came home from the War, but—it had already happened by then, and Cutler isn't man enough— Cutler watched what they did to her like I did. We all let it happen." Birdie's face was deathly white now, her eyes wide with fear. "We'll all go to hell for what we've done, Dulcie, I know we will. Nothing can save us from this."

Dulcie finally found her voice, at first able only to say Blythe's name. "Blythe? Not Blythe! What happened, Birdie? How could that happen? Blythe would never—she's so sweet. Of all of us, she was the most innocent. She couldn't become—"

"She is."

"But how?" Dulcie breathed. "I don't understand."

Birdie shrugged, her face lined with sadness and cruel memories. "The War, what else? We were getting along fairly well, even with Daddy and Glenn and Todd gone. There were enough of us girls, and Mama, and a few servants, that we could plant a vegetable garden and keep it tended. And we had our pecan trees, and a cow we kept hidden in the woods, and Daddy's bees, and the peach orchard. We knew if we were to survive, we had to keep the crops coming. We did it like the white trash we were. Working all day, filthy-dirty and stinking like field hands, but we all thought it was worth it. In a way we were fighting too. We were doing our part for the Cause. We always gave whatever we could to the Confederate Army, and we were keeping Daddy's plantation as best we could for him."

She laughed harshly, remembering. "We had such stupid dreams. Even when the world was exploding all around us, and people were dying every day, and we'd walk into Savannah and read the death lists, I think we all kept believing that someday Daddy and Todd and Glenn and Cutler and Billy Bob would all come marching home again to brass bands and pennons in the streets, victorious, and somehow one day we'd wake up and everything would be like it was before the War. I know I did. Oh, God, did I dream. I could see it wasn't true." She laughed brittlely. "All I had to do was look around me to see, but I believed anyway. And so did Blythe. Maybe more than me. Blythe was always a romantic dreamer."

Birdie stopped talking, her eyes staring blankly at the wall. Then she took a deep breath and let it out slowly. "Then in 1864 . . ." Her voice trailed off, and tears again slid down her face. She struggled with herself and went on, "In 1864, Sherman came through. The damnyankees! Oh, God, Dulcie, I still have nightmares just remembering how they came through. I don't even have to be asleep and I have nightmares."

She fell silent again, her gaze far away, seeing a brilliant spring day, soft with peach bloom, heavy with the hum of honeybees, sweet with the songs of a mockingbird high in a ginkgo tree. She could see herself as she had been that day, laying out the wash, spreading the kitchen towels and baby Teddy's diapers on bushes to bleach. She and her married sister Blossom, Teddy's mother, were chatting back and forth between the porch and Birdie's position at the scrubbing board. Blossom had been paring vegetables for dinner, she remembered.

"All of a sudden the yard was full of bluecoats, Dulcie." Birdie's eyes were wide with apprehension, as though the bluecoats might again appear from nowhere. "I—I don't know where they came from. I didn't hear them—they were just there. I screamed and ran for the house, but I ran right into one of them." She put her hands over her face. "I can still smell him. I can't forget that rank odor, and lice—he was swarmin' lice. I could see them—I mean it looked like his hair was alive—moving over his hair and his clothes—I can't forget him. It's like he's become a part of me."

Dulcie put her forehead against her friend's arm. "Oh, Birdie, I don't know what to say. It must have been so awful."

Birdie shuddered violently. "Yankees were all over —in the house, in the barn, the root cellar—stealing everything they could lay their filthy hands on. They were shoving food into their mouths. It's so odd the things that stick in your mind as being horrible—not the things that were really horrible at all, but they are what I remember. Men with juice running down their chins, laughing with food in their mouths and having missing teeth. It all seemed so—so—it was like everything was rotting; they were, and they were going to make us rotten too. They were going to touch us, and then we'd never be clean of their rot. I'm not making much sense, I know, but I can't forget—

"We had just thought we'd barely make it through spring to garden time, and then the Yankees began to take everything we'd saved. All the food—and they trampled the garden we'd just begun as if it didn't matter. And they built fires, and right there in the yard they cooked everything, even when they knew they couldn't eat it all. Some of them began to set the house on fire. Dulcie, it made no sense. None. They just wanted to hurt, and destroy. They intended to stay at our house for a time, and even that didn't stop them— they destroyed anyway. And later when they needed food and we couldn't provide it because they had ruined everything, they stole from everybody else around. They shot our cow and they burned the orchards and they even killed the bees. We were all standing there crying, begging them to leave us something to live on, but they wouldn't listen. They laughed. It was as if they had lost all human feeling. They were like devils. I—I can't even tell you how—how terrible it was."

"But your house didn't burn. What happened?"

"The soldiers who came at first were bummers. They had gone out in front of the regiment. When the captain and the rest came by they put out the house fire. It seemed even from the start that these Yankees would be different." Birdie's voice, now roughened from talking and emotion, trailed off. In her mind's eye she saw it again, the gentle spring day fled to be replaced by a night of fire and shouting and fear.

Yet the days that followed gave the Saunders women confidence. With the Yankee captain in charge and lodged in the house, there was a kind of order, and the women settled down to endure until this enemy moved on to plague someone else.

"For a while they were kind enough to us," she went on. "They even tried not to be a bother, asking us for things instead of just taking them. We didn't trust them—we never trusted them!—but I guess you could say we were at ease with them. We always tried to stay together, at least two of us together." Birdie stopped again, her eyes seeking the window and those days four years ago. "From the beginning we sensed something, but none of us knew what. I suppose we just didn't want to know, but we did. Women always know, and that's why we tried to stay together."

Dulcie's voice was thin and choked. "They wanted you."

"Yes." Birdie's voice was very low. "They all did. They were no better than dogs. But the captain kept them in line, he wouldn't give them a minute's pleasure or leisure. But he felt differently for himself. He wanted a woman to give him comfort, he said. We didn't know what he'd do, or which one of us he'd take, or maybe it would be all of us. For a while all he did was talk and look. It was awful. We couldn't move without him looking at us in that crude way when you know he was just peeling the clothes off our backs with his eyes. He said terrible things, vulgar things; I wanted to die. I knew I'd die, Dulcie, if it were me he came near.

"I couldn't sleep at night. I was petrified at every noise in the house. Every time I heard a creak or a sound, I *knew* it was him coming up the stairs for me. Every day I was surer and surer that it was going to be me." She put her hands over her face and began to sob again. "I would have sold my soul to keep him from me." She looked, stricken, at Dulcie. "And I did . . . I mean in a way, that's just what I did, only worse. I sold Blythe's soul, too, because I couldn't bear to have that man near me."

"Oh, Birdie, no. You can't blame yourself if he went after Blythe instead of you. You weren't to blame for that."

Birdie laughed through her tears. "Wasn't I? Wasn't I? Blythe tried to comfort me, to talk to me and help

me, and I cried all my terror to her. And then finally
one day he came to my room, and I knew he had
chosen me. I was going to—give him comfort. Blythe
heard me screaming at him. He hadn't even touched
me and I was screaming. She came in. I wish I could
forget her." Birdie moaned, remembering the sight of
her delicately pretty sister standing in the doorway to
her bedroom.

Blythe's clear, innocent hazel eyes shone with a
missionary's zeal. She was frightened, and her softly
smiling lips trembled, but she was going to save her
sister. Birdie remembered seeing that look on her
sister's face, and knowing, even then, that that was
what Blythe had in mind, never realizing what she was
actually proposing. Birdie could see herself as she had
been curled up protectively on the floor, her pillow
held against herself for a shield, and she remembered
feeling viciously relieved that Blythe had come. She
didn't think of protecting Blythe. All she thought was
that Blythe could save her, and she never thought for
a moment of what it would do to her fragile sister.

Blythe had walked bravely over to the blond-haired
captain and put a dainty hand on his forearm. Her
voice shook, but it was sweet and full of innocence.
"Why do you force yourself on my sister, when I am
here and willing to do whatever you ask?"

The captain had looked at her first in astonishment,
then in bemusement. He gazed down on her smirking,
his head cocked to one side. "So you're willing. What
is it you're so willing to do?"

Blythe had been confused by that. She raised her
large hazel eyes to him, her lips parted slightly, her
voice low and soft. "I . . . I don't know. I'll do whatever I'm supposed to do."

The captain glanced at Birdie still cowering on the
floor, then he turned his attention back to Blythe. He
said gruffly, holding out his hand to her, "Come here,
girl." After a hesitation Blythe stepped forward. He
grabbed her roughly, his big arm encircling her and

bending her down against him. He kissed her hard,
then stood up, still holding Blythe like a broken doll
limp on his arm, and looked straight at Birdie. "Well?"

Birdie had pulled her pillow tighter against herself.
"You bitch! You gonna let her take your place?"

Birdie had said nothing. But Blythe had. Birdie
would never be able to erase the soft, frightened voice
of her sister saying, "I don't want her to save me.
Please, sir, let me be the one and not Birdie."

Birdie pulled herself back to the present. She looked
at Dulcie, feeling a peculiar kind of pride in finally
baring her soul of the horrible thing she had done. She
sighed deeply, her breath catching. "I used to tell myself that it wasn't as bad for Blythe as it would have
been for me. He was kind to Blythe, at least as kind as
he knew how to be. And Blythe made it so easy for me
to make excuses. She never complained. She wouldn't.
But I knew, we all knew. We could hear her crying when
she thought no one could hear, and anyone could see
from the way she looked that she suffered horribly."

"If he was kind to her, Birdie, perhaps it wasn't so
bad as you think. I mean no woman can ever desire
something like that happening, but perhaps he had
some sensitivity that you didn't know about—with
Blythe, I mean."

Again Birdie laughed. "I was saving myself for Billy
Bob! I used to say that to myself over and over again.
It was so important that *I* remain untouched, undefiled
by that rapist, because I was going to be Billy Bob
Acton's wife, and bear his children. And on the rare
occasions when I'd think of Blythe and her dreams of
being Cutler's wife, I'd so easily say, oh, Blythe will
be all right. Cutler will understand. Blythe can make
anything all right. And she kept offering all her strength
to save her family from the very thing that she was
enduring. And we took it. Like greedy pigs we took
everything from her so we could be safe. Even Mama.
Her own mother! Dulcie, don't you hate me? Can you
bear to look at me?"

"Birdie, please don't say things like that. You couldn't have stopped what happened. It would have been you or Blossom or your mother. It would have been one of you."

"That captain was about Mama's age. Would it have cost her so much? Why didn't she do something, Dulcie? Or Blossom? They had at least been married. They knew!"

Dulcie shook her head. "I don't know. I don't know."

Birdie made a face, mocking herself. "We ate better after that. Everything was better. You'd never have known we were still the enemy. He stole somebody else's cow to replace ours, and made his soldiers replant our garden. Of course he couldn't do anything about the orchard or the bees—they were destroyed—but I really think he would have if he had been able.

"Do you know how selfish people can be—how self-centered?" Birdie went on without Dulcie's reply. "I finally got to thinking that Blythe liked it, that she had never really done it for me, us. She had done it because she wanted to. It was a lot easier to think that. I didn't have to feel so bad then, and pretty soon Mama and Blossom thought the same. Sometimes we'd gather outside and talk like three old crones about Blythe, bad Blythe. Instead of loving her for what she did, we all began to hate her and were hateful to her. Sometimes when one of us wanted things, we'd even go to her and ask her to wheedle it out of her captain. My *God!* Dulcie, we knew what she had to do, and we *asked.* We no longer cared for her. We used her as much as he did. More, I think. We were worse than he ever was, for she was one of our blood."

"What happened when the Yankees left?" Dulcie asked.

"Even before they left, word got around somehow—you don't know how it does, but it always does. People were talking about her. Whispering, but so there was no question who or what they were whispering about.

You know how people can do. For a while they thought we were talking about all of us, and as usual we protected ourselves at Blythe's expense. I don't even know how we did that. But somehow we let it be known that it was just Blythe and not us who was . . . with the captain. Every once in a while we'd all go to church meeting. Mama wanted the neighbors to know that we hated the damnyankees even though they were still in our house. She wanted to be sure everyone knew it was against our will. We'd sit in our pew, and one by one those near us would move. There we'd be—all alone. The whole side of the church where we were was empty. But if Blythe didn't come with us, no one would do anything. It was like always, people smiling and being friendly. That's how we knew that everyone else knew that Blythe was the bad one, and not us.

"After the Yankees left, the War was over, or almost over, and the boys began to come home. Glenn and Todd came home, and then the Whitakers. We didn't tell Glenn and Todd. Glenn was still recovering from his wound, and Todd was ill, but not as bad as now. But when Cutler came—he came to our house first thing, even before he went home. And Blythe was so happy. I really had forgotten how she was when she was happy. But when she saw Cutler, it was like a great shadow lifting off her face. We'd gotten used to her the way she had become, but Cutler remembered her the way she was, and he knew right away something had happened to change her. He wanted to know, and he asked and asked. Blythe, me, Mama, everybody. It wasn't long before he found out, either. I really think it was Blythe who told him. It would have been just like her to trust him to understand."

"But he didn't," Dulcie said for her.

"Yes, he did. He was surprisingly understanding, but that wasn't enough. His family wasn't. They didn't want him near Blythe. And the neighbors were all abuzz, everyone speculating what Cutler would do. Would he marry the bad girl? Would he ever know who fathered his children? Once Blythe had him as her husband, she'd take lovers, do anything she wanted . . . they said anything and everything.

"We all thought that the talk would die down. Glenn wouldn't talk about it at all. He just avoided Blythe whenever he could, and when he couldn't he pretended everything was all right. But Todd was furious. It was like he hated her. Todd wanted to whip her like he would one of the darkies—right out in the yard—but Mama stopped him."

Dulcie was shivering.

"Blythe kept hoping and expecting Cutler to marry her. He was still seeing her, and he loved her—anybody could see that. Then he told her one day that he wasn't going to marry her, that he couldn't go against his family, not now. Blythe threw herself into his arms, and Todd saw. After that, sometimes Cutler came to the house, and every once in a while when I was getting up in the morning I'd see him sneaking home out the back way. I hated him. I could see what he was doing to Blythe. Right then, when it was happening, I couldn't see that Mama and Blossom and I had done the same thing. I didn't hate us yet—just Cutler, and all the people who talked about her. Well, Todd found out about Cutler staying with Blythe too, and one morning he went to Blythe's room right after Cutler sneaked out and beat her with his fists—I tried to stop him, I got the broom and cracked him with it, but he just— oh, Dulcie!" Birdie broke down, sobbing.

Dulcie put her arms around Birdie. "Don't talk about it any more now. I don't want to know—it's enough."

Birdie raised her tear-stained face. "That's when she left home. We drove her out. All of us. She didn't have anyplace to go. And she really didn't even try to get away from us. She went to Savannah and tried to live decently. She tried being a seamstress, but she was starving, and she tried working as a house servant for other people, but no one would let her in. And now she's—she's—oh my God, Dulcie, it's all my fault. She lives in an awful rooming house, and I can't stand—oh, God—it's all my fault and I still can't forgive her. Even now I think sometimes that she's the one to blame, that she likes it, she wants to be that kind of woman." Birdie's sobs grew hysterical again. "And—and I can't have children, because of her. God won't let me . . . I'm so evil . . . I hate the Yankees. It's their fault! And the Whitakers! Why couldn't Cutler marry her? If he had married her everything would be all right. Everyone would have forgotten— we'd all be happy again. It's his fault."

Dulcie's head was aching. She felt miserable and helpless, and she too kept remembering what Blythe had looked like and been like when she had last seen her. Birdie's story seemed impossible to her. Blythe could not be living as a lady of the evening in Savannah, walking the streets, wearing the peculiar, gaudy clothing that marked those women. She couldn't. Not the Blythe Saunders Dulcie had known.

Dulcie calmed Birdie down. Birdie was limp with exhaustion. She had no more tears, and no more words in her. Her face was sad and drawn with fatigue. Dulcie arranged for her to be driven home, promising her she would come to see her the following day, and they would talk some more. "There must be something we can do, Birdie. I know there is."

Birdie shook her head sadly. "There isn't. I've tried and tried to think, but I never can find an answer. Do you hate me, Dulcie?"

Dulcie hugged her. "No, I don't hate you. I could never hate you, Birdie."

Birdie looked at her, and Dulcie added, "Nor Blythe. And we will figure something out, I promise. I can't think any more today, but I'm sure there is an answer somewhere. There must be."

CHAPTER FOURTEEN

The day following Ruel's funeral was an ordinary working day at Mossrose. Adam rode across the fields examining the progress of the workers as he always did. He looked in on Jothan, busy at work on the plantation accounts, and now doing his own work and his brother's. Everyone seemed to work as usual, but each of them carried his private thoughts of Ruel and what had happened to him. No one mentioned Ruel's name, but it was there in the eyes of every worker at Mossrose.

This disturbed Adam more than it would have had the workers refused to go to the fields, or had they turned their outrage and frustration on the owners of Mossrose. The anger that had run through him the day of Ruel's funeral grew. He turned his horse and rode out across the fields seeking a solitary spot, a place away from the docile bowing to a power like the Klan. He had ridden a considerable distance before he realized another horse and rider was keeping pace with him some distance behind. Suddenly wary, he slowly moved his right hand toward the Colt he carried. With a quick jerk of the rein, he turned the horse so he could see the rider behind him.

Apollo's dark eyes watched each move Adam made, the hand slipping into position near the gun, the angling of the horse's course. His face remained impassive, immobile. One part of him wanted to catch up with Adam and tell him what he knew about the Klansmen in the hope that Adam would be able to do what he could not. But a quiet despair still lurked inside him that made him wonder if after all it wouldn't be better to be dead and not have to struggle with the cruelty of life.

"Son of a bitch, 'Pollo!" Adam shouted angrily. "I damn near shot you. What the hell are you doing coming up on me like that?"

Apollo dug his heels into his horse and caught up with Adam. "Ah been tryin' to make up mah mind if Ah want to talk to you 'bout somethin'.'"

"You're damned lucky you've got the option left. I could have killed you before I even realized it was you."

Apollo's unwavering brown eyes met Adam's. "Ah was thinkin' 'bout that too."

Adam's heavy dark brows knit together. "Have you made up your mind yet?"

"Ah reckon Ah have," Apollo said unperturbed. "Ah'll talk to you."

"About Ruel."

" 'Bout the Klan, Cap'n. They killed Ruel, and Ah knows who they ah. Ah knows some of 'em anyways."

Adam reined his horse in, dismounted, and led the way to the shelter of several pine trees. He sat down and waited for Apollo to tether his horse and join him.

Apollo remained silent for some time. "Ah hates havin' to tell you."

Adam did not reply, understanding that Apollo was struggling with a sense of helplessness that he loathed. He remembered that feeling of utter impotence. It still brought him pain to recall his days on Andros Island searching for Dulcie and being unable to do anything, or even to communicate his desires to those around him. And then later he had not even been able to make Ben West understand the terrible need he had to go back to find her. He knew what Apollo was feeling, and he ached with the black man. He knew, too, that although his own trial had lasted while he had been on Andros, Apollo's trial of courage in the face of helplessness would last all his life unless something changed quickly; and they both knew it wouldn't.

Apollo stared out across the freshly mown meadow.

"Ah want to go aftah them—those men—mahself. Ah want them to know by a black man's hand what they done to Ruel an' to Kyra."

Adam spoke softly. "You can't do it, Apollo. They'd only end up killing you."

Apollo turned to look at him. "Mebbe it'd be wo'th it."

"It would, if they'd learn from your death, or if they'd understand what you were willing to die for, but they wouldn't." Adam rubbed his index finger across his mustache. His deep blue eyes were filled with a sad anger. "Even if you tell me, the most we might be able to do is stop them."

Apollo threw his head back, the muscles in his throat working, his eyes squeezed tight. "Ah want to make them hu't. Ah want them to pay like they made Ruel pay! He was moah man than Leroy Biggs ever be. Ain't right Leroy can snuff out somebody like Ruel an' not even know it was a man he kilt."

"You're sure it was Leroy?"

"Ah'm sure, an' if you need moah than mah word, Ah can make you sure." Apollo's jaw was set, his eyes were smoldering.

Adam reached out and put his hand on the black man's forearm. "I don't need anything but your word, you know that. I've suspected Leroy's involvement in the Klan from the beginning, but it isn't I who must believe, Apollo. If we're to do anything, it will be done in the courts, and the law requires proof."

"Law courts take a man's word," Apollo said, and waited with perverse smugness to hear Adam's inevitable reply.

Adam stared directly at him, his own anger now a match for the black man's. "All right, you want to hear me say it, I will. A black man's word won't be taken in court, not by a jury. Now, if you're finished punishing yourself and me with the injustice of the way things are, maybe we can get to the facts that will do some good. If you're interested, that is. You say you want to avenge Ruel and Kyra, but I wonder. Do you really, or are you merely interested in drowning yourself in pity for what has happened in the South?"

"Why shouldn't Ah pity mahself? Even if we get the proof you need, an' we stop Leroy an' his friends, that ain't gonna stop the white man from shittin' all ovah the niggers any time he gets a chance. What we gonna do if we get 'em?"

"What will happen if we don't stop this group?" Adam asked angrily.

Apollo shrugged. "Ain't gonna be a whole lot diff'unt one way or t'other."

Adam stood up. "Come on, show me this proof you have."

Still indecisive, Apollo followed Adam to the horses. Once mounted he said, "We got to ride ovah to the ol' Matthews plantation."

He led Adam past Ruel's and Kyra's burned-out house and into the woods. Half a mile farther Apollo dismounted and walked to the small stream. The horse had been covered over again, but he knew well the burying spot of that animal—a part of himself had been buried with it. Coolly he walked directly to the spot, and with a fallen branch he began to dig. After a few minutes' effort, the bloated belly of the animal showed through the mud. Adam began to help him. On the horse's now-exposed flank was Leroy Bigg's plantation mark.

Adam leaned down and cleaned more of the mud from the brand. "This proves it's a Biggs horse all right, but not that he rides with the Klan."

Apollo uncovered the horse's neck and showed Adam the wound Kyra had made with her butcher knife. "That do it, Cap'n? Or does you need moah?"

"More?" Adam asked, looking up at Apollo.

"Ah'm a nigger, Cap'n, but Ah ain't stupid. You want moah, Ah'll give you moah." Chuckling to himself now, Apollo walked a little distance from the burial mound of the horse. "That night Ah sez to mah-

self, 'Pollo, them bastards is gonna leave the mos' impohtant thing behind 'cause they the ones what's dumb,
an' they did that, an' Ah got it. Heah it is," he said,
pulling from a muddy depression at the side of the
stream the white sheet Leroy had used to cover the
horse the night of Ruel's death. "You look good at
that, Cap'n, an' see what you see."

Adam looked curiously from Apollo to the filthy
sheet.

"Take it, Cap'n. Look it ovah, an' you gonna see
how dumb a white man can be."

At first Adam saw nothing except that the sheet had
been crudely sewn into a blanket for the horse. Then
he stared incredulously at the hemmed corner of the
sheet. Darker than the rest of the muddied cotton was
a beautifully hand-stitched monogram of the Biggses.
Adam looked up at Apollo's smug, grinning face. He
shook his head, a smile coming to his own lips, then
became somber again.

"What's the mattah, Cap'n? Ain't that enuf fo' a
jury neither? You got mah word, an' Ah saw them
drag that hawss away an' hide it. Fac' is they had the
debbil's time tryin' to get that hawss. An' you got the
carcass with the brand an' the wound, an' you got the
robe. What else you need?"

Adam shook his head. "I don't need anything,
Apollo, and I don't think a jury even from around here
could fail to find Leroy guilty. I'm just wondering if
you realize what it might mean to you—and your
people."

"It mean we doan sit on ouah butts an' watch while
one of ouah men gets killed fo' nothin'. It means mebbe
we feel a li'l pride in who we is sometimes."

"It also means that Leroy is likely to go to prison
for a long time, and his friends are likely to seek revenge on every black family in the district."

Apollo folded his arms over his chest. "You sayin'
you ain't gonna do nothin' aftah Ah show you all this?
If you woan do nothin', Ah doan guess they's any

white man what will. Ah guess that mean nothin' gonna happen."

"I didn't say I wouldn't do something. I'm asking you if you realize what the consequences may be. Do you want to take the risks that will come from this? There may be alternatives we can take short of going to court."

"Like what?"

"Like putting some pressure on the Klan. Both of us belong to the Union League. Perhaps if we stir those men up, they can clamp down on Klan activities. After all, these men are all neighbors. They have influence on each other."

"An' what happens to Ruel? What's that do 'bout his death? He dead, an' nothin's bein' done 'bout it."

Adam's voice was deep and firm as he said, "You might as well accept that nothing can be done about Ruel. All the avenging on earth will not change the fact of his death, or justify it. We can do nothing about Ruel. But we can do something about the Klan. We do have a chance to make certain that no one else dies as Ruel did. It isn't easy, and it can't be done swiftly. We'll have to move in a planned, sustained, and deliberate fashion. And the Klan will fight back. Before I do anything in your behalf or my own, I want you to be sure you are willing to face the retaliation that may come."

Apollo cocked his head to one side. "Look to me like you have a doubt or two yo'seff, Cap'n. How much this retaliation you willin' to have come down on you? You sure it's me you worryin' 'bout?"

"My mind is made up, Apollo. I will fight the Klan, but I don't want to hurt innocent and unwarned people. Whatever blame I receive from the Klan will be shared by you and Kyra and perhaps some of the other Negroes at Mossrose."

"You gonna tell everybody what you plannin' to do?"

"Not what I'm planning, but that I will be doing something. If they want to leave Mossrose they are free to do so. It is a choice each will have to make. What is yours?"

Apollo grinned. "Ah want to fight. An' Kyra will fight too."

Adam looked at him from the corner of his eye, a small knowing smile playing at the edges of his mouth. "You speak for Kyra now?"

Apollo bristled, not certain how to take Adam's easy assumption of his feeling for Kyra. "Ain't nothin' wrong passed 'tween Kyra an' me. She's a good woman. Ain't nothin' loose 'bout her."

"I wasn't suggesting that there is," Adam said calmly. "Don't defend that which needs no defense, Apollo." He strode to his horse, looking back over his shoulder. "There's a Union League meeting tonight. I want to be there, and before I go I must talk with the Mossrose people. Will you come with me?"

"Ah want to talk to the Mossrose niggers mahself. You gonna make it sound like they gonna get chewed up by that damn Klan, an' Ah want them to know mah side of it too."

Adam and Apollo rode into Savannah late that afternoon, giving Adam just enough time to stop by his office on Factors' Walk and ask Cutlaw Whitaker to be sure to attend the Union League meeting later that evening.

Adam approached the meeting hall, noting with interest the guards who paraded back and forth, making a show of the Union League's ready defense against possible Klan attack. He waved as Laban Sweet caught sight of him and hurried over to join him.

"Hey, Adam, Ah ain't seen you fo' a coon's age. Hear you had some trouble out on Mossrose. You think it was the Klan's doin'?"

"I know it was the Klan's doing, Laban."

Laban made a sucking noise through his teeth, his pudgy face pained with commiseration. "They sho' are raisin' up a fuss lately. But then so ah the darkies. Ah ain't nevah had so much trouble keepin' mah people in line as Ah've been havin' of late. 'Co'se they ain't really mah people, undahstan'. Theah new blacks comin' up fum Florida an' thereabouts. Soon's Ah get 'em good jobs they'll settle down again. Y'all ain't lookin' fo' a couple or three field han's?"

"Sorry, Laban, I've got all the field hands I can use. You let me know when a good bookkeeper comes along, though."

"Ah see you smilin'. You know God-damn well darky bookkeepahs come once in a hunnert yeahs."

Adam raised his eyebrows. "I wonder why?"

"Aww shit, what you anglin' fo' now, Tremain?"

"Nothing!"

"Like hell. Ah know y'all. You got somethin' on youah mind. Bettah spit it out afo' it gags you. You ah the most agitatin' man alive."

"I was wondering if it would help us if we had a first-rate Negro school in the district around Mossrose."

"We got mo' damn groups settin' up schools fo' the darkies now than we can handle. What you want anothah one fo'?"

"Because no one has set up a school near us. The most that has been done has been done on Mossrose. I think Kyra could run a school that would take care of all the children on the surrounding plantations. You've got Freedmen's Bureau Negroes living on sections of the Matthews property. Some of those kids haven't ever seen the inside of a schoolhouse. How many families have you got out there, Laban?"

"Cain't say's Ah know. Officially theah's 'bout fifteen, but you know them darkies, they move on in 'thout tellin' nobuddy. Ah expect theah's mebbe thirty, thirty-five families out theah by now. It's harder'n hell t' keep records on 'em. The Beero says we got t'keep track o' the coloreds, but they sho' as hell doan say how. Ah'm jes' one man, an' Ah cain't be ever'wheah at once."

"I think a school would help you, too."

Sweet guffawed. "Mos' likely would. Ah nevah could write too good."

"No, I meant if the darkies could read and write they would be able to register with your Bureau and inform you of their whereabouts and contracts much better. I would guess Kyra'd be happy to keep records of the blacks in her district for you. You know she's hell-bent to reunite every black family she can. She's a stickler for records."

Laban looked at him for a while, his round, full lips pursed. "Couldn't hurt nothin', Ah doan s'pose. You tell her Ah said it was all right. Ah woan intahfere with her school, but mind, that ain't a official permit. That's only me, an' if sumbuddy highah up says huh-uh, Ah ain't nevah heard o' no school out neah Mossrose."

"Don't worry, Laban. We'll clear it with all necessary officials. But I wanted you to know my intentions before I took any other steps. After all," Adam said, clapping Laban affably on the shoulder, "we're the ones who have to work together."

Laban's eyes showed real gratitude and pride at being so respected. "Ah 'preciate that, Tremain, truly Ah do. Ah thought fo' a time theah, you an' me wasn't evah goin' t'see eye t'eye. Ah'm happy Ah was wrong. Truly Ah am."

Adam smiled in agreement with Laban, then left him to seek his seat beside Cutler. The hall began to fill up. Men removed themselves from conversations and headed for their seats. The busy noise of the room began to filter away. Arthur Redgrave called the meeting to order. Adam and Cutler sat listening to the regular order of business, Cutler with only half an ear, and Adam with unusual interest as he tried to determine how far, on this first attempt, he could persuade these men to move against the Klan. Occasionally he looked around the hall, catching sight of Apollo. He too was intent, listening for every nuance in the voices of the men as they spoke about the state of their treasury, the minutes of the last meeting, their plans and suggestions for future projects, the local political climate, and their chances for Radical victories in the next elections.

Finally, Adam rose to speak. Granted permission from Arthur Redgrave, he left his seat and walked to the front of the room. Heads turned and eyes lighted with curiosity as the people waited to hear what was of such import that they should be addressed in this formal manner.

Adam stood for a moment just looking at them. His mind was racing as he focused on one neighbor's face after another, wondering which of these men might be Klansmen as well as Union Leaguers. It wasn't unknown for a man to put his money on both sides of the table. He wondered how much retaliation he would bring from the Klan upon himself, his family, and his friends when he began to talk against them. The Klan could not withstand local opposition or legal action. To exist they had to have at least the tacit cooperation of the people.

He waited until his audience began to get restless with impatient curiosity, then he spoke, his voice deep and carrying. "By now, I am sure all of you have heard of the incident that took place on the old Matthews property. One of my most trusted employees, Ruel Jordan, was attacked at night and killed by a group of ruffians who call themselves the Ku Klux Klan. I am also sure that by now all of you have heard through one source or another the purported purposes of this Klan. They claim to protect the weak and the innocent, to uphold the Constitution, to relieve the injured and the oppressed. Among the many claims this organization makes is that they shall protect people from invasion, unlawful seizure, and from trials by other than their peers.

"There is no need for me to stand up here and draw lines from the incident with Ruel Jordan to what the Klan claims to stand for. It is obvious to all, including themselves, that what they stand for is suppression,

fear, and lawlessness. These are men who rule by terror.
They stop at nothing, hold no value for human life or
human progress.

"In recent months the Klan has been called to our
attention by their activities, but also by their own hands.
Many officials have received written messages. Any
Radical politician is subject to both written threats and
physical action by the Klan. We have posted armed
guards at our meetings—why? We all know it is to
protect us from the Klan. In our newspapers these men
have seen fit to publish their scarcely veiled threats;
yet we protect ourselves with armed guards and do
nothing that would actually stop them."

Adam paused, his eyes moving over the faces in the
room. Men who had been open, listening, now had
closed expressions; others spoke knowingly in low tones
to their neighbors. Here and there he heard the low
murmur of laughter. Some faces showed the same indignation and determination Adam himself felt, but those
faces were few, and too many of them were black.

"Tonight, I ask all of you to consider that we begin
making plans to end the Ku Klux Klan in Georgia. It
can be done; eventually it must be done. It has never
been more bold or virulent than it is now. We cannot
stand by and allow them to continue with a free hand.
We are not safe in our homes or on our plantations as
long as the Klan continues."

Adam paused, and a man called out. "How you
gonna protect us when we come out fightin' agin the
Klan? You think theah gonna take that lyin' down?"

"No, I don't. But I do know they can't afford too
much attention focused on them. They won't keep
raping, burning, killing, and pillaging if a few of their
kind land a prison term."

"Where the hell are you gonna find a honest jury to
convict one of 'em? You know sure as shit theah gonna
git off an' come right back at us. Ain't nevah been no
othah way."

"It will be, if we determine not to stop—to pledge

ourselves to the battle until we've won," Adam said
hotly.

"Youah gonna have a bunch o' stinkin' victorious
corpses!" the man hooted.

The hall burst into life with voices. Adam attempted
to gain their attention again. The noise rose. Men
shouted out comments to him from the floor, all of them
unintelligible with the chaotic noise in the room. Several
men were now in heated arguments. In the middle aisle
two men were in a shoving match, their faces distorted
with anger. Adam watched Laban Sweet and another
man move to stop the quarrel before it became an outright fight.

Arthur Redgrave came to stand beside Adam. He
took up his gavel, pounding for order. The racket went
unabated, the gavel not even heard. Arthur kept pounding, his face white with anxiety, his arm going automatically up and down, his eyes staring at the milling
mob of men within the hall. Adam took hold of Arthur's
wrist, gently but firmly stopping the motion of his arm.
"Call for a motion to adjourn."

Mechanically Arthur did, and Adam gave it. The
second was forgotten, and both men walked from the
podium into the body of the hall. Adam made his way
through the crowd to Cutler. Cutler hadn't moved. He
still sat in his seat, head down, unnoticing of the confusion around him. Adam tapped him on the shoulder,
nodding that they should leave. Cutler rose and followed Adam into the warm, moist night.

Both men were silent. They walked without destination. Out of habit they found themselves eventually on
Factors' Walk. Adam looked up at the moon through
the thick foliage.

Cutler asked finally, "Are you really going to try to
end the Klan?"

Adam laughed humorlessly. "I am. I'm not sure I
have a choice left after tonight. I'll end them, or I have
a feeling they will end me."

Cutler murmured agreement, but said nothing else.

A few minutes later Adam said, "You had nothing to say at the meeting tonight, Cutler. I expected you might. I thought you might speak out with me." He stopped, expecting Cutler to take up the conversation. When he did not, Adam sighed and said, "I suppose I shouldn't have assumed anything. We've never talked about it in so many words. You and I are generally in agreement about politics and conditions here. I expected we would be concerning the Klan. How wrong was I, Cutler?"

Cutler's long face looked more forlorn and miserable than ever. He sounded as though the words were being pulled from him. "I don't know," was all he could manage. His mind was seething with contradictions. It seemed to Cutler that there was never a time when he could say only what he himself believed without having to consider what his opinions would do to his family. He felt trapped and miserable. Above all else right now, he wanted to be drunk. Adam wanted to talk, to sort through the things that had been said at the meeting tonight, the things that were on his mind. Cutler could feel that as strongly as he could feel his own reluctance to say anything. Never before had Cutler deliberately cut short conversation or an opportunity to allow the friendship to grow between himself and Adam, but tonight he needed to be alone. He said, "I don't want to talk about the meeting or about the Klan, Adam."

Adam's blue eyes examined him carefully, and Cutler felt the pull of this new friend. It was seldom that Adam Tremain asked anything of another human being. Tonight he did, and Cutler couldn't give him the simple conversation he required. He turned away from Adam's inquiring look and walked swiftly on. He didn't know where he was going. As long as the street continued, Cutler would walk—on and on until he was finally alone.

He didn't know exactly when it was that Adam was no longer by his side, and it took him a moment to realize that he was down by the oceanside, near the place where James Oglethorpe had first landed in Georgia to begin the colony that would become Savannah. He had passed the houses and gone to the edge of the ocean, a deserted, desolate strip of sand, the end of Georgia. A place to which Cutler felt an affinity. The edge of his world.

For a time Cutler stood and gazed without seeing at the dark ocean. The steady lap, lap sound of a soft tide coming in somewhere in the darkness meshed with his disturbing repetitive thoughts and made him tired and sad. An endless sound always beating in the back of his mind day and night, day after day, week after week. Cutler was a good son, a responsible man, an upright man, a man's man, a mother's son, a father's heir—a fool without will or courage of his own.

Slowly the wet sand seeped through his shoes, and the cold moisture made him uncomfortable, a sensation that matched his state of mind. Cutler began to think of himself as he had been when he was very wrong. A vision of a towheaded boy, wild and headstrong, came into his mind. How many times had his father brought out his razor strap because of Cutler's joyfully recalcitrant ways? How many windows had he broken with thrown rocks? How many times had he been sent from the table for expressing too strongly his half-formed juvenile opinions?

What had happened to him? Tonight he had listened to Adam stand before the Union League and say the things that Cutler himself believed, while he had lowered his head so no one in the room could even read his agreement in his eyes. He had not spoken a word in support. And after, he had not had the courage to admit even privately that he agreed with Adam. What was it he feared? Disloyalty to his family. His family. How much had they cost him? His self-respect? His love? His life?

Cutler shivered as the night breeze blew off the ocean colder and damper than before. He thought of the white sheet, the decorated hood that Brock so carelessly stuffed beneath the straw in his horse's stall. Brock didn't really care who knew. After all, only the family could find out, and he counted on the family's silence. Brock didn't care about agreement. He was doing what he wished, and counted on the family for tacit approval.

Cutler's mind shifted to Cedric. He wasn't sure about Cedric. He didn't know if Cedric rode with Brock or not. Cedric seemed to be missing whenever Brock and his costume were, but Cedric was not so careless as Brock, and Cutler clung to the doubt that perhaps Cedric was not connected with the band of murdering ruffians. But he knew that Cedric, too, went with what he believed, right or wrong, while he, Cutler, stood somewhere in between in that no-man's-land called un-questioning, unreasoning loyalty. It left him unable to believe in himself, for those people to whom he was loyal were those same people whose principles and ways were in direct opposition to his own beliefs. He hated the Klan. He hated what they did. He hated the lies and the hypocrisy. He hated the aims and violence of the Klan. He hated.

With more bitterness than he knew he had in him, he admitted he hated himself, and his family for what they had done to him, and what he had allowed them to do to him. And finally, beneath all the bitterness and resentment, he faced what he truly felt most deeply. With a peculiar cognizance that he had reached the end of something, Cutler didn't try to wipe away the tears that now moistened his salt-stung cheeks.

He thought of Blythe. He remembered the scent of her, the feel of her small, supple body clinging to his, the innocence that always seemed to dwell in her eyes, and his love for her. It was a physical hurt he felt as he remembered coming home with the expectation of marrying her, and finding the whole neighborhood set against her. And it was an agony of shame he felt when he recalled how he had promised her that together they would erase the hideous memories of the Yankee cap-tain, then had later sat with his disapproving family and

talked about Blythe. He had talked about her behind
her back because he hadn't the courage to stand up before his father and mother and brothers and sister and
say he loved her.

Those days he had played a double game. Talking
one way about Blythe to his family and friends, and
talking to her, encouraging her trust in him when they
were alone. He remembered how easy it had been to
slowly shift from the promise of marriage to the nights
he had stayed in her bed with her to sneak out with the
dawn and run home like a fox fresh from the chicken
coop. It had been so easy to tell himself it had been
Blythe's choice, not his.

He had no idea how long he stood by the shore
staring out at the unseen sea, but it was long enough
for him to feel more self-loathing than he could stand.
When he turned away and began to walk back toward
his office and the full bottle of whisky he kept in his
desk drawer, he was aware of every movement of his
body. It was as if he were doer and observer all at once.
What he saw was a worthless, dirty man. And what he
felt was a worthless, dirty man. He was acutely aware
of the way the fabric of his trousers moved against his
legs, the way his arms moved, the way he held his head,
the muscles in his neck. He kept walking, a detached
viewer of this debauched, weak man who walked along
the streets heading for his lonely office and his lonely
bottle of respectable oblivion.

Cutler sat down at the desk in the shipping office.
Adam Tremain's office. His friend's office. He sat there
and pulled the bottle from the desk drawer. He held
the bottle up, squinting to see it in the darkness. He
lifted it once. To Blythe. His love whom he had betrayed and left to defend herself against hate and bigotry
and slander. He drank deeply. He lifted the bottle
again. To Adam. His friend whom he was about to
leave to the vengeance and hate and slander and vio-
lent devices of the Ku Klux Klan. He drank again, his
throat burning with the liquor and tears. He lifted the

bottle a third time. To Cutler Whitaker. The man whom
he had betrayed worst of all, for he had relinquished
all he loved and all he believed in so that he could be
respected by those whom he did not respect.

CHAPTER FIFTEEN

It was late when Apollo left the Union League meeting, angry and frustrated. Tonight he had not enjoyed the fracas, nor had he found any release in the rare occasion when he could disagree and fight with a white man on equal footing. He gently rubbed the bruised knuckles of his right hand and looked back toward the hall. The golden light that spilled from the open door was cut crazily by dashing, leaping shadows of fighting men. The pushing, shoving, hitting disagreement that Adam Tremain had begun with his speech went on. Apollo shook his head and walked away. A few days ago he would have stayed to the end, until the last angry blow had been struck, the last angry word shouted. Tonight that hot, ragged anger seemed hollow and without meaning.

He mounted his horse and headed back to Mossrose. Other times after a Union League meeting his mind had been a cauldron of thought and feeling. But he was tired of the politicking and vote buying, even of hearing the evils of the Klan. The talk seemed endless, valueless. Things didn't really change. One more election and one or two of the men in the Union League got elected. Now and then a bill to help the blacks slithered through the Legislature, but there was always someone else to see that the law was never enforced. And a new battle began. The same battle, always the same. The fighting, the struggling, never ended. Tonight he cast it aside.

He looked up at the dark night, reveled in the feeling of the soft Georgia breeze that moved over his heated, sweating body. It was an easy, mellow night, and he began to think of nothing but Kyra. It had been only

a few days since Ruel's death, and already he was
having trouble keeping her from his thoughts for an
hour at a time. She was always there, ready to spring
forward if he dared allow himself to think of her. He
laughed a little as he considered what Kyra's reactions
would be if she knew some of his favorite daydreams
of them together. His hand automatically went to his
cheek, and slowly the smile faded.

He dreamed of Kyra playful, laughing, loving, even
angry. But she was none of those things these days. He
didn't like thinking of the sadness that always seemed
to be on her face now, the too quiet way she moved
through a day, the lack of interest she displayed toward
her students and toward him. She didn't seem to care
as she once had. He understood her grief. That was
natural. But it hurt him to think that perhaps she had
buried some part of herself with Ruel. That was something he couldn't stand.

He urged his horse out of its slow, leisurely walk
into a brisk trot. He wanted to see Kyra right now. Talk
to her, stir up in her the desire to teach again, to tend
to her children—all those black children who would
never learn at all if Kyra weren't there to care and
teach. He thought of Israel Jackson's children and of
the Warrens and the Coles and so many others, all
ignorant as sin. He thought of their parents who relied
on the word of Nemo Whitelaw and Osgood Baxter to
tell them what they owed, and thought of the times
they had trustingly signed their X's to contracts, never
knowing what portion of their lives they were signing
away. Too many days, too many lives were being lost
for want of what Kyra could give in abundance.

As he rode on his ideas enlarged, became more
pressing. Adam would help him. He wasn't sure why
he trusted Adam Tremain so thoroughly, but he did.
He would talk to Adam about building a real school
for Kyra, to which all the children from the area could
come to learn. He was excited, filled with his idea, by
the time he rode up the long front drive to Mossrose.

He knew it was very late, but he didn't care. He stabled his horse and went immediately to Jothan's and Mindy's cabin, where Kyra was staying. He hammered on the door, waited for a moment, and hammered again. Then he opened it and entered the dark cabin.

Jothan raised himself in bed, his eyes squinted, his face rumpled and stupid with sleep. " 'Pollo? What you doin' here? Something wrong?"

"Nothin's wrong. Ah got to see Kyra. Kyra!" he whispered loudly.

"She's asleep, man," Jothan said, yawning. "What do you want? Go home, Apollo. Lord God, it's late, you dumb stud. Get out of here."

"Shut up, Jothan. Ah tol' you Ah got to see Kyra. It's impohtant. Kyra! Wheah ah you?"

Jothan was sitting up in bed now, his eyes blinking against the darkness, indignation slowly setting in. "What the hell's wrong with you? Get out of my house! Apollo, I swear I'm gonna beat you alongside your head."

Apollo heard no sound coming from Kyra, so he spoke aloud.

He awakened Mindy, who shrieked in fright and clutched Jothan.

Kyra lay awake listening, waiting for him to give up and go home to his own cabin.

"Kyra!" Apollo said louder, stumbling now through the dark room. "Ah know you in heah. You got to be awake. Come on, woman. Ah got to talk with you."

She finally sat up, reaching for her wrapper. "I'm awake, Apollo. Go outside and keep quiet."

"No! Ah got to see you. Ah ain't goin' nowhere till you come with me!" He took another couple of halting steps in the thick darkness. "Wheah ah you? Ah can't see nothin'."

"Go outside, please. I'll be right there."

"You sure?"

Her voice was exasperated. "Apollo, I said I'd be there. I don't lie. For heaven's sake, be quiet! You've already wakened everybody here, and if you don't hush you'll have the whole compound awake."

Grudgingly he went outside and waited. He was ready to rush back inside again and drag her out when she finally joined him.

"What is it that couldn't wait until morning?" she asked, hands on hips. "Have you been drinking?"

"No!" he howled.

"Shh! What's the matter with you, man?! You're just determined nobody is going to get a wink's sleep. Come over here, and hush your mouth!"

He followed her, talking in his loud whisper again. "Why you accusin' me of drinkin'? Ah ain't had a drop. Smell!" He huffed into her face and said proudly, "No likker."

"Lord have mercy," Kyra breathed. "You're no better'n a little child. Well, what is it that's so important?"

"Ah want you to begin teachin' again. Not like befo', neither. Ah want you to get all the chillun 'round heah, an' teach 'em all. Ah'm gonna he'p you. Ah kin build you a school, an' Cap'n Tremain'll he'p too. Ah know if Ah ast him he'll say it's a fine idea."

Kyra looked at him openmouthed. "You tellin' me that you came bustin' into Jothan's cabin and waked us all up out of a sound sleep in the middle of the night to say you want me to teach!" Her brow furrowed. "That man has to work in the morning, Apollo. And so does Mindy. You nearly scared her to death stompin' around in there. What's wrong with you? Maybe I can't smell anything on your breath, but you sure got some joy juice somewhere. You get on out of here and let me go back to sleep!" She pushed past him, her eyes intent on the cabin door.

Before he had time to think, Apollo reached out and grabbed her arm, pulling her back. He pulled hard, and Kyra twisted and whirled into him. Both his arms closed around her. Astounded, Kyra found herself clasped tightly against the long, muscular length of him. "Let me go, Apollo," she said when she regained use of her voice, but she was blushing hard, and her words did not carry the authority she meant them to.

Apollo looked as startled as Kyra, but he didn't release her. At the long-dreamed-for touch of her against him, thought fled. His face softened and his eyes filled with love. He kissed her softly on her forehead, his lips lingering, savoring the slightly salty taste of her skin, his nostrils filling with the clean, warm scent of her hair.

Kyra pushed against his chest with her hands, but it was only her arms that gave resistance. She didn't want to leave his embrace any more than he wanted her to. She stood that way, indecisive, for what seemed to her a long time. Tears slowly formed in her eyes, and she wasn't sure if they were for Ruel, Apollo, or herself. "I can't stay here with you, Apollo. You've got to let me go. I can't do this."

His voice was no more than a breath that touched and curled around her head. "We ain't hurtin' Ruel, Kyra."

"Yes, we are . . . his memory. This is wrong, so wrong."

He held her tighter, his lips seeking her neck. She let her head go back. A soft sound escaped as his warm mouth touched her skin. She lost herself in the feeling of him for a moment, then straightened, renewing her efforts at control. "I'm going back to the cabin now. Let me go now. I mean it. I won't do this. It's wrong. I loved Ruel. I did. I won't—won't cheapen his memory by—by—"

Apollo released her, but he caught hold of her hands, holding them firmly. He stood for a moment just looking at her, his feelings exposed for her to see. He spoke quietly, emotion trembling in his voice. "Ruel's dead, Kyra. You ain't gonna hurt him none by lovin' me. Nobody's ever cheapened by lovin'. Lovin's all we got in this world, and it don't come too often."

Kyra couldn't look at him. She turned away, her head down. "Ruel isn't even cold in his grave and here we are sniffing around each other like two old dogs. What do you call that, Apollo? Do you think the Lord's going to think we're good? Do you think this is what we should be doing?"

"The Lawd made us like we is, Kyra."

"He made Ruel too!" she said desperately.

Apollo pulled her closer to him. "Touch me, Kyra." He put her hand over his heart. "Feel that? Ah'm alive, an' Ah love you. Ah was meant to love you. They's blood an' heat flowin' through me like it nevah did fo' any othah woman. Mah heart's beatin' fo' you. Ain't nothin' cheap about that. Ain't nothin' the Lawd don't like 'bout that. What Ah'm feelin' is as honest as a man can get."

Kyra began to cry. She didn't fight when he took her into his arms again. "What we're doing is wrong," she murmured.

Apollo smiled gently in the darkness. "Jes' hold me," he said. "Ah guess they's some things you don't know, but Ah teaches you. You jes' hold me."

Kyra looked up at him and felt a trust for a man she had never known before. It was seldom she would relinquish her judgment to another, but tonight she knew his understanding far outreached her own. They moved in unison, walking past the cabins into the quiet night hush of the pine woods.

Apollo laid her down on a thick blanket of pine, then lowered himself beside her. Kyra's eyes never left him. Apollo stroked her softly, slowly. There was no urgency for either of them. It was their night for discovery of each other, and they did this with fingertips and reverent hands. Kyra remained passive for a time, enjoying in wonder the presence of this man, and then she began to kiss him, to discover the feel of his features in the dark, the rich texture of his skin, the scent of him which she would thereafter know as her love, making him an indelible part of herself.

Apollo unbuttoned his shirt and hers. He leaned down, letting the warm skin of their chests touch, then he kissed her, and touched her. Kyra looked at him through a haze of love and wonderment. She reached for the fastener of his trousers and did what she had never done before. She undressed him and gazed unashamedly at all of him, her hands running along the fine, firm line of his hips, over his buttocks, and across his flat, hard abdomen. And then she undressed herself, laughing, refusing his help. With each garment removed, another of her fears fell away. The strange, binding fears that she as a black woman had to be purer than purity itself, for she would be criticized so easily. That she must be sexless, for her race was thought to be lustful. The proper words of loving she left on the ground with her chemise and skirt, and she came to him freely.

Dawn was turning the inky sky purple when they came back to the cabins. Kyra stood for a moment outside the door of Jothan's and Mindy's cabin, her hands enclosed in Apollo's. She tried to speak, but there were no words for what she felt, only the longing and love in her eyes and on her body.

Apollo hugged her close to him, rocking her, then he sent her inside. He walked back to his own cabin. Five minutes later he was striding back toward the woods where they had spent most of the night. The cabin was no longer home to him. This place in the Mossrose pine woods would always, for him, be the place where he had found home.

He was not prepared for Kyra's reaction when he saw her later that morning. She no longer tried to hide from him her feelings for him, but she intensified her efforts to hide them from everybody else. Last night, she had worried that being with him would cheapen Ruel's memory and their life together. Now she worried that if anyone knew she had been with Apollo they would think she and Apollo were cheap. She protected the privacy of their love so fiercely that nothing he said or did seemed innocent enough to her, should anyone happen to be listening or see. Kyra insisted he treat her as Jothan might. It made him laugh, but it also made his heart burst with pain.

The one thing it aided was the building of the school. Kyra wanted to start on it immediately. She wanted to teach the children, but it was an acceptable reason for Apollo to be around her a great deal; and in spite of her protective propriety, she desperately wanted to be near him. By the beginning of September she was insisting that Apollo talk to Adam and Dulcie about the school.

Apollo, as anxious as she was to find a way to be alone, hesitated to talk to Adam at just that moment. "Miss Dulcie is gettin' ready to move to that new house. They ain't gonna want to hear about a nigger school now."

"But you said Captain Tremain would understand the importance of the school. You said he'd be in favor of it."

"He will."

"But you called it a nigger school. Why? Does he feel that way?"

"No, it ain't him. Ah said that. Ah shouldn't have," Apollo said, digging himself in deeper. "Ah'll talk to him first day aftah they move. Ah promise, Ah'll talk to him right away."

Kyra frowned at him, her finger waggling under his nose. "Don't you ever call it a nigger school again. How do you expect me to teach these children to respect themselves if you go around talking like that? It's bad enough they hear the white folks say it, but you shouldn't. You know better."

He opened his mouth to defend himself, but wisely realized that he was better off accepting this chastisement and not calling a worse one down on his head.

When she finally wound down, Apollo gratefully said that he had to check the condition of the drays and have them taken over to the Whitakers' to move the Morans' and Tremains' household goods to the new house. As he went to the barn, he was chuckling to himself, happy to be free of her lashing tongue, and happier that she was his.

An hour after Apollo left Kyra, the drays were on their way. Dulcie saw them coming down the drive from her bedroom window and flew into more frenzied activity. There were boxes and trunks and crates strewn throughout the upper hallway, and still there were linens, silver, and china that had not been tucked safely into containers. She called the servants to her like a battle commander, setting each man and woman to work on specific tasks.

Adam was in the lower hall, calling up to her that the wagons were ready. Dulcie glanced over the confused room. Silk dresses, crystal vases and bronze statuary, Adam's uniforms, Beau's small suits of velvet and merino, toys, playthings, knickknacks, letter paper and ink, correspondence to answer, a half-finished quilt top she was making, all the myriad things the Tremains and Morans had accumulated in their rooms for their comfort, convenience, and entertainment; all and more had to be securely packed and the containers fastened before the drays could be loaded.

Adam finally came upstairs, a rakish grin on his face as he watched his frantic wife spinning around the room trying to talk to three people at once and keep straight what was being packed. His blue eyes twinkled; his mouth curved into a smile as she caught his eye. Angrily she wiped a curling, moist ringlet of auburn hair from her brow. "Well, why are you standing there? You could help. Reverend Hooks is visiting Daddy. One of us should be there. I'm hurrying as much as I can. Why did you have the drays come so early?"

He stepped over the crates, his long legs closing the distance between himself and her. He picked her up, turned to look at Ivy Warren. "Ivy, Mrs. Tremain is indisposed. You can finish this up, can't you?"

Ivy's face split into a wide, knowing grin. "Sho'ly can, Cap'n."

Adam nodded and threaded his way back past boxes and barrels. Dulcie began to giggle, her head nestled against his shoulder. "Where are you taking me?"

He looked at her, one eyebrow raised ridiculously high. "I'm going to see to it you get exactly what you need."

In mock indignation she wiggled in his grasp, her fists hitting against his chest and back. He ignored her and strode into their bedroom, where, without ceremony or romance, he began to remove her clothing. Then he picked her up again and carried her to the luxurious, flowered-enamel bathtub. He lowered her into the bubbling, scented water. Grinning happily, he said, "Lust will always confuse your thinking."

She threw a handful of suds and water at him. "You beast! You wretched beast!"

He put his hand on the top of her head and pushed her under the water. Her legs flew up, kicking and splashing him. She came up sputtering and laughing. She threw her sponge at him, hitting him squarely in the chest, and followed that with both hands slapping the water from the tub in his direction as fast as she could. Adam came at her to push her under again, and saw too late that she was waiting for him. She gripped him firmly, and pulled with all her might. Losing his footing, he was half in the tub and half out, spitting soapsuds and laughing as hard as she.

Still giggling, she said, "The Whitakers will be glad to see the last of us." With wide, dancing eyes, she added, "We aren't very civilized, Adam Tremain. I think that must be your influence."

He kissed her. "I know. You were always such a good child before you met me."

"I was!"

He kissed her again. "I know. Glenn Saunders has told me all about you, not to mention what your mother has had to say upon occasion."

"What did they tell you?"

He chuckled evilly. "I couldn't betray their confidence."

She smiled, looking at him from the corner of her eye. "What if I bribed you?" Her hands were inside his wet shirt, then she was unbuttoning it. Happily she dunked the shirt into the bathtub then tossed it onto his head.

From between the dripping sleeves he looked out at her. "Your bribery leaves something to be desired."

"I could do better if you'd give me your trousers."

The shirt still on his head, he stood and removed the rest of his clothing, dropping it into the tub with her.

Dulcie got out of the tub. She stood before him, then slowly moved her wet, slippery body against his. Easily she took a step back and Adam followed. One step at a time they moved toward their bed, kissing and fondling each other as they progressed. They tumbled onto the stripped bed. Roughhousing in a way they hadn't since the early days of their marriage, they played and nipped at each other, laughing and wrestling until they had reached a peak of wild, heightened excitement.

Adam rolled on top of her, and Dulcie wrapped her legs around him. With an intensity that sought only release, he drove into her, and her hips rose to meet him.

Later they lay on the bed together, their hands entwined, both of them content and quiet. Dulcie looked out the window. They had lived with the Whitakers for better than two years, and never had they made love with the fun and abandon they had today. In all that time they had been sedately proper, and now she wondered why. Perhaps it was being so near to her mother again. Perhaps it had been Emma and Ned Whitaker's presence. Perhaps it was just all the old rules, never spoken to her now, but so well remembered from her girlhood. She wasn't sure.

But she did know that during the time they had lived with the Whitakers she had been grateful for every duty that had called her to Mossrose, so that she could momentarily escape having not one demanding mother, but two. Her married status had made little difference to either Patricia or Emma, who considered daughters as extensions of their own hands on a plantation where women's work never ended. She had not resented her position, but it had been restricting.

Until this minute she had not realized that the greatest restriction of all had been with Adam. She had lost the way to be young and playful with him. She now realized how badly she had missed it and what a part of their life it had been until they had come back to Mossrose. With sudden tears in her eyes, she looked at Adam's smiling, contented face, and even in his presence began to miss him in the days that were to come. She had expected to stay with Patricia and Jem for a few months; now it looked as though the visit to Mossrose would be extended indefinitely, and she wondered how many, if any, days like this they would have in the new house with her father and mother under the same roof.

She knew Jem was improving. Daily his words became clearer; daily he insisted on going downstairs, to sit in his wheeled chair and mix with the families. Patricia hovered anxiously around him, in particular when he began to attempt the conduct of his business once more. But he shooed her away. He wanted Dulcie there. Mossrose would be all hers one day, he insisted; and she should learn how to run a large plantation. There had been a time when she would have thought owning and running Mossrose the most desirable occurrence in her life. Now all she wished for was a home of her own with Adam.

But her father was far from recovered. He still required much physical care, and although Patricia's constant watching irritated him, he needed that, too. More quickly than anyone else, she observed when he began to grow tired and pale, and deftly she would maneuver him into resting.

It was a source of great satisfaction, the achievement of a dream to Jem, that the new mansion was completed. This time there would be no shells to destroy it, no Yankee soldiers to burn down the remnants. The new house faced north and was built of soft-pink brick, with white limestone lintels above the doors and windows, and six white Doric columns across the spreading veranda. Its sixteen rooms had been built to accommodate a large family of several generations. Dulcie could not keep from her mind the fact that Jem dreamed of those generations, herself and Beau, and perhaps Beau's children. It would go on and on. She turned to Adam, burying her face against his chest. She wanted to please her father, but it was this man she wanted with all her heart. Mossrose was behind her, yet she didn't seem able to pull free of it.

Adam held her for a moment, then got up. "Ivy should have everything packed by now, Mrs. Tremain. It's time we got back to work."

Dulcie clapped her fingers over her mouth. "Adam! I forgot all about Reverend Hooks!"

Adam laughed. "I'm sure Patricia can manage a sickroom call without a chaperone."

With deft fingers Patricia straightened Jem's covers and smoothed the collar of his nightshirt. She said brightly, "Jem dahlin', Reverend Hooks is heah to see you. Now Ah want you to be good this time, an' not try to argue with him the way you usually do."

Jem shook his head jerkily, which could have meant anything except humble acquiescence.

"You may come in now, Reverend Hooks," she said primly. "Mistah Moran is ready fo' visitahs."

The Reverend Jabez Hooks strode into the room, radiating confidence and good will, his slightly rusty black frock coat flapping with each long step. He placed a bony hand on Jem's shoulder and leaned forward to speak to him in a loud tone as though Jem had become deaf. "Good mawnin', brothah Moran! Ah trust youah feelin' bettah today!"

Jem made an indeterminate noise and nodded, more with his eyes than with his head.

Patricia scurried around, unable to find a servant at the moment, and finally brought a chair up to the bedside herself.

"Much 'bliged, sistah Moran," said Hooks graciously, waiting for her to seat herself.

"Weah sorry we haven't been able to attend worship suhvices lately, Reverend Hooks, but as you see—"

Hooks patted Patricia on the upper arm. "Mah deah sistah, Ah would be the fust t'say y'all have every reason t'stay right heah by the side of youah ailin' husband. As a mattah o' fact, Ah sometimes feel that fo' some folks it's the nearah to the church, the farthah fum God, if you follow me." He beamed at Jem, who was wearing a faraway, bored gaze.

Patricia fluttered. "Ah don't know jes' what you mean, Reverend." Tentatively she pulled up another chair at a little distance from him.

"C'mon right up heah, sistah, so's weah all close togethah, an' Ah'll explain mahseff. Theah now, ain't that bettah?" Again he patted Patricia, who stiffened under his touch and darted a glance at Jem to see if he had taken offense.

Jem had not; his head was nodding and his eyes were half-closed.

"The nearah to the church," Patricia reminded Hooks.

"Yes ma'am, Ah was 'bout t'say, with some folks, they go t'suhvices ever' Sunday an' ever' Wednesday evenin', but they doan truly make the effoht t'be neah t'the Lawd. They think theah hymn-singin' an' theah lis'nin t'mah sermons is enuf t'make 'em all real Christians. But them folks, they got a roof ovah theah heads, an' thoo the good fo'tune o' havin' mah sto' neahby, they kin get theah food an' necessities o' life. They ah sittin' in the catbird seat. They ain't makin' no effoht t'he'p one anothah. They ain't settin' no example fo' somebody else. They ah gettin' fathah an' fathah fum the Lawd all the time."

Patricia's face held a confused expression. "Ah don't know that Ah undahstand, Reverend Hooks."

Hooks launched into his favorite theme. "They ain't sufferin' like real Christians ought to. A real Christian knows he is one, 'cause the Lawd gives him sufferin' t'do. Take Mistah Moran heah, now theah's a man who knows all 'bout sufferin'. He has lost the use o' his left side, God gave him that so's he'd know 'bout sufferin'."

Jem said, "No!" and Patricia interposed hastily. "The loss youah speakin' of is temp'rary, Reverend Hooks, the doctah told us that. But youah right, poah Jem *is* sufferin'."

"The mahk of a true Christian." Hooks nodded solemnly. "But it hasn't broke him, sistah Moran. It has broke his pride, like the Lawd said, 'I will break the pride of your power.' But brothah Moran's spirit is still in theah standin' upright, fightin' the good fight an' showin' us all how a true Christian enduahs the notice o' the Lawd."

Patricia said hesitantly, "Whah Ah do b'lieve that's so. He—"

Jabez Hooks was never one to let another person speak too long. He continued, "An youahseff, sistah Moran," patting her on the shoulder, "now ya'll exemplify the truly Christian wife. Standin' by his bedside day an' night, fum what youah friends tell me. That's like the Apostle Paul wrote t'the Corinthians, 'Let the husband render unto the wife due benevolence; and likewise also the wife unto the husband.' Sistah Moran, you ah renderin' due benevolence unto youah husband, an' the Lawd will see you get youah rewahd."

"Oh, but Ah don't want any rewahd, Reverend Hooks, Ah only want Jem to get well."

Hooks said slyly, "Well now, sistah Moran, if Ah was you Ah'd count that as a rewahd." He was leaning toward her, looking earnestly into her eyes, little puffs of his breath touching her chin.

Jem said unexpectedly, "I will."

Patricia jumped, and turned toward her husband with a nervous smile. "You will what, Jem? Did you mean you'll get well?"

Jem nodded vigorously. "Get well."

Hooks said loudly, "Praise the Lawd. Brothah Moran

has said he's gonna get well! Let us pray." Hooks reached out two long arms, one to take Jem's hand and one to take Patricia's. He bowed his head solemnly. "O great an' gracious Lawd, we gathah heah at the bedside of ouah stricken brothah to thank Thee fo' Thy notice o' this worthy gentleman, an' to pray that Thy strictures will be lifted as soon as it be thy will. An' as fo' this lovin' wife, sistah Moran—" Patricia felt a gentle finger run across her palm and then back as Hooks went on without a break. "—as fo' her, O Lawd, we ask Thee to give her stren'th in the days t'come." Again she felt that suggestive tickling and tried to pull away, unsuccessfully. "Give her, if it be Thy will, the stren'th of eagles, the stren'th of ten women—" Another small tickle, another jerk from Patricia. "—so's she may help ouah brothah heah re-covah his full powah in the humility o' the Lawd. Amen. Amen."

Hooks abruptly raised his head and smiled into Patricia's eyes. Her face was pink with affront. Hooks said easily, "Ah hope you'll fo'give mah little vellication theah, sistah Moran. The Lawd give me a bad twitch in that ahm, an' with his he'p Ah'm tryin' t'ovahcome it." Turning to Jem he said, "Well now, brothah Moran, Ah doan want t'tell no tales out o' school, but Ah got a li'l gossip t'entertain you with. Y'all know youah black boy name Boy?"

Jem scowled. "No damn good."

"Well now, that black boy is workin' on a rock pile. The Freedmen's Beero done lease him to the govament. Ah seen him yesterday, workin' on a pile o' rocks out beside wheah they ah macadamizin' the road. He was takin' big rocks an' makin' little rocks out of 'em." Hooks threw back his head and laughed uproariously. When neither Jem nor Patricia joined in, he said, "It was right laughable, he had this big maul an' he was breakin' up rocks. Yes suh, it was a funny sight." Ostentatiously Hooks wiped his eyes. "Ah thought it was jes' 'bout his speed, bustin' rocks."

"It's jes' what he deserves," Patricia said primly, having moved her chair away from the preacher.

Jem said, "What he 'serves."

Hooks placed his hands on his thighs, elbows out, preparing to rise. "Well, brothah Moran, sistah Moran, Ah got a heap o' pas-torial calls t'make this mawnin'. Next Ah go t'see the Tweed sistahs, an' then—"

Patricia said earnestly, "Oh, Reverend Hooks, will you give them mah fondest love, an' assuah them that Ah'll come callin' on them jes' as soon as Ah can? Ah know it's hahd fo' them to get out."

Hooks held out his hand, and reluctantly Patricia gave him hers. "Ah'd be happy t'do you such a little favah, sistah," he said, and gallantly swooping down from his height, laid a kiss on the back of her hand. As she flinched he said, "Mah goodness, sistah Moran, did Ah go an' twitch *again?* Mah li'l affliction seems t'be extry bad today."

Patricia said, with spirit, "Maybe you ought to consult with the Lawd about that, Reverend Hooks. Maybe He might have somethin' t'say to you about youah—youah problem."

Hooks, his black eyes boring into hers, flared his nostrils dramatically as he drew in breath. Then he turned to Jem, shaking his hand, assuring him that the Lord would not give him any more suffering than he could bear, and promising to return soon. "Ah want t'leave y'all with this word fum the Lawd. 'When the righteous cry for help, the Lawd heareth and delivereth them out of all their troubles.' Jes' think on that, now." Bowing and nodding his head, he made his way out the door.

Patricia glared after him, her arms akimbo. Under her breath she murmured, "Filthy-minded old man!" Then, sweetly smiling, she turned to Jem and pounded his pillows into plumpness once more.

Adam and Dulcie dressed, saw to the loading of the first drays, then went to Mossrose to see to the place-

ment of the crates and barrels. The draperies and curtains had already been hung to Dulcie's approval, the
floor waxed and shined. Furnishings to fill the house
would come partly from their rooms at the Whitakers',
for gradually they had found they wanted certain
items of their own for daily use, and Emma had removed most of her furniture from their apartment.
There were also numerous wagonloads of chairs and
sofas and dressers and wardrobes, china, silver, linens,
books and stands, kitchen equipment and pans, which
had come from New York on the *Black Swan* and
waited in storage in Savannah.

All day long, wagons of household goods drove up
the sandy lane, unloaded, and departed for more. Men
from Whitakers' stables brought over the Tremains'
riding horses. Even the milk cows were moved from
Whitakers' back pasture to a pasture on Mossrose.
Servants worked with relative smoothness under the
direction of Dulcie in the house and Adam outside.
If a dusty footprint was left on the polished floor,
thirteen-year-old Cilla Warren's sole duty was to dart
in and wipe it up before the next pair of feet touched
the floor.

It had been thought best not to bring Jem over
until the excitement had died down and things were
in place. Beau, too, was left behind, crying in Mindy's
arms because he saw his dresser and toy chest being
taken. At last the moving was nearly finished. Dulcie
wiped sweat from her brow and throat and climbed
wearily into the wagon beside Apollo to fetch Jem
and his wheeled chair, Patricia, and Beau and his small
crib and his nurse.

"He's been cryin' all day, Miz Tremain," said
Mindy, looking ravaged as she handed Dulcie her son.
"I tried to tell him you'd be back for him."

Beau sobbed and hiccuped against her shoulder, his
small, plump hands patting her breast as though she
were the one needing comfort. Wisely Dulcie took him
downstairs to sit on her lap in the wagon, afraid he

would start crying afresh if he saw his crib being dismantled.

The long day came to its end. Jem had been wheeled to every room in the house, to gaze at and admire the results of his own and Patricia's taste many months before. Patricia, glad enough to turn him over to Dulcie for a few moments, directed Apollo in straightening the angle of a painting, in exchanging this chair for that, in moving the marble-topped stand to this wall instead of the other. The newly hired servants in the kitchen got together a passable meal, and it was soon bedtime.

Peggy, who was Dulcie's personal maid, found her in the parlor about ten o'clock that night. "Miz Tremain, Ah doan know where me'n Saul is s'posed to sleep. We went to go to baid an' dere ain't no baid."

Dulcie laughed ruefully. Her maid and her stableman husband had been sleeping in the Whitakers' quarters. "Oh, Peggy, I'm sorry—I never thought. We must have some place."

Adam got up. "I'll ask Jothan what cabins are available."

"They may have to double up for a few nights," Dulcie observed as he left. She put her head back against the wing of the chair and dozed. In a few moments, it seemed, Adam was back.

"Dulcie, I don't know why neither of us thought of this, but now that the house servants are here at Mossrose, we don't have room for everyone in the cabins. We had to clear out Kyra's schoolroom. By taking out the desks and other things, we can sleep eight people in there temporarily."

"Oh, no! What did Kyra say? Was she very upset?"

Adam shook his head, laughing a little. "It was very strange. Both Apollo and Kyra helped. There wasn't a word of disagreement. Those two have something up their sleeves. I wonder what it is?"

"But her school—she was so proud of it. We can't take her school away from her."

"We won't. We'll build more cabins. We can't have these people living all crowded together as they are tonight. Kyra will have her school back as quickly as it's possible to give it to her." He paused, looked back toward the door as though he could see the quarters from where he was. "I just can't think what Kyra and Apollo are up to." He suddenly yawned and turned back to his wife. "Let's go to bed. I'm sure Apollo will tell me what he has on his mind soon enough."

Dulcie allowed herself to be pulled into his arms. They embraced, sleepy and relaxed. "Oh, Adam, don't you wish we were in our own house?"

"More than you can guess, my love. But we will be, in time, soon enough for our children to play in the yard and climb the liveoaks. Right now we can't leave your mother with everything to manage alone."

Dulcie laid little kisses on the corners of his mouth. "Do you realize," she said dreamily, "that we've been married seven years . . . and we have yet to make a permanent home?"

He murmured, "Does it matter?" He bent over and blew out the lamp. In the darkness he pulled Dulcie's compliant body tight against his. His mouth covered hers and they kissed long, deeply, lovingly. Without loosing his hold on her, he moved to the tall double doors and turned the lock.

Button by button they undressed each other, kissing, caressing, until they stood naked, flesh to flesh. Leisurely he laid her down and lay beside her on the luxuriously cushioned Beidermeier sofa. With his mouth and his fingertips he stroked her, arousing her until her entire body seemed to glow with the heat of her desire for him.

Her hands pressed along the rounded muscles of his breast, the flatness of his belly, the long, smooth muscles of his inner thighs. Kissing her still, he poised his body over her. Her knowing hands enclosed him gently, guiding him to enter her warm, moist secret recess. Unhurried, sensual, he glided his length into her. They moved together minimally, prolonging the delicious glow, tantalizing each other to the height of ardor.

Then Dulcie drew in a quick breath, whimpering his name. Her strong fingers dug into his buttocks, pulling him closer into her as they rocked against each other faster and faster. Simultaneously they trembled on the brink, and then with great sighs of gratification let themselves coast shuddering to a halt.

They lay together for some minutes, both enjoying the afterglow, the closeness of one to another, the satisfying experience of giving and receiving and sharing love. He whispered, knowing that she already knew it, but still wanted to hear it, "I love you. I love you."

She let out a long breath of contentment. Tenderly, her palm came up to caress Adam's cheek.

Soon after breakfast, Peggy came to tell Dulcie that Apollo wanted to see her. "Are you sure he doesn't want to see Captain Tremain instead?"

"No'm, he said Miz Tremain. He din't say cap'n."

"Send him into Daddy's office, Peggy. I'll be waiting there."

Apollo entered the room hat in hand, but lacking the false humility that slavery had once imposed on black men who crossed a white man's threshold. In slave days, Dulcie reflected, Apollo would not have been allowed as far as the porch. Now, here in a place he had helped to build, Apollo, though troubled, was poised.

"Good morning, Apollo." Dulcie smiled, for she was nearly as fond of him as Adam was. "What can I do for you this morning?"

"Cap'n Tremain told me Ah should talk to you about the school, Miz Tremain." She noticed he had dropped the Miss Dulcie.

"This is something you've already discussed with Captain Tremain?"

"Yes, ma'am, but he said you'd be in charge, an'

Ah should come heah an' figger it all out with you."

Dulcie smiled, indicating a chair. "It looks as though we'll have a great many details to discuss, Apollo, so you'd better sit down and be comfortable. First of all, I would like you to tell me fully what you and Kyra want in the way of this schoolhouse. Captain Tremain told me Kyra is thinking of teaching the black children of the entire neighborhood. How large a building, to begin with?"

Dulcie listened patiently as Apollo talked about the school. The day slipped by as they sorted out the practical from the impractical. They made tentative lists of the supplies that would be needed in the building of a schoolroom approximately twenty by forty feet, and then began to list what would be needed to equip the school.

At length Dulcie put down her pencil, looking blankly at the paper. She was tired; her mind would no longer sort out the information. She looked at Apollo. "We'll have Kyra join us tomorrow. Neither one of us knows what she will need as well as she does. I'm sure we have items on here that will be of no use, and we have not even considered others we should have. In the meantime, I'll have Jothan look over the property and see if he can locate a good site. It might be well if you accompanied him and reported to me tomorrow."

The following day Dulcie talked with Kyra about the school and what Kyra believed she could manage. Later in the afternoon Dulcie tended to the plantation affairs that Jem seemed to want her alone to see to. She then prepared the daily reports for her father. Just before she left her office after a long, exhausting day, Jothan and Apollo came to tell her they had found a suitable piece of land, convenient to Mossrose and to the neighboring plantations as well. Black families in the area worked under contract for neighbors, or leased, tenanted, or owned portions of the old Matthews plantation. They saw no problem for the children of these workers in getting to school.

Dulcie smiled. "What a nice note to end the day on. I'll speak to Captain Tremain about it, and I believe he'll approve your choice. I'll expect both of you and Kyra here tomorrow morning. The sooner we get this project started, the better."

Adam was in the new bathroom, a convenience Mossrose had not boasted before, and one that eased the servants' lot considerably. Dulcie knocked and walked in as he was drying himself.

"You should have come sooner, Dulcie, you could have been my companion in the tub." Playfully he flicked her with the corner of the towel.

"I could have washed your back—or something," she said, smiling.

"Well, now we'll have to save it, won't we?"

"Why? Adam, where are you going? I didn't know you were leaving."

He laughed and, trapping her head between his hands, kissed her. "I'm only going to Savannah."

"But it's nearly dinner time. Are you—you're going before we eat?"

"I'm having dinner with Cutler at the hotel." He paused for a moment, thoughtful. "I'd like to talk to him—if I can get him to say anything. I don't know what's bothering him, but he hasn't been himself lately."

Dulcie thought of Birdie and the near-hysterical conversation she had had with her. Her eyes did not meet Adam's. "What do you think it's about?"

"I don't know. That's what I want to find out."

Dulcie hesitated for a moment, considering asking him if he knew anything about Cutler and Blythe, then she thought better of it. "What else are you going to do tonight?"

"Oh, nothing of interest—business."

Dulcie's face changed, became wary. "You're going to the Union League meeting again."

"Yes, I am. I'll stay in Savannah overnight and come home tomorrow."

"Adam, you aren't going to ask them to act against the Klan, are you?"

Adam's expression was closed. "Yes, I am, Dulcie."

"Why? You know they won't listen to you. The last time there was a fight afterward. What good will it do you—do anyone?"

"They may not listen this time either, or the next time, and they may fight until they have battered each other, but I am going to keep telling them. Someone has to. I'm going to keep on telling them the Klan must be brought under control. Sometime, someone has to listen."

"And if they don't?"

"They will."

Dulcie sighed softly, but said only, "You are a stubborn man, Adam Tremain. You wouldn't listen to me if all the angels in heaven told you I was right. You'd still go ahead with what you thought was right."

He looked at her in total agreement.

"Since you insist on wreaking havoc on all of us, I might as well resign myself and tell you better news. Every now and then we have some, you know."

"And what is that?"

"I talked with Kyra this morning, and this afternoon Jothan and Apollo came to tell me they've found a piece of land for the new schoolhouse, a nice clearing in the northeast field where the lane goes between the Chilcotes' and the Actons'. To my knowledge we never have used that field. Daddy always has plans for it, but nothing ever comes of them. What do you think?"

"It sounds ideal to me. Most of the children would be within close distance. Kyra should have a healthy supply of pupils. When do you plan to begin building?"

"Well, I—can we start right away?"

"Dulcie, this is your project. Don't ask me, tell me. When do you want to begin building the school?"

She followed him into the dressing room. "We'll

begin right away, and—Adam, I think it would be better if we bought the supplies locally, too. I don't think we should use the Savannah suppliers. Apollo tells me that all the people hereabouts use Seldon's general store for supplies. And from what I've heard from the Tweeds and Saunderses and some others, there is nothing Nemo Whitelaw can't get. He seems to have everything we'd need, or he can order it for us. I think if the people—I mean the coloreds—could hear and know about the school from the start, they would be more likely to send their children. It would be a kind of community project."

Adam grinned at her, shaking his head. "You have been busy. Have you considered how much of your time and energy a project of this size will take?"

"Why, don't you think I can do it?"

"Of course I think you can do it. I am asking you if you want to take it on. There are the servants' quarters to be built too, and I doubt that you'll turn that over to anyone else. You were all over the place when the first ones were going up. Don't try to make me believe your mind didn't store away everything you observed. By now, I imagine you've decided how all our early errors can be corrected."

She looked at him, smiling. "Well, not all of them, but I do think the dividing wall should be moved a foot to give more room in the bedroom. A couple of our families are rather large."

Adam laughed, and she looked startled. Then he moved to her, tipping her chin to kiss her gently on the lips. "Dulcie mea, you please me very much."

She caught his hand and held it for a moment. "You look very fine," she said at last. "Must you go so soon?"

"Not yet. Come sit with me for a moment." They took chairs by a large window overlooking the slowly greening front lawn. "It's a pleasure to be settled for a while."

"Yes, but funny, isn't it, I miss the noise all those

Whitakers make. Those loud-voiced men with their clomping boots, and Enid and Emma calling to each other from opposite ends of the house."

Adam seemed contented and peaceful as he listened to her, but his mind had gone back to Cutler Whitaker and the peculiarity of his actions lately. His thoughts merely added fuel to his determination to see the Klan ended in the area around Mossrose, in all of Savannah if he could manage it. He said, "Perhaps what we need is a little noise and excitement in Mossrose."

Dulcie made a face. "Mama and I could put on field boots and clump up and down the new staircase."

"A dinner party would serve as well. I'd like to give a dinner party, a number of dinner parties."

"Oh, but not now, Adam! Not while Daddy is so—so—"

"He'd enjoy it, you know that. And at the first blink of his eyes, your mother would cart him off to bed. Surely you aren't afaid he'd disgrace the family, are you?"

"That is unfair. It never occurred to me," she said coolly. "I was thinking only of him, but I don't really believe your purpose is to entertain him."

Adam was unperturbed. "We've been to many parties where the old people doze off in their chairs and nobody finds it remarkable. We should permit your father the same privilege."

"Adam Tremain, you are trying to lead me astray, and I won't be led. I know you are not talking about an ordinary round of dinner parties. Whom were you thinking of inviting?"

"The neighbors, of course. And perhaps a few people from Savannah."

Dulcie looked suspiciously at his bland mask of innocence. "The neighbors. Which neighbors? The ones you think might be amenable to riding against the Klan?"

"It would be nice if it turned out that way," he said mildly.

"And if it didn't—" She paused, not daring to go much further with her thought. "Adam, it is one thing to invite the neighbors socially, but to use a dinner party as a political platform—Oh, Adam, we don't even know who is a Klansman and who isn't. We can't take chances like this! You'd have them here as a captive, polite audience—they'd hate you!"

Adam remained quiet for a moment, then said, "Those who would hate me already do, Dulcie. Isn't it better to know the face of your enemy than always to wonder if he wears the guise of your friend? Have you ever considered, love, that the family we just lived with has probably one or two Klan members in its ranks?"

"But who—which? How do you know? They did us no harm. It can't be true!"

Adam sighed. "It's just a hunch, just the way some men talk. But if I am right, they have done us harm. Who do you think it was that rode against Ruel? Who do you think has robbed and harmed and burned out Negroes in the neighborhood?"

Dulcie opened her mouth to protest that it couldn't be any of the Whitakers, then she closed it, shaking her head. "I can't believe it, Adam. I can't believe those—those people I grew up with could do something like that."

Adam made a grim face. "There you've expressed one of the major strengths of the Klan. No one can imagine husbands, fathers, brothers, perpetrating the brutal acts of the Klan. Those acts are committed by hooded, hidden men. But never for a moment forget that behind those hoods are faces that you know, and I know. Theirs are the faces of men who have done business with Ruel Jordan and smiled at him, perhaps even joked with him. I imagine some even admired his ability. But they still killed him."

"But Adam, the Whitakers aren't murderers and arsonists! They are our neighbors!"

"Only without their masks. But you're right in a

way. These men feel they have a grievance, and they haven't the means to cope with it short of mob action. It's my intention to show them alternate ways of meeting this situation we're in."

"But Adam—I don't think a dinner party is appropriate for—"

He looked directly at her. "I would like to do this. One way or another I'll rouse people against the Klan, but if I can, I'd also like to help the Whitaker family. They all fought for a common cause once, and they could again."

Dulcie just stared at him, thinking of Blythe, her eyes moist, her heart beating faster than it should have. "I don't want you interfering with the Whitakers—let them patch up their own differences. And I certainly don't want you rousing the Klan members against us!"

Adam sat back and crossed his legs. "What *do* you want me to do?"

"What do you mean by that?"

"You've made it amply clear what you don't want me to do. What suggestions do you have?"

Dulcie looked away from him. "I'm frightened. I'm always frightened any more. I—I guess I just want a—a peaceful existence, with you safely at home and our children growing up in a world where—where terrible things don't happen."

Adam leaned forward, his hand caressing her arm. "Terrible things happen when people allow them to happen, Dulcie. We can't refuse to act upon our own values and beliefs, and then expect something like the Klan to disappear quietly. It will be gone only when we present a better, stronger way."

"But I'm afraid!" Dulcie said passionately. "I don't want to lose you! I want to have more babies, and—Adam, you always look at life as though you are invincible. But you're not . . . you're not. I don't want to lose you."

He spoke quietly. "I hear what you have said, but what would either of us have if I sit back in luxury, my hands folded on my lap, while people who are helpless need a voice to speak for them? What would we be to each other if we stood by watching while hooded ruffians destroyed people who have no protection? Could you even look at me, Dulcie? In a year, what would you be saying to me then? What could I say to myself?"

"Don't talk sense to me! I don't want to hear it! I don't want to know. I don't want to hear. We'd still love each other—I could never think less of you no matter what you did. I—I'd always know . . ." She put her face in her hands. She sat for a long time, silent and closed within herself.

She took a breath and let it out. "How many guests shall we have?"

CHAPTER SIXTEEN

Adam returned from Savannah with customary defeat imprinted on his featutres. The men of the League, while agreeing in principle with him, wanted no part in actually exposing and punishing their friends, family, and neighbors. Dulcie greeted him with mixed feelings. For the first time in their married life she wasn't certain whether she wanted him to succeed or fail. She wasn't sure that the outcome would be much different for them whichever way it went. He had already set himself against the Klan and all that it stood for. She knew that, yet a part of her held back, wanting to seek a security that she knew wasn't there.

They avoided the subject of his campaign against the Klan, to the extreme that it was always on both their minds. Dulcie finally said, "I haven't forgotten your dinner parties, Adam. We will have them, and I will do the best for you that I can, but I want to get Kyra's school started first."

He said little, too little, and Dulcie added his mute acceptance of the delay to her worries. It wasn't often that she and Adam could not talk openly to each other. This time there was a barrier between them that stemmed primarily from her view of the world as a woman, and his as a man. She saw the days passing and Beau growing, and thought of the safety and quality of those days. She thought of nights shared without fear and of more babies to be born, of days working, laughing, talking side by side, building something together; and she knew he saw something else. She even knew and understood what he saw, just as he understood her view. But this once, understanding wasn't enough. Somehow she had to reach a point that his world of great movements and political shifts and economics meshed with her world of feelings and principles and values.

They tended to their chores separately. Dulcie calmed her raging emotions and tried to sort out the pieces of their life that disturbed her most. Always she came back to the story Birdie had told her about Blythe. In that tragedy, she realized, were the seeds of the one she sensed storming around them. Blythe—good, innocent Blythe—had done what she thought she had to do to save her mother and sisters, but had only succeeded in becoming the sacrificial lamb. It was the ease with which the Saunders women had turned their backs to her that frightened Dulcie. Those women didn't wear hoods as the Klansmen did, but they wore hoods of piety and self-righteousness that were just as masking. And even now, she couldn't say that those were bad women. Yet, if they weren't evil, and they were still capable of such blind cruelty, what were they?

What she did not seem able to explain to Adam was the feeling she had of being beset. Adam said it was better to know the face of your enemy. He said it was dangerous to let your enemy wear the false face of a friend. But it wasn't Adam who had grown up in Chatham County, it was she. All her enemies here wore the faces of friends. Who, then, was there left to call upon in need, or in simple humanity?

She saw Birdie several times, but none of their visits was satisfactory. Both she and Birdie were restrained, and they found it difficult to recapture the honesty of their first, spontaneous conversation about Blythe. She tried also to talk with Cutler on the one occasion she saw him, but that, too, was unavailing. Cutler was his usual charming, gallant self, amusing her with small talk and inconsequential gossip. But Dulcie wanted him to talk with her about serious matters. She wanted to know about his brothers, his feelings, about Blythe, about his loyalty to Adam—all things she could not directly ask a man.

Still unsatisfied, she made a round of visits to the neighborhood women. At each house she subtly turned the subject to the Klan. Her ear keen for any nuance, any change from previous attitudes, she listened. And there was a difference. She couldn't quite define it, but there was a slight closing off. Though the women talked, Dulcie from long experience with teatime gossip was immediately sensitive to the nearly indiscernible restraint the women imposed upon themselves. The more she listened, the more hemmed in she felt, no longer able to distinguish what she actually heard in the voices from what she imagined or feared.

As if running from the gathering flood of disapproval and criticism she believed her neighbors would pour down upon Adam and herself, she threw all her energies into planning and building Kyra's school. There alone she allowed herself to express some of the defiance that was building in her against the neighbors she had always thought of as friends. If they were going to talk about her family, condemn the Tremains, let them have something substantial to whisper about. She'd give them a darky school, and put it right under their pseudo-aristocratic noses.

Once she had begun the project, she seemed unable to stop. She worked through the days and well into the early evening nearly every day. She was exhausted when she returned to the house at night. And then she often sought a time to be alone. She didn't even allow Adam to invade the solitary time she commandeered for herself, for it was then she permitted her doubts and fears to have some reign again. Blindly she was trying to find her way to standing by Adam's side bravely, and to join with him in fighting for a new order in the South. Her mind told her it must be done and that she wanted to do it. Her emotions told her she was afraid and wanted only to seek comfort and security.

And her sentiment told her that by helping Adam stir the County against the Klan, she would be cutting herself free from her past, her girlhood, the people she had grown up with and loved. Admirers who had stolen a kiss in the folly on a warm summer's night might now be among those who wore hooded sheets. She was happy in her ignorance of who the hooded men were, but she knew a part of her would be gone forever once she started to hold the dinner parties Adam wanted. She knew Adam. Once he had begun, nothing would stop him. He was one of those rare people who recognize truth and, no matter how painful it is, pursue it to the finish. She wasn't sure she had that kind of courage or vision.

The school building progressed. Dulcie took part in every aspect of it, including the buying of supplies. She told herself she went to Albert Seldon's general store because Apollo and Kyra needed her guidance, but still she admitted that she was more interested in hearing what the people there had to say. It was her way of gauging the temper of the times.

It was a hot, dry autumn afternoon. Kyra and Beau seemed to be equally excited, Kyra because she was thinking about her school, and Beau because he loved to ride in the two-seated farm wagon. Apollo was driving them to Seldon's store. "Miz Tremain, do you think those supplies we ordered have come in yet? Mr. Whitelaw promised them faithfully last week, and he hadn't received them then."

"He sent word that they are in," Dulcie assured her, reaching out automatically to keep Beau from falling as he leaned over to watch the wagon wheels go around. "He had only to make a trip to Savannah to pick them up."

"Let's see now, you ordered pencils, paper, chalk, ink, pens—"

"Not to mention readers, arithmetics, and penman-ship books."

"And a geography?" Kyra asked anxiously. "Did you tell him to get a geography? I want these children to know where they are in relation to the rest of the world."

Dulcie chuckled. "Yes, I ordered several of every-thing. You certainly are ambitious, Kyra. These boys and girls will know more about the world than most of the adults hereabouts. I still don't have a good idea where France is, even though I traveled there before the War."

Kyra said eagerly, "It has the Atlantic on one side, the Mediterranean Sea on the other, and it's bordered by Spain, Italy, Germany, Switzerland, and Belgium."

"Do-o-o-o tell!" Apollo turned to grin at Kyra, add-ing teasingly, "Sho' you didn't leave out Affica?"

"Of course I left it out, Apollo, it doesn't border on France. Besides, it's pronounced Af-ri-ca. Africa."

"Yes, ma'am, Africa." Still grinning, Apollo returned his attention to the horse.

Beau patted Dulcie on the arm to get her attention. "Mama, when I get big will Daddy take me to Af-ri-ca?"

Dulcie smiled at her sturdy three-year-old with the soft black curls and the blue eyes so much like Adam's, proud of Beau's good vocabulary and ready compre-hension of adult conversation. "It won't surprise me if he does," she said. "But that's not a promise, now."

"Peggy's granddaddy got stealed out of Africa. She said so."

"That wasn't very nice, was it, for someone to steal him?"

Beau's eyes were round with indignation. "No. It was naughty!"

They were overtaking the Tweed sisters, and Apollo stopped the wagon near them. Quickly Kyra scrambled into the driver's seat beside Apollo, with Beau squirm-ing in delight between them. Tiny Phoebe hopped up spryly, her ascent interrupted at the last moment as Zenobia gave her a boost.

"Gracious, sister," Phoebe protested. "You nearly threw me over the seat!"

"Ah just don't know mah own stren'th," said Zenobia placidly, settling beside her sister.

"How are you coming on your book, Miss Zenobia?" Dulcie asked.

"Mah book?" Zenobia looked blank, her faded blue eyes startled.

"Your book about Papa's life, sister," prompted Phoebe.

"Oh. Ah haven't found too much time to work on it lately, we've just been so busy in the house." In a whisper she added, "Housecleanin' time, you know."

As it had been a hot autumn, and most ladies chose a cooler season to houseclean, it was Dulcie's turn to be surprised. Zenobia went on, "We are just throwin' out a good many of those ol' things Papa insisted on keepin' around. It's high time we got new curtains fo' the kitchen, so we decided to walk down to the store an' order some this very day."

"White netting, with ruffles," said Phoebe dreamily.

"An' a new blue checkered tablecloth and napkins. So we can provide a little change when Mr. Miller dines with us." She cast a sly glance at her sister.

"But sister," said Phoebe, rosily, "that's only once in a while." She said confidentially to Dulcie, "We just got tired of the same old things that have been in the house for fifty years, so we decided we'd treat ourselves to new."

"*And* we are givin' serious thought to a new Oriental rug for the parlor floor."

"But we haven't *decided*. We might just *ask* today."

"How is Mr. Miller working out?" Dulcie asked, thinking of the attractive young man who now farmed the Tweed property.

"Oh, he's ever so nice to us, an' he seems to be a

good planter—is it planter now, sister, or would he be a —"

"A farmer," Zenobia said with a touch of disdain. "He is makin' very wise use of Papa's land. It takes me back to the days when Papa was still alive, with everythin' green and flourishin'. Yes, it does. He lives by himself, back in one of the cabins."

"—And we feel sorry for him, having to cook all his own meals, so occasionally we ask him to dine," Phoebe finished triumphantly. "Oh, we are very circumspect, Mrs. Tremain, we chaperone each other!"

Dulcie stifled a desire to giggle, and agreed that lone ladies could not be too careful, for the neighbors' eyes were sharp.

They had arrived at the general store. As they dismounted from the wagon, Phoebe murmured to Zenobia that there was that Todd Saunders drunk again.

"An' durin' the daytime!" Zenobia hissed. "Now Ah want you to be very careful what you say to him, sister. You know what he did to that sister of his. We don't want to inflame him."

Phoebe drew her tiny little body up to her tallest, still not quite reaching five feet. "Ah nevah inflamed anybody in mah life!"

Todd made an exaggerated bow, ushering the Tweed sisters gallantly into the store. To Dulcie he nodded unsmiling, murmuring her name.

Cheerfully Dulcie said, "Well, good afternoon, Todd. How are you feeling today?"

"Well enough, for a sick man." In some subtle way he contrived to let Dulcie know that his illness was as much her fault as the Yankees'.

She made a polite reply and stepped into the gloom of the store. At the far end was a long counter that on Saturday nights served as a pulpit from which the Reverend Jabez Hooks preached. Behind it now was Nemo Whitelaw, his wire-rimmed glasses slid down his bony nose, figuring up a grocery bill on a piece of butcher paper. Watching him closely, clasping her

fingers and unclasping them, was Lydia Saunders, and
with her was Addie Jo.

During the week the right-hand end of the counter
formed a bar, where now Cedric Whitaker and Billy
Bob Acton sat drinking. As Dulcie accustomed her
eyes to the dimness, Todd joined them, and three pairs
of eyes slued her way. Cedric and Billy tipped their hats
and spoke to her, but neither stood, or relinquished
his grip on his drink. Dulcie had almost the feeling of
interfering with something she knew nothing of. It was
an unpleasant, almost shivery sensation.

Was this a meeting of the Klan, she wondered. There
were fewer men here than she had been led to believe
belonged in the Klan. Maybe it was an officers' meeting.
No, instinct told her, none of these men had the hard-
ness, the grudge, the determination that should char-
acterize the leaders of such a vengeful group. But they
were obviously together in *something,* some activity
more binding than drinking away an afternoon.

Maybe they were united in disapproval of her, feeling that as a woman she was attending to situations
better left to the man of the house. Perhaps they were
jealous of Adam and his wealth. That might be it. God
knew they were all poor enough, even Cedric Whitaker,
who along with his brothers was land poor. And they
probably did resent a man of good looks, wealth, and
influence such as Adam had in abundance.

It could be these very men—Cedric, Todd, Billy,
even Nemo Whitelaw—whom Adam was speaking
against in the Union League. And they knew it, of
course they would know it if they had ears, and they
would hate Adam for that, and hate her too.

But these men are all my friends, she thought in dismay. We grew up together, played and flirted together.
We even lived with Cedric's family and now he's glaring at me as at an enemy.

She could not stand his silent scrutiny any longer.
She said, "Cedric, how is Pearl getting along? I hope
she's not having any more trouble now."

Cedric's face relaxed and he smiled at her. Gone was the abstracted glare, the rigid posture. He said, "She's much better these days, thank you Dulcie. The doctor was out just last week, and he says she'll be able to carry the baby to term."

"I'm so glad. Pearl has had such a hard time of it. I'll try to get over to see her on Thursday or Friday. Will you tell her I asked after her."

"I'll tell her," he said, smiling.

"How's your new leg, Billy Bob?"

Billy Bob Acton tended to be sheepish around women. Now he blushed and looked in another direction. He said, "Aww, it's too damn—too dang long. Makes me walk all hippity-hop. See?" He got down off his stool and took a few steps around the room, exaggerating his ill-fitting prosthesis, making a joke of his loss and its inept replacement. The men laughed, elbowing each other, telling him to do it again.

Dulcie, watching him walk, saw nothing funny about it. "Billy, if you'll come down to Mossrose, we have a fine carpenter who could shorten that for you and make it fit properly. Or our cobbler could build up the shoe on your other foot so you'd be more comfortable."

Todd said, laughing and coughing, "Ol' Billabob could wear high heels an' be a real la-a-ady!" Whooping, he clung to Cedric.

On Billy's face there flashed hope, then instant rejection. "Don't want to put nobody to trouble ovah me," he mumbled, and resumed his seat.

"Trouble? For an old friend? We'll be glad to help, if you'll let us. Why not come down tomorrow, and bring Birdie for a visit?"

He looked away again. "Well, Ah might." Fiercely he turned to Todd. "Jees' Chris', Todd, why don't y'all go outside t'cough?"

The Tweeds' white heads bobbed around here and there, whispering, inspecting a barrel of apples, pinching sweet potatoes for freshness.

Nemo Whitelaw said gruffly, "Hands off the merchandise!" before he looked up. Then, apologetic, he said, "Oh. Ah didn't see who it was, Miss Zenobia, Miss Phoebe. You go on an' look. Ah'll be with you in a minnit, soon's Ah get done with Miz Saunders."

Addie Joe's voice came snippily. "Mr. Whitelaw, you know I was next! I got in here right after Mother Saunders!"

Whitelaw held up his hands, his fingers spread apart for her benefit. "Ah only got two han's, Missus. Y'all goin' to have to wait a bit. Now theah's youah pahcel, Miz Saunders. Jes' carry it by that string an' you'll make it home all right." He raised his head to address Zenobia and nodded to Dulcie and Beau.

"I am next, Mr. Whitelaw, and I'll have five pounds of flour."

Whitelaw ignored Addie Jo. "What'll it be today, Miss Zenobia? Must be somethin' pretty special to bring you an' Miss Phoebe out."

"Oh, yes, it is—" Phoebe began.

"We came to order curtains an' a tablecloth," Zenobia finished. Then her face tightened as she became aware of the stares of her neighbors. Billy nudged Cedric with his elbow, grinning; Todd's eyes caught those of his mother, and something like resentment flashed between them. Lydia stopped in her tracks, the heavy bundle dangling from her hand, and looked inquiringly at the sisters.

She said pleasantly, "Well, it's nice to hear that somebody has had a windfall! Miss Zenobia, did you sell your book already?"

Phoebe started to answer for her. "Oh, no, Lydia, she's still working on it. We just—well, we *need*—"

Zenobia's full height was somewhat more than Lydia's. She stood tall and said imperiously, "We ah spendin' the Tweed money, Lydia Saunders, an' we considah it Tweed business exclusively."

Lydia snorted. "I thought the Tweed money had

gone during the War, just like the Saunders money, but I see I was mistaken. Please excuse my jumping to conclusions."

"Of course, Lydia," said Phoebe, her sweet face completely guileless. "Ah haven't seen dear Blossom for so long—is she farin' well? An' the children?"

"Oh, yes, everyone at our house has been in good health this fall—knock wood. And Jan has gotten another room added to the house, so we feel less crowded."

The sisters exchanged a knowing look. Zenobia said sweetly, "And your other daughter—Blythe? The one who lives out West. Have you heard from her lately?"

Dulcie, her attention riveted on Blythe's mother, caught the flicker of fear on Mrs. Saunders's face before she replied smoothly, "Only last month we got a nice letter from her. She and her husband are so happy together in the new land."

"I don't suppose there are any little ones on the way yet," said Zenobia.

"Well, she doesn't *say* so, but—" Her laughter trilled out happily. "—you know how girls are, they don't want to worry Mama. I wouldn't be *surprised* if any time—"

At the bar, somebody's fist crashed down heavily; Todd Saunders got up, clomped past the chatting ladies, and went outside.

"Dulcie, I didn't mean to ignore you, child," Lydia said brightly. "We're just talking a mile a minute here—" She stopped at the closed look on Dulcie's face. "How is your dear father today?"

Dulcie found herself nearly bursting with opposing emotions toward Lydia Saunders. With desperate haste she looked around the store, smiled quickly at Lydia, and busied herself at a table of whatnots and play-pretties. Her hand closed over a delicate porcelain figurine. The edges of the finely worked skirt of the figurine dug into the palm of her hand.

I'm going mad, she thought, fighting to control the agitation that thundered inside her, beating against her temples. All she could see was Blythe, Blythe as she might now be. And here stood her mother, a woman who had come through the War unscathed.

Calming slightly, she tried to be impassive, reasonable. Lydia Saunders had suffered the loss of her husband; her two sons had come home nearly invalids. Todd would never completely recover. And she had had to sell her house to a Yankee at a drastic financial loss.

Dulcie dared a quick look at Lydia. She had survived; she had good health and a tough-minded outlook; and she had had a house to sell.

The anger returned. No reason, no twist of logic could justify in Dulcie's mind what Lydia had done. Dulcie balked at the thought, then forced herself to pursue it. Lydia Saunders had sold her own daughter to the Yankee captain to save her own skin. She had survived; she had her house and her health in exchange for a young girl's innocence. She had thrown Blythe out on the mercies of a world that had no mercy toward a fallen woman. And now she dared to stand here and subtly criticize the elderly Tweed sisters for replacing fifty-year-old curtains.

Dulcie held up the figurine, amazed at her own capacity for deceit. She hated what Lydia had done, but she wasn't going to let Lydia or anyone else know it. She would maintain the façade as everyone else did. If Lydia could sell her daughter to protect herself, she could do worse to Dulcie and Adam if one of her sons was a Klansman.

Dulcie did not dare let on that she knew about Blythe, for that would tear away the mask of friendship. She began to understand for herself what Adam had been telling her. There was no way to hide from what the War had done. They still had to fight.

She turned to Lydia, made a complimentary remark about the porcelain figure, then said in as friendly a voice as she could muster, "Daddy's improving, Mrs. Saunders. Mama is very lonely for company, but she can't quite leave him yet."

"I'll get over soon, but we've been so busy lately." Lydia directed her gaze at Beau. "He looks sturdy and healthy. Just see that beautiful skin! Oh, my, Dulcie, what I wouldn't give to have some of those roses in *my* cheeks now!" She laughed girlishly.

Beau tugged at Dulcie's hand. "Mama, I don't have roses on my face, do I?"

"No, honey, it's just a grown-up expression that means something nice."

Phoebe said, her eyes twinkling, "We've been hearing about your caller, Lydia. In fact, Mr. Miller sang you very high praise only the other evening at dinner."

Lydia's tanned, leathery face acquired a pleased, embarrassed glow; and back again in his corner, her son laughed unpleasantly, ending in a spasm of coughing while his drinking companions pounded him on the back. Lydia said, "You could hardly call Mr. Miller a *caller*, Miss Phoebe, just more of a friend."

Phoebe in her innocent way said, "Oh, yes, he is much younger than you are, Ah'm sure." She leaned forward and whispered loudly, "But isn't it *exciting?* Ah have noticed mah own heart beatin' a little faster whenevah he's neah."

Addie Jo's nasal voice cut through again. "Mr. Whitelaw, while these ladies are just standin' there talking, you could be stacking up my grocery order. I'll start with six of those red apples—"

Whitelaw heaved a sigh of disgust and found her the six worst apples in the barrel. When her order was complete, he wrote down the figure in Hook's debt book and clapped it shut.

"If you don't mind, Mr. Whitelaw, I'll just have a look at that figure you wrote down. I b'lieve you made a mistake and put it down wrong."

Dulcie drew in a quick breath, still smiling as Lydia and the sisters talked around her, and listened alertly to Addie Jo and Whitelaw. His expression, she noticed, did not change. "Ah don't make mistakes. Your ordah was six dollahs an' thutty-eight cents, Missus. 'Nother round, gent'men? Comin' right up." Quickly he moved to the bar and poured more drinks, writing them down in the book.

Addie Jo stood uncertain for a while, then as Whitelaw remained to chat with the men, she reluctantly picked up her purchases. While the Tweed sisters were debating over samples of curtain material, fingering them and discussing relative wearability, Addie Jo and her mother-in-law left. Dulcie moved forward to stand at the counter.

Whitelaw reached into a large glass jar and held out a yellow-striped stick of candy, just out of Beau's reach.

"Mama, may I have it?" the little boy asked eagerly.

"Yes, Beau, you may have one stick. Mr. Whitelaw, please add that to my bill today."

"Oh, that's free, Miz Tremain. Ah got a mighty big ordah fo' you this week. Them things all come in, the books an' ink an' all."

Dulcie smiled tightly. After what she had observed with Addie Jo, she was beginning to wonder just who was the Albert Seldon who was supposed to own this general store. Was there really such a man? Or was it someone else? And what were the exact roles played by the Reverend Jabez Hooks and Nemo Whitelaw in connection with Seldon? Whitelaw was cheating someone, with his figures scrawled in a black book so quickly closed. Was he cheating the man called Seldon, or was he cheating Hooks, or his customers? Or all of them? Or was there another purpose behind this store?

Whitelaw stood poised, eager to serve, pencil in hand. "An' now what kind o' groceries y'all need today?"

"Just the school supplies, Mr. Whitelaw. And I would like an itemized bill, please."

"Oh, Ah already got it all figgered up fo' you, Missus. Comes to one hunnert an' fo'teen dollahs."

Dulcie spoke calmly but firmly, as she often had to an obtuse servant. "Possibly I didn't make myself clear, Mr. Whitelaw. I insist on an itemized bill."

"Well, you can see Ah'm pretty busy today. Why'n't you jes' have youah boy take everythin' along, an' Ah'll have the bill fo' you t'morra."

Dulcie's golden eyes flashed fire. "I want an itemized bill now. I will check it for myself."

Whitelaw's lip lifted in a sneer. "Think youah mighty high sassiety, don'tcha, Missus."

Dulcie said nothing, but her eyes never moved from Whitelaw's face.

After a few moments his gaze dropped. Hurriedly he began writing down items and figures. "It's a hunnert an' twenty-five dollahs. Ah fo'got to add in that box o' chalk."

"A box of chalk is eleven dollars? Give me the bill, please." Dulcie held out her hand insistently. He gave up the bit of paper with greatest reluctance.

Quickly Dulcie looked over the items, added up the figures, and placed the correct total at the bottom. "I'll just hold onto this while Apollo and Kyra check the order and load up everything," she said pleasantly.

"Ah need that fo' mah records."

Dulcie smiled at him. "Mr. Whitelaw, you aren't going to need this, for I'm paying you cash and you are going to give me a receipt for this itemized statement."

"Nobody pays cash heah," he said stubbornly.

"Yes, I have noticed that, and I have wondered why not." She leaned forward, her gaze intent on him, while Kyra called out the order and Apollo checked it and loaded the wagon. She became acutely aware of the men watching her from the bar. They all charged things, she knew, having seen Whitelaw write the amount of their drinks down in the book. "Perhaps you could explain to me the advantages of your system, Mr. Whitelaw. I might be making a silly mistake, paying you now. Do your customers save money by buying on credit, or—"

Whitelaw seemed uncomfortable, sweat beading his narrow forehead. "That's it, Missus, we give a discount when y'all buy on credit."

"How very considerate," she said warmly. "And when are one's payments due?"

His eyes slid away and came back briefly to hers. "Well, jes' whenevah sumbuddy can pay, is all."

"Not something regular that they must pay every week?"

"Oh, no, nothin' like that."

"Forgive me, I'm just a woman and I'm not familiar with men's business—but what happens if a person can't pay?"

Whitelaw's fingers were drumming on the countertop now. "We work it out, Missus. Now if y'all ah done, Ah'll put you right down in the book—"

"Ever' thing's heah, Miz Tremain," Apollo said.

Dulcie laid down her money. "Your arithmetic is very bad, Mr. Whitelaw. The bill is ninety-nine dollars and two cents. Plus a penny for my son's candy."

"Ah said that's free!"

Dulcie said softly, "Mr. Whitelaw, I wouldn't want to place my family in the position of owing you one cent. Here is the cash. Please count it and sign my receipt."

With angry flourishes Whitelaw did as she asked, and she left the store.

After the wagon had pulled away, Whitelaw treated himself to a glassful from the nearest keg. Billy laughed. "Sho' is a silly female, ain't she? Spendin' the Cap'n's money so free."

"I don't take to that Tremain a-tall," Todd said bluntly, sloshing down the last of his whisky. "Hard for me to believe he was ever a blockade runner. If you ask me, I'd say he was a draft dodger living in New York and coining money while the rest of us were starving and fighting Yankees in the rain."

"Rabble-rouser," said Cedric contemptuously. "Always tryin' to stir up somethin'. Hear he wants the Loyal League to ride against the Klan? Tell he don't belong here." The men snickered, exchanging knowing glances.

Billy said, "Well, what'n hell else could you expect, when his li'l woman's lost all her fem-eye-ninity? Orderin' the menfolk around, doin' men's work, she prob'ly gives him shinplasters fo' spendin' money." His dig was rewarded with guffaws and slaps on knees.

The Tweed sisters were listening avidly. Phoebe said, "Ah just don't believe she undahstands business, do you, sister?"

"Either that, sister, or she is a *very* peculiar individual."

Whitelaw slapped his glass down on the bar. Turning to the Tweeds he said, "Aha, goin' to buy curtains today, you said? Ah'll have to ordah 'em fo' you. Take about a week. Y'all goin' to charge, or you payin' cash too?"

Somehow, the men at the bar and the two white-haired sisters found that irresistibly funny, and they laughed and laughed.

CHAPTER SEVENTEEN

It was near the end of October, 1868, that Dulcie finally had the first of Adam's dinner parties. With cynical bemusement she thought it was fitting that this first party should be held near Halloween. Had it not been so horrible a thought she would have laughed to think that at her beautifully set table would be men who perhaps hours later would ride howling through the countryside with masks on their faces, the horns of devils on their heads, and torches blazing in their hands. A dinner party, she thought, with death as the dessert?

But once she was committed to the parties, she poured all her energies into the effort. On this crisp October night, an orange moon hung low in the sky, and in Mossrose the soft lights of welcome shone. There were bouquets of flowers on every table. Candles glowed in the dining room. And Dulcie awaited her guests, wondering who was truly friend and who only wore the face of a friend.

She looked at Jem and Patricia. They were excited at the prospect of having guests in their new and beautiful house. Dulcie wondered how they would look if she told them the true purpose of this gathering. Birdie and Billy Bob Acton, Glenn Saunders and Addie Jo, Brock and Cutler Whitaker; Marcia Baxter, the daughter of Osgood of the dry goods store, to be Cutler's dinner partner; Nancy Kane, Dulcie's dressmaker, for Brock; Ralph Miller, the tenant farmer on the Tweeds' property, and Enid to keep him company—her guests. She shivered slightly, not knowing if she was going to get through this evening or not.

She was wearing a second-best party gown of crack-

ling amber taffeta, frothy with cream-colored lace at
the low neckline. Her auburn hair was swept to one
side, falling in curls behind her left ear. Placed in the
curls was a spray of golden strawflowers. Even to her
own critical eyes she looked poised and in command.
She smiled at herself in the mirror, then glanced at the
reflection of Adam and her parents behind her. Looks
were so deceiving. Life was so deceiving.

The guests began to arrive promptly at eight o'clock.
Enid Whitaker and Cutler arrived first, closely followed
by Nancy Kane. With Glenn and Addie Jo was Marcia
Baxter. Glenn and Addie Jo, Dulcie decided, after a
few years of marriage not only looked alike but acted
alike. They were both ash blond, with pale-blue eyes
and dissatisfied mouths. Constantly one turned to the
other for confirmation: "And I just told her what was
what, didn't I, Glenn?" "You certainly did, Addie Jo."
Or one would interrupt the other, then, remembering
politeness, insist that the first one continue. Much of
their conversation centered on the marvelous deeds
and sayings of their sons Zane and Noel, ages six and
five.

A trying couple, well deserving of each other,
thought Dulcie, and then quickly remembering her
task, tried to imagine Glenn riding with the Klansmen.
She could not. It was too laughable to be taken seriously. Just as quickly she sobered, and remembered
what Adam had said could happen to people once they
had put on a mask and felt they had a power because
of it. Was it possible that Glenn, who could not string
three words together with grace, could don a horned
mask and become—she turned away, unwilling to complete the thought.

Her eyes sought the rest of the group. Birdie and
Billy seemed content to sit apart, Birdie and Enid
chatting on a sofa, and Billy, Cutler, and Adam discussing horses. Nancy sat on the edge of a chair, her
back straight and her expression tense, evidently un-

easy here, although Dulcie had tried her best. Brock
and Ralph Miller had come in the door together, and
Dulcie noted they still stayed close to each other. Without trying to figure out why, Dulcie was uncomfortable
at the apparent friendship between the two men.

Brock seemed very nervous, going around and shaking hands with the men, always returning to engage in
quick, whispered conversations with Miller, sitting
down briefly, then standing as Josh, the butler, handed
him a drink. His speech was slightly impaired, probably
from drinks before leaving home.

Miller was a muscular man of around thirty, with
waving black hair and a pleasant smile. He did not
seem to welcome Brock's constant attention, and diffi-
dently took a chair next to Jem and submitted himself
to a cross-examination.

Jem's speech had returned nearly to normal, with
only an occasional hesitation. "And tell me, Mr. Miller,
what did you do before the great War?"

"I was a planter, sir, not like yourself, of course. I
had a small holding, about a hundred acres, twenty
miles north of here. I grew vegetables for the city
markets. There was hardly enough land to plant one
of the staple crops, but I got along, and I had my
dreams for the future. Then I went to serve the Confederacy. When I came home there wasn't much left.
My slaves were free, and the rail and water transporta-
tion I had relied on was not available."

Perhaps it was a sound in the tone of his voice, or
a word spoken in a certain way, but Dulcie began to
pay closer attention to what Ralph Miller was saying
to her father. Almost hopefully she looked at him,
wishing it would be Miller who was a Klansman. He
did not wear the face of a friend; he was a stranger,
and strangers could be imagined to do anything.

Miller went on, his voice slightly lower and with an
edge of bitterness to it. "What can a man do when
other men have the power to take everything he owns

from him." Then he laughed a little. "You know, Mr.
Moran, I shot at Yankees for nearly four years, and I
aimed to kill every bloody one I came in contact with,
but I tell you, I never hated them like I did right after
the War. What they called peace was the damnedest
farce I ever saw. Still is."

Jem nodded agreement, and Miller said, "So now
I haven't any acreage, and not too many dreams for
the future. I work for Mr. Albert Seldon."

Dulcie's ears perked up.

"The man who bought the Saunders out and re-
named their plantation Green Vale?"

"Yes, but of course it's the Tweeds' plantation I
run."

"He owns the Tweed land too?"

Miller looked quickly at Jem, and Dulcie tried to
seem as though she were not listening. To her, Miller
looked suspicious and deceitful. He said, "I can't say
as I know. There's some arrangement between the
Tweed ladies and Mr. Seldon."

"Personally, I don't trust Seldon," said Jem, who
had never seen Seldon. "Something is wrong with a
man who doesn't tend to his own land."

"I've met him once," said Miller. "He was just
another Yankee to me. He was rather abrupt and
businesslike, had no time for talkin' or visiting, but he
gave me license to raise what crops I thought would
do best. I couldn't have asked for a fairer shake than
the man giving me a free hand. Aside from that, and
a check every month, we haven't had further contact.
So far, he lets me do my job, and he's kept his share
of the bargain."

Jem grumbled beneath his breath. "I still say there's
something peculiar about a man who doesn't see to
his own land. What's he want it for? Why? That's
what I want to know."

Patricia hurried to Jem's side as his voice rose. "Jem,
dahlin', Ah told you theah was to be no arguin' politics
tonight."

"I wasn't arguing politics, Patsy. Go sit down. This is man talk."

Patricia smiled sweetly at Ralph Miller. "Ah hope you'll excuse mah husband an' me, Mistah Millah, but it's time we retiahed." She waved at Josh. "Take Mistah Moran to his room, please, Josh."

"Patsy," said Jem, his face reddening. "Woman, I've never embarrassed you in front of guests, but if you have that buck lay a hand on my chair, I'll cause a ruckus to bring the roof down."

"Jem!"

Jem's eyes fixed hard on her until she straightened up, standing meekly beside him instead of leaning protectively over his chair. Then, as if nothing had occurred, he looked at Ralph Miller. "It's been good talking to you, Miller. Stop by some afternoon, and we'll discuss crops. My wife and I retire early, I hope you'll forgive us." He wheeled his chair deftly through the room, pausing to say goodnight to the guests along the way. Patricia followed behind him.

Dulcie nodded at Josh, and within seconds dinner was announced. With only a few mishaps, everyone found his partner for the night. Brock Whitaker seemed to grow more and more nervous. And with it his physical appearance became nearly repulsive. He couldn't stop yawning. His nose was running, and he continually ran his sleeve across his sweating face. Nancy Kane would not go near him, let alone allow him to escort her into the dining room.

Dulcie looked to Adam for rescuing and found it as he gallantly took one lady on each arm and walked proudly, complimenting them both profusely as he led them to their seats. He quickly returned to the living room for Brock.

They sat down to a sumptuous dinner of roast duckling, fresh-caught bass, peas and potatoes grown on Mossrose, hot buttered biscuits, sweets and relishes, crowned with an iced cream delicacy and small, frosted cakes. Each of the party seemed delighted at the dinner so similar to one that might have been served before the War. Dulcie relaxed slightly and basked in the compliments.

Only Brock Whitaker did not participate in the repast. He sat there with the air of a man about to fly to pieces. He barely touched food or spoke to Nancy Kane, preferring to devote full attention to his glass. Before the meal he had downed a number of whisky highballs. Dulcie had seen him take only a biscuit and a glass of wine, ignoring all the inviting food set before him. Everyone knew he drank to excess, and Dulcie had seen Brock drinking on other occasions, but never as he was doing this evening. He seemed to want, perhaps need, to be intoxicated.

As Brock's drunkenness and his restlessness and perspiring increased, Dulcie heard Adam speak, almost with relief in spite of his subject. "It looks as though we may get some unexpected aid from the Congress. I recently received a letter from Rod Courtland. He had just returned from Washington, and he tells me the Ku Klux Klan has made itself so noteworthy across the South that the Congress is talking about intervening."

Addie Jo looked up from her food, smiling coyly at Adam. "Surely you're not going to talk politics with the ladies still at the table, Adam. With all these beautiful gowns and smilin' faces surroundin' you, I'm sure you can think of something more interestin' to talk about. Don't you think he could, Glenn?"

Adam laughed. "You are unquestionably right, Addie Jo. I doubt that I should ever run out of thoughts and comments, considering the array of beauty here tonight, but I choose politics as a compliment to that beauty. Unless we return the security of road and home to Chatham County, you ladies can't be abroad safely, and then all of us men are denied the lovely sight."

Brock stood wavering, bracing himself against the table. "Wha' d'you care 'bout ladies, Tremain? All you evah care 'bout is the Klan. Can't shut your mouth— Klan."

Nancy Kane turned away.

"Sit down, Brock, you're drunk," Billy Bob laughed, rudely reaching over Nancy Kane's head, and shoving Brock back into his seat. He glanced grinning at the others sitting at the table. Finally his eyes rested on Adam. "But that don't make him wrong. What is it with you, Tremain? A man'd think you got a single-handed crusade goin' against the Klan. It don't seem to me they done much hahm to anybody. Why ah you on theah tail?"

"You don't consider what was done to Ruel Jordan much harm, Billy?"

Billy raised his hands. "Well, now everybody thought highly of Ruel. You know that. Nobody wanted t'see him dead, but sho' as hell ain't worth all this fuss. After all, it wasn't like he was a white man."

"It does seem to me," Ralph Miller added, "that a good many of the Yankee agencies are designed to help the nigger, and there aren't too many that give a damn about the white planter. I'm not backing the Klan, I want you to be clear on that, Captain Tremain, but it does seem to me that they are the only group that cares to look after white interests."

Glenn said, "I heard of a Klan den, next county over, that gave money to the widow of a Confederate lieutenant. If it hadn't been for them, she and her five babies would have been put off their property and left to starve. The Yankees don't care about women like her. What was so bad about that?"

"Glenn!" Dulcie said. "You must realize that the Klan robs and steals to get the money they so generously give. How could you ask what is wrong with that? How much would you praise their activities if they were stealing from you and Addie Jo?"

Glenn's expression was one of pained silence. "They would not be stealing from Addie Jo and me. We are white."

Forgetting decorum, Dulcie picked up her wine glass and drained the remainder in it. "Oh, Glenn, how can you even sit there and have the nerve to say something like that?"

"Like what? I said nothing that isn't true."

"Then it is all right with you if the Klan steals from the Negroes, who have virtually nothing?"

"Nothin'!" Billy chimed in. "They got themselves theah own God-damn bank, an' it's full to overflowin'. They got whatevah they want. Ah got three niggers workin' undah contract fo' me right now, an' every one o' them damn bucks got more'n Birdie an' Ah have. Wheah you been, Dulcie? Them niggers get help from the Freedmen's Bureau, they get food handed out to them, they got theah Yankee henchmen to watch out ovah theah contracts, they got that Yankee Seldon handin' out credit to 'em fo' anything they want. What's Birdie an' I got? Who's lookin' out fo' us?"

Brock Whitaker waved his glass grandly in the air and grandly sang out, "The Klan! Three Cheers fo' the Klan!"

Laughter boiled up around the table, and a semblance of a cheer rose amidst the laughter. Then it quieted, and the group was somber again, all of them looking at Adam and Dulcie.

Ralph Miller spoke first. "I make bold to speak, Captain Tremain, because we have something in common. Neither of us is native to this area. I think, perhaps, you do not fully understand the peculiar problems that beset your neighbors. Perhaps you would do better to live here for a while before you stir up the local politics over an issue that may cause more harm than good."

Adam had listened passively, his face revealing nothing. Now he looked at Ralph Miller. "I think you gentlemen tend to forget that we have lost a war. We are a conquered people. Our only choice is to get along with our conquerers, and rebuild our section of the country. There are only a few avenues open to us in accomplishing this. The primary and most powerful is through the ballot box. No one is going to hear what the South needs or wants until we have representation in Congress again. As long as some of our population continues to fight an undercover war under the banner of the Ku Klux Klan, we aren't going to be respected or heard."

"Who wants to be respected by the damnyankees?" Billy asked.

"Anyone who cares about the South," Adam shot back.

"You're an idealist, Adam," Cutler said quietly, speaking for the first time.

Adam looked at him. "Is there any man who would not, in his dreams, wish to live an ideal life, Cutler? Perhaps we can never achieve that, but if we don't strive for it, we'll never even approach it. Slowly we'll all melt back into the chaos of a primitive past."

Billy guffawed. "You sure do have purty talk a-plenty, Tremain. But Ah'm wonderin' how purty youah talk would be if you didn't have this fine house an' money to do whatevah you damn well pleased? How'd you like t'walk around in mah shoes? Think you'd be so all-fired eagah to have the Klan disappear then?"

"I hope I would. But however I'd feel personally, I believe I would still respect the Constitution of this nation, and I believe I'd want to see the South become whole and strong again, and to that end I would fight the Klan."

Brock raised his wobbling head. With great effort he said, "Klan p'tects the Cons'tution. Rights—whi' rights."

"There is no mention of *white* rights in the Constitution," Adam said.

"There is!" Brock shouted. "America's white man's land."

"Then how do you account for the presence of the black man?" Adam asked.

Billy said acidly, "We brought 'em heah t'do ouah work. We brought 'em 'cause they was meant to be the servants of a superiah race, an' that's the way nature meant it t'be."

"Well, gentlemen, ladies, I see there is little point in

continuing this discussion tonight. We are in strong opposition to each other. But I will say this. I hope all of you realize how serious a problem the activities of the Klan have become. There is talk about forming a Congressional Committee to investigate the Klan. Too many heinous acts have been perpetrated by the Klan throughout the South to allow this organization to continue. While you, our neighbors, may feel the need of protection by a force like the Klan, there are many more men both North and South determined to end this attempted reign of terror. I suggest you think about it."

Brock Whitaker stood swaying uncertainly. "I take offense, Tremain. Man has t'defend his honor." He stopped speaking, his eyes were not focused. He fought for control, squinting at the bright lamps. He was sweating profusely, his face pallid and shiny. "I—I wanna chal-challen—" He lost his balance and lurched forward, bumping the table.

Cutler jumped up from his seat and took his brother's arm. "Hey, boy, better get you outside."

Brock growled, "No-o-o! Lemme go. Challenge—'im."

"You don't want to challenge your host. Come on, outside. You'll feel a lot better."

"Outside . . ." Brock murmured. He wiped his sleeve across his face, clinging to Cutler. His other hand he pressed tightly against his stomach. "Got to get t'Tully's," he said so thickly that no one understood him.

Cutler asked him to repeat, but he wouldn't. "Well, let me help you home, Brock."

"Get your God-damn hands offa me," Brock snarled. "Take care m'self."

Clutching at chair backs and finally supporting himself along the wall, Brock made his way out, with Cutler and Adam following close behind.

Adam called to Saul to hitch the plantation buggy to take Brock home. Instead, Brock staggered out into the darkness and managed to find his mount. From the saddle he pulled a rifle. Unsteadily he pointed it toward the open doorway and the figures of Cutler and Adam. "I can take care m'self."

Cutler and Adam said nothing, then as Brock attempted to gain his saddle and failed, Cutler said cheerfully that he'd like to go with Brock for the evening.

"Huh! You? What I want you for? You don' know nothin'—can' help me." Suddenly, Brock patted at his pockets, then rooted through his vest pockets. Failing to find what he sought, he turned to Adam, the rifle once more in his hand. His ghastly pale face glistened in the flickering torchlight. "Ol' buddy," he said to Adam, and essayed a smile, "C'n you len' me tw— twenny dollars? Pay you back Tuesday, Wensdy fo' sure."

Adam looked at Cutler.

"Brock, what do you need twenty dollars for? You're goin' home, aren't you?"

Brock laughed. "You're a shit, Cutler. Dumb shit. I got me a whore—" His laughter was high and thin. "You know my whore, huh, Cutler?"

Cutler's face grew paler than his brother's. His eyes filled with pain, he excused himself. "I'm sorry, Adam, please give my apologies to Dulcie and the others. I— I—" He hurried into the darkness to fetch his horse.

Brock looked after him, then back to Adam. "Brother ain't got no balls. You gonna len' me the money? Or you jus' give t'niggers?"

Adam tossed him a twenty-dollar gold piece. "You have a gracious way of asking for favors, Brock."

"Shiiit! You freeloaded fo' neah two years offa my daddy. You owe me this a hunnerd times over." He mounted somehow and cantered away. Automatically he whipped the horse, keeping his head down to avoid low branches. Before he reached the River Road, however, he jerked his animal to a stop. Then, leaning out perilously as he hung onto the horse's neck, he heaved his burden of whisky, biscuits, and wine onto the road. He wiped his sour mouth with one hand and sat up. Better go on. He started the horse at a sedate walk, then whipped him to a gallop.

Funny. By God, it was funny, but emptying his stomach only made the feeling of sickness worse. His head pounded now, his throat felt raw. He'd give his life for another whisky now, to be sipped slowly, an antidote to the terrible shaking, griping craving he had. Just get to Tully's, they'd fix that for him. But what if Tully's was closed? Or they wouldn't let him have any? What if they were out? Oh, God, what would he do? What would he do?

Go to Baxter's, like he did during the week. Ol' Baxter'd have a box of the little opium pills for him, fifty cents for enough to last ten, twelve days. This time he'd get two boxes, see that he didn't run out this time. Damn stuff was weaker than before, one pill would hardly make a smoke for him. God-damn Tremain, keeping him at the dinner table when he had to have a pipe.

The griping grew worse, and his anxiety increased. A man could gripe to death, oh, what if he did, jouncing along this rough road, the horse's hoofs pounding up into his skull . . .

His flask. He'd rather have the pills, but sometimes whisky calmed the griping till he could get them. Clumsily, holding onto the reins, he uncorked the small, flat bottle and tipped it to his mouth. Whisky gurgled out, warming and cleansing his mouth and his parched throat. Eagerly he sucked, but no more would come out. He shook the flask. Empty. With great care he put the cork in his vest pocket, then heard the metallic clatter as the flask fell to the roadway.

His anxiety—his illness—was mounting. He had to get to Tully's. He whacked the horse, who leaped ahead in startled fashion, nearly unseating him. As the horse galloped, the trees along the black road seemed to soar toward him in rounded gray shapes, shapes that bounded dreamily up and down. He was one with the wild-eyed horse, moving swiftly, unhindered through the damp, velvety night.

There was no moon, and the darkness was cooling and soothing on his hot eyes. Light—light pained as it sparkled. Dark gave anonymity and comfort, an endless cool cloth drawn across the brow, endless. Endless. Cool. Coolcold. Cold. A cold place in the belly. A cramp, a griping cramp that called for heaving when there was nothing to heave. Ride faster, faster, get away from the clamp on the belly, let the damp wind dry the sweat. Let Tully dry the sweat.

Tully. Brock began to laugh, laugh and cry, laugh and cry until the tears streamed down his cheeks. Show Tully. Show him the money and make him hand over the stuff. Plenty of stuff. Plenty of little darkish pills, little round wooden boxes full and spilling over, pills to heat and to suck the vapor up the nostrils with an indrawn breath, suck and suck and then feel it take hold. Feel it grab the shakes like a giant hand a giant hand a giant HAND and stop the shakes. Dry the brow, dry the trickle that ran like a river down the back and the belly, kill the sharp claws that grasped the belly in a vise, just make everything easy, sweet and peaceful and easy.

The horse was lathered and flagging now, but Brock scarcely noticed, for the demon in his belly was eating him. Eating with long sharp teeth, eating him in bloody bites. Dizzily he turned his head aside and retched. Four or five whiskies in two hours had absorbed quickly into his bloodstream and the retching did him no good. Without knowing he did it, or how he did it because he had so often ridden drunk, he clung to the horse's neck and let the animal carry him into Savannah.

He slid off his horse and rushed to the door of Osgood Baxter's dry goods and general store. He tried to lift the latch. Locked. Dark. Baxter . . . gone. Frantically he pounded with his fists, pounded at the door until his knuckles were raw, pounded and cried Baxter's name, pounding with his nose running and his eyes streaming, pounding pounding pounding . . .

He stopped. He wiped his face on his coat sleeves, then doubled up, clutching his stomach, panting with pain and anxiety.

Bret Tully's house of prostitution was situated on the riverfront. Unpainted and needing repair, in this abysmal district it seemed unremarkable. Behind its tightly closed blinds it was lavishly furnished. The interior was dimly lit, the lamps few and turned low, the walls covered with dark-red brocaded paper, the draperies of black velvet swagged with gold fringe.

Soothing, Brock had sometimes thought before he became an opium eater. Here in the room where he had been shown to wait for Tully, there were no noises from the piano in the parlor, no girlishly shrill laughter or clink of glass upon glass. There were none of the cries or the pleasured moans that could be heard from room to room upstairs. Here there was only dimness, the red and black dimness, and the silence.

Tully did not come immediately. The small black boy to whom he had given a penny had promised to find Bret and bring him promptly. Brock sat huddled on a sofa, yawning uncontrollably, holding his splitting belly with both hands. Then, unable to bear inertia, he began to pace up and down, up and down the closed-in, dark room.

It was Colonel Lloyd Henry Grooms who found him there, his shaky cramping legs unwilling to carry him farther, the greasy sweat rolling down his forehead into his eyes, his mouth dry and gasping, his pupils dilated and anxious.

Grooms said harshly, "Didn't Ah tell you t'stay outta heah, Whitakah? We ain't got no use fo' boys what don't pay theah bills. Now go on, get out." But he made no move to eject Brock, simply stood waiting and watching the sweating sick man in his abject misery.

Brock pulled out his gold piece and eagerly held it toward Grooms. "I c'n pay, Lloyd Henry, see, I c'n pay. I got the money for this'n. C'mon, Lloyd Henry, I need a pipe bad." He held out a jerking hand. "I'm in bad shape, see? Please get it, Lloyd Henry, I'm so bad off I can't hardly wait."

Grooms paid no attention to either the hands or the money. Deliberately he reached into a vest pocket, extracted a small notebook, and slowly leafed the pages.

"I'm paid up, Lloyd Henry, honest to God! Just ask Tully if I ain't!"

"Tully went to N'Orleans yestahday," said Grooms absently. "Yeah, heah y'all ah. Brock Whitakah. Owes fifty dollahs. That ain't nothin' like all paid up. You jes' bettah get on out."

Brock grabbed Grooms's lapel and shook it in his anguish. "What if I paid twenny? Part on my bill, an' part—Lloyd Henry, you *got* to—"

Grooms reached out with an unexpectedly strong grip and wrenched Brock's hand away. Brock, thrown off balance, staggered against the sofa. "Don't talk t'me about got to. Ain't nothin' Ah got t'do fo' you, Whitakah."

To his own mortification, Brock burst into sobs. "Please, Lloyd Henry, please, please. I'm gonna die if you don't let me have a pipe! Look!—" He held out the gold piece again. "I got the cash—'nuff for two!"

Lloyd Henry said regretfully, "Prices've gone up, Brock. A pipe heah'll cost you twenty now."

"I'll pay! ! I c'n pay!"

Lloyd Henry capitulated, taking the money and turning toward the door. "Ah'll see if it's all right. Wait heah."

Brock waited in a restless sweat for Lloyd Henry to return and escort him to the opium den. God, how he needed that, the pale-pink lights and the men lazing on the couches, the pipes, the air damp and scented with opium, and him lying there taking his ease, puffing leisurely, all night to enjoy it in. . . .

When he returned, Lloyd Henry had a long, slender packet in his hand, not like the little round boxes Baxter supplied him with. Before Brock could protest, Grooms said smoothly, "We got somethin' a little bettah fo' you to try this evenin', Whitakah. Ah'd take you in fo' a pipe, but Ah can see what kinda bad shape youah in. This'll fix you up quick, boy. Now shuck off that coat an' pull up youah sleeve."

Lloyd Henry helped him, then positioned his arm out straight. "Now you got to hold still fo' a minute, an' then you'll be jes' fine."

Anxiously Brock watched as Grooms produced a shining hypodermic needle, held it up to the light and expelled a drop, found Brock's large arm vein, then inserted the needle and depressed the plunger.

In the moment that Brock was watching Grooms pull out the needle and stand straight, he felt the sensation. It was quick, a lot quicker than a pipe, quicker and harder-hitting. It was like a rush of warmth to his griping belly, a highly pleasurable feeling of well-being, a warmth of rapture or ecstasy, like coming in a woman only it was in his belly, and it went on and on and on. He sat there perfectly still, his lips curving up in surprise, enjoying the warmth and the relief from the cramps and the pain, and the falling away of the spiking anxiety . . . warm like a wave going over him again and again.

Grooms observed him from the doorway. "Feelin' bettah, ain'tcha, Whitakah? That's mighty good stuff we got this time. Jes' 'bout makes a man feel he can do anything he wants to, don't it?"

Brock smiled. The demons had stopped gnawing on his belly, and the earthquakes had quit making his hands and legs shake. "Yes, yes, I'm a lot better. I was awful bad. You don't know how bad, Lloyd Henry."

Grooms smiled knowingly. "Now you kin lick youah weight in wildcats, huh? Want me t'send in one o' the girls? Ah can jes' put it on youah bill. Only be anothah twenty."

Brock looked at him through a blessed, moving haze. He wondered, as he had before, why they always called all whores girls. Maybe a couple of Tully's were, but—"I don't think so, not now. Just let me sit here a while —get my bearings again."

"Aw, c'mon, Whitakah, you know these ah somethin' special. Man, you talk about tight pussy—"

"No!" Brock said too loudly. More softly, "No. Thanks. I got to get along home."

"You don't know what you been missin'," said Grooms in a last attempt at persuasion. "Bettah think about it now, bettah try a li'l bit o' that. Ain't hardly nothin' like it."

Brock found he was thinking about it; and the thinking had given him a thick swelling in the front of his trousers. He waited until Grooms left, then stood up carefully, wanting to preserve what he had for a better purpose than Tully's whores.

Unsteady and feeling sick again, he reeled out the door and into the yard. He had one thought in mind: find Blythe. He'd told Cutler he'd have her, and he would. It had to be Blythe, his dear brother Cutler's lost sweetheart. He almost laughed to think of it— himself and his helluva hard-on, and Blythe smiling and spreading her legs for him, and dumb shit Cutler banging himself by hand for love of a whore.

He nearly fell down, but grabbed the fence and pulled himself along. Only half a block half a block half a block. Then up the stairs and wait for Blythe. He felt himself to be sure he was still up.

It was going—but Blythe would bring it back for him. She'd put her little hands on it and pull on it and he'd think about Tully's whores . . . He had to stop for a while and lean on the fence. God, God, this was worse than before he got the stuff! He wasn't even sweating this time. He just had this God-awful *sick*. Get to Blythe. Get to . . .

"Why, Brock Whitaker, you aren't walkin' on by my door, are you?" He looked up to see a miraculous vision: a small, blond woman in a soiled blue-satin dress, with a set smile on her reddened lips and a provocative tilt to her sassy hips. "I just wouldn't like that if you did, now."

He wanted to cry, he was so glad to see her. He mumbled, "Blythe, it's leavin' me—it's leavin'. I had a good one—honest to God—I—but now—" He hung onto the corner of the building, a pleading expression on his face.

Blythe slid an expert hand down his trousers. "Why no, honey—it's just fine," she assured him. "Come on up, and Blythe'll make you feel real-l-l good."

He got to the door and looked up the stairs. In his drug-disoriented mind they were as steep and forbidding as the gates to hell. "Blythe—I'm sick—I can't—"

"Sure you can, lover. Just take one step at a time and lean on me. There, see? Put one hand on the wall. Like that. One step . . . that's right, one step—"

He had to stop several times, catch his breath and yield to his sickness, but he made it to the top, his heart slamming and his head hammering. He swayed, putting up a wavering hand to his forehead. Blythe reached out and pulled him with her into her room. He flopped onto the bed. She turned him over and loosened his tie and his trousers, and made him comfortable with a pillow under his head.

"Now let's just see about this," she said, her voice as always soft and tender and gentle. She exposed his limp and shrunken member, and her voice took on a new note, one of pleasure and delight. "Why, Brock lover, that's beautiful." Carefully she shielded it from his sight while her practiced fingers stroked its underside. When after some time he did not respond, she ventured a glance at him. He was lying with a small smile on his face, content in her hands.

"Come on, now, Brock," she said archly. "Don't go to sleep on me, now."

He whispered, "Good ol' Bly . . ." His eyes half closed, he imagined the power surging back into his penis, feeling it grow hot and tumid and hard, a club in her dainty fingers, a mighty machine to thrust and thrust with. He no longer felt sick, but detached, floating up around the ceiling where he could look down on good old Blythe as she leaned over him and placed her lips around him and moved her tongue along him. There was something in him that wanted to respond, some fundamental masculine urge, but the whisky and the drugs were making him float, making him sleepy, so sleepy it was almost like dying. Floating on the ceiling, he let his mouth go slack.

Blythe stopped. She kissed him and refastened his trousers. He was dead asleep now, she saw, hardly breathing; and she was dead tired. Briefly she debated going out on the street again. Her rent was due on Friday, and she didn't have it. She lay back on the bed, lethargic and tired within. She wasn't a good whore. She wasn't a good anything, she thought without bitterness.

After a while, she turned to look at the quiet, slumbering man beside her. She didn't want anybody else tonight. Not after Brock. She laughed softly at herself. It was no wonder she never made any money. All she wanted was Cutler Whitaker, and he couldn't walk on the same side of the street with her without blushing and looking as though someone was walking him to the gallows. But she still longed for him and would relish a night with his pathetic, spent, and lost brother.

She stared up at the dingy damp-spotted ceiling. What a lot they all were. All the fine people of Chatham County who had lived in such grandeur out on the River Road. Her brother Glenn had become a spineless, mewling echo of his wife Addie Jo. And Todd, who had been such a handsome swain in the days before the War, was a sick, dying man. She didn't know which would kill him first, his meanness or his cough. It was difficult for her to remember days of summer soirees when Dulcie Moran and Camille Whitaker and even Addie Jo Acton would twitter among themselves hoping for a word, a dance, even the quickest glance from the dashing, bold Todd Saunders.

And Cutler. He too had been bold. All the County had talked about the wild, rough-and-tumble Whitaker boys. What had the War done to him—or had it been the War? Had the seeds of fear and uncertainty always been in all of them? And Brock—Brock would have been better had a Yankee bullet taken him. He was no longer of use to anyone, and an agony to himself. Even she used what there was left of him. She didn't want Brock, she didn't even think of him. She accepted his attempts at lovemaking because there was still a vague physical resemblance to Cutler.

And then she thought of herself. She was a whore. And it had no meaning to her. Once, long ago, she understood what she had done and thought of it as a sacrifice. She thought that anything she might give was worth the cost. And now it meant nothing. She understood nothing. Her mother hadn't cared in the end. Birdie and Blossom had condemned her. Todd had beaten her senseless and driven her from her own home. Sacrifice. It was a ridiculous notion. She was a whore. Most likely, she thought, the seeds of that were always in me too. It wasn't the War—it was what I wanted.

Everyone got what he wanted.

Suddenly agitated beyond bearing, Blythe got up and paced the small, squalid room. She wished Brock would awaken so she could send him on his way. She no longer wanted him there. She didn't want to look upon the ruin of the man any more. With a rush of anger she blamed Tully's place for Brock's ills. "Why can't they leave him alone!" she cried aloud, then looked quickly to see if she had disturbed his sleep. She hadn't. He lay still, his chest barely moving, his face blank but peaceful.

She lay back down on the bed, softly so as not to disturb him, and rested her cheek against his shoulder.

Her compassion for him returned. His was such a quiet sleep, she wondered idly what it would be like to indulge in one of Tully's potions that would allow such a sleep. She seldom could go to bed without nightmares, and sweating fear driving her awake in the middle of the night. Brock often came to her and fell asleep as he had tonight. She lay quiet, envying his stillness. He seemed to be barely breathing, but he was often that way after he came from Tully's. As she sank into slumber, she consoled herself with what pride she had left that at least this one Whitaker had had sense enough to choose her, instead of one of Tully's . . .

She awoke, feeling cold, a few hours later when Betty's new baby cried in the next room. Something was strange, she didn't know what. It was still black outside. She tried to think if she had had one of those awful dreams, but she couldn't remember. Shivering, she left the bed and peered out the window, then stealthily opened the hall door. No one was stirring in the rooming house. She still felt peculiar and vaguely frightened. It must be her imagination. She crawled back into bed, thinking to seek the comfort of the closeness of his body, then she thought better of it.

She whispered, "Brock. Brock, wake up, it's time you went. Hear me?" When he did not answer she shook his shoulder. He was cold too. She felt immediately sorry for him. Then quickly she withdrew her hand, her eyes wide and frightened. She was having a nightmare. She huddled quietly at the foot of the bed, waiting to awaken. Then, unable to stand it any more, she moved up toward Brock again. She touched his face. Her fingers slid across his open eyes. She smothered a scream and retreated to the end of the bed. She felt sick to her stomach. She was shaking with fright. Who would believe her? How could she ever explain?

She felt another surge of sickness. What was happening to her? She shouldn't be thinking of herself. She should be thinking of Brock. Brock Whitaker, weak and

vulnerable and brother to Cutler. He came to me to be
loved—came to *me*. But for the foibles of perverted
gods, she might have been his sister-in-law.

She got up, moving unsteadily toward her washstand.
Her head reeled; she had to sit down quickly or she
would faint. She sat gingerly on the bed, rubbing her
wrists and taking deep, ragged breaths. When she felt
better and slightly more in control of herself, she lit
the lamp and found a small mirror. She tested Brock's
breath, sure now that she had herself in hand that she
would find she had been mistaken. It would be one of
those terrifying dreams of hers after all.

Not the faintest mist showed on the mirror. She
pressed her fingers against his throat where the sight
of a man's pulse had occasionally set her own to racing.
There was no pulse.

She blew out the lamp hastily and sat in the dark.
Her original fears returned. Experience had taught
her harshly. No one would believe she hadn't caused
Brock's death. God knew what she'd be accused of, of
what they'd do to her. Hang her.

"Oh, God," she moaned, her head full of the sight
of herself, her family, the neighbors. She squeezed her
eyes more tightly shut, unable to stand the horrible
gnawing feeling that inundated her body. Instinctively
she thought of her mother for solace and began to cry
soft, hopeless tears. There was no one. She was alone
—terribly and helplessly alone.

She picked up Brock's dead, cold hand and clutched
it to herself, feeling a kinship to him she hadn't realized
in life. She might have become an outcast by her pro-
fession, but Brock had just as surely been turned out
by all who claimed to love him. With smiles they had
watched his destruction. She thought of Bret Tully and
Lloyd Henry Grooms and their God-awful house. Those
drugs—the powders, the potions, the needles, the smoking pipes—they had ruined Brock. Tully and Grooms
had given him the means to ruin himself, she amended.
Those who had stood and watched had ruined Brock.

A person could stand only so much pain before he learned it was better to ignore the false, empty love of those who really didn't care.

His parents, his brothers, his friends, his neighbors, Blythe herself, they had been the ones who had stood and watched him slowly die of the pills and potions so easily obtained nearly anywhere for pennies. She thought of Brock during the last year. He hadn't been able to keep his head on straight anymore. Even needing a drink, he wasn't like he was when he needed some of Tully's poisons. He was savage then, in pain that racked both his body and his mind. She had been frightened to be near him then. But she hadn't done anything.

Steeped now in an overwhelming misery, Blythe thought morosely of Tully's whores. Children of someone. Who? Who let those poor little ones fall prey to jackals like Tully and Grooms? Where do Tully and Grooms get them? She shuddered. And people say I'm sinful! "God damn them all to hell for the sons of Satan they are!" she hissed, with a helpless fury that quickly subsided.

She put Brock's hand on his chest. Oh, Brock—why did you have to come to me when you were dying? Why couldn't you have condemned the men who did this to you? If you'd stayed at Tully's just a little longer, the blame would be right where it . . .

Belongs.

Right on Tully's doorstep.

Right there where the sun will come up and shine on you and point to Tully's house.

While her mind raged in turmoil, Blythe was moving quickly. She tugged at him—oh, God, he was so heavy —and how slight she was, and how weak she was now. She thought of the long flight of stairs, and the half block she would have to drag him to Tully's house. It seemed impossible. She sank to the floor, hopelessness shrouding her again. She wept tears of self-pity and frustration.

"I can't do that to you," she cried, her head resting on Brock's arm.

I must do that—for you.

I have to do it for myself—for both of us.

She got up again, looking frantically around the tiny room for anything that might ease the burden she would have to carry. Roll him in the bedclothes—one quilt looks like another. No one would know it's mine. Besides, I can bring it back home. Wrap him tight, tight, say good night. Wrap him right, right, like a mummy bright—no, tight. Wrap him . . .

She fought back a frightened, hysterical giggle and rolled him onto his face. Thank God his hands were on his belly and his legs were out straight. She'd have to tie the bundle he made with something. She'd steal Mrs. Minch's clothesline—she'd bring it back. No one would know. She giggled again. Pad, pad softly down the stairs, untie the clothesline feeling the knots in the dark, pad back upstairs and wrap it over and under Brock. Over and under, over and under. It was like a child's game. Her head kept making up little rhymes, like a child's game.

She left her only pillow under his head—she could drag him downstairs, but could not risk the bump bump bump that his head would make. She pulled the pillowcase down around his head and tied it around his neck. It brought her momentarily back to sober reality. She stared breathless at the grisly horror of the trussed body. Her stomach heaved. She ran to her washstand, breathing hard, her head hanging over the bowl.

Then she went back to Brock. She could hardly move him at all. She pulled frantically. His dead weight thudded onto the floor and she listened heart in mouth for a neighbor in the rooming house to call out for quiet. When she heard nothing, she summoned courage to start down the stairs with him. She tried it several ways. Pulling him, she was frightened that he would start sliding and make her fall. There was no way to push him. So she sat on the stairs with one stiff leg on each side of her and she pulled him down a step at a time after her. There was noise but it was not unseemly.

She breathed a sigh of relief when she got him out of the house. She could not abandon him yet, but there was a plank in some trash near the fence, and she could roll him onto that and pull him down the street.

That plan failed. The plank itself was too heavy for her to move. She would have to drag him on the quilt.

The sky remained dark, although the birds were awake and making their morning racket. It took her a long time to pull and rest, pull and rest, and finally to get Brock's body up against the porch of Tully's house. But she did it. Panting and trying to stifle the sound of her heaving lungs, constantly peering around in fear that she had been seen, yet she had done it.

Streaks of palest gray broke the dark and she worked with terrified speed now, rolling him out of the shredded quilt, untying the pillowcase, salvaging the rope.

Brock Whitaker lay on his side, that little smile still on his face, his body stiff, but unmarked by the roughness of his final journey. She hesitated a few seconds saying good-bye to him, then turned to run back home —and ran into the portly person of Laban Sweet.

It was nightmare come true. She gasped, her heart drumming in painful cadence, her eyes and her mouth wide with fear. She could not move, though everything in her told her to run, run . . .

Laban's grip on her arm was like handcuffs. "Ah bin watchin' y'all, Blythe," he informed her. "Ah stood right ovah theah round that corner o' the house. Saw you drag 'im up, saw you undo that blanket. Now git ovah heah an' le's see who he is."

She wanted to say, "But it's *Brock!*" in a combination of protest and disbelief.

"Well, if it ain't Brock Whitaker," said Laban. "Son-ofabitch! Now what in hell did ya'll go an' kill 'im fo'? He beatin' you? Was that it?"

Violently Blythe shook her head. Had she been

guilty of Brock's murder, her mind would have been swift with denials, would have leaped to her own defense. But she was drained from her severe efforts to lay Brock at Tully's door. Her shock at knowing him dead had been postponed, and now it was upon her. She shook her head incessantly, little whimpers forcing themselves out her opened lips.

Laban jerked her roughly. "Won't talk, huh? You God-damned 'risteracrats, think you can do any ol' thing you please, don't you?" He jerked her again. "Yo' daddy'd be pretty proud o' you right now, woon't he? Whorin' 'round with every Tom, Dick, an' Harry, an' now killin' somebody. Somebody impawtint! Didn't know wheah t'stop, did y'all? Think because you was rich once that you kin still get away with anything y'do." He shoved her toward his wagon, which she had not seen hitched around in front of Tully's.

"Git up on that seat," he ordered. When she stood unable to mount, he grabbed her and swung her up. Her bundle fell open to the ground, and he pulled the rope out of it. "Hol' out youah han's, Blythe. I got t'tie y'all t'the wagon."

Mutely Blythe put her hands out, her large eyes wide with fear, but also with a pathetic resignation that was not lost on Laban.

Laban placed the ropes around her small wrists. He thought of the times he had tried to mount the steps to Blythe's room and hadn't been able to do it. Even when he'd worked up a head of steam about the cussed 'risteracrats hereabouts an' how they'd treated him like shit till the Yankees made him impawtint, he hadn't been able to take out his resentment on Blythe. He knew she was a whore, but God damn it, there was somethin' about that female no whore should have. He didn't know what name to put to it, but he sure knew the feelin' of bein' dirty it gave him when he thought about fuckin' her an' payin' her for it.

He looked up into the soft, sad pools of her eyes. "Aww shit, Blythe, why'n hell'd you go to whorin'?

Y'all doan belong down heah. Ah jes' doan get it. Son-ofabitch if Ah do."

Blythe bit her lips, her eyes moving upward to stare at the space over his head.

"Did you kill him?" Laban asked her suddenly.

Blythe shook her head. "You know Tully killed him, Laban. He just came to me to die. Where do people like Brock and me have to go to die, except to each other?"

"Kee-riist!" He wrapped more of the rope around her wrist, and loosely tied it to the side of the wagon. "Blythe—" he said and then stopped, his face working as though a great struggle was taking place. "Yeah, Blythe, befo' Ah take you in, Ah got t'take me a leak. You wait right heah, y'heah? Y'all heah me, Blythe?" Laban walked backward away from her, his eyes searching hers to be sure she understood him.

Blythe sat where he had left her. She didn't try the ropes or move.

A few moments later Laban peeked around the side of the building, to see her still sitting there. He waited a bit longer, and when she still didn't move, he whispered loudly, "Blythe, God damn it, Ah cain't leak all day!"

Finally understanding, Blythe moved her hands slightly and the rope slipped from its mooring. She stood up, looking toward the building where Laban had disappeared. Then she got down from the wagon, took up her things, and hurried down the street back to her rooming house.

Laban watched her leave, his thick arms akimbo, fists planted firmly on his broad hips. God knew why he'd done that. He looked at Brock Whitaker, his mouth turned down. "Ah doan know what happened t'you t'night, you damn sot, but Ah sho' hope sum-buddy's ass gets kicked fo' this. An' fo' once mebbe it'll be the right ass."

Laban climbed back onto his wagon and moved off toward his office. Most likely, first strong light would bring word of Brock Whitaker's end, and then maybe he could walk right into Bret Tully's house and clear them out once and for all. No bribes, no influence in high places, no deals could save Tully from answerin' for a dead man on his doorstep.

Laban Sweet felt good when he sat down in his well-padded chair in his office, thinking to catch a quick nap before hell broke loose in the morning.

CHAPTER EIGHTEEN

It was mid-morning before anyone disturbed Laban snoozing at his desk. A group of blacks wanted him to read their new work contract for them. Discomboomerated, Laban rubbed his eyes and tried to shake the vague feeling that things were all topsy-turvy. He read the contract, his lips and forefinger working their way to the end of the paper, then he hurried the men out of his office.

He went to the back room to the washbasin and tossed cool water over his face. "Sonofabitch," he muttered, wondering what he was going to do now. His impulse was to hurry back to Tully's door, but he knew Brock's body wouldn't be there. He must have been half crazy last night. A two-year-old could have figured out that Tully wasn't going to get caught by a dumb trick like propping a body on his doorstep. But what did he do now? Brock Whitaker was dead. Something had to be done, but damned if he knew what it was.

Laban strapped his Colt around his ample middle, adjusted his trousers and the heavy gun-belt, then walked out of his office into the street. His small, bright eyes, all but buried in the puffiness of his cheeks, darted this way and that. Immediately Laban was sweating. He'd never felt so self-conscious in his life. It seemed to him that everyone he saw or greeted could see for the looking that he had done wrong last night. He knew he shouldn't have helped Blythe. Now he was in a tight fix.

All morning long Laban peeked in alleys and dark corners, hunting for the elusive body of Brock Whitaker. By lunchtime he was miserable and for the first time in memory, uninterested in eating. He returned to his office and sat morosely at his desk, trying to sort through what might come of this misadventure. He finally decided to ride out to Mossrose. He had to talk to someone, and he was reasonably sure Adam Tremain would understand and not take action against him.

The Reverend Jabez Hooks caught up with Laban just as he rode from the stables toward the River Road.

"Brothah Sweet! Brothah Sweet!" Hooks's deep voice called, making the hair on Laban's neck stand on end.

Laban slowed his horse and turned in his saddle watching Hooks approach. "Ah'm on official business, Rev'end," Laban said quickly. "What you got on youah mind?"

Hooks dramatically put his hand to his brow. "Ah am so relieved that Ah caught up with you, brothah Sweet. Ah am sent on an errand o' mussy fo' ouah deah Whitaker brothahs an' sistahs."

Laban squinched up his eyes. "What about the Whitakers?"

Hooks dropped his head until his long chin rested on his bony chest. "We have all known the vale o' tears, the sorrow o' death in ouah midst, an' now that black angel has come t'rest upon the hearts o' the Whitakers."

Laban's jowls were shaking. "What the hell ah you talkin' about, Rev'end? Ah ain't one o' youah darky congregations—talk sense t'me, man. Ah tol' you Ah'm on official Beero business."

"Brock Whitaker was found this morning—dead."

Laban took so deep a breath he puffed up like a blow fish. "Whitaker—dead," he said on a long stream of exhaled breath. "What'd he die of?"

"Ah cain't say—most likely he jes' died." Hooks suddenly seemed unwilling to talk, so Laban prodded at him.

"Ah got t'know if Ah'm t'do mah duty. Where'd he die?" A long pause followed, then Laban added weakly, "At home?"

"He was found on the Rivah Road, 'bout midway

between town an' the Whitaker place. Po' soul must
have died as he was tryin' to regain the comfoht o' his
lovin' family."

"Do tell," Laban said with more than his usual acid-
ity. "Mebbe you bettah take me t'wheah you found him.
You were the one t'find him, weren't you, preachah?"

Hooks's eyes flashed to Laban's for a moment, then
he said, "Yes, brothah Sweet, the Lawd saw fit t'call
upon me fo' this painful duty. Ah shall accompany you
now, an' bring comfoht to the Whitakers." His narrow
head moved from Laban to indicate the road. "Shall
we tarry no longah, brothah Sweet?"

Hooks took Laban directly to the spot a couple of
miles outside of Savannah. Brock's body lay on the
ground, on his face, strangely stiff for a man who might
have fallen off his horse. The animal grazed placidly
on the rich grass meadow several yards away.

Laban sucked air noisily in through his teeth. Damn,
he thought. Ah musta been clean off mah head las'
night. Nevah gave the damn hoss a thought. Ah made
it as easy fo' them bastards as Ah coulda. He walked
over to the fallen body, businesslike and official. "Looks
like he could killed hisseff fallin' offa his nag, what
d'you think, preachah?"

Hooks followed close behind Laban. "Ah would
considah that a strong possibility." Hooks posed then,
his hands folded piously, his face mournful. "An' it
would be a kindness. Even in death the stench of demon
rum wells up fum his body an' taints the nostrils of the
innocent. Bettah that this soul should have perished
by the hand of God reachin' from the sky to knock
him fum his beast of burden than to have the evils of
perverted pleshuh drive him to his grave."

Laban snorted, then made it seem that the odor
coming from Brock was the cause. "Ah 'speck, seein'
it was a natcheral death, we oughta jes' take him right
on up to his mama an' daddy. Doan see no reason
t'haul him back to town, do you, preachah? Ah mean
theah ain't no sign o' foul play or nothin'. He didn't

have nothin' in his pockets, but then Brock Whitaker didn't often have nothin' in his pockets. Don't s'pose anybody hereabouts is dumb'nuf to rob a Whitaker— 'cep' maybe Cutler."

Reverend Jabez Hooks and Laban Sweet placed Brock across the back of his horse, and led their grisly burden up to the Whitaker plantation house. Laban had in mind to make his announcement as quickly and quietly as possible, leaving the Whitakers to their sorrow, and perhaps even acquiring for himself a small token of gratitude from Ned Whitaker for bringing his son home with so little fanfare.

But it was not to be that way with Jabez Hooks along. Hooks dismounted immediately, leaving Laban to tend to Brock's body, and sprang up the steps of the veranda. He pounded noisily on the door, demanding of the serving girl admittance on an errand of mercy.

The girl called Emma to the sitting room, but Hooks would not speak a word until Ned was present also.

Emma Whitaker sat nervously folding her handkerchief, her eyes searching Reverend Hooks's mournful face for some sign of reassurance. "My goodness, Reverend Hooks, why won't you just tell me whatever's on your mind?" she asked brightly. "I am sure I can take care of whatever's botherin' you. You're upsettin' me, keeping this a secret like you are."

"Mah good woman," Hooks began soothingly, "Ah know how strong you fancy you ah, an' you may be right, o' co'se, but at a time like this, Ah b'lieve youah lovin' husban' should be at youah side to suppoht you in youah houah of need."

Emma glanced at Laban, who stood uneasy, turning his hat 'round and 'round in perpetually moving fingers. She jumped to her feet as soon as Ned came through the door, and hurried to him, her arm entwining for comfort in his. "Ned, somethin' awful has happened and they won't tell me what it is."

Ned escorted his wife back to her seat, and greeted the two men. "Well, Reverend, Laban, what brings you out here? I haven't been having any trouble with any of your darkies, Laban."

Sweet looked apologetically at him. "Ah'm sorrier than Ah can tell, Ned. Ah woon'ta broke it to you this way, if Ah had mah druthers."

"Ah shall tell brothah Whitaker, brothah Sweet," Hooks intoned. "It is mah sad duty to infawm you an' youah true an' lovely wife, brothah Whitaker, that the Good Shepherd has seen fit to call home his lamb, brothah Brock Whitaker."

Emma let out a cry, and covered her face with her hands. "Oh, no, no, not my baby!"

Ned glared hostilely at Hooks. "What in the hell are you gibbering about, Hooks?"

Emma said tearfully, "Now I can see, Ned, why they didn't want me to know, not till you came to stand beside me in my hour of need."

Laban cleared his throat. "Rev'end Hooks heah claims he found Brock layin' at the side o' the road, Ned."

"Brock's dead?" Ned said, the full idea finally coming through to him.

"He is with the good Lawd," Hooks said, undaunted. "Ah come t'you an' his mothah t'bring what comfoht Ah can. Ahh—the pain o' womanhood, the pain o' mothahhood." Sadly Hooks shook his head.

"Where is he?" Ned asked numbly. "What happened? Was he robbed—did he suffer?"

Laban's mouth opened for speech, but Hooks intervened, gentle but insistent. "It was not by a human hand he died, brothah Whitaker. It was the hand o' the Almighty Lawd. He reached out fum the heavens an' took ouah brothah to himself. Praise the Lawd. Praise the Almighty Lawd."

"That so, Laban?" Ned asked.

Laban's eyes did not meet Ned's. "Can't say as Ah know, Ned. The preachah heah come an' got me in town, an' all Ah know is what he told me. Ah didn't see no sign o' harm done him. He looks peaceful."

"Where is he now?"

Laban was apologetic. "Ah took the libbutty, Ned, o' tellin' youah man t'lay him out propah in his room. Ah hope Ah ain't been unduly presumpshus." Sonofabitch, he thought, if Ah ain't talkin' like that pious scarecrow now.

"My God, no, not at all. I thank you, Laban. It was thoughtful of you." Ned seemed to lose his train of thought. He looked at his wife, crying quietly in her chair, then helplessly he looked back to the two men.

Laban said, "If y'all will excuse us, Ned, Ah think it's time we took ouah leave."

Hooks drew himself up, his Bible clutched against his breast. "Ah shall be happy to put off my pressin' duties fo' the day, an' give what small comfoht Ah can t'you an' the grievin' little mothah."

"Thank you, no," Ned said firmly. Taking Emma by the arm, he nearly lifted her from her chair. "Laban, I thank you again. Good day, Reverend Hooks."

Ned and Emma Whitaker called Brock's brothers and sisters together and told them of his death. Among them it was decided that he should be buried quietly, with only the family present.

Brock Whitaker was buried in the family plot on the plantation beside his grandparents on November 2, 1868.

Cutler Whitaker spent most of the next week in town, working and sleeping in the shipping line office. He didn't want to be near the rest of his family. He was discomposed; he no longer knew what he thought, or what he wanted to do. There seemed to be no place left for him in the family. He couldn't believe that none of the Whitakers knew that Brock was an opium eater, that he drank too much as well, and that he had become entangled with the Klan. He couldn't believe or understand what he considered the callousness of their determined ignorance of Brock's restless existence. He had sought deadly peace with his opium and, unable to stand that, had sought excitement with his alcohol. Never knowing what he wanted, he sought after something, always something beyond his current state, whatever that was.

Cutler's dissatisfaction grew with his family and with himself. It was easy to say that his father and mother and Cedric and Enid were callous and cold for ignoring what had been happening to Brock, but he had been no better. Perhaps they hadn't known.

Perhaps they didn't realized how bad off Brock was. Most men drank alcohol, and some to excess; and opium and its derivatives were in common use. Some of the ladies were opium eaters, with their handy little bottles of laudanum and paregoric for female pains and household malaises. Opium eating as Brock had done it was considered immoral yet forgivable, a vice akin to men's gambling or sexual promiscuity. Opium eaters pursued their daily duties with a serene efficiency that had to be applauded. An opium addict would not be released from his employment for his addiction; nor would his wife consider it reason enough to leave him. Most addicts continued to participate fully in their community life, still regarded as respectable people entitled to their rightful place in family and society.

But Brock had been different, heavily abusing both alcohol and drugs, not carrying his share of the family burden. Still they hadn't appeared to realize that something might be wrong with him.

He, Cutler, had. What defense could he offer for himself? His cowardice? That was all. Cutler Whitaker was not his own man, and never had been, he decided. That was his defense; and it made him sick.

On the sixth of November, after he had closed the door to the Tremain-West shipping office for the day, he sat behind his desk thinking, remembering himself and his brothers in the years before the War. He sipped slowly at a glass of whisky. Tonight was not so bad as the other nights he had sat and brooded. He was remembering the good things, all the hopes that had seemed so close to reality before the tin gods fell and the toy soldiers marched off to a glory war.

Automatically he lit the lamp on his desk. Puffing a cigar, he leaned back in his chair, allowing himself to relish the old memories that were so much more pleasant than reality. His eyes were half closed. He neither heard the door to the office open, nor saw the woman enter.

She stood for several seconds watching him. She was small and covered by shadows. Cutler, washed clean by his daydreams, felt the warmth of her presence and placed it as part of the lost past. Several moments longer he kept his eyes closed. Then, as his thoughts of her grew stronger, he slowly opened his eyes and met hers.

His expression remained impassive. He wasn't sure if she was a figment of his mind, a phantasma of the whisky, or just a wish.

She looked at the blankness of his face and thought he was disgusted by her. Her voice was small and sad. "I'm sorry, Cutler. I shouldn't have let you hear about it from others. I wanted to tell you right way, but I didn't know how. You know I cared for Brock. I would have done anything to help him—but it was too late. When he came to me, he—he was already dying."

Cutler slowly sat up straight in his chair. He didn't know what she was talking about, but he knew it was important and that he should marshal his mind to take it in. "Blythe. What are you doing here?"

"I'll leave," she said. "I knew I should have told you right away. I don't blame you for being angry. I should—" She turned to go out the door.

Cutler got to his feet then and rounded the desk, barring her way. "No. Wait. Blythe—" he said, and could think no further. Finally he managed to ask her to sit down. He held the chair for her, letting his hand linger as she leaned back and her shoulder touched it. He ran the back of his hand close to her head, so that her hair touched his skin. He could barely keep his hands off her, and he couldn't think at all.

He sat at his desk again, offering her a drink, then realized that one did not offer a lady whisky. Fretfully he refuted his offer.

Blythe placed her hand on his. "I'd like to have a drink with you, Cutler. I am not a lady. I am just myself, and there is no one to care."

When he finally regained his composure and could talk with her normally, she told him everything she knew about the night Brock had died. She left out nothing, and Cutler listened with horror and fascination. The life she spoke of that she led and the side of Brock she described so easily and with such familiarity were sordid and hideously empty to him. Once again he was sickened by himself. He loved these two people, yet the world Blythe described was as foreign to him as the African Gold Coast, a decadent world of sickness and evil. And both she and his brother had known it well.

He walked Blythe home that night and saw with clear, unshaded eyes where and how she lived. He kissed her chastely at her door and said good night to her. Then he walked through the darkened streets past the houses, out of the city proper, down to the ocean as he had the night he had failed Adam at the Union League meeting.

He stared out at the water, seeing nothing, seeing everything. Since the War, everything he had done or not done had been a failure. He thought long, hard thoughts, knowing that it was better to be dead than to be as he was. Death by whatever means could never bring him the pain that his life the way he led it was bringing. Cutler presented himself with the only alternatives he could stomach. Either he would die that night by his own hand, or he would vow to live and change the things he hated about himself.

He wondered if, in the morning light, he would have

the courage needed to stand up to his family, to his neighbors, to his friends and say he loved Blythe Saunders and was going to marry her. Would he, in the cruel light of the sun, have the strength to protect her from the questioning eyes, the harsh words, the subtle slights; and could he defend her against those from whom he couldn't protect her?

Cutler began to walk quickly back toward the town, and then to run. He would have to succeed this time. It was his only chance. And it was Blythe's. Both of them had run out of time and hope, except for this one last chance. Cutler's chest ached as he ran, but he didn't stop until he had turned the corner by Tully's house, run the last half-block and up the flight of stairs to Blythe Saunders's room.

CHAPTER NINETEEN

The large single-room schoolhouse smelled of fresh pine lumber. Its floors and desks gleamed creamy white with the afternoon sun streaming in on them. The soft patterns of the wood grain made pictures, designs that Kyra and Apollo stared down on lovingly.

"Who do you think will be the first to carve his name on a desk?" Apollo asked, running his fingers across the smooth wood.

Kyra slapped playfully at his hand. "I know who it'd be if you were sitting in class."

He took her head in both his hands and kissed her nose. "It is gonna be me! Come on, Kyra Jordan, Ah'm gonna write you mah first love note."

"Not in my new schoolhouse! Apollo, don't you dare! 'Pollo!" She ran after him into the small alcove at the front of the room that was to be her private place, a place to keep her records and the special books Adam was having sent to her all the way from England. She grabbed at his arm, trying to pull him back.

"Leggo mah ahm. How'm Ah s'posc to carve in this wood if you holdin' onto me?"

"Apollo, stop it! You're worse than a child. You can't carve in my new schoolhouse. You just can't! I'll never forgive you—I mean it! Apollo—!! What will the children think?"

He made a face, his mouth opened wide in a smile. "So that's youah objection. You afraid to let the chillun know Ah love you? Why? They'd be happy. Anyways, mos' of 'em already knows."

Kyra blushed. "Apollo. Please."

"No ma'am. Ah built this place with mah own two han's an' somebody's gonna know why Ah did it." He carved his name and Kyra's on the lintel, then stood back to look at it proudly. "Schools is s'pose to teach the truth, an' that's the truth."

Kyra stood back beside him and look at the carving too. Reluctantly she smiled, and let him put his arm around her.

His eyes were warm on her. He placed his hand gently under her chin and turned her face to him. "How 'bout you an' me jumpin' the broom?"

"Jumpin' the broom?!" she said on a high pitch. "Jumpin' the broom! Apollo, I don't know what I'm going to do with you."

"Tomorrow's the first day of your school. You could teach them chillun a lot bettah iffen youah name was Kyra Justus Sherman."

"When will you ever be serious?" she asked, and walked into the schoolroom.

"Ah am serious. Ah want to marry you. Ah know you care fo' me. Ah know it, so why can't you jes' come out an' say it's so? Why we al'ys got to play aroun' like two kids in a hopscotch game? One day we jump into the bushes, an' the nex' day Ah can't touch youah shirt-sleeve without you blushin' an' carryin' on. Ah want to marry you, Kyra."

The pulse at Kyra's neck was beating furiously. "I don't want to discuss this now, Apollo. It isn't proper. Ruel—"

"Ruel been dead fo' a yeah now."

"Some say two years is the proper mourning period."

"White folks say so. You ain't white. Ah ain't white. An' God din't say nothin' 'bout no yeah. It don't say a thing about a yeah in mah Bible."

"You've never read the Bible!" she shouted back at him.

"How you know what Ah read an' what Ah ain't?"

"Apollo, I want to go home."

"Ah got a chore to do first."

"No you haven't, and we aren't going to talk any more about this subject today. All we'll do is disagree."

"Ah say Ah got a chore to do!"

Kyra crossed her arms, glaring at him. "What could you possibly have left to do? Everything has been done. The schoolhouse is in perfect order."

"It ain't!"

"It is!"

He walked out the front door to the wagon and returned with a paint bucket.

"Apollo! What are you—"

"Ah'm paintin' the front door blue. That's fo' good luck." With broad strokes he began to cover the door, muttering to himself, "An' it look like Ah'm goin' to need lots of it. You ah the damnedest stubbornest woman alive."

When he had finished he stood up, looking at his door with the same pride he had for his carving on the lintel in the teacher's alcove. "Now say, Kyra, ain't that the prettiest door you evah seen?"

"It's pretty," she said grudgingly, then couldn't help adding, "Of course, that business about blue doors is superstitious nonsense."

"You jes' a iggerant Nawthun darky."

Kyra giggled and pushed at him. "You always get the last word. What shall I do with you?"

"Well, if you won't jump the broom with me, how 'bout goin' to the frolic on Satiddy night?"

Kyra danced away from him and back, then curtsied. "I'd enjoy that, Mr. Justus Sherman. Thank you very much."

Kyra opened the door for the first day of classes in her new schoolhouse long before any child could be expected to appear. The sun had barely begun to warm and brighten the dawn sky, but she was too excited to wait. She laughed at herself—this was worse than her first day of teaching in that small, dingy school in New York City—but she didn't care. This was her own school. Hers and Apollo's.

She walked around outside, admiring the fine lines

of the building, the wide windows that would let in air
and light. Mentally she noted what the children would
see when they gazed out the windows. It was beautiful
country. Nothing like the closed-in crowdedness of the
city, windows staring out onto brick and soot, doorway opening onto cobbled streets cluttered with refuse
and discards. Her children would learn well here.
Progress would be made.

She returned to the front of the school, smiling at
the brilliance of the blue door. It was still early. Kyra
sat down at her desk and immersed herself in her plans
for the day, dreaming of and wishing for the things
that would occur in this classroom in the hours and
weeks to come.

She was startled when the blue door opened and
Adam Tremain came in, followed by many women,
men, and children. She looked with amazement into
the faces of Jesse and Ethel Cole, Curly Jones being
towed in by his wife Welthy, who had formed a chain
with their children Otis, Opal, Olette, and Oriole. Tim
and True Crosby came with Viola, Lulu, and Bonny.
The Meadows family, the numerous Jacksons, the
Warrens all jammed into the room, rapidly shrinking
its proportions.

"Mawnin', Miss Kyra," they all chorused, smiles
abundant and broad.

"Kyra," Adam began, and motioned Ivy Warren to
come forward. "We bring you this gift as a token of
our good wishes for your endeavors here. If your past
accomplishments are any indication, we will surely have
the finest school in all the South."

They all cheered, clapping and laughing.

Ivy Warren stepped forward and with both hands
presented their gift. "God bless you, Miss Kyra," Ivy
said, love and pride twisting her features.

Kyra unwrapped the peculiarly shaped gift and
brought forth from the gaily colored paper a large
brass and ebony school bell. She stood up, smiling,

reaching across her desk to shake hands and hug whomever she could reach.

The children were milling about in the back of the room. Some were already trying out the delights of the slate chalkboard that Kyra had given a prominent position on the west wall. She glanced at the children giggling as they made shaky circles and stick figures on the dark surface. Tupper and Tammy Jackson, she observed, were as close together as cockleburs, as usual. Tupper, with his piece of chalk, drew a head, and Tammy, seeming to know her brother's mind, drew a body onto it and they shrieked with joy.

Kyra looked back at Adam, her eyes warm with pleasure and gratitude. "You've gone to all kinds of trouble for me and my pupils, Captain Tremain," she said. "We will all do everything we can to make sure that our work is satisfactory to you."

Adam smiled. "The President of the United States could hardly do more, Kyra." They laughed together easily.

Then, holding the brass and ebony bell high so all could see, Kyra stood in front of the blue door and rang the bell long and loud. Little stragglers came running down the path; those who had already found their dire enemies left off their fisticuffs in the schoolyard and came too.

As they entered, Kyra demanded from all of them some semblance of order. The adults edged out, some back to their labors, others to peek through the windows. Kyra sorted children, seated them, and clapped her hands for attention. Thirty small black faces looked up to the front of the room to their first teacher. She waited, letting them take in who she was, and allowing them to absorb some of the excitement and delicious fear of a new experience. When they were all quiet, she led them in prayer. With two more claps of her hands, school had begun.

Those first days Kyra struggled with the alphabet,

and with the sounds that seemed so difficult for children
who had learned a tongue that was a combination of
African dialects, American English, and Southern col-
loquialisms. Their greatest fascination was with the
large globe Adam and Dulcie had given the school.
Kyra smiled as she ignored the adult faces that as often
as not appeared at the windows when the globe was in
use.

One afternoon when all the children had gone home,
Kyra was pleased, but not surprised, when Ivy Warren
shyly entered the schoolroom. Ivy smiled, her head
down, her eyes not meeting Kyra's.

"Well, Ivy," Kyra said, "have you come to see how
Cilla's doing? I certainly hope so, for Cilla is one of
my best reading pupils. She works very hard."

Ivy's smile deepened. Her eyes were watery. She
nodded, then said, "Cilla been showin' me her lettahs.
She know so much . . . things you learned her . . .
things Ah ain't nevah hearda."

Kyra indicated one of the pupil chairs for Ivy to sit
on. "It is wonderful, isn't it, how fast children learn?"

"Wunnerful?" Ivy repeated pensively. "Cilla puttin'
on airs, Miz Kyra. She woan lissen to me no mo'. She
know mo'n her mama. Same wid de odders. Chester
ain't wo'th nothin' to his daddy."

"Have you been having trouble with Mabel and
Frances also?"

"No, ma'am. Mabel's a good girl. She take keer o'
de odders fo' me—mos'ly without Ah ast her. Whut
Ah gwine do 'bout 'em, Miz Kyra? Chillun got to have
'speck fo' dey mamas an' daddies."

Kyra took Ivy's hand sympathetically. "It's hard for
you, I know, Ivy, but you should also take pride. These
are your children, and they are quite bright. I believe
Chester is going to be the best scholar. Think of that,
Ivy. Chester—your son—a little black boy—and he
could be a scholar."

"Is mah skol'ah gwine chop cotton an' fetch fiah-
wood?"

Kyra laughed. "I think a touch of the hickory stick might convince Chester that chopping cotton and gathering wood is part of a scholar's life. You must try to understand, Ivy, all this is new to Chester and the other children. New worlds are being opened to them. Right now learning is exciting, but you can take my word for it, it won't be long before school begins to feel like work too, and then Chester will be right back to normal."

Ivy shook her head. "Ain't nevah gwine be normal agin, 'cause he kin read. An' Cilla allus goin' roun' an' tellin' me an' her daddy whut we doan know. Nevah be de same." She paused for a moment, then went on more stubborn than before. "Ah doan wan' it to be de same. Cilla right. Ah's iggerunt, nuthin' but a ol' scrubwoman."

"Oh, Ivy! You were never taught! You could do everything your children are doing if you had been allowed to learn. Just think what this means. More than the War, more than Mr. Lincoln's Proclamation, more than anything else, this—education—is going to free the black man. The white folks, down here at least, don't even know we have minds. We can train ourselves and use our minds. We can begin to change our lives now. We can do it ourselves."

Ivy frowned. "Ouah chilluns mebbe. Not us. We too iggerunt."

Kyra sat back, a smile playing around the corners of her mouth. "Ivy, are you asking me to teach you to write, read, and count?"

Ivy drew back, shocked. "Whut you talkin' 'bout, girl! Me, read?" She giggled, waving a disdaining hand at Kyra. "You gwine mek me laff mahseff sick."

"You could sit in the back of the classroom," Kyra suggested.

Ivy looked at the back of the room, seeing the slight shadows.

"I'd put a chair back there for you. The children

would probably pay no attention to you after the first few days."

"Ah cain't read," Ivy said, still giggling.

"You could learn."

Ivy stood up to leave. "Ah come in agin to talk to you 'bout Cilla. Ah got some worries 'bout her."

Kyra said no more about Ivy attending class. Instead she took Ivy's hand and walked to the door with her. "You come talk to me whenever you like. And don't worry too much, you have fine children."

Ivy came to school the following day. Neither she nor Kyra said a word. Ivy went quickly back to sit in the chair in the back of the room.

Cilla Warren turned in her seat, her eyes wide, her hand over her grinning mouth. "Mama? You goin' to school!"

Ivy frowned, and hissed at her daughter. "You hush, you heah! Ah box youah eahs fo' you, you doan tu'rn 'roun an' heed Miz Kyra."

That settled, Kyra began her lessons. Ivy sat in her seat working diligently, occasionally craning to see Cilla's paper. If Cilla's work was neater than her own, Ivy began again, painstakingly forming her letters.

At the end of the month Kyra was well satisfied with the beginnings of her class, and ready for some fun. Apollo, breathing a sigh of relief, asked her to go to the Saturday night services at the general store. There was always a frolic afterward. But he couldn't suppress his grin, and Kyra immediately bristled. "Any more of those sly looks of yours and you'll be going to the frolic alone!" she scolded.

"You sho' do talk a lot, woman."

Kyra's eyes twinkled. "What are you going to do about it, *man?*"

Apollo started forward, and Kyra ran for the schoolhouse, closing the door and bolting it before he could reach her. She peeked at him from the window.

* * *

At the general store, Nemo Whitelaw stood in the doorway, his arms crossed, keeping order as the Reverend Jabez Hooks wound up his regular Saturday night sermon. He stood in front of a good-sized congregation of whites, seated closely together on chairs between rows of boxes and barrels. Behind them, squatting on their haunches or sitting on the floor, was an equal number of blacks. Several mothers held small children, rocking them with a preoccupied gentleness, their attention rapt on Hooks's words and gestures.

His long, bony finger jabbed at first one in the congregation and then another. "Now Ah'm gonna use the words of ouah Lawd Jesus hisseff, who said, 'Lead us not into temptation, but deliver us from evil.' As Ah have said many, many times befo', ouah Lawd Jesus knew what temptation was. You heah me? Ah'm tellin' you the Lawd Jesus *knew* temptation! Pondah on that, you heathens! The Lawd *knew*, an' bein' the perfect bein' He was, He *shunned* it! *Shunned* it! He reckanized temptation an' He turned his back on it. He kep' His covenant with the Fathah! An' that is ezackly what y'all heah today need t'learn t'do. Long as y'all cain't say you uphold the Covenant—the almighty Covenant o' the Old Testament, y'all ain't no better'n heathens. Heah me good! Heathens! With youah almighty souls teeterin' on the brink o' the inferno! Teeterin'! Teeterin' while y'all learn t'avoid the temptations o' the world an' the flesh.

"Mebbe *you*, Israel Jackson—" Hooks's finger unerringly exposed the small, shrinking black man. "—or *you*, Ivy Warren, or *you*, Duck Meadows—mebbe you think it wouldn't hurt a thing if y'all snuck a cracker outta that barrel an' jes' put it in youah mouth an' *ate* it! Mebbe you think the Lawd ain't a-lookin', an' the Recordin' Angel ain't recordin' today! Or little Viola Crosby, mebbe you think the Lawd doan heah if you sass youah mammy. Otis Jones, mebbe you think the Lawd God ain't gonna know if you lay up drunk on a Monday mawnin'! But brothahs an' sistahs, that's *temptation*! An' the Devil's down theah jes' stokin' up the fiahs waitin' fo' y'all t'tumble right ovah into his Pit! He's a-waitin' an' a-stokin'. Them fiahs o' Perdition is smellin' up the whole world with the stink o' temptation. Temptation t'steal, t'sass, t'be lazy. Now the Lawd Jesus said it, an' y'all kin say it too—He says, 'Satan, git thee behin' me. Temptation, go 'way an' doan come back.' That's what you got to say. That's what you got to do if you gonna be like Jesus, an' if you ain't, then that ol' Satan fellah, he jes' a-layin' fo' y'all stokin' up his fiahs.

"Nemo, pass the plate. Amen to y'all."

"Amen, amen," came a mutter from the congregation. Nemo moved in and out among them collecting coins, mostly pennies, and a few wooden tokens.

Satisfied that Nemo had done a thorough job of collecting, Hooks raised his hands for attention. "Now brothahs an' sistahs, brothah Albatross will lead us in the closin' hymn. Lift youah voices to the Lawd. Satan," he shouted, "Satan, git behin' us, Satan! Lawd, weah callin' you! Lawd, heah ouah voices!"

From the back of the room Albatross sang the first phrase:

"By cool Siloam's shady rill . . ."

The congregation echoed after him, and line by line they completed the graceful hymn:

". . . How sweet the lily grows,
How sweet the breath beneath the hill
Of Sharon's dewy rose!"

"Rise, brothahs an' sistahs, stand an' bow ouah heads in humble prayah. Ouah great an' gracious Lawd, we cast ouah burdens on You, knowin' that You will sustain us, fo' You have promised that You will nevah puhmit the righteous t'be moved. An' so as we

depaht Thy house, O Lawd, we place ouah trust in
Thee. Amen."

"Amen," the congregation echoed.

With clearings of throats, scraping of chairs, and
shuffling of bare black feet, the congregation slowly
departed. The blacks were out first, in a flurry of
whispered conversations. Neighbor greeted neighbor,
fellow workers who had parted only hours before. They
disappeared around the back of the general store, waiting while the whites made their leisurely, talkative exit
into the cool spring night.

When the last shod footstep could no longer be
heard, the blacks reappeared, eyes shining, their
laughter enlivening the air, full of horseplay and ready
for Saturday night. Sleeping babies had been laid all
together on the ground with a ten-year-old girl to tend
them. Out from under shawls and out of shirts came
the cups: tin, gourd, chipped granite or porcelain, held
out to each other in imitative toast, playfully drunk
out of.

At last Nemo Whitelaw had straightened his store;
the chairs for the service were put away so as not to
interfere with the new activities. He came to stand by
the whisky barrel. Suddenly all the jostling pretense
was dropped, and the blacks lined up to get their cups
filled and see their names written on Whitelaw's ledger.
The Reverend Jabez Hooks stood to the side watching,
talking amiably and encouragingly to the people as
they moved closer and closer to the tangy-smelling
whisky barrel.

Apollo dispensed the whisky, exactly the same
amount no matter how large the cup. He announced
each allotment as Whitelaw scribbled rapidly. "Jesse
Cole, one cup. Ethel Cole, one cup. Curly Jones, one
cup. Welthy Jones, one-half cup. That's right, Mistah
Whitelaw, Welthy brought 'long a li'l cup this time.
Won't take a whole po'tion. True Crosby. How's that
least baby, True?"

The small black woman's face lighted. She answered softly, "He doin' right well now, thanky, 'Pollo."

"Glad to heah that. Bring him 'long to church?"

True smiled. "Ah sho' did. He out back, wid Polly Meadows sittin' right by him."

"Me'n' Kyra'll have to take a look at him, see how strong he is. Maybe it'll give her ideas." Apollo grinned, winked devilishly at True, then went on. "Tim Crosby, one cup."

Tim leaned forward and whispered something into Apollo's ear. "Mistah Whitelaw, Tim say he want to put a li'l somethin' on his credit. How much you want to pay, Tim?"

Again Tim whispered. "He want to put a dollah an' fifty cents down agin his credit, Mistah Whitelaw."

Whitelaw waved the hand holding the pen. "Oh, that's all right, Tim, it's Saturday night an' you don't need to pay now. Let it wait till Monday."

Tim whispered again to Apollo. "He want to do it now, he say."

Whitelaw waved the ledger and his pen angrily. "This ain't no time t'be talkin' 'bout youah credit, Tim. Look behin' you, boy, you holdin' up the whole line. You do youah bizness with me some othah time, y'heah?"

Tim didn't move from the line. He leaned toward Apollo again.

Apollo repeated Tim's request. "He want to know how much do he owe, Mistah Whitelaw."

"Tim, youah makin' me mad," Whitelaw declared. "Now git on, git on, youah roonin' mah bizness."

Tim's head went down, he didn't dare speak again. Apollo put his hand out and held Tim in his place. "He ast you a reasonable question, Mistah Whitelaw, suh. How much do he owe you?"

Whitelaw ruffled angrily through the pages. "Tim Crosby. He owes me sixty-one dollahs an' ninety-five cents. An' five mo' cents fo' the whisky. Now Ah hope youah satisfied, 'Pollo, 'cause Ah sho' as hell wouldn't want t'think you was tryin' t'make trouble or nothin'."

Apollo held Whitelaw's eyes with his own. "When kin he pay the dollah an' fifty cents? Soon as everybody gets whisky?"

Whitelaw sighed gustily. "Oh, all right, 'Pollo, but this ain't none o' youah bizness an' Ah don't want you buttin' in again. An lissen t'me, y'all, Ah don't want none o' you makin' a practice o' this. Satiddy night ain't bill-payin' time, y'heah?"

"We heah," Apollo said, and the others chorused affirmation after him. "Tim, you want to stand ovah heah?"

Tim nodded, his face showing Apollo his gratitude. He stood to one side as Apollo had indicated, carefully holding his cup.

Apollo called out, "Clem Clinton, one cup. Vere Clinton . . . Abel Clinton. Cilla Warren, y'all know you is too young fo' whisky."

At thirteen, tall and gawky, Cilla Warren was slightly built, with more rear than bosoms, but she was beginning to fill out the front of last year's dress, and very proud of her accomplishment. She cocked her head to one side and slued a glance up at Apollo, hoping to charm him. "Aw now, 'Pollo, you woon't keep me fum a li'l fun, would you?"

"You bet Ah would. Youah daddy'd have mah hide stretched out on the bahn door."

Cilla batted her eyes in an unpracticed gesture. "Mah daddy gib me a taste o' his'n when Ah ast him."

"Then you bettah go'n ast him."

"Ah arready did," she pouted.

"Cilla, why doan you jes' go an' talk with youah teachah fo' a while. Go see Miz Kyra, Cilla, go on now. Duck Meadows, one cup. Ruby Meadows . . . Israel Jackson. That's a right purty shirt there, Israel. Like to have one like it mahseff. Pauline make it fo' you?"

Israel Jackson flushed and looked pleased at being the center of Apollo's attention. He said proudly, "She done dye it."

Pauline Jackson, standing behind her husband, held out her cup. She said, "All Ah done was what Israel want. He tell me he want blue an' red an' gol'. Ah tell him he a cross 'tween a rainbow an' a flash o' lightnin', but it tuhn out right nice. Ah make you one, 'Pollo. You bring Kyra ovah some evenin' an' Ah measure you up."

"Thanky, Pauline, Ah'll do that. Link Jackson, one cup. Buster Jackson . . . Annabelle Twoshoes. How are y'all this evenin', Annabelle? Ah thought Ah hear you an' Link was thinkin' 'bout gettin' married."

The sultry Annabelle, long-limbed and the color of *cafe au lait*, cast Apollo a knowing look from under long, dark lashes. "We was, 'Pollo, but Link been sniffin' 'roun' dat Delia Jackson." She tossed her long, curly hair. "Ah got me a bettah idee. How 'bout you 'n' me dancin' a li'l bit latah on?"

Apollo for once looked embarrassed, and quickly sought Kyra's approval. "That's a mighty han'some offah, Annabelle, but Ah got to think some 'bout that. Mebbe Ah come an' ast you, huh?" Apollo smiled, promising nothing.

Annabelle turned away, pouting prettily as Link Jackson glowered from a corner. The second-oldest Jackson youth, Buster, caught up with her as she turned. Cups in hand and laughing, the couple wandered out into the night.

On the bare earth to the north of the store, Lester Warren and Curly Jones were turning their gourd fiddles, and Tim Crosby was setting up his drums. Soon Abel Clinton joined them with his pipes, and ten-year-old Tupper Jackson begged to be allowed to play his cigar-box mandolin. No one objected, and Tupper's twin Tammy snuggled down close beside him, both of them smiling hugely while Tupper plinked valiantly to keep up with his elders.

As a young spring moon climbed the sky, by couples the dancers began to drop out awhile, then return, giggling and glancing roguishly at each other. Hooks abandoned his conversation with Nemo Whitelaw. "Well, Nemo, Ah guess Ah'll do a turn around the premises now; it's nigh onto witchin' time. An' then Ah got to hurry on so's Ah'll be in time fo' mah church in the mawnin'."

Whitelaw laughed coarsely. "Evah figger out wheah that church is, Jabez?"

Hooks said irritably, "Ah tol' you, go down the road jes' ten mile an' theah it is. Seminole Junction Church o' God."

"Ah'd be mo' inclined t'believe it's Tully's house."

Hooks spat onto the floor. "Nemo, youah iggerance is ex-ceeded only by youah good looks."

Nemo raised his head, his mouth turned down. "It ain't mah iggerance, Jabez. Ah know what Ah know." He snorted. "Seminole Junction, huh!"

Hooks's narrow face was somber. "Jes' lemme give you a kindly piece o' ad-vice, Nemo, an' as a man o' God, Ah suggest you take it. A feller that totes up figgers in a li'l book ain't hard t'replace. An' a feller that can't keep what he knows t'hisseff ain't nobody's friend. Get mah meanin'?" He gave Nemo a studied look, then clomped across the floor and went outside. Once there he seemed in no hurry, taking a turn dancing with two little black girls, who clung to his bony hands as they giggled and twirled to the fiddle music.

Hooks wandered around the edges of the dancing area, long arms folded over each other, watching the dancers and occasionally looking into the darkness outside the torchlights.

Apollo and Kyra had been dancing; now they sat side by side with his arm around her, talking softly about the success of the new school and some of her quicker pupils. In the months since the building had been completed, she and Apollo had cajoled parents from all over the neighborhood to send their children. Now the schoolhouse was full, every seat occupied, with nearly forty pupils coming every day. Kyra still

wrestled with the problem of parents keeping their
children home from time to time to do chores or to be
hired out, but she tried hard to convince them that their
children's best chance in this new era was to be educated. More often than not they looked at her as if she
spoke an unknown tongue. In a sense she did, but Kyra
merely redoubled her efforts, offering to teach the adults
the rudiments of reading, writing, and figuring in the
evening.

To this end she had moved out of Jothan's cabin and
made the teacher's alcove of her school into her own
home, doing her cooking in the fireplace, concealing
her bed and few pieces of clothing behind a curtain.

Apollo tried more than once to persuade her not to
live so far from anyone, or better still, to allow him to
move in with her and protect her. "Kyra, ain't you
afraid o' ghosses an' boogers out theah?"

Kyra chuckled. "I never even knew what boogers
were until you started trying to scare me with them.
No, Apollo, I'm not afraid. And it's good to have my
own quarters. If I hear somebody snoring in the night,
I know it's myself."

"Ah doan snore," he said hopefully.

"Hint, hint," she said, looking at him and laughing.

His eyes held hers, he said smiling, "Cain't blame
me fo' keepin' on tryin', can you?"

"That's the sign of a true hero, Apollo, a man who
keeps on trying against all odds."

"The odds," he said significantly, "favah me."

She had to laugh. "Maybe they do, after all. I'd
probably be disappointed if you gave up now."

He squeezed her against his side briefly. "Ah'm not
givin' up, no way."

At their back, a little distance away in some bushes,
they became aware of soft laughter, a pleading tone
followed by a gentle slap, then long murmurs, the
sound of a kiss, more murmurs, and then small snap-
pings of twigs as someone lay down. After a while the

bushes began to shake, their leaves rhythmically moving, although there was no perceptible breeze.

Apollo found that his mouth had gone dry and he could not speak a word. He became acutely aware of Kyra, so close beside him that they could do what that other couple were doing. If she, too, lay down, he could roll right over onto her, join his mouth and his body to hers. He wanted to move, leap up and get out of there; he wanted Kyra's hand on him to ease the bursting ache in his groin; he wished . . . Oh, God, how he wished . . .

Kyra too had fallen silent, waiting like Apollo for the shaking of the leaves to reach a crescendo, waiting for the sighs or moans of rapture to be uttered and to die slowly away and the leaves to be still once again. She did not know how her grip had tightened on Apollo's hand, or that she was hardly breathing, listening for the small sounds that to them soared over the music.

The sounds they awaited came, and diminished. The music stopped while the fiddlers went to fill their cups.

Apollo took a deep breath to fill lungs that hadn't known air for long moments. "Guess we bettah get on home."

She nodded. "Whatever you say, Apollo."

Hooks loomed up beside them, his face gaunt in the torchlight. "Havin' a good time, folks?" he asked genially. "Still plenty o' whisky left in theah." Without waiting for an answer, he strode over to the bushes, parted them, and peered in.

Annabelle Twoshoes gasped first, hastily putting down the long, slim legs that were wrapped around the bared bottom of Lincoln Jackson. Link pulled away from her, jerking up his trousers as she pulled her dress into place. "Rev'und, we wuz jes'—jes' tryin' it on fo' size," Link explained glibly.

"Oh, no, suh, we ain't doin' nothin' *wrong*," said Annabelle.

Hooks's avid eyes had seen it all: Annabelle's full,

pointed breasts with their erect nipples, the dress rolled up around the midriff, not concealing the small, delectable navel; her soft, flat belly, the hipbones showing palely through the cream-and-coffee skin. He saw the tightly curled mound of pubic hair and the way it ran down each side of the moist cleft at the beginning of her thighs, and the tight way those smooth, rounded thighs fitted together even as she hastily closed them. He put the sight away carefully in his mind, to be taken out, gazed upon, and caressed at his leisure.

His voice was mild. "Guess you two made up youah diffunces, huh?"

Annabelle was sitting up now, with Link squatting beside her. Through the thin material of her shift he could just glimpse her nipples, see her rapid breathing. "Oh, yassuh, we done make up, doan we, Link?"

Link, having advantageously combined the hardening of his desires with the softening of Annabelle's attitude, was more cautious. "Well, mebbe we do dat, Rev'und. We is sho' thinkin' 'bout it anyways."

Hooks's voice carried readily to Apollo and Kyra. "Guess you two wasn't lissenin' when Ah was talkin' 'bout temptation theah in church."

"*Ah* was lissenin'," Annabelle declared, "but Link done temp' me too fah."

"Link, it doan make me proud t'heah that Ah been talkin' t'the air," Hooks said in mild severity. "Now Ah ain't gonna say nothin' t'y'all this time, but nex' time Ah catch you like this, Ah hope it's right aftah Ah jes' marry you up."

Annabelle said boldly, "Well, mebbe we gwine 'head an' do dat, huh, Link? You done say we will!"

Link's answer was mumbled, and Hooks said, "Doan you fo'git what you say, Link, 'cause the Lawd done heah an' he woan fo'git, an' Ah woan fo'git. Ah'm gonna remembah." He turned around to return to the dance area.

Briefly his eyes caught Apollo's and slid away. This black man disturbed him. Then, annoyed that any black should have an effect on him, he looked at Apollo again. This time his gaze was studied and unflinching. "You folks ain't leavin' now, Ah y'all? Ah might need somebody latah on fo' shaparoons—somebody that woan give in t'the weakness o' the flesh. Bein' a schoolmarm Ah guess makes you jes' 'bout as pure as a woman kin git, doan it, Kyra? Ah might jes' call on you t'look aftah these people whilst Ah go 'long t'mah Sunday church."

Kyra's eyes glittered in the darkness, then she calmed herself, trying to remember that a Southerner's idea of a compliment to a Negro was a far cry from her own ideas. She said regretfully, and respectfully, "I'd like to help you, Reverend Hooks, but we are both quite tired. It has been a long day for us."

Hooks stared at her for a moment, then waved a long arm toward the dancers. "They ain't tired." He paused, then added, smiling, "But you go on, Ah know you got t'git youah rest." The innuendo was plain.

Kyra said with dignity, "Perhaps the Coles would act as chaperones for you. I believe you should find them sufficiently upstanding."

Hooks's gaze sought Apollo once more. Apollo watched the preacher with brooding dark eyes. He remained silent, his face unreadable. Hooks, at a loss for words, moved awkwardly. Abruptly he said, "Well, g'night then."

Kyra and Apollo watched him walk among the dancers, smiling and making amiable conversation. Then they got up and started back to Mossrose.

The crescent moon was high now, casting a dim light along the dirt road. Neither of them had spoken since they had left the gaily torch-lighted area of the frolic. Apollo felt the need to say something, anything, to fill the void that seemed to yawn between them; yet he could think of nothing to say that did not pertain to those bushes and their shaking.

Kyra was preoccupied, struggling to understand the Southern mind. Had Reverend Jabez Hooks been a

Northerner, she wouldn't have trusted him for a minute;
but he was Southern, and try as she would Kyra still
misjudged the kindly meant Southern insult for the intended one. Very little that was said to Negroes in the
South was uplifting. She couldn't get the speech he had
made at Ruel's funeral out of her mind, yet only she
and Adam had seemed to see anything amiss. The
other blacks and the few whites who had attended
seemed to accept his sermon as fitting, even complimentary. It had taken her a long time to find herself
able to forgive his remarks. Now, trying to be fair to
the preacher, because he had annoyed her again tonight, she tested a sentiment on Apollo. "That Reverend
Hooks is a mild and gentle man, don't you think,
Apollo?"

Apollo caught his breath and let it out partway. "Ah
guess so . . . Ah doan know jes' what you mean."

Kyra thought for a moment, then said tentatively,
"He could have been quite severe with Annabelle and
Link tonight, you know. But he was lenient."

Apollo, at that point, possibly understood more
about Reverend Jabez Hooks than Kyra did; for just
a moment as Hooks had turned away from Annabelle
and Link, Apollo had glimpsed the lascivious expression on the preacher's face and the bulge in his trousers.
Then he thought of his own reaction to the sounds that
came from the bushes. He replied carefully, "Yes.
Mebbe he was."

Kyra flared up immediately, as though she had been
waiting for any excuse. "Oh, Apollo, don't be so quick
to judge people! Reverend Hooks preaches hell-fire and
brimstone sometimes, and he says things that are ill-
advised, but deep down he is—a—a very humane person, forgiving and understanding."

Apollo, with his lately acquired knowledge of white
men and their privileges, had an uncomfortable twinge,
wondering what it was Hooks was up to. Remembering
again his own reaction, he tried to quell his suspicions
that a white man becoming excited by viewing such a

scene was more sinister than a black man doing the
same thing. He swallowed his dislike and distrust of
Hooks and said lamely, "Ah—we need mo' people like
that, doan we, Kyra?"

Kyra laughed, amused. "Now you're quoting me,
Apollo, turning my own words on me. I knew I should
never have taught you to read, or talked about my
philosophy with you. I have handed you a sword to use
against me."

"Ah wouldn't use anythin' aginst you. Iffen you say
Rev'und Hooks is a good man, Ah'll try to see it that
way."

Kyra looked away, then she leaned against Apollo's
arm as they walked. "I don't know what I think about
him. That is why I said I had given you a sword. I say
Reverend Hooks is humane and kind, but when I hear
the same words come from your lips, I'm not sure I
can believe it."

"Then why you sayin' it?"

She laughed at herself in light mockery. "Because I
don't care much for white Southerners. I can't tell when
they're being kind and when they're not. Oh, Apollo,
don't you see? They are ignorant—some as ignorant as
we blacks are. I can't tell when they are simply mouthing stupidities they have believed for years because they
know no better, or when they are deliberately making
fun of us, insulting us."

Apollo stopped walking and turned her to him. "Ah
doan know fo' sho' 'bout Rev'und Hooks neithah, but
Ah ain't nevah seen that he did anythin' fo' any of
ouah people." He paused. "But Ah ain't seen him do
hahm eithah. Ah jes' doan like him."

Kyra began walking again, feeling better now. The
Reverend Jabez Hooks, for all he was a man of God,
was not an easy man to like. If Apollo felt that way
too, she could not be entirely wrong about him. Her
mind greatly eased, she began softly to sing, "In the
sweet bye and bye, we shall meet on that beautiful
shore . . ."

Apollo, hearing the languid sweetness of her voice and feeling the warmth of her body as his arm encircled her, let his mind drift back half an hour. Now in his imagination they sat once again on the little grassy hill beyond the torchlights, watching the dancers, hearing the fiddles and . . . those other noises . . . the bushes shaking . . . the rapturous moans . . . He shuddered, the delicious and terrible tension upon him again.

"Apollo, are you cold?"

"Mebbe. A li'l bit."

"We'll hurry on, then."

But it was a long way to her schoolhouse, and as they spoke casually of many things, Apollo's mind was in turmoil, remembering the very few times he had made love with Kyra, the gentleness and sometimes the fierceness of her giving, the feeling of completion he had with her in his arms. On this night, with her voice making music in his ears, he ached with longing to make love with her again.

Now they were at the door of her cabin. The thin moon and the stars were brilliant in a black velvet sky. In the nearby woodland, a whippoorwill called. A faint breeze stirred and touched Apollo's cheek. He wanted to reach out for her, but he could not, for tonight he knew he had little control over himself, and he would ruin all that they might someday have together.

He stood with his hands in his pockets glumly waiting her dismissal. But she said casually, "Would you like to come in for a cup of coffee? It may be spring, but that long walk made me chilly too."

"That'd be fine," he said, reaching past her to open her door. As her skirt brushed his hand, he pulled back, his breath feeling a little short. It didn't mean nothing, he kept telling himself, she might ast him in but she didn't mean nothing by it.

They made their way past the desks, which had been perfectly lined up and tidied before the children had left for the weekend. Kyra lighted a lamp and stirred the ashes in the fireplace, finding a few glowing bits that were enough to start the shavings Apollo kept ready for her use. In a few minutes the flames were licking at the bottom of the coffeepot she had set on a small tripod. "There now, it won't be long," she said.

Apollo squatted on his heels, his back to the small fire, watching the way it lighted Kyra's beautiful cheekbones and her full, pleasant mouth. "We doan need that lamp now, Kyra."

"I guess we don't," she agreed, and rose to blow it out. The room acquired a pleasant, warm dimness, with the desks retreating into shadow. The room, Apollo noticed, had the faint, clean smell of lemon verbena that clung to Kyra's clothing and her person. It erased the impersonality, made this Kyra's stronghold. It gave him, Apollo Justus Sherman, someplace to keep coming to, a place of wisdom and courage and peace. And for him, that place would always be wherever Kyra was.

He said, "Kyra, why ain't we married? Ah think we ought to be."

She looked away from him, uncomfortable.

"We git along, doan we? An' right well, considerin' Ah was bawn a slave an' you wasn't."

"Yes, we get along right well."

"Then why ain't—why *aren't* we married?"

"I'm—I'm not ready yet. I don't want to—to commit myself so soon after—" Once she had been able to say "Ruel's death," but now, now that she was mostly over it, it seemed such a harsh and emotionless phrase for that terrible period in her life.

"It ain't soon, Kyra. You ain't bein' disrespec'ful."

Kyra rose from her chair and pulled the pot off the fire, putting just the right amount of cream and sugar into Apollo's cup before pouring. They sipped for a few moments in silence.

"Iffen Ah was sumbuddy else," Apollo began, "sumbuddy edjicated like Ruel was, an' with good speech an' fine clo's, would that make any diffunce with you?" He still squatted, staring out into the shadows, fearing her reply yet hoping . . . hoping.

She did not answer him directly, instead saying, "I knew a man like that once, before I met Ruel. He had all that and was a rich man besides. We—we were going to be married—until one day he became angry with me over a trifle. Then I saw him for everything he was not, and I asked him to give my promise back."

"Ah doan need to know things like that, Kyra."

"What I'm trying to say, Apollo, is that the outward symbols do not make a man more manly, or give him a truer heart, or make him strong when a woman needs him for a rock to shelter under. It would make no difference to me if you had riches and education. I would be very pleased for your sake, but I would feel the same toward you as I do now."

"Youah sayin' Ah'm fine the way Ah am?"

She smiled. "You're just fine, Apollo, the way you are."

"Theah's times Ah been wonderin' mahseff," he said, shaking his head. "You think mebbe you might—commit youahseff soon?"

Her smile faded. "I—don't know."

Apollo finished his cup and set it on her table. "Ah bettah go now, Kyra."

She looked up at him, her face soft in the dying firelight. Her eyes held his for a long moment, during which Apollo's heart began to race hopefully. She said, "I don't want you to leave, not yet."

He knelt beside her, his hands on her arms, his face close to hers. "You know what youah sayin', Kyra?"

Her head moved in a small nod. "Yes. I know."

He kissed her tenderly. "Ah doan want to leave you. Not tonight, not in the mawnin' gloam, not any time." He pulled her up into his arms and their lips met, tentatively, then passionately, hungrily; and her lips were as eager as his.

Her hands touched his shirt, and her fingers flew, unbuttoning him; then she pulled off her own clothes and they stood naked before each other, tall, proud, loving and wanting love. She held out her hand to him and led him to her bed, shutting the curtain after them.

They woke up together. He was lying on his back, holding Kyra, whose mouth was pressed against his shoulder, her arm around his neck. The springtime sun, mid-morning bright, streamed in over the short curtain that enclosed them. Kyra gasped, her eyes wide seeing Apollo and the angle of the sunlight.

"Lawd God, what day is it?"

Apollo chuckled, holding her to him as she tried to struggle out of bed. "Sunday, Kyra," he said, and joyously pulled her back half on top of him. She collapsed, laughing in relief and trying to pull the sheet to cover them. Apollo protested, "Woman, you gwine try to hide from me now, when Ah spent all night lookin' at you?"

"How you gwine see black woman in the dahk?" she said, imitating him, and they laughed again. Then she sat up on the narrow bed, winding the sheet around her. "Oh, Apollo, I'm so embarrassed. What if somebody comes and finds us? What will they think of me, of us?"

"If that's all you got to worry 'bout, then quit worryin'. We ain't none of nobody's bizness."

She was serious as her eyes met his. "And what must you think of me? I—"

He interrupted her, putting his fingers over her lips. "What Ah think of you is Ah still want you to be Missus Apollo Justus Sherman. An' then Ah doan nevah have to git up an' go home." He added hastily, "That ain't the only reason; the main reason is Ah love you—which mebbe Ah has said befo'—an' would like to have the oppahtewnitty t'say agin from time to time."

With dignity despite her nakedness, Kyra stood up and began to dress. "I—I can't talk about that now, Apollo. I'll—get breakfast."

He pointed out reasonably, "You got to talk about it sometime."

But she had gone out, still fastening her skirt, to start the morning fire. He followed her partly dressed. "Kyra, you ain't 'shamed?"

She did not meet his eyes. "Of being with you? Of waking up with you? No, I'm not ashamed."

He pointed to the corner where the bedding lay tumbled. "How 'bout that? What we did in baid?"

"I should be," she said obliquely. "Excuse me, I'll go get water."

He took the bucket out of her hand and stood squarely before her. "Ah ast a reasonable question. Doan go hidin' youah eyes from me."

"I—don't know."

"Kyra, you ain't one o' them womans that use a man 'cause he's a good stud, ah you?"

She looked horrified. "Is that what you think I am?"

"Well, Ah doan know. Is that what you think Ah am?"

"A good st—?" She gulped. "Sweet Jesus, Apollo, how are we ever going to have breakfast if you keep standing there?"

"Iffen you doan ansah mah question, breakfast is gonna be the las' thing Ah want."

"Which question? You asked so many."

"What we did."

She looked him straight in the eyes. "I should be ashamed, but I'm not, because I didn't *use* you any more than you used me. I—wanted you to stay. I just didn't think it would be—all night."

He burst out laughing, and she had to laugh with him. As he went out the door he turned and shook the bucket at her, saying, "Befo' the sun goes down this evenin' Ah'm gonna go ovah to Mossrose an' git us a big ol' roostah. He git us up fo' sho'."

Kyra shook her head as she turned back to her small table that served as desk and kitchen counter. She began to slice pork fat to fry with the potatoes and eggs. To herself she muttered, "A big ol' rooster! A good stud! A woman who uses a man—Kyra, you've let yourself in for something now, he expects you to let him stay tonight too!"

She looked up as he came back in, carrying the full bucket with utmost care. Then she thought, *Why is it that I'm holding back?*

She answered her own question: Because I'm so mixed up with wanting him, I don't know if I love him too!

And if I don't . . . then I am using him, and he is too fine for that.

Kyra, decide. Soon.

CHAPTER TWENTY

Cutler Whitaker had never felt better. For once in his life he knew what it was to get up in the morning, look at his reflection in his shaving mirror, and know he was his own man. After a struggle of wills, past hurts, and current doubts, he managed to make Blythe believe that this time he would stand by her. She had put him through a particular kind of hell, insisting that he know all the details of her fall from grace. He remembered, without pain now, his protests, "I don't care about your past. It is the here and now that counts. We won't ever look back—the past doesn't exist for us."

"It does exist," she had insisted. He hadn't known how much iron there was in that small body of hers. She wouldn't consider a future unless both of them had raked over their pasts, hiding nothing, admitting and recognizing all the faults and mistakes and weaknesses that had been a part of both of them.

It had taken months before he could convince her of his sincerity, and even then she had not allowed him to live with her. He had spent miserable days and even more confused and miserable nights trying to fathom her reasoning. He recalled the day he had cried in frustration and anger, "But you have made a living by sleeping with men! Why won't you allow me to stay here? I don't understand!"

As placidly as if she had never known the life she had led, she replied, "For you and me, it will be marriage or it will be nothing. I won't live with you. I won't make a business of love. Of sex, yes, but never of love."

She had been right, he now admitted. For them she

had been right, for they now rested in a world with each other that had no dark, hidden secrets, no private worries or doubts. He didn't question her feelings for him, nor would he ever have to.

Cutler smiled at himself, straightening his shoulders, looking forward to the day ahead. With a final approving glance at himself, he left his room behind the shipping office and went to the stable to hire a horse for the day.

"Hey theah, Mistah Cutlah, wheah you goin' all spiffed up?" the stableman asked with a laugh.

Cutler, feeling jaunty, tossed the man a coin. "Visitin', Jeb, a real important visit."

Jeb's old face screwed up into a grin, his eyes almost squinted closed. "She sho' mus' be a purty one."

"She is. Second prettiest woman livin'—my mama." Cutler wheeled the horse and headed through town for the River Road, leaving Jeb to wonder who came first.

He kept his horse to a steady trot, enjoying as he never had before the ride to the Whitaker plantation, and thinking that it was strange he should learn to appreciate it at the same time he had resigned himself to losing his place there. His mother and father would be scandalized when he told them he planned to marry Blythe Saunders.

He turned into the long drive. Ned had planted new trees along the road to replace those that had been ruined or used for firewood during the War. They were small, golden rain trees, almost mockeries of the old, tall, straight-trunked maidenhairs he remembered from his youth. Looking at them, he wondered what it was that tied a man to his family long after it was time he should have cut those ties. Had it been the War and the uncertainties they had all faced? Or had it begun long before that?

He thought perhaps it had. Perhaps it came from the sense of continuity that so many old families seem to have. Families that were a long chain living through time, lending to each other a sense of identity and purpose and importance; but also chains that held one to a future determined generations before.

Now he was about to break that nice, neat chain of Whitakers who had lived and fought and planted in this county for over a century. He was going to break the tidy vision of a single family forging together through the years. And he thought of his brothers and sisters. Andrew and Camille would go down as hero and heroine of the Whitaker family. Andrew had died in battle in the War. Camille had died a heroine's miserable death, also a fatality of the grand War. Brock's mistakes would be forgotten in time, and he too would fit nicely into the family memories of those who had died too young.

Perhaps he too could be listed as a War victim. He would be known as the black sheep, the ne'er-do-well who had married the fallen woman and left his responsibilities behind. That left Enid and Cedric to carry on for the Whitakers. And he wondered if they didn't also represent the end of the Whitaker line in Georgia. Neither had married, and neither was likely to, not now. Cedric was content to live his days like a good old boy of times past, spending his money on women, gambling, and horseplay. He reveled in the past and carried it with him into a time in which it no longer existed anywhere but in his own mind. And Enid, at twenty-seven, was an embittered old maid. She had loved once and lost; Enid, stubborn and cynical, would never risk her love again.

He looked up to see the dark-red brick house, its windows gleaming clean and welcoming in the early afternoon light. He wondered what part of himself he was losing now as he came to its doors to say good-bye. Lester Warren, the Whitakers' stableman, came up to him. "Aftahnoon, Mistah Cutlah, been a while since we see you. Missy be mighty glad you' heah."

Cutler handed him the reins and clapped him companionably on the back. "It has been a while, Lester.

I let myself get a mite too busy in town, I suppose. It's good to see you. How's Ivy—she still bakin' up a storm?"

Lester, grinning, patted his stomach, which protruded noticeably over his belt. "She sho' is. Ah tells her she otta open up a li'l shop an' doan do nothin' but make them good cakes. We be the riches' niggers in the County." He giggled, shaking his head. "But you knows wimmen, Mistah Cutlah, they doan lissen to sense."

Cutler laughed agreeably. "I'll put in a word for your idea. Maybe if we gang up on her she'll do it. Sounds good to me."

Lester looked at him, surprised and pleased that he had been taken seriously. "Why Mistah Cutlah, Ah'd sho' 'preciate that. Ah would 'ndeed."

"Consider it done." Cutler leaped up the front steps and opened the front door, calling loud, cheerful greetings to his parents. Ned Whitaker poked his head out from his study and broke into a large grin when he saw his son.

Emma came hurrying from upstairs, her arms outstretched long before she had reached him. He embraced his mother heartily, lifting her from her feet and planting a kiss on her cheek. As soon as he put her down, Emma smoothed her skirt and hair and ushered him into the living room. She immediately rang the bell and asked Ivy to bring refreshments.

"Ivy," Cutler said, "I hear you and Lester are thinking about opening a bakery."

Ivy looked hastily at Emma. "Dat Lester, he all mouth an' no sense. Ah likes mah job heah."

"Aww, come on now, Ivy, give Lester his due. It's a good idea. No one in the County can bake like you. Ask Mama if every lady hereabouts wouldn't patronize your shop if you had one."

Ivy smiled, her eyes cast down. "Ah wouldn't want to work nowhere but fo' Miss Emma."

Cutler was undaunted. "Mama, tell her that she

could make a success of a bakeshop. Tell her she'd have more customers than she could handle."

Emma looked at her smiling son, shocked. "Cutler," she said severely, "this is not the time or place for this kind of discussion. Please recall who you are and act accordingly." She looked sternly at Ivy. "You may bring our refreshments now, Ivy."

The embarrassed woman scurried from the room. Cutler said no more until she had vanished from sight. "Why wouldn't you tell her, Mama? She could be very successful, you know."

Emma sat stiffly in her chair. "Cutler, you forget yourself."

He feigned surprise. "But why? How? It is true, isn't it? Ivy is the best baker around—everybody would come to her shop."

Emma's lips were pressed so tight they looked bloodless. She spoke in stiff-lipped fashion. "We do not discuss such matters with a *servant!* I believe you have been in Savannah too long, Cutler. Apparently city ways have made you forget your upbringing. It's no wonder, associating with the hoi polloi as you do. Please, we will have no more of it."

"But surely you want what's best for Ivy," he persisted.

"Ivy has no part in this!" Emma snapped. "She works for me, and I need her. Remember that, please. I am your mother. If you must exhibit sympathy, save it for me. Good help is difficult to find these days, things being what they are. I try my best to keep some semblance of order and charm in this house for you children and your father. How can I be expected to do that with my own son undermining my efforts?"

"Your mama is right, Cutler," Ned said, as though that closed the matter. "We all know you've turned Radical and you're in pretty deep with that Loyal Leaguer, Captain Tremain. We've kept quiet about his influence on you, trusting your good judgment and breeding to pull you out. But now you've gone too far,

trying to start trouble with the house servants. I won't
have it. Leave them to your mother. And you're not to
say another word to Ivy, do you hear?"

In spite of himself, in spite of the fact that he had
known his parents' attitudes, Cutler was disappointed
and hurt. He smiled grimly, nodding his head. "I see.
Of course you must understand that this does not
change my opinion, and that we are in total disagreement."

Ned looked at him kindly, the elder statesman viewing the young, untested upstart. Casually dismissing
Adam Tremain's reliance on his son to manage a large,
busy shipping office he said, "When you've carried
some real responsiblity for a while, I think you'll see
things more clearly." Eyebrows raised, he smiled. "That
won't be very long now. I'm getting older, you know.
It's time I began turning over the workings of the plantation to you—a little at a time, so it won't be too much
for you. When you go back to Savannah tomorrow, I
want you to tell Captain Tremain to look for another
man to run that office of his. I'm going to be needing
you out here."

Cutler felt the familiar sinking feeling of entrapment
in the spidery family web. Almost as if it had never
existed, the buoyant strength he felt when he was with
Blythe was disappearing. He was thirty-one years old,
and suddenly he was a child again, a grown child who
couldn't quite fathom or contradict his father's authority. Cutler sat listening to his father, his new-found
voice lost to him. He began to feel panicky and helpless. He hadn't even mentioned Blythe's name and
already he felt himself slipping back to where he had
been—a perpetual, ineffectual child.

Emma was saying, "Since you'll be staying, Cutler,
we'll send to town for your things. You can just send
a message to Captain Tremain that you'll not be working for him any longer. I never did like the idea of a
Whitaker working for an outsider."

"An outsider?" Cutler asked hesitantly.

"Oh, well, you know what I mean. It's true he's married to a Moran, and that certainly makes him eminently acceptable, but nonetheless, he doesn't come from this county, and we really don't know that much about him—only what Dulcie has told her mother. When you think about it, he's no more than an adventurer. There's even some question as to which side he was on during the War—and just look what he's done to politics here! Why, Cedric tells me that much of the unrest between the darkies and the planters can be laid right at his door."

Cutler looked at her, wide-eyed. "You offered him the hospitality and comfort of this house for nearly two years! You never said you felt this way about him."

Emma looked mildly uncomfortable, but recovered quickly. "I would never refuse my home to the Morans. Why, Patsy Moran is one of my dearest friends. I couldn't very well refuse her son-in-law, now could I?"

"If you could have, would you?"

Emma looked at Ned. "I rather doubt the question would have come up. Perhaps you didn't notice, but that is one of the differences between our kind of people and Captain Tremain. I don't believe he would have asked for the hospitality of his neighbors. He most likely would have housed his family in a public establishment."

"A hotel?" Cutler asked.

"Yes," Emma said primly.

"And that is wrong?"

She glanced knowingly at Ned. "New rich. Strainers."

Cutler didn't know what to say, and a heavy silence descended on the room. It wasn't broken until Ivy returned bearing a tray laden with pastries, lemonade, and wafer-thin sandwiches.

Emma thanked her, and served her husband and son. Cutler looked at his plate of small delicacies, and couldn't eat. He watched his father and mother happily consume the sandwiches and felt that they consumed a part of him with every bite they took. He was slipping away, being lost again, and knew that if it happened today, there would never be another day when he could work up the courage and self-esteem to free himself. In a sudden burst of desperate self-preservation, he put down his plate with a clatter and said baldly, "I'm getting married."

Emma's sandwich was poised mid-bite. She sat ridiculously frozen in place staring at Cutler. Ned managed to clear his throat and force a congenial laugh. "Well, now! Married. Who's the lucky bride?"

"Cutler," Emma finally said, aghast. "What do you mean you're getting married? Why didn't I know about this? Why haven't you brought her home as you should? Where is she? Who is she?"

Cutler took a deep breath. "Blythe Saunders."

Emma clutched her chest, her head thrown back pathetically. "No-o-o, oh, no, no! Ned . . . my salts . . . my salts . . ."

Ned Whitaker glared at Cutler, then quickly went to Emma's side, pulling her smelling salts from the pocket of her skirt. He wafted the odoriferous bottle under his wife's nose. "Cutler, look what you've done. What the hell's got into you, boy? You been drinkin'? Why'd you say a damn fool thing like that. If you weren't a Whitaker I'd say you're off your head."

"I am getting married, Daddy—to Blythe."

He jammed the smelling salts into Emma's hand and turned to face his son. "I heard what you said the first time. Now it's time you hear me. No damn fool man would marry Blythe Saunders. No man, hear me! You don't buy the cow when you're gettin' the milk free."

Cutler, red in the face, stood squared off to his father. "I won't hear you slander her name, Daddy. She's goin' to be my wife."

"She's not going to be your wife! I'll see you dead before I'd stand by and see that!"

Cutler shouted back, "Then you'll see me dead!"

"By God, I will," Ned screamed, red-faced as his son. Ridiculously, he marched around the room in a furious, futile search for his Army Colt. "Where is my gun?" he shouted to no one. "Emma! Where'd I put my Colt?"

Emma's head lolled. "Cutler," she moaned in a high, weakened voice, "you can't do this to me. You're my son, my baby. You won't do this to your mama, will you, darlin'?"

"Where's my Colt!"

"I'm marrying her. I love her. I've always loved her."

"She's a God-damned whore!" Ned roared at him.

Emma shrieked, and slouched over the couch again. Ned shoved the smelling salts under her nose. "Can't you see what you're doing to your mama? You're killing her."

"Why can't any of you ever listen to me—see my side of it?" Cutler said in angry frustration.

"Because you haven't got a side! I'll disinherit you, by God. You'll never set foot on Whitaker property again. I'll see to that. You're no son of mine."

Emma rallied again to turn her fear-filled eyes on Cutler. "We'll be the laughingstock of the County, Cutler. You can't do this to us. Your daddy and I won't be able to show our faces in public. Oh, blessed heaven, what will Patricia say? She'll laugh—she'll never talk to me again!"

"Is that all it means to you?" Cutler said. "Don't you care about me at all?"

"Of course we do!" Emma declared. "Why else would we be trying at this very moment to prevent you from making this awful mistake? Think what you're doing, Cutler! You know the sort she is. Think what this will do to your sister! Oh, my dear merciful Lord, make him think of poor Enid. Cutler—" She reached out a languid hand toward him, pleadingly. "Cutler, tell me you've already given up this foolish notion."

Cutler stood for what seemed a long time looking at his mother and father. Then he said quietly, and finally, "Good-bye, Mama, Daddy."

By the time he was once more on the River Road

heading back to Savannah, his stomach was roiling with nausea. He stopped near the edge of the woods and vomited. Afterwards he lay in the long sweet grass beside a small stream, thinking about today and about his family. With a sadness sharpened by relief, he knew he was done with them. Finally, he banished them with thoughts of Blythe.

He remounted and continued his journey. He had one last task to accomplish before he and Blythe could leave Chatham County behind them, leave Georgia behind, leave the whole stinking, decaying South behind them forever.

CHAPTER TWENTY-ONE

"Adam! Adam!" Dulcie called, laughing, her voice high as she burst open the front door and ran across the veranda to interrupt the serious conversation he had been having with Beau.

The little boy clutched Adam in confusion as he saw his mother running and shouting, then he bagan to smile and laugh with her.

She ran into Adam's free arm, momentarily buried her face against his shoulder as she caught her breath, then said, "You'll never guess what has happened!" Her golden eyes were dancing, inviting Adam to share her joy.

Adam chuckled, knowing he and Dulcie were both thinking of the same thing—for several weeks now, there had been reason to believe that Dulcie was carrying another child. "Beau, your mama is a silly girl. What do you suppose she is talking about?" His eyes smiled into Dulcie's.

Beau smiled, uncertain of this adult nonsense, then he shrugged, his small hands turned dramatically upward.

"Oh, Adam, I'm talking about something *else!* I have the most amazing news—and I got it before you did. I *think*. I did, didn't I?"

"How can I answer until you tell me what it is?"

"It's Cutler!"

He said blankly, "Cutler?" and Dulcie giggled in triumph.

"There! I did surprise you! He's marrying Blythe Saunders, and the Whitakers have disowned him, and Emma thinks she is dying, and Mama is upstairs now with a wet cloth on *her* head—a sympathy death, I think. Isn't it the most wonderful news in the world, Adam? I want to go see her. Let's have a party for them. Oh, please! I want to do *something!*"

"Slow down. Tell me this again—slowly. Beau, go see Mindy. She'll take you for a walk—tell her Daddy said so."

Dulcie told Adam her news again, this time more slowly and calmly. He listened, then asked, "Will they be staying here?"

He stopped Dulcie cold with that. "Wouldn't they? I don't know, Adam. Mama didn't say anything about that. I suppose it would be difficult, wouldn't it?"

"I would say so, especially with feelings about Blythe running as they do."

Dulcie bit her lip, thinking quickly. "Then we must have a party right away. I want to do something to show them that we are happy for them. If they are going to leave here, I want them to know—"

"Wait a minute. No one has said they are leaving here. I just said I thought it would be uncomfortable for them."

"Whom do you think I should invite?" Dulcie asked.

Adam threw his hands up. "You're not listening."

"Yes, I am, but I know you are right. They'll leave. And we'll have a party before they do. I want to buy them a marvelous wedding gift. Help me think of what we can give them."

"Dulcie, have you considered that perhaps no one would come to a party for Blythe and Cutler?"

"Maybe they could be married here at Mossrose. Just think, a wedding right here in our garden!"

"Dulcie!"

She looked up at him, her golden eyes sparkling with merriment and a tinge of sudden doubt. "Don't you want to have them here, Adam?"

"Damn it, woman, you know very well I do. But I—"

"Good. Then help me plan the party."

In the days following, Adam and Dulcie went about

their plans for Blythe and Cutler. Dulcie tackled Mossrose, polishing it until it shone, driving the yardmen
like an overseer of old to get the gardens into immaculate shape. She had new bushes planted, flower beds
enlarged. The yard furniture was moved about dozens
of times, until she had the most pleasing arrangement
for dancing and conversation. She had the household
staff frantic with new recipes and cold-drink mixtures.
The house buzzed with chandeliers being washed, silver
being polished, china and linens being matched to perfection.

Adam spent his time in Jem's office writing letters
and sending telegrams to New York, New Orleans, and
San Francisco. The desk was piled with replies from
Rod Courtland in New York, Ben West and Tom
Pierson in New Orleans, and a Louis Boyce in San
Francisco. Though Dulcie asked him innumerable times
about his hasty activities and the constant trail of telegrams going to and fro, he just smiled and told her
this was his half of the surprise; he would tell her when
he was sure it would work out.

Dulcie fretted only briefly about his stubborn secre-
tiveness, for she was experiencing some problems she
should have anticipated, but had not. Replies to her
invitations were coming back, but only to express re-
grets. She didn't tell Adam how many there had been,
nor did she tell him that the only positive reply she
had received had come from Birdie, and she would be
coming without Billy Bob. Unwilling to admit defeat,
she sent out more invitations, and said nothing. Too
well she remembered Adam's warning.

With the day of the party nearing, and still no one
coming, Dulcie did something she had never thought
to see herself do. She went personally to the homes of
the men and women who had refused to come, and
asked them why. Humiliated and embarrassed almost
past endurance, she stood her ground and demanded
that their judgment and condemnation of Blythe be

spoken aloud to her. She did not succeed in changing any minds, but she did manage to tell her neighbors what she thought of their behavior. In the process, she decided that in her own way she had now made herself as much an outcast as Cutler Whitaker.

Finally, appalled and more than a little frightened, she confessed her actions to Adam. She curled up beside him in the private darkness of their bedroom and told him with merciless honesty what she had said and done.

He held her close, his hand gently caressing her back, but he said nothing.

She went on, "I've probably ruined your business, and I've certainly blackened our name and reputation."

He kissed her forehead, but still he said nothing.

"They probably will never speak to me again—Oh, Adam, they may take it out on Mama, too. What have I done? Adam . . . ? Adam, say something. I'm sorry. I shouldn't have meddled—but they made me so mad I didn't think— I didn't realize how badly this could affect your shipping until I'd already started telling people off. Adam, please say something."

"I love you," he said softly.

She pulled away from him slightly, trying to see his face in the darkness. "But I've made a terrible mess for all of us. I don't think you know how much I upset people, Adam. I even told Lydia Saunders that she made me ashamed to say I was a Southerner. I told her it was people like her were ruining the South."

"I know how bad it is, Dulcie."

"You mean they've already—? Then why aren't you angry? These people will never ship another thing on one of your ships. They'll say awful things about us, and gossip, and—"

"And I'm very proud of you."

"But Adam—" she protested, then, "Are you? Are you really?"

His lips caressed her cheek. "Very proud," he repeated. With one arm he hitched her body closer to his, thinking how slender she was, how fragile she seemed.

Dulcie pressed herself tight against him, her troubles receding. She sighed, happy once more. Somehow, in Adam's arms, the worst situations could be met and made light of; refreshed by his strength, she would find new strength all her own.

She murmured, "Adam, I'm so glad I'm going to have another child of yours. I know he'll be a wonderful person, just like you are."

He kissed her tenderly, holding her gently, wanting to possess her, yet aware of the tiny life that grew within her and fearing that he who had planted the seed might snuff it out.

Dulcie said, "Adam, please—come inside me. Now, so I can hold you, feel you a part of me. I need you— not to be loving and gentle—I just feel elemental, earthy, wanton. I need to be *had*—as though you are a big, rough stranger, and I—"

In spite of himself, his thoughts flew to the bayous of his youth, to a woman called Johnnie Mae and her games of pretense. *Play loike ye be a big ol' bear, an' ye wud wrostle me down,* she had said. *Play loike Oi be a lady, an' ye be makin' me do it wie ye. Play like . . .* "I don't want to hurt you, love," he said.

"You won't hurt me. Please, Adam, I need that." None too nicely, her teeth nipped his shoulder before she shoved him away.

His memories of the sunny-haired swamp girl fled to oblivion; gone were his fears for their unborn child. Roughly he grabbed her and jerked her back against him, his hand tight in her hair as he pulled her to meet his lips. She did not seem to yield to him; rather, she stiffened her body and tried to bite him with her open mouth.

Rudely he took hold of her nightgown at the neck, and yanked. A wide strip of cloth came away clear down the front of the garment. Dulcie, exposed, tried to roll away from him, but he pinned her in place with one hand. With gentle teeth he nipped down her breasts and her belly, even though her fingernails were clawing at his arms and back, and her hands were jerking at tufts of his curly hair.

He tried to part her legs, but she resisted. Finally, using both hands, he forced his knee in between them. His hands, exploring her now, were far from soothing. He ran them hard up her inner thighs, pressing the tender flesh at their joining. He drew his fingertips away wet. She was ready for him. She had abandoned even her token resistance.

Kneeling, steady, he pulled her hips up toward him and entered her as she balanced against him, her arms around his neck and her legs wrapped around his body.

Her mouth came to his, moist, eager, and their tongues met and tasted each other. He had hardly moved within her, holding her against him, and yet they were both climaxing in a sweet, intense flood of ecstasy. When after a long time it had finished, he moved slightly, or she moved slightly, and they felt the blissful little tremblings grow and fade again and again.

He laid her down on the bed once more and lay breathing heavily, his cheek pillowed on her thigh. In his nostrils was his own scent, and hers, and they mingled strong together, but he was too content to move. With one hand he stroked her leg lightly.

"Thank you, Adam," said Dulcie, and he could hear the pleasured huskiness in her voice.

He chuckled briefly. "You've welcome, my love. Pleased to oblige."

In the days that followed, until the night of the party, Dulcie made innumerable trips into Savannah to the new apartment Cutler had found for Blythe. After an awkward beginning, Dulcie and Blythe had renewed their old friendship. Dulcie learned where Blythe and Cutler intended to live after their wedding, and because Adam would not reveal what he was

working on so laboriously with his telegrams, she wrote
to Ben West herself and, unknown to Adam, made a
special arrangement of her own. Fairly bursting with
curiosity about what he was doing, and dying to be
able to see the look on his face when she announced
her own surprise to Cutler and Blythe, Dulcie spent a
seemingly endless afternoon before Blythe and Cutler
and Birdie were to arrive for what was now to be an
intimate dinner party for five.

For the evening, Dulcie had had Peggy dress her hair
in the popular waterfall style, smoothed back, and
brushed shining over a horsehair loop which hung low
on her neck. Her gown of peach silk featured great
swags of material forming the overskirt. The bodice was
cut low, with blond lace at the breast and trimming
the ruffles on the fitted sleeves. With it she carried an
ivory fan imported from the Orient and bought in
Nassau on one of her famous shopping trips with Glory
West.

She was nervous when she entered the softly candle-
lighted parlor on Adam's arm. The two of them sat
stiffly on chairs near each other, waiting for the arrival
of their three guests. Adam asked Josh to bring him a
branch rickey, and suggested that Dulcie have a glass
of sherry or plum brandy. Dulcie took a hesitant sip
of her brandy, then looked worriedly at Adam. "Do
you think Birdie will actually come?"

"She said she would be here." Adam took Dulcie's
hand reassuringly. "You have no reason to doubt her
word, do you?"

"No—not her word. She was hurt and angry that no
one else would come when she accepted. But she'll be
coming all that distance unescorted. It's different, you
know, when the time actually comes that one must dress,
leave the house, and get into a carriage alone. Perhaps
she'll be afraid, or maybe Billy Bob will try to talk
her out of it—she *is* defying him."

Adam acknowledged the possibility, then smiled at

her. "Let's not borrow trouble. Most likely she will be here. Perhaps it will be the other way around, and Birdie will persuade Billy he should come with her."

Dulcie laughed a little. "I'm not sure that would be an advantage. As a conversationalist, Billy leaves a lot to be desired. I really don't know how Birdie ever came to marry him!"

"She probably says the same thing about your marrying me."

Dulcie's eyes danced. "Not on your life. Just give Birdie a chance to change places."

"Ahh, I'll keep that in mind. Tonight may be more interesting than I had hoped."

"Adam Tremain, if you so much as look askance at Birdie Acton, I shall do damage to your ankle under the table with the very pointed toe of my hard little shoe."

Adam laughed. "The prospect seems to cheer you, my dear."

Both of them grew instantly silent when the doorbell sounded. Their eyes met, and they listened intently as Josh opened the door.

Dulcie breathed a sigh of relief. "It's Birdie!" She got up immediately and hurried to the hall to embrace her friend. "Oh, Birdie, I'm so glad you're the first to arrive."

Birdie giggled and returned Dulcie's hug, then turned her cheek up for Adam to kiss. "Thought I wasn't coming, didn't you?"

"Of course not! You said you'd be here," Dulcie protested.

Birdie playfully pinched her cheek. "Liar! You know I'm a coward at heart. I had the most awful time getting myself into that carriage all alone. I wasn't sure myself that I'd get here until we were past halfway, and then I knew it would take me as long to ride back home as it would to go on." She laughed again, then eyed Adam's and Dulcie's drinks. "Well, aren't you

going to offer me anything? Surely you two aren't going
to be nervous all alone and leave me out."

Birdie remained determinedly gay and lively as the
three awaited Blythe and Cutler. She took a bourbon
and branch water from Adam, a man's drink, he noted,
and then smiled at his own resistance to the many
changes the War had brought. She drank a little too
fast, and too often she would seek the understanding
comfort of Dulcie's eyes, only to turn nervously inward
at this meeting between herself and her sister.

It had been a long time since Birdie had seen Blythe.
She had written letters occasionally, but had been too
afraid to go to Savannah to seek her sister out. If she
were truthful, it hadn't been the fear of going to the
awful neighborhood where Blythe had lived for so long
that frightened her, but of being seen by someone who
would then later talk about her. She fought down the
quickly rising feeling of self-loathing and took another
healthy gulp of her drink. one couldn't afford to think
such thoughts. She was here. And tonight had to be a
nice, gay time.

Both women jumped when the doorbell sounded
again. "They're here," Birdie breathed.

Birdie stood up and turned to face the door just as
her sister entered the parlor. Blythe, slender and lovely
in a soft ochre gown, stopped just inside the room.
Neither woman said anything. Their eyes met and held,
searching each other for signs of forgiveness and love.
Birdie burst into tears and a smile all at once and ran
to embrace her sister.

Cutler immediately sought the security of Adam's
side. He wiped his hand across his brow. "I didn't
think I'd get her in here. We've been outside sitting on
the River Road for the last fifteen minutes. She was
afraid to see Birdie again."

Adam took him by the arm and led him to the small
cart on which Josh had placed several bottles and
mixes. "What you need is a drink. I have a feeling

we'll be left to our own devices for a time anyhow. Thirty more seconds should pass a few more tears, and all three ladies will head upstairs for talk and repair." Smiling, he looked over his shoulder at Dulcie, who had now joined the two sisters. Then he pulled his watch from his pocket and showed it to Cutler.

Dulcie said, "Adam, Cutler, please excuse us for a minute, will you? We have need of the powder room." She smiled and wiped at her eyes in explanation.

Adam managed to say something polite before he again looked at Cutler and began to laugh.

By the time the ladies returned, dinner was waiting, and they all went to the dining room. Cutler was fortified by three highballs and much reassuring talk from Adam. Blythe was much her old self, her friendship with Dulcie already reestablished, and the love reaffirmed between herself and Birdie. Talk around the dinner table was light, filled with memories and stories of times gone by.

After dinner there were several rounds of toasting. Then Adam, with an air of purpose, asked Cutler if he planned to remain head of the Savannah shipping office.

Dulcie's eyes riveted on Adam. Blythe looked in stern amazement at her fiancé. "Cutler Whitaker! You said you had taken care of everything!"

Cutler again mopped at his brow. "I meant to tell him—I just never found the right—"

Adam laughed. "Never mind, Cutler. I am taking unfair advantage. I've known for some time you wouldn't be staying here."

"I'm sorry, Adam, I truly am," Cutler said. "I've wanted to tell you—no, I haven't. The one difficult thing about leaving here is that I liked running the shipping office. It's the first time I've ever truly enjoyed and felt competent in what I was doing. I didn't know how to tell you. Now I'll be leaving you in a pickle. Who will you get to take my place?"

"Oh, I'll find someone," Adam said lightly. "But I don't like losing a good man. Would a shipping office in San Francisco have any appeal for you?"

Blythe was beaming, and Cutler was spechless.

"Adam!" Dulcie cried. "You knew all along! How did you find out where they're going? Now you won't be surprised at my gift, and here I thought finally I was one step ahead of you."

"You're steps ahead of *me*," Birdie said. "Tell us your surprise."

Dulcie rose and took from the serving table a small packet. She handed it to Blythe. "Passage on the *Black Swan* with Captain Ben West at the helm," she said proudly, and made a face at Adam as if to say, "Top that!" Then she couldn't resist telling him, "I've been in touch with Ben for weeks arranging this."

Cutler looked at Dulcie, then at Adam. "I—don't know what to say."

Birdie giggled. " 'Thank you' might fit the occasion. Now all you two need is a house, and I wish I could give it to you. I'm almost ashamed to give you my gift, Blythe." She took out a very small, carefully wrapped package.

Blythe unwrapped a delicate shell cameo and drew in a long, shaky breath, her eyes growing misty.

"It was Grandmother's. Remember it? Remember Mama used to let us pin it on our dresses sometimes when we were small? I always thought the cameo looked like you."

Blythe hugged the brooch to her breast with one hand and reached out for her sister with the other. Once more they were crying and laughing in each other's arms. "Oh, Birdie, I'll treasure it. Always. Always."

Cutler Whitaker, smiling at everybody at the table, reflected that for himself and Blythe, life had not begun until he had swept away dependence and deceit, and become his own man. Yet without the example of the consistent strength of Adam Tremain, he might not have done it even for Blythe. In a sense, he owed Adam his life.

"Adam," Cutler said, "thank you is a very short phrase, but from the bottom of my heart, I thank you. For everything."

CHAPTER TWENTY-TWO

Kyra worked long hours in her school, and by the next year was beginning to see the fruits of her labor in the children's progress. Nearly all had learned the alphabet, and many had begun to read elementary books. Those who had not, she realized, probably never would. They were not capable of learning, at least not by the methods she knew. Too many years of poor food, poor care, and dire poverty had robbed them of faculties; and others had been born robbed of any hope of ever learning. These children Kyra kept busy, allowing them to make primitive pictures with the wonderful chalk Adam provided, and teaching them simple games and repetitive tasks at which they became reasonably proficient. It was all she could do. Often, she had to begin by teaching them the simplest things, such as buttoning their garments or coordinating the motions of their arms and legs. These children perplexed her, but she refused to give up on them.

To Apollo's consternation, she refused to give up on anything. She worked all day in the school, and too often spent long hours deep into the night at related tasks. She planned her classroom hours; she visited the homes of the children, talking with them and teaching their parents. She worried about the welfare of all her families.

She was busy devising a special exercise for Lulu Crosby when she heard a soft noise. She lowered her head to hide a smile. Tupper Jackson and his shadow, Tammy, she was sure. Even after the long school day, the twins were far from satiated with learning, and they often stole back in the late afternoon, smiling and eager for more lessons.

But it was Cilla Warren, nearly fourteen and glowing with an innocent sexuality, who edged into the schoolroom. Cilla stood by the blue door poised for flight, her eyes focused on her bare feet.

"Cilla?" Kyra said, waiting for the girl to enter or say something.

Cilla's eyes met Kyra's for a moment, then resumed the examination of her feet.

"Come here, child. Sit down beside me," Kyra said companionably. Cilla obeyed, but still said nothing. Kyra talked easily and pleasantly about the work she was doing, asking Cilla if she thought Lulu would enjoy playing with the simple abacus she was making for her.

The girl shrugged her shoulders, and Kyra laid down her work. "I think you have something very important on your mind, Cilla. Would you tell me about it?"

Cilla shrugged again. "Ain't nothin' to tell."

Kyra cocked her head. Uncritically she said, "You know that isn't true. And you also know how wrong it is to lie, especially to those who care about you."

"You won't thing it's nothin'. Mama say it's growin' pains."

"What are growing pains?"

Cilla quickly turned and flung herself into Kyra's arms. "Ah's skeered, Miss Kyra. It ain't growin' pains, an' Ah ain't thinkin' it in mah haid. It's real."

Kyra patted her and held her close. "What is real? Tell me."

"They's a big fat ol' white man aftah me. Ah knows he is. Ah ain't 'maginin'. Ah ain't! He al'ys on the road when Ah comes home fum school."

Kyra straightened and moved Cilla so she could look more closely at her. "A white man has been bothering you? Has he tried to touch or asked you to go with him?"

Cilla shook her head.

"What exactly has he done? Tell me carefully, Cilla; it is very important. Do you know him? His name?"

She shook her head again, and Kyra repeated her

request for Cilla to tell her everything the man had said or done.

"He gib me candy fum the gen'l sto' sometime. But Ah didn't take it, hones' Ah din't, Miss Kyra. Ah loves candy, but Ah say no. Ah did!"

"What else?"

"He say Ah'm gwine be purty when Ah'm bigger."

"Did he try to touch you?"

"No'm, he jes' look. He do a lot a lookin', an' smilin'."

"Have you ever seen him before, Cilla? Is he one of the men from around here?"

"No'm. Ah ain't nevah see him befo' he wait fo' me on the road."

"Well, from now on, you don't walk home alone. Not ever, you hear? This afternoon I'll walk you home, but every day, you make sure someone is with you. And if you see that man, you stay far away from him. Come back to school, or go to someone else's house until he is gone. Don't go near him, Cilla."

Kyra walked the girl home. When they reached the spot in the road where Cilla said the man usually waited for her, no one was there. Kyra went to the Warrens' house and waited until Ivy had come home from the Whitakers' for the night.

"Miz Kyra, what you doin' heah?" Ivy asked in surprise. "Which one mah kids been bad?"

"No one has been bad, Ivy. But I want to talk to you about Cilla." Kyra told Ivy an abbreviated version of what Cilla had told her.

Ivy waved her hand at Kyra in deprecation. "Cilla gettin' to dat age, Miz Kyra. Ah thinks she been foolin' 'roun' wid dem Stuart boys, Ozro an' Shadrack. She jes' makin' de odder up. What white man gwine mess wid a li'l pickaninny like Cilla. Why, she ain't even full growed yet. She makin' up stories fo' you."

Kyra remembered occasions at the Saturday night frolics when she had seen Cilla trying out her newly developed femininity on several of the boys. Harry

Woodfork, a big, attractive boy Cilla's age, came to mind. She said, "Perhaps you are right, Ivy, but I am a little concerned. I don't think either of us should take what Cilla says too lightly. Please try to keep an eye on her. If she is telling the truth about the man waiting for her, it could be serious."

"Ah do what you says, but Ah doan b'lieve it. She thinkin' 'bout de bucks, tha's all. Purty soon, you see, she doan al'ys come to school."

Kyra looked doubtful, and Ivy smiled. "Wait till you get a gel like Cilla, then you knows. She's all'ys busy figgerin' out 'bout how to git a new dress fum her mama, when her mama ain't had one herseff fo' de longes'."

Kyra murmured sympathetically, still doubtful.

Ivy was quick to hear that doubt. She went on, "Ah go down to de gen'l sto' de odder day an' Mistah Whitelaw tell me Cilla done come in an' buy a dress an' put it on Lester's credit. Ah ast him what he let her do dat fo', and he say she tol' him her mama say she kin. But she doan bring no dress home. Ah ast her 'bout dat an' she look funny, but she say she doan git no dress. Den she staht in on me agin. Ah whup her good dat time. Wait till you have a gel like dat one, den you unnerstan's."

"Maybe she didn't buy a dress," Kyra suggested. "Maybe Mr. Whitelaw was the one who lied about it."

"How he gwine know Cilla been at me an' at me?"

"She could have admired a dress or asked its price."

"Mebbe she hide it someplace so Ah doan know 'bout it."

"Ivy, have you and Lester any idea how much you owe Mr. Whitelaw?"

"We'ns doan owe Mistah Whitelaw nothin'. He say so hisseff. We owes Mistah Seldon, an' he ain't nevah been 'roun' to see what we owes." Ivy giggled. "Long's he stay up Nawth we'uns doan worry none." She saw the stern expression on Kyra's face and was reminded of the feeling she had sometimes when Reverend Hooks caught her in some misdemeanor. "Well," she added quickly, "we owes it anyways. An' it enuf, Ah say dat. Ah bin at Lester to pay de bill, but he say we doan haf to now."

"Hasn't Mr. Whitelaw or Reverend Hooks ever asked you for at least a partial payment?"

Ivy shook her head, but she didn't seem sure, so Kyra pursued it. "Has either of them ever asked you or your family to do favors for them—bartering for payment of the bill?"

Ivy's black eyes were two points of suspicion. "Lak whut?"

"I—I don't know. Perhaps he'd ask Lester to plow for him or have you do some cleaning, in exchange for what you owe."

Ivy considered for a moment, then said, "Gracey, dat's mah oldes' gel, she work fo' Rev'und Hooks. She doan come home nights no mo'." Ivy's gaze slued off to the side. "She got a heap o' work to do, she say. Ah go ober dere yestiddy an' we visit an' carry on, den Rev'und Hooks come in de do' an' he pat her on de ahm an' he tell me Ah got to git on home now. An' Gracey ain't lookin' her mama in de eye no mo'." Though Ivy's expression said she knew perfectly well what was going on between Gracey and Hooks, she added, "Ah doan know what dat gel up to neider. She jes' all full o' herself. Dey growin' up too fas' fo' me."

"How old is Gracey?" Kyra asked casually.

"Fifteen years ol', bawn a yeah befo' Cilla."

Kyra thought a few moments. "Cilla wouldn't be spending some of her time with Gracey, would she?"

Ivy shrugged. "Dey fight like dog an' cat when Gracey lib at home. Cilla a good gel," she said defensively. "An' Gracey a good gel too." She stood up. "Ah 'preciate you stayin' heah wid de chillun, Miz Kyra."

Kyra had the feeling that Ivy had said more than she intended. She said reassuringly, "I'll see Cilla in school tomorrow, Ivy, and I'll talk to her and see if I can find out what's bothering her."

"She too smaht fo' her britches."

On the way home, Kyra was thinking. If Lester and Ivy still owed the general store so much, why wasn't Whitelaw trying to collect it? With every family, the story was the same. Whitelaw seemed to be offering credit to everyone without limit, and he never asked for payment of debt. And why would Cilla charge a dress on Lester's account, when she knew she would get into trouble and likely have to give up the dress anyway? Cilla was a headstrong young girl, but Kyra had never seen any evidence that Cilla was malicious or dishonest. She tested the thought that perhaps Nemo Whitelaw had placed the purchase of a dress on the wrong account.

Then she remembered how Tim Crosby's money had been refused the night of the Saturday church services, until Apollo had intervened. What she knew made no sense to her. She had heard Ruel talk about business often enough to know that no business is run the way the general store was run. But what purpose could the mysterious, never-seen Mr. Seldon have in letting the blacks, and maybe the local whites, run up big bills?

Her thoughts went back to Cilla Warren. Then she discarded her suspicion. Cilla was a young, boy-crazy girl, it was plain to see, flirting at the frolics, always making eyes at the boys at school, rubbing up against them sometimes. Kyra shook her head, annoyed with herself for making something sinister out of nothing. Cilla Warren was learning some things that weren't taught in school. But some girls were like that.

Kyra closed the blue door behind her, lighted a lamp, and began putting the reading books back into their case. She was here to teach these children to read and write and figure and to know a little about the world. She could not see to the welfare and morality of each child. And sternly she told herself that, of these children, she was going to lose more than she saved. Too many years of degradation, ignorance, abuse, and deprivation had gone before for one black teacher in Georgia to make a significant difference. She was only a teacher, not a savior. It was time she started thinking more about that.

During the rest of the month, Kyra kept her mind on schoolwork. She was kind and open with children, inviting them to talk to her, but she tried diligently not to think about Cilla Warren, or the white man who waited for her to walk home. Recently Kyra noticed that Cilla was dressing better and, at the recess period, was often surrounded by a bevy of girls, all chattering and looking at whatever treasure Cilla had brought to school on a particular day.

Ivy Warren no longer came to school, either for lessons or just to talk. But obviously, her problem with Cilla was becoming more pronounced. Kyra finally approached the girl. She took the brightly colored string of beads around Cilla's neck in her hand. "These are very nice, Cilla. Where did you get them?"

Cilla, of late, had become quite withdrawn from Kyra. She now looked at her teacher with dark, suspicious eyes. "Mah man gib 'em to me," she said defiantly.

"Your man," Kyra breathed, impressed. "Well, Cilla, you are certainly growing up in a hurry."

"Yes'm."

"Is Harry Woodfork your man?"

Cilla put her hand over her mouth, smothering a burst of giggles. "He a boy!" she howled. She stood up, and posed a little for Kyra, then said haughtily, "Ah got to be goin' now. Ah'm vurry busy, Miss Kyra."

Kyra stood at the door, hands on hips, her lips compressed into a tight line as she watched Cilla sashay alone down the lane away from the school.

Apollo found her standing thus. "Missus schoolteachah, it looks like you ain't too happy with youah students today," he said happily.

Kyra managed a smile and a kiss on his cheek. "It's that Cilla Warren. Ivy told me she'd given Cilla a couple of good whippings lately, but I'm beginning to think she could use a couple more. Oh! That little girl is impossible!"

Apollo laughed. "Ain't so li'l now. What's she been up to? Into the bushes with all the boys?"

"Apollo! Nothing of the sort!" Then Kyra sighed, her shoulders slumping as she sat down hard. "More than likely that is exactly what she's up to. I almost hope it is, at least that would be better than some of my darker suspicions."

"Now, now," Apollo crooned, still not certain if Kyra was serious or just showing the exasperation of a difficult and long day. "What dark thoughts you been havin'?"

Suddenly weary with keeping the problem pent up inside her, Kyra launched into a description of Cilla's recent behavior, her conversations with Ivy Warren, the mysterious white man, and the misgivings she had about the general store.

Apollo listened carefully and quietly, asking an occasional question. When she had finished, he put his arm around her and drew her near to him. "Ah doan think you been imaginin' anything," he said. "Cap'n Tremain been talkin' to me lately too. He thinkin' along the same lines you are, jes' diffunt people."

"Who?" Kyra asked, looking up into his frowning face.

"You know them two funny ol' ladies—Miss Phoebe an' Miss Zenobia?"

"The Tweed sisters?"

"That's them. They got themseffs into some trouble too, 'bout that gen'l sto'."

Impatient now, Kyra sat straight, looking directly at Apollo. "Well, tell me! Why are you so hesitant?"

"Ah doan know jes' what to say. It doan make a whole lot o' sense. Even the Cap'n say it doan make sense."

Kyra made a noise of exasperation through her closed teeth.

Apollo looked up. "Ah' gwine tell you, Ah'm jes' thinkin'. Miss Phoebe an' Miss Zenobia been chargin' things at that sto' fo' near three years now, an' it ain't all butter an' eggs neither. They been havin' stuff sent from New Yawk—sofas an' pier glasses or somethin' like that. Cap'n say those things cost a whole lot o' money, an' Miss Phoebe an' Miss Zenobia doan have nothin'. Onliest payment we kin figger is that theah crops is gwine pay off some o' the debt, but spendin' like they do, even that ain't gwine covah it."

"Then the credit is extended to the whites as indiscriminately as the blacks," Kyra murmured. "But why? I don't understand—what does this Mr. Seldon want? You don't suppose he is a philanthropist?"

"A phila—a whut?"

"Someone who is charitable—gives things to others who are in need—there are some very wealthy men who give away vast sums of money to charities."

Apollo shook his head. "Uh-uh. Cap'n Tremain thought of that. He wrote to his daddy in New Yawk an' had Mistah Albert Seldon checked out. He ain't hurtin' fo' ready cash, but he ain't this kind o' rich neither."

Kyra's eyes were wide. "Then how can he allow all this credit? If it isn't Mr. Seldon, who is it?"

"That's what the Cap'n an' me was wonderin'. An' it looks like we jes' might find out purty soon. Mistah Seldon ain't givin' the Tweeds no mo' credit, not even fo' necessities."

"No butter and eggs, huh?"

"Nothin', lessen they pays up theah account in full."

"They can't!"

"Ah knows that," Apollo growled. "So does everybuddy else, an' so does the Cap'n. So he's gwine do somethin' 'bout it so's this man, or mebbe them mens, behind all this is got to show theirseffs. He's gwine make a suit, an' take it to co't."

Kyra looked puzzled for a moment. "Make a suit? Oh! He's going to take the people who are now demanding payment from the Tweeds to court—how? What have they done? The Tweeds do owe the money."

Apollo's eyes twinkled. "Yeah, but Mistah Whitelaw is sayin' he is the offishal rep'sentive of Mistah Albert Seldon, an' by his authority he is demandin' the Tweeds turn ovah all theah plantation to him as payment fo' debts. Cap'n Tremain is gwine say the ol' ladies was cheated, an' they got this big bill 'thout knowin' what was goin' on."

"Lord, Lord," Kyra sang. "Chatham County is going to be buzzing about all this. I suppose the general store will close."

"Nobuddy say nothin' 'bout it yet."

"Now all those debts will have to be paid. Oh, my! We may all be in for hard times this next year, Apollo. I'll just bet I lose half my class, too. Every child big enough to work is going to be working for his family." Suddenly she looked up at Apollo. "You said earlier that what I was thinking about the store and Cilla and that white man she told me about all was part of the same thing as the Tweed business—I don't understand."

"Ah doan neither," Apollo admitted. "Jes' seem like it all smells like the same rat, don't it seem like that to you?"

"This whole thing seems impossible. I guess we'll find out when Mr. Seldon has to come to court and explain everything. If one man is behind all these things, then they will all stop when Captain Tremain gets one thing cleared up. I know that I'm going to have a very hard talk with Cilla Warren tomorrow. I want some straight answers from that child."

The following day Cilla was not at school. Kyra was annoyed, but not too surprised. Cilla's attendance had always been irregular, and of late it had become worse. When she failed to show up all week, Kyra sent a message home with Chester for Ivy to come to the school to talk with her. Ivy didn't come, and when

Kyra walked all the way out to the Warrens' cabin, Lester self-consciously said that Ivy wasn't there. Kyra knew perfectly well that Ivy was somewhere about, but she returned to the school temporarily defeated, telling herself that it served her right for not minding her own business.

Days went by, and still Cilla did not attend school. Kyra went again to the Warrens', and this time refused to leave until she had talked to Ivy. Mabel and Chester acted cowed. They too had been irregular in attendance, and those days they came, they had been reluctant to talk with her.

Ivy came into the front room about fifteen minutes after Kyra arrived. "Whut you want?" she asked rudely, her eyes avoiding Kyra's.

"Ivy?" Kyra was not sure what to make of Ivy's unusual unfriendliness.

"Y'all sees me standin' right in front o' you, doan you? Whut you want, Ah got things t'do."

"I want to know why Cilla has not been attending school," Kyra said sharply.

"Cilla gone. She move away."

"What do you mean she's moved away! Ivy, what are you talking about? Where would she go? She's not fourteen years old yet. Now you listen to me, Ivy Warren, I'm at the end of my patience with you. I want to know where Cilla is. I'd like to talk to her myself."

"Ah tol' you! She ain't heah! Now Ah got things t'do." She began to walk from the room.

Kyra was angry and upset. This was so unlike Ivy. She grabbed the woman by the arm. "Ivy, why are you acting this way? Please, if Cilla is in trouble, let me help. You know I care about her—and you. We're friends, aren't we?"

The color of Ivy's eyes deepened with feeling for a moment, then she looked away. "Ah ain't got nothin' else t'say. Cilla gone—she got a job. She fine—got a fine job. Leave me alone now, heah? Ah got things t'do."

"Ivy—I won't give up this easily. I can tell something is wrong—terribly wrong."

Ivy's jaw jutted out. "Well, miss high-ass school-teachah, mebbe you ain't got no say in the mattah. Mah kids doan haf t'go t'youah schoolhouse no way, an' mebbe dey jes' woan fum now on."

Kyra tried again to soften Ivy's hostility, and failed. Finally, she turned to leave. At the doorway she stopped and said, "If you change your mind and decide to tell me what is wrong, Ivy, I'll be at the school. I'd like to help. Honestly I would."

Kyra returned to the schoolhouse tired and disturbed. Apollo was waiting for her, and for once without provocation, she walked directly into his arms, seeking comfort and secuity.

"Hey, honey, what's wrong," Apollo crooned, holding her tightly.

" 'Pollo," she said, sliding into the darky way of saying his name, "I'm frightened. Something is happening. I don't understand it or know what it is, but I can feel it, just like the night Ruel died. I can feel it. Something bad is happening."

He held her and caressed her, trying to reassure her before he even knew what had upset her. Slowly Kyra told him what had happened at the Warrens'.

"She mebbe tellin' the truth. Mebbe Cilla got a job— it do happen. Cilla a big strong girl."

"I know, I know, and I'd believe her, I really would, 'Pollo, except that she's acting so strange. If Cilla really had a job her mother was pleased with, wouldn't she be happy to tell me about it? Wouldn't Ivy be proud and want me to know how well Cilla was doing? She wouldn't even tell me where Cilla is. And she was awful to me—it was as if *I* were the enemy. I just can't bring myself to believe her. I think something has happened to Cilla, and Ivy doesn't want to say."

"Like what? What happened?"

"I don't know, but I can't forget that white man Cilla kept talking about. Suppose he really did wait for her to come home from school? Remember, I told you that Cilla had all kinds of new clothes and trinkets the last few days she came to school? Maybe it was the white man who gave them to her. Maybe Cilla never was making up stories."

"Nobuddy evah saw that man. Cilla jes' told you."

"That doesn't mean he wasn't real! Someone gave her those things!"

Apollo said nothing for a time. "Would it ease youah mind iffen Ah was to 'scort the girls home aftah school? Ah could do that—be a guard, kinda."

"I can't ask you to do that."

"You ain't astin'. Ah'm offerin'."

Kyra's problems with the schoolchildren continued. To all but her it seemed, Cilla Warren was forgotten. No one, not even the children, mentioned her name aloud. And Cilla wasn't the only student to disappear from the classroom and the customary schoolroom gossip. Annabelle Twoshoes had stopped attending, not that she had come often to start. Kyra had spoken to her mother and had been told curtly that it was none of her business, but if she must poke her nose in where it wasn't wanted, Annabelle had had a fight with her beau, Link Jackson, and had gone to visit Mrs. Two-shoes's sister in Alabama.

Kyra didn't believe the mother's story any more than she had believed Ivy Warren, but she could get no one to admit to anything different. The more Kyra prodded and tried to get the parents of the missing children to talk, the more reticent and suspicious they became. A wall of conspiratorial silence grew daily between the teacher and the parents of her children. Attendance became very irregular. Her only ally besides Apollo was Link Jackson. She had been teaching the young laborer.

"Ah din't have no fuss with Anabelle," he pouted. "Her mama tell you a fib. We wuz gettin' married come Chris'mas."

"Then you have no idea why Annabelle might have hurriedly decided to visit her aunt in Alabama?"

Link's face twisted with hurt anger. "She ain't got no aunt in 'Bama. She ain't got no aunt noplace. She got her 'nother man, that's whut she got. Her mama doan like me nohow—betcha her mama make Anne- belle get her 'nother man."

Kyra placed her hand on his arm. "I'm sure Anna- belle wouldn't do that to you, Link. Please, think—try to remember if Annabelle said anything to you, or was acting strangely in some way that might have indicated she was in some sort of trouble?"

Link straightened immediately and took a step back. "We ain't doin' nothin' like that. She ain't in no trouble. We tells Rev'und we waits till we's married. Ah ain't done nothin' wrong to Annabelle. It ain't mine!"

Kyra sighed, her eyes closing for a moment. "I didn't mean that kind of trouble, Link. It's all right. But when you go home, I want you to think, and try to remember if there was anything Annabelle said or did that would make you think she was having some other kind of trouble—maybe someone pestering her, or maybe she was afraid of something. Please—try."

Link eyed her suspiciously, then nodded his agree- ment. He quickly left, and Kyra, tired and worried, began to prepare the lessons for the following day.

At dusk, just as she had pinned the last well-done paper on the bulletin board, Tammy Jackson's small, wildly braided head popped around the corner of the schoolhouse door. Kyra smiled and welcomed the child. She was one of the few students who had not acquired a cautious, silent manner with her of late. Tammy ran across the room and hugged Kyra's waist.

"Well, Tammy," Kyra said, holding the child and swaying back and forth to her eager, loving motions.

"What brings you back to school? Haven't you learned enough for one day?"

Tammy giggled and squeezed her harder. "Ah jes' loves you, Miss Kyra."

Kyra placed her hands on either side of Tammy's face, turning it up to her. She kissed the child's forehead. "And I love you, Tammy. Come along. Would you like to help me pin the new bird pictures around the room?"

"Yassum," said Tammy eagerly. "Kin Ah put extry neah mah seat so's Tupper an' Ah kin look at 'em?"

"No, we will be fair and put an equal number around the room so everyone can look at them. Anyway, you aren't to be looking too much. How will you and Tupper get your work done if you're looking at the pictures?"

"But Ah wants Tupper to have somethin' nice to look at. He sad."

"Oh, I'm sorry to hear that, Tammy. What has made Tupper sad? Did he get into trouble at home?" Kyra was reasonably sure of the answer, considering the impish Tupper who was far prettier than his twin sister. Kyra couldn't hold back a smile when she thought of the scamp, but Tammy was very serious and concerned for her brother.

"Ah doan know," she said, her braided head turned down so far her small, pointed chin rested on her chest. "Mama an' Papa is al'ys talkin' 'bout Tupper an' sayin' he could work an' he'p the fam'ly. Tupper doan wanna work. Him an' me doan like to work—'cep' in school. We like that," she said, brightening at the last statement.

"I wouldn't worry too much then, Tammy. Tupper is pretty young to work. But you do realize that it is the duty of everyone in a family to try to help the others. You come here to help me, and you must remember that your mama also needs help sometimes, and Tupper must think of his daddy, too."

"Ah does the warshin'!" Tammy said indignantly.

"And I bet you do it very well. I am proud that you can be such a help, aren't you?"

Doubtfully, Tammy nodded. "Ah gots to go home, Miss Kyra. Mama get mad at me." She began to skip toward the door.

"Tammy! Wait a minute. I don't want you walking home alone. Apollo will be here in a minute, and he'll walk with you. You wait for him."

"Why Ah got to wait? What he gwine walk me fo?"

Kyra thought of the mysterious white man Cilla had told her about, and didn't know what to tell Tammy without unduly frightening her. After an awkward pause, Kyra smiled and said, "Why, you're getting to be quite a young lady now, and you know that ladies are always escorted. This is good practice for you."

Tammy looked balefully at her flat chest and her protruding, little-girl tummy. "Ah ain't gittin' t'be nothin'. Mama say Ah got the shape of a ol' pinto bean."

CHAPTER TWENTY-THREE

Cutler Whitaker and Blythe Saunders were married at twilight in the new folly at Mossrose. More spacious and elaborate than the old one had been, it was a place where Dulcie enjoyed entertaining guests on summer and fall evenings. It was a romantic setting for a wedding, with its nine pillars entwined with fragrant hothouse flowers and colorful ribbon streamers, and masses of pale yellow and apricot African daisies and ferns on sands and tables throughout the room. High up near the arched roof, clinging to a pillar and peering out impishly from a hiding place of wisteria vines, was a white-marble Cupid that Adam had had especially carved in New York as a present for Dulcie.

Blythe, alternately blushing and paling, walked on a delicate, green-velvet carpet strewn with white rose petals. Dulcie and Birdie, as her attendants, wore identical apple-green silk gowns with low necklines and puffed sleeves. Dulcie, to mask her six months' pregnancy, wore a small hoop pulled high under her gown. Birdie and Blythe wore the latest fashion, the dress improver or bustle, a horsehair cage made plain and flat in front, and giving an elegant, high, rounded shape just below the waistline in back.

The bride's dress was of natural-colored silk pongee, cut low across the neckline and shoulders, lavishly trimmed with blond satin folds and false panels outlined with blond lace and loop fringe. Under a cream-colored silk gauze mantilla, Blythe's blond hair was parted in the center and brought in waves over her ears, with curls piled high on her crown and a single long curl hanging on each side of her face. At her décolletage was pinned her grandmother's shell cameo. She carried a small bouquet of yellow chrysanthemums and baby's-breath atop a white Bible, a sardonic last-minute gift sent by her mother.

Beau had been pressed into service as ring bearer, and he stood remarkably still in his moss-green velvet suit, holding the cream-velvet pillow on which the wedding ring reposed.

Looking more distinguished than he felt in evening clothes, Cutler watched the self-possession of a child not quite four and felt sweat trickle down his back, in spite of the cool blessing of the evening breeze. Trying to excuse his own nervousness, he reflected that Beau could damn well be calm, he wasn't the one getting married here.

As her bridesmaids took their places and Blythe's hesitant footsteps brought her nearer, Cutler's heart began to hammer so loud in his ears that he glanced hastily around to see if anyone else heard. Adam stood quietly nearby, so elegantly handsome in his evening clothes that Cutler, had he been less a man himself, might have felt inferior. He took a deep breath and, catching Blythe's steady gaze through the mantilla, managed a little smile.

Patricia and Jem and the Tweed sisters were the only guests. No one except Birdie had come from Blythe's family; and Blythe had avoided the chancy friendships of other prostitutes, so there was no one to represent the bride's side. Cutler's severance from his family had been complete. No gifts, not even scornfully bestowed, and no goodwill messages came from the tight-closed Whitaker clan.

Early in the afternoon, the Tweeds had sent over a long note, tear-blotched in places, explaining that they had talked it over and felt that they had been wrong to refuse Dulcie's dinner-party invitation and that Blythe was actually a dear sweet child and that Cutler, although he might be a *little* bit wrong to have parted so irrevocably from his family, was still the same lovely boy he had always been and that if Dulcie and Adam and

Blythe and Cutler would forgive them for being two
doddering old fools, they would consider it a privilege
to attend the wedding this evening. On the other hand,
since they could hardly forgive themselves, they would
understand *perfectly* if the others could not forgive
them. In either event, along with the note they were
sending a small token of their affection and esteem,
which they hoped the happy bride and bridegroom
would find useful in their new life in San Francisco.
Their gift was a silver teapot with matching tray,
creamer, and sugar, decorated lavishly with a chased
design of apple branches and blossoms.

Blythe had read their note three times, tearful and
then laughing, and dashed off a reply saying that they
absolutely must come or there wouldn't be a wedding.
Dulcie sent a message too, telling them that Adam
would send the carriage for them at half past five.

Now the two sisters sat twittering in low whispers
beside Jem and Patricia, stealthily dabbing an eye
as the musicians played the "Wedding March" from
Lohengrin.

Suddenly the music ceased. The minister from Savannah stepped forward and placed Blythe's hand in Cutler's. Cutler felt a great peace descend on him, so great
that he did not hear the words the minister was saying,
so deep that he wondered if Blythe felt it too. He
turned his head to find her looking at him with awe.

They floated through the ceremony, making all the
proper responses in the proper tones, kneeling together
gracefully, and when Cutler lifted the gauze veil to kiss
Blythe as his wife, his fingers did not fumble or falter.
Her lips were warm and yielding under his, and he reflected that tonight—tonight!—the long waiting for her
would end at last. Tonight their life together would
begin.

They turned away from the altar together, and the
triumphant music followed them past the guests to the
doorway formed by two pillars. Hand in hand, they
turned again to face the room, and Cutler saw for the

first time the tall candelabra with fat, flickering candles, the masses of fragrant flowers, the smiles on every face.

As the others came to congratulate Cutler and wish them well, the servants were noiselessly moving the improvised altar, covering it with a starched, white linen cloth, and laying plates and table service. From the kitchen other servants were bringing platters heaped high with cold sliced ham and relishes, serving dishes heavy with salads and fruit compotes, and sweating silver bowls brimming with iced drinks. When the company was ready to eat, then would come the hot roast beef and pork, the hot biscuits and spoon bread, the steaming vegetables swimming in butter sauce, the two-handled serving urn of coffee.

"Mah, that was jes' the loveliest weddin' Ah think Ah evah saw," Patricia exclaimed, prettily wiping her eyes. "Didn't you think so, Jem dahlin'?"

Jem looked at his daughter and winked. He said, "Yes—yes. Lovely indeed. Like Dulcie's."

Dulcie's wedding had been held aboard the *Independence*, one of Adam's first two ships built for blockade running; and her parents had not been present, a fact on which Patricia commented occasionally. Seeing her mother about to contradict him, she said hastily, "Yes, Daddy, mine was a beautiful wedding too." As Patricia started to protest, Jem said, low, to Dulcie, "Whatever it was, you married well, daughter. Our Adam is a fine man, and don't forget I said so."

"Oh, yes indeed," Patricia agreed automatically. Turning to the Misses Tweed she said, "Well, Zenobia, it's very pleasant to have you heah. Ah been meanin' to get ovah to visit soon. Jes' seems like all the time Ah get busier an' busier. When Ah was a li'l girl, Ah used to wondah whah mah mama was always workin' so hahd, when we had plenty o' suhvants. Well, now Ah know."

Phoebe said, "But Dulcie should be helpin' you, Patricia—isn't she old enough? Or—" She lowered her voice to a whisper. "—can't she manage servants?"

Patricia laughed, putting her hand on Phoebe's dry, thin arm. "Of co'se, Phoebe, she is a fine help. But we both work ouahselves to the bone every day an' still it doesn't all get done."

"We do too," Zenobia declared briskly, "and the same thing applies. Ah don't know *how* we managed when dear Papa was alive." Self-consciously she looked down at her hands, roughened and calloused from the scrub board and the broom. Then tears came to her eyes, but she quickly blinked them away. "But we're just thankful that we've been able to keep Great Grandpa's home as long as we have." Brightly she turned to Cutler. "Well, young man, we've been hearing some very good things about you in your job in Savannah. What are your plans for San Francisco?"

Cutler smiled at Adam before replying. "Well, Miss Zenobia, thanks to Adam and Dulcie, we have passage on the *Black Swan* around Cape Horn to San Francisco. And when we get there, I'll open up a new branch of Captain Tremain's shipping line."

Blythe, her arm linked lightly in Cutler's, said, "And we expect to have lots of guests, so we'll have ample opportunities to use that beautiful gift you sent us."

Phoebe leaned toward Blythe and whispered. "Well, dear, to tell you the *truth*, we ordered that through the general store, thinking we might use it ourselves. But it just *happened* that we nevah did—and we felt you would get a lot of good out of it instead. Ah hope you won't think of it as secondhand, now that you know."

Blythe hugged Phoebe, saying, "Never! I'll always think of it as a dear gift from two dear ladies who came to my wedding when—" She had been about to say, "when my own mother wouldn't come," but she thought that might make her cry. Instead, fumbling, she made things worse for herself by saying, "Mama wasn't well today, and so she couldn't come, but she sent me a gift, a white Bi—" Her voice broke, and she looked away. For the hundredth time she wondered, would her

mother have sent it—sent *anything*—if she hadn't forgiven her, a little bit?

Dulcie had been talking with Beau, complimenting
him on his reliability as a ring bearer. Now she came up
to announce that dinner was served. When they were
all seated, Jem proposed a toast to the bride and groom.
Holding his glass first to Cutler and then to Blythe, he
said, "To your continued business success in the land
of the Gold Rush—and to you, Miss Blythe, may you
have many happy children gathered about you and your
good husband!"

Blythe turned scarlet but smiled tremulously, looking
up at Cutler as though for permission.

Cutler replied, "And may we have an old age as fine
as yours, sir—with our children to comfort us as yours
do!"

Dulcie, thinking of and longing for her and Adam's
home she had never seen outside New Orleans, felt a
twinge of disloyalty for even wishing. *But we'll go someday,* she thought.

The dinner proceeded merrily, with the servants,
overseen by Josh, smoothly replacing one course with
the next, and conversation flowing. Once Dulcie looked
at Adam to see him whispering quietly to Zenobia, and
her nodding assent. Perhaps he had new information
concerning his suit for their property. She must remember to ask him tonight.

At last Cutler and Blythe cut the towering wedding
cake, a dark fruitcake layered with crusty white icing.
Blythe fed him a piece, and he her, then the servants
cut the servings for the other guests. The minister was
staying overnight at Mossrose, as they were, so when
they were finished, Cutler felt it would not be unsociable
to excuse themselves. They left the folly in a shower of
rice and flower petals.

In their bedroom, Cutler slid the bolt home and held
out his arms to his bride. "Oh, Blythe," he sighed, as
he folded her in his embrace, "I have waited so long
for you."

"And I for you, my love," she said softly. They kissed again and again, their passion mounting. Then he let her go, sighing for a different reason.

"What's wrong, Cutler? Is there something—"

"No—it's just—well, damn it, I've got to call the maid to come and undo you. I'm no good with button-hooks and things."

Blythe laughed and took off her veil, shaking out grains of rice which ticked across the floor. "There isn't a button on my gown, darling—Dulcie saw to that. She started to explain about her own wedding gown—something about forty buttons on the cabin floor—and got to laughing so hard she never did tell me. My gown is put together with snaps, so all you have to do is hold both sides firmly and pull it apart."

"Like this?" He pulled experimentally, and her gown parted, with sinister little popping noises.

"Yes. Isn't that fun?"

"It certainly *is*," he admitted, pleased with the effect, and pulling some more. Magically, Blythe's gown opened down the back to reveal the horsehair cage of her bustle.

"Lawdy Lawd, what's that thing?"

She giggled. "Surely you didn't think it was all me back there, did you?"

"I had rather hoped it wasn't."

She whirled around to face him, still giggling. "Oh, darling, you are so innocent—and that's just the way I love you."

His arms went around her again, and his lips pressed hers. "Whatever it is you love about me, it won't be my innocence for long."

"No, it won't," she murmured, then pulled away again. "Do let me shuck this off, Cutler; I'm just a mass of layers of clothing."

Instinctively he turned his back, watching her shadow move on the wall in the lamplight. She said, "It's all right, turn around, darling, I'm not modest at all."

"But I am," he said through clenched teeth, trying

to keep himself in check and wondering if he would
look silly if he went into the dressing room to disrobe.
Then he realized that she had taken off everything.
His breath was getting short now; he moved uneasily
toward the door. He saw her drop a long nightgown
quickly over her head. She was coming toward him.
Her voice was not that of Blythe, the woman he loved;
it was the practical voice of Blythe the prostitute.
"Stand still, please," she said. "I'll have you out of these
in a moment."

"But I—" he began to protest and realized that his
tie was undone and she was moving expert fingers down
his shirt buttons. Going around behind him, she took
off his coat and his shirt. He could feel the skin of his
chest blushing. Next she removed his boots. As he
stood up she undid his fly and asked him to be seated
again. Before he was seated she had his trousers down
to knee level and was working the first leg over his foot.

He was totally naked now, handsomely cockaloft;
but he mumbled, "I—a nightshirt—don't want to embarrass—"

She knelt before him, her palm resting on his inner
thigh close to his crotch. One finger moved slowly back
and forth. Her face in the lamplight was Blythe Whitaker, the woman he loved and who loved him. "Dear
Cutler," she said softly, "we don't need clothing now."

She rose, and the nightgown fell from her fingertips.
She smiled at him lovingly.

Cutler caught his breath. He had had a few women
in his life, and even Blythe before, but he had never
been naked, or the women had never been naked before. Always, in his experience, there had been clothing
in the way—a nightgown, however thin, that had kept
breast from meeting breast; or trousers, that hindered
and pinched him; or dresses and petticoats pulled up
hastily and let drop afterward. Never, he thought as he
rose and reached for her, had he felt the thrill of flesh
pressing against flesh, of bare nipples rosy and hard
against his chest, of a cool belly against his throbbing

penis; of all that, and willing lips open to his own and
a tongue exploring his mouth, and arms that gently
tugged him on top of her on the bed.

He had wanted to make more of this, their wedding
night, had hoped to touch her with his hands, even
through her nightclothes, had wanted to kiss her throat
and the soft inside of her arms . . . but she had taken
hold of his penis and placed it at the opening of herself . . . and moved against him so that he was gliding
into her . . . was tightening and relaxing her inner
muscles in a way that he had never felt before in his
entire life . . . his breath became short, short, as he
drove frantically into her, clutching at her like a drowning man, intent on nothing but his own pleasure.

He felt the sweat popping out and cooling on his
back, heard his own uneven breathing, felt her teeth
against his opened lips and her fingernails digging into
his buttocks. It was like an explosion of joy, with
colored lights dancing before his eyes, feeling the immense release, feeling the rapture going on and on.

Then as his head began to clear a little, he realized
that she was feeling it too. She was panting as he had,
she was as frantic now moving against him as he had
plunged into her; he felt the little spasms of her joy as
he had felt his own. He kept moving in rhythm against
her, until at last, with gasping breath, she went slack
under him. Drenched with sweat, he let his weight onto
her and kissed her gently on the mouth.

Her hand caressed him tenderly, on his arm, on his
back, on the back of his neck. At last she murmured,
"Oh my love, that was so good. It was the thing I always searched for, but I never could find. I tried to
pretend—but I never found it until tonight, with you.
Oh, my darling, my darling."

He opened his mouth to speak, and closed it again.
He hadn't known that women experienced what men
did—he hadn't even known they dreamed the same
dreams men did, dreams of being with someone with
whom to share such an experience. He hadn't known

that a woman could dare to want that too. If she hadn't told him, he might have blamed himself for clumsiness in making it happen to her.

He said, "I wanted to take more time—kiss you more—but I—"

To his amazement and delight she said, "You can do that. Kiss me more, do anything you want to tonight. We have the time—and the door is locked."

"I didn't think you'd want—I mean I thought that once tonight—"

"Once is only the beginning, my love. We're not limited to once, or even twice, tonight or any other night. I'm here because I love you, and I want to make love with you as often as you like."

He knew he was very limp now; he could do nothing that way. "But it's no good now—"

"It comes back, darling, didn't you know?"

Still he thought that he should withdraw from her; but her hands held him. "Not yet, don't go yet," she said. "When you do, take it out very slowly. And notice how it feels."

He did; and even limp and covered with his own ejaculate, the sensation was extremely sensual. He almost thought he might become hard again. Once or twice before, when he had paid a woman to lie with him, he had had that happen; but she always wanted a second fee, and at no time had he had the money. So then there had been nothing to be done about it.

He lay close beside her, hiding his limpness between them until it would grow useful once more. But her hand reached for him and held his penis lovingly in her fingers. Her relaxed body told him there was no need to hurry, that he could take as long as he needed. Meantime, he could touch her—maybe not her breasts tonight, though he longed to feel them under his fingertips, perhaps even against his lips someday.

He caressed her arm and let his fingers move up the smoothness of her shoulder to her throat and her cheek. He turned her face toward him and kissed her mouth lovingly. He started his hand back the way it had come; but her position had changed, and before he was quite aware of it, he was caressing her breast. And she was not only letting him, she was arching against him, as pleasure-loving as a cat being stroked. He swallowed an apology, and dared to feel her nipple. Then he thought he had been bold enough, so he placed his hand on her arm again.

Blythe said lazily, "Cutler, I love it when you touch me. I want you to touch my breasts, all you want to, caress me and rub me and touch me anywhere, everywhere you want to. I want your hand on me. I want your hands to know me, just as I want your lips to know me . . . everywhere." As if to demonstrate, she ran the flat of her palm down his shoulder, over his breast, feeling the little erection of his nipples, caressing his belly and the inside of his thighs.

Cutler lay back, with sensations rippling through him like running water, as she caressed him now with both hands, her lips moist on his erect penis making kissing motions that roused him almost unbearably.

With diminishing caresses she stopped. Stretching, she lay on her back beside him. "Now you do things like that to me. Do anything you want to do, anything you think you might like to do. Caress me for all the years we've been apart, my love."

He began awkwardly, feeling a little silly, a little afraid he was being too bold, that he might do something to displease her. But she placed his hands where her experience told her that he wanted them; and under his hesitant motions she rolled a little; first one place and then another fell deftly under his fingers. Although she made no move to touch him simultaneously, he knew his penis was hot and hard. If this went on much longer—

"Blythe, I'm afraid I can't wait—"

"Then don't, darling. Let me help you a little."

Once again they were joined, and she wrapped her legs over his back, placing her body tight, tight against his, again flexing her inner muscles to provide him the maximum sensation. He was proud of himself this time; he did not have to let himself go the minute he was inside her. The terrible urgency which had seized him before had less strength, and he was able to wait a few seconds until he thought she was letting go too. They moved in perfect rhythm, reaching a long, satisfying, simultaneous climax.

He had entertained notions of trying for a third time; but before he could put his notions into effect, he had fallen asleep. Blythe slept too, for the first time in years without any nightmares at all.

The following morning Adam and Dulcie drove them into Savannah. As they neared the docks Adam's heart gave a glad leap, for there, waiting at anchor in the busy harbor, was the *Black Swan*. Drawing closer he saw a familiar figure standing at the rail, holding his cap in one hand and running his fingers through blond, wavy hair with the other.

Adam leaped out of the carriage, yelling for permission to board.

Captain Ben West started toward Adam, hand outstretched, and they met in the middle of the deck, shaking hands, laughing, pounding each other's shoulders.

Introductions were acknowledged all around, and Ben gave the order to have the Whitakers' trunks brought aboard. "Let's go below," he said, again slapping Adam on the back. "We've got a lot of catching up to do."

They settled themselves in the captain's mess, and the steward brought them coffee and an assortment of fresh pastries.

"I don't suppose Glory came along," said Dulcie. Then she turned to Blythe explaining, "They have four children."

Ben grinned, obviously pleased. "All red-haired like Glory, and all girls. Don't know yet if they're going to be *entirely* like Glory used to be or not."

Adam chuckled, remembering Glory as he had first known her, formerly Miss Eleanor Brooker of Boston, formerly governess to little Johnny Packer whose parents had suddenly packed up everything and left their governess stranded and owing their hotel bill in Nassau. He had seen her first in the dining room of the Royal Victoria Hotel, a lushly built woman in a harlot's dress. Yet she had a little-girl face and a wide smile to go with her engagingly frank manner.

She had changed her name to Glory Hallalooya, she said, and she was going to become a dancer. She had been like an irresistibly frisky puppy, affectionate and funny.

"Glory," said Dulcie, who had later become her fast friend in Nassau, "is a prize. Is she staying well?" Dulcie was thinking of the baby-a-year that Glory had borne to Ben.

"Oh, yes, she takes everything in stride. The girls have had chicken pox, measles, pneumonia, all that, and she sails through everything with colors flying. We're going to have another baby girl at Christmastime. How about your family, Dulcie?"

"Beau will soon be four, and the new baby is due in February. We're hoping it's a girl. With black hair like Adam's."

"What do you hear of Tom, Ben?" Adam asked.

"He bought back his family mansion on Clio Street, and he's blended himself right back into society where he belongs, scars and all."

Adam chuckled. "Good old Tom," he said affectionately. "Maybe he's finally let go of his determination to kill Ravanche."

Ben shook his head slowly. "He used to make me shiver sometimes, the things he said, and the way he'd say them."

Adam said, "I know. After Revanche murdered Ullah, I thought Tom—"

As Adam realized what he had said, Ben's gaze, startled, went to Dulcie. She was sitting bolt upright, her face white, her eyes wide. In a whisper she said, "Adam—did you say that Edmund—"

"Holy Mother, Adam, didn't you ever tell Dulcie?"

Adam shook his head, then rose to pull Dulcie to him and hold her securely in his arms. "I'm sorry, Dulcie mea, I'm sorry. For so long I couldn't tell you— and then it no longer seemed important—"

Dulcie was sobbing hysterically, trying to push Adam away, hating making a scene in front of the Whitakers. Cutler rose, taking Blythe with him as he made his excuses to leave the room.

Then, blowing her nose and apologizing, she asked Adam and Ben to tell of the day of Ullah's death and Tom's disfigurement.

Adam had thought himself immune to it by now, the harrowing memory of that brilliant December day seventeen years ago, the sight of the grotesque Mardi Gras masks, the Boar hitting and kicking Tom again and again, while the Snake and the Bear held him. But he felt it all over again in beads of sweat and the rise of hair on the back of his neck, as he remembered the reluctance of Ullah's flesh to let go the knives that had killed her.

"I shot at the Boar," he related haltingly, "but the bullet only creased his mask on the right side. Then a few weeks later Edmund came to our house to threaten my mother, and he had a fresh bullet scar on his right cheekbone. It proved to me what Tom had only intimated, that Edmund Revanche, his old friend, was the Boar."

Dulcie forced words from her tight throat. "What's wrong with me? I thought Adam was dead, and I agreed to—to marry that—that murderer. I had my eyes open, but I didn't see—"

Ben said, "We've known Edmund for years now, Dulcie, and I don't think any of us has seen all there is to see about him. I doubt if any one person knows the depths of his degradation."

Dulcie said, looking wildly at Adam, "But he told

me he was going to rebuild the South! I was going to help him! I—I thought I would be making *Adam's* dream come true!"

Adam's arm around her was comforting. "I've forgiven you long ago, Dulcie mea. Have you forgiven me?"

Wordlessly, her eyes full, Dulcie nodded.

"I thought you were dead too," Adam said. He went on talking, holding Dulcie's hand, recounting his fevered days after they were shipwrecked, finding the food where natives had ritually placed it, his nightmare visit to the Gilmartin house, and the monster boy on his dogcart. He told of waking to a ring of fire, of waking again to find Dulcie's gown and a skull decorating a cross at his feet, and of the Androsean natives coming at him in an unbroken line, forcing him into the sea.

They sat quiet for a few moments, each thinking his own thoughts. Dulcie, very slowly recovering from her feeling of shock, was looking at Adam and realizing anew how much he loved her, how great a part she played in his life. Thinking of Edmund, she shivered violently. Adam had told her how Revanche had tried to kill him, in Tom's cabin in the swamp, and that had so horrified her that she had made herself forget it— until today, when she learned about the death of Ullah Pierson. And now she could not forget either occurrence for now it was rumored that Revanche had interests in Savannah.

CHAPTER TWENTY-FOUR

With Blythe and Cutler's departure, Dulcie anticipated that some of the hectic activity around Mossrose would abate. She was wrong. If anything, the pace intensified. She had no time to herself, nor did she want it. These were days filled with worries and work, but finally, when the spring of 1870 had come, she felt that some of the vague haze of hostility and the unspoken threats were being forced out into the open.

She helped Beau dress and sent him out to play in Mindy's care; then she turned her attentions to the new baby. She became fascinated with tiny red-haired Jenny as she always did, letting the infant grasp her finger, and laughing as the small, groping hands wrapped tightly in her glossy auburn hair. The baby curled up in delight, her laughter unpracticed but her grin unmistakable. Dulcie winced a little as the baby grasped the tender hair at her temple and pulled, trying to get it into her mouth. Regretfully she ended the few precious moments of play she had with her daughter, and disentangled herself. She dressed Jenny and placed her in her crib, once more leaving her child to the care of another as she went downstairs to see to the business of Mossrose.

She looked back at Jenny for a moment, content in her nurse Lolly's arms, and she thought ruefully how short a time ago it was that she had longed to be recognized for her talents and had insisted that she be given responsibility, that she could take over plantation duties that had ordinarily been a man's. Now she had the responsibility, and two children, and not enough hours in the day.

Jem was waiting for her in the study. He was busily

fumbling through the stack of papers and correspondence she had left neatly stacked on her desk the evening before. It was now a disheveled pile spreading out across the surface and onto the floor.

"Daddy," she said, a frown on her face but her voice cheerful, "I had those in order for you to look at. You know, if you weren't so impatient, this would be much easier."

"Good morning, Dulcie Jeannette," he said happily. "I thought I'd get an early start. You weren't here— I thought maybe you wouldn't be coming down this morning."

Dulcie gave him a quick hug. "You fibber! You know there isn't a morning that I don't come directly here after I've tended to the children."

He grinned crookedly, his eyes twinkling. "Well, since I've been so busy, what do you say we call Peggy to bring us coffee, and you can tell me all the goings on."

"Goings on?" Dulcie asked innocently. "Whatever can you mean by that?"

Jem leaned forward, touching her arm. "Now you listen here, daughter, I want to know all there is. Don't you be like your mama and try to keep things from me."

"Poor Daddy, Mama does work awfully hard to protect you."

"Then you'll tell me?"

"Yes, I'll tell you, at least as long as you don't let it upset you."

Jem rubbed his dry hands together in anticipation. "All right, first tell me what it is Adam has gotten himself involved with concerning the Tweed sisters."

Dulcie's eyes were wide. "How did you know about that?!"

"I have my ways, and I won't be telling you, or they will mysteriously vanish like everything else around here. Your mother finds out everything."

"All right. Adam feels that there is something amiss with Seldon's general store, and—"

"Tell me about the Tweeds, Dulcie. I don't want to hear about that Yankee's business."

"Daddy, you are the most impatient man! I *am* telling you about the Tweed sisters. Adam thinks the general store, or rather the men who are backing it, are involved in some sort of land scheme. You know the Tweed sisters are not the only plantation owners who have accepted extensive credit from Seldon. There are at least three others we know about, and Adam suspects that there are several store owners in Savannah who owe Seldon too. So far they have been very close-mouthed." Dulcie looked out the window, her mouth drawn into a tight line. "Foolish men! They won't talk to Adam about it, because they don't trust *him*! But they trust Seldon—a Northerner—a man they have never seen, and who is likely trying to bilk them out of everything they own. Foolish, foolish men. As long as I live, I will never understand why—"

Jem laughed. "Not everyone knows Adam as you do, Dulcie."

"They don't need to," she said sharply. "One needs only to look at him, to talk to him, to know the kind of person he is."

Jem sat back in his chair. "I haven't always been fair to him myself. The first time he visited Mossrose I said to you that he was a cold-blooded man who would snap your heart like a fiddle string—well, I was wrong about him. He's a good husband and father to your children. And though I don't always manage to display my feelings, I'm deeply grateful that he has remained here. I may be an old blowhard, and stubborn, but I do know what it costs him to stay at Mossrose when his heart is with his ships and his life is in New Orleans."

Dulcie's face lit up. "Oh, Daddy, you do understand." She jumped up and hugged Jem fiercely. "Thank you, thank you for saying that. I watch Adam and know what he's doing, and sometimes I think that no one in the whole world really appreciates him. This isn't his fight! The Tweeds are Chatham County people, and Adam certainly gets no thanks from the people around here for what he does for them, but he won't give up. Wherever he is, Daddy, he does what he thinks is right . . . I didn't think you understood that. I'm so happy you do!"

Embarrassed, Jem looked away, cleared his throat, and said gruffly, "Enough of this sentimental nonsense. Hurry and tell me about the Tweeds. Your mother will be coming down any minute to cosset me, and then I'll hear nothing of interest the rest of the day."

Dulcie laughed and poured him a final cup of forbidden coffee, then told him that Adam had gone into Savannah early this morning to talk with Sam Hartman, the lawyer who was handling the Tweed case. "He wants to move as quickly as possible, in order that the identity of Seldon's backers, if he has any, become known. Adam doesn't feel that Seldon could possibly be doing this on his own." She explained Rod Courtland's findings about Albert Seldon. "So he has a minor fortune, but nothing which would support the general store as a charitable activity. Adam thinks he is only a figurehead for some other man or group of men."

"Does he have any idea who it might be?"

Dulcie shook her head. "He says not—but I'm sure he's not telling me everything. I suppose it is just my imagination, but I keep remembering the agreement Edmund Revanche proposed to me. Do you remember that?"

Jem fell silent, and Dulcie's eyes took on a faraway look, but she was alert, alert to a past that was as vivid in her memory now as it had been years before. She remembered the cold, frosty Christmas Eve that Edmund had come to see her at her Aunt Mad's house in New York. His voice rang clear in her memory:

"Dulcie, my dear, you are more beautiful than I had remembered." He took her hand and admired her gown of green silk. Later he had handed her a lavishly wrapped Christmas present. "Open the package," he had said, "and tell me if I must return it."

Dulcie had slid the bow off the gold-foil-wrapped box. Inside a satin case, nestled on white velvet, was a bib necklace of teardrop emeralds, each surrounded by small diamonds. There were earbobs to match.

Now, with the safety of years separating her from that evening, she felt a shiver creep down her back and across her arms. Even then, when she was actually allowing Edmund to court her, she had known. Some instinct, some intuition truer than any facts had made her say that night, "You're . . . trying to buy me."

And he had not denied it. "Is the price insufficient? You haven't heard my terms yet."

She had closed the box and held it out to him. When he did not take it, she put it on the floor. "I don't want your jewelry, or your terms. Just—just take them back."

He had sat across from her, watching her keenly, enjoying her distress and bewilderment. "It's an honorable offer. I'd advise you to take it." He withdrew a smaller case from his pocket, snapped it open, and held it out to her. An emerald and diamond ring glittered there, beside a wide, gold wedding band.

She had felt hypnotized.

She remembered the cool confidence of his smile. "After this war is over," he said in his assured voice, "there will be opportunities to make staggering amounts of money in the South. Railroads are going to have to be rebuilt. New lines will be established. Someone will have to furnish materials. There will be plantations upon which taxes are overdue. I propose to pay those taxes and make the owner a decent offer. The South is going to change . . . I'll be rebuilding the South. No, Dulcie, I'll be leading it. Perhaps as governor."

He had gone on to describe the kind of marriage he

was offering—a business arrangement devoid of love and children and warmth—to further Edmund's plans to "lead the South."

Slowly her eyes returned to Jem and focused in the present. "I don't know how I could have been so fooled by him, Daddy."

"You weren't yourself in those days, Dulcie Jeannette. And we were all fooled by him. All of us but your Aunt Mad. She saw through him from the first—didn't even want the scoundrel in her house."

Dulcie nodded. "I wish I had listened to her. She was right about a lot of things. And I'll bet that if Aunt Mad were here right now she'd say this whole thing smells of Edmund Revanche. You know how he hates Adam—he'd do anything to harm him."

"Now, now, I understand your feelings, daughter, but what is happening to the Tweed sisters isn't directed at Adam. In any case, Revanche would be more likely to be looking for Adam in New Orleans. Most likely he doesn't even know Adam's whereabouts."

"He knows everything! Nothing escapes Edmund. Daddy, you can never think of Edmund as you would other men. He isn't like others. He has a coldness that eludes rational judgments of him. He has spies, he hunts for people's weaknesses, and he uses what he learns without the slightest remorse. He knows Adam is here. He knows where I am."

"Dulcie darlin', you're letting your imagination run away with you. Without question Edmund Revanche is a rotter, but he can't know all you give him credit for. No man can. And anyway, he isn't interested in Georgia politics. Louisiana is his plum. Adam himself has told me that, and from what I hear, Edmund is making some healthy inroads in Louisiana politics. What would he be wanting with one Georgia plantation?"

"It isn't just one! There are many people in the same difficulty as the Tweeds. And it isn't just plantations either. Kyra has been having trouble in her school. The children's attendance is very irregular and the blacks are acting very strangely. Some of them won't even talk to Kyra about their children, and—"

Jem began to laugh. "Come now, surely you're not attributing those troubles to Edmund Revanche, too? Of all men, he is the least likely to trouble himself with darkies. They mean less than the dirt under his feet to him. No, you've let your fear and imagination take hold of you and run wild."

She looked at him hopefully. "Do you really think so? I wish it were so, Daddy." Dulcie went quickly to the papers on her desk, sorting and straightening them. "These really should have your signature, I think. The rest you need only look at, and I will take care of them this afternoon."

"Where are you off to now?" he asked, as she went toward the door.

"To the school. I promised Kyra I'd stop by. I can't help worrying and wondering what is happening. Woman's intuition may be something men scoff at, but until it is quieted, I am going to try to find out what is going on." She smiled at him and blew a kiss. "After all, you'd follow a hunch, and is there any real difference?"

Dulcie met her mother as she came into the front hall. Patricia insisted on having lunch with her daughter, claiming she never saw her these days. "Whah, weah all but stranjahs, Dulcie. An' Ah want youah word that we'll go shoppin' next week. We can make a day of it in Savannah. Ah sweah, Ah haven't a thing to weah. Ah can't even be seen visitin'. Ah been neglectin' mahself since youah daddy's been ill, but Ah think he's well enough now to be left fo' a day or so." Patricia paused only for a moment, then went on. "Dulcie, Ah been thinkin'—maybe we could go all the way to Cha'ston, an' make a real trip of it. Sho'ly Adam could put us on one o' his ships, an' we could shop, an' shop, an' see a play, an' have a good time."

"You've stayed home too long, Mama. I think it

sounds like a marvelous idea. I promise we'll do it . . . soon."

Patricia looked dismayed. "Ah told you, you should leave men's work to the men. Ladies must be free to tend to themselves. Heah you ah tied down to plantation mattahs that shouldn't even bothah youah head. Why, Dulcie, it might bring on gray haih befoah youah time!"

Dulcie giggled. "I don't have a gray hair on my head, Mama, and when I do, I am going to color it."

She talked with her mother for some time longer, then went to see her children again, treasuring the few precious hours she had with them. It was hours later by the time she had talked with Jothan about the new storage for the animal feed and was on her way to Kyra's school. She arrived at the school in the soft springtime afternoon, just after Kyra had sent the children home for the day.

The two women embraced. "Oh, it's good to see a grown-up face for a change," Kyra said, laughing.

Dulcie walked around the classroom, looking at the papers Kyra had hung on the bulletin board. Her hands ran across the smooth surfaces of the desks. "It must be very satisfying to come here every day. There is a special, warm feeling in this room."

"You can feel it?" Kyra asked, delighted.

"Of course I can feel it. Not only that, but I could easily envy you. I think I'd enjoy teaching, Kyra." Then she laughed. "I might have some difficulty, however; I don't know enough."

"Nonsense! You'd do just—" Kyra whirled at the sound of a screaming child.

Tammy Jackson burst through the blue door and ran straight into Kyra's arms. "Tupper gone!" she screamed. "They gibbed him away, an' he ain't nevah comin' back."

Kyra held her close, trying to soothe and quiet the child so that she could be understood.

Tammy continued her high-pitched wail. "He gone, Miss Kyra! He gone. Tupper gone!"

Dulcie knelt down beside Kyra and Tammy. Tammy buried herself deeper into Kyra's lap. "Tammy, where is Tupper?"

The child's cries hit a higher pitch. "Ah doan know. He gone. Mama an' daddy gib him away."

"Now, Tammy, quiet down, child. No one has given Tupper away." Kyra's hand moved gently over Tammy's tight braids.

"They did!" she screeched. "They gone gib me away, Miss Kyra? You keep me? Ah doan want to be gib away! Miss Kyra! Ah wants Tupper!"

Dulcie's and Kyra's eyes met over the woebegone huddle that was Tammy. Dulcie said, "She can't be right, can she? The Jacksons wouldn't—oh, that's ridiculous, children aren't *given* away."

Kyra's eyes were burning, her mouth a straight, hard line. "Not given away, perhaps, but they are sold sometimes."

"But not the Jacksons! Not our d—"

"Not Mossrose darkies, Miss Dulcie?" Kyra asked quickly, hostility flooding her voice. "What's so different about Mossrose darkies? They're just as poor. You don't see any of them sporting new carriages or dresses. They don't spend a whole lot of time giving yard parties and teas, now do they? Poor is poor, Miss Dulcie, and all darkies is poor an' iggerunt. They do a lot of things white folks don't think is right."

Dulcie stood up, her face pale, shock imprinted on it. "Kyra . . . I'm sorry. I didn't mean to offend you."

Kyra pulled Tammy away from her and sat the girl on her lap. "Now Tammy, you stop that crying right now, you hear? What happened to your brother? You've got to tell me nice and clear."

Tammy hiccuped, still sobbing. Her eyes were puffy almost to being closed, her nose and lips were swollen. "Ah doan know wheah he go. Mama an' Daddy gibbed

him away. They say Tupper has to work an' he ain't
comin' back no mo'."

"Tammy, I want you to be sure you are telling me
the truth, because I am going right now to see your
mama and daddy, and if you've told me an untruth you
will be in a lot of trouble. Your mama won't like it a
little bit if I go to your house about Tupper if nothing
is wrong."

"Ah tells the truth, Miss Kyra. Ah al'ys tells the
truth."

"Kyra, please—" Dulcie began. "I want to help.
That's why I came here."

Kyra put her hand out to Dulcie. "I know. I had no
business talking to you like that, Mrs. Tremain. I'm
sorry." She looked at Tammy again. "I've had my mind
on so many things— Tupper is the third child to disappear."

"What can I do?"

Kyra laughed, a trace of the angry bitterness returning. "I don't know what anyone can do. I've tried
to talk to the parents. It's gotten so that they all turn
and walk the other way as soon as they see me coming.
But I don't give up that easily," she said on a deep
breath. "Tammy, you come along. I'm going to see
your mama. Maybe this time we'll find out something
about your brother."

"May I come with you? I'd really like to."

Kyra looked at her uncertainly. "I don't know if you
should, Mrs. Tremain. I'm through being polite about
this. I don't know what is going on, but I sure know
something is, and it isn't nice. Tammy's mother isn't
going to want to talk to me, and I am determined that
I am going to talk to her."

"I think I can stand up to that."

"Well, don't say I didn't warn you."

Dulcie held out her hand to Tammy. "Come with
me, Tammy; we'll ride to your house in my carriage,
and if you'd like I'll even let you hold the reins. Would
you like that?"

Tammy looked for Kyra's approval, then nodded and jumped down from Kyra's lap. She placed her small dark hand into Dulcie's white one. The child started at the startling contrast for a moment, then her face broke into a huge grin. "Look at that, Miss Kyra!"

The trip to the Jacksons' house that took Kyra an hour on foot was no more than a few minutes in Dulcie's carriage. They drove into the front yard, scaring the Jacksons' three scrawny chickens into a flurry of feathers and squawks. Pauline Jackson looked up from her labors in her garden and made a hasty dash for her house. She slammed and barred the door as though she expected a siege.

Kyra dismounted from the carriage and marched to the door. Out of the corner of her eye she caught sight of Pauline peeking from behind the front curtain. She rapped on the window and called out, "Pauline Jackson, you come on out here. I'm going to talk to you today or know the reason why!"

"Ah ain't gwine talk to nobuddy!" Pauline screamed back. "You go 'way, Kyra! You ain't got no call to pester me! Ain't none o' yo' business! Go 'way!"

Kyra crossed her arms, planted her feet apart on the porch, and said, "I'm staying right here, Pauline. You might as well talk now, because I'll be here until you do. Where's Tupper?"

"He gone! Go 'way, Kyra!"

"No! You talk to me!"

Pauline, screaming, opened her door. She stood blocking the doorway, her eyes wild with anger, her hair standing on end where she had been pulling at it. "Woman, you git offen mah propitty, or Ah gwine cut you open like a big ol' melon, y'heah?"

"Don't you threaten me!" Kyra said, equally angry. "I asked where your son is, and I want to know. What's happened to him?"

Pauline brought a butcher knife from behind her back. "Ah'll cut you!"

Kyra held her ground.

"You gwine gib me a fit, woman," Pauline cried, her free hand again going to her hair, pulling frantically at it. "Tuppah gone! Ain't youah business! Ain't!"

"Mama an' Daddy gib him away to the white mans," Tammy yelled, and raced forward, beating on her mother's belly with her small fists. "Ah wants Tupper back!"

Pauline back-handed the child across the porch, but her eyes rested on Kyra. She waved the knife around. "Ah feels a fit comin'," she said breathlessly. "Ah feels it." Suddenly Pauline began to twitch, her body seeming to move of its own accord, her eyes rolled back in her head, the knife slicing the air coming closer and closer to Kyra.

"Pauline! You stop that. I know you, and you're not having any fit. Are you going to tell me about Tupper, or do I have to find out some other way?"

Pauline began breathing in and out very fast and loud. Spittle rushed in and out of her mouth, gathering on her lips in bubbling white foam.

Dulcie jumped up from where she had run to see to Tammy and grabbed hold of Kyra, pulling her away from Pauline.

Kyra jerked her arm free. "She's not having any fit! She doesn't want to talk and she thinks this will frighten me. It doesn't. Do your hear that, Pauline? It doesn't scare me at all!"

"Kyra, please," Dulcie insisted. "Leave her alone. She isn't going to talk to you."

Tammy popped up, unhurt, apparently accustomed to battering. "Ah already tol' you, Miss Kyra, Mama gib him to the white mans to work. Kin you git him back?"

Dulcie looked at the child. "Kyra, please, Tammy is probably telling you all you're going to learn here. Let's go before something happens. It's time to let Adam and Apollo take care of this. Please, come with me—Adam should be back from Savannah by now. Let him handle this."

Kyra reached quickly out and knocked the knife from Pauline's wavering hand. She took the woman by the shoulders and shook her hard. "I'll be back here, Pauline Jackson, and I will find out about Tupper and Cilla and Annabelle, you hear me? I'm not going to stop until I know what is happening to those children."

Pauline let out another awful, animal scream, then she yelled after Kyra. "Min' youah own business, Kyra! You be sorry you mess wid us, you be sorry!"

Dulcie ran for the carriage, pulling Kyra with her. She brought her whip down on the horse's back as soon as they were seated, and didn't look back until they were well away from the Jacksons' house and the sound of Pauline's wild voice.

"My Lord," Dulcie breathed.

"She's hiding something," Kyra said. "That means Tammy is most likely telling the truth. Damned ignorant darkies!" Kyra spat.

Dulcie looked at her in surprise.

"Well, it's different when you say it." She smiled at Dulcie, then they both laughed, but there was no mirth in it.

Dulcie drove back to the school, where Apollo joined them after returning from his duty of walking the children home. Then the three of them went directly to Mossrose and Adam.

CHAPTER TWENTY-FIVE

As plantation houses went, The Willows was small and dainty, like an exquisite jewel prized for its brilliance and subtle color rather than for its size alone. Now, in the summer of 1870, it had been restored to its pre-war grandeur. It stood on an acre of perfect green lawn, poised on the bank of the Great Ogeechee River, a few miles from Savannah. Outside, it was white-washed brick, with four slender, white columns hold-ing up the roof over the veranda from which the waters had a silvery look. Inside, the walls were papered in shades of gray and blue and old rose; there were prismed glass chandeliers and polished silver, and Oriental rugs on the polished floors.

Tonight there was a small party in the dining room. Six men, all well dressed, partook of pheasant under glass, with wild rice, glazed new carrots and peas, a crisp garden salad, and fresh fruits and cheeses. They were served by three attentive black waiters, correctly uniformed and wearing spotless white gloves. No man sat in front of his finished plate for so long as a breath before it was deftly whisked away and a clean one placed in its stead. Wines and liquors were freely poured. Fresh white linen napkins were laid anew with each course.

"Edmund, you sho'ly do know how to set a fine table," said Bret Tully admiringly. He was a small, slender, wiry man, with gimlet eyes and a hard mouth. "Ah thought mah sainted mothah knew everythin' about a home, but you get the grand prize."

Edmund Revanche inclined his head graciously. The light from the chandelier gleamed on his black hair, delicately shot with gray. "I . . . have led a cosmo-politan life," he admitted.

Albert Seldon speared a bit of cheese and popped it into his mouth, chewing rapidly. "I had one hell of a time findin' this place when I come down yesterday. Almost had to give it up an' go back North." He chuckled at his own joke, his bald head shining with perspiration. Then, as no one else found it amusing, he added hastily, "But I didn't want to miss the oppor-tunity to get to meet everybody we been dealin' with for the last four years."

Edmund gave him a brief basilisk stare. He said coolly, "Albert, I believe we agreed not to talk busi-ness over dinner, did we not?"

Seldon looked around guiltily. "Nobody said any-thing to me about that, but you're the boss, Edmund."

Talbot Channing, who had come earlier so as not to be seen arriving here with Albert, said, "This is an ex-cellent angelica, don't you think so, Reverend Hooks?"

Jabez Hooks sipped at his wine and ran it through his teeth twice. "Jes' a touch too sweet fo' my palate—no, *no,* doan take that away, boy! Ah intend t'drink it all up anyway. Is this youah fust trip, Channin'?"

"Why, uh, no." Talbot glanced at Edmund tenta-tively. "I, uh, came here on vacation last year." He cleared his throat.

Hooks said brusquely, "You, Colonel Grooms? How do you like it heah in ouah paht o' the country?"

Lloyd Henry Grooms, the spurious Louisana col-onel, was fat. Fatter than Albert Seldon, more mus-cular and menacing-looking. Yet his smile was cherubic. He beamed that smile at Hooks. "Well, Jabez—will it be all right if Ah call you Jabez?—Ah doan mind sayin' Ah puhfuh mah own territory. But theah ah compensa-tions heah." He smiled at Edmund.

Revanche did not see fit to return Lloyd Henry's smile. He glanced around the table. "If we are finished, gentlemen, let us repair to the library. I have quite a collection of the best authors—Rabelais, Chaucer, Maupassant, Omar Khayyám. The works of the Marquis de Sade I have found especially edifying and instructive."

No one seemed to know how to respond. Edmund allowed himself a smile. They progressed leisurely down the hall, austerely decorated with erotic sculpture and paintings on which he commented at some length. Talbot Channing, always uncomfortable at the prospect of his name and reputation being damaged should he be connected with his compatriots, began to fidget. He tugged nervously at his tight collar, succeeding only in creating a rumpled appearance. He stoically refused to engage in the conversation, or permit himself a smile or even eye contact with the others, as if by this means he could dissociate himself in the eyes of a world that was not even watching. Edmund glanced at him occasionally, his expression one of venomous amusement. His descriptions of the artwork became more detailed.

Finally, closed in the library, Edmund saw no reason to waste more time upsetting Talbot Channing or the others on subjects too fine for the minds of his henchmen. With an air of grand superiority he said, "You might prefer that leather chair in the corner, Lloyd Henry, since it was built for a large man. Jabez, I'll appoint you barman for the first round, as I think we all agree we prefer to have no ears but our own privy to this conversation. Gentlemen, what will be your choice?"

More drinks were poured and the men seated themselves. They waited for Edmund to speak.

"We will have done with the business first, before we go on to the problem at hand, gentlemen. I feel our operation is running smoothly. Reverend Hooks, with the aid of his hired man Nemo Whitelaw, is succeeding in accumulating considerable debts through Seldon's general store. Lloyd Henry and Tully are doing the same at the house. Tab, you are falling behind with supplies, but we will discuss that later. Albert is maintaining contact with all our different business aspects in an adequate way. Bret, I'll expect a report from you on the business in Louisiana."

As Edmund paused, Tab Channing burst out, "I'm having a lot of trouble getting supplies, Edmund! The opium producers have learned of our operation here in Savannah, and—" Channing gulped, meeting Revanche's cold eye. "They've raised the prices and they're saying that supplies are short! And the cantharides—we thought they would be a popular item, but some foul rumor has—"

Edmund said coolly, "And how have they learned of this business here in Savannah?"

Talbot Channing's usual dignified appearance had deserted him. His forehead glistened with sweat; his light-blue eyes were harried. "I said nothing to anyone! Believe me, Edmund! You know how I feel about secrecy. You know that! You agreed at the start that I was not to be involved in this in any way. All I have done is to order supplies and see to their shipping myself. You know I'd never say a word—my family—my God! If word got out I was involved—I never said a word," he finished, mopping at his brow and doing further damage to his rumpled shirt collar.

Revanche's cold gaze met that of every man in turn. "Someone has had a loose tongue. Who is it?"

"It couldn't be me," Hooks reassured him. "Ah didn't know 'bout Channing till right now. He's not the only one has a reputation to protect, eithah. Ah doan take to him implyin' he's lily pure whilst the rest o' us is undah-handed thugs. What's he got t'lose the rest of us ain't?"

Lloyd Henry's booming voice said, "Well, Ah've talked to numerous local gentlemen, tellin' them about the house, an' hintin' at the variety of excitements we offah. But like Jabez heah, Ah didn't know 'bout Tab. Even had Ah known, it wouldn't sca'cely be to mah advantage t'reveal ouah so'ces."

Seldon laughed nervously. "Come on, Edmund, be

fair. You been around, you got to realize there's spies everyplace. Why, it might even be one o' Tab's employees. Or former employees."

As Channing renewed his protests, Tully alone sat silent and watchful. Revanche noticed this. "What do you have to say for yourself, Bret? Is your lack of denials to be taken as admission of guilt?"

Tully looked up with a smirk, then said shortly, "No. Ah doan know what has happened, but Ah might tend t'side with Albert were it not fo' anothah thought that comes t'mind. Theah's spies all ovah, undoubtedly, but it seems t'me mighty strange that Mistah Channing is havin' all this trouble. Why can't he get othah suppliers if these are givin' him difficulty? It's not like opium is hard to come by. Even ol' ladies get it fo' theah daily case o' the vapors. All he's got t'do is make sure we got a steady stream of it comin' in when we want it. Now, that don't seem all that hahd t'me."

Talbot Channing sat upright in his chair, his thick jowls quivering in his reddened face. "Would you like to replace me, Mr. Tully? You make it seem quite simple, and the availability of opium is not the problem, it is that small item you slide right over—a consistent, reliable supply!"

Tully was unimpressed; his eyes bored into Channing. "What's the rumor about the Spanish fly?"

Channing looked to Edmund. "I don't have to listen to this man talk to me so. He's—"

"I believe we'd all like to know, Tab."

"You tell him not to talk to me like that." Channing sat back, stubbornly silent and sulky.

Edmund scrutinized the manicured perfection of his fingernails. "Bret, you have a point about Talbot's handling of the supplies. He could be replaced quite easily, and with no threat to ourselves."

Channing said hastily, "This rumor goes around periodically—perhaps you've heard it before. It is said that an overdose of cantharides can cause a man to—to fuck himself to death—to—"

The men's laughter drowned out his words, but Channing protested, "I'm sure all you gentlemen know better, but the man on the street is ignorant. He may like the idea of a permanent hard-on, but he doesn't want to die with one."

Hooks wiped his eyes, still chuckling. "Boys, that's the way t'go. Mebbe Ah ought t'try some o' that Spanish fly."

Edmund sat unsmiling, waiting for the vulgar chuckles to die down. Into the chilly silence he said, "Reverend Hooks—Jabez—will you give us a brief report on the debts, and the collection of same?"

Eagerly Hooks reached into his pocket for his small ledger. "Ah got it right heah, Mistah Revanche, an' mah news is good, *good* news! The manna is fallin' right outta heaven an' into mah saintly han's! Amen, brothahs, amen!" he said, enjoying his moment in the spotlight. He smiled broadly, showing his long, yellowed teeth, then looked to his ledger. "Mah biggest debtah by fah is Israel Jackson. Stupid nigger, he ain't got the leastest notion 'bout what it means t'pay off somethin'. He has owed me money fum the word go."

"What are his assets?"

"Mostly his chillun ah too big to be int'restin'. Delia an' Flo, they 'bout fifteen, sixteen, an' ugly as homebrewed sin. His othah boys whup y'all in any kind o' fair fight. But theah's twins." Hooks's black eyes gleamed lustfully.

"Of which sex?" asked Revanche.

"Both. Tammy's the girl an' Tupper's the boy. Ten yeahs old an' the boy is purty as a spotted pup. The girl ain't nothin' yet. Now, heah's the fust o' mah good news. Lloyd Henry heah told me we was needin' boys fo' the house mo' than the girls, so Ah called Israel's debts due. He din't know fo' shit what that meant, so Ah told him Tupper was t'work fo' some wealthy white family down in Alabama an' what he made would come t'Mistah Seldon t'pay off the debt. Ah had t'go home an' bathe mahseff, the stupid nigger damn neah kissed the skin right off mah han'. The boy is in the house right this minnit, an' fum the repohts Ah been gettin' he's gonna be a mighty profitable piece o' black ass."

Revanche drew a breath, his lips drawn back in a rare involuntary smile. "Go on."

Hooks, thoroughly pleased with himself, smiled broadly and raised his arms as though he were preaching a sermon. "Ah got mo' good news, brothahs. You kin feel it, cain't you? Feel it in the air we breathe. The good news is comin'."

"Oh, my God," Channing moaned. "He's a blasphemous gorilla!"

"Lissen, Yankee boy, he's gettin' the job done," Tully reminded him.

Hooks waved his long, bony hands for silence. "Ouah next acquisition was a joint effoht," he said, winking at Lloyd Henry. "Cilla Warren. Now her daddy doan owe me too much, an' try as Ah might, that darky jes' wouldn't run his bill up. But Cilla's gettin' ripe, an' that's when Lloyd Henry come to mah aid. He begun t'meet Cilla on her way home fum school, an' give her li'l treats—pretty ribbons, an' sweets, and latah even gave her a dress. Befo' you know it, we got Cilla Warren eatin' outta ouah han's."

"Not quite," Lloyd Henry interrupted. "Bettah tell Edmund everything, Jabez."

Hooks waved Lloyd Henry silent. "Aw, *she* cain't do nothin'. It's no 'count."

"I prefer to know everything," Edmund said coldly. "What is it you consider of no account?"

"Oh, the darkies have got themseffs a schoolhouse. The teachah is a long-nosed bitch lookin' in wheah she doan belong. She come neah to gittin' Cilla t'think agin 'bout workin' fo' Lloyd Henry."

"Cilla Warren knew who she was going with?!" Bret said loudly.

"Hell, no! She thinks she did," Lloyd Henry growled.

"What about this teacher?" Edmund asked. "Who is she? Does she work for the Freedmen's Bureau? Where does she fit in?"

Hooks shook his head. "Ah'm tellin' you it ain't nothin' t'worry youahseff 'bout. She's jes' a Mossrose nigger. She was raised up Nawth an' they cain't do nothin' with her, so they let her—"

"Mossrose—you say she's a Mossrose woman?" Edmund sat forward in his chair. "She's Adam Tremain's woman?"

"Hell, Ah doan know—Tremain's or Moran's. Doan make no diffunce, she cain't do nothin'. That ain't even a real school. She's jes' out theah playin' schoolmarm."

Edmund remained quiet as Hooks rambled on, discounting Kyra's influence. His eyes burned, his face was drawn and hard. When he spoke it was with a quiet voice, so quiet that the others strained to hear. "Never discount woman, man, or child who has access to Adam Tremain's ear."

"But he doan care what his niggers do in that schoolhouse," Hooks whined. "He's got biggah fish t'fry. He's up to his neck with this fool suit he's bringin' on behalf o' the Tweed sisters."

Edmund's hand slammed down hard on the arm of his chair. He jerked himself upright, his body a taut line as he stalked across the room. "Tremain does care!" he shouted, as though trying to inform the wind.

All of them fell silent, their faces wearing expressions of surprise, wariness, even fear. None of them had ever heard Edmund Revanche raise his voice or betray emotion of any sort. Their eyes followed his pacings apprehensively back and forth across the room.

"You forget too easily!" Edmund ranted. "It could bring us all to grief. Never forget the War we fought— never forget the nature of the men who fought it!"

Lloyd Henry found his voice, soft, placating. "We haven't forgotten, Edmund. Why Ah remembah distinckly hearin' that Tremain nevah got his boots wet.

Nevah could make up his mind, an' even at the end he wasn't wearin' the Confederate Gray or the Yankee Blue. He was still fence-sittin'."

The veins on Edmund's forehead stood out, making his pale clear skin look a grayish white. "The Black Swan!" he said with venomous emphasis. Sneering crookedly he added, "You haven't heard of the Black Swan?"

"Sho'ly we have—jes' anothah war story 'bout a hero bringin' in gewgaws t'save the South—"

Edmund's fist crashed down onto a small table, causing a priceless Sung vase to smash to bits on the gleaming oak floor. "Tremain!" he ground out through clenched teeth. "Tremain! He is the Black Swan! He is the man who stole slaves—who burned plantations— who brought beggary and ruin to many a proud Southern family. Adam Tremain is the Black Swan!"

Silence enfolded the room. Lloyd Henry rubbed his forehead with a beefy hand. Without sound his lips formed an apology.

Edmund went on relentlessly. "Who doesn't listen to his niggers, did you say? The Black Swan? There never was a bigger nigger lover alive than Adam Tremain. And you are idiot enough to tell me your news is good, good—that this nigger teacher is no threat to us!" His black eyes raked his captive audience. His breathing still erratic, he said with a faint semblance of his usual icy calm, "Have any of you remembered who it is who's going to try to force our identities out into the open in a court of law over the Tweed arrangement?"

"Co'se we remembah," Hooks assured him hastily. "Ah jes' mentioned it mahseff. Ah jes' didn't make the connection between—"

Edmund Revanche's hands clenched and unclenched, as though he would like to have them on Hooks's skinny windpipe. Though his voice came softly, it was frigidly sarcastic. "You didn't make the connection." His voice began to rise again. "Our business—our secrecy—*our success* depends upon your making the proper connections! Connections are *everything*. Money is made by the shrewd! Power comes only to those with the insight to make the connections. To see and comprehend the minutiae that others overlook!"

Nonplussed by Edmund's unwavering glare, Hooks nervously smoothed his waistcoat over and over. He cocked his head to one side and then the other, began twice to speak and finally stammered, "Ah'm—Ah'm sorry, Edmund—Mistah Revanche. Mebbe—mebbe theah's still somethin' we kin do 'bout the teachah." He looked helplessly at the others, who avoided his gaze. "She's all the time wanderin' 'round at night seein' the families o' the pickaninnies. She—mebbe she could have a accident. Or mebbe she jes' doan come back one time—or some man takes a likin' to her an' is jes' a li'l bit too amorous. Could be she nevah recovahs fum all that lovin'."

Edmund, back in control once more, said softly, "Or it could be that we simply leave the teacher to her own pleasures. It could be that we eliminate the *source* of our problems instead."

They looked at him with breath-held attentiveness. Tully's thin lips curved upward.

Edmund smiled, the familiar, controlled, cold smile they were used to. "Making connections with information, gentlemen," he said. "I shall demonstrate what I mean. Haven't I heard you mention a man named Leroy Biggs, Jabez?"

Hooks's uncertain gaze was everywhere, not sure if he should admit to knowing Leroy. Hesitantly, he nodded. "Everybuddy knows ol' Leroy," he said, defying them to deny it.

"Good. Did you not also tell me it was rumored that this Biggs is involved with the Ku Klux Klan, may even be the leader of the local chapter?"

Surer now, Hooks nodded more vigorously.

Edmund, hands behind his back, head up as if drawing inspiration from the ceiling, continued, "And the

Loyal League is one of Captain Tremain's favorite organizations. Correct me if I am in error." He whirled to look at Hooks, who moved farther back in his chair. "The Loyal League and the Ku Klux Klan have displayed strenuous animosity toward one another hereabouts, so one might surmise that a Klan leader would welcome the demise of a Loyal League leader, might one not?"

"Oh, God!" Lloyd Henry breathed in relief, his cherubic smile spreading across his face. "There goes most of our problems—nobuddy to defend the Tweed bitches, nobuddy to look out for the niggers!"

"Exactly!" said Edmund sharply. "Now, Jabez, how willing do you think Biggs would be to perform the duty of ridding us of Adam Tremain?"

Jabez grinned evilly. "Like a houn'-dog smellin' a bitch in heat. Now Ah wasn't heah at the time, but the locals say theah was bad blood 'twixt them two long befo' the War evah got fought. Leroy purely hates Tremain."

"Arrange a meeting between me and Leroy Biggs, Jabez—tomorrow."

"Ah'll do it! By God, Ah'll see to it yet tonight. Heah? You want to meet him heah?"

"No. I don't want any local besides yourself and Lloyd Henry to know about my presence in this house. Have him meet me at Tully's."

"Right theah in the house?" Jabez asked.

"In the parlor—it's an excellent place for gentlemen to do business. And Hooks, don't come to me with excuses. Make certain he is there at eight o'clock and not a moment later."

"Ah will, he'll be theah, Ah'd bet mah life on it. Wait till that ol' boy heahs what you have in mind! Nothin's goin' t'hold him back—except—mebbe—"

"What?" Edmund asked sharply.

"Well, Ah think he'd do it fo' the pleasuah it'd give him, but jes' mebbe he's goin' t'want t'know what's in it fo' him."

"I thought you said he hated Tremain."

"He does, he does, but it ain't easy killin' a man as well-known as Tremain. It might take some plannin', an' theah's the risk. Biggs ain't stupid, he's gonna know right off you got reasons o' your own fo' wantin' Tremain out o' the way. Ah know Leroy, he's got a nose fo' lookin' out fo' hisseff."

"What would tempt him?"

"Mebbe he woan need no temptin', but Ah know he's havin' one hell of a time holdin' onto his propitty, an' his buddy, Lyman Matthews, has got niggers all over his. Give 'em theah propitty, an' Ah know they'll do it. Shit, they'd kill theah own daddies fo' less'n that."

"Lloyd Henry, you know Laban Sweet, don't you?" asked Edmund.

"Sho'do, damn li'l prick! But he's as honest as a dishonest man can be. Ah don't think we want t'mess with him."

"No need to involve him in anything he will understand. If coloreds are on the Matthews property, the likelihood is that the Freedman's Bureau is behind it. Laban Sweet is, if I recall correctly, susceptible to bribery. Arrange it so that the Matthews land is found unsuitable for niggers. Sweet can manage that. If you do it well, he should make no connection between the transfer of that property and the demise of Captain Tremain. As to Biggs's monetary problem, an anonymous contribution to his bank account should take care of that. Is there anything further, gentlemen?"

They looked at each other blankly, then shook their heads. Edmund, smug and pleased, rocked back and forth from his heels to his toes. "I hope you have all refreshed your minds to the value of making the proper connections among facts, small pieces of information that when strung together properly place power—" he put both of his cupped hands before him—"power in one's hands."

CHAPTER TWENTY-SIX

Leroy Biggs stepped out into the street. Behind him glowed the mellow golden lights from the window of Tully's house. He hooked his thumbs in his belt. His hat was pushed far back on his head, and on his face was a tenuous smile, a mixture of bafflement and satisfaction. He looked up into the soft blue velvety night, and the smile was transformed into a satisfied smirk. He took a deep breath, his eyes on the incongruously cold disc of a moon that seemed to ride higher in the sky tonight. Even as he stood staring at it, relishing the surprising turn of events this night had presented to him, the moon seemed to retreat, brighten, and sail still higher in the endless void of soft night blue.

With a jerky motion he broke his fascination and walked toward his horse. Unable to help himself he would occasionally halt, shake his head, flash the strange baffled smile, then go on. All that had happened during his meeting with Edmund Revanche did not yet have the feeling of reality to him. It was more like a dream—a good dream. His belly was full and warmed with fine brandy, his nostrils still quivered with the pungent aroma of the best, most expensive cigar he had smoked since before the War, and his ears still rang with the sound of Edmund's voice offering a means to the end of all his troubles.

He laughed aloud. Sure enough, he had heard Revanche's words, he understood their meaning, but it sure as hell still felt like he was lying in some scented bed with satin sheets wrapped all around him. He swung his leg over the saddle, and sat on the horse's back gazing up into the stars. It was as though he had been transported back home and was lying in his own bed staring up at the ceiling hating the people who now stood in his way, and wishing so hard for the good old days before the War to return that he had made it happen.

His mind jerked quickly to the old darky mammy who had taken care of him for his mama. She'd told him tales of the powers of the mind, powers that came from the force of will, powers of wishing and hating and sometimes, only occasionally, loving. He wondered for a moment if that old woman with all her talk of drums and dolls and pins and chants and curses had anything to do with him now. Had he somehow conjured up powers of his own, unwittingly made his own chant of hate and longing? Edmund Revanche's cold, marblelike face floated in his mind. Roughly he jerked on the reins, making his startled horse jump forward out into the road.

The cold moon lit the road home, making it shimmer with an eerie blue haze. Leroy shivered, looking around him, luxuriating in the pleasurable fear that his thoughts of conjure-men and the words Edmund Revanche had spoken aroused in him. He glanced with an eager wariness at the tree-shrouded roadside, his eyes scanning the dusky darkness for movement, listening for strange howls and calls from that phantom world of power he had begun to relish. He smiled, thinking. It should have been a cold night with its little globe moon and the blue haze creeping out all over the ground, but it wasn't. It was clear and warm and summery, the kind of night that should make a man's mind turn to such things as moonlight swims, and making love in the open. There was barely a breeze stirring. The leaves were silent. Everything seemed strange and new. His mind would not hold thoughts of love or softness. Instead they held red vibrating images of blood and revenge and finally a release from so much of the angry agony Leroy had lived with for so long.

With laughter tinged with a nervousness that he wouldn't admit to, Leroy thought that this was a night much like Edmund Revanche himself.

It had been a long time since Leroy had had the opportunity to sit in a saloon like Tully's and enjoy the company of gentlemen. He hadn't realized how much the amenities had meant to him. Before the War he had never taken the opportunity to consider the feeling that eating from a table covered with real linen gave a man, or what it meant to taste and relish food prepared by talented black hands, to be served by darkies who still recognized the superiority of a gentleman. And Edmund Revanche had that all the time. He had lost none of his command over his own superiority, or of his dominance over the blacks. As far as Leroy could see, Edmund Revanche had been unscathed by the War or its aftermath.

He admired Edmund Revanche. He admired him and envied him. He wanted what he saw the man had. He smiled now, knowing that he might not have had Revanche's good fortune in coming through the War whole, but he had the know-how to use Edmund's position and Edmund's offer to get for himself all that he wanted in this world. He might have been defeated once, but no more. No sir! Leroy Biggs was on the rise again.

Unknowingly he leaned forward, caressing the neck of his horse as he spoke aloud, more to himself than to the animal.

He was now in a world of his own, a world that had already gone beyond Edmund Revanche. He dreamed now of a world devoid of Adam Tremain. A world that would come into existence when Edmund had deposited a considerable sum in Leroy's new bank account. A time to come after his property was free of liens and restored to its former splendor, a time when he would again have the respect of all the local planters including Jem Moran. A time when he'd have the power to make his word law. Leroy laughed harshly, the sound intrusive on the unnaturally still night. Revanche might have his henchmen, but he, Leroy Biggs, had something even better. He had the Invisible Empire.

CHAPTER TWENTY-SEVEN

Adam shrugged into his jacket as Dulcie sat watching, a look of consternation on her face. "I still think there must be a better way," she said. "You know, of course, that after tonight every darky in the district will be stirred up."

"They ought to be," Adam said complacently. "And so should every white."

"I hate it when you talk to me like that. You are deliberately ignoring the intent behind what I'm saying. If black children are being sold into . . . whatever, then the blacks have to have something to do with it too. And those who do and those who don't are going to be at each others' throats. What is that going to solve?"

"In the first place I don't agree with you. There have not been many involved. Right now we are talking about two or three children, and this is the time to stop it. Two or three families are not going to stand up against the opinion and pressure of the rest of the blacks."

"And I suppose the people who are buying the children are going to sit back and let you ruin their business?"

"I hope not. I want them out in the open."

"Well, why can't Apollo go to the meeting and talk to them? Why must you always be involved? You're not a cat, you know. No one gave you nine lives, but the way you seem to enjoy accumulating enemies, anyone would think you believed it."

He came over to her, kissing her quickly. "Apollo is going to talk to them. I will be there only to lend my support and encouragement. I promise, I'll be as charming, as sweet as Beau. Not a single enemy will I cultivate."

Dulcie snorted at him. "You?! Go somewhere and not talk? Never! Be careful, and come home early—please. I have a few plans for tonight too."

He grinned at her and walked from the bedroom.

Apollo and Kyra were waiting in front of the house in the buggy. Adam rode beside the carriage. It was a crisp, warm night with a light breeze keeping them cool. The sky was a brilliant red—a sailor's delight, Adam thought as he watched the sun dip beneath the horizon, leaving behind its vivid array of color.

"It's a good night for the meeting," Kyra said distractedly.

"Yeah, a church meetin' with fun after," Apollo said, grinning, "not the kind o' meetin' you've got in mind fo' them."

Kyra turned toward him scowling. "Don't you make light of this, Apollo Justus Sherman! This is no laughing matter!"

Apollo's jaw set. "Ah ain't goin' 'round with no long face fo' nothin'. You do ser'ous things, doan mean a body got to stop smilin'."

"Use correct English!"

"You use it. Ah likes laughin'."

"You two better save some of that spleen for the meeting tonight."

Apollo waved his hand. "Oh, it ain't nothin', Cap'n. This woman cain't handle nothin' impohtant without gettin' all pouty-faced about it."

"Apollo, I may forget I'm a lady and throw you right off this buggy if you dare say another word!" Kyra snapped.

They arrived at the general store in stony silence. Adam approached the small groups of whites who had gathered outside to talk before the Saturday night meeting, and informed them there would be no regular service, but a meeting of the blacks. As the whites left from across the fields the blacks could be seen coming, some on foot, some on horseback, some in wagons, alone and in groups. Shrill bursts of children's laughter jabbed at the evening calm. The lower sound of adult talk and muted laughter gave a background hum. It seemed so incongruous to Adam, in the midst of this cheer and good-spirited greetings, that the reason for his being here was one of such horror and degeneration. Apollo was right, no one was really going to be prepared for tonight's meeting even though Mossrose people had been sent to every home, urging, demanding that everyone attend. With quick remembrance he glanced around and noted that he did not see any of the Jacksons. "Kyra, didn't someone go to the Jacksons' to remind them to be here tonight?"

"Not a family was missed. But I didn't expect the Jacksons, and I doubt very much that we'll see the Warrens. Maybe no one else knows what we have in mind tonight, but you can bet that the Warrens and the Jacksons and the Twoshoes do. They won't show their faces."

"You must be right. I don't see any of them," Adam said. "It's too bad. I was hoping they'd cooperate."

"They 'shamed," Apollo said.

"They ought to be!" Kyra said quickly, then held out her arms for Apollo to help her down from the buggy. Safe on firm ground, she marched up to the general store, pausing to glare at Tim Crosby until he opened the door for her.

"Evenin', Miss Kyra," he murmured.

Nemo Whitelaw looked up from his ledger as Kyra entered with Adam close behind her. "Well now, what have we heah? Cap'n Tremain, it's a privilege to have you join ouah humble prayah meetin'. Reverend Hooks'll be mighty pleased to see you heah."

Adam nodded his greeting. "When does the meeting begin, Whitelaw?"

"Y'all gotta be patient, Cap'n. Weah jes' plain ol' country folks heah. We get 'round to things, but in ouah good ol' time. It ain't like we got pressin' matters like the gentry."

During the next fifteen minutes the people slowly moved toward the interior of the store. When they were finally assembled, Reverend Jabez Hooks made his entrance from the tiny back cubicle that was Nemo's private room. He walked in three long strides to the center of the room. Like a great beaked hawk, his head turned almost mechanically this way and that, his eyes narrowing as he noted the absence of the whites. Out of the corner of his eye he caught sight of Adam. A quick look of apprehension crossed his face. He remembered well the last time Adam Tremain had been in the congregation when he spoke. He'd never forget the humiliation of Ruel Jordan's funeral as long as he lived. He decided to take the bull by the horns and perhaps silence Adam before he ever had a chance to speak. "Well, Cap'n Tremain, Ah see you have had a change of heart. We welcome you t'ouah suhvices an' shall offah special prayahs foah you tonight, an' special praise t'the almighty Lawd that he should have guided you t'us. We ah all sinnahs befoah him. Yes, suh," he cried, warming to his talk. "All sinnahs come t'beg his evahlastin' all mussiful, all bountiful, all holy forgiv—"

"I actually came this evening, Reverend, to beg your indulgence to allow me and Apollo Justus Sherman to talk to these good people."

Blustering, Hooks pulled his handkerchief from his pocket, wiping the spittle from his lips and chin. "This is a prayah meetin', suh! We ah heah t'give praise t'the Lawd God. You blaspheme!"

Adam cocked his head to one side. "Come now, Reverend, you exaggerate." Without further talk, he walked to the center of the room and stood so near Hooks that the man backed away, giving him room.

Apollo sauntered up to stand beside Adam. From her place by the door, Kyra smiled encouragement. "Ladies and gentlemen, what Apollo and I have to say is not pleasant, nor do we take pleasure in having to be the ones to say this, but it is time you were all aware of some of the things that have been happening right here in our own neighborhood. We will begin with this general store. Hasn't it struck some of you as strange, and perhaps a little too generous, that Mr. Seldon, whom you have never seen, would extend to any and all of you unlimited credit?"

Apollo moved forward slightly. He looked at Adam, a little smile on his face. "What he's sayin' nice-like is y'all's gettin' cheated. Mebbe it look like you gettin' anything you want, an' doan hafta pay till you can, but that ain't the way it's goin'."

Nemo Whitelaw shoved between the two men, his face red with anger. "Who the hell do you think you ah, comin' in heah an' sayin' lies like that to these people? Mr. Seldon ain't nevah been nothin' but good to all of 'em, ain't that right, folks!"

A chorus of agreement went up. Then a few loud voices could be heard, saying, "We ain't lissen to 'Pollo. What he know?"

"Ah know when it come time fo' Ivy Warren t'pay up, her li'l girl disappear!" Apollo shouted, and gained a stunned silence from the crowd. "Ah know Tupper Jackson doan come to school no mo'. An' Link, what happen to Annabelle? You knows she ain't got no aunt in 'Bama. Where'd she go jes' at the same time her mama an' papa doan have no mo' debt at Mistah Seldon's gen'l stoah? You tells me that!"

"You shet youah mouth!" Nemo shouted. "You shet youah mouth an' git out! Liah! No-'count liah!" He shoved at Apollo, trying to drive him out through the door.

Adam ignored these proceedings; Apollo could handle Whitelaw. He looked back to the alarmed and confused congregation. "We believe that what has been happening to the children in Chatham County is very serious, and involves men of the lowest character. Reverend Hooks here has been your shepherd all right, but not for God. He has led you to his compatriots, led you to trust men who would take advantage of you, cheat you, and eventually take from you your farms, your homes—even your children. Mr. Whitelaw not only sold you goods and let you build up a debt, he sold you a false life. No one gets anything for noth- ing. No man is rich enough to give credit indefinitely. And if you remember, many of you have tried to pay off your debts a little at a time, and that payment was refused. You remember that, don't you, Tim Crosby?"

Crosby looked down at his feet. When he spoke he was barely audible. "Ah 'membahs."

"Are there any of you here who have been told in the last day or two that you will now have to pay what you owe?" Adam asked. "Raise your hands."

Two hands went up.

Slowly, cautiously, Jabez Hooks edged against the wall until he gained the door. He shoved aside the child he met running up the walk, then hurried to his horse.

Tammy Jackson picked herself up off the ground. With muddied hands she wiped at the tears that streamed down her face. She ran to the front door, then stopped outside, frightened by the loud sounds of shouting, angry men.

Apollo had Nemo Whitelaw imprisoned in his grip. Whitelaw's arm was twisted behind him. He screamed like a demented bull as he struggled against the larger black man. Over the noise Apollo shouted, "Did Hooks or Whitelaw tell you mebbe they'd let you work off that debt instead o' takin' hard cash? Mebbe did they say one o' youah chilluns could work it off fo' you?" Apollo gave Whitelaw's arm a vicious wrench, and Nemo screeched. "Did you say that, Whitelaw? Didja? Tell 'em! Tell 'em what you gonna do with them chilluns! Tell 'em, or Ah breaks this ahm."

Tammy stood in front of the door for some time, her eyes streaming tears. She reached for the hem of her dress and rubbed it across her nose, then tenta- tively she placed her small hand on the knob and pushed the door open just enough that she could see inside. The main room of the general store was crammed full of people, many of them she called auntie or uncle. Others she knew only as masters, mysterious pale-faced people who owned everything and had something to say about everybody's life including hers and her mama's and her papa's—even Tupper's. Tammy's face screwed up again, and she held her breath so no crying sounds would leak out of her. She grabbed her dress in both fists, hanging onto the rough cloth for comfort.

Her eyes roamed over the room once more, and this time she caught sight of Kyra standing not four feet from her. The air came out of her with a gasp, and she scuttled across the room. When she neared Kyra she hurled her small body into the comforting protection of Kyra's long, soft skirts. She buried her face against Kyra and stood there for a moment taking the first deep breath she had dared since running from home.

Kyra looked down and enfolded the small girl in her arms, holding her fast for a few moments. Then she squatted, to be on a level with the child's face. "Tammy, what are you doing out alone? Isn't your mama with you?"

Tammy shook her head. "You gotta come, Miss Kyra. You gotta he'p Tupper—he gwine die fo' sho'."

The noise in the room reached a new level. Kyra placed her hand over one ear to hear better.

"Is he tellin' true?" a voice yelled at the struggling Whitelaw.

Kyra took Tammy's arm and led her outside. She asked the child again what had brought her out alone.

"Tupper dyin'," Tammy wailed. "You come, please you come wif me, Miss Kyra. You kin do somethin'. Please come."

"What happened to Tupper?" Kyra insisted.

"He come from Mistah Tully's all beat up an' bleedin'. Mama cain't mek it stop. Tupper bad hu't. Please come."

Kyra stiffened. Her face became hard. "He came from Tully's, you say? Are you sure, Tammy? How do you know?"

"Tupper say so!" she screeched. "Mama an' Papa sell him to Mistah Tully. Ah tol' you!" Tammy began to pull on Kyra's hand, trying to make her start down the path that would lead to the Jackson house.

Kyra looked back at the general store. "I should tell Apollo where I'm going . . ." She raised her head. "No—they want proof in there. Well, this time I'll give it to them. Tammy, come along. You and I will take the buggy."

Kyra snapped the whip over the horse's head with more vehemence than she had intended. As the minutes passed, the more incensed she became. She thought of Tupper, remembering his pixie face full of deviltry and intelligence when he heckled her during class; and then she thought of Tully and his establishment, and of the Reverend Jabez Hooks and his pious preaching, and of Nemo Whitelaw and his ever-ready account book with its endless credit, and of all the ignorant and trusting black people who still believed that somewhere in this world there really were forty acres and a mule that some benevolent white man was going to bestow upon them. She shuddered. She hadn't known it was possible to feel such pity and such hatred simultaneously.

It took her ten minutes to reach the Jackson house, but it seemed hours since she had left the meeting. She dismounted from the buggy and walked quickly to the front door. Pauline Jackson, haggard, her face streaked with tears, blocked the way. "You git outta heah, Kyra. You ain't comin' in t'see mah mis'ry, you heah? You git. Leave me t'mah sorrows."

Kyra took Pauline by both shoulders. "You listen to me, Pauline Jackson. This is no time for pride. Tammy said Tupper is badly hurt."

Pauline burst into fresh tears and fell against Kyra. "He dyin'. They done kilt him. They used him bad an' they kilt him."

"Let me see him, please. Perhaps I can help."

"No-o-o!" Pauline howled.

"For God's sake, Pauline, I'm not here to judge you. Don't you understand, what hurts you and Tupper hurts me too? Please let me try to help."

Israel Jackson came to the door, standing in the shadows behind his wife. "Pauline, let her in. Ain't nothin' lef' t'hide now. The evil already been did."

Obediently, Pauline stepped aside, and Kyra walked into the one-room home. Jackson children sat silent and unnatural against the walls, as though trying to make themselves a part of the chinked wood. The room was dim, little light coming from the single guttering candle on the rough wood table. Hearing a sound, Kyra moved toward the darkest corner of the room. There on a pallet Tupper Jackson lay moaning, his legs drawn up against his abdomen. Though she could see little, Kyra could smell blood. Her hand went down on the sodden and sticky blanket that Pauline had laid the boy on. "Bring me that candle," Kyra ordered.

The Jacksons all remained still, blank looks fixed on their faces.

Kyra repeated her order.

Tammy moved toward the candle. Her mother began to wail. "No doan, doan—doan look at him. No-o-o, doan look."

Tammy's eyes went from her mother to Kyra to the candle. Slowly she took the candle in shaking hands and walked over to Kyra. The child began to tremble violently as the light touched the edges of Tupper's blanket. Kyra reached out quickly and took the light from her. "Go back, Tammy, go to your papa. Hurry now, do as I say."

Tammy's teeth were chattering, her eyes were huge and fixed on her twin brother.

"Israel, come get her. Can't you see she's terrified?"

"Tammy, come heah," Israel said, but didn't move. Kyra realized then that he would not look or move in the direction of Tupper. She got up and led Tammy to her father with some difficulty. The child moved stiffly, her arms and legs reluctant to obey. Kyra went back to the pallet and for the first time took a look at Tupper Jackson.

The boy's face was swollen almost beyond recognition. Gone were the delicate pixie features, and in their place were the distorted irregularities of a battered head. Both of his eyes were swollen shut, with blood oozing from cuts on his eyelids. His lower lip had been ripped; it hung in a swollen blob on his chin. Burn marks scarred his torso. Yet none of these visible disfigurements accounted for the amount of blood that seeped and filled the blanket and then dripped steadily to the floor. Kyra, eyes blurring with pity, looked at Pauline.

Pauline's face was screwed up in queasiness and horror. "He all tore up on de inside—dey done terrible things to him, Kyra. Ah din't know—Ah woon'ta let 'em have him iffen Ah knowed."

Kyra glanced back at Tupper, then realized what Pauline was saying. Quickly her hands went to her mouth and her stomach. She fought down nausea.

Tupper began to moan again. "Mama . . . hu't me, Mama . . . dey hu't me, Mama . . ."

As Pauline came and took her son gently in her arms, Kyra moved about the shabby room collecting any piece of cloth that was clean. She went to the well and soaked them. She came back in and began to pack the cool rags around Tupper's small body, as Pauline held him. The rags turned brilliant, warm red as fast as Kyra put them against his hips.

"It ain't no use, Miss Kyra," Israel said quietly.

Kyra put the remaining rags against him, determined not to give up; but as Tupper's moans became softer, weaker, and less frequent, she too slumped against the wall in the darkness away from Tupper Jackson, instinctively disassociating herself from death as the others had done. She cried in heartbroken, hopeless sobs, also as the others had done.

Then her anger began to rise again, and she thought of Cilla and Annabelle and Lord knew how many other children she knew nothing about. She thought of Tully and the men who supported him and made this kind of horror possible. She stood up quickly, with a look of purpose on her face.

Israel Jackson was instantly alarmed. "What you gwine do? Wheah you gwine?" He followed her rapid footsteps out onto the porch of his house.

"They aren't going to get away with it. Captain Tremain may have them all in jail over the Tweed property, but that will take weeks, maybe months, and not one more child is going to suffer like this. Not one more! I'll see to that myself."

"Miss Kyra! Wheah you gwine?"

"I'm going to Tully's. It's time somebody cleaned that nest out."

"You cain't do dat! Dey'll git you fo' sho'!"

Kyra walked steadily to the buggy.

"Miss Kyra, you come back heah," Israel shouted, but he did not move off the porch.

"What she gwine do, Papa?" Tammy asked, clutching her father's hand.

"She gwine git herself kilt, jes' like Tupper."

CHAPTER TWENTY-EIGHT

Adam stood to the side of the main meeting room in the general store, fascinated by the slowly changing atmosphere. The defensiveness of each individual was giving way, and they were beginning to form a cohesive group. They no longer looked upon themselves as individuals who had been cheated, but as a group who had been victimized by a common enemy. Now they were becoming a unit whose collective power would root out and defeat the Whitelaws and the Seldons.

Adam crossed his arms over his chest, a smile on his lips. It was the first time since he had begun his campaign against the kinds of things taking place in Chatham County that he had seen the people actually become a unified force. He knew that this time, tonight, something would come of his crusade to end the power of men like Seldon to take advantage of the blacks and struggling whites under the guise of kindness.

Apollo had warmed to his new role as leader of his people. He stood in the center of the room, his strong-featured black face glistening in the warmth of the candlelight, his eyes bright and filled with fervor and purpose as he talked. With all the heat of a man who has known despair, he told them of life. As a man who had once been tied and bound, a sacrificial victim to be shot in order to make other slaves give up one of their own who had made free, to a master who believed only in ownership, he spoke of freedom and education and choices.

Around him the faces of the gathering of people listened first with curiosity, then with interest. Now their eyes lit with passion, and knowledge of injustices, and a sense of power that said, "I no longer must take

anything that is handed to me. I need no longer do what
I am told, but may do as I want, as I know is right.
I can do something. I am free."

Adam let Apollo talk on for some time, and then
moved to stand beside him, judging the moment when
the congregation was prepared to deal with the main
problem, the children. Apollo easily deferred to him,
stepping back, his eyes alight with pride. Adam repeated to them what had happened to each of the children about whom he had any information. He added,
"So far we have not been able to prove what we suspect,
but the best thought tells us that Bret Tully has received
these children as one might accept stolen property. As
there are women and young people among us tonight,
I cannot say at this meeting to what uses these children
have been put, but I think we are all knowledgeable
enough to know what kind of house Bret Tully runs."

Link Jackson spoke up then. He stood silently for a
moment, his face working, his eyes filled with anger.
Finally he said, "Mah Annabelle got took by them.
Whut we gwine do 'bout it? Talk? We gwine talk an'
talk?"

"No," said Adam quickly. "These people have used
the law and the law enforcement officers to hide their
schemes and businesses. They have made themselves
look to be generous and concerned about the welfare
of your people. We are going to turn their own weapons
against them. We'll use the courts and the laws, and the
firsthand information each of you has. It may take
more time than any of us would like to give, but there
will be no more Bret Tullys or Albert Seldons preying
on the people of this county in the name of charity.
With your cooperation, I will begin proceedings against
them tomorrow morning."

Link remained standing. "Ah doan want no co't t'do
mah work fo' me. Ah wants t'feel mah han's roun'
Tully's neck fo' whut he done t'Annabelle."

"We don't know what he has done to Annabelle,
if anything," Adam said. "We only suspect—we are

guessing what happened. In a court we can make those guesses become evidence."

Tim Crosby shouted out, "S'posin' dey doan think it's ebidence? Whut den? Tully keep on takin' ouah chilluns."

"It's youah job to keep watch on youah chilluns!" Apollo said.

"Who gwine plow mah fiel' iffen Ah'm bein' mammy to mah kids?" Jesse Cole said. "Ah say we do somethin'. Ouahseffs!"

Tammy Jackson stood outside her house in the dark for nearly an hour, staring down the empty road Kyra had taken. Though the night was warm and clear, Tammy's teeth were chattering. Her dark eyes strained against the thick darkness that gathered in clumps along the road, trying to see Kyra emerge. Several times she looked so hard and wished so hard she thought she saw Kyra, but the darkness held only tantalizing shapes that never became Kyra. At eleven o'clock Tammy moved off the porch and took several quick steps toward the road.

She stopped and turned back, seeing the comfort of the faint light that showed in the front of her house. She was terrified. Ghosts were about tonight. Tupper's spirit was somewhere nearby, wandering about in the darkness hurt and unsettled. She knew no one could die as Tupper had and be able to find his way straight to heaven. He had hurt too much and he was wandering, she knew. And perhaps there were others. Perhaps even Kyra.

Tammy could not imagine what had happened to her teacher. Papa had said she was going to be killed, just as Tupper had been. Tammy was horrified at the thought that she might run headlong into the battered, bloodied spirit of Kyra Jordan wandering about the earth tonight. Yet she knew that there was a chance that Kyra had not died. Perhaps if she could find the courage, she could send help to Kyra. Perhaps the men at the meeting could avenge Tupper, and then Tupper too could go on to Jesus, and not have to wander.

She felt strangely close to Tupper, as if he were there somewhere close beside her telling her she must go even if she was afraid. He had always called her a scaredy cat. He had always been bolder than she. Tupper was not afraid of the dark. She wasn't too sure what he thought about ghosts; somehow they had never got around to talking about that, but she guessed that he would have laughed at the idea of her being afraid of his ghost. He was her twin, and he loved her. She knew that. Now she seemed more aware of him than ever, and before the feeling could leave her alone and frightened again, she began to run, her arms and legs pumping hard, propelling her down the dark path through the woods that would bring her out near the field that led to the general store.

This time Tammy did not hesitate on the porch; she shoved at the door with both arms, still running full tilt. She burst into the room, a small, frightened girl, her hair standing on end. Wild-eyed, she looked fom one adult face to another, then ran to Apollo. "Tupper daid! They kilt him, an' Miss Kyra gone t'git them mens. Papa say they gwine kill her too! You got to stop her, Mistah Justus, you got to git her!"

"Whut she mean Tupper's daid?" Link Jackson cried, and ran to his frantic young cousin. "You tell me, girl, whut you talkin' 'bout?"

Apollo let Link take Tammy from his grasp. He craned over the heads of the people in the room, his eyes moving rapidly, looking for Kyra. He didn't see her. Again, he scanned the room, sure he had missed sight of her. "Kyra! Kyra! Wheah ah you? Ansah me, woman!"

"She ain't heah," Ethel Cole said. "She lef' wid de chil' a long time 'go."

"What child?" Apollo asked, baffled.

"Dat chile. De one you talkin' to, fool."

Apollo looked once more to Tammy. He shoved a

crying, grieving Link Jackson aside and took the little girl by her shoulders. "Tammy, did Kyra leave here with you?"

Now, nearly paralyzed with fright and exhaustion, Tammy made a high humming noise through clenched teeth, her small head with its wild braids nodding frantically.

"Why?! Wheah'd she go? Tell me!"

With a tremendous effort to speak, Tammy wailed out Tupper's name.

Beside them Link Jackson lamented in a high keen, the pain and hurt coming from deep within. Suddenly he roared, a shrieking, cutting sound that alarmed everyone in the room. A large man, he jumped to his feet, then onto an empty chair. Above all the others in the room, he gestured, his great arms reaching upward, then down, his whole body curling forward in pain. "Dey kilt him!" he howled. "Dey done tek his guts out! Tully! Tully!" The man's name sounded like an animal cry from deep within some primitive jungle, and like electricity the hatred and agony within Link's voice ran through them. Slowly a chant of mourning began to hum in the background, and then the movement of bodies unable to quietly contain what they felt added to the sound. The chant became a keen, and the pain and the anger began to well and foam, boiling up from deep within all these people as though they had become one.

Sensing the volatility of the situation, Adam stepped forward to calm them, but he never managed to say a word, because already the group had merged into one mind, one lusting mind that wanted blood for blood. As though the thoughts of one were automatically the thoughts of the others, the blacks were on their feet, swaying, chanting, talking in a heightened, emotional way. Their movements seemed to be directionless, but they were moving toward the door. The thought had not fully formed yet, but the minds were already prepared to receive and act upon it as soon as one made a suggestion. Apollo moved through the room, still unwilling to believe that Kyra had really gone to the Jacksons' and then into town to deal with Tully on her own. Finally, unable to do anything but believe, Apollo, his face gray, said in a deep voice, "We got to he'p her. Tully's gonna kill her iffen we doan kill him first."

Adam felt the waves of hate push against him, swell and burst out the door of the general store with the mass of blacks that streamed forth. They covered the road in front of the store. As they went, they picked up fallen branches from trees, or broke off green limbs. Some had had knives concealed on their persons, and now that steel gleamed in the faded, pale moonlight.

They surged over the fields and across the roads, the sound of their keening and chanting filling the night, moving toward Savannah and Tully's.

CHAPTER TWENTY-NINE

Leroy Biggs took extra care and derived unusual satisfaction as he carefully donned and arranged the garb of the Klan that marked him as the leader—the Cyclops —of the local chapter. He stood in front of his mirror moving his head so that the cut-out eyes of the hood seemed to change shape and appear more menacing. He had always been proud to be Cyclops, but that leadership, and in fact the local Klan, had taken on an aspect of added importance since Edmund Revanche had come into the picture.

It was one thing to harass a bunch of no-'count darkies, and keep a few poor whites in line and understanding of the way things were done in Chatham County. But with Edmund Revanche behind them, and even asking favors of the Klan, there would be money and a certain prestige and power that had been starting to slip away from them lately. The folks around the County took them seriously enough because they all knew the consequences, but it had become a kind of tongue-in-cheek respect. No one bucked the Klan outright—they obeyed its dictates all right—but it was beginning to be looked upon somewhat as a club of the good old boys who had all been friends and hell-raisers before the War. That would end tonight. They'd be starting anew. Once Leroy had accomplished this night's work, no one would ever look down upon him or smile knowingly and pityingly behind his back. He'd have all the money in the world and the power to make its force felt.

He adjusted the belt he wore around his robe tonight, then went to his closet, rooting beneath a pile of old blankets and linen tablecloths, until he came up

with a well-polished wooden box. He ran his hand
across the smooth surface, then unfastened the latch.
He took from it the Klan flags and carefully unfolded
them. Behind the mask his eyes glittered. He couldn't
help smiling.

He looked at the clock on the mantel, noting that it
was eleven-thirty and that he had just enough time to
get to the meeting place in the cemetery. Tonight he
wanted everything prepared when the others came in.

The first to arrive were the Lictors and the Night
Hawks. Leroy immediately sent them outside to inter-
cept all other members as they arrived.

"Aww, c'mon, Leroy," Osgood Baxter complained,
"we don't have t'do that any moah. We all know each
othah."

"Naw!" agreed Silas Ormond, a former planter,
turned distiller since the War.

"You do as you're told, boys, y'hear? This is a special
meetin', an' we're goin' t'do everything right. Now git!"

The Lictors went outside, muttering and catching
each other's eyes.

One by one the members came into the small caretaker's hut in the cemetery and very formally gave
Leroy the Klan secret handshake. With unusual solem-
nity they took their places around the room and waited
until all their members had gathered. All of them were
tense. There was something indefinable, but certainly
different, about Leroy. There was not a man in the
room who did not expect trouble to come of this night,
this meeting that Leroy had called with such urgency.
The tension mounted as Leroy kept them waiting for
nearly half an hour before he strode to the center of
the hut.

He performed the ritualistic opening of the meeting,
then gave a short, formal talk about the purpose of the
Klan. "We are formed to protect the innocent." Dramatically he pointed to his white robe. "And here's the
color that reminds us—white, the symbol of purity."
He held up the bottom of the robe and touched his

sleeves, pointing out the red trim. "Red—red, the color of blood, our blood that we're willin' to shed to protect those who can't protect themselves. I don't often remind y'all about these things, but tonight is a special meetin' with a special purpose."

"Git on with it, Leroy. Ah'm in a hurry—Ah got the purtiest li'l gal waitin' fo' me you evah did see," Billy Bob said.

"Ahh!" Lyman cooed. "I'm goin' t'tell Birdie!"

"You shet youah mouth!"

"All o' you shut up!" Leroy roared. "We're holdin' a trial tonight, an' it's most likely the most important action this den will ever take!"

"Oh, hell, Leroy, quit kidding yourself," Todd said, and began to cough. "The Klan in Georgia is finished. We all know it. Shit, we can't do anything now with that Congressional Committee investigatin' everything an' breathin' down our necks."

"Nobody's breathin' down our necks. Most likely nobody even knows we exist. We ain't called the Invisible Empire fo' nothin', Todd boy."

"You tell that to Gen'rl George W. Gordon," Billy Bob said, snickering and elbowing Lyman in the ribs.

"Listen here, General Gordon did fine by us. He ain't told that Congressional Committee a thing worth hearin'. He's protected the Klan, an' you can count on him doin' it every time. Congress is always pokin' its nose in where it hasn't got no call for bein'." Leroy stood taller, pushing his chest out. "An' I've heard about all the tomfoolery I'm gonna listen to. I told you I got news an' a special task fo' this den."

"Gawd, youah a hahd-ass!" The muttered comment came from the back of the room. Leroy's hooded head swiveled around, but he could not identify the speaker.

"Hard-ass, shit!" Leroy snarled. "Y'all're so damn dumb, it ain't no wonder you're all piss poor. We got us the chance of a lifetime, and you can't even hold your tongues long enough to hear it out."

"We need only to read the newspapers, Leroy,"

Glenn said timidly. "The Congressional Committee means business. We could all end up in prison for continuing Klan meetings."

Leroy glared first at Glenn, then at Todd. "What is this? All you Saunderses chicken shit cowards or what?"

"You can count in a Whitaker too, Leroy," Cedric said, standing up and making himself the center of attention. "When the Klan had a purpose and some honor to it, was one thing, but all we're doing is scaring off a bunch of no 'counts. We aren't accomplishing anything and we're risking prison for it."

The mask on Leroy's head bobbled as he pushed his face toward Cedric. "You God-damned coward! You don't know what you're talkin' about. Nobody's gonna come get you! Who'd have the balls to put us in any prison? Who's gonna convict us?"

Cedric bellowed, redfaced, "The United States Government!"

"They can, Leroy! I read in the paper this committee has the power to act," Glenn said.

"Shi . . . it," Leroy intoned. "You don't even know what's goin' on with this meetin' and you're turnin' tail."

"I don't need to know," Cedric said, and looked at the rest of the group. "Y'all feel like goin' along with this it's your ass, but I'm not. Anybody here gonna leave with me?"

Lyman said loudly, "I'm with Leroy."

Glenn stood up and edged to Cedric's side. Cedric waited a few more moments, then the two men left.

"Talk," said Lyman to Leroy, before recriminations against Cedric and Glenn could begin. Then he stood and looked at the others. "Leroy always guided us right. It ain't gonna hurt t'hear him out. Leroy gets *some* good ideas."

"That's more like it," said Leroy. "Now everybody knows what counts in this world is who you know an' what they're gonna do for you. It looks like this here li'l ol' den has got itself a big ol' sugar daddy, an' he can do a-plenty."

The other men in the crowded room began to pay attention.

Leroy's eyes glittered behind the mask. He began to pace back and forth in the small space at the front of the room. "Nat'rally I got to keep his name quiet, but he's a mighty pow'ful man, an' he wants a li'l favor from us that jes' happens t'be in our interests as well. Fo' that li'l favor, he's willin' an' ready t'see there is money an' opportunity comin' our way. For instance, if we see our way clear t'do this favor for ourselves *an'* him, there is fifty dollars comin' to each an' every man seein' fit t'help out! When was the last time any o' you seen fifty dollars at one time?"

Leroy allowed the men to crow and hoot a little. A murmur of interested and excited voices talked of nights on the town, whores, and more practical things like mules and plows and picks. He allowed the talk to continue a while, then said, "Ain't there a one o' you smart enough to want t'get on with this? Y'all gonna talk the night away an' lose the first opportunity you had since the War t'see a little daylight?"

There was a chorus of excited comment.

Sure of himself, Leroy's voice became louder and stronger. "We-all are goin' t'have a trial—right here an' now, accordin' to the laws an' rules o' the Invisible Empire!"

There was a moment's hesitation, then a chorus of *yeas!*

Leroy moved faster back and forth in front of the men. He opened a case he had brought in earlier and took out three whisky bottles, which he handed to men in different sections of the room.

"Hey, that's agin the rules!" Caleb Wells objected.

"When'd you evah turn down a free drink, Caleb?" asked Bufer Tate.

"This here's a special meetin', a very special meetin',

an' as your Cyclops, I say we all need clear heads for it!" Leroy burst into the general laughter. Most of the others joined in and eagerly reached for the bottles.

Again Leroy gave them time, talking only occasionally and then only to raise the pitch of the excitement and to encourage them to think about what they had been deprived of since the War and what was now within their reach if they performed the small favor their benefactor wished done.

When the liquor bottles had made several circuits of the room, Leroy said, "All right boys, I hereby call to meetin' the trial in absentia of Cap'n Adam Tremain, alias the Black Swan, alias the enemy of all decent folks in Chatham County, Georgia!"

For a moment the room fell silent. All eyes stared stunned at the hooded man at the front of the room. Then a chorus of wild, intoxicated revelry broke out. It had become a game, and no longer were the Klansmen thinking of consequences or Congressional Committee investigations. There was a fifty-dollar gold piece and a benefactor to help them out of anything.

Leroy's berobed arm stretched out straight, pointing at Lyman. "You, sir! By authority of my office, I appoint you defender o' the accused!"

Lyman spewed out a mouthful of whisky and stood up unsteadily. He bowed to the others, then, head thrown back, he said in a wailing voice, "Sir, I beg the in-dulgence o' the court, but my client ain't got no defense. Whatever you good men think he done, he done it an' lots worse!"

Leroy slammed his fist down on a rickety table. "We ain't playin' 'round here, Lyman! The Klan is sworn to uphold justice, an' we will! You defend him!"

"Shit, Leroy, I can't! I hate the damned bastard!"

"Ahh, c'mon, let's just say he's guilty and get on with it," Todd said. "What's the point in foolin' around, we all know he's guilty."

Arvin Mitchell, sitting in the back, asked, "What's he accused of?"

"Conspiracy!" Leroy shouted. "Incitin' the niggers to riot! Thievin' other people's stuff—like their slaves! An' gen'ral meddlin' 'round where he ain't wanted!"

"Well, shit, theah ain't no question he done all that," Osgood Baxter said.

Ignoring the collective feeling that everything was already accomplished, Leroy tapped twelve men on the shoulder and called them a jury. Hooting and laughing now, and progressively more inebriated, the men shouted guilty as soon as Leroy moved from one to the next. The room rang with the loud, laughing shouts.

"Guilty!"

"Hang the bastard!"

"Whup 'im!"

"Burn the son of a bitch to hell!"

Leroy, still stubbornly holding to the "proper" form of the trial, announced the verdict, then pronounced the sentence of death by hanging upon Captain Adam Tremain of Mossrose Plantation.

No one heard him, or seemed to, until he had announced the sentence. The noise in the room rose still higher. The men were all out of their seats milling around, punching at each other, telling stories of abuses they had heard or knew firsthand that Adam Tremain had committed.

Leroy looked over what was now a mindless mob, and he smiled behind the mask. Without comment, he brought out the last five bottles of whisky Edmund Revanche had provided him with. Three he set aside to be put in his saddlebags to be used later, the other two he passed around the room. In a few minutes he shouted for those who were dressed in everyday clothes to don their robes, then go to their horses.

It was nearly one o'clock in the morning by the time the noisy, excited band of forty men was assembled and mounted. Leroy held his horse under control at the front of the mob. When they all seemed firmly seated, he raised his hand, then brought it swiftly to his side. En masse, the Klansmen's horses shot forward, making the noise of thunder on the hard-packed road from the cemetery. At the River Road Leroy turned his mount, and they galloped, their robes beating in the wind, toward Mossrose.

CHAPTER THIRTY

Kyra Jordan turned onto the street on which Tully's house stood just after midnight. She wasn't frightened, nor had she any care or concern for her own safety. She didn't know when she had lost it. Perhaps it had died with Tupper Jackson, and though she hadn't stayed to see him die, she was sure he had, or would. Her only concern was the lateness of the hour. She knew little of establishments such as Tully's. Would Tully still be there? Where would she find him? Would she dare walk in the front door, or would she be thrown out before she crossed the threshold? She wasn't even sure if women, black or white, were allowed in there if they did not belong to Tully.

Her mind raced in furious circles trying to decide whether she should brazenly approach the front or walk through the back posing as a servant. She supposed they did have servants. Didn't all white men have servants?

Kyra brought the lightweight buggy to a halt at the back of Tully's house. She tied the horse, and took a moment to smooth her hair and straighten her skirt. Satisfied that she could pass as a servant, she walked boldly to the back door and entered without knocking. She felt only a small surprise when the door gave and she came into the well-lighted kitchen. She stood for a moment, her eyes scanning the place, taking in the layout. Four women who appeared to be cooks, and·two men, most likely waiters, were talking at the far end of the long, narrow kitchen. None of them looked up or seemed aware of her standing near the door. On the big wood stove stood a large copper teakettle. She looked at the shelves and saw a stack of silver trays.

Quickly and silently she walked across the kitchen, picked up the steaming kettle from the stove, then took a tray as she passed the shelves on her way out through the only other door to the kitchen. Either the blacks hadn't noticed or didn't care. Kyra let out her breath and paused in the murky, dark hallway, forcing herself to breathe normally. She felt ill. Her whole body ached and she felt sick to her stomach. She hated this place, the man who ran it, and those who frequented it. She hated the women and men she had seen who would work in a place like this. It made her feel dirty just being here.

Worst of all—because they had been her children, her students whom Tully had taken and defiled—Tully had made her as diseased as himself. She hadn't really seen what was happening. She was a reasonable person; it had been reasonable to take little action until a child had died, because one could not bring oneself to believe or defy evil. Her hands clutched the tray until she shook and had to calm herself consciously, lest she spill the steaming water all over herself. Oh yes, she said silently, he had made her one of them by her wanton ignorance, and there was only one way to cleanse herself.

With purpose and an enforced calm, she walked steadily down the long, narrow hallway, wondering only mildly where it would bring her. Whatever she had to do, if she had to go into every room of this house carrying her kettle of water, she'd find Tully.

She came to the first door in a series that opened off the long hallway. She would open it boldly, as someone who worked here all the time would do. Her mouth set tighter as her hand closed over the crystal knob. She was unprepared for the brilliant glitter of light shot about the room from the many prismed chandeliers. She stood momentarily blinded and blinking inside the salon. When her eyes adjusted, she was again dazzled by the overpowering opulence in which she found herself. Rich brocades covered windows, while deep blood-red plush couches and chairs were arranged in private seatings about the enormous room. Tables wrought and covered in gold leaf sparkled richly in the crystal light. Mirrors twinkled reflections of luxury back at her from all over the room. The scents of leather, fine tobaccos, and aged brandies swirled around her, and there were other less definable odors that overwhelmed her and made her feel giddy.

Kyra stood unable to move or decide what to do next. The room had ripped away from her her sense of reality. This was a hedonist's fairyland, a place of gossamer castles and demonic dreams. For the first time she felt a tingle of doubt and fear creep along her spine. She sucked in her breath, trying to regain the feeling of purpose that had carried her through the dark night to Tully's house. She forced herself to think of Tupper Jackson wandering around these rooms, mesmerized by the richness, being called upon to do the most degrading and horrifying things whenever the men who occupied these rooms wished him to.

It seemed to her that she stood for hours fighting her doubts and the idea that she had been wrong about everything, though it was only seconds. She lowered her head, staring at the steaming copper kettle sitting alone and ludicrous on the etched silver tray. How could such evil exist in a place of such overbearing beauty? Again she felt sick to her stomach at the peculiar forms men's perversions took. Then she raised her head, squared her shoulders, and looked around the room. Only then did she remember that she did not know what Tully looked like. How would she know him? Once again panic and doubt assailed her. Could there be right, and God, if she could not find the man who was responsible for the horror of Tupper Jackson's death?

At a secluded table, partially hidden by a red-velvet swag, she saw Reverend Jabez Hooks. In her mind she could hear Adam Tremain standing at the meeting tonight, his finger pointed first at Nemo Whitelaw and then at Hooks, accusing them of being partners to Tully and his schemes. Tully would be there at that table, hidden by the drapery. Hooks had no doubt ridden straight here to warn him. Her back straight, she walked directly across the room and over to the table.

She said, in a loud clear voice, *"Tully!"*

Jabez Hooks was the first to look up. His eyes widened, and Kyra felt a surge of strength as she saw fear in them. He leaped up from the table shouting, "Tully! Who let her in heah? What you doin' heah, woman? Git out!"

Kyra instinctively moved toward him, and he jumped aside, bumping into the table. The snowy white linen cloth that covered it caught on his watch fob and ripped from the table, spewing wine and cigars across the floor. The slender dark-haired man seated nearest Kyra and across from Hooks threw out his arms, flinging from himself the tumbled wine glasses and decanter. His arm hit her in the abdomen. Kyra doubled, her tray and the steaming hot kettle flying from her hands.

The man's shriek cut through the room. The other men at the table leaped to their feet, hurrying to the aid of the one whose clothes now steamed hotly with the scalding water. The man's voice narrowed to a high, shrill moan.

Horrified, Kyra backed a few steps away, her hand over her mouth, her eyes watering. She could nearly feel the stranger's pain. Then she began to laugh, sure somehow that the man was Tully. Hysterically, she laughed, with the strange delight of vengeance.

Tully, Albert Seldon, Jabez Hooks, and Lloyd Henry Grooms mopped and waved at the man's steaming flesh and clothing.

Edmund Revanche emitted the wail of a wounded animal, his voice high and thin; and then a rage unmerciful and powerful filled him. He tore at his hair, his burning body stiffening against the soft, red plush of the velvet chair. His chest, his belly, his groin and his legs were in a fiery vise. He could feel the skin shriveling and tightening. He could feel where the water had eaten deep into him, and he alone seemed aware of the woman's hysterical, mocking laughter. The sound filled his skull and burned deeper than the scalding water had done. Not knowing he was incoherent, Revanche screamed for his friends to get her. He beat at himself, at them, with weak, flailing fists. He struggled to his feet, then fell over the table, his face in the spilled wine. "Bitch!" he screamed. "Bitch! Bitch! Bitch!"

The other men understood that, understood the hatred the single word carried. "Get her! Get her! Kill —kill that—" The effort was too much and the pain took over again. He lay across the table, once more howling in his thin, high whine. Then, with greater effort, he gasped, "Stop her laughter! Stop it!"

Grooms placed his hands on Revanche's shoulders and tried to ease him back into his chair. "Tully, we got to get him to a doctah."

"No-o-o!" Revanche howled. "No one must know I'm here!"

"Tully, someone discreet . . ." Lloyd Henry continued.

"Get the bitch!" Revanche gasped, his eyes murderous with pain and rage.

"She's gone," Jabez Hooks said in best funereal voice. "She will plague you no longah."

Revanche's eyes disappeared into his head, the whites staring blindly at Hooks, then he suddenly lurched forward, his hand reaching wildly for Hooks's thin throat. "The bitch! Get her!"

Hooks grabbed at Revanche's clawing fingers, prying the fingers loose one at a time. Choking, struggling for breath, Hooks clawed at the air, his mouth working and sucking.

Albert Seldon's chubby face was pale and wet with perspiration. He clutched at Lloyd Henry's beefy arm. "What should we do, Colonel? What the hell are we gonna do? Somebody's got t'get him to a doctor!"

"Oscar Weston—a doctah—a couple streets over," Tully said. "We've never used him but he's got his shingle out."

Grooms stood watching Tully frantically putting ice on Revanche, and Edmund as quickly throwing the sparkling frozen bits off himself. Then he looked at Hooks quietly vomiting onto the thick-piled Oriental rug, and at Albert Seldon holding to his arm like a small child, his face slick and sickly looking.

"Seldon," Lloyd Henry said, "you take Mr. Revanche over to the doc's. Tully, you get some men togethah and we'll carry out Mr. Revanche's ordahs. We'll get that woman. An' we'll do it legal-like. Let the law hang her. No nigra can get away with doin' this to a white man, 'specially not one the calibah o' Mr. Revanche." He placed his thickly muscled hand on Edmund's shoulder, squeezing gently. "We'll take care of everything fo' you, suh."

Revanche's response was a snarl, but Lloyd Henry, perhaps better than any of the others, understood his boss and knew that he was pleased.

A dray was brought to the rear of Tully's house and layered with blankets and carpets so that Revanche could be laid as comfortably as possible in the bed. The black waiters Kyra had seen in the kitchen now scurried to Grooms's orders bellowed out with military authority. Neither man made a sound. They had never seen an occurrence like this in Tully's house. Many had been the time that they had carried out a drunk, and some that had looked and felt more dead than drunk, and they had buried the small body of a child more times than either liked to remember, but they had never seen Tully and his important guests in such a state of panic and disruption. Neither man dared to look at the other, for both of them knew who had done this to Mr. Revanche, and both of them knew that some-time Tully or Grooms or one of the others would question how the woman got into the house. As soon as they were clear of Tully and his house, both of them would disappear into the night and never return here. But until they were away and free they didn't dare look into each other's faces, for fear the white men would also see their guilt and their knowledge.

Revanche was bundled into the wagon, and Albert Seldon was hoisted up into the dray bed with him. "Y'all watch him good, Albert," Lloyd Henry said loudly so Revanche would be sure to hear. "Y'heah? Now repeat fo' me—wheah y'all gonna take him?"

Seldon mopped at his brow. He licked at his lips. "To—to Dr. Oscar Weston's—and—and I pay anything he asks. He's not to know who Edmund is, an' he's not to tell anyone we were there—or—or Tully will come after him."

"Not Tully, you idiot! No names! Tell him it'll be the Klan!"

"Yes, yes—I won't say a name to him—you know that, Colonel Grooms—it was just to you I said the name. You know I wouldn't use a name! You know that."

"Ah know you bettah not. Weston ain't the only man Tully kin find if he goes aftah him. Doan fo'get that, Seldon. Noo Yawk's not so fah a man kin hide when somebody like Tully wants him."

"Oh, Jesus, don't talk like that, Colonel. You know I'm as loyal as can be. I've always done my job!"

Lloyd Henry clamped his teeth down on his thick cigar and grunted what Seldon took to be agreement.

After the dray carrying Revanche to Dr. Weston's house disappeared around the street corner, Tully, Grooms, and Hooks returned to the saloon. Tully poured each of them a generous glass of whisky and sat down wearily. He took a deep drink from the glass and exhaled slowly, letting the tension run from him along with the breath. "Lawd Gawd, this has been a night! Ah sho'ly am glad to see it ovah. What d'you s'pose is gonna come o' Mistah Revanche? He didn't look none too good t'me."

"Ah reckon he'll be jes' fine," Grooms said. "An'

this night ain't hardly begun, mah friend. We still got work t'do. Mistah Revanche is goin' t'be askin' fust thing what came o' that woman, an' we bettah be able t'tell him she ain't in this purty ol' world any moah."

"Aww shit, Colonel, you ain't really gonna bothah with that nigra, ah you? We can tell Revanche anything we damn please. How's he gonna know the difference? That woman won't evah show her face 'round heah agin. She's mos' likely halfway to Ohio by now."

Grooms laughed harshly. "Tully, Tully, y'all got a shawt mem'ry. 'Membah who youah talkin' about. Mistah Revanche is goin' t'know every dee-tail o' what happened to that darky. An' y'all bettah be prepared to tell him, or staht runnin' youahseff."

"Well, we sho'ly can't take care of it legal-like. Ah don't care what y'all promised, it can't be done that way."

Grooms snapped, "Why not?"

" 'Cause Revanche don't want his name fouled up in it, an' what ah we goin' to tell Laban? We ain't got no injured pahty t'give him. Laban Sweet's got a itchy palm, but that don't make him no fool. He can't charge nobody with the crime o' assault with intent t'kill if he ain't got a injured pahty."

Grooms chewed mercilessly at the end of his ragged cigar. "Then we got to do it some othah way."

"How?" Tully wanted to know. "Ah sho' as hell ain't trampin' aftah that wild nigger all by mahseff."

Grooms was silent, continuing to work his cigar until the dark liquid oozed from the corners of his mouth. With a ringing thwang he shot a wad of tobacco and saliva into the brass spittoon.

Hooks, still pale and shaken from his earlier fright, winced, his hands going protectively around his midsection.

Finally Grooms looked from one man to the other. "Rev'und, you got a mighty gift fo' stirring folks up. An' Tully, you got a house full o' randy, achin'-for-a-fight men. What we need's a mob, an' right heah, undah this roof, we got the makin's. Now Ah'll tell you what weah goin' t'do. Ah'm gonna staht screamin' about that woman doin' me hahm, an' you two ah goin' t'git this houseful o' men on the move. Fust, you git all the rope we need fo' a good ol'-fashioned hangin', an' then preachah, you staht talkin'. Hurry now, that nigger's got a good half houah staht."

Grooms waited until Tully had placed one rope in an obvious spot in the saloon, and one in an entryway, just in case the first should be overlooked. Then, in good imitation of Revanche's anguish, Grooms began to howl. Tully and Hooks looked on in horrified shock as the huge Grooms writhed in mock pain. Then, like puppets pulled by an invisible cord, they each went in different directions, shouting frantically about the crazed negress who had attacked the white man.

Hooks, caught up in his role, went wildly through the halls, his long, bony arms waving, an authentic ring of hysteria in his voice as he shouted about damnation and evil and the demons of the black skin preying on whites in the night.

Tully, less dramatic, was nonetheless as effective as Hooks. He appealed to the vigilante in the men. He brought out in them the desire, under the guise of justice, to vent some of their hostility and gain a sense of raw power over the workings of their world. A Southern justice, an eye for an eye. Hooks and Tully, without being aware, worked hand in glove stirring up men, who wanted only the right time and the right cause.

The lobby swarmed with angry men. The small black girl at the front desk, where Tully insisted that all firearms be checked, was terrified as the men demanded their guns, some of them thrusting the weapons into her face and shouting at her as though she had been the one who had "harmed the white man." None of them even asked who the white man was, or what had been done to him.

Colonel Lloyd Henry Grooms took his place at the head of the mob, his deep voice carrying over the confusion and threats and angry expletives. Hooks was beside him, his long arms still waving, still spewing his fevered credo of fear and damnation and retribution. Tully too was there, his face somber and filled with purpose.

In seconds they shoved and pushed their way out the door and into the street alongside Tully's house. A cursing, haphazard posse, they spread out in threes and fours covering the area around the house, all looking for Kyra. They shouted back and forth to keep in touch with one another as each of the groups moved down the side streets.

Kyra had left Tully's and mounted the small buggy. Once in the buggy, she hadn't known where to go or what to do. By now she realized that the man she had scalded was not Tully, but who he was she didn't know. She shivered with fatigue and a deep tiredness that went far beyond the physical. It had been a night of horrors, and she felt sick and dirty inside. She no longer had a desire for revenge, or anything else. Some things are too evil even to avenge, she thought. She wanted only an end to it.

She drove the horse aimlessly up and down streets, her mind blank. Where was she to go? As often happens when one cannot face the present, she began to think of past days and times. She thought wistfully of the hopes and dreams she and Ruel had had when they had first come South with Adam Tremain. She thought of the plans they had shared for a family. She skipped over his death and began to think about Apollo and how she had first met him and taught him to read. She even managed to smile and laugh a little when she thought of his battles with proper English and pronunciation. In spite of herself, she rather hoped he would never completely lose that rather odd and endearing distortion of the language. Apollo is a good man, she thought, and again began to remember.

She thought of the day he had told her of his brother,

Jupiter, and how much he wanted to find him. Together they had written innumerable letters that had been sent through the Freedmen's Bureau to various churches across the South, but Apollo had never heard from Jupiter. She sighed and let her hands go slack on the reins. The horse slowed to a stop along the side of the road, chewing contentedly at the long grass. Kyra sat for a few minutes thinking of nothing, wanting to do nothing. She arched her back, running her hands along the sides trying to ease the tension and tiredness. Something had to be done, she thought. One cannot do harm to another and not pay—at least she could not.

Once more her mind sought a memory—the Freedmen's Bureau. She knew she could go to Laban Sweet and tell him what had happened. Laban would know what had to be done, and still be fair to her. He'd at least listen to her story.

She picked up the reins again and guided the horse through the streets to the darkened Bureau office. Laban's rump-sprung rocker sat outside on the porch. Kyra dismounted from the buggy and sat in the rocker. She put her head back, her eyes closed, her face immobile. She looked to be asleep, and perhaps she was. There was at least one part of her that would not permit thought or feeling to penetrate her consciousness any more tonight. She sat and rocked and waited.

Kyra heard the sounds of the men shouting and occasionally what sounded like a gunshot, but she thought nothing of it, and in no way connected the raucous activity with herself. She sat and rocked and waited.

The men had moved into the squares of Savannah. They met in the center of each, listened again to the haranguing of Lloyd Henry, Hooks, and Tully, and once more they moved, hunting for the darky bitch who had maimed the white man, the castrating bitch, the demented black whore, the woman.

Melvin Wickes, husband of a wife who ran away with great regularity, father of twelve, eight of whom were not his own, saw Kyra first. He tiptoed toward the woman who appeared to be asleep, then stopped, leaning forward, his watery, prominent eyes straining into the darkness. Then he took three loping steps closer and began to yell gleefully. "Hey, hey, hey! Hey, hey, hey, boy! Ah got 'er! Ah got 'er!"

Kyra continued to rock. She heard the man, but felt no fear. She was too tired. She sat and rocked and waited.

One by one the other men appeared in the street, then approached the spot where Wickes stood grinning madly at the seemingly sleeping woman. Guns were shot off in signal to those who had searched farther afield. Soon the street around the Freedman's Bureau office was clogged with men. They formed a semicircle around Kyra, none of them venturing too near. Brave with words, they jeered and called her names, but none actually approached, none touched her. From the back of the crowd Grooms shoved a path through the men. He was followed closely by Tully and the ranting Hooks, who seemed no longer able to keep from babbling his blasphemous credo.

Grooms stood a little inside the semicircle, his beefy arms folded across his barrel chest. He looked at the woman rocking peacefully on the porch of the Bureau. He tugged dramatically at the sides of his mustaches, then looked at Tully. "That's her. Ah'm sho' of it as Ah would be if it was mah own mothah. What do y'all say?"

"Le's jes' get this ovah with, Grooms."

"Now Tully, we got to be fayah. Ah say Ah'd know her anywheah—you seen her befoah?"

"Ah seen her in mah place pourin' scaldin' watah on a poah hapless customah."

Hooks put his hands up to his eyes as if in dread. "Ohh, Lawd, this heah's youah faithful suhvant beggin' you save him fum the eye of the evil one! Delivah us, oh Lawd. Guide us in the destruction o' Satan an' his demons! Yea, Lawd, we heah you! We heah you, Lawd, an' ah brave an' blessed, ready t'do youah work! Rid the Lawd o' the sight o' this evil woman, men! Y'all heah?! Rid us of her!"

The men broke the neat regularity of the semicircle and lunged toward Kyra, each eager to be the one to drag the woman to the tree where they would hang her. Hands reached from everywhere, pulling at her dress, ripping it, catching handfuls of her flesh and hair. She was jerked in several directions. She fell to her knees and was dragged along the street amid the groping hands and the excited shouts and curses.

As they dragged her from the porch and down the street, Kyra was limp, making no attempt to protect herself or fight them. For a time, it seemed too much of an effort to fight, too much of a nightmare, too much like everything that had happened this night to be real. She hurt, she felt the clawing hands, but she did nothing until finally her sluggish brain began to scream to her who these men were and that she was letting them do to her what they had done to Tupper Jackson, and Cilla Warren, and Annabelle Twoshoes. These were the very men! And it was herself, Kyra Jordan, they were going to destroy now!

Kyra suddenly came to life, wresting herself from her captors with all her strength and weight. Surprised, they fell back and let her go. "Animals!" she screamed at them as she ran into the darkness. "Filthy, evil animals! Child eaters!"

Kyra ran through the streets without thought or direction, hunting for shelter and safety. She ran across the streets into the back yards, across the prettily wrought verandas of elegant stuccoed houses, and through gardens. The light summer scents of night flowers swept past her on the wind. The sounds of the night insects came to her in those moments when the pounding feet of the following men retreated or fell into confused silence. She ran past the front of a beautiful Greek Revival house on Bull Street, then across Madison Square, touching the Jasper Monument as she raced toward the safety of St. John's Episcopal Church.

From the southwest, Tully's men pounded from the grounds of the home of the Savannah Volunteer Guards. They spread out across the square, easily outrunning her, cutting her off from the sanctuary of the church. This time there was no resignation in Kyra. She fought them, kicking, scratching, clawing. She pelted anyone near her with her fists and bit those who dared let her mouth near them. Her fury fueled their own, and they beat at her not as human, but as some hated object. They dragged her prone through the streets back to the tree. Now even the most timid of the men had no doubt that what they were about to do was justified.

Groom's mammoth elbow dug into Tully's side as the Colonel winked in pleasure, knowing that the deed was done.

"Bring youah hawss ovah heah!" A man shouted to another.

"Git her up on it!"

They struggled with Kyra, and she fought back with every ounce of strength she had.

They had finally got her astride a horse with the rope around her neck, when from down the street they heard a gun reporting. Momentarily they paused, all turning to see who had shot the pistol, and why.

Laban Sweet, his face red from running, puffed toward them. "Sonofabitch! What the hell you boys doin'?"

"Git out o' heah, Laban! This heah's a killer witch!"

"That's mah bizness, God damn it! What she done?" Laban stood gasping as he finally came to a halt in the midst of the mob. "Y'all git on home, y'heah?! Ah'll take care o' any law-breakin'!"

"Ohh, Lawd God, don't let us be turned fum ouah mission!" Hook's ripping voice pierced the noise.

"Lord God, blast him to hell forever, child eater that he is!" Kyra screamed.

"Y'all shut up!" Laban shouted as he pulled his gun from its holster again. He raised it over his head and shot it once. "Now y'all bettah lissen, 'cause that's the last shot Ah'm wastin'. What in the hell is goin' on heah? What'd this woman do?"

"She killed a white man!"

"No, she didn't—she castrated him!"

"That ain't what Ah heard! She—"

Laban shot his gun again. "Now jes' hold on! Ah'm takin' this woman into the jail, y'heah? Y'all come in an' tell me what she done. You got a complaint, Ah'll lissen. Now git outta mah way, 'cause Ah'm Jestis o' the Peace, an' this heah's mah prisonah till we know what she done or ain't done."

Tully and Grooms edged back to the perimeter of the mob. "What're we gonna do now, Grooms?" Tully asked.

"Jes' hold tight. We can't do anything right now. Let him take her. She won't be the fust that evah died in her cell. Jes' hold tight."

"Youah sayin' weah gonna—"

"That's what Ah'm sayin', Tully, so shut up an' walk easy-like back to youah place. Ah wouldn't mind a bit if ol' Laban nevah seen we was heah."

Laban walked through the uncertainly milling, angry men to Kyra. He helped her down from the horse and removed the rope from her neck. When they were some distance from the still-clamoring men, Laban asked, "What the hell did you *do,* woman?"

Kyra told him exactly what she had done and why.

"Sonofabitch!" Laban exclaimed. He began to put together some of the peculiarities of the night. He had been happily visiting at Dr. Oscar Weston's house playing cribbage, five pegs ahead of Doc for once, when a dray carrying an injured man had driven up. Some Yankee man came to the door asking the doctor's help with his friend. Laban had heard mutters of conversa-

tion. Doc Weston had refused to treat the man, something Laban had never before known him to do, but
then you could never tell exactly what Doc Weston
might do. A crusty old bachelor, Doc was a man who
played his own hunches. All Laban knew was that the
doctor hadn't wanted to finish their cribbage game and
hadn't been fit company for bears. His evening unaccountably spoiled, Laban had left to go back to his
office when he heard the yelling and shouting around
Madison Square. Then he had found the mob surrounding Kyra.

"Tully's place again," he said aloud.

"They killed Tupper Jackson tonight, Mr. Sweet,"
Kyra said. "Maybe I did hurt that man, but it was an
accident. What they did to Tupper was no accident.
Are you going to do anything about it?"

Laban rubbed at his cheek until it hurt. Was he going
to do anything about it? "You got anything to show
this is true, Kyra?"

"Tupper's body."

"That doan prove nothin'. Can't tell who did what
to him."

"Then what do I have to do, Mr. Sweet? Take you
in that house while they are right in the act of mutilat-
ing some child?"

Laban was silent for a moment, then said, "That
ain't the worst idea Ah evah heard, Kyra. Mebbe we
could do that—jes' walk right into one o' Tully's
private rooms when nobuddy's thinkin' about it.
Mebbe."

"Then for God's sake, man, do it! Do it now!"

"Ah got t'lock you up first."

"I'm not going to run away. You know me better
than that."

"Yeah, but you ain't safe on the street. Ah'm gonna
lock you up befo' Ah do anythin' else."

"Then let's get on with it," Kyra said, and began to
walk faster, leading the way to the jail.

Laban put her in a cell, locked the door, and went

out again. He stopped at the home of his massive deputy Clyde Kinney, and presently they walked on together. Laban hadn't realized until now, but he was frightened, not only of what he'd find at Tully's, but of what he'd have to do when he did find it. Lord knew what men, maybe even prominent men, he'd find in that hell-house. One thing no town ever thanked a man for was exposing its respectable residents and most often it wasn't the prominent who paid for their crimes, it was the man who exposed them. In spite of the additional security offered by Clyde's taciturn presence, Laban nearly turned back. One thing he had always been was cautious; but he kept on going. Maybe he had been able to take their payoffs only so long as he hadn't had to think of what they were doing. It was all beyond him. All he knew was that he was scared, and he was going to raid Tully's house anyway.

CHAPTER THIRTY-ONE

Adam strode along with the mob of blacks, keeping pace with their ever-increasing momentum as they neared the outskirts of the city. As they gained the Savannah streets they walked nine and ten abreast, their massive, angry line stretching from curb to curb. Adam had no idea how many there actually were. As they had moved across the countryside their numbers had swelled until now, looking back, he was unable to see the end of the march.

Apollo marched at the head of the column, often going ahead of the main body, scouting, asking questions, gathering information as he had done during the War. He moved like a sleek, graceful animal through the dark, nearly deserted streets.

With each garnering of information he melted back into the mob and found Adam Tremain. "Near everybody's heard somethin' 'bout a woman bustin' into Tully's tonight. Lem Dobkins told me they was a lynch mob," he added in a near-breathless whisper.

"After Kyra?" Adam asked.

Apollo gave one quick nod of his head, his face screwed up in fear. Then quickly he controlled it, turning it to anger. "Ah'm gwine kill that Tully—with these two han's. He touch Kyra an' Ah kills him." He glared at Adam, defying him to disagree, then he turned quickly and disappeared into the mass of dark, purposeful bodies. A few seconds later, Adam heard his voice loud and strong somewhere closer to the front of the crowd. "Move—faster! We get Tully! We get Tully!"

Sound exploded from the blacks, all of them taking up in unison the cry to get Tully. The pace grew until the whole pack was going at a dead run, clubs overhead and ready to strike. They rounded the last of the squares, headed down the side street, and managed to run harder when Tully's house came into view.

Human battering rams, they slammed against the house as though it too were an extension of Tully's own person. Their clubs beat against the frame exterior. The full weight of their bodies and momentum crashed against the doors, splintering them.

Inside the house, the men who had been part of the lynch mob earlier milled about the saloon. Tully had generously provided the first round of drinks upon their return to the house. However, no one had been satisfied with one round. They were too fired up. A vigilante fervor had been awakened, and none of them wanted to leave the company of the others. The room rang with tales of might-have-been glory, justice that should have been done, and evil that always won out—at least since the Yankees had won the War and had their noses in everything.

Lloyd Henry Grooms took his pocket watch out and was swinging it dramatically at Tully. Tully raised his hands and nodded his head. He went to the bar and with the help of an eager customer clambered on top of it. He stood there, hands raised for attention. Quickly the room began to quiet as the men stopped mid-conversation and looked toward him. "Gentlemen!" he cried loudly. "Gentlemen! I think we ah all of one mind. Laban Sweet ain't got no right interferin' in ouah business! The Freedmen's Bureau is a niggerlovin' bunch o' traitors! They doan know an' doan care what happens to us! We know! Weah goin' back out on those streets an' get us the nigger wench! Weah gonna finish what—"

"Hey, wait! What's all that shoutin'?" a man in front yelled.

"Ah you goin' to listen to me, suh?" Tully fired back indignantly.

"Ah'm tellin' you somethin's goin' on out in the street! Christ, lissen!"

"Ain't nothin'."

"Like hell—" The man ducked, his arms protecting his head as the leaded bottle-glass window behind him shattered, admitting a huge black body. The window to the east exploded, and men leaped into the room, clubs upraised, and then brought them down with indiscriminate ferocity on any white head or shoulder. Through the splintered doors and windows a black tide poured into Tully's house.

Black and whites grappled and tore at each other. Angry black men swung their clubs in righteous fury, destroying the opulent interior of the house. The floor of the saloon was slippery with shattered crystal from the chandeliers. Tully's pride, the magnificent mirror that covered one whole wall with gilt and glitter, splintered into millions of tiny shards as Apollo Justus Sherman beat against it with a log four inches thick. The plaster wall behind the mirror crumbled, and then the lathing gave way, until Apollo glared through the battered wall into the next room.

Three naked young black children huddled in fear against the outside wall. Apollo stared in momentary shock. He had known it; he and Adam had been talking about this all evening long at the general store; but to see it was a different matter. Across from the children an obese man struggled to find and don his clothing. With a cry of strangled rage, Apollo smashed at the wall until he had broken a large enough hole to go through. He pushed into the room and stalked the man, whom he now recognized as a federal soldier, Sergeant Jeremy Rimner, a man who hated the conquered Southerners and abused his power over them.

Apollo bared his teeth in a mockery of a smile and walked in a low crouch toward the naked Rimner. Rimner grabbed for his trousers, clutching them modestly against himself, but Apollo leaped forward and grabbed them from him. He tossed the trousers into the corner of the room, and gradually edged his way toward the window, his eyes never leaving Rimner. He opened the window with one hand, and motioned to the three children.

The three little boys looked at Rimner, back to Apollo, then back again to Rimner; then, as one, they darted to Apollo's side.

Apollo said in a low voice, "Get on outta heah. Y'all go to the Beero, knock on the do' an' keep knockin' till somebody let you in. Get on, now!"

The three children scrambled up to the sill and jumped the short distance to the ground. Apollo kept his eyes on Rimner, but listened to the soft sounds of their feet running along the street. He began to chuckle, a low menacing sound. "Now, white man, le's go see youah frien's. Move 'em out, Sahjint!"

Rimner looked at Apollo in horror. "Gimme my pants, man—lissen, we can make a deal. I can make it plenty easy for you around here—anything you want, hear? Anything—money—liquor—women—any-thing—"

Apollo laughed harder, the sound rising to a thin, high pitch.

"Oh, Jesus, listen to me—you ain't thinkin' clear. Come on, let's you an' me get outta here. I'll pay you good—"

"Weah goin' to get outta heah, Sahjint—right out that do', an' into the light so's everybody can see what kind o' man does things to li'l chilluns what can't help themseffs."

Rimner didn't move. Apollo took two swift steps and thrust his club into the small of the man's back. "You *move*, Sahjint, or youah goin' t'bust into that room with this heah log right up youah ass!" Apollo lowered his club and viciously jabbed at Rimner's rear.

As they passed through the broken section of the wall, Apollo let out a bloodcurdling Rebel yell. Then he thrust Rimner into the flailing, angry mob. He stood back and watched with satisfaction as the man dis-

appeared beneath the pounding fists of three or four
blacks. The man's screams were like music, wiping
away some of the horror of the terrified cries he
imagined had come from Tupper Jackson. He watched
as the man's straw-blond hair streaked with blood, then
became brilliant red all over. Then he walked away,
moving through the melee with his fists doubled, seeking any target but always taking himself closer and
closer to the door.

Tully's house was a shambles. The great expanses of
red velvet were torn from the walls, and there were
gaping holes in the plaster. Not a window was left in
the place, and from all the doors of the house small
children both black and white, and young girls were
streaming, some in fear, some escorted by the pack of
black men who had come into town to end Tully's
reign.

In Tully's office, Adam Tremain fought as he had
not done since his prewar years in the bars and back
alleys of the world. Bret Tully had started as a worthy
opponent, but now was reduced to mewling, whining
fear, willing to tell Adam anything, do anything to end
his onslaught. "It wasn't me!" he cried. "Revanche—
he made us do it—it's his house—oh, God, don't hit
me again—Ah didn't mean no hahm, Ah sweah!"

Adam's big fist flashed forward again, hitting the
man in his stomach with such force as to lift him off
his feet. "Where's Revanche?" Adam rasped. "Where
is he?"

"Ah don't know!"

Tully's head snapped back as Adam's hand smashed
across his face. "Where?"

"Doc's—Doc Weston—Ah sweah—stop—please—
Ah can't take no mo'—please—" Tully slumped to his
knees when Adam's hand stopped supporting him.

Adam took a handful of hair and pulled the man's
head back. "You sure he's at Weston's? You wouldn't
lie, would you, Tully?"

"Ah sent him theah mahseff. Ah ain't lyin'." Tully

fell forward when Adam released him. He lay face down on the floor moaning and crying, "Ah ain't lyin'. Oh, Jesus, Ah huht."

Lloyd Henry Grooms managed to avoid almost all personal damage by lying on the floor pretending to be unconscious. When the opportunity presented itself he rolled and crawled toward the servants' hallway, where the least amount of fighting took place. Two or three others followed his example, among them Jabez Hooks, who had not been as clever as Lloyd Henry, but had survived with only a broken nose and bruises. When the four men got outside and were relatively safe from the battle that raged inside, Jabez Hooks broke down and cried gulping tears of rage and hate. He was ruined, no matter how this night ended, he was finished in Chatham County. Jabez gave full vent to his overwhelming emotion—he had never felt such consuming passion as he had this night when hatred swam over him, swirled around him and inside him.

Lloyd Henry picked up a rock and threw it at the discreet sign that marked Tully's house. "That bitch did this! Revanche told us t'get her! She done this to us!"

Jabez choked on his own spittle, then coughed in an effort to speak. His eyes blazed into Lloyd Henry's. "She did it," he managed. "We got to git her—she ruined me, Colonel, she ruined me!"

Without more being said, the four of them walked briskly away from the house, toward the jail.

Apollo left the house as soon as he was certain his people were having the best of the fight. He smiled in grim satisfaction when he saw the condition of the house, and of the men who had run and frequented it. Then he left, running across yards and through the darkened, peaceful squares. In the back of one of the mansions he found a stable unattended. Gently and quietly he hitched two fine stallions to a dray. He smiled again, thinking how nice it was to know, with

the knowledge only an ex-slave could have, which was
the house of a merchant likely to have a dray. He
mounted the heavy wagon and pulled out into the
streets, laying the whip across the horses' flanks. He
went directly to Osgood Baxter's store. With satisfaction he took a box from the back of the dray and
heaved it through Osgood's plate glass window.

Apollo wasted little time on this pleasure, but hurried into the store, carrying out sacks of flour, meal,
all the canned goods he could find, blankets, yard
goods, personal items, shoes, coats, and all the smoked
meats in the place. He took several more precious moments to run his hand along the counter, hurling everything to the floor. Then he knocked over all the dis-
plays and scattered the papers that lay on Baxter's
desk. Last he took a huge crock of molasses and spread
that over the entire mess. "That's fo' you, Ruel," he
said aloud in the empty store. He threw the empty
crock and listened to it shatter against the wall as he
ran back to the dray and leaped onto the seat.

Adam Tremain gave Bret Tully one last, cruel blow,
which knocked him unconscious; then climbed through
the window of Tully's office out into the street. After
several frustrating minutes he found a horse he assumed
to be Tully's. He rode to Doc Weston's house.

The house was dark, quiet; there was no sign of the
dray Tully claimed to have sent carrying Revanche. He
jumped up the steps to Weston's porch and pounded
on the door. The house remained dark, and Adam
hammered against the solid oak door until his knuckles
pained. "Weston!" he shouted, hammering again.

Upstairs a lamp gleamed. The window opened and
Weston stuck his head out, seeing nothing, as his view
of Adam was blocked by the porch roof. "You get outta
heah! Ah told you Ah wouldn't treat any scum from
Tully's. Get on out, or Ah'll shoot you wheah you
stand!"

Adam stepped down from the porch and out into the yard. "You didn't treat Revanche?"

"Get outta heah! Ah don't have anythin' t'do with Tully's soht!"

"They aren't my friends!" Adam shouted. "Doctor, where is that man? I want him arrested and brought before the law!"

"Who ah you?" Weston asked, now peering curiously into the darkness. He ducked his head inside a moment, then reappeared with his spectacles perched on the end of his nose. "Don't Ah know you?"

"Yes, sir—Union League. I'm Adam Tremain."

"Well, damn it all, Tremain, y'all woke me up. Ah didn't treat any o' that riffraff. What the hell ah you doin' this time o' night beatin' on mah doah?"

"I'm looking for Edmund Revanche—the man who came here earlier for your help. Can you tell me where he went?"

"Ah can't tell you anythin'. Ah sent him an' his Yankee boy packin' outta heah. An' Ah don't give a spit in hell wheah they went."

"Did you see which—"

Weston shouted, "No!" and slammed his window down. The light in his bedroom went out.

Kyra sat on the edge of the hard, narrow bed against the wall of the jail. Leban had forgotten to give her a candle, and the poor thing he had lit and left on the desk had long since guttered and gone out. It was dark and cold in there now. Fatigue and fear had taken their toll, and Kyra shivered. She lay down and shut her eyes, hoping she could fall asleep and make the waiting shorter, but it was useless. Sights and sounds of this awful night filled her head. She got up again, pacing the small cell, listening for Laban's return, or for men shouting, searching for her again. If Laban failed in surprising Tully in his house, she had no doubt that sometime this night Tully's men could come for her again, and she would die.

Laban had tried to quell the riot in Tully's house alone with only his deputy, Clyde Kinney, to assist him. Neither his gun nor his badge nor his authority meant anything tonight. After having been heartily punched in the belly and battered across the room, Laban struggled back to Clyde and sent him for the federal troops. From the time Clyde left, Laban concentrated on protecting himself and avoiding farther damage. He finally made his way into Tully's relatively quiet office, where he found Bret sprawled unconscious on the floor. With the toe of his boot Laban rolled the man over onto his side, grimaced at what he saw, and let Tully fall back onto his face. He picked up the slashed cushions, placed them on the legless, broken sofa, and sat down to wait for the federal soldiers.

It was here Adam found him. After leaving Weston's, Adam returned to Tully's, thinking to get more information about Revanche's whereabouts if Tully were able to speak.

Laban's hand shaking, he drew his pistol. His voice quaked as he said, "Y'all bettah stop wheah youah at!"

With one leg in the room and his body outside, Adam yelled, "Laban? Is that you?"

Laban blew breath out his fat cheeks. "Sonofabitch, Tremain, Ah was all set t'blow off youah private pahts!"

Adam climbed the rest of the way into the room and went directly to Tully. He began slapping the man's face to bring him to consciousness.

"Woan do no good," Laban said. "Sumbuddy done a job on him. He ain't likely t'see daylight a-tall till next week."

Adam sat back on his heels. "Laban, I want you to get busy—there are at least a dozen men here we need warrants for, and one other—the leader of this whole hellhole. It's in Tully's name, but Edmund Revanche is the real boss and brains."

"Who—Emmun' who?"

"Revanche. He's from New Orleans." Adam told him briefly of Edmund.

"You say he's the real ownah heah?"

"Yes," Adam said, urging Laban to hurry or Revanche would be gone from Savannah and lost to them.

"Tremain, Ah cain't go 'restin' a man 'cause sumbuddy tol' *you* what he looks like—"

"Tully admitted it!"

"Shit, Cap'n, Ah'd admit anythin' y'all ast iffen you was doin' t'me what sumbuddy done t'him. Ah cain't 'rest a man on that."

"Grooms! Grooms knows Revanche was here—and all about this place."

"Then we bettah git Grooms. An' Hooks too, y'say?" Laban stood up. "Well now, Ah heah mah boys a-comin'. Looks like we kin git this li'l ol' fight settled now, an' then mebbe we can look into what youah sayin' about this-heah Revanche boy." Laban walked into the main room, his pistol drawn and held over his head. He shouted for order. Not getting it, he paused only long enough to see the soldiers coming to the door, then shot repeatedly into the ornate, scrolled ceiling.

Apollo sent the dray careening around the corner of the street on which the jail was located, just missing four men walking along the side of the road. He returned their shouted obscenities and drove on. He pulled the dray around to the back of the jail, dismounted and ran to the front. There was nothing furtive in his motions, nor was there fear. His course of action was set. He pulled his Colt from his waistband and placed his hand on the doorknob. He gave it a sharp twist, and smiled when the door opened easily. He quickly stepped inside.

The jail was murky dark. Kyra peered into the gloom. She knew it wasn't Laban returning, the tread had been too quick and too light, and Laban would never have entered silently. She put her hand up to her throat and moved back to the far corner of her cell.

Apollo stumbled into a chair, swearing under his

breath. He groped his way toward the desk, knocking objects and papers to the floor in his search for a candle.

Kyra held her breath, hoping the man would speak again, even in that low whisper. Her throat ached to make some sound so that he would respond, but she was too frightened to chance his being one of Tully's men. With all her might she willed him to speak, to tell her it had been Apollo's voice she had heard and not a trick of her yearning for him.

Apollo gave up his hunt for the candle, cursing in frustration. Something smashed as he swept the desk clear; other noises filled the room. "Kyra, you in heah?" he asked belligerently. "Ansah me, woman!"

"Apollo?" Kyra said softly.

"Wheah ah you?"

"In the last cell. Laban put me here to keep me safe from those men. Apollo, he's at Tully's. He's clearing that place out, you hear? Tully's going to be all finished after tonight."

Apollo groped along the wall hunting for the keys that Laban always kept on their ring hanging from a hook. Thinking of Kyra's safety, he laughed bitterly. "Laban's ain't gonna get nothin' at Tully's 'ceptin' maybe a broke haid. Every darky at the gen'ral sto', an lots mo' long the way, is down theah tearin' Tully's to pieces."

"A riot? Apollo—tell me, are they rioting?"

He said with dignity, "Folks in New Yawk riots. We jes' seein' Tully don't take no mo' chilluns." He worked at the lock, trying each key until he found the right one and the door swung open.

She clutched at him. "Apollo, we must go to Tully's and stop them. You know this will only bring more trouble to them. All the white people will back Tully. All those black families will be in terrible trouble."

"Hush!" Apollo commanded; then he went hurriedly to the window. "You keep youah mouth shut, woman, an' do jes' what Ah tell you."

"I'll do no such thing! I—"

He grabbed her by the arm and shoved her face to the window. "Kin'ly tell me what you sees."

Kyra looked out and saw and heard a mob of people moving down the street, flanked on either side by blue-uniformed federal militia. "Oh my God," she breathed. "They've already been arrested."

"An' so will Ah iffen you don't do what Ah say an' get outta heah."

Kyra looked at him stubbornly for a moment, then pursed her lips and nodded.

"Ah'm goin' out fust. They was fo' men walkin' this way when Ah came in. Ah don't want to chance them bein' paht o' youah lynch mob. Wouldn't they jes' love to get us runnin'."

He moved toward the door, and Kyra took hold of his arm, pulling herself to him. "Apollo, I'm scared. I don't want to die now—I want to be with you."

He hugged her fiercely, drawing in his breath. "You finally tellin' me you love me?"

Her words tumbled out. "Oh, yes, yes, I am—I do."

He laughed aloud. "You bettah do as Ah tells you or we both goin' to hang, an' Ah got bettah things on mah mind. Now le's go."

Kyra waited in the dark doorway, listening to the approaching sounds of the Federals and their captives. When she finally heard Apollo's whispered signal she ran, staying close to the side of the building. As she came round to the back, Apollo's hand reached out for her. She stifled a yelp. Before she had identified the vehicle, she found herself being lifted onto the front seat. Apollo climbed up beside her. Neither spoke. Apollo snapped the whip, making the horses jerk, then slowed them down to a walk. Carefully he drove the team down a narrow alley, then onto the quiet residential streets, slowly making his way as unobtrusively as possible toward the outskirts of Savannah.

CHAPTER THIRTY-TWO

Leroy Biggs rode like a demon at the head of his pack, the Klan banners snapping imperiously in the night air, his torch high over his head. The battery of pointed hoods bobbed up and down against the dark sky, and the night shattered with the shrill, fierce Rebel cries coming from the spectres.

Their horses' hooves sounded like thunder as they pounded down the long, gracefully curving Mossrose drive. With shouted orders and frantic arm gestures, Leroy deployed his men into a single line circling the plantation house. He waited, his eyes wild with excitement, until the Klansmen had made several circuits of the house and he was sure that all inside were aware of the Klan's presence. Then he rode to the front door of Mossrose, stationed his bannermen behind him, and shouted, "Adam Tremain! Adam Tremain! We call you! The noble dead of the Confederacy call to you! Adam Tremain! Show yourself!"

Figures, dim and veiled, were seen behind the curtains, but no sound came from the house. Adam Tremain did not show himself.

"We call for the third time! Adam Tremain! Show yourself! Come out to us, or we shall come to you!"

Still there was no response from the house. The left bannerman whispered to Leroy, "What do we do if he don't do nothin'?"

Leroy shrugged. "We have us a li'l more fun, that's all. We go get him."

"What the hell ah y'all talking 'bout? He doan ansah the do'—how we gonna get him?"

Leroy laughed madly and dug his spurred heels deep into his horse's sides. The animal twisted and raised himself onto his hind legs. Leroy again dug into the horse and bolted him forward, clattering up onto the veranda. Repeatedly the horse reared on its hind legs, each time beating the front door with its forehooves. The door splintered, then gave way. Leroy looked back over his shoulder and signaled that the others should follow him. With another vicious thrust at the horse and a mighty heave forward, he burst into the foyer of Mossrose. He threw his head back and emitted a bloodcurdling yell that echoed through the downstairs and wrapped around the upper corridors. The sound was followed by the other Klansmen, bursting through the ruined doors.

Mossrose rang with the sounds of madness and horror. Dulcie ran barefooted across the hall to her children's nursery and gathered Beau and Jenny to her. Not knowing where to go or how to escape, she took the children and sandwiched all three of them in the closet. Frantically she pulled everything from the shelves trying to hide them.

With Patricia's help, James Moran struggled from his bed and got into his wheelchair. Keeping Patricia silent and right by his side, he rolled his chair to his bureau. Jem opened drawers wildly, tossing the contents out. "Where's my pistol, Patsy? Where is it? I know I put it here!"

Patricia began to cry brokenly. "Jem . . . oh, Jem, Ah took it away. Ah was so afraid you'd do youahself hahm when you were so sick an' despairin'. It isn't theah anymoah, Jem."

Ten horsemen had managed to crowd into the foyer and front parlor of Mossrose. Men urged horses up onto sofas and into tables and stands. Crystal and porcelain shattered. Amid the shrill animal shrieks were the sounds of tearing cloth and splintering wood. The room glowed brightly with the smoking lights of the Klansmen's torches. Enjoying himself thoroughly, Leroy called for the men to make cavalry formations. Laughter, yelling, and drunken confusion abounded as the men maneuvered their mounts in the confines of the room. Relatively orderly, Leroy thrust his arm forward and charged with his mount through the foyer and into the dining room, making a circuit of the room and then back to the entrance hall, riding through the ranks of those who had not yet entered the room.

Riders lost control of their mounts, and then pandemonium broke out among the animals as flames from a dropped torch shot up along the heavily draped west wall of the dining room. The men frantically turned their horses in an attempt to exit through the big, double front doors they had entered. Flames licked ominously along the edge of the carpet in the parlor. Leroy shouted orders and pushed his way through the jostling animals. He smacked the horse in front of him smartly on the rump. The animal screamed in a crazed whinny and bolted forward and through the front window in a shower of glass and screams from his rider.

Outside the house the majority of the Klansmen were still circling the building, now with diminished enthusiasm. Then their speed and interest increased as Mossrose began to glow brilliant and hot with inner fires. Thinking a plan had been set, they began to gallop again, tossing their flaming torches into every window of the house.

A group of five Klansmen broke away from the main body and rode to the middle of the lawn. Quickly they erected a cross and doused it in kerosene. A torch touched the foot of the cross, and fire began to climb and spread out across the arms of the cross.

Mossrose pulsated in gold and orange flame. The night was filled with a horrifying, deep roar as the fire fed upon itself, exploding into new fury. Lyman rode over to Leroy. "Jesus, Leroy, what we done? We never meant this t'happen—nobody said this'd happen. God, Leroy, I can't stand it! People's screamin' in theah!" Lyman jammed his fists against his ears and began to pant like a winded dog.

Leroy said shrilly, "Shut up, Lyman. They're gonna get out. You'll see—everybody's goin' t'get outta there."

"They're burnin' alive!" Lyman sobbed.

"No they ain't! You hear me? They ain't! They're all right!"

Dulcie, Mindy, and the two children stood paralyzed at the top of the main staircase, staring in horror as the flames leaped up, touching higher and higher on the stairs, only to drop back down and burst upward again still nearer to them.

Dulcie clutched Jenny to her breast. Beau clung to her skirts. "The servants' stairs," she murmured, horrified and fascinated by the fire. She stood for seconds longer, then seemed to shake free, and took Beau's hand, nearly dragging him behind her toward the servants' stairs at the back of the house. From the top of the steps they could see the ominous glow at the turn of the stairs.

"We can't get down!' Mindy wailed.

"We can!" Dulcie said. "There's a window at the landing. We can get there if we hurry."

"We can't! I'm scairt! We'll die, Miz Tremain!"

"We'll die if we stay here! Hurry! Beau, show Mindy what a brave boy you are. Come on, Beau, come with Mama and Jenny." Dulcie ran down the stairs to the landing. To her right she saw the licking flames creeping slowly up from the first floor. She put Jenny down on the floor, and worked hastily at the window latch. The window was seldom opened; it was stuck shut with paint. Dulcie pulled, shoved, and pounded with all her strength, always aware of the moving flames out of the corner of her eye. "Mindy! You must come down here! I can't do this without help!"

Mindy looked behind her and watched a thin trickle of fire snake across the hall carpeting, then she looked down the stairwell at the hot glow coming from Dulcie's right. She was going to die. She could feel it, and now she could smell it, invading her nose and throat. The thick, curling smoke swirled around her, moving inside her, stopping her breath and making her eyes water.

Dulcie, choking, called to her again, and Mindy realized she could barely see Dulcie and the children. From somewhere down the hall, Mindy heard an agonized scream that seemed to go on forever. She ran from that scream, no longer seeing the steps, her feet simply finding the right place to be. Dulcie jerked the window free as Mindy came down. She crawled up onto the ledge and looked down the eight feet to the ground.

"Mindy, I'm going to jump. You drop the children out to me—Jenny first, then Beau." She leaned down and kissed Beau. "You be Mama's brave boy. We'll be all right, I promise you, Beau. You do what Mama tells you." She pulled free from his grasp and jumped from the window. Her legs gave way as she landed, and she fell hard. The frightened tears she had been holding back burst free. She took a deep breath forcing them away again. Coughing, her eyes streaming from the thick, acrid smoke, she shouted. "Mindy, I'm ready! Drop Jenny from the window." Dulcie bit her lips, trying not to think what would happen if she wasn't able to catch the now screaming, wriggling infant.

Mindy leaned out of the window as far as she could, holding Jenny by her arms. She lowered Jenny, stretching and pulling. Dulcie's arms stretched upward, but could not touch Jenny's churning feet. "Drop her, Mindy! Drop her and get Beau out! I can get her, I can!"

Mindy closed her eyes and let go of Jenny.

Beau stepped forward and climbed up to the windowsill by himself. "I can do it myself, Mama. I can jump."

"Mindy! Get him! Lower him to me. Get him!

"I can jump!"

"Beau!" Dulcie screamed, her control breaking and the wicked tears coming again. "Do as I tell you!"

Beau placed his hands in Mindy's, and allowed himself to be lowered to his mother's outstretched hands. She couldn't grasp him, however, and when released he fell onto Dulcie, both of them sprawling painfully on the ground.

Mindy, her eyes on the nearing flames, which had now reached the last step before the landing, jumped and landed in a heap beside them.

The screaming inside the house rose to an unearthly pitch. Dulcie shuddered, not having allowed herself until now to think of whose screams those were. She began to cry, her fists dug against the sides of her head; but once again, her eyes wild and sunken, she forced control on herself. "Mindy, take the children somewhere—to a neighbor's—anywhere, but to safety."

"Miss Dulcie, I'm not leavin' without you! You can't do anything—you can't go back in there—you can't!"

"Take the children!" Dulcie screamed, and ran around to the rear doors. She knew the fire had already consumed the front of the house, she had seen its inexorable progress up the front staircase, but perhaps the back . . .

Leroy saw the pale, filmy-garbed woman race from the side of the house. "See, Lyman! What'd I tell you? She's out an' safe!"

"They're dyin', Leroy. I can hear 'em screamin'!"

"No, there's Dulcie, I saw her—I jes' saw her—Oh, God—" Leroy lashed at his horse, and sent the animal toward the house and Dulcie. She was on the back veranda, her arms up across her face, her body twisted as she tried to force herself through the flaming doorway. "Mama! Daddy!" she screamed, crying and sobbing hysterically. "Adam! Help me! Mama! Daddy!"

Leroy's hands were so tight on the horse's reins that he threatened to break the animal's neck as he forced the fear-crazed beast toward the flames.

The sky glowed a hazy pink, a great rainbow entirely of reds and golds and pinks spreading in an arc over

Mossrose. Plantation bells from all around began to sound, adding their clangor to the madness.

The heat was blistering, unbearable. Leroy shouted at her, but Dulcie didn't seem to hear or see him. She inched closer to the door. He pulled and ripped viciously at the horse's mouth, and grabbed Dulcie under her arms, dragging her out onto the lawn. "You can't go back in there, you fool! He ain't worth savin' anyway, y'hear me? Tremain ain't worth you!"

She had no idea what he was saying, but she struggled and fought him, wanting only to get to her parents. He dragged her to the edge of the driveway, and was met there by a group of the Klansmen.

"We bettah get the hell outta heah—everybody fo' miles around'll be heah in a minnit."

"Shit yeah, an' we bettah be here too. Take the robes to the cemetery, an' get right on back here," Leroy ordered.

"Hell no! Ah'm goin' t'be as fah off as Ah kin be!"

"You're a neighbor! You got to be here helpin' put this out, or you're goin' t'look guilty as hell!" Leroy rasped. He pulled Dulcie a bit farther, then let her fall to the ground. Somebody else would take care of her until he could get back here as himself.

CHAPTER THIRTY-THREE

Adam left Savannah as soon as he was assured that most of the blacks who had been jailed would be released in the morning. He had Laban's promise that he would be notified immediately if there was any trouble. He sighed tiredly, regretting that Edmund Revanche and his Northern partner had managed to escape, but at least Hooks, Tully, and Colonel Grooms were now under house arrest in the hotel. It was better than nothing, and Adam admitted that it would likely end the traffic in children in the area, but he knew that as long as Revanche was free another house like Tully's would thrive in another city.

He sat on the porch of the Freedmen's Bureau in Laban's rocker, waiting until Laban came back with a horse he could borrow tonight. Adam leaned back, letting his eyes close, barely able to think of this long and exhausting night. Tomorrow would be just as long. Vaguely he made plans to come into Savannah early in the morning to see that none of Tully's men managed to bribe or lie their way out of the charges.

Laban stomped up onto the porch and shook Adam's shoulder. "Y'all git on home, Cap'n. Be a while befo' all the dust settles on this'n. We woan know what we got fo' a day or two."

Adam's blue eyes snapped open. "We'd better know, Laban, and right now. None of those men is going to slip away this time."

"Now that ain't what Ah meant," Laban whined. "Y'all too tard t'be talked to. Ah'll see you in the mawnin' when you bring the hawss back. G'night, Cap'n. Give mah best t'youah purty wife, y'heah?"

Adam smiled, conceding his exhaustion. He took

Laban's proffered hand, mounted and rode away without looking back. Savannah was quiet again, its streets giving no hint of the activities that had taken place there tonight. But for an occasional dim light in an upstairs window, most houses were dark and peacefully silent.

He rode slowly to the River Road, too torn by confused thought to urge the horse to any speed. Once on the River Road he let the horse do all the work, dozing for minutes at a time as he rode.

As he neared Mossrose he heard the sound of a single plantation fire bell still tolling its message into the night. He looked at the sky, black and heavy before false dawn, and saw the wavering arc of pink and red staining the night. Before his reluctant mind could realize the direction of that glow, his heart began to pound furiously. He slapped at the horse, bringing it to a gallop. He knew, he knew with all logic that he was frightening himself for nothing. Whatever planation it was, it was not Mossrose. It wasn't. It couldn't be.

When he was still some distance away, riding across the fields, he still told himself it was not Mossrose. It was a nightmare that had begun early that evening. He had been thrust into a world gone mad, trapped there and not released, but he would be now, for the embers that still glowed rose-red like the fire on a forge just before the smith works his bellows on it, was not Mossrose. Heavy black smoke still billowed from the blackened brick shell. Adam ran the horse into the front yard and leaped from the saddle just as a section of flooring broke loose and fell with a rumbling slam to the ground. Men and women, not real people but blackened shadows that hurried to and fro with buckets and shovels, yelling and coughing and crying, kept coming between him and the nightmare grotesquerie that seemed so similar to Mossrose.

A long, painful negation ripped from him. In the rubble he could see the hideously crumpled outline of

Jem's and Patricia's brass bed, and beside it one of the
metal wheels of Jem's wheel chair. At the front of the
house, now a nearly quiet pile of ash and ember, a sudden spitting, sizzling sound came; and like a geyser, a
column of flame shot up and quickly died. His voice
breaking on a sob, he cried out "Dulcie! Dulcie!" And
the earth took up the echo, Dul-see--ee--ee! "Dulcie!
Where are you? Dulcie! Answer me!" He ran blindly,
wildly toward the spitting geyser of flame that died and
rose again, hissing at him.

At the steaming, smoking veranda he was driven
back by heat still so intense that it blistered his face
and seared his throat. He backed up into the yard,
gasping for air; then, soot blackened, his face streaming
tears of anguish, he drove himself back to the house.

Ned Whitaker raised his shovel once again. His arms
and shoulders burned with their own fires of exhaustion, but Jem's screams, the screams of his best friend
and neighbor, still rang in his ears, and he couldn't stop
working now if he dropped dead. It might be better
that way, he thought desperately, his mind trying to
find some reasonable spot of solace. "He told me it
was fireproof," he said aloud to himself, remembering
Jem saying he had been burned out once and would
never be again. Somehow Jem telling him Mossrose was
fireproof should have made it so. He and Cedric and
the other neighbors should not have been here tonight
putting out this fire. It wasn't supposed to happen. It
couldn't happen. Jem had built Mossrose to be fireproof.

Mechanically he kept tossing shovelfuls of dirt on
the ashes, trying to salvage whatever might be salvage-
able. Occasionally he wondered who would be there to
salvage . . . would Jem appear as he had always been
tomorrow morning? Would he, Ned, have saved some
part of Mossrose for his friend? He remembered again
the hideous screaming that had gone on forever and
might never again be stilled. He shook his head, and

from the corner of his eye saw Adam attempting to enter the blistering hot ruin.

Ned flung aside his shovel and ran, yelling Adam's name. As he raced past, others looked too, and dropped their efforts with the fire. Four men converged and ran up to the crumbled veranda. Ned hurled himself at Adam, throwing the larger, younger man off balance. Cedric and Jan Chilcote wrapped their arms around him and pulled him from the house.

Adam wasn't aware of who they were or what they were doing. He wrestled with them, his fists striking out. "Dulcie! Let me go to her! Dulcie—my children! Let me *go!*"

Jan and Ned pinned him to the ground. Ned, his voice choked with smoke and his own tears, said pathetically, "We're doing everything we can to damp it down. But it's going to take days before you can go in there, Adam. Days . . . days . . ."

Adam broke into sobs, his voice as pained and agonized as Jem's had sounded earlier. "Dulcie—"

"We're doing all we can," Ned assured him, and himself.

Adam suddenly cried, "No! No, we'll put the fire out. We'll find them. They're alive. The well—we'll put the fire out—water—"

Jan Chilcote said, "The well went dry half an hour ago."

"No, there's water, Jan—I'll help—we'll find them—"

Jan put a hand on his arm. "Take it easy, Adam. You can't do anything—but wait."

"Wait?! No—Dulcie needs me!" He sat up, then jumped to his feet. He smiled at Jan. "She wasn't in there—she left. I'll find her." He ran to the servants' cabins. Frantically he opened cabin doors, his face bright with expectation each time. "Dulcie, where are you? Answer me! Beau, Daddy's home. Beau, where are you? Jenny?" He saw tumbled beds, clothing piled in casual nighttime heaps on the floor, all the debris left by people who have quit their dwellings hurriedly. Sometimes thinking a lumped shape might be Dulcie, he would rush in to touch it, only to have his hands identify a chest, a wood box.

He was becoming less coherent, less capable of rational or sequential thought. He examined some cabins three times, others he skipped entirely. Then he remembered the well. He had been going to put out the fire.

He ran from the cabins back to the well, pumping madly until he managed to bring up a thin trickle. "Jan, there's water!"

Jan didn't answer and Adam ran once more to the cabins, then to the barn. No one in the cabins, no one in the barn. The woods. She might have gone to the woods. She had been frightened and had run with the children to the woods. Beau and Jenny loved the woods. He was out of breath now, his long legs were leaden. He had to slow his run and stop frequently to suck in a deep breath. His voice was hoarse, but he called her. "Dulcie! Dulcie! Answer me!"

His heart began to thunder anew when a ghostly figure walked slowly, dreamily toward him. The figure was clad in a flowing nightgown, its hair hanging in deep waves down around its shoulders. "You don't need to shout, Adam," the figure said in a calm voice. "I've been right here all the time."

His eyes widened, and sobbing he grabbed her and crushed her against his hammering heart. "Oh, Dulcie, oh, God, you're safe," he panted, running his hands clumsily down her shining hair. "I was so afraid—and now you're safe, I'll take care of you—"

She struggled to get away from him. "Don't squeeze so hard," she said complainingly. "Nothing's happened. I just went for a walk—"

"Walk?! Dulcie—" He grabbed her by the shoulders and shook her. "Where are they?" he ground out.

She stared at him, then said, "I—Mindy—I told her to take them."

"*Where?*"

She cringed away from him, her face screwed up in pain. "I—I don't know! I can't remember! The Klansmen wanted them, but I—"

His hands on her tightened again. "The cross. Oh, my God, I forgot the burned cross."

Wordlessly, she nodded. He dropped his hold on her and turned away, his shoulders heaving, his heart feeling as though it might burst. Through his confused mind ran all the events of the evening—the destruction, the violence, the madness.

Dulcie's soft crying returned him to the present. He turned to her, opening his coat so that it might provide shelter for the two of them. He held her slender body pressed tight against his, and his lips sought and found hers. Then it was as though the flames from dying Mossrose swept over them, flames fanned by the realization that death had come and passed them by.

He laid her on the hard ground, his hands hot and rough. Her fingers were claws on his back. Savagely they took each other, used each other to the fullest.

When they had done, their faces were wet with tears. They lay there a long time, holding each other with the tenderness they had spurned only minutes ago. They used no words, for there was no need for them. When he rose, he held out his hand, and still touching they walked across the fields to the ashes of the house.

Ned Whitaker saw them coming and went to meet them. "You'll need a place to stay. We'd like to have you with us."

"Thanks, Ned," Adam replied, his voice betraying his desolate exhaustion. "Will you—can you help me find my children?"

Ned held Adam's arm and said quietly, "We'll find them safe. We will!" He strode away.

Cedric watched Adam put Dulcie on his horse, and mount behind her. He would take her back to the Whitakers's home, Cedric thought, but what would he do then? He had known Adam too long to believe the man would let this night pass unavenged. Thus far Adam

had not mentioned the Klan, but Cedric feared his silence more than he would have feared threats.

He turned quickly and ran, catching up with his
father.

Ned Whitaker touched his son's arm. "We got to
find those children safe," he said. "A man can take
only so much."

"Daddy," Cedric said gently, "I'm goin' to round up
the Union Leaguers hereabouts and go after the Klan.
You know Adam isn't going to let this night rest, and
like you said, he doesn't want more trouble."

Ned nodded slowly. "You think he's likely to go
after them alone?"

"I think so. And I want to get there first. I know you
know I've ridden with the Klan, but Daddy, I swear,
I've never done anything like this. They got to be
stopped, and not by Tremain." Cedric looked hard at
his father for a moment, then ran off shouting Arthur
Redgrave's name.

"God go with you, boy," Ned said quietly.

When Adam and Dulcie got to the Whitakers', the
women servants were in an uproar, preparing food for
the hungry firefighters. In a corner was Mindy, looking
pale and sick. Beau was sleeping, spent, with his head
against her leg. Jenny lay on her lap, the picture of
sweet repose.

Dulcie and Adam flew to their children and picked
them up and held them and cuddled them. Then Adam
brought Mindy a stiff whisky highball, which she
downed obediently with a sour face. Within a few minutes they were all in bed, and Dulcie and his children
were safely asleep.

Adam got up and quietly put his clothes back on. He
had one more thing to do tonight, one more piece of
the nightmare. He was going to kill Leroy Biggs.

CHAPTER THIRTY-FOUR

Adam rode away from the Whitakers, not knowing where to find the Klansmen. He had heard rumors as everyone had: The Klan met in a burned-out farmhouse that bordered the Matthews' land, they met deep in the woods several miles south of Mossrose, they met in the cemetery off Thunderbolt Road.

He rode until he came to the place in the road where he had to choose whether to go due south or continue toward the Matthews's land.

He brought the horse to a halt and sat rigidly still for a moment, his mind seething with opposing thoughts. He turned the horse toward Mossrose. Someone there still trying to put out the fire would know something. As he rode he considered each of the men in the vicinity, sorting through all he knew about each. Who was likely to be a Klansman? Who was likely to know or be related to a man who was? Over and over he came back to Glenn Saunders. Glenn, too weak and spineless to do anything on his own, but too easily influenced to withstand the pressure of friends to join the Klan.

When he rode up the road to Mossrose, the trampled lawn was deserted. The shell of the house still smoldered and stank, but no one was about. He brought his hand down hard on the horse's rump, and rode across the fields toward the Actons' plantation where Glenn lived on his brother-in-law's bounty.

The house was dark when Adam rode up. He hammered on the door. When Birdie opened the door a crack and asked apprehensively, "Who is it? What do you want? My husband isn't here," he shoved her aside.

He pushed his way in and stood in the entry, glaring at her, unresponsive to her fear. "But your brother's here, isn't he?"

"Yes," she whispered. "But Glenn didn't do . . ."

"Where is he?"

"Captain Tremain, please, Glenn . . ."

Adam made an impatient gesture, silencing her, then took the steps upstairs two at a time. "Saunders!" he shouted, waking children.

Cries and scurrying feet accompanied the heavy staccato of Adam's boots as he opened one door after another until he found Glenn and Addie Jo clinging to each other in their bedroom.

He pushed Addie Jo aside and grabbed Glenn by his shirt front, pulling him to his feet. "You've got thirty seconds to tell me where I can find Biggs."

"I . . . I don't . . . know," Glenn stammered.

"Learn, Saunders, or there won't be anything left of you." Holding fast to Glenn and dragging him along, Adam ripped everything out of the closet and the bureau drawers. He pulled open the chifforobe, tossing out shoes and clothing until he came up with Glenn's robes. "Tell me, or you'll take Biggs's place. One Klansman is just as guilty as another."

"I . . . I . . . can't," Glenn wailed.

Adam smashed him across the face with the back of his hand.

Blood spurted from Glenn's lips and his nose.

"Ten seconds, Saunders."

"Please . . ."

Adam hit him again. Glenn doubled up, clutching his stomach.

"Don't tell him!" Birdie cried from the doorway. "He'll kill them!"

Addie Jo lay crumpled on the bed sobbing uncontrollably. Adam shook Glenn like a rag doll. "Tell me!"

"Cemetery," Glenn choked out. "But they're gone. They aren't there! They're gone!"

"Thunderbolt Road?" Adam asked, and when he didn't get an immediate response, slapped Glenn's head from side to side.

"Yes . . . yes!"

Adam whirled Glenn around and shoved him at Birdie and Addie Jo. For a moment he stopped in front of Birdie. "You call yourself Dulcie's best friend."

He ran down the stairs and back into the night. He mounted and began the ride to the cemetery meeting place.

Apollo had not allowed the horses to slacken their pace since he had left the outskirts of Savannah. He kept them moving as fast as he dared, north and west. Kyra, beside him, constantly looked back, always fearing to see the flickering light of a torch.

"We gonna be all right," Apollo said, assuring himself and her for the hundredth time. "We gonna make it. All's we got to do is git in them Carolina uplands and nobody ever be able to follow us. We be all right."

"I know," Kyra said, her hand on his arm. She ran her fingers over the soft skin and hard muscle of his forearm. "I'm learning, Apollo, I'm learning. With you I'll be all right."

Apollo made a soft sound deep in his throat.

"Where are we now?" she asked.

"Don't know 'xactly. Somewheres in South Carolina. The mountains cain't be more'n a few miles off."

"The Blue Ridge?"

"That's what youah books say."

"Then what do we do?"

Apollo turned to look at her. In the faint light given by the moon she could see the twinkle in his eyes. "Ah beds you down, woman, an' then we runs and keeps on runnin' 'til we runs right into the ocean on the other side of this U-nited States."

Kyra leaned over and kissed him. "I love you, Apollo. I love you! We're going to be just fine."

Fifty Union Leaguers on horses made quite a lot of noise going down the road, Cedric noticed, although they were trying to be quiet. As they approached the cemetery he saw one of the Lictors vanish from his post. He heard the alarm go up and some commotion in the caretaker's shack.

Three of the men hastily dismounted and poured kerosene all around the shack. Arthur Redgrave called out, "Bettah come on out with youah hands up, boys."

He was answered by a warning rattle of gunfire. Leroy's voice rang out. "What fo'! We ain't done nothin'! What the hell d'you want?"

Arthur nodded, and the three men bent and lighted the kerosene. In a few seconds the little wooden shack was surrounded by a ring of fire. Flames were already creeping up a corner post. "Come out with youah hands up!" Arthur called. "Drop youah weapons by·the first tombstone."

A single shot rang out from inside the building, and Arthur Redgrave clutched his shoulder and fell to the ground. Almost immediately a white handkerchief showed, and Osgood Baxter came out leading most of the other men, coughing, their eyes streaming. Obediently they discarded their weapons.

With Arthur wounded, Cedric took command. He shouted, "Leroy! Lyman! Todd! Billy! Come out, or we'll come in after you! I'll give you ten! One—two—"

"Go fuck yourself!" was Billy Bob's reply, punctuated by Todd's terrible racking cough.

"You want t'burn to death like Jem Moran?" Ned Whitaker jeered. "It'd serve you right! Just stay in there and we won't have to bother about you!"

"Five—six—"

Suddenly Billy Bob ran through the door, his back afire. Without even stopping to put his weapon down, he rolled over and over on the ground, grunting and moaning. One man took charge of him, taking his gun away and making him stand under guard with the others. Todd's cough was unceasing now, and soon he stumbled through the door, doubled over in paroxysms. Smoke was rolling heavily through the small building.

"Eight—nine—" Cedric said, and motioned four men to follow him into the burning building.

At the count of ten they rushed in and found Leroy and Lyman lying on the floor, groggy with smoke inhalation. They showed a semblance of resistance, but in seconds the Union Leaguers came out with their prisoners. The war between the Klan and the Loyal League had been short but decisive.

The Union Leaguers had plenty of rope with them. They tied the Klansmen together, two on a horse, and started them down the road toward Savannah and jail, surrounded by a heavy guard of Union League men.

Adam Tremain, riding hard toward the cemetery, met them halfway. His blue eyes were wild with fury, his curly black hair roughed by the wind. He pulled his horse to a halt and leaped off. Unerring even in the dark, he ran toward the horse carrying Leroy Biggs and Caleb Wells, and tried to jerk Leroy to the ground. Caleb began to yell, and the horse, skittish anyway with the unaccustomed load of two men on its back, reared and threw them both off.

Adam leaped on Leroy, and began to punish him with his fists. Several Union Leaguers got down off their horses. Adam had the strength of ten men, but after a great struggle, he found himself with his hands bound behind his back.

"Let me go!" he cried, twisting to get loose from his bonds. "He tried to kill us all—let me have him!"

Ned Whitaker said, not unkindly, "No, boy. I know how you feel, but this isn't your right. It's the law's right. And if the law don't take care of it, the Lord'll take care of it. Now you're going back home, Adam, back to Dulcie and your younguns. Cedric and Jan, you and Earl and Leonard see he gets there and stays till morning."

Adam was helped onto his horse and accompanied to the Whitakers' under guard. Though he was unbound before they reached their destination, he was informed that if he tried to get away from them, he would be shot. The Union League, whom for so long he had tried to persuade to disband the Klan, would do its utmost to see that Leroy Biggs and his den of Klansmen were given the full extent of justice.

CHAPTER THIRTY-FIVE

The trial of the Klan for the burning of Mossrose was over. Everyone on trial had been guilty in some way, yet no one had been convicted.

Adam Tremain, his eyes burning with bitter anger moved through the crowd to Laban Sweet.

"I want you to arrest Biggs right now."

"Son of a bitch, Captain, he jes' got free. I can't arrest him two times for the same thing. I'm sorry as hell, you know that, but sometimes there ain't nothin' you can do."

"I'll do something," Adam snapped. "You just arrest him."

"Fo' what?!"

"Ruel Jordan's murder."

"Ah cain't! There ain't nobody lef' who seen anythin'. Kyra Jordan an' 'Pollo's gone. Aw shit, Captain, he'll get free."

"Then I'll find another way to put him behind bars."

Laban stared at him, then shrugged. "Ah guess you gotta do it, but Captain, he's gonna go free agin, an' be laughin' like hell at you."

"Arrest him," Adam repeated flatly.

Outside the courthouse, Leroy, Lyman, Billy Bob, and Todd were talking, slapping each other's backs and making jokes about the night of the fire.

"Damn that fool judge," Billy said. "He as much as accused us o' bein' there—an' then he had t'let us all go!"

"Well, what did I tell you?" Leroy boasted. "Billy Bob, don't you know we're the Invisible Empire? Nobody could see us, so nobody could testify against us! Now does that make me a leader or don't it?"

"It sure does, Leroy," said Lyman admiringly. "Jes' like when your horse dropped that big turd right on Miz Moran's parlor sofa!"

They laughed uproariously. "Shoulda had somebody come an' take a picture o' that," said Todd. "Preserve the sight for posterity."

"An' Lyman, I ain't forgot what a wondrous thing you was, rammin' your bay'net through that big dish cabinet. Glass an' china cups an' saucers flyin' 'all over the place." Leroy laughed again, nudging Lyman.

"Leroy, don't fo'git Ah jerked down that big chand'-lier in the liberry," said Billy Bob. "That made one hell of a crash, wouldn't you say?"

Todd said suddenly, "Hold on, hold on. Here comes Fatso Sweetso."

Laughing again, they turned to watch Laban striding down the sidewalk on his short, thick legs, closely followed by his deputy, large, muscular Clyde Kinney. "What in hell's he up to now?" Lyman asked.

Leroy turned around. "P'tend you ain't seen him. Ain't nothin' t'do with us." Loudly he said, "Well, boys now that we been found *not guilty,* 'spite o' Cap'n Tremain an' his God-damn lies, how's about we get us a dri—"

Laban had walked directly up to Leroy and put his ham-sized hand around Leroy's bicep. He said formally, "Leroy Biggs, in the name o' the law heah in Chatham County, you ah undah arrest."

Leroy jerked away, but still found his arm held fast. He attempted elaborate gestures of disbelief and humor. "Laban," he said, laughing hollowly, "you sho' know how t'scare the livin' shit right out of a man. If you didn't p'rade around bein' the law all the time, I'd sock you one right on your fat jaw."

The others laughed; but Clyde Kinney moved menacingly nearer. Leroy realized that in Clyde's hand there was a pistol pointed at his gut. "Tremain don't think it's no joke, boy," said Laban. Deftly he placed a handcuff on Leroy's wrist. "You ah charged with murdah, the murdah o' Ruel Jordan."

"Aww Laban," Leroy protested.

"Jes' shet up an' c'mon with us, boy," said Laban shortly.

Leroy attempted to stand rock still, resisting; but Clyde's knee came up behind him, severely jarring the end of his spine. Leroy moved, protesting all the way into his small jail cell.

He sat there, surprised and apprehensive, for over an hour. Laban had clanged the door shut behind him and then left him there all alone, probably going out sucking up to Adam Tremain. Leroy had never felt so deserted in his life. Even out scouting during the War, he had known where the others in his party were, had known that Lyman was waiting exactly where he told him to wait, or was going exactly where he had told him to go. Sometimes, he thought dolefully, he missed the War. There was something *reliable* about a war. You hunted the enemy or he hunted you, finally you met and you fought and killed him, and then you could rest a little maybe till the next skirmish. And all the time your men were with you, obeying your orders and backing you up. A man could count on their loyalty.

But now—with Tremain undermining him—immersed in self-pity, Leroy felt tears coming into his eyes. Jesus Katy! This was what being deserted did to a man, impaired his manhood, made him feel uncertain of himself. Wasn't he Colonel Leroy Biggs? Well, no, he only said that to people. But he was as good as Tremain. Wasn't he the Cyclops of his den of the Klan? Yes, by God and by Jesus, he was! He was the *leader,* he gave the orders and the rest of them just followed what he told them.

And what good was it doing him now? Stuck in a tight little cell with nothing in it but a cot and a pisspot, who was he going to lead now? The treacherous tears kept wanting to return, and he kept fighting them.

"Psst! Leroy!" It was Lyman, calling to him from the high, barred window.

Leroy, caught in his moment of weakness, snarled, "Where in holy hell ya been?"

"Waitin'. Laban mighta caught me. I don't wanta be in jail too—"

"All right, all right, jes' shut your mouth an' lissen to me. We got t'find me a alibi, Lyman. And it's got t'be watertight. I got it! Why don't *you* be my alibi?"

"Sure, Leroy, what d'you want me t'say?"

"Lemme think. What we need is you t'tell the story, me t'swear to it, an' somebody else jes' happenin' along that could back it up. Lessee, we were out in the woods —naw, that ain't goin' t'do."

"I'll jes' say we were home all evenin', drinkin'."

"The judge'd b'lieve that all right, but Tremain would jump right on it. *You* don't always remember things you did when you got drunk, Lyman, everybody knows that. What if somebody conter—conterdicted what you said?"

"How 'bout sayin' we were workin' the still that night?"

"A whorehouse! That's it! Lyman, we went to a whorehouse, me'n'you an' Billy Bob, an' never got outta each other's sight."

"Jeez, Leroy, I ain't never fucked a woman with somebody watchin'."

"The judge don't have t'know that."

"I don't know about Billy Bob—Birdie ain't gonna like it if she thinks he's been whorin'."

"You stoopid asshole, he can tell her he ain't, can't he? Quit arguin' over dee-tails, the important thing here is me. If y'all can't get me out of it, I might have t'go to prison fo' killin' that high-talkin' black sonofabitch."

"Aww, Leroy, nobody's got anything on you. That nigger schoolteacher didn't reckanize anybody that night. She was too busy."

"Yeah. Too busy stickin' her bread knife into my horse. Don't you see where that puts me, Lyman?" he asked tiredly.

"It don't put you nowhere, Leroy. We buried that horse an' he's all rotted away by now. They can't prove a thing with a rotten horse."

"That horse didn't string hisself up in a tree, did he? Some sonofabitch knows 'bout that horse, an' I'm thinkin' it's Tremain. He's been talkin' t'Laban. An' there's Dulcie; she might remember somethin' or she might not."

"That little redhead hates your guts, Leroy, she'd say anyth—"

"Shut up! I don't want to talk about her right now. I need my mind for somethin' else. Now the Klan's got to have a leader till I get out. I don't think jes' a hell of a lot o' Osgood, but he's next in line, so we got t'use him. He can get all our stories together, think up things for everybody t'say so's it'll come out soundin' natch-eral. An' jes' t'make sure he don't double-cross me, we'll put him in court, too. I'll make him say he saw us."

"Leroy, how you gonna make him do anything when you're locked up? He likes Tremain."

"I'm leader, ain't I? We swore a mighty oath, didn't we, t'stand by our brothers in trouble? Osgood'll do it, or he'll pay. You go find him an' tell him he's got t'come right here after dark. Me'n'him's got t'do some plannin'."

"Seems like t'me what you got t'do is get you a lawyer, Leroy."

Leroy snapped his fingers. "A lawyer! That's right, Lyman. Good thing you thought up that one. An' the Klan'll pay for it!"

"Who d'you want us t'rob? Morans was the only ones with real money."

"Let Osgood figger that'n out."

Leroy lay down on the lumpy bunk, hands clasped under his head, feeling good about himself again. Jailed he might be, but he was still the leader. Lyman would do everything he had told him to do. Osgood would be here tonight.

Osgood did not come. Next morning Laban brought some sorry-looking fried eggs. "The jedge is workin' real fast fo' you, Leroy. Youah trial's all set fo' next Wensdy."

Leroy looked up from his cold, gray biscuits. "Wednesday!" he squawked. "Laban, I ain't even got me a lawyer yet!"

Laban chuckled.

"Well, boy, when *an'* if y'git one, bettah have him make out youah will too, 'cause youah gonna be in the penitentiary fo' a long, long time." Laban turned and walked away.

To his fat retreating back Leroy shrieked, "I ain't in yet!"

The long, chilly, hungry day went by. By God if he couldn't use a drink. He'd give ten days off his life if he could just have a jug of that smooth whisky from his own still. That sonofabitch Lyman was probably drinking it all up and not even working the still when it was gone. What in the living hell was he *doing,* anyway? Here it was Friday already with Tremain putting a noose around his neck. Where was the lawyer the Klan was going to buy? Where *was* everybody?

"Herr Leroy Bikks?" The owner of the voice was small in stature, with a mild, unimpressive face, nondescript brown hair, and a matching business suit. Leroy looked him up and down, hostile. "I am Dutch Harbach. I am your attorney."

Leroy's next reaction was suspicion. "Who sent you?"

Harbach's small eyes behind his wire-rimmed glasses hardened a little. "Herr Baxter sent me. Now, Herr Schveet has said ve may speak for a liddle vile, so come closer, *bitte.* I haff no vish to be oferheard."

Leroy came to stand at the bars. "I'm innocent. I swear it. That bastard Tremain's tryin' to get me hung."

"I belief you. I always belief my client even ven I know he is lyink."

Dutch Harbach shifted his briefcase from one arm to the other. "Let us understand each other, Herr Bikks. Tremain is making the effidence against you look very stronk. If I may make a liddle choke, the dead horse is stronkest of all."

"That's not my horse!"

"The horse vears your *brandmarken,* shall ve say. Further, there is the matter of a vound in his neck. Furthermore, there is the matter of a Klan robe mit your family monogram in vun corner. All dese t'inks vill be held against you in court. I must varn you dot der man who vill be testifyink against you is wery conwincing."

"Tremain!" It was almost a sob.

"You know *Kapitän* Tremain, then." Harbach sniggered. "Goot. You know vot ve are defending ourselfs against."

That night Lyman came, standing on a goods box in the alley so he could look into Leroy's cell. "Did he come, Leroy? Harbach?"

"Yeah, he came."

"Osgood says if any anybody can git you off, it'll be Dutch Harbach."

"Lissen, Lyman, you tell Osgood I want somebody else. I don't want no harelip foreigner doin' my legal work for me. I gotta have the best."

"You ain't got time t'switch around now, Leroy, the trial's hardly four days off. 'Sides Tremain's been out in the County snoopin' around everyplace."

Leroy paled. "Oh, God, Lyman, you gotta help me."

"Leroy, I'll do everything I can. You b'lieve me, don't you, ol' pal?"

"Layin' around here in jail, with nothin' t'do an' nobody t'talk to 'cept the walls, I don't hardly know what to b'lieve, Lyman, an' that's a fact. The only thing I b'lieve fo' sure an' certain is I don't wanta go to no penitentiary."

"I don't want you goin' neither, Leroy. You're the truest friend I'll ever have." Lyman's voice showed signs of breaking, then he cleared his throat and went on. "They won't do it to you, by God! I'm not goin' t'let 'em."

Leroy said gratefully, "I'll never forget this, Lyman. I'll remember you did this the rest o' my natcheral life."

Dutch Harbach came to see Leroy at eight o'clock Wednesday morning, an hour before the trial was to start. After inquiring into Leroy's health and receiving brusque snswers, Harbach said, "Your case has been dismissed, Herr Bikks."

"Dismissed! I thought you were gonna get me off, you lousy—"

"Be kviet, Herr Bikks, vile I explain. I haff talked with the prosecutor. *Kapitän* Tremain vas not present ven Herr Chordan vas killed, nor ven your horse vas found. The effidence he vould giff is hearsay, second-hand. As there are no other vitnesses, the prosecutor agrees it vould be useless to press your case. Therefore, you vill be set free today."

Leroy sat stunned for a moment, then broke into a jubiliant Rebel yell. "Free! That'll show that dumb shit Tremain—and I won. I won! Now, I don't have to pay you anything, do I? Since you didn't have to do anything?"

Harbach smiled. "I always collect my fee in adwance, Herr Bikks."

Half a million Southern men were Ku Klux Klan members; but in 1869 General Nathan Bedford Forrest, reportedly the Grand Wizard of the Klans in the eastern South, had ordered the societies disbanded. Scattered local groups continued active. In 1871 Congress had passed the Ku Klux Act, making it a crime to attempt, by "force, intimidation, or threat" to deny a citizen the equal protection of the laws. For several months following, Congress was making intensive investigations into Klan activities.

At the end of March, 1872, the law enforcement arm of the federal government descended on South Carolina, making five hundred arrests in a number of communities. Methodically the arresting officers located the men named in warrants and took them into custody. The Ku Klux Acts suspended the right of *habeas corpus*, implying that all those accused were guilty. Countless prominent men were arrested—lawyers, clergymen, physicians, and imprisonment of ten percent of their numbers served to quell Klan activities for the following four decades.

On a bright Sunday afternoon in early April, 1872, Leroy Biggs was working at his still when he became aware of the sounds of marching men. Marching men. Horsemen. Old instincts still quick from the War made him seek concealment up a tree until they had passed, whoever they were and wherever they were going. He watched them approach, a cordon of blue-clad infantry from one direction, a line of blue-clad cavalry from another. In moments federal soldiers had surrounded him and forced him down from his tree. A sergeant read the charges, conspiracy to deprive American citizens of their rights, and the murder of several persons. "Leroy Biggs, in the name of the federal government, you are hereby placed under arrest."

His shocked protests were in vain, as were those of his fellow Klansmen who were also arrested at their homes that sunny day. The color drained from Leroy's face, his head throbbed with Adam Tremain's haunting presence. He had escaped imprisonment twice; he would escape this time, too. How many times could Tremain have him arrested?

The trials were thorough. A few men were convicted. Leroy had retained Dutch Harbach again, at a scandalous fee; but the witnesses were many, and positive of his identity. Leroy Biggs was found guilty as charged.

He looked wildly around the courtroom, his eyes

locking with Adam Tremain's. He took a deep breath, to let it out in a primal cry. "Why me? Why me, Your Honor? There was a whole slew o' boys in that den an' they're goin' free—why do I hafta go to jail? Why me?"

The judge's face was dispassionate. "Ah will now pronounce. Leroy Ethridge Biggs, Ah sentence you to life imprisonment in the penitentiary. The case is closed." He pounded once with his gavel, and quickly left the courtroom, undoing his judicial robes as he went.

Leroy went berserk. "I'll get you!" he screamed at Adam. "I'll break out, an' I'll get you if it's the last thing I ever do!" Then as the deputies moved in to seize him, he whirled around, shaking his fist at the alarmed and fascinated spectators. "You heard me! I'll get him—I'll get Adam an' Dulcie—jes' wait! You'll see! I'll make 'em so damn sorry they'll wish they never got born!" Raving, he was led out into the hall to go back to jail for the night.

Lyman was waiting for him, tears in his eyes. "Leroy, I'm sure sorry," he began. "We-all did everything we could—"

Leroy, with the brute strength of rage, broke away from the startled deputies and grabbed Lyman by his throat. His voice by now was hoarse, croaking. "Lyman, you got to swear! Swear! God damn it, swear to me!" When Lyman instead began to sag, his face turning crimson, Leroy let him go and put his arms around him. The deputies tried to grab Leroy, but were not quick enough. "Lyman," he said, his voice lower, "swear you'll get me out! Swear it, oh, Christ." He began to blubber, "You got to swear you'll get me out! Swear you will, Lyman, please swear you will!"

The deputies had him now and quickly handcuffed his hands behind his back. Lyman, gasping for breath and clutching his throat, his eyes wild, met Leroy's equally wild and stricken gaze. He nodded. He whispered, "I swear it, Leroy. I'll find out where they send you— I'll get you out. I will."

"Never meant t'hurt you, Lyman—good ol' buddy —" Half-crying, still raving, Leroy was forced through a door. Lyman, wanting to get the last possible glimpse of his idol, heard Leroy's hoarse howl, "God-damn fuckin' sonsabitchin' bastards to hell! I'll get 'em! I'll get even with 'em all!"

Lyman, raising his eyes heavenward for possibly the only time in his life, whispered softly, "An' I'll help you, Leroy. Swear to God I will."

CHAPTER THIRTY-SIX

Leroy's arrest and imprisonment brought little consolation to either Adam or Dulcie. Dulcie's world had been shattered in Georgia. She could no longer view neighbors as she once had. Though she tried to call back the memories of her growing-up years, and the warmth and love she had previously counted on, the night of the fire, the Klan, and identities of the Klansmen haunted her. Jem and Patricia haunted her. The sounds of their terrified, agonized voices called out to her over and over. And though she couldn't bear the sight of the ruins of Mossrose, neither could she keep herself away from them. Adam had found her there crying and staring into the burned hulk on so many occasions he dared not count them. She walked around and around the building, examining the crumbled walls, trying to find some way she might have got back into the house to save her parents had she only been smart enough or brave enough.

For Adam, remaining in Georgia was frustration and pain. He couldn't stand daily watching Dulcie going back over the night of the fire, always coming up with more questions and never any answers. More and more he found himself longing to return to his own home, New Orleans. The city beckoned him as it always had. Though the ills of Reconstruction had dealt as harshly with New Orleans as they had with Savannah, there was an excitement, a bawdiness about that city that no other in the world could match. It was a vitality that Adam understood and thrived on. He missed his friends, and needed them as he hadn't remembered needing anyone since the War years. Tom Pierson and Ben West and Glory filled his mind, and often his dreams.

He began to talk to Dulcie about Holly Hill, the sugar plantation in St. Mary's Parish he had bought right after the War, when he had thought their stay in Savannah would be a short one. At first, Dulcie listened politely, but showed no sign of interest in leaving Savannah. It wasn't until she realized that she was pregnant once more that she began thinking of life in preference to that night that meant only death and ending to her.

At the first sign of renewed vitality from her, Adam's hope revived.

"Dulcie, Holly Hill would be something entirely of our own making. We'd be starting anew . . . on our own."

Dulcie laughed, responding to the boyish enthusiasm in his voice.

"We would be," he assured her eagerly. "St. Mary's Parish was nearly abandoned. The cane had all run out, and there was no seed cane, and no one wanted to put money in land where the return would be slow—not when there's so much easy money to be had."

"But of course you do," she said, her eyebrows raised as though disapproving.

Too intent on his dreams, he missed the twinkle in her eyes. "We may have to wait for a while, but we'll have something that will last—something we have built and done the right way."

"Oh, Adam, just what you've always wanted, your own little world!" This time he did not miss the mischievous twinkle, and rushed to her, taking her in his arms in a bear hug and rolling with her across the bed.

Determined he would show her the best of Louisiana while they were settling at Holly Hill, he took her along the bayou country, to all the places he had hunted, played, and swum as a boy. They picnicked and played with the children along the low, dark-wooded shores of Lake Ponchartrain. Adam stared out across the lake, remembering the night so many years ago that he and his mother and Tom had fled for their lives, leaving New Orleans and Lake Ponchartrain behind. He thrust the memories aside, for they, like so many of his memories, led him back to Edmund Revanche. He quickly looked for Beau and found him playing in the mud along the bank. For several minutes, until the thoughts had disappeared, he played with his son, and would have continued doing so had Dulcie not declared it time they return home.

She smiled at him, then gathered up the picnic paraphernalia, still smiling, and thinking that Holly Hill was beginning to feel like home. She and Adam had both thrown all their energies into the sugar plantation, and slowly it was beginning to feel as though it was theirs, a part of them.

Adam had a sense of well-being as he drove up the long, winding drive. The brick house, white-pillared and vast, stood on a hill. Designed for generations of gracious living, the center portion was three stories high, the wings two stories. Windows in all the front rooms looked out on a tender green lawn shaded with moss-hung live oaks and bald cypresses, the whole reflected in a series of pleasant pools bordered with marsh plants and stocked with golden carp.

To his left Adam could see the newly painted sugar mill with its long gallery. He had already paced the length of that gallery so often it felt as familiar to him as the deck of his own ship. He had to smile at the similarity of the feeling he got from it. From the gallery he could see all that went on in the main building. He could watch the cane crushers working and the four large vats that received the juice, the kettles and clarifiers, the steam pumps and the filtering process. There was an order, a feeling of propriety in seeing everything in its place and producing as it should. Since the War this was the first time he felt he and Dulcie and the children were where they belonged, doing something that in time would make a difference to themselves and the South.

In September 1871 Adam and a crew of hired men, both black and white, took cuttings and made their seed cane. Across his prepared fields the seed cane was laid in mats to protect it from frost. By October, he was in the fields with the men, doing the daylong, back-breaking work of planting the seed cane in straight rows with a seven-foot spread between the rows. As the next year passed, and Adam was working outside, Dulcie was arranging the interior of their new house. From her windows she could look out on the lines of new cane covering the fields, spreading out farther and farther from the house. She too was beginning to feel pride, and confidence in the future, as she envisioned the mature cane looking in June as Adam had described it for her, acres and acres of green stalks as tall as himself, waving in the soft breeze, shining in the warm sun. A future full of promise was something she thought she had lost in the ashes of Mossrose. She placed her hand on her belly, and as she felt the young life within her stir, she felt her own sense of destiny, so long asleep, stir too.

Dulcie and Adam developed a closeness and unity of mind they had never before reached. During the last weeks of her pregnancy, she was confined mostly to her room, cumbersome and mildly uncomfortable. On May 10, 1872, she gave birth to full-term twin boys. They were dark-haired and looked identical. At one month they woke and slept and became hungry as one. And by the New Year, Dulcie was eager to show her new additions off to her friends.

So the months passed. On a hot August afternoon in 1873, Adam took Dulcie and the four children to visit Glory and Ben West. In the soft, damp air there was the scent of greenness, a fresh, pure fragrance of tropical plants that grew in profusion in all the gardens, and that Dulcie had come to associate with happiness and home. She felt particularly good this afternoon and was looking forward to a long weekend brimming with laughter and gossip and children with Glory. As Adam helped them out of the carriage and Glory and her tribe of five children could be seen tumbling eagerly out the door and down the front steps, Dulcie took a pride-filled critical last look at the perfection of her children before she turned them over to the eyes of the Wests.

Beau, at seven and a half an earnest child with his father's sense of fun, was a chronic reader with a lively, investigative mind. Jenny was three, as red-haired as Dulcie and with a temper to match her curly tresses. Matthew and Michael babbled happily, and worked with tremendous energy to remove their shoes and stockings. Pleased with what she saw, Dulcie turned them over to the squeals and tears of Glory. Dulcie turned to Ben, hugging him and remembering the years that seemed so long ago and nearly lost, when Ben and Beau LeClerc and Adam had first begun running the blockade. Again she felt the surge of warmth and rightness well up in her. Though she had been born in Georgia and had lived most of her life at Mossrose, Holly Hill and Louisiana were her home, and these people were her family.

The two families talked and ate and reminisced all afternoon and well into the night, with oversized plans for Glory and Dulcie to put on a small dinner party on Sunday, and Adam and Ben to make a much-needed trip into New Orleans the following day. Not the least of their business was the promise to bring back delicacies and flowers for the Sunday party.

The quiet, sandy streets of the Crescent City were shaded by magnolia trees and live oaks festooned with Spanish moss that waved gently in the lazy, sun-drenched breeze. Adam and Ben drove slowly past old houses of brick and stucco, some with frothy ironwork decorating open archways and balconies, some of stark architecture standing tall and straight with palm trees shading their windows.

Adam halted the horse and waited while a mule-drawn streetcar crossed their path. The car was filled with laughing young girls in gay ginghams and dimities. On their laps were picnic baskets and parasols, shawls and pet lap dogs.

Ben glanced over at Adam. "I can remember a time when we'd have abandoned the horse and leaped on that streetcar and gone with them."

Adam laughed. "Have you ever noticed how difficult it is to leap with four children clinging to your legs?"

"And instead of a strange woman's head on the pillow next to you when you wake up, it turns out to be somebody's babydoll. And the seductive creature who asks to get in bed with you usually has wet diapers."

Adam, laughing, looked up, and realized they were nearly at their destination. He stared for long moments at the elegant Greek Revival mansion built of dark brick with white window frames and front door. The wide veranda was graced with six white Doric pillars sparkling with new paint. Around the veranda were closely manicured bushes and shrubs. All was order, showing the touch of caring hands. Even the outbuildings, glimpsed through a gate in the hedge, were well maintained.

"Tom's Clio Street house," Adam said softly, his voice warm with affection. "It certainly looks as though Tom has completely recovered. This is the home of a man who wants to be seen. You say he entertains here now?"

"Lavishly. Glory and I came to a ball once. Everything was so well managed you'd have expected a woman's hand in the preparations."

Adam looked at Ben, his eyebrow raised. "Think he's been holding out on us? Let's go in. I'm eager to see the old monkey."

Adam knocked on the front door. It was opened by a respectful black butler, who said regretfully that Mistah Tom was not expected back until late in the evening, and could he give him a message?

"Tell him, please, that Captain West and Captain Tremain called on him."

As they got back into the buggy Ben said, "Let's go to the St. Charles. By dinner time you can find anybody in the world over there."

They pulled up in front of the portico of the St. Charles Hotel. With the sense of excitement that good times remembered brings, they walked into the hotel's great rotunda, which nightly welcomed a motley throng of gamblers, sharpers, planters, merchants, drummers, overseers, travelers, riverboat men, Yankees, Rebels, and politicians of every persuasion. As Adam and Ben entered, the evening crowd was already gathering, standing in groups, chatting, and promoting deals of every kind.

They saw Tom standing with another man, a drink in his hand, both of them watching the crowd intently. Adam approached from the side, putting out his hand and waiting for Tom to shake it.

Tom shifted his drink and grasped Adam's hand before he even realized whose it was. "Adam! You sonofagun, you're finally down here where you belong!"

"Here to stay," Adam assured him. With a delighted grin, he noted the fit of Tom's brown frock coat and his elegant waistcoat of watered silk embroidered with medallions. He noted too the twinkle in the mild blue eyes, the smile lines etched around Tom's pleasant mouth. "You're looking about two hundred percent, Tom. Where'd you get those glad rags? You make me feel like a farm boy."

"I thought you were," Tom said, and winked. "Anyway, God blesses some of us with looks and others—" He turned quickly to Ben. "How's yourself? Glad to see you again."

"Glory sends her love, Tom, and wants to know how soon you're coming out."

"Sunday's her preference," Adam added, and briefly explained the grandiose plans of Glory and Dulcie.

"Tell the ladies I'd be honored." Tom took the fourth man by the arm. "I'd like for you to meet a pal o' mine, Geddes Ingraham. Adam Tremain and Ben West, Geddes."

Adam shook hands and smiled at the tall, slender mulatto man, who returned Adam look for look in a fashion friendly but self-possessed.

"Geddes b'longs to more clubs an' organizations than you can count, Adam. A good man for you to get to know. He holds offices in every group that'll have him. What he doesn't know isn't worth knowin', right, Geddes?"

Ingraham looked amused. "Your friend Tom is much too modest, Adam. He knows more scandal, and has more influence, than I can ever hope for. When I need information, Tom is always my first source. However, he has told me some about you. Perhaps we will prove to be of service to each other."

Adam made a pleasant reply, and studied the man with interest.

Geddes Ingraham gave him an enigmatic smile. "This is not the time, but we shall talk, Captain Tremain, and see if your entry into the mainstream of activity in New Orleans cannot be facilitated. I happen to know another friend of yours. Rosebud McAllister serves on many committees with me." Smiling again, Ingraham bowed slightly and excused himself to join four well-dressed whites.

"Let's go sit down," Tom suggested, adding in a low tone, "See that? Those sonsabitches ain't fit t'clean Ingraham's boots, but they're carpetbaggers, an' right now they got the upper hand in Loosiana."

"Politics and New Orleans," Adam said musingly. "Bedmates."

Tom laughed. "There ain't hardly a man in this

room that's not tryin' to shave somebody else. Wheelers an' dealers—every one of 'em. And these Yankees think they died an' went t'heaven here. They're jes' now learning what we always knew. Jes' bein' here's a ticket to whatever makes you smile. You want girls? Go on down to the House of Mirrors, or Mahogany, or Les Belles. You want to buy a public official? They're all for sale, even got a price list. You want to line your own pockets? Get in the right political party and buy a federal job. Or get a gover'ment contract for doin' the printing for Governor Warmoth. Better still, *be* Warmoth. Some say he came down here with his hat caved in, but what I hear is he's gettin' eight thousand a year as Governor, an' 'round a hundred thousand a year for practicin' the open hand policy."

"Does he control the Legislature?" Adam asked.

Tom and Ben exchanged looks and burst into laughter. Before speaking Tom signaled the waiter to refill their glasses. "Nobody controls the Legislature, includin' the Legislature."

Puzzled and amused, Adam looked at both his friends. "What?"

"Boy, the Legislature is the curiosity of the city when travelers come here. It's our main entertainment attraction. I don't guess it's any worse than some others, but it sho'ly is a mess. Down in Mechanics Hall the lobbies are chockablock with darkies straight off the fields, and their women have sweets they're sellin'. Such a racket you've never heard in all your days."

"We'll have to go in someday, Adam," Ben said. "It's a regular circus. You know how the darkies like fancy names and big words? I had the pleasure of hearing Abraham Abiather Wilmot Proviso introduce a respected colleague as his 'venomous bruddah.' And Jimpsey Leander Rabishaw said he hoped the visitors would consider the Legislature a house of call, and that their every want would be 'disarumgumptigated'."

Adam chuckled. "Surely it isn't still that bad."

"Oh, it's gettin' better all the time, but it's still bad.

The blacks are bein' used on one hand an' fightin' so hard to take their place on the other that they get used anyway. There's a lot o' drunkenness, an' a bunch of 'em can't read an' don't understand what's bein' voted on. I saw one senator sittin' on the floor rockin' an' shakin' his head like somebody in an insane asylum. Then when a bill came up for vote, giving away a hundred fifty thousand dollars for some fool thing, he raised his hand for yes, and his vote was taken serious. All this has a funny side to it, but honestly, Adam, I don't know what's gonna happen to Loosiana if this keeps up indefinitely."

"Warmoth's young—only thirty-one right now. But he's got influence in high places," Ben said. "He came here with the Army during the occupation, a member of General McClernand's staff. Then he was made a judge of the provost court for the Gulf."

"He sounds like a formidable man."

"In some ways he is, and in others he *was*. Time's going to tell what'll happen. One sure thing, we haven't seen the last of him. Jes' last year, he tried to switch sides an' back a Democrat for governor. He ran into trouble between blacks and whites, and we had a real donnybrook goin' on down here. Republicans split, an' blacks were fussin' with whites, an' the Conservatives were encouragin' all the battles an' tryin' to form an opposition party made up of ex-Whigs an' moderate blacks. Called themselves the Unification movement. So Warmoth thought he saw the handwriting on the wall and backed the Democrat. He didn't read it right though, an' the Radical Republicans up an' impeached him. Black man named Pinchback acted Governor, an' then they bought up more votes than Warmoth and 'elected' Bill Kellogg. So we're still fightin' it out an' keepin' the military busy."

Adam sat straighter, his blue eyes bright and alert. "Wait a minute, who's this Pinchback? I know the name, but—"

"Pinchback's a pretty good man, smart anyway,"

said Ben. "Got himself in the Constitutional Convention as the first black state senator. This man may be the first and best black politician we've ever seen. Anyway, when Warmoth made his mistake, Pinchback was ready for him."

"So what happened?" Adam asked.

Tom took over, smiling and enjoying his story. "Well, it was one o' those nights made in heaven—warm, pleasant, a good New Orleans night. Federal troops were all over, the statehouse had the whole place surrounded. They looked real impressive standin' there, backs all achin' straight and the bayonets ready. But the Yankes ain't never gonna learn how things happen down here. The streets were packed with folks. Baronne Street, Canal Street, Royal and Rampart, Lafayette Square, all of 'em were full o' whisperin'. Trouble on the way. Everybody knew it an' everybody was waitin'.

"And it came. Time for election returns and we got us two election boards, and they had elected different governors, one Republican an' one Democrat, plus two different legislatures. Both sides appealed to the courts, but that's not where it was going to be settled. Everybody knew that. It was all gonna happen right there in the Legislature. It was one big power struggle. Ol' Warmoth had put his balls in the vise, and Pinchback, as actin' Governor, had his hand on the turnscrew. Nobody was gettin' off the streets till they found out which legislature Pinchback was gonna allow to be seated."

"Nothing really happened until about midnight," Ben said. "Then Warmoth and C. A. Weed, the principal owner of the *New Orleans Times,* visited Mr. Pinchback at home. Seems like an offer was made, but Pinchback had the game in his yard and wouldn't let it go. He told Warmoth that he'd answer him in the morning."

"Mornin' came," Tom went on, "an' Warmoth is coolin' his heels in his quarters here at the St. Charles.

No word yet from Pinchback. So Warmoth wrote a letter an' sent it by messenger to Pinchback. With that, Pinchback shoots back a reply and hurries over to the Legislature, and fast as you can sneeze installed the anti-Warmoth body. He was the coolest thing this side o' ice. Warmoth men were jumpin' up and down tryin' to get recognized so they could hold off Pinchback from installin' the old senators, bceause they were all against Warmoth. Pinchback stood there and time an' time again said, 'The chair will recognize you as soon as the roll is called.' 'Course, when the roll was called it'd be too late. So he installed his bunch, then played his trump card. He stood up there in the Senate and says there's a conspiracy to overthrow the state gover'- ment. He tells how Warmoth come to him in the middle of the night an' offered him a bribe, fifty thousand dollars, and the right to name any number o' state officials in return for a pro-Warmoth Senate. Then he read Warmoth's letter. That same afternoon they impeached Warmoth."

Adam smoothed his mustache. "I don't suppose this was an unusual occurrence."

"Nope, not a bit. That's politics in the good ol' Crescent City, flower of the South. Got to admit, it's never boring."

"No, but it is dirty. And Louisiana is paying one hell of a price for it. All that money the Legislature and the politicians are raking in is coming from somebody's pockets."

Tom nodded. "We're hurtin'. The boys tell me it's that way all over the South. I never did ask, Adam, how long've you been in the city?"

"We just came in this mòrning, Tom."

"Then you haven't seen Angela yet."

"No, not yet. How is she?"

Tom shrugged and gave a sad smile. "Fine. Prospering. I wonder sometimes what Ullah would think o' that."

"What do you think of it, Tom?"

"I think my daughter is about the highest class prostitute in New Orleans, with the lushest place around, and it don't sit easy with me. I had hoped for something—else—for her."

"She owns Les Belles," Ben explained. "It's got a good reputation, and some of those girls are sure beauties. Angela is careful who she takes in. Some of them are as sweet ladies as you'd find anyplace—soft-spoken, refined, educated. They're all colored girls, handpicked."

"Her clientele?" Adam asked. "Is it for blacks, or whites?"

"Look around you here in the St. Charles," Tom said. "Any shade you see here, you'll see at Angela's. She's not prejudiced."

Angela's house, Les Belles, was on Basin Street. It was a large, yellow, frame building with ruffled curtains in all the windows and lanterns strung across the invitingly wide veranda. As Adam went up the steps he could hear a piano and a sweet soprano voice singing. He nodded to the three or four well-dressed ladies and gentlemen who sat decorously in wicker chairs on the porch. Through the window shades discreetly drawn in the front parlor, could be seen shadows of men and women moving around, talking, dancing.

A smiling mulatto butler took his hat. Adam glanced around. Hepplewhite chairs, with shield backs using the Prince of Wales's feathers as motif. On a dainty Hepplewhite sideboard was displayed a fine collection of large cloisonné vases and incense burners. Paintings and sculpture were in the most modest classic styles. A crystal chandelier of proper proportions for the size of the room. On the polished oak floor, Turkish rugs in muted colors.

"Come with me," said the butler. "What name shall I say to Madame?"

"Let's see if she recognizes me," Adam replied.

The parlor was softly lighted, warm and friendly,

decorated in shades of rose. Comfortable leather arm-
chairs and slender-legged side chairs were scattered
around the room. In the center was a grand piano. A
blond woman, her hair done in fashionable waves and
ringlets, and wearing a lightly draped gown of cream-
colored silk crepe, sang:

"Wilt thou not, relenting, for thine absent lover sigh?
In thy heart consenting to a prayer gone by!
Nita—Juanita! Ask thy soul if we should part—
Nita—Juanita! Lean thou on my heart."

Concluding with a delicate arpeggio, the woman
stood to face her audience and curtsey to their applause.
As she rose, her dark eyes caught Adam's.

She saw a tall, black-haired man, muscular and
handsome, whose blue eyes shone with gladness and
devilment and whose white teeth flashed beneath a
piratical mustache.

On Angela Pierson's beautiful face there played a
symphony of emotions: joy and surprise at seeing
Adam, hope that he had come to visit her, and anticipation of the pleasure that visit might bring. Involuntarily, she took a step toward him, her arms lifting to
him.

Then, with a flicker of her long eyelashes, the naked
emotions were veiled. She held out her hand to Adam
to kiss. Her voice did not sound like her own. "Well,
Captain Tremain, how good it is to see you! It is so
nice of you to come."

Adam ignored her proffered hand, took her in his
arms, and kissed her. As he let her go he smiled and
said, "Angela, you're beautiful."

Flustered, she let her trembling fingers almost touch
her mouth. "Adam—" hurriedly she turned her head
from one side to the other—"Ladies, gentlemen, may
I present the famous Captain Adam Tremain, the dashing blockade runner also known as the Black Swan."
Hastily she began reeling off names as people came

up to greet him, the girls clustering around him and touching him lingeringly, the men clasping his hand and murmuring remarks according to whether their sympathies lay north or south of Mason and Dixon's Line. In the press he nearly lost sight of Angela.

Abruptly he excused himself from the gay company and followed her down a dim hall, to a bedroom with a small sitting room. He closed the door behind them.

She whirled, her eyes wide. Her hand went to her breast in a graceful yet startled gesture. She let her breath out in a sound of exasperation. "Adam, you—you surprised me!" Her eyes had turned cold and hard. "What did you come for? One of the girls?"

He gazed at her for some time, until her creamy flesh began to grow rosy, and she turned away from him. He said, "I came to speak with an old friend. Somehow we seem to have started off with both feet in our mouths. Angela, look at me."

Reluctantly, after some time, her eyes rose as high as his mouth.

He said softly, "Hello, Angela."

"H-hello, Adam."

"May I stay awhile, and talk with you?"

"Well—" With a jerky, awkward gesture she indicated the sitting room. She seated herself gracefully. She seemed to be back under control. "That chair is comfortable for a tall man, I believe. Shall I ring for drinks? Brandy?"

"Yes, if you'll join me."

She pulled a bell cord and presently a servant entered. When the girl had gone, she said, "Are you in New Orleans on business?"

He was watching her face. "I live outside New Orleans now." Her eyes widened ever so slightly. He added, "With my wife Dulcie, and our four children."

"Fou—" she said, and stopped. "And is your family well?"

Adam smiled. "We're all very well. I hope you'll come to visit us sometime."

Angela looked at him from under lowered lashes. "Do you? I wonder if your wife would share your— desires."

Adam remained silent for a moment, then said, "No cat and mouse, Angela. I told you I came here to talk with an old friend. Because you are my friend, Dulcie will welcome you; and given an even chance, she'll like you."

"Still arranging everything and everybody to suit yourself, aren't you, Adam?" She refilled his snifter from the decanter, then sat back. "I'm afraid you will no longer have much success with me. I am not interested in your idyll of domesticity, or your wife. You haven't changed, and neither have I. You want your own way, just as you always did, and so do I. I wonder which of us will win?"

"There is no contest, Angela—there can't be one without at least two contestants, and I am not competing with you. I am your friend now, as I have always been."

She looked hard at him, then said bitingly, "There has never been only friendship between us, Adam. I loved you and wanted you—and you had the same feelings. I could feel them pouring out of you, but you didn't want to bed a nigger!"

Adam looked away from her, a quick flash of her warm, inviting body next to his. "You still won't understand, will you?"

She smiled at him enigmatically. "Would you care to bed me now, Adam?" Slowly, sensually, she slid her gown off her shoulder, baring one creamy breast, the nipple pale brown and tautly erect. She whispered, "Touch me. Caress me, Adam. Take me—and then tell me how much *she* means to you."

Adam sat perfectly still, his expression frozen. He knew then, as he had known before, what underlay his affection for Angela. He had watched her grow up from a child of three years. Now it seemed as though he had never known that child, only the woman she had become early in her teens, the woman she was now at twenty-five. Always, the woman in Angela tempted him.

He rose, his heart beating fast.

She smiled. "You're afraid. You were always afraid!"

"Yes. You're right. Good night, Angela."

She watched him stride down the hall, her eyes bleak. In a few moments, a determined smile on her face and her head high, she rejoined her guests in the front parlor.

CHAPTER THIRTY-SEVEN

It was midweek before Adam and Dulcie finally left the Wests' house. Tom, too, had stayed on with them until they were packing the carriage to return to Holly Hill.

"Next time we'll all gather at Holly Hill," Dulcie said happily.

"But Dulcie honey, you've hardly had time to settle in," Glory said.

"I've had plenty of time, and if I knew we'd all be together—perhaps over the holidays—I'd have the incentive to have the house decorated and prepared for anything."

Glory laughed. "With all these children of ours, you'd better be ready for everything. Well, that settles it! We're coming, aren't we, Ben?"

Ben grinned, his arm around Glory's waist. "We're coming."

"Don't leave me out of this!" Tom roared. "I'm comin' too, and by virtue of my advanced age, I claim the role of Santa Claus."

As soon as they had returned to Holly Hill, Dulcie threw herself into preparations for the holiday season. Plans grew as she had the house painted and guest rooms took shape. The guest list now stood at about twenty, including Geddes Ingraham and Rosebud McAllister and their families.

As the weeks passed and the holiday season grew nearer, both Adam and Dulcie became busier. Adam's fields flourished. His first year cane was called "plant cane" and required close attention and work. The men went to the fields hoeing and plowing around the cane as though it were corn. It gave Adam a sense of pride and progress, however, for it was from these shoots that the ratoons, or new shoots, would come. From this "mother cane" Holly Hill would really begin.

By December the guest list had grown to include Dulcie's New Orleans cousins, Robert Tilden and his sisters Jenny Tilden Morgan and Gay Tilden Richards and their families. Adam laughed as she told him that all had accepted happily.

"We'll have to build a new wing. Where shall we put all these people, Dulcie mea? We'll have them hanging from the chandeliers."

Dulcie giggled. "Rings on their fingers and bells on the bores, we shall have music whenever they snores!" Adam grimaced, but she doubled over, vastly amused with herself. "Oh, Adam, I'm having such *fun!*"

The week before the guests were to arrive Adam spent several days in New Orleans on business, the final two devoted to some special Christmas shopping of his own. He bought dolls for Jenny and a train that ran on a track with houses and water towers of its own for Beau. For the twins he collected an assortment of tiny clothes, and oddments that Dulcie seemed to fancy for them. The last and the most exciting purchase he would make was a gift for Dulcie. He entered the finest jewelry store in New Orleans and emerged the proud possessor of a diamond and topaz collar with matching earrings. Thoroughly pleased with his purchase, he decided that he couldn't give it to her so easily. He had to tease—just a little—to whet her anticipation.

So mid-morning of this December day found him in a specialty shop on Royal Street, curiously examining ladies' hair accessories and heartily wishing inspiration would strike. The clerk patiently laid out feathers, ribbons and stars, artificial flowers in nosegays and cascades. Nothing seemed quite right. Everything seemed either too ridiculous for her not to guess something of greater importance was yet to come, or too serious, and would make her think it really was her only gift. He was about to give up.

A rather imperious voice said to the clerk, "I should like to see your best bone combs, please." Adam's eyes lit up. He turned, sensing help at hand. It was Angela. "Angela! You're well named. I think you've solved my Christmas shopping problems." He turned quickly to the clerk. "Do you have hair ornaments in tortoiseshell?"

Angela laughed softly. "I haven't any idea what you are talking about, Adam."

"I'm hunting for a gift for Dulcie, and have managed to find nothing. That is, until you came in." He pointed to an ornately carved tortoiseshell comb. "I'll take that one, please."

As the clerk lifted the comb from its velvet bed, Angela took it, turning it in her hand for close examination. A slow, knowing smile touched her lips. "Her Christmas gift?" she asked, then before he could explain, added, "I'm sure she'll be very pleased with this, Adam. It's quite lovely—and appropriate. How is your wife, and your family?"

Adam laughed. "Busy." As they made their purchases, he told her of the holiday plans. Together they walked out of the shop.

Angela said, "It all sounds such marvelous fun. I think I am jealous."

Adam looked at her, enchanted as always by the smooth beauty of the woman and charmed by the warmth that he felt just being near her. He thought how proud his mother would be to see the polish and the easy manners this Angela had. Zoe Tremain had reared her after Ullah's death and had put her all into giving Angela every chance at success.

"What ever are you thinking about? You're hundreds of miles away. I certainly thought my charms could at least hold your attention through a simple conversation." Angela's lower lip curled in a pretty pout.

It was on the tip of his tongue to ask her to come to Holly Hill for the holidays, but he bit back the urge, and smiled. "I was simply allowing myself the luxury of losing myself in your beauty. Forgive me."

"You said that very handsomely, Captain. I shall indeed forgive you. I would like to see more of you, Adam—as your . . . friend. Perhaps one day I shall meet your wife. We might even like each other. Or perhaps I'll take you up on your invitation, and visit your home. I still have that invitation, do I not?"

"Of course! I'll talk with Dulcie about it—we'll make arrangements."

Angela had a strangely alluring smug smile on her face. "Yes, do that."

Adam gazed at her curiously. "You look mighty pleased with yourself about something."

Angela's laughter tinkled. "One of my triumphs," she said. "I am merely savoring it. Will you celebrate a little with me? The Chez Renee is close by."

He helped her into his carriage, and hers followed them to the small restaurant a few blocks away. They were seated at an intimate table in the corner. Angela laid her spotless white gloves in her lap.

"Are you going to tell me about your triumph?" he asked when their drinks had been served. "Or am I to celebrate in ignorance?"

"In ignorance, dear friend, in ignorance."

He looked at her mildly nonplussed. He was now very curious, fascinated by the small game they were playing. Then she became serious, her smooth brow creasing into a frown. "Oh, Adam, I'm such a fool!"

"I couldn't disagree more, Angela."

"Don't deny it. I am! And I'm trying to apologize for my behavior when—when I saw you last. I was so offensive!" she hissed.

"You did nothing that offended me." He smiled.

"You were right, of course, you always have been. There is too much between us to allow my—my imaginings to interfere. Sometimes I say or—or do things that are outrageous—just to test people—to get a reaction."

He said nothing and she went on, watching him closely. "I was so annoyed with myself after you left. You were so kind, and I'd been such an idiot—Adam, do you think you can forgive me?"

"There is nothing to forgive. I am your friend," he assured her. "I've never been anything less."

"Oh, are you, Adam?" she asked wide-eyed, tears forming. "Are you really? Even now? I so need friends who don't have any ulterior motives. You know, in my—my business, friends are not common. Not real friends."

"Well, I am one. Now let's talk of your triumph. What is it?"

"Not yet. There's one more thing. I haven't—haven't made it so that you won't come to see me anymore, have I? You will visit me."

"I promise."

"Oh, I am so relieved!" She stood up, gathering her gloves. Quickly she walked around the small table, kissing him gaily on the cheek. "Now, dear friend, I must run. I am late already to a meeting of the Philharmonic Society." She smiled brilliantly at him as she walked away, then paused, turning and posing. "I'm sure that is a wonderful gift for your wife. She'll love it."

Adam sat for a moment shaking his head in delighted amusement. As the waiter hovered nearby, he asked for the check, still chuckling.

On the way home, Angela was much in his thoughts. He wasn't sure what it was that he kept trying to bring forth from the back corners of his mind, but he never grasped it, and once he arrived at Holly Hill the incessant activity and gaiety drove away all thoughts of Angela.

Two days after Adam's return from New Orleans, guests began arriving. The house was constantly filled with laughter and noise, and the merry clink of glasses raised in toasts.

With nearly all the guests present except Tom, Geddes Ingraham, and the McAllisters, who would not arrive until Christmas Eve, the whole party went out to the woods on a crisp Demember day searching for mistletoe and the Yule log. Adam stood on the veranda for a moment watching his guests race like the children across the lawn on their quest for the joyful things of Christmas. He looked too at the children, not even daring to count how many there were. Small bodies ran and gamboled, squealing with laughter and sudden anger as minor battles broke out between little boys, who wildly tumbled each other to the ground. Mamas with skirts flying ran to separate the combatants, and then they were running again, crying out whenever they saw anything resembling mistletoe clinging to the trees. Adam's crew of workmen was kept frantically busy hurrying from one excited group to another, cutting the mistletoe free.

That evening there was dancing, much talking and much drinking of eggnog. The Yule log burned brightly in the fireplace, making them all too warm, but increasing their delight in the season. Children's bedtimes were ignored, and one by one the small ones found sleep on chairs, under chairs, on the steps leading upstairs. This time Dulcie's crew of household help found them, undressed them lovingly, and put them to bed to dream of the next day's festivities.

It was difficult, but that evening Adam managed to find a moment alone with his wife to give her the Christmas gift he had taken such pains to select for her. Eagerly he gave her the velvet-covered box. She sat speechless looking at the sparkling jewels glinting up at her from their satin bed. Then she sprang up, thrusting herself into his arms. Adam picked her up, spinning around with her. The other box containing the comb lay forgotten on her vanity.

"Oh, Adam, they're so beautiful!" she said happily. "I love you!"

She clasped the necklace of topazes and diamonds around her neck, patted it into place, and turned to show Adam. "Oh, Adam, I think it is the loveliest present you ever gave me. Don't I look splendid?" She was grinning, delighted with her reflection.

"Yes, my love, you look splendid, but you don't need any necklace for that."

She wrinkled her nose at him. "Do you think I'll knock them dead tonight? I do want to make a good impression."

"Of course you will, Dulcie. The only time I can recall when you did *not* make a good impression was the night you and I were being shot at in the ballroom of Mr. Clyde Lewis of New York City."

Dulcie chuckled softly. "That was the night I forced myself on you and we ran away together, wasn't it?"

"Something like that." They smiled at each other reminiscently. He rose, devastatingly tall, and handsome in evening dress. Dulcie, elegant in moss-green velvet, took his arm and they descended the stairs.

The music had already begun, and below them in the large, decorated rooms of Holly Hill, Dulcie and Adam saw an array of gaily colored gowns twirling and mingling their colors, as formally garbed men whirled and courted their ladies. They stood on the stairs for a moment, enjoying the sight. Dulcie found Adam's hand. He clasped hers gently, and the smile that was deep in his blue eyes said all she wanted to know. After a moment, she asked, "Has Tom arrived yet?"

Adam laughed. "No, but if you recall, Tom has insisted on playing Santa Claus, so don't be surprised if he arrives via the chimney on the stroke of midnight.

"He wouldn't!"

"Oh, but he would if he were so inclined."

"Honestly, Adam, don't you have any conservative friends?"

"One."

She looked at him.

"Glory Hallalooya," he said, and chuckled, his hand gentle on her back as they entered the main hall. In seconds they were swallowed up by many eager friends. Dulcie found herself in her cousin Robert Tilden's strong embrace. "Before anyone else can steal you from me, I'm taking you to the middle of the dance floor and not letting you go until we have caught up on all the news," he said, his eyes gleaming with admiration and amusement.

"Not in so short a time, Robert! I intend to have many lovely afternoons and evenings of talk with you and Gay and Jenny. I want to remember and laugh about all the terribly ornery things we did as children. We were the worst little demons, weren't we?"

Robert held her tighter. "I'm not so sure about us, but you were. You always brought life and frivolity with you, Dulcie."

She giggled. "Surely not all the trouble was attributable to me alone!"

"Mmm, well, certainly the lion's share. But, little cousin, I must say it has agreed with you. You look marvelous, and so does Adam."

Dulcie looked up at him still smiling, but her eyes clouded a little. "We are—now—but it hasn't been easy, Robert."

"I know," he said softly. "I know. I thought not to talk of Uncle Jem and Aunt Patsy tonight, but I am aware."

"Did you know that Leroy Biggs led that horrible mob?"

"Yes." Robert's word was barely audible.

"I still find it difficult to accept that, Robert. He was my friend—I grew up with Leroy. How could he do—how could he—"

"The War, Dulcie. It has done strange, awful things to so many of us. None of us is what we once were, and some—well, some are hardly men at all. Honor no longer exists for those—civilization is gone."

"I know—at least my head knows—but Robert, I can't think how he could have done that—my parents! He's known them since—"

"No more talk of it now, Dulcie. It's Christmas Eve, and you are looking magnificent, and your husband glows with pride, and your children are cherubs. Tonight is no time for the past. Look ahead. Jem and Patsy would want it that way. At least you have the satisfaction that Leroy is in prison, likely for the rest of his life. No doubt it will be a short life."

Dulcie nodded. "I have thought so too, and I don't like myself for it. Sometimes I think that he will die there, and his death will be as horrible as Mama's and Daddy's."

"Shh, shh, not tonight. Think good thoughts tonight. It is a festival!"

"You're right. No more tonight, but Robert—thank you. Sometimes it helps to talk just a little."

Robert whirled Dulcie through a waltz, then released her into the arms of Geddes Ingraham. The tall, distinguished mulatto smiled genially into the warm golden eyes of his hostess. "You honor us, Mrs. Tremain. It is a privilege that you should entertain and dance with one of my color."

Dulcie blushed uncomfortably. "Mr. Ingraham, I am embarrassed that you should say that to me. You of all people are accustomed to mixed groups. Adam has told me often of your entertainments."

"Ah, but for a select few, Mrs. Tremain, only a select few."

"It will change," she said seriously. "It must."

"Yes, it must, but I fear it will not before much more heartbreak and hatred passes. We make much false progress, but I cannot say I see much of a lasting nature. The causes, the great humanitarian causes of the War are already forgotten. The true crusaders are few now, and not powerful."

"I hope you are wrong!"

"So do I, Mrs. Tremain. Thank you for the dance."
He bowed to Ben West as Ben took his place with
Dulcie.

Ben had scarcely taken her in his arms when the
room burst into a cacophony of merry sound and
laughter. With a raucous flurry, Santa Claus burst
through the front door dragging a bulbous, bulging
sack behind him.

"Ho! Ho! Ho! Children! Children, where are all the
children in this house?"

As Tom hopped and pranced about the room, followed by a vision in red, Glory bounded to her husband's side, her wide eyes full of questions. "Look at
Santa's helper!" she hissed in Ben's ear. "What's she
doing here? Ben! She'll cause trouble!"

Nervously Ben glanced at Dulcie standing on the
other side of him only feet away. "Glory, will you hush!
You'll cause more trouble than she. Tom probably
asked her to come."

"In a pig's eye!" She turned and walked away. Ben
leaped after her.

"Glory! Don't you say a word to anyone else, you
hear? Glory?"

"Ben?" she mocked sweetly, then made a face at
him and said even more sweetly, "You know how to
shut me up, don't you, Ben?"

His mouth opened, then he closed it.

"Oh, well," she said, and moved a little farther from
him. "If you don't care . . ."

"Damn it, Glory, not now!" he whispered.

She grinned, irresistibly engaging. "Why not now,
Ben?"

He grabbed her hand and dragged her toward the
staircase giggling triumphantly. "Now," he said. "All
right, woman, now!"

Dulcie watched Tom's progress through the room,
fascinated by the woman with him. Tall, blond, slender,

she was of regal stature, a woman of authority, yet ultimately feminine.

As she watched, Angela seemed to sense the gaze upon her, and coolly, the disdain barely hidden, her eyes locked with Dulcie's. Without self-consciousness Tom's daughter assessed her rival and felt conflicting thoughts. Her confidence in herself and Adam's latent desire for her was high. But Dulcie was more beautiful and warmer than she had expected. She recognized in the smaller woman qualities she did not have, and it made her uncomfortable. Angela was accustomed to getting her own way, and this of all times it was of greatest importance to her. She wanted Adam Tremain, and she would have him. Other times she had tried and given up. This time, there would be no defeat. She would have him.

After a cold midnight supper, the children were put to bed, and the adults returned to conversation and dancing. Dulcie, having danced with all the men, as the hostess should, allowed herself to melt into the background for a moment to assess her party. As she chattered with some of the other women, her eyes found Adam. He was dancing with Angela.

"If I had known elves are so lovely," Adam was saying, "I'd have volunteered to be Saint Nicholas myself."

Angela smiled secretively. "I had to come along, Adam; isn't this Christmas Eve? A woman wants to be with family on Christmas. And you and Tom are the only family I have."

He squeezed her affectionately. "We're glad you were able to come."

"I've never forgotten the Christmases we used to have at Aunt Zoe's." She smiled mistily. "When you used to tease Mammy and call her your woman. I was only a little girl then, but I wished I was Mammy." She sighed, looking away. Then her dark eyes met his fully. "And I remember sometimes going to sleep in front of the fire, and you carrying me upstairs to put me to bed at the end of the long, beautiful day."

As he struggled for recollection, she added, "Those days are all a dream now, aren't they? Your house is so warm—so pleasant, Adam. I feel—quite welcome in it."

He smiled again. "And you are, Angela."

Dulcie realized that a man had been standing nearby, just out of her range of vision. He, too, had been watching the dancers. She turned and he put his warm hand on her arm. "Dulcie, you are lovely tonight."

Tom stood smiling at her, dressed now in a well-cut evening suit. She gave him an affectionate kiss. "Where have you been? I thought you were going to play Santa Claus all night."

"I am." He looked at the group of women. "Ladies, I hope you'll forgive me, but I'm gonna steal your hostess away from you for a few minutes. Ol' Santy has one more gift to give to Captain and Mrs. Tremain."

"Tom?" Dulcie asked, clinging to his arm. "What is it? Don't make me wait!"

He clucked at her. "Dulcie, I'm ashamed of you! Are you one o' those who peeks in all the packages before Adam even gets a chance?"

She slapped playfully at his arm. "You're as mean as ever."

Excusing them, he took Adam and Dulcie aside where they could be private. "On my way in," he said, "I ran into a messenger on his way here. Well, bein' Santy, I said if it was good news I'd deliver it, an' if it was bad, he was to come back tomorrow. He gave me this letter, an' not bein' a trustin' feller I took the liberty of scannin' it."

He handed Adam the letter. Adam opened it, and together he and Dulcie read it. "Oh, Adam! They're safe!" She jumped up and kissed Adam, throwing her arms around his neck and clinging to him.

Tom stood back watching, his eyes alight, his face

beaming. "Looks like we all got a fresh start. Like I said, I only scanned the letter. Where did Kyra say she and Apollo were settling?"

"She doesn't say exactly," Adam replied. "When she wrote, they were in New Mexico Territory, on their way to San Francisco."

"Well, they can't go much farther, can they—not unless they swim."

"Oh, Adam, this is the best Christmas gift of all! I want to run inside and tell everyone."

Adam hugged her. "Most of these people don't even know Kyra and Apollo."

"Does that matter? They're safe and they're together! Oh, Adam! Adam! I was so afraid we'd find out that they were dead too!"

Dulcie felt as though she were floating several feet above ground for the rest of the evening, and seeing the mood she was in, her husband stayed by her side.

By three o'clock the party was over. Tom, who had danced with nearly every woman there and had drunk all the men under the table, collapsed into an armchair in the library and fell asleep between words of a sentence to Adam. Adam, who had been waiting for the moment when the last guest retired, took Dulcie's arm.

Gently he steered her out of the library while she was still saying, "—best party we ever—can't remember so much fun—" and started her upstairs. On the third step she stopped, smiling sleepily up at him. "Adam, carry me."

He chuckled softly and swooped her up into his arms. He carried her to the door of their bedroom, went in, and shut the door behind them. Then he let her down lightly on her feet.

Dulcie leaned against him. Her voice was pleasantly slurred. "I feel *mar*-velous, Adam. Not a bit tired. Not even sleepy. Are you?"

He ran his palms up her deliciously rounded bare arms. Lightly he kissed her. "Think of your head in the morning, my love. We can stay up all night, but you'll be sorry."

"No I won't," she said reasonably. "I feel like being naked. Just stark naked—and dancing. Dancing with you, Adam. Will you unhook me so I can—I can dance with you?" Like a little girl she turned her back to him so he could unfasten the many hooks on the back of her dress.

He had some trouble, for she kept leaning against him, kept turning her head around to see how near he was done. Finally the troublesome thicket of fasteners was undone, and the moss-green velvet dress slid to the floor. She lifted one foot, then the other, and stepped out of it. She left the dress lying where it was. With astonishing swiftness for one seeming somewhat tiddly, she shed her camisole and one petticoat after another, leaving them in lacy heaps just where she dropped them. Adam was reminded of nothing so much as Miss Glory Hallalooya in their days together in Nassau.

Stark naked except for her new necklace, she looked up and down herself, front and back, to see if she had forgotten anything. The green silk slippers sailed one by one over toward the closet. She looked at Adam, giggling, then cried, "But you're still dressed! How can you dance naked with me if you're—"

She approached Adam, her fingers out toward his buttons, but his mouth stopped her words. After quite a long time he said, "I didn't have dancing in mind . . . not really."

Her face changed, her amber eyes smoldering with desire for him. In seconds she had his frock coat and vest undone and was working on the studs of his shirt. His garments fell to the floor, and she danced lightly away from him, inviting him to join her.

Adam, struck by the idea of dancing naked, bowed before her and they solemnly waltzed a few steps to some unheard melody. Deliberately, Dulcie let her nipples brush his arm. He responded by stroking her breasts with his fingertips until the nipples stood erect. Dulcie, holding his hand, essayed a pirouette, then swayed dizzily toward him.

"Woo," she murmured. "I don't see how they do it."

He pulled her to him "Do what?" he murmured in her ear.

She rubbed gently against him. "Dance when you're tipsy. I keep wanting to lie down."

"A superb notion," he said, but did not immediately move toward the bed. "Let's try it this way." He held her tight and they took a few steps.

"Try dancing?"

"Try whatever you like." He bent her backward over his arm and she let her hands and arms float while he whirled her around a few times. When he straightened her up, her arms went around his neck and her body melted yearningly to his.

She nibbled with her lips at the corners of his mustache; her tongue went in tantalizing strokes across his mouth. His arms went around her hard, raising her off the floor so that his penis was held warmly between her thighs. Ever so slowly she rolled her hips from side to side, creating a motion they both found pleasurable.

He began kissing her, starting with her eyes, moving to her lips, to the hollow of her throat, bending her away from him so that his tongue moved freely around her hardened nipples while she still held him, caressing and pulling him with expert flexings of her thighs.

He said against her cheek, "Dulcie, I love you so," and the saying made his blood race more madly. He wanted to feel his penis against her cool belly; he wanted to feel it touching her firm breasts. He wanted to run his fingers over her smooth flesh, teasing, awakening her to an ardor that matched his, until her hands enclosed him and she guided him into her.

He did the things he wanted, and more besides, and she caressed and fondled him and pressed her opened lips against him. His passion drummed in his ears, a wild thing crying out for rapture. Then slowly she placed his penis at her entrance and slowly, slowly, let him travel its delicious length. He lay absolutely still on her, feeling the heat and the moistness of her, feeling the little spasms that spoke of their eagerness for each other.

With careful deliberation he withdrew almost his entire length from her, and went into her slowly again and again. In a few strokes he felt her shudder, felt her contractions faster and faster, heard her respirations come hard. His own arousal surged powerfully, to a tense high pitch of excitement. Into his ear she sighed his name, not so much a sigh as an undertone of fulfillment that murmured of her love for him. He continued to move within her, acutely aware of her every sensation, of her beginning to build to the pinnacle again, of her ardent striving, her fingers pulling him closer into her, of his own aching, suspended need.

He relaxed, let go. He had the sensation of the two of them climbing a long hill, of poising, breath held, at the top, then of cascading downward together in a warm rush of sudden well-being.

Dulcie's moans were soft, their urgency diminishing. She lay panting beneath him, sometimes taking a deep breath and letting it out contentedly. Her hands began to stroke his back, kneading all his muscles she could reach, making him very drowsy. Presently she stopped, and they fell asleep together.

CHAPTER THIRTY-EIGHT

Leroy Biggs smiled meanly. He shifted his weight and continued staring at the man he was tormenting.

The huge black tensed, drawing in his breath, his muscles flexing ready to spring. Through tight lips he said, "White boy, you takes dat back, whut you say, befo' Ah kills you. Nobuddy gwine call me dat an' lib."

It was 1874. Leroy had been in the penitentiary for more than two years. Having no legitimate outlets for his normal aggressiveness, he had fallen quickly into convict behavior—hectoring, harassment, persecution, and malicious abuse of his fellow prisoners—simply to lay claim to his own space in this confined place.

He lived in a small, stinking cell with three other men, constantly revulsed by cockroaches in his clothing, waking at night screaming to find himself being bitten by rats. His ankles stayed raw and bleeding from the shackles blacksmithed on for his labor on the chain gang, and worn day and night. His hands, still unused to the rigorous labor of breaking rocks and of digging out earth for a roadbed, were cut and blistered. His muscles were wracked and aching. He was incredibly sore in mind and body; and he needed someone to take it out on. A good fight would be the one thing to make him happy just now.

Leroy stayed tensed, alert for the black man's premature swing which might throw him off balance. Grinning now, he repeated his filthy insult and backed it up with a strong right to the other man's jaw.

He returned to consciousness aware of a hideous ringing in his ears. He lay on his back in the foul-smelling muck of the cell floor. He couldn't figure out how he had got there, or why he had chosen to be there.

Jupiter. That black son of a bitch had knocked him flat. He lay perfectly still a little longer, working out a strategy to get up.

He stiffened. Something was crawling on his hand—something as long as his hand, something soft and creepy—slowly he raised his hand in the dim light, then sat up with a strangled yawp as he flung away a six-inch centipede.

Raucous laughter greeted him from big Jupiter, spindly little Luke, and Quillin. "Great big boy's scared of bugs," Quillin jeered.

Leroy rose, ready to thrash Quillin, then the pain in his head made him reel and clutch the wall. "Kee-rist," he muttered.

"Hu't y'seff, Whitey?" asked Jupiter with mock solicitude.

"Naw, stupid, it's jes' my time o' the month," Leroy growled, and they all laughed again. But this time the laughter was less jeering, more in appreciation.

He felt awful, as though he might have to puke; and his head and neck hurt worse than any pain he had ever known. He had to sit down somewhere. He reeled back to the bunk he was temporarily sharing with the black man, and sprawled half-sitting, his mouth hanging slack and his ears filled with the buzzing of a thousand hornets.

Jupiter said softly, "Dat ain't only de beginnin', white boy."

Leroy had no reply. He was trying not to be sick. Without warning he vomited up his thin supper, fouling his clothes and his side of the bunk.

Luke giggled uneasily. "Looks like ol' Leroy git t'sleep in his own puke t'night, don't it, Jupe?"

Jupiter made a noise of disgust and rolled over with his back to Leroy. But Leroy was too sick to care. All he wanted to do was go to sleep, not to wake up before

morning. And then he was going to pound Jupiter to a
bloody pulp.

Leroy's health was not too good for some time afterward. The injury he had sustained to his neck muscles
plagued him like a ten-ton weight on his head, keeping
him half-nauseated and in considerable pain. But he
got no sympathy from his gang-mates or from the guard,
who had been an overseer on a plantation before the
War, and was consequently at home with a whip in his
hand. When Leroy faltered, he felt the tails of the
whip cutting him through his rough shirt.

He was constantly nagged by pain and the rude injustice of it all. Here he was, a white man, owner of a
large plantation, the elected leader of a powerful den
of the Klan, an ex-Colonel in the Confederate Army,
a man among men, respected in the best society. And
now he was chained between a spindle-assed woman
killer and a freely sweating nigger, both of whom could
outwork him, and he couldn't get away from them even
at night.

This was the kind of thing the Klan had tried to
stamp out, the inequities in the court systems that
would convict one man for the crime of twenty and
send him to prison to rot his life away. Why, if Osgood'd
had them on their toes the way *he* would have, they'd
have spirited him out of jail and up into the South
Carolina hills where no arm of the law could hope to
reach. He'd be sitting on his butt this minute, laughing
his head off.

"Watch dat maul, white boy," said Jupiter sharply.
"Y'all 'bout mash mah toe."

"You jes' shut your mouth an' do your job, nigger,"
Leroy flared.

The whip cracked over their heads. "No talkin', I
said," the guard cried.

Jupiter's lips hardly moved, but his voice came
quite clear. "Y'all gwine hafta learn t'talk lowah, white
boy, lessen you wants ol' Woof whuppin' you all de
liblong day."

Leroy, seething bitterly, said nothing. His head hurt so bad he could hardly hold it up. All he wanted to do was lie down. But he kept on breaking up rocks, the heavy maul lifting and dropping automatically.

A thought struck him, and he turned to Luke. "What's that guard's name?"

"Wolf," said Luke out of the corner of his mouth. "Brags about used t'be a overseer on Mossrose, whatever the hell that was."

Leroy's spirits rose so hard they made his head hurt. Wolf. Mossrose. Wolf'd remember him, sure. He'd remember the day of the insurrection when he, Leroy, got the idea to shoot a nigger every hour till Dulcie was found and brought back from being captured. Wolf might help him get out of here. Didn't look like Lyman was going to.

He straightened up and turned around to smile at Wolf, who happened to be looking the other way. He'd never have recognized the man. Bearded now, gray and balding, he looked like a wreck till you caught that glint in his eyes.

Those eyes were everywhere. "Turn back around there, boy," said Wolf harshly, gesturing with the whip. "Nothin' back here y'need t'see."

"Jes' thought you might reckanize me, Wolf," said Leroy pleasantly. "Leroy Biggs, of near Mossrose."

For answer the whip stung his back. "Shut up an' git back t'work."

Jupiter's face suddenly closed. Sho, he 'membered Mossrose. And ol' Simmon, his shrunk-up daddy, and his mama. Dey had a passel o' pickaninnies, dem two did, most of 'em younger'n him. He 'membered 'Pollo an' him roughin' each othah up when dey was boys. 'Pollo nevah did whup him, but he come close sometime. An' 'Pollo was smart, yeah he was. An' han'some, mebbe mos' as han'some as ol' Jupe. Mastah Jem was jes' stahtin' t'use 'Pollo fo' a stud when Jupe got sold down de ribbah. Dat was a bad time aftah dat, a bad mastah an' a mighty po' plantation. 'Specially aftah Mossrose.

Jupiter wiped his sweating forehead with one hand. Wondah whut mighta happen to 'Pollo. He a good boy, didden gib his mama an' daddy no trouble, been good to de pickaninnies. Be a mighty fine man dese days, iffen he go on like he staht. He was de one Jupe 'member bes', de one Jupe work wid an' sleep wid' an' play wid.

'Pollo mos' likely daid, he told himself, erlong Mama an' Daddy an' all de res' of 'em. Wull, mos'ly he jes' member Simmon an' Mama an' 'Pollo. But he ain't let on yit 'bout knowin' Woof, no sense in attractin' de whup no mo'n he had to.

Leroy. In the way of convicts, Jupiter had long studied Leroy's face and mannerisms—partly for weaknesses, partly to see if he was some enemy previously recognized. Hearing his full name for the first time, he tried to recall if it meant anything, and it did not. Leroy was a mean one, but he, Jupiter, could be meaner, when he took a notion. He decided to keep quiet and see what else he found out. That Leroy might take a notion to bust out, and if he did, Jupiter would be busting out right behind him.

Dark had fallen, and most of the prisoners were asleep when Wolf came to the cell door. "Biggs! C'mere."

Leroy heaved himself up off his bunk, barely able to move for pain, his mind groggy and his arms and legs feeling numb. Jupiter went on breathing heavily with his mouth open, listening hard to catch their words.

Wolf did not trouble to lower his voice at first. "Say you come fum 'round Mossrose?"

Leroy said eagerly, "Yeah, Wolf, yeah. Don't you remember that insurrection? When I was goin' t'shoot that nigger buck 'Pollo?"

Jupiter's breathing stopped for a few seconds.

Wolf laughed. The years had done nothing to improve the appearance of his broken, tobacco-stained teeth. "Like it was yestiddy. I bin sorry ever since, that Moran din't let you do it. I'da like t'see him crawlin' 'round gut-shot, beggin' on his knees fer y'all t'shoot 'im in the haid."

"Been many a time since I wished I had, Wolf. He got too big for his britches durin' the War, an' the South wasn't hardly big enough t'hold him after."

"How so? Did he kill somebody?"

"Must've. He went over to the Yankees an' they made him a cap'n in their army."

Wolf snorted, and spat tobacco juice near Leroy's boots. "Whut the world ain't comin' to," he said disgustedly. "Hear you're in for murder."

"You couldn't hardly call it that, ol' pal, mo' like the Yankee gover'ment wants somebody for a showpiece t'tell they stopped the Klan. I'm payin' fo' what the Yankees hate most—bein' Rebel."

Wolf chuckled.

"How's the South been treatin' you lately?"

"Purty well, Biggs. After I left Moran, I come right here an' picked up a job, nothin' to it. I make out all right. Good thing I quit, too, I heard Mossrose got burned out by the Yankees."

Leroy said with a satisfaction that was lost on Wolf, "Can't hardly find where it was any more."

"Moran had a daughter—feisty little redhead. I sho' woulda like t'git up her petticoats." Wolf sighed, not noticing the flash of anger in Leroy's eyes. "Guess I jes' missed my chanst." Wolf shook his head. "Whut were you a-doin' in the War, Biggs? Hidin' out in the swamps?"

Leroy damped his anger down. It wouldn't do to get Wolf riled, not yet. "Naw, I got lucky. I went into the Army early an' come out a colonel." Not wishing to create any more envy than he already saw on Wolf's face, he added smoothly, "But I lost my land anyway."

"How so? Yankees burn you out too?"

"Naw. They wanted me t'sign their fuckin' Iron Clad

Oath, an' I refused," he lied. "Now a friend o' mine,
Lyman, he signed it right away, an' they give him his.
But mine's got niggers livin' all over it, prob'ly a couple
hunnerd." He thought of Lyman, getting his own land
back now, probably still living in *his* house, passing the
idle days in pure enjoyment, and never giving a minute's
time to getting Leroy Biggs out of the penitentiary. He'd
get even with him, too, when he got out; he'd see to
that.

"God-damn niggers takin' over the country," Wolf
growled.

"Yeah, I got a big one in bed with me," said Leroy,
hoping Wolf would take the hint and put Jupiter somewhere else.

Wolf glanced at the bunk where Jupiter lay sprawled
in noisy sleep. "Oh, him. That's jes' fer the time bein',
Biggs, till they get some more cells built. Don't want
t'pay no 'tention t'Jupe."

"Hell, Wolf, he's as fat as a train," Leroy complained.
"Kinda hard t' igganore."

Wolf changed the subject. "You gittin' enuf t'eat? I
c'n git you lots more. Providin' you got money." Wolf
lowered his voice now. "Food'll cost extry."

Disappointed, Leroy said, "Naw, not a red cent. But
I got friends. They'll be comin' to visit pretty soon, an'
I'll have all kinds o' cash money after that."

"I don't give no credit," said Wolf. "I git the cash or
I don't do any bizness." He started to leave.

"Hey, Wolf, don't forget t'come back now an' then.
We'll talk over ol' times. An' when I get some money,
we'll—" But Wolf had passed around a corner out of
sight.

Jupiter was chuckling. "Whitey, save yo' cash t'light
yo' see-gars. Ol' Woof ain't gwine keep up his end o'
no bahgain."

"Mind your own business, nigger. An' for Chrissakes,
can't you move over? Sleepin' with you's like sleepin'
on a two-by-four."

Jupiter made himself wider on the bunk. "Dat dere is too bad, white boy. Ah got heah fust."

Leroy considered taking action, but his head was pounding again and he wanted to lie down before it split right in two. Not speaking, he lay down on the edge of the bunk. After a while he noticed Jupiter was giving him a little more room.

He was asleep when his bedmate whispered, "Leroy. Leroy."

"What the hell do you want?"

"Tell me 'bout dis 'Pollo. Seem like I heard 'bout him."

"What do you want t'know for? He's jes' another nigger."

"You say he a real bad-ass. He git in a lot o' troubles?"

Leroy was struggling with sleep. "Naw, I guess not. He tried t'make some trouble but nothin' came of it. Then he run off with the nigger schoolteacher on Mossrose."

"When all dis happen? In de War?"

"Jes' fore I got sent up. What d'you care?"

"Ah doan. Ah doan eben know him."

On the verge of asking why again, Leroy slid into slumber. But Jupiter lay awake, thinking.

At first Leroy had been sustained by hope. Hope that Lyman would come to visit him. Hope that Lyman would outline a clever scheme by which he would be sprung from prison. But the months passed, a year, two years. Lyman did not visit, or send messages either. Leroy's hope, which had lent him daily courage, began to be replaced by the same desolate feeling of abandonment that had been his when he sat alone in Laban Sweet's jail. And from feeling abandoned, his next sustenance became hate.

He hated Lyman, who had called him his truest friend and promised to get him out, and had failed in that promise from the moment Leroy had set foot in prison. He hated Adam Tremain, who had stolen Dulcie from him, who had riches and power and had sent him to the penitentiary. Most of all he hated Dulcie Tremain, who had filled his dreams for years with her red hair and golden eyes and that smile he had always thought was for him alone—hated her for making him stay away from her, hated her for not loving him the way Camille had loved him, for not wanting him the way he had always wanted her.

He would have Dulcie. By God he would. He'd get out of here somehow, and he'd find out where she was now. He'd wait outside, in the dark, looking in through her windows where the lights were soft on her creamy skin and her rosy mouth, and he'd find out her habits, when she went shopping and when she went visiting. He'd be in his carriage then—a big fine carriage, finer than Adam Tremain would ever own—and he would follow her wherever she went.

He'd wait for his opportunity, and when it came, he'd kidnap her. Kidnap Dulcie Moran right out of sight. He'd have a place all fixed up to take her, a place where nobody could ever guess he was holding the wife of Adam Tremain. And it would be there he'd have her.

Oh, God, he thought, feeling the surge of lust, would he ever fuck her. Fuck her every way to Sunday, turn her every way but loose. He would fuck the living daylights right out of her, and when he was done he'd fuck her some more for good measure. He'd make her forget she ever knew of Adam Tremain, fuck her so much her head would swim, so often she wouldn't even lose the shape of him before he had it in her again.

He had his penis out now, running his hand up and down it, thinking of Dulcie and the ways he would have her. Then a fresh sensation of power came to him as he thought of the way he'd punish Adam Tremain. His hand slowed, keeping up the tension but not wanting to go off yet, wanting to think of cruel and unusual ways to punish the man before he killed him for stealing the only girl he had ever loved.

Cut off his balls, he thought, pulling out his own and fingering them. One at a time, with a dull knife. Stand and watch while Tremain begged and begged him not to take his cock too. Then cut that off—one stroke, whack with a big cleaver and let the blood fly. That shouldn't kill a man, only maybe in his mind, so there were lots of other things he'd do to Tremain when he captured him.

Do it in front of Dulcie. Let her see his power, let her see what a real man was like for a change. And then, when Tremain lay dead on the floor, he'd have her again.

His hand was moving faster now, along the shaft and up over the head of his penis, back and forth, back and forth, while in his mind he had mounted Dulcie, and when he came it was in her sweet body. He lay there quiet for long afterward, holding himself tenderly, still dreaming of Dulcie.

"Man, she must be some pussy to bring you on like that," said Quillin.

Leroy turned his head, seeing his surroundings with some surprise. Leisurely he refastened his trousers. "Sho' is, Quillin, sho' is. Tightest one I ever knew."

"She waitin' till you get out?"

"Oh, hell yes. Las' thing I told her was, now honey, don't you do it 'less it's by hand till ol' Leroy gets back. An' you know what she said?"

"What'd she say, Leroy?"

"Says she's gonna use a candle. A church candle, 'cause they're the only ones big as me."

The men laughed. "That girl's gonna have a real sanctimonious hole for you, Leroy," said Quillin. "She got a name?"

Leroy lay contented on his bunk. "Dulcie. Dulcie Moran."

In the dark, Jupiter's eyes moved swiftly to Leroy's

face. He remembered Miss Dulcie, a sweet, pretty little thing who made friends with all the slaves. Leroy lied a lot, he reflected, most likely it was all in his mind. A man who hated niggers wasn't going to take up with a girl who loved them the way Miss Dulcie had, no sir. Well, it was more like she wouldn't take up with *him.*

They were all awake now, stirred up by what Leroy had done, all thinking of women they had had sometime.

"Hey, Jupe," said Leroy. "What was it like when you raped that white woman? Did she give in to you easy?"

"Ah din't rape no white 'oman."

The men jeered. "Aww shit, Jupe!" said Quillin. "It's what you're in here for."

"Jes' de same, Ah din't do it. Ah din't go nowheah neah dat 'oman."

"No bull, now? Honest to God?" said Luke.

"Ah'd sweah it on a stack o' Bibles. De onlies' kin' o' meat Ah goes fo' is black."

"You never said so before," Leroy complained.

"Nobuddy heah nevah ast befo'," Jupiter replied quietly.

"Then huccome you're in?" Luke demanded.

"Black boy ain't got much chanst when a white boy lie 'bout whut he done, an' when de white 'oman's husban' might be gonna fin' out. She got t'blame sumbuddy. De only thing Ah did was spade up de gahden, but Ah was in de wrong spot at de wrong time."

"That ain't fair," Luke protested. "Naow Ah kilt mah wife, but she was a-layin' with the hire-hand. It's plumb silly t'put a fella like me in prison. Ah ain't a-gonna kill nobuddy else." As Luke was weedy, frailly built, and peaceable, his statement was not argued.

Quillin seemed to have more education than the rest; he was able to view events more philosophically. "Now I know I ought to be in here," he said. "I been in before, and when I got out, I did the same thing all over again. I got me a gun and I went and robbed someone. It's like I'm not home till I get back in prison."

Leroy was appalled. "Kee-rist, Quill, spendin' your entire life with shackles rubbin' your ankles? Never seein' a light from supper to breakfast? Fightin' the rats for your half o' the bunk? You musta had some hell of a home."

Quillin said laconically, "This is better."

Jupiter had waited a long time for the conversations to turn in this direction. Now he said, low, "Any you boys evah think 'bout bustin' out?"

"All the time," Leroy whispered back. "You got any ideas?"

"Yeah. Dis yere wall is smack on de prison yahd. Iffen we kin git a shubble, we kin tunnel out undah de yahd."

"What are you gonna do with the dirt, Jupe?" asked Quillin.

"Take it out in ouah pockets. Dribble it out erlong de road."

"You can't dig through stone walls with a shovel, Jupe."

Jupiter reached under the bunk, fumbling for a long time. Finally he passed an object around. "Feel dat," he whispered.

Leroy got it first: a long-bladed knife that Jupiter could have killed him with anytime. He shuddered and passed it to Quillin.

"Not bad," Quillin pronounced. "I don't know what it'll do with mortar, but it's worth a try."

"It'll break," Luke said.

Leroy could feel the old power of command on him. "All right, boys. We're all agreed, we all want to break out?"

"Not me," said Quillin. "I don't want to know anything about what you do. I been in solitary, and if you hate rats and cockroaches you're gonna lose your mind in solitary. And that's just where they'll put you if they catch you trying to escape."

"Lissen, I stay here another six months, my brain'll be cold mush anyhow," Leroy declared. "No matter what happens t'me, it's better'n bein' in here the rest o' my natcheral life. Jupe, you want out?"

"Ah sho' do, white boy."

"Luke?"

"Don't make no difference t'me. Whatever you an' Jupe think."

"Then we're gonna try it," Leroy said. "Who wants t'start diggin'?"

"It's mah knife," Jupiter reminded him.

"Okay, you start."

"Not yet." Quillin's voice was authoritative. "Wait half an hour."

"What in hell *for*?" said Leroy.

"You'll see."

Jupiter touched Leroy on the shoulder. "De gahd, Leroy. He come 'round mo' less any time."

Leroy could have kicked himself for not remembering this basic rule of prison life: you didn't do anything if it was time for the guard to come around. In silence they waited, trying to assume natural-looking positions of sleep in case the guard flashed his lantern into their cell. Once he had been gone for a seemingly sufficient length of time, Jupiter lay under the bunk and began to chip away at the mortar.

Quillin whispered, "Jupe, you're sure makin' a racket."

"Cain't he'p dat," Jupiter replied. "Knife on mortah make noise."

Luke said, "It ain't only the guard you want to look out fo', it's the boys in the next cell. If sumbuddy hears you scratchin', they're a-gonna rat on you. Better cover yourself up an' muffle that noise."

Quillin said, "We need to post a guard, to listen in case they start changin' their routine. We don't want to count on two hours at a time and all of a sudden look up and they're watching outside the cell door."

"You better throw in with us, Quill," Leroy said. "When we get out, if you're asleep in your bunk, they'll put you in the hole for not tellin'."

"It's gonna wind up the same," said Quillin philosophically. "I'll take my chances along with you boys. I'll stand guard."

That first night they were able to work for an hour, and succeeded in breaking the knife blade twice. They had chipped away a heartbreakingly small amount of mortar. In the light of morning Jupiter trampled into the filth on the floor. For weeks they kept at it, lying in the cramped position under the bunk, hacking away with an instrument that grew shorter and duller. But after much frustration, the magic night arrived when two of them were able to draw the stone entirely out.

"Something's wrong," said Quillin. "We should've hit dirt. That's fresh air coming in that hole."

Luke got down on his belly for a look. "Hell yes, it's the yard. We opened up a door right into the yard! Put that stone back fast, boys."

Leroy, standing by the cell door, whispered urgently, "Guards!"

They got the stone back in place, and themselves into their bunks, just before two guards came by, flashing lanterns into every cell, peering long and hard at every occupant. After they had gone, Quillin said, "They know something's up. When it comes daylight, we'll be in for it."

Leroy said urgently, "Le's get out now. Take our chances runnin' through the yard. I been shot at an' missed a hunnerd times before."

"No," said Quillin. "We're staying right here."

Leroy's whisper was indignant. "Who the hell's leader around here, anyhow? I say we're goin'. Pull that rock out, Jupe."

"Leave it there, Jupe," said Quillin. "There's four of us in this, not just one hotheaded country boy who wants a bullet up his ass. Not one of us'd live through it if we go out that hole."

"I'm goin'!"

"Want me t'give you anodder headache, white boy?"

Jupiter asked. "We ah hearin' de man whut know. Now shet up an' lissen."

"We can't use that hole to get out, so we've got to try to fill in around the stone and work out another plan," Quillin said.

"I'll be old an' gray before I get outta this pen."

"Better that than be young and dead and go out in a plain pine box."

The next evening as they came clanking in from labor, six guards plucked them out of line. "You're comin' with us," said one, and shoved the men ahead of him roughly with the bayonet on his rifle.

"Where we goin'?" Leroy asked. "What about supper?"

"You're goin' to the hole," the guard answered. "Supper's bread an' water."

"The hole?" Leroy's voice rose. "How long? What for? What'd *we* do?"

"Six months."

He was put in first, shoved through a narrow barred door, where he literally fell into a dark hole. Picking himself up off the floor, he suddenly felt sharp teeth on his bare chafed ankles. He screamed, flinging his feet up off the floor in a desperate dance to escape the ravenous rats. Above him, he heard the chuckles of the guards as they moved down the hall.

After a long time the rats seemed to have gone away. He no longer heard their little conversational squeaks. Soon his eyes became accustomed to the dark. There were none of the comforts of his former cell here, only a plank platform a few feet off the floor, and as he ran his hand over it, he realized it was covered with rat dirt. If they thought he was going to sleep in that filth—

He would have to. The only other place was the floor. But that night he did not sleep, nor the next day, nor the following night. He was busy killing rats. Or trying to kill rats and only maiming them, and then hopping around on one shod foot chasing the injured rat to kill him with the heel of his shoe. He scarcely had time to eat the two meals a day that were lowered to him at the end of a rope. Mostly, it was rank-smelling bread and thin, cold gruel, or sulfur-tasting water. He would stuff the bread into his shirt, looking wildly around to see if a rat was going to try to get inside the shirt after the bread. He had to keep one bare foot swinging all the time, for fear the rats would try to bite his toes.

By the end of a week he had a stack of rats in one corner, nearly a hundred of them, starting to decay and stink up the place, as if it hadn't stunk already. These attracted roaches by the thousands, roaches and other unmentionable bugs crawling on the floor and the walls, bugs he squashed whenever he put foot down.

And he was itching, bitten all over his body by the fleas that had deserted the rats and now came to crawl on him in swarms. There was no way to combat this new peril, except to try not to scratch, and that was impossible. Some of the flea bites became infected, and he spread the infection to other raw places on his body.

There was no water for washing or bathing. Some days there was hardly enough for drinking, let alone a few drops left to dribble on the worst bitten areas. As the months dragged by, he suffered from constipation, followed by a bloody flux. His gums became so sore that even running his tongue around his dry mouth caused him pain. A few of his teeth became so loose that he was afraid they would fall out. The old neck injury that Jupiter had given him gave him fresh pain; and every long-forgotten injury from hunting, playing, or fighting resurfaced to nag him night and day with arthritic pangs.

He could not tell a rainy day from a sunny one, for his hole remained constantly bone-chillingly damp. He could tell night from day only by the merest gradation from one shade of black to the next.

Leroy, who had always been surrounded by people, usually of his own choosing, and who did not care for his own company, was now totally, completely, abys-

mally alone. The guard who lowered his inadequate
meals to him never spoke, not even to tell him to shut
up. After a few months, Leroy gave up trying to speak
to him. And after that he was afraid to break his own
silence.

Somebody had to be to blame for this. Leroy's elastic
conscience had long ago forgotten that he had played
any part in the deaths of Ruel Jordan or James and
Patricia Moran. He did not even remember being on
the scene except as spectator, and that memory was
being erased by the justification that such accidental
deaths were no longer anything to do with him.

It was Dulcie to blame. Dulcie, and Adam Tremain,
and Lyman. If Dulcie had married him, he would never
have felt any emptiness after the War, never have felt
any need to fill that emptiness with the Klan, never
gotten into trouble in the first place. If Dulcie had been
his, he would have been contented and happy. If he'd
had Dulcie—but that thought, here in the black, vermin-
infested hole, had no power to arouse his lust. When
he thought of Dulcie now, it was only with hatred.

Hatred like he held for Adam Tremain. Tremain
was a braggart, a show-off, a thief and a liar and a
nigger lover. A man who did not deserve to live in his
fine house and wear his fancy clothes and sleep with a
beautiful woman.

Hatred like he held for Lyman Matthews. Completely
forgotten were Lyman's years of unquestioning obedience, his patience and dog-like devotion, his cowardice
transmogrified into bravery because Leroy had told
him to perform a particular deed. Those years had been
washed away by the deluge of Lyman's failure. With
tears coming from his eyes Lyman had sworn a mighty
oath to rescue Leroy from prison. And he had not done
it. He had sworn an oath, and he had broken that oath.
Things like that could make a man hate his best friend,
hate him enough to want to kill him.

But he didn't hate anybody the way he hated Dulcie.
When he got out—and in the very depths of his dis-

integrating soul he knew he *would* get out—he would get even with all of them.

He would torture them, one at a time.

Then he would kill them, one at a time.

When he got out.

CHAPTER THIRTY-NINE

1874 was a year of hard work and progress for Adam and Dulcie. Beau had become quite a little man and was proud that he was now able to accompany his father and give his "advice" on what should be done with the cane. Adam looked upon his son with amused pride and often found himself amazed at how much Beau actually had learned. For the first time Adam Tremain began to look to the years beyond his own life, and it gave him a feeling of permanency he had never before thought about, of Holly Hill going on into Beau's generation, and then to his grandchildren.

It gave him a sense of purpose and renewed his desire to be an active part of the development of postwar New Orleans. It also gave Tom and Ben ample fodder with which to tease him. Tom took every available opportunity without the slightest hesitation.

"Geddes, my friend," Tom said, grinning at his companion, "I deliver to you a man ripe for the political picking. He has begun to look to the ages—sees his son and his son's sons walking in his footsteps through time. Now, has there ever been a time when a man is more likely to fall for any scheme handed to him? Recruit him, Geddes, recruit him before that rosy glow leaves his vision."

Geddes laughed. "Tom, you are going to ruin my whole approach. Adam, ignore our friend. I sincerely wish to convince you that your expertise and influence are desperately needed in Louisiana politics."

"I don't doubt your sincerity for a moment, Geddes, and I am listening to you. I've heard Tom and his ill-formed jokes for years." Adam laughed with them and jabbed Tom lightly in the arm. "You can buy the next round, and the next."

They were in their favorite dining room of the St. Charles. Tom waved at a waiter and without missing a word of conversation reordered for all of them.

Adam was saying, "I have been particularly concerned about the rise of the White League. It smacks too closely of the Ku Klux Klan. I realize that it is parliamentary and not secret as the Klan is, but the mentality and the sense of purpose and cause are similar —too similar for my comfort."

"I share your concern," Geddes said. Tom had told him of Adam's tragedy at the hands of the Klan. "I am sure your fears and wariness must surpass my own. I must admit that I, like so many others, paid little attention to the rise of a new group in the beginning. It wasn't until the occurrence at Coushatta in Red River Parish that I realized how fearful a group this could be."

Adam nodded, then sat silent for a moment sipping at his drink. He said, "The terrifying aspect is that events such as that at Coushatta can be caused by rumor alone—that people are so ready to turn to violence that they will take any excuse, founded or otherwise."

"And that the most virulent of all rumors is that of black men planning to attack whites," Geddes said.

That had been the rumor at Coushatta—that a group of blacks was planning to attack some white Democrats.

"Yes," Adam said. A call for help was sent out and men—many of them White Leaguers—came from as far as Texas. They put the white Republican officeholders under protective custody and had their word to resign if they were given a guarantee of safe passage from Louisiana. As they were on their way to Texas under this protective custody, a mob met them and shot the five officeholders and a friend who had accompanied them.

"Jee-zus!" Tom sighed.

"That won't be the end of it," Geddes added. "Everyone I know says something is afoot. It wouldn't surprise me if we get a taste of this White League politicking right here in New Orleans. There has been a lot of activity among the White Leaguers in the city. They're buying arms from the North and bringing them in here by the shipload."

"Then there will be trouble," said Adam, thinking of the militia loyal to the McEnery government, and those loyal to Kellogg's. With the support of the federal government, the Kellogg regime was able to hold office, but Louisiana still had two legislatures and two governors, with some of the people following John McEnery's orders and the others following William Kellogg's.

"Oh, yes," Geddes agreed, "bad trouble. The problem for men like us is to know which side to be on. No decent man can call himself Republican or Democrat these days. Each party has its good men, yet each is grasping and using the hatreds of the War and of color and of politics to get the prize plum—power, control, wealth. What are you, Adam?"

He looked up at Geddes, his eyes clouded and sad. "I don't know. When my wife and I first lived in Georgia, I was a Radical Republican. There were a few devoted men who wanted the two races to work together. Then the only men I knew who were working for that were Radicals. I joined them despite some being carpetbaggers and Scalawags. But now—here— I don't know. Are there any honest politics or politicians left?"

The men talked on until the small hours of the morning, solving nothing, but giving to each other the preparedness of the wary. Too tired to make their ways home, they all stayed at the St. Charles, each going to his own room, each occupied with his own thoughts.

Adam was filled with ghastly memories of the Klan and their kind of violence. He thought of Dulcie and of his children, and of New Orleans and their White League, which was different, yet too similar. He had hoped to put all that warlike hatred behind him, but here it was again, rising up, threatening him and all

that he loved. A lesson he had learned repeatedly in
his life, he realized again: Evil can never be ignored.
When one wants a certain tranquility in one's life, there
must be a continuous vigilance to maintain and guard
it. Before tonight he had not made up his mind whether
he would remain a sugar planter and stay away from
politics, or if he would once more involve himself in
something distasteful, and too often futile or tragic.
But he knew now he couldn't sit back and let this time
that was his pass by. He would be involved. As he had
told Geddes, he no longer knew if he was a Republican
or a Democrat, but he'd find out and he would fight,
as he always had, for himself, his family, and his South.

Tom lay on his bed fully clothed. He thought of
Edmund Revanche. He hadn't mentioned Edmund to
Adam this evening; in fact, he had not done so since
Adam had returned to New Orleans. But saving Adam
from pain didn't prevent Tom from thinking of Edmund, dwelling on him, making him his obsession. For
so long he had followed Edmund Revanche from city
to city with only one thought in mind: to kill him as
soon as he could lay hands on him. But he no longer
felt that urgency. He had become more deliberate as
the years had passed. He'd kill him, but not just anytime. No, he knew now he'd wait for the right time,
the time he'd choose, the time when he sensed Edmund
would most want to live. It was funny with men like
Edmund, Tom had learned. In a way they were dead,
and only came to life when their peculiarly hideous victories were in hand. That was when Tom wanted Edmund—in the elation of one of his perverted victories.

Geddes Ingraham thought of the trouble that was
coming, and he wondered where it would strike and
whom. He thought of the black men who had died,
and whose deaths would never be avenged or even
recognized as crimes because no jury in Louisiana was
going to convict a white man of killing a black.

The following day Adam met Ben West for lunch,
and the two of them returned to the Tremain-West

shipping office. "Do you ever wish you were still captaining the ships, Adam?" Ben asked, his eyes on the broad expanse of the Mississippi.

"It was a simpler life," Adam said.

"But do you miss it?"

Adam didn't answer for a long time, then he said softly, "Yes, I do."

Ben nodded, then looked down. "I guess I just wanted to hear you say it. I feel the same way. I wonder if there will ever be a time again when we'll go back to the sea?"

Adam left the shipping office with the same feeling he had had the night before, after having talked to Tom and Geddes about politics. Much had to be sacrificed in order to have a place worth living in. He didn't often think of his ship or the sea, because when he did, he longed for it, missed it, missed the sense of command and of peace he had on the bridge of his ship, a feeling that he could not seem to grasp fully on land. He walked along the waterfront, pacing back and forth, tracing and retracing his steps past one warehouse, onto another wharf, and back again. He could not shake the discontent that had settled on him. Suddenly he felt lonely and in need of conversation that would take him no deeper into waters such as these. He turned abruptly and walked hastily toward Les Belles.

He did not permit the butler to announce him, but asked if Angela was alone. Finding that she was, he went directly to her room and opened the door.

Startled, and annoyed at the rude intrusion, she whirled from her vanity, the hairbrush in her hand poised as though she might throw it. "How dare you enter here withou—Adam! Adam, what are you doing here?" She got up from the seat and stood staring at him.

"I'm sorry—I was terribly rude, Angela, I didn't think . . . I just wanted . . . needed to talk to someone, and came right here."

She cocked her head to one side, wondering at the

uncertainty in him, something she couldn't remember having seen since he had come home to recuperate after he had lost Dulcie on Andros. She sensed his vulnerability, and her own power. Her brow furrowed in anger, anger with herself, for this was one night she could not take advantage of the opportunity he was presenting to her.

"I've made you angry," he said, and walked over to her, touching her brow, smoothing out the frown line. "And you should be. What I did was unforgivable."

"Oh, no, it isn't that—I am angry for—for circumstances." She sighed. "This is the one evening I cannot spend with you. I'm afraid I have an appointment, and unfortunately I must keep it."

He looked away from her. "Oh, I see. I should have thought of that—I seem to be walking on two left feet tonight."

Angela laughed softly and stroked the side of his cheek. "No, Adam, not *that* kind of business. This is quite different." She forced him to look at her. "Are you jealous, Adam—do you so dislike thinking of me with clients?"

He hesitated, then said, "Yes, I do dislike thinking of you with clients—you're—you're too much of a person for that."

"Well, rest your mind, I am not going to be servicing a client. This is merely a meeting, but one I must attend. I am truly sorry, more so than you realize, and worse yet, I must ask you to leave, as I am already late."

Angela stood at the balcony and watched as Adam walked downstairs, through the salon, and out her front door. Then she walked with quick angry steps to the small office at the other end of the hall. She opened the door and looked coldly at the slender, elegant man seated with legs crossed in the leather chair behind her desk.

"Don't you have the courtesy to rise when a lady enters a room, Mr. Revanche?" she snapped.

"But of course, when a lady enters, but certainly not when one of my own pickaninnies comes in."

Angela glared at him. "Get out of my chair."

Revanche laughed softly, deliberately. He looked at her through narrowed eyes. "I wonder what it is that has the notoriously frigid Miss Angela Pierson so heated. If I paid you enough would you sell me that piece of information, as well as the other delectable tidbits you collect from your clients?"

"If you continue to play your asinine games with me, I'll sell you nothing. Now, shall we talk business, or shall you indulge your perverse sense of humor, *Massa*?"

Revanche laughed, this time more heartily. In a way, he enjoyed his encounters with Angela. She loathed him as much as he loathed her, but between them was a grudging respect. When she sold him information, it was always accurate, and usually worth the exorbitant prices she charged him. "Have you found out about the next arms shipment?" he asked.

"I have."

He pulled out his wallet, fingering the crisp bills resting inside it. He looked up at her expectantly when she didn't speak. "Well?"

"Well," she mocked, "I don't like you, Mr. Revanche, nor do I like being called your pickaninny. Tonight, if you want information, you'll pay once for the information, and once again for the insult."

His eyebrows went up. "Double the price! And just because I told you the truth? My, my, I so rarely use the truth, isn't it ironic that it should cost me so much." He said nothing for a while, then smiled at her again. "All right, I'll pay you double, but recall that having paid, I am free to remind you that I own you."

Angela snorted. "You own no one, Mr. Revanche. You live with illusions and delusions, and you come here to me—your *pickaninny*—to buy information of other men's illusions and delusions. Put the money on the desk, get out of my chair, then I'll tell you as much as you have paid for."

Revanche did as he was asked. He had pushed her as far as he dared, and still wondered what it was that had her so agitated. He made a note to himself to find out what had happened, or whom she had seen, before she came to him.

Angela waited until he stood by the door. "A shipment will arrive on the *Mississippi* this coming week. It is said to be large. Rumor also has it that General Longstreet is going to make a stand and put an end to the White League's purchase of arms. The Metropolitan Police may also be involved."

Revanche smiled, then reached out, cupping Angela's chin in his hand. "You have outdone yourself, my dear."

Angela slapped his hand away. "You want to touch me, you pay more! Now get out!"

Revanche left her office and sauntered down the steps to the main salon. His eyes roved about the room until he found Angela's butler; then he had the man brought to him. Slipping a twenty-dollar bill into the man's vest pocket, he asked who Angela had seen earlier that evening. Having received his answer, he handed the man an extra bill and jauntily left Les Belles.

Adam, Ben, and Tom were at the Tremain-West shipping offices the September morning the *Mississippi* came into port. As with most ships and shipping in the area, the men had a good knowledge of who was shipping what. They also knew that the Kellogg government wanted a stop made to the shipments of arms. The three of them stepped outside and watched from the front of the shipping offices.

The streets were lined with spectators, and every window in the area held curious occupants looking down on the scene in the streets. The whole city was expecting a confrontation. With two governments—one recognized by a segment of Louisianians, the other recognized by the United States Government—the political fighting was a three-ring circus, usually with a lot

of spectacular bluster, but which occasionally exploded
with blood and battle. No one was quite sure what today was to bring, but it was sure to be exciting.

General James Augustus Longstreet, commander of
the state forces, had the Metropolitan Police and some
black militiamen barring the way to the waterfront. It
was meant as a message of strength informing the White
League that no more arms were to be brought in from
the North and that the *Mississippi* was not to be unloaded of its cargo. It took the White League almost no
time at all to accept the challenge.

The river became thick with boats filled with more
of the curious, anxious to be safe, yet see what was
taking place. Almost immediately it became clear that
this was not to be a small confrontation, a mere show.
The White League had been buying arms for some
time, and it now hauled out onto the streets a dazzling
display of determination and power. The Battle of
Liberty Place, New Orleans, began with masses of
armed men formed into opposing armies. Artillery was
brought down into the square.

Adam, Ben, and Tom looked on with sorrow and
could not help wincing and drawing back at the rapid-
fire sound of the Gatling guns. The battle raged throughout the day, and they watched. By evening they had
seen all they could bear. Men now lay in the streets,
some dead, some uttering the peculiar cries of the
wounded and the dying. The air was filled with the
sharp, acrid sting of battle smoke.

The White Leaguers had the best of the fight, having
the most men and being better armed. In Adam's mind
he saw the Klan all over again. As he watched he began
to understand what had hurt and confused Dulcie so
thoroughly—how one neighbor could deliberately mas-
sacre another. These men in the streets were neighbors.
Likely there were some of the same family fighting on
opposite sides, but no one in those streets was thinking
of family or love or of anything but winning, of gaining
power.

The men tried to leave the offices as darkness approached, but found themselves prisoners of the shipping office unless they chose to fight their way through the waterfront. None of them did, but neither did any of them want to see more of the battle, or hear more of the dying. They closed up the office as though preparing for hurricane, the windows shuttered, the doors barred.

The conversation was short, and avoided the subject of the Battle of Liberty Place. The White League had won without question, and rumors were now circulating that federal troops would be arriving in the morning to restore order. Adam knew that the federal troops would accomplish that without effort, but the important point had already been made. A Radical Republican administration could not survive anywhere in Louisiana unless the United States Army was on hand to guard and protect it. The federal government might be able to put in office whomever it wanted, but they could not make the Louisianians live by their rule peacefully.

Adam spent a sleepless night sitting in his chair behind his desk. Tom and Ben slept on cots in Ben's office, but Adam's mind would not allow him rest. He thought of his own role in New Orleans and questioned without finding satisfaction what he could do. The only thing clear in his mind was that New Orleans—all of the South—had to have relief from the pressures and the abuses of Reconstruction, whether it be the Radical Reconstruction or the Democratic Reconstruction. The country could not stand much more of this.

It was anybody's guess how it would end. The only thing that had become clear was that battles such as this one would go on, and organizations such as the White League, the Knights of the White Camellia, and the Ku Klux Klan would keep on rising. They could be silenced for a time, officially ended; but time and time again they would surface, more hostile, more righteous, more virulent than ever before.

CHAPTER FORTY

It was a bright summer day when Leroy Biggs was released from solitary confinement. He kept his eyes shut against the light while he was being fumigated. Not a sound escaped from his mouth while the prison doctor examined him, treating his sores and pulling the teeth he had tried so desperately to keep fastened in his gums. He had lived so long with dark and fear and silence that it had become a part of him. Even the feeling of clean clothing and new shoes robbed him of the minor security he had had.

He was placed in a cell with only one cellmate, as pale and emaciated and silent as himself. When they were herded down the corridor to supper, Leroy was cowed by the light and the men and the clatter of tin plates. The food the men wolfed down looked discolored and fuzzy to him. He ate nothing but the familiar bread and drank a liquid he recognized as lukewarm coffee. Shrinking from the men crowded so close around him, he sat with his thin hands on his thighs, staring down at his plate.

The man next to him elbowed him. "Hey, boy, if you ain't eatin' t'night, I'll take it." He reached for Leroy's plate.

Leroy's old instincts struggled to the surface and he lifted his hand for combat. Then, catching his breath, he put his hand in his lap.

"Jes' got outta the hole, din't ya?" his companion asked.

Leroy did not answer. He did not want to be noticed, and silence was the only way to avoid notice.

In this way he spent several more weeks. Too weak

to work, he was left in his cell. Gradually his eyes became accustomed to light. His sores were a long time healing. The doctor saw him once in a while, and applied fresh salve and dressings; but malnutrition and living in filth had lowered Leroy's resistance to infections. He was visited by a new plague—boils. They came in ones and twos, they came in clusters, they flared up and died down again. They were at his waist, on his neck, under his toes. They began as a small red spot uncomfortable to the touch that rapidly grew large and painful and swollen purple. After endless days they drew to a head, and he learned to lance them with a splinter from his bunk.

In spite of his afflictions, he was starting to get well again. He began to eat, and sometimes to venture a look around him. By autumn he was speaking occasionally, if approached first. His fears of dark and solitude would never leave him. Always at the back of his mind would be the spectre of being alone in blackness.

By September, 1874, he had been put back at light labor, making chairs in the prison workshop. At first he resented his duties and was sullen and watchful of his fellow prisoners, fearing that they plotted him harm. But as the months went by, and he continued to regain strength, he began to want to rejoin the living. He especially liked the feeling that after rotting in the hole he was still capable of accomplishing something.

But he would never be his old self again. He would never be as strong physically or mentally. Prison had done to him what the War and years of semi-starvation could never have done. Prison broke him. He lost initiative. There were men here who needed a leader, but those he knew had nowhere to go. Breaking out again made Leroy think of the rats and vermin and darkness. His daring exploits of yesteryear seemed to have been performed by someone else, not Leroy Biggs.

In the back of his bitter mind was still the image of

revenge on Dulcie and Adam and Lyman, but even that seemed far away, the product of some other imagination given to him to carry as burden.

He had been in prison for three years when Wolf came again to visit him. Wolf was gaunt and hollow, but the fires of contempt still burned in his jaundiced eyes. "Biggs!" he said, as before from the darkness outside Leroy's cell. "Biggs, c'mere."

Leroy started violently, his heart hammering. He had not heard Wolf's approach, was not aware of anyone standing there staring through the bars at him. He hated noises from out of the darkness.

"Wha—what d'you want?" He was ashamed of his stammering.

"C'mere. Want t'talk a minnit. Ain't you got the time now, boy?"

Reluctantly Leroy came and held the bars that separated him from the prison guard. "I was—uh—sleepin'," he lied.

"I brang you a New Year's present." Wolf handed him a package.

Leroy feared to touch it. He did not know why Wolf would bring him anything but bad news.

"Well, take it, dummy, lessen you don't like ham fum yer own hogs." The package was heavy enough to hold ham, a good big chunk of it.

"Why are you givin' me this, Wolf?"

"You got a friend on the outside, ain't you?"

"After three years, the only friend I got is me."

"This boy says t'give you the package an' there might be mo'."

Leroy's mind was refusing to work. "Who?" he asked suspiciously.

"Sure you don't remember Lyman?" Wolf grinned, pleased with the way he had built up suspense before he gave away the secret.

"Where'd you see him?"

"Here. He come to the prison yestiddy."

Leroy discovered that he was holding the package to him with both hands. He looked at it and then at Wolf. "What did he say?"

"A few things," Wolf admitted. "Mostly he ast how you're doin'."

Leroy shook the bars in agitation. "What else? How did he look?"

"Prosperous, I'd say. Well fed an' prosperous."

"On my money," Leroy muttered to himself. "Why in the hell ain't he been here to see *me*? Where in God's name's he been since eighteen seventy-two? Three fuckin' years an' he acts like it was yesterday!"

"No use a'yellin' at me, boy, I ain't bin the one that screwed you. Reckon if he was missin' you he'da come before."

"Didn't he say *anythin'*? Give you a message?"

"He gimme 'bout a dozen messages, Biggs, but he aint gimme the cash t'carry 'em to you. Get me, boy?"

Leroy had buttoned the package inside his shirt, where it lay cold against his skin. "I ain't got a red cent, Wolf. Every damn penny I have is on the outside, prob'ly settin' on Lyman Matthews's back. Is he comin' back, or what?"

"Get some money," Wolf said, and slouched off down the corridor.

Leroy tore open his package. A feast lay inside: tender pink ham, pecan meats, dried peaches, cookies, and pralines, that sweet Southern candy that had once been Leroy's favorite. He sat staring, a lump in his throat. Everything he liked. Everything he hadn't seen for over three years. Echoes of home and his sassy old mother and of boyhood delights long since vanished. And Lyman had sent them, like a lover wooing his beloved with sweetmeats and flowers. Lyman . . .

He bit into the ham, sweet and juicy, and followed it with some pecans and a praline. He sat on his bunk chewing slowly, breaking into a smile every now and then. Old Lyman. Good old Lyman.

Between two cookies pressed together he found the note and read it eagerly:

> Dere Leroy, I bin tryin to get in to see you but they said you was in sollatary. I aint never forgot my promise. But I bin bizzy runnin to farms an tryin to get ahead a little. I got a plan for us wich will take sum time to work out. So hold on an dont give up I am cumming to keep my sworn othe. Your friend Lyman Matthews

The note roused more questions than it answered. Why hadn't Lyman been here since he got out of solitary? What two farms? What kind of plan? Did he mean to get him out? And who fixed the food? Had Lyman got married while his friend rotted in prison? And who had he married? If he's the one that killed Tremain and married Dulcie, I'll murder him, thought Leroy savagely. Takin' my girl—

Cool good sense finally took over. Lyman did not have the interest in Dulcie Moran that he had. Lyman's taste ran to poor white girls, most of them his cousins. Had one of them fixed this elegant repast? How would she know what he liked? Whoever had prepared the food, Lyman had had his say in the doing.

And maybe from now on Lyman would get more packages to him, maybe something with a file in it, or dynamite. And maybe a note, too, slipped into the package, notes that would outline the great plan Lyman had cooked up for the two of them. He resigned himself to thinking in terms of months and not in days.

Then one cold November 1875 morning a guard he did not know came to the wood shop and marched him out, down the long corridors to the warden's office. "Tell me what I did," Leroy pleaded. "What'd I do? I didn't try to break out or nothin'—" His heart was in his mouth, his face was sweating at the thought of more months of solitary.

\ Mutely the guard prodded him into the outer office of the prison warden. Other men stood waiting. He did not recognize them—except the big black. Jupiter! Their eyes caught and quickly slid away, but on Jupiter's face he did not see fear. Maybe Jupiter wasn't going to the hole again. Maybe it was only him.

Then the warden's door opened, and a bearded, well-dressed man came out. Casually he looked over the prisoners. "These men'll do," he told the warden. "My wagon's outside." Quickly the guard manacled each man to the next.

Leroy's head throbbed. Where were they being taken? Lyman wouldn't be able to find him—he'd be gone. Dry-mouthed, he asked the prisoner on his left, "Where we goin'?"

"Labor crew."

"No talking," said the guard.

Silently they were herded out through the gates and loaded into a wagon. Leroy sat stunned. He felt like crying. He knew what a chain gang was like—long hours and as little food as would keep a man alive. It meant good-bye to Lyman's little treasures—

Leroy's head snapped up. His eyes widened and bored into the back of the bearded man. He had scarcely looked at him before. He was a little heavy for Lyman. Lyman could have gained weight; he could have bought those fancy clothes and grown that dark beard. He could have bought the wagon too. Leroy studied the man, waiting until he turned around or moved in some way like Lyman. Or unlike Lyman.

They stopped beside a stream for a frugal lunch. The guard, sitting apart with his rifle across his knees, allowed them to talk. Leroy said, "Can we ask 'bout this place where we're headed?"

The bearded man looked up, and Lyman's eyes met Leroy's across space and time. In Lyman's there was a look that transcended triumph, a look that shouted, *I figgered it all out by myself.* A look that sang of old loyalties and of adversities shared and overcome.

Lyman said, "We're goin' t'Sweetbrier. I own two farms, an' you men'll be helpin' me farm 'em. An' I need somebody t'work in the house, t'fix up the furniture some. Things ain't in such good shape."

Leroy held up his hand. "I can do it, if you got tools."

The guard said, "He's got to work where I can see him. I'm the one responsible for these men—"

Lyman interrupted. "We'll work all that out when we get there."

They arrived at Sweetbrier a few days later. As Lyman had promised, their first meal was good, and plentiful, brought out by the fat arms of Diza, the black cook. Leroy wondered if he would ever eat in the dining room of the house. Would he ever get the chance to talk alone with Lyman?

His chance did not come for several days. He had begun to wonder if Lyman was deliberately putting him off. Lyman seemed to be mighty damn self-important, always running here and there and stopping only to check with Coker, the guard, as to how well the men were doing their work. Leroy had no chance to talk with him. Besides, he did not want the others to know of their prior friendship. While he waited, he was careful not to start ruckuses or to offend Coker.

Lyman finally ordered Leroy to his study one evening after supper. Once the door was shut behind them, Lyman gripped him by the hand. "Leroy," he said with tears in his eyes, "I was afraid we'd never see this day."

"Me too, Lyman, Kee-rist! You got any idea how long a day is in solitary?"

"That was your own dumbness, not mine," Lyman said, withdrawing a little. "If you'da had sense enough t'wait on me, 'steada bustin' out—"

"How the hell long's a man s'posed t'sit around waitin' with no word? Why didn't you send me a letter?"

"I *did*, Leroy. Every month."

"Like shit you did. I never got a one."

"Well, I sent 'em. An' I got you out, didn't I?"

"Yeah, but how 'bout when we got t'go back?" Sullenly Leroy poured himself the first drink he'd had for four years. He was trying to figure out what was wrong with this scene. He and Lyman should be happy to be back together again, after all this time; instead they were bickering like ninnies.

The bottom rail is on the top, and we're gonna keep it there.

Now why in thunderation did he think of that fool thing, the thing those niggers chanted at him and Lyman when they were running them out of their shack city?

"Ain't you drinkin', Lyman?"

"I had t'cut down, Leroy. It was interferin' with my work."

Leroy snorted. "Never did before."

"Well, I had t'take charge o' things if I was gonna get you out, an' when I was drunk I wasn't in no shape t'do nothin'. Then I heard about this here Sweetbrier, an' I scraped up enough cash t'buy it for taxes. And I'm runnin' the farm next t'this'n. I'm doin' all right, Leroy. In fact, I'm pretty proud o' myself."

"And what in the hell were you doin' 'bout *my* plantation while you're foolin' around with this stuff? Is that where you got the cash?"

Lyman burst out, "Leroy, I don't unnerstand you a-tall any more. I thought you'd be *happy* t'be out o' prison. I thought you'd be *glad* we can be friends again. What you got to yell about?"

"Well, I don't know, but things don't seem right someway. An' where's my plantation?"

"Right where it's always been, back o' Saunderses old place. You didn't think Tremain was gonna let me save it fo' you. Leroy, the minnit you went to the pen, somebody was buyin' it for taxes. An' Tremain didn't leave fo' New Orleans 'til he was sure it wasn't me that got it. There wasn't no way in God's world I coulda saved it for you then."

"But you saved your own, an' bought this'n."

Lyman scratched his head; his face was wrinkled in concentration. "Your place went up for back taxes, an' the Freedmen's Bureau took mine right back again, so I didn't have no place to go. Billy Bob took me in, but that there Birdie hates my guts. She didn't want me in that house. Hadn't been for Billy I don't know what I'da did. Him an' me robbed a house, an' my split was enuf t'buy this place."

"Why wasn't the Klan helpin'? They swore t'help a brother."

"The Klan's gone, Leroy."

The whisky was taking hold of Leroy; his stomach glowed with warmth, and his head had a pleasant, faint buzz. He smiled. "Well, I'm back now. We'll start the Klan up again. Lyman, I'm gonna take over this county. Run it like it oughta be run."

Lyman rubbed his beard. "Uh, Leroy, you forgot one thing."

"Like what? You want t'be leader? I didn't see you doin' it while I was away."

"You can't do nothin'. You're still a prisoner."

"Christ, Lyman, what the hell difference does that make? You can get me away from that gang any time y'want to. We can go on night rides together—lissen, Lyman, we'll rob *another* house, or maybe a store this time—and I'll get enough t'buy my plantation back. You can help me run it, see, and we'll make money hand over fist, like you're doin' here. Don't that sound fine? We'll be back in business again!"

Lyman was just staring at him, his face sad.

"What's wrong? Somethin' I said don't set right with you? Maybe you've got a little bit too fine for old friends while I been gone! Maybe you got a *better* friend!"

"C'mon now, Leroy, you know that ain't so. No-body's ever been a better friend t'me than you. I told you that before."

Leroy stared at him dubiously.

"It's true. We been friends since we was boys an' nothin's gonna change that for me. But you ain't in no position t'start up the Klan again, or t'go night ridin' or anything like we used t'do. In fact, I'm s'prised that guard ain't come in by now an' said you got t'go out t'the shack."

Leroy leaned forward. "You won't let him do that, Lyman, will you, ol' buddy? Don't let him take me out there—I want t'sleep here in the house—with you! Now you tell him that, hear? Tell him I don't hafta go back out there an' stay!"

Lyman drew his shoulders up and spread his hands helplessly. "I ain't in charge, don't you know that? I tell the guard what work you do, but—"

Leroy rose, fire in his eye. "You do what I say, or I'm gonna choke the livin' lights—"

Suddenly there was a foot in his stomach, shoving him, and he flew backwards across the study, to land sprawled on the floor. He scrambled up, to find Lyman out the door, shouting, "Coker! Guard! Guard!"

In seconds he was a prisoner again, his hands manacled, struggling to free himself, shouting obscenities at a white-faced Lyman as he was being strong-armed down the path to the convicts' shack. "You'll be sorry!" he yelled. "I'll make you sorry for takin' over—"

Lyman, watching his friend being taken away, was slowly shaking his head. Maybe it wasn't goin' t'be so easy, havin' Leroy around again. Seemed like he was touchier than he used to be. Still thinking, Lyman poured himself a small amount of whisky and added water to it. Mebbe it was the whisky that done it. That was it, Leroy had to get his head for booze back, then he'd be all right again. After the way he took on, though, that guard wouldn't let him go for some long time. Well, he had figured it all out how to get Leroy here, he sho' oughta be able to figure out how to keep him.

* * *

In the shack, Leroy sat holding his head with his manacled hands. His left leg was shackled to the iron bedstead. If there was one thing he purely hated, it was being tied up so he couldn't move anywhere. At least on a chain gang, you could swing a pick.

After a long time Coker went outside to relieve himself. Jupiter whispered, "Whut happen, white boy? You git in a tussle wid Mistah Lyman?"

"Hell no, he ain't no fighter," Leroy declared.

"What he want wid you?"

"Wants me t'fix some furniture. I told him I can't work 'thout the proper tools. He's goin' t'have me back in when he gets 'em."

"Meanwhiles, you choppin' crops like de res' of us."

Leroy lifted his head and glared at Jupiter. "What're you gettin' at, you black bastard?"

Jupiter smiled beatifically. "You knows, an' Ah knows, an' it ain't nobuddy else's beeswax." He leaned over and whispered. "You was asshole buddies befo' you got sen' up. Ah ain't tellin', but Ah ain't fo'gittin' needah. An' wheah you goes, Ah goes. Git me, Whitey?"

Leroy tried bluffing. "Go ahead an' blab t'the whole world, see if I care."

"When de time come, Ah will." Jupiter laid back on his bunk, hands behind his head, a little smile on his lips. He wanted out of doing field work; his hands were more skilled than that. And he could see that if they stayed here long enough, the guard who had been sent along with them would be getting careless, not watching his prisoners so closely. When that time came, he, Jupiter, would make his escape.

He would go West, he thought; from what he'd heard it would be possible for a man to lose himself among the others bound for the Pacific Coast. He might work his way on a riverboat, take on any job he had to till he got as far as St. Louis, wherever that was. It was the place he'd been told made the dividing line between civilization and the wilds. Once he got there, he'd look around a while. A Georgia boy ought to be safe on the edge of the wilderness. He might even find his brother Apollo.

That was what he'd do. He'd keep leaning on ol' Leroy, to make sure he got to do work inside that house too. It meant he'd have to keep his temper, for convicts lost their privileges if they talked back to Coker, or hit somebody who had it coming. Jupiter dearly loved a fight, especially one with Leroy, who made him a nearly even match. But for now he'd just fasten his mind on getting loose when Leroy did.

Several weeks passed before Lyman was able to bribe the guard sufficiently to let Leroy begin work on the household furniture. Lyman had objected strenuously to Leroy's insistence on having Jupiter in the house. "What the hell d'you need that big buck for, Leroy? There ain't hardly enuf work for one person, say nothin' 'bout havin' a helper. You an' him got somethin' goin'?"

Leroy drew back his fist. "Y'wanta say that again, Lyman?"

"Aw, Leroy, don't always get mad. I take it back, c'mon now."

"I told you, Jupe's gonna tell the guard we're friends if I don't get him in here. And I'll get sent back to the penitentiary."

"Well, I can't hardly give that t'Coker for a excuse, Leroy."

"An' if Coker finds out, he's gonna want a lot more bribe money. 'Course you can afford it—"

"I can't, that's the whole trouble. You oughta know I don't see any cash money only 'bout once a year. Barter don't buy Coker."

"Well, y'must have somethin' he wants. Whisky, tobacco—girls! Women! Coker'd go for that!"

Lyman sighed. "I'll be a son of a bitch, Leroy, if you don't get me in more damn trouble. The only girls'd have Coker would be Caleb Wells's girls, an' they're clappy. That ain't gonna do."

"Well, jes' ask Coker anyway. He might let Jupe go."

"Leroy, that big nigger gives me the fantods. If he's in the house he's goin' t'know everything I'm doin'. And he'll steal me blind."

"Naw, Lyman, he ain't in for stealin'. He's in for rapin' a white woman. The only one in danger'd be Diza, an' she looks like she could use a piece. Hey! Mebbe you could get her an' Coker together—"

"Jes' let me figger it out, willya?" Lyman turned his back and walked away.

Leroy took his hammer and pounded on a chair leg until it was smashed to splinters.

Within a few days, Jupiter came to the house. He proved surprisingly able, and found many additional jobs to spin out their time. Still, Leroy hated having him around. He continually made gibes about Jupiter's abilities, his future, and his ancestry. Jupiter remained sunny and sweet-dispositioned.

Finally Leroy exploded. "What in the hell's the matter with you, Jupe? You yella? Seems t'me a man'd take offense. If he *was* a man, 'steada a yella-livered black-assed ape that his mama—"

Jupiter's hands were like lightning, catching both Leroy's arms and pulling them painfully behind his back. He said tensely, "Lissen to me good, white boy, 'cause Ah ain't gwine say nothin' no mo'n wunst. You'n'me gotta stick togeddah, iffen we likes it or we doan. One dese days when de time is ripe, we's gwine 'scape fum heah. An' we got t'leab togeddah, so's de one lef' behin' doan tell nobuddy nothin'. Dere be a time fo' me'n'you to fight, an' mebbe one of us'll lay daid when it all ovah. Meanwhiles—" He twisted one arm, to make sure he had his victim's attention. "Meanwhiles, you'n'me's gotta git 'long. You heah me?"

"I can't help but hear, Jupe, you got them big lips right up against my ear. All right, I'll get along with you."

Jupiter released him and stood alert, hands at his

sides, ready to fight if Leroy broke his promise. But all Leroy said was, "Hold this board while I nail it, Jupe."

When the spring crops were in, Lyman found other chores for his convicts until chopping time. On two farms there was plenty of work. And Lyman found their labor remarkably cheap, having only to feed and house them.

In Leroy, working each day with Jupiter and having to keep his peace the steam was building up. All during their long years of friendship, it had been he who was the boss and Lyman who had followed unquestioningly. Now the bottom rail was on the top: it was Lyman whose property it was, Lyman who gave him instructions for the day, Lyman who owned the good suit of clothing and who was free to chase the women and go somewhere and play cards and hell around all night if he wished. Leroy looked down resentfully at his prison garb, which he had to wear because *Lyman* said he didn't dare get him anything better.

"I'm gettin' sick an' tired of it!" he shouted, one afternoon.

Lyman eyed him wearily. He had seen the friendship between Leroy and Jupiter, and Leroy growing away from himself. It had been lonesome enough for him, having to drag himself up by his own bootstraps, having to make his own decisions for the first time in his life. Now, with Leroy here and spending the livelong day with Jupiter, and never a cross word between them, Lyman found himself helpless to assuage the loss he was feeling. He took a deep breath. "Jupe, you jes' go on with what you're doin' there, 'hear? Somethin' I want t'talk to Leroy about."

"Yassuh," said Jupiter, and when they had closed the study door, he moved to eavesdrop. He was worried, yet exhilarated, at the prospect this day held. Coker and the men were miles away, working on the other farm. The day was mild, clothed in milky sunlight, with a few birds hopping and twittering in the trees. A fine day for traveling.

Jupiter, down on his knees varnishing a baseboard, looked around the room with pride. They were almost done with this room, fixing, painting, until it gleamed with beauty and newness. There was one last room to tackle, then they'd have to go back out to the fields again. Unless Mistah Lyman thunk up some other chores for them.

He leaned toward the door; the murmur of voices was reassuring. In the months that they'd been here, he and Leroy had filled out again, regained that alert healthy look of men who work hard and are well fed. He had long been ready to make the break; but Leroy was waiting for something, he didn't know what. Waiting for the next meal, waiting for Lyman's notice, waiting for a day like today when everybody was gone far off.

Lyman's voice was conciliatory. "Now what's the matter, Leroy? What're you gettin' sick an' tired of? I thought you wanted t'be here. I thought you wanted Jupe workin' with you."

Now, faced with the opportunity to voice his resentments, Leroy hardly knew where to begin. "I'm jes' gettin' sick o' bein' a prisoner! Havin' t'sleep with one leg locked to the bed! Sick o' wearin' these damn darky clo's! Look at me, Lyman! A man in the prime o' life, an' I ain't had a woman for damn near five years. Shit, I don't even know if I *could* any more!"

"Sure you could, Leroy," Lyman said positively.

"And another thing, I'm sick o' bein' told what t'do! It's Leroy fix this table, Leroy paint this wall, Leroy kiss my butt—where in the livin' hell do you get off tellin' *me* my business?"

"Well, it's my house. An' you're here 'cause I got you out o'—"

"That wasn't fair in the first place!" Leroy shouted.

"I wasn't the only one at Mossrose—an' here I'm takin' the blame for the whole kit an' caboodle o' you!"

"You ain't eggzackly innocent—" Lyman held up both hands, waving them before him as though to stop a herd of cattle. "Now don't go gettin' riled, Leroy. It ain't *my* fault how it turned out, is it? I done the best I could for you."

Leroy's mind had shut off the words Lyman was saying. His expression was faraway. "Lettin' me rot in prison for years," he muttered. "Promisin' you'd have me sprung in two months. Sellin' my land, an' my daddy's house on it. Sellin' it so's niggers can sleep in *my* bed. Layin' up drunk all the time. Takin'. Takin' from me an' mine so's you can get yours."

"Leroy. Now, Leroy," Lyman began, afraid of this man he had idolized all his life and whom he did not know anymore. "We—we talked about all that—"

"I was *it*, wasn't I? I could run faster, yell louder, fight better; I could love the women longer an' make 'em happier. Couldn't I, Lyman?" Lyman's hasty nod of agreement went unnoticed. "I was the leader. I was Colonel Biggs o' the Confederate Army—the Cyclops o' the Invisible Empire. Anyplace I went, anything I wanted to do, men followed me, 'cause I was smarter, foxier than any of 'em."

His gaze was focused on the distance; his eyes were boring into Lyman's. "You was my second in command. What I said, you did it. What I didn't know was how you was workin' behind my back." Suddenly his eyes became aware of Lyman, sitting dumbstruck in his chair, a half-finished drink in his hand. "YOU sent me to prison! You, Lyman! YOU let me rot in the hole! All those rats—and the flea bites—and the boils—" Leroy had risen now, and was approaching the mesmerized Lyman.

"Leroy—Leroy!" Lyman begged. "Cut it out now, you ain't yourself. Leroy, hear me?" He shrank back in his chair as the taller man drew close to him.

Suddenly Leroy's hands shot out and gripped him

by the windpipe. He never stopped talking, did not
even know what he was doing, except that in his
dreams, waking and sleeping, he had done it all before.
Telling Lyman off, putting the blame where it belonged,
taking hold of his neck and choking his friend. All, all,
he had dreamed of. He scarcely heard Lyman's glass
clatter to the floor or the gasping noises he was forcing
from his throat, did not notice the purpleness of
Lyman's face. He stood over Lyman who had gloried
in his leadership all of his life, and his strong hands
squeezed and squeezed until that life was ended.

He was king now. All that Lyman owned was his,
his to rule over, his to manage as he pleased, as he
thought best; it was all his now.

And he did not want it. Lyman was dead; his triumphs had died with him. He, Leroy Biggs, was alive,
with other dreams to fulfill as he had this one. He was
alive, throbbing and pulsing with a lust as strong as
he ever had for a woman, thrilling as he had during the
War when he had killed a Yankee. That was the ulti-
mate triumph, to know and murder your enemy.

The War had not ended for Leroy Biggs. It had
scarcely begun.

He came out of the study, shutting the door behind
him. He said, "Let's go."

Jupiter, cleaning his varnish brush on a piece of rag,
glanced up. "Go wheah?"

"Go. Before Coker brings the men back."

Jupiter stood up, glancing hastily at the closed door,
then at Leroy's jubilant face. "Whut you do wid Mistah
Lyman?" His eyes widened at Leroy's smile. He looked
into the study. Lyman Matthews was sprawled in an
easy chair, his complexion florid, his head lolling to
one side. On his neck were ugly bruises. Jupiter gasped.
"Git on outta heah," he said, and began to run.

"Jupe! This way! Get a horse!" Leroy said, and
Jupiter changed course.

Within minutes they were mounted, Leroy on Lyman's mare, and Jupiter on the back of a startled work-

horse with a lame leg. They pounded down back lanes and across fields and finally slowed down within a thin wood.

"Think anybody saw us, Jupe?" Leroy's smile was carefree; his wavy brown hair was floating in the breeze.

"Mama Jesus," Jupe muttered. "Ev'ybuddy sees us. Whut you think, Leroy, dey blin'-eyeded? We got to git mo' miles behin' us. Dey gwine be aftah us wid dogs an' all."

"Go down a streambed then," said Leroy, and plunged his horse into a shallow creek. They followed it for half a mile until it ran out. The horses were blowing, and Jupiter's horse was limping badly. Still they moved as fast as they could.

"We got t'stop an' get us some clo's someplace," said Leroy. "We ain't eggzackly dressed for the sport we're engaged in."

"Whut you got in min', Leroy? We boff so big, we got to fin' us some big man t'rob."

"An' we got to get a gun, too."

"Oh, no!" Jupiter's eyes bulged. "Ah doan want nothin' to do wid no gun. Ah's skeered o' guns, they goes off in you han's."

Leroy laughed. "Sho' do, Jupe. That's the idee. Now lessee, where are we?"

"Out in de County someplace. Doan look like noplace Ah evah been."

"Me neither. That means nobody'll reckanize us."

Silently Jupiter looked down at his prison garb.

"We'll fix that when it gets dark. We'll find us a house an' go in an' get what we need."

"Ah think we oughta hide till it gits dahk. Soon's we fin's a place. Mah gizzard is tellin' me t'git outta sight."

"We got t'keep goin'. We got t'keep our head start." They rode on in silence, Jupiter's mount traveling more and more slowly. Finally Leroy said, "Get off that nag an' let him go. I c'd walk a faster pace than this'n."

"Wull, Ah cain't. Kin Ah git on wid y'all?"

"Oh, all right. Hurry up."

At dusk they came to a neglected farmhouse. Weeds grew in the patch of front yard. A stake, a chain, and a circle of worn earth showed there once had been a dog. A tall horseweed within the circle said that it had been some time ago. The house was unpainted and uncurtained, but a dim light showed in a back room.

They stood there looking for a few moments. Leroy whispered, "Jupe, get down an' sneak 'round an' see who's there."

Jupiter slid down off the horse and tiptoed stealthily around the house, peering into windows. He held up a finger to indicate one, and imitated a curtsey. Leroy beckoned him back. Jupiter said, "Leroy, go knock on de do' polite-like. Mebbe we kin git some food an' clo's an' git on outta heah. Dis is too quiet. It spooks a pusson."

"You do it, Jupe. If she's scared o' you, an' yells for somebody else t'come an' help her, I'll tackle him."

It was ridiculously easy. The old lady lived alone, crippled with rheumatism and off in the head. She mistook Jupiter for her own servant. In a cracked, penetrating voice she said, "Sambo, git on in heah. Mah goo'ness, boy, wheah you been? Ah send y'all out foah wood an' youah gone the livelong day. Now Ah want you t'cook me a dish o' tunnups. Ah'm hongry fo' tunnups. They keep mah blood good an' thin. Well, git stahted, boy, youah slowah than—"

Jupiter entered the slatternly kitchen. Dirty dishes littered the table. A rat scuttled under a filthy bed. He smiled briefly. He knew how Leroy felt about rats. He said, "Ma'am, Ah need some new clo's."

The rheumy old eyes looked him up and down. "That'll have t'wait to nex' week, Sambo. Leroy'll be out nex' week."

Jupiter felt the hair rise on his neck. "Who dat Leroy, ma'am?"

"My boy, Leroy. Fine boy. Youah ol' massa."

Jupiter's eyes slid to Leroy, standing behind him. The old lady had not noticed him yet. Jupiter whispered. "She's think Ah's Sambo. You already Leroy."

"Gives me a idea. Hey, Mama, how you been?"

"Leroy, is that y'all? Doan hardly look like you, son. Ah been wantin' to tell you, this-heah hip's been achin' me like fury. Ah want y'all to carry me ovah to the yarb woman today. She—"

"Mama, where'd you put my clo's?" Leroy was prowling around the room, gingerly lifting up the bedding and a box or two that might conceal clothing he and Jupiter could wear. He let out a yelp as a rat ran past him, and red with fury, he turned on the old lady. "Where's my britches, ol' woman?" he yelled into her face.

"Mah goo'ness, boy, y'all git moah like youah daddy ever' day. Theah behind the do'."

Leroy found a ragged pair of overalls, thick-laden with dust and cobwebs. He shook them out and exchanged them for his prison trousers. "There, that's better, ain't it, Jupe?"

"Ah's gwine look fo' me some. Gimme dat lamp, Leroy."

"I'm comin' along. She might have a gun we could take."

To the accompaniment of the querulous old voice, they prowled the other rooms. Leroy found an old shirt, which split when he put it on. Jupiter claimed a moth-eaten gray sweater. There was no gun. They went back to the kitchen, where the elderly lady was still complaining.

"Jupe, you stay here with her. I'm goin' t'take a look 'round outside. There might be a horse back in that shed."

"A daid hawss," Jupiter said glumly. But something about Leroy warned him. "Ah's comin' 'long. She ain't gwine raise no ruckus."

"Look, she's got t'have food some place. Cook it. I'm starvin'."

"Cook youah own, white boy," said Jupiter. "Ah ain't lettin' y'all outta mah sight."

Leroy glared at him. They went out into the darkness. "What's the matter with you? You don't trust me any more?"

Jupiter said softly, "Ah nevah did. Not fo' long, anyways. Not aftah you done brag 'bout whut you done to 'Pollo."

" 'Pollo?! Hell, he wasn't nothin' but a nigger."

"Wull, iffen you ain't notice', Ah's a nigger too. 'Pollo, he's mah bruddah. Ol' Simmon was mah daddy. How you like dem apples, Lee-roy?"

"You black son of a bitch, I oughta kill you."

"Go 'head an' try, Whitey. We got one hawss an' one suit o' clo's 'tween us, an' Ah wants 'em."

"Why, you—" Leroy lunged at Jupiter in the darkness, and his fist connected with Jupiter's jaw. Jupiter's massive arm described an arc, and his fist hit Leroy on the side of the head and made him reel. Jupiter went down the three steps to the back porch. He said tauntingly, "Come an' git me, Lee-roy."

As Leroy roared down the steps, Jupiter stuck out his foot and tripped him. But Leroy, as he fell, grabbed Jupiter by the legs and brought him down heavily onto the ground. They rolled around in the weeds, first Leroy on top and then Jupiter, their fists and knees working. Then suddenly Leroy lay still, not breathing. After a minute Jupiter got up off his chest, only to have Leroy spring up and grab him by the neck.

Leroy's strength had returned in the months at Lyman's house, and his thumbs on Jupiter's windpipe pressed desperately. But Jupiter, stronger to begin with, felt a desperation of his own, to live and conquer this deadly companion of his. Gasping, he pried Leroy's fingers away, and threw Leroy on his back. For several seconds he stood there, watchful, getting his breath back and the bright spots out of his vision. Though it was full dark, both men could see better now.

Leroy watched Jupiter. Slowly he began to rise, shaking his head as though knocked senseless. He got halfway up, only for Jupiter to kick at his chin and graze it.

Quick as a cat, Leroy grabbed Jupiter's leg and threw him off balance, bringing him down to the earth again. With his fists he pounded Jupiter's eyes and nose. Then Jupiter turned his body, spilling Leroy off, and he scrambled on top of him.

Jupiter had never killed a man, but he was fighting for his life. If he did not kill Leroy, he would be the one to lie dead in the widow's yard. He sat heavily on Leroy's solar plexus, Leroy's arms pinned next to his body, and with his big fists he struck Leroy on the temple again and again, until Leroy's body grew slack under his own.

He stopped. He lifted himself on his knees. The man who had once shared his bunk no longer moved. Cautiously Jupiter got up. For some time he stood over Leroy, alert for tricks. Then, aware by the pricking of his neck that he was in strange territory standing by a dead man, he quickly undressed Leroy, changing his prison garb for the stolen overalls, shirt, and sweater.

On silent feet he moved toward the still-tethered horse. He looked back, but Leroy lay as he had left him, on his side in the weeds. It might be a month before he was found. But if that other Leroy, that old woman's son, came out—

He mounted Lyman's mare and dug his heels into the horse's sides. By morning he would be miles west of here, well on his way to St. Louis where he might find Apollo.

Leroy Biggs was not dead, but for days afterward he lingered near death. The old widow's son came to visit and found him lying in the yard, groaning with the pain in his neck, out of his mind with headache, suffering from exposure to the evening dews and the daytime sun on his nakedness. That other Leroy took

him in to his mother, who in her absent-minded fashion
nursed him adequately and fed him broth whenever
she became hungry herself.

He came back to consciousness in a strange bed,
sure that his neck or back was broken, and knowing
that his skull was split clean across. But within a few
weeks his determination had helped him recover enough
to start walking. Walking a step at a time, an hour, a
half day at a time. Walking down the steps and back
up them. Walking back down and out into the yard and
out to the dusty road that shimmered away in the summer heat. Walking down that road toward New Orleans, walking toward Dulcie Moran and toward Adam
Tremain.

CHAPTER FORTY-ONE

Leroy Biggs arrived in New Orleans at the beginning of August. The city was lethargic, still gasping from the last waves of summer heat. Leroy could not help being taken with its moist beauty. Nor could he help being intimidated by the city. It throbbed with life; people moved with lackadaisical elegance, purposeful and mannered as they went about their business; and New Orleanians had business—of every nature. After his postwar years of poverty, then the years in prison, Leroy found that New Orleans was more than he could absorb.

He found a small room on a back street behind Gallatin Street and felt somewhat comforted by the meagerness of his quarters. He knew far better now how to live with austerity than with opulence. New Orleans was going to take some getting used to. He walked the streets, mostly at night, when he expected them to be empty or near empty—but they weren't. Still, it was better than in the daytime.

Most of the time he spent in his claustrophobic room daydreaming and laying his plans. Though he tried not to think of Lyman or of what had happened in the past he was not entirely successful; Lyman's distorted, purpling face often haunted his nights. In his overwrought, confused state of mind, plans were difficult to formulate; consequently, much of his time was spent fantasizing about Dulcie. His thoughts of her temporarily became his "plan."

His heart beat faster as he thought of the culmination of that plan. She would be his at last, pretty Dulcie with that long, red hair and those eyes that looked the color of sun on rocks in the bed of a clear stream. Her smiles would be for him now, him alone. He'd look at her, and she'd smile for him.

He thought of her smile always on him, always for him, and then his mind traveled down to her neck, her shoulders. Her body would be his too, and like her smile would always be for him, him alone to use in any way he wanted, his to bend to his every whim. She would be his . . . he stuck on the word, couldn't bring himself to use the word for her—those women were not for one man alone. Dulcie was for him alone. She'd be like his—no. She'd *be* his wife. She was his wife, and he had come to claim her. His wife, he mused. His thoughts turned to Adam, and he began to laugh aloud. The funny part of his whole plan was that when he got Dulcie, he'd be getting Adam too. It wasn't often a man could combine carnal pleasure such as he'd know with the revenge he'd inflict upon Adam.

He let his mind wander now, no longer thinking of "Dulcie," but of the red-haired woman, and the sea captain, and him. He let his mind race free, reveling in Adam's imagined pain, and the excitement of being with the red-haired woman. He was breathing rapidly, and he stirred restlessly on the bed, his agitation and need growing. His riotous mind continued to torment him, and his body ached for release. He rubbed his hand across himself and felt a deep inner discontent, knowing that what he wanted was a woman, and not his own hand.

He got up and went quickly down the stairs to the street. It was very late, but there was a house, Les Belles, that was open all night long, as far as he could tell. He'd walked past it many times, peeking in the windows, trying to see between the slender opening of the draperies. He had never had the nerve to go into the place, but then he had never felt the need so strongly as he did tonight. He paced back and forth along the side street near Les Belles, gathering the courage to present himself as a normal man wanting a normal service. The visions of Dulcie and Adam and occasionally Lyman continued to flash through his mind, tormenting, exciting, making his body hungry beyond bearing. He crossed the street and entered Les Belles.

Janet Robbins, a shapely black woman, was Angela's assistant and friend, who took over for Angela at times. As soon as Leroy entered, she sized him up. She approached him before he had managed to reach the center of the main salon, and determined what girl to put him with. She didn't want him seen in the main part of the house, nor did she want to chance his mixing with the regular clients.

Pleased with the attention he got, and the alacrity with which it was given, Leroy didn't even notice that within seconds he had been hustled off to the back of the house far from the excitement and revelry of the front rooms. And being more comfortable with, and less fearful of plainness, he didn't think it extraordinary that the room Janet showed him to was small and nearly devoid of decor. She took his jacket and hung it on a clothes tree, smiled graciously at him and told him his lady would be there in a few moments. She poured him a generous shot of bourbon and left him alone to wait.

Upstairs in her private suite Angela Pierson was spending a sleepless, restless night as well. She had taken the evening off, leaving Janet in charge so that she could plan an intimate dinner and evening for herself and Adam Tremain. She walked through her rooms agitatedly, a highball in her hand sloshing over as she turned sharply. She placed the glass on a table, and sat down for the twentieth time, only to get up again. She had never known such frustration as she was now experiencing with this man.

It seemed that no matter what she did, she managed to fall into one trap or another with him. She was near her wits' end. She could feel his attraction to her pour from him, could feel the effort it took him to restrain

it, and yet he did manage to do so. She didn't know
what approach to take with him anymore. When she
had been direct and honest about her feeling for him,
he had talked to her as if she were a child who did not
know her own mind. And now that she had established
a more casual, friendly relationship with him, he came
more often and seemed to enjoy their evenings together,
but she might as well be spending the time with a girl
friend.

He used his wife's name like a shield. No matter how
affected he might be, and she knew that he nearly
always left her in an excited state, he did indeed leave.
And he left her craving for the touch of his hand on
her breast, her thighs, the vulnerable places of her body.

She didn't know what to do, but she did know that
she could no longer tolerate being Adam Tremain's
"friend," and nothing more. Somehow it had to change,
or she might never again have a night of peaceful
sleep, or a day of pleasurable anticipation of her next
meeting with him. He was coming to spend the evening with her and have dinner again the next week,
and then, she vowed, things would change between
them. It had to be.

The evening, when it came, went exactly as she had
planned it. Adam was on time, handsomely clad in a
wine-colored coat and silver-gray trousers that fitted
him precisely. He smiled when she opened her door,
and his kiss of greeting was warmer, less wary, than
usual. She let her fingers trail down the fine broadcloth
of his sleeve, reluctant to lose the touch of him; and
he responded by tucking her hand under his arm, patting her and saying, pleased, "Angela, how lovely
everything looks!" His eyes told her that she was
loveliest of all.

She had no need to glance over the perfection of the
appointments, for she herself had chosen them all. The
two love seats faced each other, so that if he chose, he
might sit beside her as they shared the regal repast.
She had agonized longest over her gown, choosing a

silk pongee in peach, a fluid garment that clung sug-
gestively to her delightful curves, and intimated nakedness where nakedness was covered.

As the evening progressed, she constantly reminded
herself to go slowly, not to press, not to be obvious.
In all things she would lull him into feeling secure, at
ease, and at one with her. They sipped their drinks,
talking and smiling. She served Adam's plate herself,
sometimes feeding him from her spoon, sharing with
him the dishes she especially favored. Infrequently she
touched his hand, his sleeve.

In time he came to sit by her, and occasionally, sitting with knees wide as men do, his thigh accidentally
touched hers. Angela pretended not to notice it, although the deep-laid burning she felt for him was im-
measurably heightened by that meeting of flesh through
cloth.

He wanted her. And tonight he was yielding to his
desire, her desire. The air was electric. She had only
to make the right moves now, to seem to follow where
he led, when from the first moment it was she in the
lead.

Her voice had subtly become softer, her laughter at
his sallies more subdued, the meeting of their eyes more
meaningful. She kept the wine flowing, though Adam
had an excellent head. Then, as he raised his glass to
propose a toast, she placed a warm hand on his and
softly quoted the words of an old, old song. " 'Drink
to me only with thine eyes.' " With her long-lashed
dark eyes, she spoke to him of her love, and her wanting him.

Adam murmured, " 'And I will pledge with mine.' "

Angela, seeing the leap of flame that she had so long
hoped for, leaned toward him. " 'Or leave a kiss but
in the cup—' "

Their faces were close; Adam's arms went around
her; Adam's mustache tickled her; his lips were on hers,
hot, open, decisive. Angela felt the thrill tingle throughout her entire body as she responded with all her being.

He pulled her tighter; yet she was lying on her back with Adam lying half on top of her, his mouth seeking, one hand gently cupping her breast, which had fallen free from the flimsy gown, his other hand gripping her bare arm with excruciating strength. She yielded all to him, her body crying out, take me, take me.

It was over before it had begun. Adam had sprung up from the love seat and was standing with his back to her, his head bowed. She came up behind him to put gentle arms around him, but he flung her away so that she hit with a plop where she had been seated before. He said, from between tight lips, "I am two fools, I know—for loving you, and for being here. You . . . have my apologies."

"Apologies!" she flared. "Shall I go to bed with apologies? Cool my fevered blood and still my racing pulse with your apologies? You've been leading me on for months—now you owe me this, Adam!" She tried to press her body against his again.

His face, flushed with desire and self-reproach, had closed. "I owe you nothing, Angela. We will not do this. Not you and I. Not now, not ever." His eyes left hers, and he pulled himself from her grasp.

The anger that gripped her was more searing than ever her desire for Adam Tremain had been. Her hand came up, and the sound that it made on Adam's cheek echoed in the suddenly hushed room. He turned to look at her once more, and on his face was love, passion, anger, sorrow. He said, "Good-bye, Angela," and went out, closing the door.

He paused momentarily when he heard the vase smash against the other side. Bereft of Angela's kind of relief himself, he felt like turning back, flinging open the door, and confronting her. He stood in the hall, leaning on the balcony rail staring blindly down into the salon below. He envisioned himself walking back into Angela's room, taking her by the shoulders and shaking sense into her. Sense? Was that what he would do? The thing he wanted to do? He would never leave Dulcie, didn't want to, but Angela's passion for him flattered him. It paid him compliment in a way that no wife, no matter how well loved, could ever manage, simply because she was his wife.

Slowly the salon came into focus and the inner views of himself conquering Angela's passionate, rebellious nature dimmed. He stood up straight, then walked down the stairs, through the salon, and out of Les Belles.

Angela raged around her room in a fury of frustration. He *had* responded—with a passion to match hers —had almost taken her! But as always, there was Dulcie, standing between her and what she wanted most. "Dulcie! *Always* Dulcie!" she screamed, and hurled a wine decanter against the wall, taking pleasure in watching it shatter, and its violet-red contents stain the pale wallpaper. She picked up the wine glass from the tray and hurled that after the decanter, and another. By now each piece of glassware she broke was Dulcie Tremain, shattering, splintering, being hurled out of the way, out of Adam's life—out of Angela's life.

Poised ready to fling the last of the wine glasses, instead she ran across the room and tugged hard on the bell pull. Seconds later a servant entered. "Send Janet to me immediately," she said curtly.

As soon as Janet appeared, Angela asked her urgently, "That man—the strange one who comes here sometimes—what's his name?"

Janet looked at her puzzled.

"You know!" Angela said impatiently. "He's too rough with the girls and he brags about knowing Edmund Revanche. Quickly, tell me his name!"

"Ohh! The crazy one. Oh, what is his name—Biggs, something Biggs. Leonard—Lee—Leroy, I think, something like that."

"Has he been here recently?"

"No, not for a couple of weeks, maybe longer."

Angela smiled. "Good. He's about due then. The next time he comes here, send him directly up here to me."

"Here?" Janet said. "Oh, Angela, you don't want anything to do with him!"

"Let me be the judge of that. You just make sure you keep an eye out for Mr. Biggs, and send him right to me. And now, I want you to send a message to Edmund Revanche's house and tell him I need to see him immediately—tonight."

Janet looked at her with concern and worry, but didn't argue. When Angela was like this, there was no point in trying to talk with her. She left and did exactly as she was ordered.

When Edmund Revanche appeared in her office an hour later, Angela came directly to the point. "You will be running for office in the coming election, won't you?"

Edmund nodded, his curiosity already piqued.

"Well, Mr. Revanche, who in this city could be your best popular supporter if he were willing?"

Edmund studied her for a moment, then mentioned the names of several well-known politicians.

"I said popular supporter, not some hack politico."

Edmund's eyes glittered in understanding. "I sense that the serpent has reentered the garden. What is it you have in mind, Angela?"

"I propose to sell you a plan that will guarantee Adam Tremain's support of your bid for election. Does that appeal to you, Edmund?" she asked coquettishly.

"Not particularly," he said coldly. "I don't like being summoned from the comfort of my home in the middle of the evening for nonsense, Angela." He got up to leave.

"It is not nonsense! I am telling you Adam Tremain will be a parrot for you, say anything you ask, do whatever you need to be elected. What better man for the coloreds and the lower classes to trust than him? Sit down, please—at least hear me out. I've never directed you wrong in all the information I've given you."

"I'll listen," he said, but remained standing.

Angela hesitated. "Before I tell you how this can be done, we'll talk about price. This one has a special tag on it."

Edmund laughed, and turned again to the door.

"Wait! It's not money—I want something different this time."

Once more Edmund looked at her curiously. "What is your interest in Tremain?"

"That is none of your business and not part of the deal. Will you talk price now?"

"All right," he said wearily. "I said I'd listen—what is it?"

"There is one part of this plan that I want done my way, and without your word on that, I won't tell you any of it."

Revanche laughed, and sat down. "What confidence you have, Angela Pierson. I tell you I am not interested in your impossible scheme; then your price includes the stipulation that I must execute this scheme in accordance with your wishes. Well, my dear, you have planned well so far, because you now have my ear and my curiosity."

"Will you agree to my conditions?"

"Why not? Of course, I may not do any of this, but if I should, then your conditions will be met. Is that good enough for you?"

Angela bit her lower lip, considering, then said, "I suppose it must be. We seem to be at a stalemate if it isn't."

"Indeed we are."

"All right. Adam Tremain would never support you if he was able *not* to. But—if there was something he wanted more than he hates you, he would do whatever he had to in order to gain his own objective."

"My dear child, I can see you do not know Adam Tremain well. He would cut off his hands and give them to me before he would do anything he considered . . . wrong. In his narrow mind, I am the epitome of evil."

Angela laughed smugly. "No, Mr. Revanche, it is you who do not know him. Of course, he would harm *himself* in preference to helping you; but would he harm someone else? Someone like his wife?"

Edmund's eyes opened wide.

Angela's soft laughter filled the room. "Now we will bargain over my condition, Mr. Revanche. When this is accomplished—and I can tell you how it can be done without ever coming back on you—you must promise me that Dulcie Tremain will never come back to me, that once she is gone, she will be gone for good."

Edmund's tongue swept across his lips. "Agreed."

As Angela outlined the details of her plan, Edmund leaned forward, listening with rapt attention.

Leroy did not show up at Les Belles until the end of the week, and none of Angela's efforts earlier on had located him. Janet Robbins took him immediately to what he now considered "his" room, and sent bourbon and a girl to him. She then hurried upstairs to Angela's suite.

Edmund Revanche was summoned and present at Les Belles within the hour. Angela's people hurried through the halls, preparing a midnight collation, crystal glasses, and decanters for the moment when Leroy was finished with his girl; Edmund Revanche would then walk into the room to enlist Leroy's aid, and thus put Angela's plan into action.

Leroy Biggs left Les Belles a new man. His plan was no longer a fantasy of Dulcie. Now he had money in his pocket and a set of tasks to perform. It was all so methodical, so orderly—so certain to succeed. And best of all, Edmund Revanche, his mentor, knew just as Leroy did that Dulcie was his alone.

The next day he began looking for a house, a particular house. After all, this perfect revenge of his was not a thing of a moment—it was the rest of his life, and it was going to be good. No ordinary cabin was good enough for the wife of Leroy Biggs. She'd have a house. One worthy of her, one she would stay in and keep nice for him. It had to be near the city but not too near neighbors. He wouldn't want her blabbing her story to someone. It had to be a house that didn't belong to anyone, but that didn't worry him—there were plenty of abandoned houses around New Orleans.

Edmund became impatient, but finally, in early September, 1876, Leroy found the place. The house was perfect, miles away from everything, almost buried in undergrowth and trees that hid it from the dirt road. It had been abandoned for some time. The rooms were full of dusty furniture, and the closets held mildewed linens, as if someone had just given up and walked out, never to look back or come back. There was even a broom still hanging on its hook behind the kitchen door. Everything a wife would need was already there—even her husband. Leroy let his laughter ring through the untenanted rooms.

Hacking away at the briars that had spread over the back walk out to the privy, he imagined how it would look through Dulcie's eyes. There was a chicken house. They'd have chickens, and a few ducks. On Sundays he'd have Dulcie fix roast chicken and dumplings. There were wells, an old abandoned one and another. When he primed the pump the water tasted all right. There were a few acres with the house, grimly bare or festering with scrub growth. In the back the land sloped away toward a body of water.

He needed more than the house. He wanted things like the ones he had once owned, a gold pocket watch and rings and fine clothing to show him to be a man of substance. A gentleman fit to be Dulcie's husband. Those Edmund Revanche would not provide. So over the weeks he watched her and waited for her, he became quite an accomplished burglar. Sensing when it was safe to enter a dwelling, he obtained the accoutrements of wealth, even a gold-headed cane and a straight razor for when he got ready to shave off the beard he'd

been forced to let grow. He took money, too, when he
found any, and hoarded it against need.

In one man's barn there was a decent carriage, so he
hitched two horses to it and drove boldly away. It was
miles to his new abode, but every man knows his own
horses and carriage. Leroy altered some of its distinctive features and repainted it. The horses he covered
with fly-blankets.

He was busy all the time, doing things to the house.
He nailed the windows shut and the front door. The
weather was cooling a little, and he could go in and out
the back door. It wouldn't do to make it easy for her
to leave. He might go to sleep and she'd be gone.

He did not neglect his primary objective, to fix in
his mind the habits of the Tremain household and the
comings and goings of Dulcie and Adam. Many a time
he stood barely concealed beside the road as Dulcie's
carriage was driven by. She had plenty of freedom out
here, he observed. One of these days she'd be driving
herself, as he had seen her do, and he'd seize his opportunity.

This wasn't the way he had wanted it. It seemed to
him Revanche had taken over his dream, cut it up into
one little act after another, instead of the one grand
vengeance he had always visualized. But he had to
admit Edmund had had a point when he impressed him
with the need for watchful patience. Finding Revanche
was a bit of luck he hadn't expected, but now his whole
plan had come alive, seemed fated to happen. And the
more time it took, the more it seemed right to move
slowly and steadily. Anticipation, when Dulcie was all
but within his grasp, was heightened to a point of sheer
delight.

CHAPTER FORTY-TWO

Dulcie was happy today, feeling lighthearted and giddy and—and *free*. She wanted to dance, to sing, to float in the air like a gone-to-seed dandelion. Her feet could not move fast enough, her fingers could not fly swiftly enough as she did her hair. Her borrowed maid could not hook up her buttons quickly enough—for she longed to be away, away.

Glory Hallalooya West's bubbling voice came from the next room. "Dulcie, aren't you ready *yet*?"

"No!" Dulcie called. "Aren't you?"

"Nearly! Two minutes! —Oh, *damn*, make that ten minutes, I just ripped the buckle off one of my favorite shoes."

Dulcie was ready at last, and she came to Glory's door to watch her toilette. "I'll never make it," Glory groaned, holding still with effort while she was being hooked together in back. "Find my hat, can you, Dulcie? I know I put it somewhere—"

Dulcie glanced around. Glory hadn't changed at all since the days in Nassau—stockings and shoes and petticoats and stays and feathers and furbelows all over the floor, all left for the maid to put into order later. Dulcie overturned the bright heaps of clothing and from under one of them extracted a wide-brimmed hat of horsehair, trimmed with black-velvet ribbon and a full brown feather.

Glory pounced on it and jammed it onto her hairdo. Ignoring possible peril to her skull, she rammed in two wickedly long hatpins. "There!" she said, whirling to show herself to Dulcie. "We hardly look like two housewives off on a spree, do we? Oh, I like that gown, Dulcie. That rust color is so becoming to you. Are you packed? Harvey can take your cases down if you are."

"I had him do it earlier. After all, I didn't have the children to tend to this morning as you did."

"Bless their six little red heads," Glory said, patting her protruding stomach. "If Number Seven isn't a boy, I'll just give up and quit. Do you realize I've spent five years in pregnancies? Do you realize what that does to your tummy?"

"Right now I'd say it makes it stick out," Dulcie said, and they laughed wildly. "Oh, Glory, won't this be *heaven*? Two nights and three days without seeing a single child? How on earth do we stand that constant prattle?"

"If I ever found time for self-examination, I'd have to be locked up," Glory giggled. "There—last thing in the trunk—now to see if we can close it."

"Did you put that stuff in there yourself?"

"Of course. Myra's so slow—"

"Mind if I fold a couple of things over?"

"Oh, Dulcie, what's a few wrinkles? They'll hang out. Let's *go*!"

They did not actually get on their way until some time later, by the time Dulcie and Glory had kissed all the children and Glory had found Ben and bade him good-bye. As the carriage rolled along, they laughed and chatted, talking as women do of their absent children from the moment of parting. There were other vehicles on the road, so when a maroon carriage drawn by two brown horses followed them at some distance, they did not consider it curious.

"It's been *ages* since we raided the shopping district, hasn't it, Dulcie?" said Glory enthusiastically. "I wonder if I have my list—" She scrabbled her fingers through her reticule and came up with a mangled slip of paper. "Aha! Saved! Now let's see—flannel, bird's-eye cloth—oh, drat, this is last year's list!" She collapsed against the cushion as Dulcie began to laugh.

Dulcie said soothingly, "You can spend more money

if you forget your list. You always have to add on things so you won't run out."

"Of course! How could I fail to remember that? And just think, we won't even see Ben and Adam for two whole days either. I don't know if I can stand it, Ben and I are so much a part of each other. I'm glad he married me, Dulcie. I fell in love with him the first time we went to bed together." She added pensively, "Of course I fell in love with other men for the same reason. But it wasn't the same. I warned them all that I was very fickle—which I used to be. Except with Ben, we just kept coming back together."

"He certainly has stayed crazy for you, Glory; I was noticing that last night."

"Like Adam is for you. But Adam's more—more aloof than Ben is. I always know what Ben is thinking, and with Adam I'm not sure I would. Does that make sense? What I mean is, Adam's a complete person all by himself. And you're complete all by yourself. And you make a perfect couple. But Ben and I—we're only half complete unless we're together. I like it our way, but when I see your way, I like that too. I don't know why I go through this every time I'm with you, Dulcie, all I do is look at the four of us and I get all confused."

Dulcie giggled. "Don't think about it, Glory. Just concentrate on gowns and laces and hats and gloves— do you think we'll actually come home with anything new?"

"I'd better. I'm so sick of everything I own. Oh, we're going to have a marvelous time!"

"I wonder what the children are doing today at Holly Hill. Oh, I don't miss them, not too much. And I'm sure Mindy is spoiling them to make up for their mother being gone. And Adam is stalking around hunting something I left out in plain sight for him."

They giggled together, as happy and carefree as schoolgirls.

By late afternoon they had accumulated a pile of

boxes and packages, clothing and toys for the children, presents for everyone at home. Glory's patient driver followed them around, carrying everything, and occasionally making a trip to store items in the carriage.

Glory sat slumped on a chair in the men's suit department, her feet sticking out awkwardly. "I am worn down to a nub," she declared.

Dulcie was looking at shirts. "Do you think I should have bought that green hat?"

"I told you so at the time. Why don't we go get it, Dulcie? Tomorrow it'll be gone."

"Why don't I go? It's only over in the next aisle and down a little bit. You sit and rest your feet, and I'll be right back."

"Fine. Then let's head for the hotel. Meantime I'll have Harvey take a load outside and just wait for us."

Dulcie left Glory comfortable in her chair, turned left at the coats, and headed toward the front of the store. That green hat had been in the window, hadn't it? She peered through the display, but could not see it. She stepped out onto the sidewalk for a better look. There it was, dark velvet with a black marabou feather. Now, having looked at hats all day, this one seemed just—

"Hello, Dulcie."

She swung around, startled. A bearded man was standing near her, looking at her, but he did not seem familiar . . .

Then she recognized him, and her heart rose in her throat to choke her. What was he doing here? Why wasn't he still in prison? Had they let him go? How did he find her, coming all the way from Savannah—

She turned to run, and he caught her.

"You're coming with me. Get in this carriage."

She twisted and squirmed, trying to break his grip, wishing frantically that someone, anyone, would come along the banquette, or would look out the window of the store. She opened her mouth to scream, and a leather-gloved hand moved swiftly up to stifle her. Half carrying, half dragging her, Leroy maneuvered her into the carriage. This was his moment; he had known it would come today, and he was all ready for it. Every last detail had been tended to just as Edmund told him. Even the straps were ready, to buckle over her and hold her in. And the black silk handkerchiefs—one over her eyes, one over her mouth. In the swiftly growing dark, and in the depths of his carriage, no one would be able to see what he was doing. Dulcie might struggle as they went along, but once they left Royal Street, no one would care.

As he whipped the horses into a run, a dark carriage loaded with packages came around from the back of the store. The black driver sat waiting for his passengers.

CHAPTER FORTY-THREE

Dulcie was nowhere to be found in the store, on the street outside, or in the neighboring shops. Glory was frantic.

"Perhaps it is best if we notify Captain Tremain," the store manager suggested.

"He's all the way out in Holly Hill," Glory moaned. "We've got to find her now! Something awful's happened. I know it has."

"Now, now, Mrs. West, your friend has probably met an acquaintance and is happily sipping café Brulôt at this moment. We'll just send someone out to Holly Hill, and I'll have Maxwell take you back to your hotel. Why, I wouldn't be at all surprised if you found Mrs. Tremain there waiting for you—perhaps wondering what has happened to you!"

Glory glared at the man. "You old windbag! Don't you think I know you want me out of your store! You don't care what happened to Dulcie. Call the police! Call someone who can help! Don't just stand there patting me!"

"Maxwell," the manager said with some force, "see Mrs. West to her lodgings."

Messengers were sent both to Holly Hill after Adam and to Mimosa summoning Ben to New Orleans, but Glory wasn't satisfied. Something had to be done—*now*. Adam and Ben would take too long getting to the city. The police took her fears of kidnapping only half-seriously, and Dulcie had now been missing for three hours. Glory's first thought was of Angela, and then Tom. Tom Pierson was right here in New Orleans. He'd know what to do.

She caught him at home just as he was preparing to

leave for an evening at the theater. "Tom," Glory said breathlessly, her hand clinging to his coat sleeve. "Tom, you've got to do something right away. Dulcie's been kidnapped, I know she has, and Adam's clear out at Holly Hill and Ben isn't here, and no one else will listen to me! Please, do something!"

Tom took her into the parlor and sat her down. As he turned to ring for his butler to bring her something to drink, she popped out of her seat again. "We're wasting time! Tom, please, we've got to find her."

"Now, damn it, Glory, you sit down and tell me slow-like what happened. I can't make heads or tails o' what you're sayin'. Now, right from the start, tell me. What makes you think Dulcie's been kidnapped?"

"What else?" Glory asked.

Tom rubbed his forehead. "Tell me everything you know."

After several frantic false starts, Glory recounted the whole day. "Tom, I'm sure someone took her away. You know Dulcie, she wouldn't just go off, and she hasn't been in an accident, and no one saw anything of her, and she doesn't know very many people here— just you and me and her cousins. If she were with them, they'd let me know, wouldn't they? Dulcie would never just go off and let me worry like this."

"No, no, she wouldn't, but kidnapping—why? Who'd want to do a thing like that?"

Glory shuddered. "Oh, Tom, it could have been any awful—any derelict—that's why we can't wait until Adam and Ben get here. Think what she may be going through. Oh, please, there's got to be something we can do."

Tom looked at her for a moment, then said, "We'll do something, Glory, don't you worry about it." There was nothing he could do tonight, and he knew it. He knew she wanted him to ride out into the darkness and hunt Dulcie down and bring her safely home, but he couldn't. "Right now, you're gonna go to bed an' rest, and then I'll go and see what I can find out."

"But I want to come with——"

"I know you do, Glory, but I'm going places where you can't come. If you really want to help, you'll stay here."

Glory looked up at him, her eyes large in her pale face. She nodded. "I just want so badly to help her."

Tom went to every dive and brothel in New Orleans asking questions, trying to find out if anyone had heard about the abduction of a lady. His questions were met with curiosity and a mild excitement, but no one had heard of any such doings. He finally stopped in at the St. Charles for a drink before he made his way back home. There was nothing further he could do before morning.

The bar was nearly empty, and Tom took a seat near the end of the room. Tiredly he leaned on the bar. The barman glanced at him and began mixing his drink. Tom sipped, thinking of what Glory had told him, trying to figure out why Dulcie should be abducted. Was it a chance thing? Had it happened at all? Or was it a deliberate act? Was she merely a woman taken, or was it Dulcie Tremain taken? They were futile questions to which he had no hope of finding an answer tonight, but he couldn't keep them from circling around his mind.

He pulled his elbows in closer to himself as a man sat down in the seat beside him. He didn't look at the man until he heard the low laughter of Edmund Revanche.

"Hello, Tom. It's been a long while since we've sat and had a drink together."

"We're not having one now," Tom said harshly, and stood up.

Edmund put out his hand, stopping Tom. "I want you to deliver a message for me."

Tom snorted and hit Edmund's hand away.

"To Adam Tremain."

Tom stopped again. This time he looked carefully at Edmund. "What business do you have with Adam?"

"Let's just say I have certain information I think he'd like to have. Tell him I'll receive him tomorrow afternoon at four in my suite here at the hotel." Edmund laughed again. "I assume he will be here by then, won't he? Someone has notified him?"

"You son of a bitch! What the hell do you know about Dulcie?"

Edmund's eyebrows lifted. "Dulcie? Why, very little, why do you ask, Tom?"

"Holy Jesus, you *did* take her. It never ends with you. I said it, but I didn't really believe you were behind this, Edmund, till now when you denied it."

"Denied what? Really, Tom, I do think your age is catching up with you. Well, old man, I must be going. You will deliver that message for me, won't you? For once I think Captain Tremain and I may find ourselves on the same side. Isn't life strange—suddenly the worst of enemies can find themselves allies. Politics. It can achieve anything."

Tom stood at the bar and watched Edmund make his way through the room, shaking hands with anyone whose notice he could gain, talking about the coming election, always reminding that he, too, would be running for office. Tom's eyes glittered with hatred. He placed a dollar on the bar and walked out of the hotel.

Glory had been right. Dulcie had been abducted. Tom no longer doubted it at all, but his fear for her rose. God forgive him, but he'd rather see her at the mercy of the derelict that Glory so dreaded than in the hands of Edmund Revanche. His mind flooded with the horrifying visions of the grotesquely masked Boar, Goat, and Bear prancing around the yard of his home so many years ago, prancing in a devil's dance as they slowly and painfully murdered Ullah and nearly killed him. Edmund Revanche had led them, had been the Boar, had been the one to take pleasure from the agony and the pain and the death.

He thought until his breath was coming in hard, painful gasps, and he was nearly blind with the memory

and the hatred he felt for that man. Though he would
not, could not put it into words, he had no hope that
they would find Dulcie alive. But one thing was clear
to him—Edmund Revanche would not live to enjoy her
torment. This time nothing on earth, nothing in heaven
or in hell would stop him from killing Edmund. He
would kill him. When the fruits of victory were within
Edmund's grasp, he would kill him. Perhaps he could
not save Dulcie, but he could destroy Edmund Revanche.

Adam arrived in New Orleans early the following
afternoon. He went first to the hotel where Dulcie and
Glory had been staying and found a message there to
go to Tom's house. He ran up the front steps and
pounded on the front door.

Tom answered it, and before he could speak, Adam
asked, "My God, Tom, what's happened? Where is
Dulcie? Is she all right? No one seems to know—they
didn't say—is she ill?"

Tom felt as though someone were squeezing the wind
from his chest. He ached. "We don't know where Dulcie is, Adam." He stopped, all but unable to tell him
Edmund Revanche was behind her disappearance. "He's
got her, Adam. I don't know if Edmund took her himself, or had it done. He wants to see you this afternoon
in his suite at the St. Charles. Four o'clock. Says you
an' him are gonna be allies."

Adam sank weak-kneed into a chair. He looked up
at Tom wordlessly.

Tom looked away from his unspoken question. "He
says it's politics. I expect it is."

Adam's bleak eyes moved aimlessly around the room.
"I'll never see her again," he said in a voice not his own.

Tom said nothing. There was nothing to be said.
Both of them knew the man they were dealing with,
and they knew he was ruthless when he had the upper
hand.

"I've got to take the chance he'll—I'll do whatever he asks, Tom."

"I know, boy, there ain't anything else you can do."

They sat in near silence, speaking only to make a dread-filled comment based on past experiences with Edmund, until it was time for Adam to leave.

Edmund escorted Adam into a well-appointed study, then offered him a seat and a highball. Adam sat down, but refused the drink.

"I think we should drink together, Captain," Edmund said, his eyes bright on Adam.

Adam accepted.

"Now," Edmund said, pausing and holding his drink up, gazing at its warm amber color. "I suppose, on this first meeting of ours, you'd prefer to stick with business."

"Yes, I would."

Edmund allowed another span of time to pass, drawing Adam's nerves out thin. Finally Adam asked, "What have you done with my wife, Revanche? Is she all right?"

"What makes you think I've done anything with her? As a matter of fact, I haven't. I have neither seen her nor touched her."

Adam looked up at him, unable to hide the anguish in his eyes. "Where is she?"

"Oh, now, as to that—I might have information of that sort. But first we shall talk business, Tremain. I want to be elected," he said flatly. "Of course, I can be given a political appointment, but I want to be elected by the people in my own state. And I want you to help me do it." Edmund sat back, musing. "Your sentimentality has always been your weakness, Tremain, and my, ahh, accumulation of enemies has been mine. Now, however, all these years later, here we are, each of us able to provide what the other needs. You want your wife, and I want the popular vote."

"I campaign for you, and you return Dulcie to me."

"Precisely! It works beautifully, doesn't it, and to

both our advantages. Equitability—one of your favorite themes, is it not, Captain?"

Adam winced. "You'll guarantee her safety—that she won't be harmed?"

Revanche's eyebrows went up. "I shall return her to you alive and sound."

"What does that man? Where is she? Who has her —Revanche, you do have her someplace where she is being well cared for?"

"She is in an adequate place, Tremain—a house. And someone is there to care for her."

"A woman? Someone who'll look after her well?"

"We have talked enough of that, Tremain; what now of your end of the agreement? Can I count on you to speak in my behalf?"

"As long as I know Dulcie is alive and well—and not being harmed, I'll do as you ask. But how will I know you'll bring her home when this is over? You're going to have to give me some regular signs that she is all right. What happens if you lose the election in spite of my efforts? There is no way to guarantee that people will listen to me."

"Oh, I think there is. You aren't precisely alone. Rosebud McAllister has a way of convincing people it is in their best interests to do as he suggests. And you and Geddes Ingraham are quite close. Geddes is a man of considerable influence. I am quite sure of success with men like the notorious Black Swan, Ingraham, and McAllister backing my cause. And of course, I also have considerable support from my fellow Republicans."

"But if it isn't enough—if you lose the election in spite of everything—what happens to Dulcie?"

"Then, my dear Tremain, we shall both be bitterly disappointed men."

CHAPTER FORTY-FOUR

Leroy lounged in a chair he had dragged into the kitchen as he watched Dulcie prepare supper. He began to speak as though he could read her mind. "I been waitin' a lot o' years for this, Dulcie. Sometimes it didn't seem like me'n'you'd ever be together. I first noticed you when you was fourteen—'member?"

Dulcie said nothing, nor would she look at him.

"Honey, I don't b'lieve you been lis'nin." His voice came at her soft, reasonable. "Now ol' Leroy has went to a lot o' trouble jes' for you, an' he likes t'be appreciated. He don't want you gettin' him mad, 'cause he does some pretty bad things when he's mad."

She turned to face him, drying her hands on the apron he had thrust at her. "Leroy, you say you—you care for me, have for a long time. Then stop this now, please. Take me back to New Orleans. I won't say a word to anyone. You could go on—get away. No one would ever know."

"Oh, but you're goin' with me, Dulcie. Anyplace I am from now on, that's where you're goin' t'be."

"Adam will find me, Leroy. And when he does he'll have you arrested for this. You'll go back to prison."

His smile was terrible to see. "When ol' Adam gets here—an' that ain't gonna be soon—I'm gonna kill him. It's all part o' our big plan."

"Whose? Yours and Lyman's?" she asked, sneering.

His face clouded fleetingly. "Lyman died. Back las' spring. Naw, me'n' Edmund's plan. Edmund Revanche."

Fear swarmed over her, stifling her. She had thought, months ago, that Edmund might be connected with the things that had happened around Mossrose—and he had been. And now here he was again. He was right there with them, with her and Adam, dogging their steps, plaguing them, blighting their happiness. She watched the smile on Leroy's face. "Edmund?" she whispered.

"He said you'd remember him. An' if you didn't, I was to remind you 'bout a set o' emeralds an' diamonds. You like them jools, Dulcie? You want me to git you emeralds an' diamonds?"

"No—no! I can't stand them!" Nervously she turned back to the stove. "Leroy—you—you want your supper. Tell me where the wood is, and I'll go out and—"

"An' run away? Wood's right there. Kindlin's beside it. Shavin's in that box. You don't need t'go outside fo' nothin'. Do you HEAR ME? NOT FO' NOTHIN'!"

Dulcie backed away from him. "I hear you."

He grabbed her by the arm and swung her to look at him. "Then lissen t'this, Miss Dulcie Smartass Moran. You're gonna do what I tell you, get that? I got everythin' all planned, an' you ain't gonna spoil it for me, unnerstand? First you're gonna get my supper, an' then I'm gonna eat it, an' then we're gonna set 'round the cookstove like two ordinary married people, an' when I get good an' ready then me'n'you's goin' t'bed." He gave her a hard shove. "Now get that fire started."

Silently she prepared the fire. While the stove was heating, she rummaged around for plates and tableware. She could not find a sharp knife anywhere. "Leroy, I can't cut ham without something to cut it with. Where have you put the butcher knife?"

He took a key from his pocket and unlocked a drawer. He said, "I'm goin' t'watch you every minute you have that in your hand, Dulcie."

She managed a smile. "Don't be foolish, Leroy."

She worked noiselessly, coring apples and slicing them to fry; slicing the ham, stirring the cornmeal into hot water to make mush.

"Why ain't you singin'?" he asked plaintively. "I

want you t'sing fo' me. Somethin' nice an' soft. Like a
—a cradle song. That's it. Sing that."

After a moment Dulcie began,

"The dearest spot of earth to me is Home,
    sweet Home!
The fairy land I long to see is Home, sweet Home!
Home, sweet Home! There how charm'd the
    sense of hearing!
There where love is so endearing!
All the world is not so cheering as Home,
    sweet Home!"

He frowned. "I don't like that one. Sing what I said."

Obediently Dulcie sang, hardening her heart against
treacherous thoughts of little Matthew, whose favorite
song this was:

"Lullaby and good night, with roses bedight . . ."

"Now that there's nice. Do that one some more."

So she sang and hummed as she worked, while Leroy
sat basking in her attention and the warmth and the
good smells emanating from the stove. "This is jes' like
I thought it would be," he said happily.

She sat down at the newly scrubbed table, leaning
toward him. "Leroy, it's not like you thought. It never
can be. Don't you see?"

He patted her on the arm. "Sho' it will, Dulcie honey.
We jes' take one step at a time, jes' do one little thing
an' then another, an' it all works out fine."

"But it's all false! This is not your house—not our
house. I do not belong here. I belong at—"

His fist pounded the table, making the plates, and
Dulcie, jump. *"You belong here!"* he shouted. "Don't
say you don't! I dreamed you here an' you're gonna
stay! Do you hear that?"

"I hear you," she said meekly.

She put his meal on his plate. He stared at it, then at her accusingly. "Where's the spoonbread? The beans? I said—"

"They're soaking on the stove right now. They take hours to cook. And you don't have any eggs to make spoonbread, so I made mush."

Reluctantly he took the first forkful, then began shoveling it in while she tried not to watch him. "Ain't you eatin? I want you t'eat with me."

She served herself. He took second helpings and noisily devoured them. Then he sat and picked endlessly at his teeth while she did the washing up. She was getting more and more nervous.

"If you don't hurry up with them dishes, we ain't goin' t'have time t'sit around," he said fretfully. "My maw an' paw always sat by the fire of a evenin'. C'mon, Dulcie, I want to do that."

She did not reply, and this angered him. *"Hear me?"*

"I'm coming." She hung up the rags she had been using for dishcloth and towel. "Where do you want me to be?"

"Right there. Push your chair right over there. See, ain't that nice?"

She managed a smile. She had not known, as perhaps Leroy had not, how much his home life had meant to him. Whenever she had seen the Biggs family together, at parties and barbecues, they had always been bickering among themselves. And now he was trying to bring back those days . . . with her.

"Sure wish I'da thought t'git me a cigar," he said wistfully.

"Leroy . . . are you—did you bring me here because —because you're fond of me? That is the reason?"

He looked embarrassed. He said, hesitant because he feared she would laugh, "It was 'cause I wanted you t'act like my wife. An' you *are*. You're Dulcie Biggs now. Unnerstand?"

Without answering she went on, "And when you're

fond of a person, you want to do things for that person, and make her happy, don't you?"

"That's jes' what I'm doin' right now, makin' you happy."

"What would be better for both of us is if you'd take me back to New Orleans. Before—"

Abruptly he stood up. "You don't say that! You're mine now! Come on, I'm ready t'go t'bed." He jerked her up into his arms.

"Leroy, please let me go—I don't want to—" He stopped her pleas with a long kiss. His hand fastened on her breast, squeezing and kneading in an access of desire. Then suddenly he picked her up and carried her, squirming and pounding on his back, to the bedroom. He dumped her on the bed and locked the door behind them. Thin moonlight seeped into the room, enough to show her that he was tearing off his clothing. He said, "Better get them clo's off right now, 'cause ol' Leroy is *ready.*"

She had never hated herself, or him, so much. With shaking fingers she undid her buttons and slid down her dress. Then, naked, he was at her, his hands ripping at her fine silken lingerie. Appalled and frightened, she tried to get away, but he only laughed, grabbing at her again until she stood naked with the rags of her underclothing hanging from her. She cringed as his teeth nipped at her bare breasts. She jerked away as his rough fingers slid down her slender hips, and coarsely violated the tender flesh between her thighs. Still standing, making a noise halfway between chuckling and quick, hoarse breaths, he tried to force himself into her.

Terrified, her breath coming painfully, she kept turning her head from side to side, moaning incoherently, "Please, please, no, don't Leroy—"

His right hand let her go long enough to come up and slap her, sending her senses reeling. Whimpering, she kept shaking her head. She could not do this . . .

His other hand came up and he slapped her on the

other cheek, with a harsh, cracking sound. After a few seconds he said, "There's plenty more where that come from. Now what're you gonna do?"

"Wh-whatever you say—"

"Leroy honey."

She forced the words out.

"Now that's more like it. I want you t'take hold an' help me. Spread them legs out, honey, I can't put nothin' in this way. Like that, that's fine. Now—"

Not letting herself feel or think or reason, she obeyed his commands. Bitterly reserving what she could of her private self, she was making the years-long dreams of Leroy Biggs come to glowing life.

Leroy, striving hard, was as triumphant as a king. All those nights in prison when he had romanticized her, letting his rampant fantasies have full sway . . . those other women he had had in his life . . . always wishing it was Dulcie he was plunging himself into . . . in dreams feeling her arms and legs curling around him . . . around him warm and loving like they curled around Adam Tremain . . . Adam Tremain whom he was going to torture and kill . . . arms and legs curling around him like they . . . what the God-damn hell was this . . . he was losing it . . . it had been hard as a rock . . . hard as it had ever been . . . and all for Dulcie . . . and now . . . desperately he tried to revive himself by thinking of her being beneath him . . . he was slipping out of her . . . she lay so still, not moving with him the way she should . . . not helping him like a good wife . . . he tried to enter her again but it was a fumbling effort and impossible . . . couldn't do it 'cause o' that God-damn Adam Tremain. . . .

Harsh desperation took over his voice. It came out in a whisper: "Dulcie . . . get me back up again. Hear me?"

She did not have the courage to refuse.

Within minutes he was powerful again, in command of himself and her. This time he found completion, but it was an empty victory, leaving him with a feeling as hollow and lonesome as he'd known in prison. It was as desolate as making love to himself.

He ought to do something to her for this, punish her some way for crippling him at a crucial moment, making him ashamed of himself, making him beg. For making him feel lonely and lost when he was in her. Not tonight . . . maybe . . . he was growing sleepy . . . maybe pretty soon . . . after a little shut-eye . . .

He rolled away and lay with his back to her, and soon he was snoring. Dulcie waited, letting her heartbeat slow to normal and trying to throw off the feeling of ravagement. Then she slipped out of bed and began hunting through Leroy's pockets for the key to the door.

It was not there.

Desperately she felt around on the floor, on the dresser top, slipping her hand into his boots. All the time she was listening to Leroy's breathing. If it changed, she would have to slip back into bed beside him, pretend she—

She had not reckoned with the sleeping habits of a man who had spent long years in prison. "All right, Dulcie, that's enough."

She jumped in the dark, knocking into the dresser. "I—I can't go to sleep naked," she said lamely, trying not to remember the countless times she and Adam had slept blissfully skin to skin the whole night long.

"Get on over here an' rub my back. I like to have my back rubbed."

Later she awoke from a doze to realize that he was standing over her, looking down at her. The moon had moved on, and there was little light to see his expression. "What's the matter?"

"Nothin's the matter. I'm jes' lovin' you with my eyes, is all."

Her mind flashed to something Leroy had let drop about Lyman's death. Had Lyman been asleep when Leroy— She began to shiver, and could not stop.

As the dawn was breaking, he used her again. Then, pleased with himself, he demanded breakfast.

After they had eaten he went outside, locking the door behind him. She did not care if he saw her, now that it was light outside and she could see where she might run to. She tried every window. On the last one she saw hammer marks where he had pounded in the nails. Nothing, not even a crowbar, would reach into the wood and grasp those nailheads. There was no chance to get out that way.

But if he went far away and could not hear her, she might break a window.

When he came back in she had stripped the bed and brought the tick out into the kitchen. "May I go outside, Leroy? I want to air the bedtick."

"Snakes out there, Dulcie. Saw one jes' now."

She dragged the tick back to the bedroom. Under his admiring eye she spent the morning cleaning up the kitchen. She hated the idea of catering to his fantasies of home, but a filthy kitchen she could not abide.

He took her on the living room carpet, but was very surly afterward.

At the end of the long day she was exhausted, wanting only to sleep until Adam came for her. But again they sat by the stove. Again, he tried to mount her. This time he was overtly angry.

"Damn it, Dulcie, what in the hell is it you do to a man that he can't have you good? You ain't put a spell on me?"

"I don't know how to make a spell," she said shortly. "Maybe your conscience is bothering you."

"My conscious ain't botherin' nobody," he asserted. "It's somethin' you do, to turn a man soft."

She did not answer him.

"There ain't nothin' wrong with me!" he cried. "It's you!"

There was no calendar to tell the days, but each morning Dulcie made a mark behind the kitchen stove. A few weeks passed, and there was no indication that

Adam had tried to find her. Nor had Edmund communicated with Leroy. Their food supply was running low. One evening he said that he would have to be gone a while. She was relieved, yet scared of the alien dark and the snakes that he mentioned from time to time. She had not been outside, and except for a few minutes at a time had not been separated from Leroy. The constant association, his constant striving to make love to her and consider it successful, was grinding them both down. She began to know what it had been like for him in prison.

He was ready to leave; hand on the doorknob, he looked her up and down. "You look all right," he said. "Put your arms around my neck, honey. Hang on now." And he carried her outside and put her in the carriage. "I know what you're thinkin', Dulcie. But you ain't goin' t'get away from me. You ain't even gonna step one foot away from your lovin' husband. All you're gonna do is smile an' look purty."

Dulcie entertained a hope that she would see somebody, anybody, who would recognize that she was being held by force and would be willing to help her.

Leroy said, "But if you did pull a fast one an' get away from me, by the time you could get home, Adam'd be dead."

"You'd have to locate him first," she reminded him.

"Jes' so happens Edmund is keepin' his eye on him." He turned to smile at her in the dusk. "I thought you'd enjoy knowin' that."

She burst out, "Leroy, why won't you tell me what's going on?"

" 'Cause it didn't make no difference, long's you're in the house with me. But now you're goin' out to be showed off in public, an' this is a good time t'tell you, 'cause you'll remember it better. You're with me 'cause you're my wife. But Edmund ain't interested in you that way—he told me so flat out. He says I can do anything I want to with you long's I keep you alive. Edmund's usin' Adam, see. He wants Adam to stand up an' speak for him, he says."

She whispered, "The election." Edmund would use Adam's reputation for integrity, trade on it, in his election campaign. Adam Tremain's honor and position would seem to be solidly behind Edmund Revanche— and the people would believe what Adam said about Edmund. Then once the election was over—

"What happens after the election?"

"He tells Adam where he can find you, an' he comes an' finds you. And me."

Oh, she had to get away—to save Adam's life and honor. She stared at Leroy, her mind churning. But no usable plan of escape evolved.

They rode through the dark to a small general store. Leroy, cursing as he banged on the door, kept shouting, "Open up! Open up!" Eventually a light appeared, and there was the noise of the latch being undone.

"Fer the Chris' sakes, what y'all poundin' on mah do' foah this time o' night? Ah ain't open till six in the mawnin'.'"

"We want some provisions," said Leroy, pushing his way in.

"Well, y'all jes' come back—" His voice changed, became deferential, as Dulcie entered behind Leroy. "Oh—well, good evenin', ma'am, didn't see y'all theah. Now jes' gimme a minnit till Ah set this lamp on the table. Theah now, what kin Ah do foah y'all?"

"This here's my wife," Leroy asserted.

The man chuckled foolishly. "Yeah, Ah kin see that. Purty li'l woman, she sho'ly is. You jes' tell me what-all you need, ma'am, an' Ah'll have it foah you in a mattah o' seconds."

Dulcie said softly, "We need eggs—" The chickens Leroy had dreamed of had not worked out well; they kept getting themselves slain and eaten by some marauding animal. She went on, listing numerous things they would need. The planter scurried around, gathering all the supplies Dulcie asked for. He looked up with a smile. "What else, folks? Pickles? Flour? Now how's this goin' t'be paid for?"

Leroy dug into his pocket, and flashed a wad of bills. "I got cash. Le's get this stuff out to the carriage an' I'll pay. Honey, I want you t'wait outside. Jes' stay right on the porch, y'hear?"

Apprehensively Dulcie waited while the men loaded the carriage. Of all the desolate spots, this was it. Not a sound for miles except crickets. And Leroy was up to something.

As he carried out the last bundle he muttered, "Go get in that carriage. An' don't get any fancy notions."

This was her chance. She would have only seconds, for she was certain that Leroy meant to knock the store-keeper unconscious and then they would run. She fumbled with Leroy's left-handed knot around the hitching post. Finally she got it undone, and touched up the horses with the whip. Startled, they took off running. Behind her, she could hear Leroy shouting, "Hey, come back here! Y'hear me, Dulcie?" as his feet pounded down the road after her. She flicked the whip again. Leroy had once been a good runner, but he'd have to go some to beat a pair of high-spirited horses.

The country dirt road was bumpy, but then it became smoother. Then Dulcie noticed there were sounds she hadn't been hearing before—the horses' hooves and the carriage wheels were echoing off some surface that wasn't trees or bushes.

She had made a wrong turning somewhere in the blackness, and was driving right up some planter's fenced lane. And ahead of her was a white-painted gate. She could hear Leroy, still following.

She was trapped.

If he caught her, he would do terrible things to her.

She jerked the horses to a stop and scrambled out of the carriage. In agonizingly slow motion she went over the fence, only to be raked all over by brambles, and in trying to get away, find her skirt caught fast in a dozen places. Panting, she tried to extricate herself.

His footsteps were much nearer now, only a few yards away. She dared not go on trying to free herself. The noises would give away her hiding place. Quickly she crouched, putting her face down and covering her pale hands with her skirt.

He found her, by accident. When he caught up with the horses, he quickly tied their reins to the gate, and vaulted over the fence that had seemed so difficult to Dulcie. He landed right next to her.

With one hand he jerked her upright, and with the other hand he slapped her face repeatedly. "That's for openers," he assured her. With another jerk he had her free of the brambles and was shoving her over the fence. "Now you get in that buggy and don't you move a muscle or say a word. We're still in trouble, thanks t'you. I got t'back us up outta here."

As they passed the general store, the proprietor came out to meet them, a pistol in his hands. He fired two bullets through the back end of the carriage. Dulcie screamed and bent forward with her hands over her eyes.

Leroy laughed and whipped the horses harder.

When they reached the house, Leroy made her carry in everything. When she faltered under the weight of heavy bundles, he booted her. After this had happened several times, Dulcie was so furious she took no thought for her future. The next item was a small bag of salt, and pretending to stumble, she swung it and connected with Leroy's jaw. To her great surprise, he fell over backwards.

She stood frozen in place astonished, watching him until he got up and came for her. She ran up the steps and into the house, slamming the door behind her. She ran to the drawer and got the only weapon she could think of—a heavy wooden potato masher. She was tired of being a meek, frightened mouse just to keep Leroy's temper from flaring.

He jerked open the door and it flew back and banged against the wall. His fury would have been a terrifying thing if she hadn't been so angry herself. He roared, "Dulcie! You better come here right now! Dulcie! Hear me? I'm gonna find you, an' when I do—"

From a crouching position behind the cookstove, she swung the potato masher with all her might and cracked him on the shin. He shrieked, startled, and began hopping around hanging onto his shin. Meantime, she swung her weapon once more and hit him on the arm.

He did not yell this time; he simply put out both hands and caught her. Frantically she waved her weapon, hitting him in the ribs, until with a lightning cat-like motion he twisted her arm, breaking her hold on the mallet. Dulcie screamed with the pain, but she was beyond caution. With one hand she raked his cheek with her nails. She bit his arm, hard. And she did something she had not done since she was six years old and wrestling with Jothan—she spat in his face.

He growled like a wild animal and, taking her in his hands, shook her until her teeth clicked together. Then he threw her against the wall, knocking the breath out of her, and when she lay on the floor half-conscious, he kicked her. Groggily she considered getting up, but the effort of thought was too much. She surrendered to the inevitable.

She regained consciousness a few minutes later with the cool breeze on her. Sprawled on the kitchen floor, her hair out of its pins and her neck feeling broken, she was being raped. And Leroy, from the sounds he was making, was enjoying it very much. Her anger returned, but not good sense with it. She would not stand for this. Death was better than further indignity.

She twisted her hips at just the right moment, and Leroy slipped out of her. "Aaawww!" he cried in disappointment and pleading. Failing to make a new connection, he sprawled on her and finished.

Afterward, they lay still, Dulcie trying to get her breath beneath the weight of his body. Still panting like a man in great distress, he said, "Maybe—we oughta—do that every time."

In disgust she said, "Get off me. I can't breathe."

He did not move. "Look who's bein' nicey-nice now. You was lovin' it jes' as much as I was."

"I hate it!" she burst out passionately.

"Dulcie," he said wistfully, "don't say that. You don't mean that."

They were back at taw. Leroy still had the upper hand. She said, defeated, "No. I don't mean that."

He chuckled in relief. "That was pretty fun, wasn't it?"

Thinking of when she had hit him with the potato masher, she said, "Yes, it was pretty fun. Maybe—sometime—I'll do it again."

Leroy had gone out to attend the horses when a knock came at the back door. Dulcie had been making beaten biscuits and did not hear the carriage wheels. She was surprised to hear a Negro voice call, "Leroy! Oh, Leroy! Y'all home?"

He had not locked the door this time, so she opened it, to greet a small black man with a gold tooth. She started to speak, but stopped at the look of shock on the man's face. "Why are you staring? Didn't you expect to see a woman? And who are you?"

The hat came off, and holding it in front of him like a shield, the man said, "Ah'm Tyrus Washin'ton. Mistah Edmun' Revanche sent me to inquiah 'bout y'all. Fo'give me fo' starin', missus, but dem is two beeyootiful shiners. Yes, dey is."

She said excitedly, "I am Dulcie Moran Tremain. My husband is Captain Adam Tremain. I am being held here against my will. Anything you can do to get me out of here will be richly rewarded, I assure you. Please—help me."

He looked confused. "Ah'm bein' paid a'ready, missus. Mistah Revanche say Ah'm his man, or Ah'm a daid man."

Leroy stepped in the door. " 'Bout time you showed up, Tyrus. I was startin' to think Edmund'd give up on us."

"Nossuh, he gimme some instructions fo' y'all." His eyes slid over to Dulcie.

"C'mon," Leroy said, and took him out to sit on the back steps in the late fall sunshine. With the door closed, Dulcie could not hear what was being said. After some time they returned, and Tyrus handed her note-paper and a pencil.

"He wants you t'write a nice letter, Dulcie honey," said Leroy.

She sat down, eagerly obedient. "Who will be getting this letter, Mr. Washington?" She looked up at him, unable to keep the hope from her eyes.

"Youah husban'."

Leroy said loudly, "*I'm* her husband now!"

Tyrus's eyes rolled from Dulcie to Leroy and back; with a small shrug he said, "To Cap'n Adam Tremain. Ah am well an' happy an' you doan need to bodder 'bout me no mo'."

Stunned, Dulcie sat with tears in her eyes until Leroy's heavy hand smacked across the back of her head. "Write!"

Tyrus continued. "Ah am vurry pleased with mah present a-bode an' am bein' treated jes' fine. An' sign dat wid youah name, missus."

Leroy snatched the letter and read it over, taking a long time. Then he threw it back down on the table. "You sho' ain't very edjicated, Dulcie. *I* can spell bet-ter'n that. An' what's this 'bout Jothan?"

"You want Adam to know it's from me, don't you?"

"I want you t'sign that Dulcie Biggs!"

"But my name is—"

"DON'T TELL ME WHAT YOUR NAME IS! Do what I say!"

She did it, and showed him. He seemed to get much satisfaction from that.

"How is the election campaign going, Mr. Washington?"

Tyrus beamed. "Fine, fine. Cap'n speakin' ebbery night. Mistah Revanche say he gwine win fo' sho'."

CHAPTER FORTY-FIVE

For weeks Adam had slept only fitfully, falling asleep to dream of Dulcie and waking minutes later to realize anew that she was not there. Alone in their large bedroom, he turned from one position to the other, punched the pillow, then gave up. Getting out of bed for the hundredth time, he paced the carpeted floor from one window to the other, standing for a while to look out, then resuming his endless steps through the long night.

Sometimes at dawn he would fall asleep in a chair. Within moments there would be a light tapping on the door. Beau or Jenny or Matthew and Michael, clad in nightclothes, their hair tousled, would pad in. Jenny or the twins would go to Adam and crawl into his lap. Beau, growing fiercely independent at nearly age eleven, sat at his father's feet. A soft, small voice would say, "Did Mama get home yet?"

Adam would have to answer, past the pang in his heart, "Not yet. Very soon now."

One morning Beau, all alone, found Adam in bed and crawled in beside him. Adam put out a long arm and scooted the boy toward him so that he lay sheltered in a light embrace that would not offend his son's sense of what was manly and what was not.

"Dad." The young voice was tentative.

"Yes, Beau."

"Dad, what if Mama doesn't come home?"

"She'll come home, son."

"Do you s'pose Mama likes it wherever she is? Do you think she might like it better than here?"

"No, son, she misses you children and me."

"I was thinking about that in the night. I couldn't go

to sleep for worrying. It would be—terrible if she forgot us."

Adam said matter-of-factly, hearing the quaver in Beau's voice, "Yes, that *would* be terrible."

"When do you think we'll know something about her?"

"Just as soon as election is over."

"Could I go with you to get her?"

"I'm afraid not, Beau. It might be dangerous for a boy."

"Do you think that someone might try to steal us? Me and Jenny, and Michael, and Matthew?"

Adam saw no reason to mention the twenty-four-hour guard he had stationed around Holly Hill. "You are safe here, Beau. Nobody will try to steal you from here."

"Jenny's afraid she'll get stole. I heard her telling Mike and Matt."

"I'll talk to her. There is nothing to be frightened of."

"Dad, you know something? You answer questions good. You don't make me feel like a little child."

Adam chuckled. "You don't ask questions like a little child, Beau."

Now, surveying the sea of black and white faces before him, Adam was thinking of that conversation. He was seated on a platform beside Edmund Revanche and several in his political train. They were addressing the Société des Artisans tonight; last night it had been the Jeunes Amis, and the night before . . . His head lolled, and he jerked it up, trying to keep himself awake while the introductory speaker finished.

Adam had learned some time ago how to submerge his fury at being placed in this position. Automatically he gave a set speech, responded to standard questions with pat solutions, graciously turning over to Edmund the answering of issues that provided scope for Edmund's grandiloquent rhetoric.

He wondered why the Pinkerton men had not been

able to turn up any clue to Dulcie's whereabouts yet.
Surely half a dozen men, even from Chicago, should
be able to locate one eyewitness to Dulcie's capture.
Surely those men would soon stumble on the hotel, or
house, or old warehouse where she was being held.
Edmund would hardly be the only one to know her
hiding place.

"—and with us tonight is that noble hero of the
savage sea, that daring blockade runner who slipped
past many a Union gunboat just to come here and give
his support to Edmund Revanche—Captain Adam
Tremain!"

Adam stood up, bowing to thunderous applause and
directing the attention of the audience to a smiling
Edmund. He cleared his throat and gripped the lectern.
This was the worst part, starting. When he had been
Adam Tremain the Black Swan, he might have been
taking half these blacks in the audience to freedom.
Now, to his eternal shame, he was advising them to
cast their votes for the one man he knew would soon
enslave them afresh, snatch from them the rights of
freedom.

"Fellow New Orleanians, ladies and gentlemen. I
want to thank you for your kindness in inviting me
here this evening to say a few words on behalf of your
friend and mine, Edmund Revanche. Edmund and I—
have known each other for many years. I venture to
say there is not a man in New Orleans, or the entire
state of Louisiana, who will do for you and your neighbors what Edmund will. Never in the course of history
have New Orleanians so badly needed a man like Edmund. Some men in public life might be all for the
white man, and some might be all for the black man,
but it is very rare to find a gentleman of Creole extrac-
tion, which Edmund Revanche is, who is so just, so
equitable, in his treatment of both blacks and whites.

"My friends, let me give you just one example—"
Adam talked on, his mind so accustomed to the speech
that he could give it without thinking. Yet he dared

not relax, dared not give in to the overwhelming temptation to shove over the lectern, jump down into the audience and start screaming at them what a bastard Edmund was . . .

Angela Pierson, seated near the front between a wealthy white stockbroker and his bejeweled wife, had come only because Adam would be here. There were few men she didn't see at least occasionally at Les Belles, and from her clientele she knew perhaps better than anyone what the feelings of New Orleanians were. That was why she had been so valuable to Edmund Revanche as an informant. But what she had been hearing lately was disturbing, and of no value to anyone, particularly not herself. Adam Tremain on the campaign trail for Edmund Revanche had caused quite a stir. To those who had believed he was too honest ever to play politics, and especially the dirty, repressive politics of Edmund Revanche's sort, Adam was a disappointment. These men didn't understand; they voiced their disenchantment. A man with the makings of a true hero had turned out to be no more than just another smooth operator with his hand out waiting to put it in someone else's pocket.

Others, having greater faith, merely questioned. Why would he do it? Why would he support Edmund Revanche of all people? These men talked of deals and blackmail, and came closer to the truth, but still there was nothing they could do except watch and see Adam, the man, and the Black Swan, the image, crumble under Edmund's influence.

A third group were men of Edmund's own persuasion. Not only were they pleased with the opportunity to use someone of Adam's popularity and stature, they busily plotted how his sudden turnabout, for whatever reason, could be used to their future advantage. A few expressed worry that his conversion to Revanchian politics might be sincere, in which case they would have to pay him in kind, and that price tag would be high. No one wanted to pay—not really.

Angela settled back in her seat, decidedly uncomfortable. When she had set him up, she had never bargained for this, or wanted this. She didn't want to hurt Adam, she wanted only to free him of Dulcie. She watched the play of light on the planes of his handsome face, the occasional smile on his mobile mouth beneath the piratical black mustache. She scarcely heard his words, for she knew they were of Edmund's composition.

She had difficulty holding back her tears. Inside her there was the horrifying desolation of knowing one has done wrong. It filled her, made her fearful and hurting. He looked ravaged, she thought. There were deep shadows around his eyes, little lines of haggard worry cleft around his mouth. She listened to the strain that came as he forced sincerity and cheer into his statements. And this she had done to him because she claimed to love him. This was what she had to give him. *No,* her mind rebelled. This was not what she had to give, but it was what she had chosen to give; and it was making her ill, physically ill. She looked around her, trying to see how difficult it would be to get out of her seat and leave.

The audience burst into applause, some of them standing, whistling, and stamping their feet. Edmund Revanche had risen and was about to begin his talk. Angela's eyes remained on Adam. He clapped and smiled with the others on the platform, but he glistened with a sheen of sweat, and she knew he felt as ill as she did right now. And she had done this. She had chained him to Edmund Revanche. She now understood that no matter what he wanted for himself, he would never willingly leave Dulcie, nor could anyone take her from him.

Already crying, Angela pushed her way toward the aisle, no longer caring whose feet she trampled on or how rude she might seem. She had to get out of there. Perhaps she could not undo the past, but she could repair some of the damage. She couldn't bear doing this to Adam. Perhaps she would never be with him as his woman, as she had wanted to be, but neither would she have him if Dulcie were killed. In an effort to get Dulcie back, Adam was slowly destroying himself.

Angela commanded her driver to take her back to Les Belles. She ran up to her suite and called for Janet Robbins. "Janet, have Tyrus Washington brought here to me, within the hour. And send a messenger to my father's house—if Tom isn't there, have them look for him at the St. Charles, or at Geddes Ingraham's home. I want him here tonight too. Quickly!"

When Tyrus arrived, he stood awkwardly with his hat in his hand, never before having been admitted to Angela Pierson's inner sanctum. Mr. Revanche had often sent him here on errands, but the people at Les Belles had always treated him as the servant he was. It unnerved and flattered him that tonight Angela, herself, had called him, and he was here as a man. His admiration for her knew no bounds. She was the best-known and most-admired black woman in New Orleans—he smiled at the term. Angela was as fair as the heavenly creatures she was named after. That gave Tyrus a good feeling too.

Angela tried to keep herself calm, and not hurry. She wanted Tyrus's cooperation on a matter that would be delicate and dangerous for him to grant to her. She knew Edmund would never tell her where he was keeping Dulcie, but Tyrus would. No matter what she had to do, Tyrus Washington would tell her within the hour where Dulcie Tremain was being held captive.

And then she would enlist Tom's aid. Finally she felt she and her father would be allies. After all these years she understood Tom's hatred of Revanche and his love for Adam. Amazingly, just now when she had nearly destroyed it, she had found what love for Adam was, and how much it meant to her.

CHAPTER FORTY-SIX

A few days after Tyrus's visit, Dulcie counted the marks on the kitchen wall. In three days the election would be held. Three days during which Adam would be making more speeches, shaking more hands, reiterating campaign promises for Edmund Revanche. She had three days left in which to escape, to fly to Adam and attempt to undo the fearful harm Edmund had forced her husband to do.

Only three days.

She said pleasantly, "Leroy, can't we sit out in the sunshine for awhile? Or could we go for a walk? It's such a bore being in the house all the time."

"All right," he said unexpectedly. "But watch where you're steppin', now."

She got her shawl. The late autumn afternoon was a medley of clouds and sunshine, and the breeze over the gently rolling landscape seemed cool. He held her arm tightly as they strolled out the back, past the barn and the empty chicken house, and up the hill. She had never seen this before, and she commented on the weedy sandy land as though it were a thousand acres overlaid with pure black bottom dirt. To be able to walk the earth, after weeks on board floors, lent her renewed strength.

Leroy beamed on her like a lover. "You're sort of happy here, ain't you, Dulcie?"

The fine day sharply dimmed. "I—I miss my children, terribly."

"Aw, forget them, Dulcie, me'n'you'll have younguns of our own!"

She shuddered. *Not if willpower or justice has anything to do with it.* She said dully, "We'll see."

"Wish I'da thought of it, we coulda carried a picnic with us."

Another chance if I miss this one. "Let's do that to-morrow!"

"Sho', honey. We'll do that, anything you want."

They strolled on down the hill and sat in the sand beside the little lake. Out several feet into the water, a family of ducks was quacking noisily, swimming and diving for food. Watching them, they laughed as the drake, larger than the rest, dived repeatedly, his curly tail barely showing above water.

Leroy's arm was around her possessively. He said, "Every so often I get to thinkin' an' wonderin' how it might've been if my younguns woulda lived. My boy Royal'd be fifteen now. Think o' that, Dulcie. Fifteen years old. Wouldn't he be a hell-raiser for sho'? Chasin' the girls, an' knowin' how t'shoot a rifle an' a shotgun, an' goin' huntin' with his daddy. But he'd be a fine boy, he wouldn't be a dumb jackass like I been sometimes. I'm gonna be better, Dulcie, you jes' wait an' see."

Thinking of a lifetime spent as Camille had spent her years with Leroy, waiting for him to change, Dulcie's eyes grew bleak.

"You'n'me's gonna get along fine. I know we will. An' that little girl o' mine, she'd be as purty as a spotted pup under a red wagon. With curly hair an' ruffly little dresses, an' comin' t'kiss her daddy on his cheeks whenever she wanted somethin'. Yeah, I'da been a lot different if I'da got a chance t'be a real daddy. 'Steada comin' home an' findin' out the damnyankees had did one more thing t'me."

Her mind clamored with accusations of the things he had done to innocent others—Ruel, Jem, Patricia, herself. But her throat closed and she could not speak.

He turned to look at her, his eyes full of tears. "For you, Dulcie, I could change. I know I could. We'll have a family—" His voice broke, and he put his head down. After a while he said, "I been cravin' you an' lovin' you as long's I can remember, Dulcie. I ain't

been sorry for a minute for stealin' you. An' I'm beginnin' to b'lieve you got some feelin's for me too.
Ain't that right, honey?"

She dared not tell him the truth, that her feelings
for him were of loathing, for the volatile man he was,
and fear, for the same reason. A man who considered
a fist fight to be the same as lovemaking revulsed her.
She was Adam Tremain's woman. But Leroy awaited
an answer.

She shook her head. "I can't—say—yet, Leroy."

He squeezed her arm. "I know you're bashful,
honey, but you'll say it one o' these days."

They had been outside the whole afternoon; now
the sun had fallen behind some live oaks and the air
was chill. He stood up, reaching out a hand to her.
"Time t'get on back." When she stood up, he pulled
her into his arms and kissed her long and lovingly.

It was that act, so like and so unlike him, that
clinched her decision. She could not, would not under-
go another night with Leroy. So long as he was alive,
he'd never give her a moment out of his sight. That
big butcher knife—he let her use it now, didn't even
lock the drawer any more. She'd slip it into the bedroom—and when he was asleep—

She felt the cold chills of fear crawl up her spine.
But it had to be done. And she had to do it.

They walked back leisurely, but Dulcie's brain
seethed with the details of her plan. She was gathering
courage to do the thing that had to be done, for otherwise she would be Leroy's captive until she died.

Dusk was starting to fall as they strolled into the
little hollow that held the house and the outbuildings.
She was relieved when he let go of her arm, heading
for the woodpile. "I'll jes' get an armload so's you can
cook supper," he said. Being the man of the house,
doing the heavy outside work, seemed to fulfill another
of his needs.

Dulcie considered running now; but he would catch
her before she got out onto the road. And she did not

want another beating. Her time would come. She must wait for it.

Idly, from the doorway, she watched him pile up three or four logs on his arm; then as he picked up another, a stick seemed to catch on his bare arm. Oddly, it terrified him. He leaped backward, drawing in his breath in an awful gasp, dropping the wood and nearly losing his balance.

For long seconds she could not think what was wrong; then as he waved his arm frantically, trying to dislodge the thing that had caught him, she recognized the distinctive splotched markings of a pygmy rattlesnake. An ugly-tempered reptile at best, they were known to strike merely upon being approached. Warming itself in the woodpile, it had not happened to make any sound, but struck at the nearest part of the object which had disturbed it. Dulcie's hands flew up to her mouth in fear.

Leroy was yelling now, the snake as frantic to let go as he was to get rid of it. Finally the fangs came free, and the snake was flung off into the undergrowth.

Leroy, his face drained of color and his eyes bulging with fear and horror, staggered toward her through the brush. He moved awkwardly, like a man under sentence of death. His stare was almost cataleptic. With one hand he was gripping his bleeding arm. He said hoarsely, "Dulcie—get the knife—cut—got to suck out the poison—"

Suddenly there was a rotten crushing sound, and he disappeared into the earth.

He cried out as he was falling, then his cries turned to screams of intolerable revulsion. Dulcie stood rooted in shock. His words echoed out of the ground as from a soul in the bowels of hell. "Ohh, *God!* God! There's a nest of 'em! God, Dulcie, get me out! Get me out! They're bitin'—oh, God!" Then she realized she had been hearing the faint hollow rattling sounds, as of a dozen angry rattlers.

Leroy's horrified screams went on, and on, and on . . .

Stiff and shrunken into herself with terror, she tried to think. She found herself in the house, her hand shaking as she tried to light the lamp. The chimney fell from her nerveless fingers and splintered on the floor. Mindlessly she left the lamp burning on the kitchen table and flew to the dark bedroom. She tore off the bedclothes and tied two sheets together. As she rushed through the kitchen she remembered the lamp, and had to slow her pace to carry it without its being blown out.

She approached the old well fearfully, fervently praying that there were no stray rattlesnakes about. His screams were hoarser, more agonized, sounding thicker as though his throat were closing.

Something was aiding her to help this man she had been planning to kill. She was incapable of rational thought now. By the back door she had grabbed a long iron bar once used to dig post holes. Now hastily shining the lamp all about her, she knotted one corner of the sheets over the center of the bar. She got as near the hole as she dared, using her light and testing the ground gingerly, until she stood on reasonably firm ground and could look down a few feet.

His voice came to her, weaker. "Dulcie—Dulcie—get me out—please Dulcie—jes' get me out—"

She could not see him. She let the bar fall across the hole, and with a stick shoved the sheets in so they dangled toward him. "Leroy, can you pull yourself up? I didn't know where a rope—"

"I can't—Oh, God, I'm so sick—can't reach—Dulcie—" He was panting now, his voice an eerie whisper. "Dulcie—I'm afraid to die—down here—get me out—please honey—get me—"

Then she heard nothing more. His hoarse breathing had ceased, and the scrabbling sounds he had made trying to get up out of the pit. There was only the sound of the rattlesnakes.

After a while even they were silent.

Her terror returned. With it came a realization of her utter helplessness, alone beside a caved-in well where a man lay dead; alone far out in the country where only Edmund Revanche knew where she was.

Lamp in hand, she ran stumbling to the house. She shut the door behind her, intending to lock it; then she remembered that Leroy had the key. She could not lock the door. Moving with haste born of fear, she shoved the kitchen table in front of the window. She pulled all the blinds. She would have to stay here by herself now.

She was sweating from her efforts, but the cold that seized her seemed to start in her very bones. A fire. She had to have a fire. Shakily she lit shavings, put on kindling, put on wood when the kindling had caught. When the stove was roaring, she closed the damper and looked about her. She would never get warm enough. She had to have a cover. Carrying the lamp with care, she went into the bedroom again and brought out a quilt. Wrapping herself in it, she sat in a rocker near the stove, shivering.

She did not try to sleep that night. She sent up continual prayers for Leroy's soul, and for her own, for she had wished him dead. After hours had passed, her stunned mind could accept that he was dead and that she was free.

Free, as soon as dawn broke, to make her way home.

CHAPTER FORTY-SEVEN

It was two days before the election when Angela talked with Tom. He listened, his face grim, but he could not criticize her. In a way it seemed fitting to him after all these years that it should be Ullah's and his daughter who would be the catalyst to the downfall of Edmund Revanche, and that as her instrument she had chosen Tom. Life does have its small equities, he thought, then looked squarely at his daughter.

"You sure you want to do this?" he asked. "This time there won't be any chance to change your mind. Think about it—be sure. I've wanted Edmund's hide for a long time, and I can get him now."

Angela, finally seeing her father, had the feeling that she was learning to know this man for the first time. She felt much as she had when she had watched Adam on stage speaking for Edmund. She had not known the depth of her father's pain, his hatred, or his love for her, her mother, or Adam. She wondered if she hadn't spent all these years of her life in a kind of oblivious torment of her own devising. Whatever the answer, she knew that now she wanted it to be different. "I'm sure," she said. "And if you'll allow me, I'd like to help you. I have many things to make right. I'd like to begin with this."

Tom smiled. "You couldn't have picked a better place. You might say, it all began with Edmund. If it hadn't been for him, your mother and you and I would have lived a very different kind of life—a happy one, I like to think. I know your mama and I were happy."

The hard veneer of Angela's cool sophistication broke, and tears formed in her eyes. Tom saw traces of the girl he had lost years ago, the girl who had grown up sweet and innocent and loved.

In a small voice she whispered, "I'm sorry—I'm so sorry, Daddy." Her eyes reached out to him, but she didn't know if she dared truly reach out for his embrace. She was new at this business of loving and forgiving and didn't know how others did it.

Tom, with tears in his own eyes, crossed the small space between them and took her in his arms, holding her as he used to do when she was very small and still his.

Much later they returned to talking of what they would do to free Dulcie, and what would be done about Edmund Revanche. "First off, I don't want Adam knowin' anything's in the wind. If we fail, he never needs to know, and to be truthful with you, I don't hold out a lot of hope for Dulcie, but we'll try. Now, did you get the word from Tyrus?"

"Yes. She's being held in a house a number of miles out of town—it's very secluded. Leroy Biggs, a man Dulcie apparently knew in Georgia, is holding her. He is the only man there. The worst problem we face, according to Tyrus, is getting to the house without being heard."

"Maybe we won't have to," Tom said. "Supposing we get Tyrus to go out there—kind of lead us in. If Biggs is doin' what Edmund orders, he'll expect to see Tyrus now and then. Think you could get him to do it?"

Angela hesitated, thinking of the particular cost to herself of the additional favor. Then she smiled and said, "Yes, if the price is right, I think Tyrus will cooperate."

Tom assumed she was talking about money, and she let him. "Good. Then we can turn that little chore over to Rosebud McAllister. Dulcie knows Rosebud, and anything smaller than a locomotive, Rosebud can handle with one hand and one foot tied behind him."

"And Revanche?" Angela asked. "Who will take care of him?"

Tom's smile widened to a grin. "Why, you an' me an' a whole bunch o' happy bystanders, Angela."

She looked at him curiously. "What *are* you thinking?"

Tom chuckled. "Let me keep it to myself a bit."

"I will not!" Angela said in mock indignation. "I want to be in on this every step of the way."

"Well, then, it seems only fitting to me that Edmund have a victory celebration. He's worked mighty hard to achieve his elected office. Why, he's been talking about this since way back before you were born."

"Tom, I can't make one ounce of sense of this—what are you saying?"

"I'm sayin' that I'm going to hire us a suite in one of the finest hotels in this city, and we're gonna give ol' Edmund a victory party he'll never forget."

"He hasn't even won the election yet; besides, why celebrate with him?"

"He'll win. He's too crooked to lose—shoot, even if he doesn't get enough votes, those thugs down at the Legislature will just write up new ones for him. He'll win, take my word. He's already paid his dues, and nobody's goin' to cross Edmund when he's paid."

"But why a celebration?"

"Well, jes' between you an' me, we could call it a wake. Now, for your part, think you can round up a band o' hungry, wanderin' gypsies who'll work for passage outta here and ask no questions no matter what?"

Angela was still frowning, trying vainly to catch his train of thought. "You're not going to tell me."

"I will, I will—a little at a time. Let me see if it will work out first. Can you get the gypsies?"

"Do they have to be gypsies?"

"No, but a troupe that can sing and dance and make a hell of a lot of noise, and won't ask questions."

"I can find them—when do you want them hired?"

"The night of the elections—the telegraph wires will be humming right from the start. We'll know the results that night. Remember, you got to make sure they're willing to take off outta here that same night. I'll get Ben to assure them passage anywhere they want to go on one of the Tremain-West ships. They must agree to that. We want no trace of them the day after."

"I understand—or at least I think I do."

"All right, little daughter, I've got some gathering of materials to do. I'll see you tomorrow. Let's have lunch. I think you an' me oughta start celebratin' right now. I'll talk to Rosebud tonight. You send Tyrus to my place tomorrow. They can leave from there. We want Dulcie safe an' sound before we start stirrin' up things here."

Tom hurried from Angela's to the theater where he had been paying mild and frivolous court to one of the actresses currently performing. After they talked for a time and Tom promised her a late night supper after her last performance, she introduced him to the stage manager, who took Tom to see several people involved in the backstage workings. When he left the theater, his buggy was loaded down with sandbags, colorful decorations, and many feet of piano wire.

From there he went to several major hotels in the city, examining each of them from the back, finally hiring a suite that had a back entrance, with back stairs leading to the suite.

Next he went to Rosebud McAllister's home and told him of the plan, and asked him to go with Tyrus Washington to free Dulcie. "Before you say anything, an' I know you're jumpin' to get at it, I want you to understand it ain't likely this Leroy is gonna give up easy. Angela tells me he's not right in his head. You can't tell what somebody like that is gonna do. And you know Edmunud isn't gonna trust him with somethin' like this if he wasn't pretty sure Biggs would hold out to the last."

"He try to hol' out wif me, an' Ah step on his haid

like a squish melon," Rosebud said, and rose to his full height.

Tom leaned back, looking up at the man as he moved closer and closer until his chest was pushing into Tom's jaw. Tom began to laugh. "Rosebud, you are the most formidable, intimidatin' man I ever seen. You jes' be careful, hear? Anything bad happens to you or Dulcie, an' Adam'll skin me."

"Ain't nuthin' bad gwine happen to nobuddy 'ceptin' Mistah Leroy Biggs."

"Remember, you've got to let Tyrus lead you in. Biggs won't be alarmed at his appearance at the house. But watch Tyrus, too."

"Ah watches him. Tyrus gwine do whut he told. Ah knows Tyrus good."

Tom grabbed Rosebud's arm and felt as though he had hit rock. "Take care now, I'll see you election night. You take Dulcie straight to my house and guard her. I'll have Ben send Adam there, and I'll be there the minute I finish with Revanche."

"Yassuh," Rosebud said, a broad grin on his face as he saluted as he had done aboard the *Black Swan* during the days he had sailed with Adam. "Dis is jes' like sump'n de Black Swan woulda did. Ah sho' likes dis job." He made a motion with his hands. "Squished melon," he said, still grinning.

Tom rode home to wait. This was the hardest part. He was very pleased that he had promised to take the actress out for a late supper. It would help him pass the hours and perhaps forget for a few minutes what was coming in the next days.

Tom was nearly bursting with impatient excitement the morning of the election. He and Angela went to the hotel early in the day and began hanging festive decorations around the attractive, masculine room. It was a white, softly stuccoed room with stained glass windows along one wall. Heavy, dark beams crossed the room in latticed squares. At the far end there was a small alcove. Tom rubbed his hands together as he looked at that.

"Very romantic," Angela said, noting the small table and curved sofa that was meant to provide a secluded, intimate place for dining.

"Let's get all that junk out of there," Tom said, beginning to pull out the table and the sofa into the body of the room. When the alcove was empty he spotted a large ornately carved chair, fit for a king's throne. "There it is! Jes' what we need." He dragged the chair over and put it in place. Then, standing on the chair, he worked a strong eyehook into the tight grain of the beam overhead. Then he implanted another. "Jes' to be sure," he said. Through the eyehook he threaded the thin, strong piano wire and attached it to two weighty sandbags used to lower and raise heavy stage settings. He stood back, admiring his handiwork, smiling so broadly and incessantly that his face hurt.

Angela watched him, unsure what to make of this side of her father. She shivered slightly. "You hate him so much," she said softly. I don't—"

Tom took her by the arm and sat her down. "It's time your education went a little further, Angela. I'm going to tell you a little about the man you've been selling information to. I can't tell you all I know about him because you and I aren't gonna be alive for the hundred years or so it'd take to detail all the malicious, dirty acts Edmund's done or been involved in.

"When we were young, he started out with simple little things like stealin' plantations from poor widows he could outwit, and murderin' his young wife. About the time I married your mama, he was ready for bigger things. Now, you know your mama was one o' Edmund's slaves, and when Edmund found out I had bought her from him to marry her, he was ready to kill, an' that's jes' what he did. Nobody ever told you how your mama really died, or how I got to be the bent-up ol' cripple I am, but I'm gonna tell you now.

We hid ourselves away from everybody, found a little place in the bayou, and we were happy there . . ."

Tom spent a good portion of the afternoon telling Angela of the short time he had spent with her mother and how happy they had been until Edmund had found them. He let her cry and beg him to stop as he recounted Ullah's death, but he went on, holding nothing back, letting his daughter feel and understand why his hatred of Edmund was so strong and so unwavering. He told of Edmund's attacks on Adam, and on Dulcie and the children at Mossrose. Finally, emotionally drained, he said, "And tonght, it's all gonna come to an end."

Angela was capable only of nodding. She got up slowly, her eyes swollen, burning, and red, her heart tight and painful. She finished putting up the decorations, the trappings of a Mardi Gras celebration that would mark the end of Edmund Revanche's life. On great pedestals around the room stood the huge, monstrous masks in gay colors: the Boar, the Goat, the Raccoon, the Bear, the Snake, the Alligator. Between them hung brilliantly colored streamers; balloons dropped prettily from the beams. A long table had been set up with bottles of every kind of liquor, a large punch bowl sat in the middle waiting to be filled, and large silver platters stood empty in the places where hours later that night they would be filled with food and pastries and delicacies.

On election evening, when the returns were beginning to come in over the telegraph wires, Tom went with Geddes Ingraham to the St. Charles Hotel where he would find Edmund. Fearing that Edmund would refuse to come outside if he requested it, he asked Ingraham to do it for him. Tom waited in the shadows with two men from Les Belles, Noah and Rufus, men Angela had assured him could be trusted and would ask no questions later. Edmund stuck his head out the back entrance to the hotel, annoyance written on his face.

"What kind of nonsense is this, Ingraham? Where are you?" He looked outside, but did not leave the doorway.

Perspiration broke out on Tom's face. Suppose that he didn't step out and let that door close? Everything would be lost. They couldn't allow themselves to be seen abducting him from the St. Charles. He had to step outside. Come on, Edmund, Tom kept repeating in his mind. Jes' come on out. Come on, now. One step. One more step.

"Ingraham!" Edmund came onto the walkway, peering into the dark, then reached for the door knob to go back in. "Damn black fool!"

Noah and Rufus leaped from their cover. Noah grabbed both his arms, pulling them tightly behind his back while Rufus stuffed a dirty handkerchief into Edmund's mouth. Tom tied on a gag, then pulled a hood over his head. Noah and Rufus completed tying him up, hand and foot. He was thrown into the carriage on the floor with Rufus and Noah sitting over him keeping guard. Tom drove with shaking hands to the hotel where he had rented the suite of rooms.

At the rear entrance Tom dismounted and went ahead, making sure no one had wandered into the back stairwell. Checking each step of the way, he called softly for Rufus and Noah to follow, bearing their struggling burden. Tom barely breathed until they had gained the safe privacy of the suite.

Angela was there waiting for them. As they entered, she closed the door, making sure the lock was set. Then she followed Rufus and Noah as they carried Revanche to the chair Tom had set in the alcove. Tom ripped off the hood and glared down into Edmund's glittering eyes. Seeing the annoyance there, but no fear, Angela began to laugh.

Edmund struggled against the strong hands of Noah and Rufus as they secured him to the chair. He tried to kick them as they passed. His glance at Tom and Angela was murderous.

"Are the gypsies here yet?" Tom asked.

"No, they are due in five minutes.."

"Then we'll jes' enjoy a five-minute visit with my ol' friend here." Tom pulled up a chair in front of Edmund, as though they really were going to have a nice chat. Tom put out his hand and Rufus quickly poured him a sparkling amber tumbler of bourbon. Tom held it to the light, and then toward Edmund. "To you, ol' friend. To days that will be no more." Deliberately he drank the contents down. "I s'pose you haven't had time to notice your surroundings, Edmund. Look at them. They should bring back old times to you."

Involuntarily, Edmund's eyes left Tom and moved around the room. At each pedestal he stopped. He looked at the Alligator. The Bear. The Raccoon. The Snake . . . what had these crude representations to do with him? Then he remembered. The Snake had been Ross Bennett. The Goat, his overseer Sleath. And the Boar, himself. They were all there, all mounted death-like on pedestals, all staring at him. His head swiveled back to Tom. Fear was in his eyes now, and he fought to control it. He hated fear. A man lost when he feared. He squinted, trying to bring the cold calculation back into his expression. He fought hard against the gag and against his bonds.

Tom began to laugh. "Don't much like it when it's you, do you, Edmund. Have you figured out yet that you're not gonna walk away from this one? Look around again, Edmund, enjoy this party. It's your victory party—and mine."

"And while you're looking, Mr. Revanche, look too at me. Tom told me all about the day my mother died. People say I look like her. Do I? Am I as pretty as she? Do I have her face? Her eyes? Her body? Look at me, Edmund Revanche, and know you couldn't kill her, because I'm here! You lost, Edmund. You lost!"

Tom glanced up at a sound in the hall. "Let the merrymakers in, Rufus. Our party is about to begin."

Rufus opened the door to admit thirty or more gypsies, all dressed for a ball in the clothes Tom had provided. Tom pulled the heavy red drapery that closed off the alcove from the rest of the room.

Just as they had been instructed, the gypsies broke up into groups. Six of them began playing violins, tambourine, drum, and horn. Though it was not melodious, it was gay and loud. Others began dancing. Still others filled the room with ancient Romany songs, and the food was passed and liquor was put into every hand. The sounds in the room were happy, cheerful—a celebration, and it would go on without stop for three hours, at the end of which they were to leave by the back way and go directly to the docks where Ben West would have a ship waiting to take them to Mexico.

Edmund squirmed frantically now, trying to keep eye contact with Tom as he moved behind him. Tom nodded at Rufus and Noah. On command, each lifted one of the sand bags up from the floor behind the chair. As the sand bags lifted, the piano wire lowered down through the eyehooks. Tom took the wire and slowly, deliberately placed it around Edmund's neck. He made sure the loop was secure, then he came to stand in front of Edmund. "You'll have to wait one more moment before I free you, Edmund. My daughter has a touch of her own." He waited while Angela took a sheet off a mirror that she had had placed in the alcove earlier that day. "We all know how you admire yourself, an' how you enjoy watching fear and pain. We couldn't deprive you of that on this last night. It's here for your pleasure, Edmund." Tom bowed, and again moved behind the chair. This time he began to work at the fastenings that held the gag in place. "If you'll hold still I'll have this loose in a minute."

Edmund kept his head still, and showed no surprise when Tom freed him of the gag. "Now that you've had your little charade, I hope you have the good sense to release me. You realize, Tom, you'll pay for this. I'm not just anybody."

Tom laughed. "I have out-stepped myself, haven't I? Jes' like I did when I married that little darky slave o' yours."

"You're a madman, and shall be put where madmen belong!" Edmund snarled. "Hurry up and untie these bonds!"

"Yes, *sir!*" Quickly Tom cut Edmund's legs free, jumping out of the way of being kicked. He glanced at Rufus and Noah, then cut his arms free.

Edmund immediately jumped from the seat, only to be pulled violently and painfully back, a thin trickle of blood immediately appearing along the line of his white shirt collar. He let out a strangled scream.

"Sit down, Edmund," Tom advised him.

Edmund fought against the wire, his hands now at his throat, clutching at the thin, deadly wire. The more he pushed and pulled at his throat, the lower Rufus and Noah let the weights go, although they still held them. Gasping and strangling, Edmund sat down.

Outside the red drapery the dancers whirled past, their full skirts touching the drapery, making it billow in and then fall straight again. The drums beat steadily and the tambourines jingled. The dancing became more active, and the odors of the room became more heavily saturated with the rich, heady smell of good bourbon and wine.

"You can't dislodge that wire with your hands, Edmund. If you want to go on tryin', you can, but you'll merely lose your fingers before your head. That's your choice. You can also scream for help. Nobody'll come, and nobody'll do anything to help you. That's how it was with Ullah. That's how it's gonna be with you. You're alone, and nothin' can stop what's gonna happen, short of an act of God. We'll find out how you stand with Him. Angela and I will say good-bye now, Edmund. When we leave, Rufus and Noah will carefully release their hold on those weights. They're a lot heavier than you are, so any struggling you might choose t'do will only hasten what's inevitable."

Edmund gave a mighty enraged surge forward, his fingers clawing for Tom. Tom turned away from Edmund's face, already purpling, the trickle of blood coming from his neck heavier, his eyes popping in fear and burning with fevered hatred. He took Angela's arm and turned her away. He looked back only to nod at Rufus and Noah.

As Tom and Angela left the alcove, the two men lowered the weights and let go of them. Edmund's head was immediately pulled upward. His hands clawed at the wire that was cutting into his flesh. All he could see were the sparkling black and red spots that had begun to form on his image in the mirror that Angela had set before him. A terrified purple-faced man whose tongue was lolling out and whose mottled face was wavering dimly with the bright spots that gathered and flickered in his head.

Tom and Angela stood in the main room for a moment and watched the merrymakers dance and sing. The women had their long heavy ball gowns pulled up above their ankles and were now doing the dances of their own folk. In a line across the room, men tossed pastries to one another and back again. Another juggled a swiftly moving and uncountable number of shells. Laughter and music filled the room. A woman with a beautiful, deep contralto set a contrary mood as she sang a slow, moving song of pathos. In the background, barely discernible, could be heard the strangled cries of a dying man.

Only half an hour after Tom and Angela left, Edmund Revanche's head rolled silently, unnoticed, into the midst of the merrymakers. Around it they danced, and danced and sang until finally one of those too drunk to know what he was doing, picked up the grotesquerie and said, "Ah, poor lost creature, you have fallen from your pedestal." With that he took a huge slap at the Boar's mask and knocked it from its stand, to replace it with Edmund's still bleeding head.

The revelers left.

Alone in the room Edmund Revanche stared blindly at the masks of his compatriots. They were all there just as they had been in the beginning. The Alligator. The Bear. The Raccoon. The Snake. The Goat. The Boar.

All there. All alone. All dead.

CHAPTER FORTY-EIGHT

Dulcie drove the carriage in the direction she had seen Tyrus Washington take. Several times she had to stop and ask her way, for she was going to Tom's house. As badly as she wanted to see Adam, she knew that such sentimentality might prove fatal to him if Edmund was indeed watching him as Leroy had said. If she could only get to Tom, he could get the message to Adam that she was safe.

The late-autumn evening was hot and still. Leaves hung limp on the live oaks; the Spanish moss dangled like an old man's tattered beard. Its wings seeming to pump in circles, a mockingbird flew up into a magnolia and sat there flicking its long tail feathers.

She drew near Clio Street, looking with hungry eyes for Tom, a servant, anyone. She saw no one, and her heart sank. Had she come here for help, only to find Tom gone? She got down out of the carriage, feeling all the strain of the past weeks and their hideous culmination. Then suddenly the door burst open and a tall black-haired man ran with long strides toward her. He crushed her in his arms, murmuring over and over, "Dulcie, you're home. Dulcie . . . Dulcie . . ."

Now she could let the tears of relief flow; the tears of totally unexpected, totally unnerving grief for Leroy Biggs. She could stop being brave and self-dependent; she had someone she could lean on, someone larger than life, bigger than love itself.

She cried, "Yes—I'm home—I'm home!"

"Are you all right? Are you—" His look took in her blackened eyes, the torn clothing, the bruises and scratches and abrasions. "Did he do this—"

She clung to him, pressing her entire being against

his dear, familiar body, burying her head in the blessed haven of his shoulder. "Leroy's dead—oh, Adam, I'll tell you—after a while—but please—never, never ask me—"

Over and over, his hand stroked her roughened hair. But he made no reply.

Rosebud and Tyrus Washington had been surprised and disappointed upon arriving at Leroy's house to find no one home. They went through all the rooms, calling Leroy and looking for him and Dulcie.

Rosebud suggested, "We bettah look 'round outside."

It was then they saw the caved-in well and Dulcie's makeshift rope. Rosebud, lying on his stomach and peering downward, saw a man's huddled swollen form. Then far below he heard a warning rattle and hastily scrambled to his feet. He put his cupped hands to his mouth and in his carrying quarterdeck bellow called several times. "Miss Dulcie! Rosebud is heah! Miss Dulcie! Kin you heah me! Ah's Rosebud McAllister!"

They searched the barn, the chicken house, calling. Then Rosebud said, "Tyrus, she ain't heah. Le's get on back to Mistah Tom an' tell him, an' get some boys out heah wif grapplin' hooks to pick up Mistah Leroy Biggs."

Returning to Tom's, and finding Dulcie still in the embrace of her supremely happy husband, Rosebud's broad face crumpled. He remembered a long time ago when he and the Captain had battled all odds because the Captain loved this woman more than life itself. He put ham-like fists to his eyes and let out a gusty sigh. He turned to Tom, who had just come back from the party.

"Dey sho' does look like dey's wheah dey belong, doan dey? Dat li'l ol' firebird an' de big Black Swan."

Tom, as shaken as Rosebud, managed a grin. "They sure do."

* * *

The time came when Dulcie had to answer questions, and a great many of them; for even as she had greeted Tom and was being hugged again, Adam had sent a messenger on horseback to bring several men to the house.

Dulcie, wiping away the tears of strain and joy, declared, "The very first thing I want to do is get into a hot tub and soak for an hour."

Adam said gently, "Not yet, Dulcie, please. I want you to look just the way you are."

She turned bruised eyes on him in astonishment. "That's ridiculous! I look awful, and I feel so filthy and stained—"

"I know that, my love. Can you possibly stand it for another hour? It's quite important."

"Well—why?"

He put his arms around her. "Because you are my only proof that Edmund Revanche had you captured and then used me to advance his campaign. The returns are coming in, and he's winning."

Dulcie's hand went to her face. She had escaped too late. Counting only marks on a wall, she had lost several days.

Adam saw her consternation, but went on. "You can help me discredit him before he takes office, and do it in such a big way that no one can possibly doubt the story. I want his entire history publicized to such an extent that he will be forever ruined, if indeed he does not hang for his crimes. Are you willing to go through this one more thing?"

"Who—who am I to talk with?"

He held her a little tighter, as though to protect her from what he knew was coming. "The police. Reporters from all the New Orleans newspapers. I will answer as many questions as I can, but your plight is bound to be of interest."

She wailed, "I can't—! Adam, don't ask me to!"

He said nothing, rocking with her gently.

After a while she said, "Very well. What has to be done, has to be done. Oh, Adam, stay near me—I don't know if I can do this!"

"We can do anything—together," he assured her.

Within the hour, two dozen men were assembled in Tom's drawing room—the chief of police, who told Adam that even now his men were closing the net on Edmund Revanche; reporters, artists, and photographers from all the New Orleans newspapers. Rude and interruptive in their eagerness to get the story and be first to publish it, they thrust questions on Adam and Dulcie, told her to pose with her head this way, now that way, to hold out her arms to show her cuts and scratches, stand up so that her disheveled state would be fully revealed. The photographers exploded several pans of flash powder, temporarily blinding everyone and sending clouds of acrid smoke toward the plaster rosettes on the ceiling. The artists sat perfectly still, making quick, competent lines on their sketch pads. The reporters became louder and louder in their efforts to overshadow their rivals.

Adam's commanding voice rang out. "That will do!" He stood without moving until the room had fallen silent. Then he went on. "I understand your zeal, boys, but this is a private home, not a barroom. And the exhausted lady with me is my dear wife. We have a story of major importance to give you, but there will be no more shouting. And no more flash photographs. I will tell you, in my own words, the story you came here to get. If you have questions as I go along, raise your hand. If we have any more commotion, you will all be asked to leave."

A discontented murmur broke out, but Adam quelled it with a casual glance around. "There is one matter upon which I must have your word, gentlemen. For the safety of my wife and my children, I am asking you to promise that you will not publish this story until Edmund Revanche is behind bars." He waited until the

shocked murmurings died down. "Yes, Edmund Revanche. Until I have your promise, we will remain
silent."

Tom glanced quickly at Rosebud, silently warning
him not to reveal what he knew about Edmund. Adam
would learn soon enough.

Having received individual promises, Adam went on.
"As a matter of fairness, I am requesting the chief of
police to notify all reporters present the minute Edmund
has been arrested."

Then, giving as many corroborating details as possible, Adam began by telling them of Edmund's murder
of Ullah. He went on, revealing everything. Reporters'
hands flew up and the questions came rapidly, but Dulcie, despite her inner turmoil, answered everything with
poise and dignity. Reporters made scribbled notes on
the closeness of the couple, and on the haggard appearance of Captain Tremain. The artists drew the scene,
portraying the tenderness between Adam and Dulcie,
while not leaving out a detail of their worn faces.

She had thought she could never relive the moments
of Leroy's death, but she did, reserving details of the
location for the police. Even the stolen horses and
carriage came under mention, as they added weight to
her story. One reporter asked Dulcie, "Now that you're
safe again, Mrs. Tremain, what is your first wish?"

Dulcie's eyes filled with scalding tears. The reporters
noted this avidly, jotting down her answer, "I want to
be with my children."

When they were finished, everyone galloped off, and
the Pierson house was quiet. Adam held Dulcie close
against his heart. "My love, you were magnificent. I am
so proud of you."

"And I of you. Oh, Adam, after all these years, is
Edmund actually going to be exposed?"

"You know Edmund's influence as well as I do—
but this time—this time, I think we have him."

*   *   *

Tom Pierson lay alone in his bed. His old friend, his old enemy, Edmund, was dead. He had a feeling of contentment he hadn't known for years. Adam and Dulcie were asleep in each other's arms in another room in his house. And Angela, his daughter, was home again, under his roof and his protection. Content with his lot now, he allowed the other side of the coin, the bitterness and the pain, to surface and drain away. Not that he was going to dwell on Edmund, but old pains from the past washed up in his mind and needed cleansing. In this time of dying, he wanted it all to be washed out, never to return.

He was fifty-three now, an old man, although he didn't feel like one. He had mourned for his Ullah for nearly a quarter century. Now he would expunge his grief and begin to live again, while there was still time. Edmund was dead. He could do that.

EPILOGUE

Edmund Revanche's beheaded body was found the morning after elections, seated in a chair, his severed head ensconced on a pedestal. The newspapers flamed with the stories: DISCREDITED ELECTED OFFICIAL FOUND RITUALLY MURDERED IN HOTEL; MY DAYS AND NIGHTS OF ABUSE AND TERROR, AS TOLD BY MRS. ADAM TREMAIN; THE FAMOUS BLACK SWAN TELLS OF THE SECRET CRIMES OF MURDERED LOCAL POLITICIAN; WOMAN'S CAPTOR MEETS HORRIBLE FATE IN DISUSED WELL; HOLDING HER HUSBAND'S HAND, SOCIALITE TELLS BIZARRE TALE OF BEING HELD HOSTAGE; I DID IT ALL FOR LOVE, REVEALS CAPTAIN TREMAIN OF HIS POLITICAL TURNABOUT; THE DREADFUL SECRETS OF A LOCAL POLITICIAN'S DARK PAST; SATANISM SUSPECTED IN REVANCHE MURDER; WAS EDMUND REVANCHE MURDERED TO SEAL HIS LIPS?

For days, Adam's story and Edmund's death made headlines that grew smaller and smaller, eventually being cast aside in favor of a much more exciting topic, the disputed 1876 national election.

The monumental scandals of the two administrations of Ulysses S. Grant were not over; they were merely exchanged for other scandals. By 1876 the public had become thoroughly disillusioned with Republican rule. Their alienation had come through several factors: the extreme measures of coercion used upon the South to enforce constitutional amendments; the constant military interference with Southern self-government; and the indifference to administrative demoralization evident under Grant's regime.

In Louisiana the State Returning Board, which certified election returns, was under the absolute control of William P. Kellogg. Kellogg, the Republican Governor, had been recognized by the federal government and supported during his administration by federal troops. Kellogg's board refused to comply with the law in several respects, and declared that Republican electors had been chosen. Kellogg himself signed the certificates of election.

In the Louisiana Presidential election Samuel Tilden, a Democrat, had actually received a majority of six to eight thousand votes over Rutherford B. Hayes. But Hayes supporters claimed intimidation of Negroes had forced them to vote for Tilden in significant numbers. Tilden's majority could hardly be ignored; it could only be overcome by throwing out votes. At one point Tilden was offered the election for the sum of $200,000. In the end, the Returning Board declared 13,250 votes improperly cast, handing Hayes the electoral vote.

In Florida and South Carolina there were dual returns of votes, each Returning Board claiming victory. The entire matter was referred to the Congress.

The Congress appointed a fifteen-man Electoral Commission, whose composition had a Republican majority of one. By a predictable vote of eight to seven, this Commission accepted the statements of the Republican Returning Boards. The famous Compromise of 1877 gave Rutherford B. Hayes the election, in return for his agreement to end Reconstruction in the South. All this took months. It was the morning of March 3, 1877, before Rutherford B. Hayes was declared elected.

The Democratic party had opposed Hayes; yet his policies, nearly following Democratic lines, quickly gained popular acceptance. He withdrew federal troops from the South, trusting whites and blacks to work out their own destinies. The very thing for which Adam Tremain had fought so hard came at last into being.

* * *

It was the autumn of 1877. Dulcie sat at her desk, writing a letter to Adam's parents. In a bassinet nearby, Rebecca Tremain slept on her stomach, showing her small head covered with fine black curls. She turned, making a grunting noise, and Dulcie broke her concentration to glance at this most welcome child. Rebecca had been the result of a New Year's resolution to increase their family, a resolution that had gone into immediate effect.

Smiling, she picked up her pen and wrote: "Rebecca is two weeks old now, and the center of family atten—"

Adam came in. Hugging Dulcie, he peered over her shoulder.

"You're writing to Ma and Rod? Good. Why don't you tell them that we'll be sailing the *Black Swan II* to New York next month, on our way to Europe?"

Dulcie jumped up from her chair. "Europe! Marvelous! How long have you been planning this? Why didn't you tell me?"

"I've worked on plans for several months. I thought maybe you'd enjoy a little peace and quiet for a change."

Her face fell. "We're not taking the children?"

"Who said that? Of course we're taking them."

Dulcie laughed, and threw her arms around him. "Peace and quiet, with six children on an ocean voyage?"

"Plus Ma and Rod, if they've decided to come."

"They'll come." She laughed again, feeling joyous and lighthearted the way she always did with him. "Oh, Adam, how I love you!"

Beaming, Adam suffered himself to be hugged and kissed. He hadn't told her everything yet. He'd wait until they got to London.